W9-BGA-723

NOWHERE-LAND

NOWHERE-LAND

A STEPHAN RASZER INVESTIGATION

A.W. HILL

COUNTERPOINT
BERKELEY

Library of Congress Cataloging-in-Publication Data has been applied for.

ISBN-10: 1-58243-498-0
ISBN-13: 978-1-58243-498-8

Cover design by Natalya Balnova
Interior design by Megan Cooney
Printed in the United States of America

COUNTERPOINT
2117 Fourth Street
Suite D
Berkeley, CA 94710

www.counterpointpress.com

Distributed by Publishers Group West

10 9 8 7 6 5 4 3 2 1

FOR P.K.

PROLOGUE

SCOTTY DARRELL STOOD in the field of winter wheat and felt the wind stab the wet spot on the front of his corduroys. He let out a sob. Somewhere along the last leg, he'd wet his pants. *I'm nineteen*, he thought, *and I peed my pants*. He hadn't done that since the age of seven, and had vowed then that nothing would make him do it again.

Scotty didn't know where he was or how he'd gotten there, but that was the point of The Gauntlet, an alternate reality field game that made Dungeons & Dragons look like Simon Says. It began on the web and moved with disorienting speed onto a global gameboard, where the moves were determined by fate, the *I Ching*, and the kindness (or malevolence) of strangers. After a certain number of moves, you couldn't retrace your steps to the trailhead. Chaotic play was built into the game; no algorithm could map its logic. The GamesMasters had studied everything from aboriginal rites of passage to Stockholm syndrome, all to fashion a separate reality to which the player would ultimately surrender.

Then came the good stuff. Then came God, whatever that was.

Scotty had bought into The Gauntlet when the call for "pilgrims" had traveled through cyberspace to the Middlebury College library server, attached to a piece of stealth spam with the heading "WE KNOW WHO YOUR DADDY IS." Though his nominal father was a tenured professor at Middlebury, Scotty had always suspected he might be adopted. He couldn't resist opening the potentially viral attachment.

Now, thirteen months later (maybe fourteen—he wasn't sure), he was playing the Seventh Circle, two ranks from the top level of the game. His last contact with the Masters—not counting the fake-out—had been from an Internet café in Butte, Montana, but that had been ages ago in gametime. He was "riffing," and not that well. He had no money and no ID, and had moved into winter without a coat. If he didn't find his next Guide soon, he would have to admit defeat. Although his status was transnational, it panicked him that he didn't know what country he was in. If it was the United States, then he supposed he was in Kansas, but it could just as easily have been the Ukraine.

Beyond all that, Scotty Darrell had done some very bad things in the real world. And although these things had been done in the person of his game avatar, he couldn't shake them. Guilt draped him, but lightly—a clammy discomfort like the dampness in his trousers.

He stopped and remembered. The wind rose and cooed through the grain. His mother's voice: *little Scotty's soul has flown, lights are on but no one's home.*

Stumbling through the wheat, his sneakers suddenly hit blacktop. He dropped to his knees and offered a prayer. He stood up, and had not been walking the median strip for more than fifteen minutes when the black Lincoln Town Car rolled up on his right and he was invited inside. "Get in, Scotty," the man said. "It's a new game now."

ONE

IT HAD BEEN RAINING in L.A. for ninety-six hours, and still no floating cars. For Stephan Raszer's young daughter, Brigit, who knelt on a high-backed chair in the dining area with her palm pressed against the streaming picture window and her eyes trained on the Cahuenga Pass, this was a disappointment. Her father had told her fantastic tales of how in "old L.A."—in the days before flood control—the winter rains would spawn such currents that automobiles cresting the hills would be rafted into Hollywood like logs on a theme-park ride, coming to rest only once they'd hit the flats of Hancock Park. Like god Shiva, children take a certain careless pleasure in catastrophe.

Raszer himself was not enjoying the rains. In years past, he'd welcomed them as a recess from the unrelenting sun, an excuse for skipping the California gold rush. This year, they seemed a nagging reminder that his Argonautic enterprise—a very private investigative service specializing in the retrieval of lost souls—was on the reefs. He rose, foul-tempered, from the futon in his room and grimaced at the stained-glass Grail window he'd installed at great cost four years earlier. Its Book of Hours colors had bled to shades of gray in the joyless morning light. He cursed his extravagance. Raszer had always spent what he earned; now there was nothing left to spend.

"Damn the rain!" he growled in an Ahab voice, partly for Brigit's benefit. He lit a cigarette. The last affordable vice—and, at seven bucks a pack for his brand, barely.

"Oh, Daddy," she chided as he entered. "I want it to rain harder. I like it."

"Yeah, I know, sweetheart." Raszer padded over and kissed the top of her head. "Rain makes kids feel safe and grown-ups feel helpless." A muscle twitched in his right temple. *There it was again.* Each time he kissed her, he had call to remember how he'd nearly lost her, and cause to pledge that he would never risk losing her again.

✦ ◆ ✦

IT RAINS WITH A VENGEANCE in Los Angeles, gray battalions of storm rolling in from eight hundred miles offshore like the skyborne funeral of a defeated warrior, drummers beating out mad, insistent rhythms on the flat rooftops from Venice Beach to San Bernardino, the swelling ranks of mourners contained only by the mountains that flank the basin like shrugged shoulders.

The rain paints a different city, a conquered city of empty, mirror-surfaced streets. For as long as he'd lived there, Raszer had looked forward to this annual transformation. Transformation was, after all, his stock in trade. This year, it was only bringing unwelcome hints that the corpse in the funeral cortege might be his own.

He stumbled into the kitchen, where there were other things that evidenced his short-lived affluence. He owned one of those big, professional chefs' stoves with a gas grill on top, and a collection of cast-iron skillets and cooks' knives that would have done Escoffier proud. Cooking was Raszer's only real hobby, as the others comprised his work. He had neither an investment portfolio nor a retirement plan. Until the crash, he'd had three savings accounts: one was a backup for his chronically overdrawn checking account, the second for the little place he wanted to build someday in Baja, the third was for Brigit. All but the third had now been exhausted, and that one he wouldn't touch. He'd taken out a second mortgage on his Whitley Heights home instead, and was consulting for the LAPD's Missing Persons Unit.

He pressed himself a thickheaded cup of Ethiopian coffee, scooped up the telephone, and stalked out the back door to the covered pine deck overlooking his meditation garden and the canyon chaparral. The garden, watched over by sentinels of polytheistic statuary placed amid the rosemary, thyme, and purple ice plants, was another product of good fortune. He punched in a phone number while watching beads of water run down all four of the goddess Kali's arms. The rain had let up, but not for long. The call was to his twenty-nine-year-old research assistant, Monica Lord.

"Monica?" he said after three rings.

"I see you made it through the night."

"You coming to work today?"

"Not if you're gonna be as cranky as you were yesterday. Besides, the pass is flooded. You want me to hire Charon to ferry me across?"

Raszer's silence drew a sigh from her. She knew he needed to maintain the ritual of work, even when there was no work to be done.

"Listen," she said, "I'll come, but you gotta promise you'll let my chiropractor adjust you. It might restore your balance."

"I'm not sure that's the sort of adjustment I need," he said. His mood darkened further when he noticed the hillside mud oozing like lava into his hot tub.

"You want me to stay with Brigit tonight so you can prowl the roadhouses?"

He leaned heavily on the wet wooden railing.

"Damnit, Monica," he said. "I can't shake this funk. I lost a stray. He's off the grid, and this fucking rain of bad luck is God giving me the waterboard."

He heard her blow the bangs out of her face, a prelude to straight talk. "Let go of Scotty Darrell. You lost your game on *one* job. One in seven years. You used to do it regularly in the old days."

"Yeah, but then I only hurt myself."

"Check again, Raszer. There was always collateral damage."

Scotty Darrell was a stray. *Stray* was Raszer's term for the runaways, cult adherents, and other lost sheep whom he'd been—until recently—paid handsomely to return to pasture. The runaways were usually running *to* as well as *from* something—most often to the fire from the frying pan. The others had been "taken" in one way or another. This they had in common: all had lost their way, and all had gotten mixed up in the Devil's business.

Tracking strays was a specialty within an already specialized field, and Raszer got nearly all jobs on referral. If someone near and dear had gone missing, if a spiritual swindle was suspected, if you feared physical harm, and moreover, your fears had risen to that inexpressible conviction that a human soul was at risk, you might find yourself eventually on Raszer's doorstep. If he took your case, it would be because the evidence suggested that an abuse of faith had indeed occurred, and that it was critical that your loved one be restored to "the grid." By the grid, he didn't mean some Cartesian straight and narrow, but something more like the lattice of a quartz crystal.

Raszer was nobody's idea of orthodox, but he did hold fiercely to one article of faith. He believed that sanity and spiritual health required that we be wired into a circuit which had as its power source the dynamo of the Godhead. He could see it, everywhere, spinning out its fibers. The Tantrists conceptualized it as a mandala, the Taoists as a path, but for Raszer it was a net woven of grace.

If he was aware of being cradled by that net now, it was because he could still recall a time when it hadn't been there for him at all. It was the one safe place to be; everything else was what the kabbalists called *sitra ahra*: the other side. Perversely, that was exactly the borderland to which his jobs took him. He guessed he had a score to settle there.

Scotty Darrell had strayed off the grid by way of a trail no police agency could follow. His loss troubled Raszer deeply. Like any good shepherd, he wanted his sheep in the fold. Like any knight errant, he wanted the dragon good and dead.

Scotty was the only child of a Middlebury College sociology professor and his mercurial wife, a former Balanchine dancer. The mother had struck Raszer as fine but unforgiving, as if the rigors of ballet had hardened her to human failings. Scotty was fey, in the old Gaelic sense of "touched," and beautiful, with fine hair the color of wet sand and a beauty mark above his lip. There had been developmental issues in childhood and suicidal tendencies in adolescence, and some of the signs had pointed to a high-functioning autism. He'd disappeared as a result of his participation in an Internet-generated role-playing game known as The Gauntlet, but Scotty's folks had inexplicably failed to contact the police until he'd been AWOL for nearly three months.

The Vermont police gave the case to the FBI when files found on Scotty's hard drive suggested sympathy with Islamists and global anarchists, and the FBI had contacted Raszer when The Gauntlet's authors turned out to be two divinity students at UNC, known by the web names Frater Vanitas and Frater Ludibrium, who'd reportedly kept a goat's head on dry ice in their dormitory bathtub.

The Fraters were questioned and released pending further investigation, upon which they disappeared from both the Chapel Hill campus and the known universe, but the labyrinthine game they'd devised and the spyware that carried its evangelical Call to Adventure onto thousands of hard drives lived on long after operations in the dormitory had been shut down. It was what gamers called a persistent world, and it burgeoned in that same anarchistic demimonde as Internet cafes and global positioning devices that allowed for stateless terrorism, but with a markedly different purpose.

The Gauntlet sought to prove the existence of God by revealing the cosmic determinism that hid behind seemingly random events. The game's design showed an understanding of both chaos theory and Christian evangelism, colored by Chinese wisdom and quantum mechanics. Moreover, The Gauntlet went well beyond its forerunners in moving play into the theater of human history. Once you were in deep, all realities were conditional, and each move affected a hundred others.

The game found its mark among the kind of brainy, introverted kids who might once have spent after-school hours at the chess club and purchased sleep with dreams of heroism—children whose futures seemed all too prefigured. The object of the game was to "ride the snake," and the means to this end was to give up all attempts to shape events and allow events to shape you. You could buy in for a limited run as a Pilgrim or you could enlist all-in as a Peregrine (in the latter case the university would sooner or later notice your empty desk). Scotty had opted for the full tour and gotten seriously sidetracked, which was why his case had wound up in Raszer's lap.

This was the thing: The game was defined as a form of service to God, but the moves that got you there might as easily entail gunrunning as good works. The goal was a kind of heaven on Earth—freedom through servitude—but along the way, there were tales of jackpots hit, sexual feats performed, and enough exotica to rival the pitch of any timeshare huckster. *Adventure! Mystery! Intrigue!* Irresistible to bright but underactualized kids like Scotty. A chance to be real in a different reality. The words not mentioned in the product description were deception, duplicity, and *death*.

If only he'd gone deeper, Raszer thought, second-guessing himself for the hundredth time. His advertised skill was missing persons retrieval, but among a certain clientele he'd earned a reputation as a street-wise shaman, adept at descending to underworlds in pursuit of his quarry. He was known as a man who'd go to Hell and back to bring someone safely home.

In order to accomplish this, he had often to do what shamans had always done: wear masks. These masks might take the form of a deep cover, a foreign language, or the adoption of an odd habit or tic. They gained him entry and served to confuse both his adversaries (the deceivers) and his quarry (the deceived). The trick was to not confuse himself, and to remove the masks in such a way that the stray would come to see him as a more trustworthy steward of her soul than its present keepers.

It was a risky business, but until Scotty Darrell, he'd beaten the odds and had been recognized by local and international police agencies as an exotic bird dog who, despite his knack for sniffing up the wrong cracks, was worth giving considerable leash.

He hadn't gained his expertise by way of an advanced degree in criminal psychology or counseling, nor through years of police work, though studying all things germane to his vocation was a constant activity. He'd dropped the only course he'd ever taken in cult deprogramming (now euphemistically called exit counseling) when it became apparent to him that the core of the art was a contempt for faith, and the methods all too similar to those of the enemy. Raszer's occupation came closer to being a "calling," for before undertaking it, he had been—of all things—an actor. A failed actor, to be sure, but not thereby a bad one. In any place but Los Angeles, where fake it 'til you make it is the rule, he might have had more difficulty earning his PI license.

The one thing required of all shamans, from the Arctic Circle to the stark, dusk-painted mesas of the Southwest, was that they die and be reborn, and Raszer had. His heart had stopped, just short of bursting, seven years earlier. It had been a tragedy of his own making in more ways than one. In those days of cocaine and cold gin, Raszer had courted heart failure the way a $50 hooker courts HIV, pissing away even the sweet wine of fatherhood. His death had been a penance: the propitiation of a deity from whom he'd grown distant. Monica, barely out of college and making a hundred a week as his press agent, had been at his bedside in the hospital. Even his adulterous wife had shown up to see him off. It was she who'd screamed first when his vital signs returned, not because it meant she'd have to endure the divorce proceedings after all, but because, along with the heartbeat, there was a beam of light pulsing from his left eye.

Now, Raszer felt cause to wonder if the intervening years hadn't been some sort of extended NDE, a lucid dream waltzing him to this moment of sad truth. He leaned over the wooden railing, feeling old ghosts rush in with the fennel-scented updraft from the canyon, and realized that he was probably depressed enough for meds. The wind shook the eucalyptus trees, freeing the raindrops to mat his chopped, ash-blond hair. He lit a cigarette and walked into the garden.

It wasn't just losing Scotty that had gotten him down. It was the reprise of his oldest terror: that the earth was, at root, a place of loss. On that signal day seven years ago, he'd thrown dice with a goddess, gambling his own life in exchange for Brigit's when a childhood illness had ravaged her kidneys—his way of making up for being a lousy dad. The bet paid off, Brigit recovered, and in gratitude, a reconstituted Raszer had made a vocation out of leveraging his own soul to save others less durable. He placed ads in the personals and the trade papers even before he was fully licensed:

SOMEONE YOU LOVE IS MISSING. CALL STEPHAN RASZER, INVESTIGATOR OF SPIRITUAL CRIME.

This being Hollywood, capital of religious flim-flam and a place where people came to be lost and then found, the ads were answered. He walked through fire for each client, and with each gig, the heat cauterized his old wounds. It was bliss while it lasted, it was redemptive, and it didn't hurt that he'd gotten a nice house in the bargain.

Just beyond the small plots of mint, mandrake, and *Salvia divinorum* was a statue of Diana, goddess of the hunt, carved from coral by an old sailor on Santorini. On the pedestal, beneath her drawn bow, Raszer had placed a small, jeweled box, and in the box was a lock of wheat-colored hair. It had belonged to the only woman who'd loved him for all he was and wasn't, unconditionally and to death in his service. She'd been beheaded in the Moroccan desert by a man Raszer had pursued, and Raszer had in turn disemboweled the man with a seven-inch knife.

He picked up the box and held it as tenderly as if it housed the clockworks of the universe, and as he opened the lid, a single tear fell from his eye into the little nest of human hair. From a nearby live-oak tree came the offended squawk of a California blue jay, whose nesting routine he'd intruded upon. On the ground beneath its perch lay the beakful of twigs and fennel stalks it had been carrying. Raszer set the box down and walked softly to the place. To his eye, the twigs formed a rough pattern of long and short, as meaningless as tea leaves to anyone not looking for meaning. He saw for an instant a connection with Scotty Darrell's plight. Advanced Gauntlet players were not allowed to take maps, compasses, or written directions on the road. The only navigational tool permitted was the *I Ching*, the ancient Chinese oracle of broken and unbroken lines. The Gauntlet's guiding philosophy was drawn from the text accompanying hexagram number twenty-five: "It is not favorable to have a destination in view." Raszer looked for a sign in the scattered twigs, but saw only confusion.

He tossed his cigarette onto the saturated ground and cursed. Raszer's divinatory powers, which could be considerable when he was at his best, went to shit when self-doubt came to town—his goddess abandoned him.

He felt a tug on his trousers. It was Brigit. She'd been nosing around his library again and come up with a gold-leaf Tantric text that he'd bought at auction two years earlier for $350. It had first been translated for the English-speaking world by Sir Richard Francis Burton, and was highly prized for its scandalous full-color plates. Brigit had happened on an illustration of the "plow" technique of sexual intercourse.

"Is *this* . . . " Brigit asked with artful innocence, "what sex looks like?"

"That's the sacred union of Shiva and Shakti, the joining of male and female energies. Powerful mojo."

She cocked a chestnut-colored eyebrow. "That how you and Mommy did it?"

"If we had," said Raszer, taking the book just in time to dodge a raindrop, "things might've gone differently." He indicated the hand-stitched binding. "And this, Pandora, is a very rare book. If you're gonna browse, stick to paperbacks."

"They don't have pictures," she replied, then tossed her head and went back inside, leaving Raszer a bit lighter. He could see the woman in her already in that little toss of the head—or, rather, he could see how her greatest charms as a woman would be those qualities of childhood she retained. After a moment's pause, he followed her inside and went to return the volume to its stall.

Raszer's library commanded the largest of three bedrooms. Although it contained nearly three thousand titles, the library was devoted to just two subjects: the history of man's fevered pursuit of divine secrets and cosmic truths, and the lesser history of how that desire had been manipulated by darker agencies. There were selected volumes on forensics, criminal psychology, and international law, but these were subservient to the grand topic of spiritual hunger and the lengths to which human beings would go to satisfy it.

Raszer had at first tried to organize the whole in subsets—alchemy, astrology, Buddhism, Catharism, and so on—but found so many overlaps and crosscurrents that it worked better to arrange them associatively, that is to say, in the manner of his thought processes, which were those of a detective. Thus, each section of the library became a history of the cases he'd taken on, and of the person at the nexus of each case, and this system gave him a convenient mnemonic device for locating any volume at a moment's notice.

The categories dealing with world religions and wisdom traditions were so broad that they merited their own shelves, but individual books had a way of migrating to the matter at hand. The entire library had been ingeniously and continuously cataloged by Monica, who was not only his researcher, dispatcher, and de facto publicist, but the woman who knew his mind and methods best. Her organizational method utilized links that, in aggregate, yielded more than 462,000 cross-references.

Natural light in the library was provided by a set of north-facing French doors. These opened onto a cloistered patio and an herb garden, within which a number of the species owed their cultivation to the library's small but definitive section on the husbandry of medicinal and psychoactive plants. Although Raszer was a coffee drinker by nature, he was also celebrated among close friends for his teas.

To Raszer's hard-won erudition and reckless curiosity were added a set of categorically feline physical attributes. He'd been a somewhat awkward and ill-adapted boy, but had managed to overcome his handicaps with a punishing regimen. He was a reasonably skillful rock climber, could handle a combat knife well, and had managed to collect a black belt in karate before bridling at the sensei's authoritarian mindset. At this stage of his life, the youthful ugly duckling had at least now achieved the grace of a swan. The sharp features that had seemed too roughly sculpted in youth had emerged from the stone, chiseled by both his Celtic and his Semitic ancestry.

He was still no Adonis, but the women Raszer desired were not interested in pretty boys anyway. He was as fit as a formerly dissolute and still nonabstaining forty-two-year-old could rightfully ask to be, and he had acquired with the onset of his second life an exceptionally high tolerance for pain. One doctor had pegged it as an overproduction of endorphins. A different kind of doctor had once called it "Dionysian masochism"—a diagnosis that still made Raszer laugh out loud.

His most singular physical attribute, however, was—in a word—metaphysical. There was a light in his eye. To the amazement of L.A.'s most skillful opthamologists, this luminance wasn't metaphorical, nor was it caused by some lodged shard of glass or accident of shape. Raszer had, just inside the stone-blue perimeter of his left iris, a "second pupil," a dwarf companion to the central orb. In bright sunlight, it contracted to a dull, clay-colored fleck, no larger than the head of a pin. On gloomy days it oscillated faintly, sometimes causing him headaches and vertigo. But in the darkness of true night, and only when the flame of desire—sacred or profane—had been fanned, it spun open and reeled out light like a strand of golden thread.

Raszer rose from the library shelf at the *click-clickety-click* of a pair of high-rise sandals and turned to see Monica come in, her streaked surfer-girl hair attractively damp and her trench coat spattered with mud.

"I crossed the Jordan for you, Raszer," she said. "Now whaddaya have for me?"

"It's bad out there, huh?"

"The major intersections are all flooded. Another kid drowned in the L.A. River last night." She regarded her dappled coat. "And there's mud . . . everywhere."

"Christ," said Raszer, "it just gets worse." Defying the gloom, she still looked sunny, and that, as always, got a little smile out of him. "Sorry about your mac. Now take it off and sit down. I want to pick your fine, feminine right brain."

"About why there are currently no women in your life?"

"No. About Scotty."

She shook her head and released a sigh that was almost a moan. "Don't you remember telling me that obsession kills creativity? Why don't we just spend a rainy afternoon combing the society columns? Somebody's kid has gotta be missing."

"I think I lost him because I played it like a man," he said, ignoring her. "I was linear. I followed leads, not scents. How would you have—"

"I dunno," she said. "The Gauntlet is a boys' game. And anyway, boss, you have as good a nose as most women."

"Not when I'm in close. I had him. I was inside the game. I offered him his exit . . . his goddamned 'DX,' for chrissakes. I had him on the phone and I lost him."

"Look, Raszer," she said, peeling off her coat to reveal jeans and an extra-large sweatshirt with a SEX WAX logo. "The guys who invented this game may be divinity students, and they may call their out clause a deus ex machina, but what if the player's already found God? Why would he quit just because the ref blew the whistle?"

"Because those are the rules. The ref is the game's puppet master."

"Well, that's where I *might've* done it differently . . . " She bit her lip. "*Rules*. Women don't follow them. The Gauntlet is an immersive-reality game, as opposed to just an ARG or an RPG. Once you're out there, *you* write the rules."

"Yeah, but you're still bound to the contract. Otherwise, the game's CURTAINS would open up and the Masters would be exposed. The whole gaming world operates on that deal. The DX clause is mutually binding. If the player calls for it, the Masters oblige. If the Masters ordain it, the player has to come home. It should've worked . . . "

"Except that—"

"Right," Raszer snapped. "Except that there was an exception." Almost a year after the fact, after the headline-grabbing lawsuit filed by Scotty's angry parents had nearly leveled him, Raszer was still churning. His anger was aimed at The Gauntlet's sly creators, who'd duped him and still come out clean, and directed inward, for thinking that anyone played by the rules anymore. "A hitch," he muttered.

Monica spoke softly. "You trusted them, Raszer. I think—under the circumstances—you had to. How could you have known they'd given him Extreme Unction?"

Some of the argot they now used as familiars was peculiar to the arcane world of The Gauntlet—*Extreme Unction*, for example, meant that the player had "died to the world" and was beyond recall, like a bomber pilot trained to ignore any instruction once the target was in sight, or an undercover agent whose existence was denied once he was active—but much of it belonged to the broader arena of alternate reality games (ARGs), an outgrowth of web-based role-playing games (RPGs) like The Beast, which in turn traced their origins to the fantasy games of the pre-Internet 1970s.

No amount of post-Columbine controversy could shake the popularity of these flights from a numbing existence, a popularity that now persisted well beyond college years. It wasn't difficult to understand why. After all, the motto of the gaming universe was "Remember, in an alternate reality, you always have a place to go."

But The Gauntlet was different, and Raszer had known it, even if he *hadn't* known that a month before he'd finally managed to hammer his way into the game's nerve center and convince its makers—under threat of exposure—to let him pull Scotty Darrell's strings, the GamesMasters had already given the boy Extreme Unction.

Scotty had been set free to "ride the snake."

The Gauntlet's trailhead, or point of entry, was located—as most RPGs and ARGs were—on the web, but with an immediate distinction. The "avatar" you took on as your gaming persona was not simply a powerful mutant, a buff guy or better-looking girl, but a saint or scholar, like Augustine or Aquinas or Avicenna. What followed were role-playing scenarios that posed hundreds of ethical quandaries, leading ineluctably to the conclusion that the only valid ethical choice was no choice at all. If God existed and you submitted, the result would be good. Once you got this, you went offline and began your pilgrimage with instructions as simple as:

1) Walk three miles due east from the Student Union to the junction of County Road HH and Hwy. 67. Board the first northbound bus. Do not carry cash, credit cards, condoms, or identification. These are *ballast*. Bring breath mints. Do not wear sunscreen.

The instructions were to be expressly followed. There were dire warnings about what might befall the player if he failed to "play out his line," sought outside aid, or revealed the identity of the GamesMasters.

2) Sit next to the most accessible-looking person on the bus (someone roughly the age of your parents). Don't worry—the seat will be open. Offer this person a mint. This is your first Guide. Leave bus with the G and say, "By the way, do you know of anyone who could make use of a keen mind and a steady heart?" If the G does not respond, get on the next bus and try again.

Following these initial moves, which put the player on unfamiliar ground and with uncertain footing, the plays became more difficult and potentially riskier. Some players came running back after one night. Others, the floaters, found themselves thousands of miles from home in the first week. It was amazing what could happen once you'd put yourself at the disposal of others.

Raszer had found the game fascinating, in principle. It was postmodern evangelism, played incognito and without preaching. It was dharma. Ordinary people might encounter these young mendicants and be subtly transformed by them—the way hardened hearts had once been softened by the Franciscans—and if so, God might show Himself in a fashion. But from the start, there were problems. The game aimed for the best and the brightest, but drew many whose moral fiber was less than firm.

Some players too eagerly followed the game's admonition "to make observations, never judgements"; some guides employed their acolytes in less than godly ways.

When Raszer had at last connected with Scotty, the boy's wariness had seemed to give way to relief. They had four contacts, the first two via The Gauntlet's message board, the last two by telephone. By then, Raszer smelled a rat, and so did his stray, who left the phone dangling at a Mobil station in Las Vegas. Scotty hopped a bus for Hollywood and was captured on a surveillance camera when he hijacked a tram at the Universal Studios tour, shooting and wounding the driver and holding the terrified passengers hostage for two hours. To the theme park's embarrassment and continuing economic distress, he'd managed to escape—vanishing almost literally into thin air—and was now on Homeland Security's Most Wanted list.

There had been something confoundingly gratuitous about the whole escapade, as if Scotty's instructions had been nothing more than, "Shake people up."

The story was tailored for the tabloid media, and Raszer was identified as the deprogrammer hired to rescue Scotty Darrell from the sinister game. He remained enmeshed in a legally dubious but debilitating lawsuit brought by Scotty's parents, who'd initially endorsed his unconventional strategy but had now hurled the weight of two lawyers against him. His reserves had dwindled, his reputation had been devalued, and his phone had not rung with new work in six months.

"So *you* wouldn't have played the GamesMasters gambit?" Raszer asked.

"Maybe not, but if I had, I might have thought of offering Scotty a new game."

There was a whisper of stocking feet in the hall, and Brigit came sliding in.

"There's a really weird old man out front, Daddy," she said breathlessly.

"What do you mean, honey? At the door?"

"No. Out front. At the end of the walk. He's just sitting there in the rain. He looks sort of creepy to me. Like the bogeyman."

"Jesus," said Raszer, tight jawed. "Another one. They all know where I live now. I'm gonna have to sell. And I love this house." He crushed out the cigarette. "You stay here with Monica, muffin. I'll go see who's come to call."

two

RASZER WASN'T SURE why his heart was in his throat. Hired killers don't wait at curbside, and neither tabloid journalists nor subpoena servers hang around in the pouring rain. There were, however, two types that did behave this way: cuckolded husbands and crackpots. Raszer had seen his share of both. In his line of work, not altogether different from that of a parish priest trying to mediate a witch hunt, passions ran high, judgments nearly always bordered on the irrational, and men were driven by a zealotry born of primal drama they could no longer remember well enough to use as an excuse for their consuming madness. Now seven years of scrupulously maintained anonymity had evaporated, and the cranks had his number.

The bedroom hallway led to a small, sunken living room with a low Moroccan tea table and a well-used hearth, up two steps to the bar and dining area from which Brigit had been watching the Hollywood Freeway flood like the Nile, and finally into the converted front room that had been Raszer's office from the beginning. There, hard drives and paper files kept dossiers on dozens of snake oil salesmen and spiritual racketeers he'd either exposed or driven back under the rocks. Any one of them or their associates could be waiting outside. A big bay window faced the cul-de-sac; Raszer stepped to the side and gently drew back the curtain.

The visitor was seated, as Brigit had described, on a low concrete pillar at the end of the short driveway, the steel toe of his work boot anchored against the right rear tire of Raszer's rebuilt 1966 Avanti. At first glance, he looked like a rag peddler—if rag peddlers still worked the streets. Too proud for a bum, too straight spined and stalwart for a junkie. On second look, he was John Brown at Harper's Ferry, complete with nineteenth-century attire, motionless as a figure at Madame Tussauds. It was on that reappraisal that the man, without shifting his broad shoulders an inch, spun his head like an old barn owl and aimed his gunmetal eyes straight at the bay window. The hair bristled on Raszer's neck, and his diaphragm contracted sharply enough to force the wind out of his lungs, but he stood his ground and did not flinch. He returned the stare with reciprocal severity, then took a very deep breath and let go of the curtain.

"I told you he was creepy," Brigit said.

"And I told you to wait in the library," he replied, and glared at Monica, who stood wide-eyed, her hands on Brigit's shoulders.

"God," Monica whispered. "He looks like that anti-abortion nut. The guy with the fedora and the raincoat who was always there before a clinic got bombed."

"He's pretty old-school, all right," said Raszer. "I haven't seen a hat like that since my grandpa died. I'd pay good money for his brown duster, though."

"I don't recognize him from any of our photo files, do you?"

"Nope. Hey—"

Brigit, who had the cunning of a sprite, had slipped out from under Monica's fingers and stood at the window.

"He's crying, Daddy."

"Come away from the window, Brigit. *Now.*" Raszer stepped to the door and peered through its single pane of glass. Sure enough, the old man held his big, bearded head in his hands while his broad shoulders quaked with grief. "I'm gonna go out and talk to him," said Raszer. "Just be ready to call the sheriff if he pulls a sawed-off shotgun out of that coat."

Raszer himself did not keep firearms in the house, and had only rarely found it necessary to carry a gun on assignment. His skills were those of a tracker, not a hunter. As he walked down the rain-slicked driveway, however, he felt distinctly unarmed. He was the perfect target for an act of vengeful mayhem, and the stranger's torment was as potent a threat as anger. Raszer came to within three yards, then halted.

"Are you all right, friend?" he called out.

The old man lifted his head from his left hand. He had a large, aquiline nose, thin lips, and gray eyes with whites the color of beaten egg yolks. His right hand was parked inside his coat, where there was a visible lump. Raszer moved a foot closer.

"I'm sorry for your grief, sir," he said steadily. "This weather's having the same effect on me. But this is a private home, and there's a child inside. Unless you have business with me—"

"*Stefan Razzer?*" the stranger said, his voice deep and clotted.

Raszer cocked his head. "It's *Stee-van* with a long *e*. Makes it simpler. And the last name is *Ray-zer*. Believe me, it was even more unpronounceable before my grandfather changed it." He took a breath. "And who might you be?"

The man said nothing at first, just held his bloodshot stare. Raszer determined at that moment that this haggard patriarch was not on the trail of a renegade wife. Up close, the look in his eyes was more haunted than accusatory. He was somebody's father or grandfather, and he was not, despite the sagging brim of his old fedora, a vagrant. None of this made him any less a threat. The lump inside his coat shifted, and Raszer knew that Monica must be growing alarmed. He moved in another step. The old fellow was beginning to teeter like Humpty Dumpty, and Raszer reasoned that if he got close enough, he could unseat him before he had a chance to pull out a weapon.

"Don't mean to be ungracious," he said, "but we've had some trouble lately. Would you mind showing me what you've got inside your coat?" Raszer put one hand behind his back, where Monica could see it from the window, and dialed an imaginary phone. "Why are you here?" he insisted.

"To save my daughter's soul," the old man said, lips trembling, and suddenly rose up to a height exceeding six feet. Raszer's mind raced through the possibilities. Was this an oath of blood vengeance or a plea for help? Abruptly, there was no time for thought. He drew his hand from his coat. Raszer feinted right, crouched, and delivered a well-aimed kick to the funny bone, disabling the grip and dislodging the concealed weapon, which fell to the wet sidewalk with a dull slap. As the man staggered, Raszer stepped back and cast a wary glance down. At his feet was a bound stack of *Awake!* magazines, the publication of the Watchtower Bible and Tract Society.

"You're a Jehovah's Witness . . . " Raszer said, incredulous, staring at the bundle of soggy pulp while his heart settled. The stranger backed away, his offended arm raised in defense. For a moment it looked as if he might turn and run.

"I'm sorry," said Raszer. "Truly sorry. I thought . . . are you all right?"

"Perhaps I've come to the wrong place," the man replied.

"No, no . . . I don't think so," Raszer countered, palms raised in peace. "Tell me what's on your mind. Tell me about your daughter. Did—did you say her name?"

"Katy." A small spasm caused the corner of his mouth to twitch. "Please," he added. "If I can trouble you for a few moments . . . "

Raszer stooped to pick up the stack of magazines and handed them back to his visitor, whom he now assayed to be no more than sixty-two, behind the full beard and parchment skin. "Of course," he said.

"You're the detective. The cult man from the papers."

Raszer winced. "Don't believe everything you read in the papers."

The stranger sputtered and doubled over in pain.

"Easy there," said Raszer. "Let's get you out of the rain." He hoped he hadn't broken any bones. The last thing he needed was another lawsuit. He put a hand on the man's back, but the intimacy was unwelcome. The man shook off his pain stoically.

"My Katy has been taken," he said, once his wind had returned. "Will you help me find her?"

Raszer looked up at the window and gave Monica an "all clear" nod.

"I may be able to do that," he said. He paused for a moment in the driveway and regarded what the rain had brought in. *Redemption comes in strange packages*, he thought; this one wrapped up more like his typical adversary than his average client. "If you'll tell me everything you know about her." He offered his hand. "I've told you my name," he said. "May I have yours?"

"Silas Endicott," the man replied, extending a bony hand. A patrol car rolled up the steep, wet street from Franklin Avenue and executed a U-turn in the cul-de-sac, coming to a stop ten feet away. The cop riding shotgun leaned out.

"Everything all right here?" the cop asked.

"Yeah, we're fine," Raszer answered. "This is Mr. Silas Endicott of the Jehovah's Witnesses. Just here to make me repent for my sins. Sorry for the false alarm, Officer."

The cop smiled and gave the old man a once-over. "He'll have a long list of 'em to work through with you, Mr. Raszer. No problem. Uh, stay dry."

"I'll do my best," said Raszer, who was by now soaked to the skin. "You too."

Silas Endicott, after a few restorative sips of hot tea, explained that he was an Overseer in what the Witnesses called the Watchtower Society—the herald of the Apocalypse on Earth. If a sect was—by standard definition—small, then the WTS had long since exceeded the standard. Raszer knew that in many nations of the West, it was the second-largest religious denomination. Endicott's designation made him an elder of the church, but even the elders were obliged to hawk the *Watchtower* and *Awake!*, and the fellow asserted he'd knocked on every door on Whitley Terrace on his way up the hill, sowing seeds of faith as he aimed for his destination. It was—to Raszer—clear that his guest was in a highly agitated state, and possibly not at all well.

"Your daughter," Raszer asked. "Is she also a church member?"

Endicott winced and wrapped his shaky hands around the teacup for warmth.

"She . . . was raised at my knee in the Kingdom Hall," he replied. "There never was a more pious little girl, or a better daughter."

"And Katy's mother?"

"Left us when Katy was six," Endicott replied, with more than a trace of bitterness. "It was for the best. She was a whore." From the corner of his eye, Raszer saw Monica lift her pen from the legal pad, not in shock as much as out of curiosity. In the background and just out of sight, Brigit slid down the hallway doorjamb and parked herself on the threshold, all ears.

"So you brought up Katy on your own?" Raszer continued.

"Myself and the Elders," the old man replied. "And there were *good* women in the congregation who helped when she came of age and became a pioneer. She was accepted into the Little Flock when she was thirteen."

"The Little Flock," Raszer repeated, rifling through his mental files. "Those are the folks bound for heaven after Armageddon, right? The anointed class . . . "

"You've studied our faith, Mr. Raszer?" Endicott raised an eyebrow.

"Any faith with twenty-two million subscribers worldwide is worth studying, wouldn't you say? Faith's too important to be left to the preachers. What *motivates* it is what drives my work . . . especially when that motivation is suspect."

"Do you judge our motivation suspect, Mr. Raszer?" Endicott asked with a glare.

"I don't judge, Mr. Endicott. That would only get in the way. I start from the presumption that people need to believe, and as long as what they get back doesn't harm or bankrupt them, I'm fine with it. But I do question, and I think it's only reasonable to question a gospel that allows only 144,000 privileged souls a berth in heaven. Those odds would make even a high roller cool his dice."

"Perhaps," said Endicott. "But look around this abode of Satan, Mr. Raszer. Can you honestly say that more than one in four million deserves paradise?"

"I've never doubted the Devil's reach, Mr. Endicott. I just don't happen to think that God assigns quotas for salvation." He tapped his fingers on the table. "But that's beside the point."

"Yes," said Endicott. "If I were looking for a man of my own kind, I wouldn't be in Hollywood. I'm looking for someone who understands . . . the other side."

"Right," said Raszer. "Let's talk about your daughter. How long has she been missing?"

"As the police in Azusa have it, she was last seen on this earth on February first of last year. But she was lost to me long before that."

"We'll talk about that," said Raszer. "But let's get some basics first. Azusa—that's a fair distance. Is that where you—and Katy—live as well?"

"Yes. For nineteen of her twenty years. Our lives revolve around the Kingdom Hall. Hollywood is a fifty-minute bus ride away. Not so very far, but then, in three decades I've not had cause to descend to this . . . gutter. Not until now."

"Well, at least we've had rain to wash the garbage away," said Raszer, neither expecting nor getting a smile. "Tell me about the physical circumstances of Katy's disappearance. Were there others involved—a boyfriend, girlfriend? Did she pack a bag, leave a note? Is foul play suspected? Tell me what the police know."

At that prompting, Silas Endicott remembered to remove his hat, perhaps moved to courtesy by the gravity of what he was about to relate. He set it before him on the table, maintaining a tight grip on the brim. Raszer read the gesture as playing for time, and possibly also as that of a man who feared his daughter was dead.

"She was up in San Gabriel Canyon," he began, his head lowered. "On a fire road. An abandoned dance hall from one of those resorts they built back in the 1920s."

"Up there past the Morris Dam, right? On the way to Crystal Lake."

"On the east fork of the river," Endicott said. "Closed down years ago because of the mudslides, but the kids . . . that never stops them. They were having—what do they call it when they dance all night, like pagans? All those drugs, all that depravity."

"A rave," said Raszer. "At least, they did in the '90s." Uneasiness fell over him like a toxic dew. "I remember this story," he said. "I was on a case, not paying much attention to the news, but I remember. Kids were hurt. How did Katy fit in?"

Raszer was suddenly aware of a tremor, like that immediately preceding an earthquake. Instinctively, he glanced up at the overhead lamp to see if it was shaking, then to Brigit, whose toes were visible just inside the hallway, and finally to Monica, whose eyes directed him back to the table and to Silas Endicott's hands. The source of vibration was in the old man's breast, transferred through his arms to the solid oak.

"She'd fallen in with a bad crowd, Mr. Raszer, but why, and by whom, she was taken is not clear." Endicott's voice thickened with a mixture of grief, shame, and rage. "The boy who witnessed it was high on pills, and whatever he saw must have . . . " Endicott released his grip on the brim of his hat and folded his hands in a moment's silent prayer. After that, he spoke with odd, third-person detachment.

"Katy left the dance hall with four boys. It was cold up there—the altitude is about thirty-six hundred feet—but she didn't have a coat on." He stared blankly, right past Raszer's left shoulder. "One of the boys was the witness. The other three were animals. They tempted her, plied her with liquor. Lured her up the road to an old Dodge convertible. Told her they had pills in the trunk. Then they . . . they—"

Monica cleared her throat.

"I understand," said Raszer. "Did she manage to escape?"

"No. Not . . . in the way you are thinking. The fourth boy, the one who gave the story to the police, backed out. He ran into the woods while the others pinned her on the trunk. He testified that while the first boy was assaulting her, a black car came up on the left and stopped. It came out of nowhere, he said. Out of the fog. Three men in dark business suits got out. One of them pulled the boy off her; another picked up Katy and tossed her into the backseat. He stayed with her. The other men threw the boys against the trunk and . . . snapped their necks. One, two, *three*." Now, finally, Raszer's unexpected guest looked him in the eye. "I don't know, Mr. Raszer, if my daughter met with avenging angels or with a fate even worse than what those hooligans had in mind."

"And the boy, the witness . . . was he able to describe her abductors, or rescuers, or whatever they were?"

"All he could or would say was that they wore dark suits and had dark hair. For all intents, they were without faces."

"What about voices?" Raszer asked. "Accents, a foreign language?"

"No. They didn't speak."

"Any indication whatsoever that Katy knew them?"

"The boy couldn't say. It happened too fast."

"And the car? I don't suppose he got a plate, but what about make and model?"

"It was a Lincoln Continental," said Endicott.

"A Lincoln. On a fire road at thirty-six hundred feet."

"The police have nothing. Nothing . . . after a full year. My daughter is a face on a milk carton."

Raszer squinted, a habit whenever something didn't fit. The tic, along with his tight-lipped smile, lapis lazuli eyes, and a certain impishness of face, accounted for the fact that even strangers sometimes mentioned his resemblance to Steve McQueen.

"If this were solely an abduction," he said, "that wouldn't surprise me. L.A. County has the most undernourished investigative force in the country. If your child is missing, you might as well be in Somalia. But we're also talking about a rape and a triple homicide." He turned to Monica. "What's been on the wires over the past year? Why hasn't there been more noise about this story?"

Monica leaned forward, a strand of streaked hair falling over her right eye. She blew it away with a practiced blast. "The boys' parents"—she glanced at Endicott—"if I'm not mistaken, Mr. Endicott, were all Jehovah's Witnesses. The local press, even Fox News, camped out up there for a few weeks, but they got nothing. No interviews, no public statements. And because the assailants were . . . deceased, there were no charges filed, except against the organizers of the rave."

Endicott kept his eyes on Raszer. "We are a close community," he said quietly, "and we take care of our own. This—this event—was a grievous wound. None of us wished to pour salt in it. The Overseers addressed the matter. Twelve young men and women were disfellowshipped, along with two parents who had prior knowledge of the . . . the *rave*, and said nothing. The bodies of the three . . . the bodies were cremated. We closed the books and we closed our doors, and waited for the plague to pass over." He sighed deeply and clutched his chest. "The only one left outside was my Katy."

The blood was quickly draining from Silas Endicott's face. Raszer telegraphed a look of concern to Monica and, after a beat, pushed back from the table.

"Let's get some air, Mr. Endicott," he said, standing. "Bring your tea. I have a deck out back. Covered." He came around the table and took Endicott's arm, and this time, the proud man did not refuse the assistance. "Brij," he called to his daughter as they reached the door. "How about you and Monica heat up that minestrone? Maybe our guest would like something warm."

They had been on the deck for fifteen minutes before Raszer returned to the subject of Katy Endicott. They stood at the rail, at first in silence, then talking about the ceaseless rain, the local flora, and finally about Silas Endicott's faith. About the Witnesses' rejection of the Trinity, their strange insistence that Christ had been put to death, not on a cross, but on a single upright beam known as a *stauros*. About the sect's proscription against the mixing of blood, and hence its members' refusal of blood transfusions, even in critical circumstances. Raszer was curious about all these things, and considered them as important to the case as forensic evidence. Endicott addressed his queries without the slightest hint of doubt, and all the while could not take his eyes off the bare-breasted, wild-eyed statuary in Raszer's garden.

Brigit came out, bearing a tray with two steaming mugs of homemade minestrone. Endicott declined, but Raszer spooned into his with relish. His appetite, dormant for weeks, had returned with the prospect of a mission. After keeping a respectful silence while Raszer ate, Endicott posed a question of his own, though it had more the tone of a challenge.

"And you, Mr. Raszer," he asked, "are you a man of faith?"

Raszer set his mug on the rail and lit a cigarette. "If you're asking whether or not I believe in God," he said, directing a bluish stream of smoke toward Aphrodite, "the short answer is yes."

"Do you believe in the power of Christ to lift mankind from its sin?"

"I believe that if men followed Christ's example, sin wouldn't be an issue."

"Then why," Endicott pressed, sweeping his arm out over the garden, "do you surround yourself with pagan idols?"

"Because, Mr. Endicott, every one of these images is a testament to man's itch for the divine. And by the way," he added, aiming a finger east, "I think the Virgin over there in the eggplant patch might take offense at your, uh, characterization."

"And this 'itch' is something you can scratch with just any stick?"

"No, sir. Although I do think that faith of any stripe—even misplaced faith—opens doors that are closed to the faithless. That's why I tread lightly on people's beliefs. I only step hard when risk exceeds benefit." Raszer rested his forearms on the rail and watched the smoke carried skyward on the updraft. "I've been thinking on this for a while, and there are just four tests I hold any church to."

Endicott folded his hands. "May I hear them?"

"It shouldn't charge admission. It shouldn't ask you to give up anything but your vanity. It shouldn't substitute one authoritarian regime for another."

"And the fourth test?"

"That's the hardest," said Raszer. "I haven't found a church that can pass it yet—not when it comes down to the bone. If anything were ever to happen to my own daughter, Mr. Endicott, I'd want my church to tell me why I should keep living."

Moments passed, with only the drumming of the rain to mark time. Raszer's cigarette burned down to the flesh between his fingers, and he didn't budge. The blue jay reappeared with a new beakful of straw, and Silas Endicott spoke his piece.

"If you think you can help me find my Katy, Mr. Raszer, I'd like to hire you."

"Okay," said Raszer, flicking away the cigarette. "Good. I assume you won't mind my talking to the police, and to the boy who witnessed her abduction."

"Of course not. But I'm not sure what more you'll learn."

"I'd like to speak with the parents of Katy's assailants. And with the other elders of the church."

"I don't know, Mr. Raszer. I—"

"Tell me, Mr. Endicott: You said Katy was a pious girl. But she was also nineteen. Was there a point—before all this happened, before the rave—maybe even some years back, when she started to question the faith . . . and your authority?"

Endicott drew a labored breath. "I guess it happened longer ago than I like to admit. She was led astray." He shuddered again, and a pungent odor came off him. "Katy has a sister. Ruthie. A girl I can't accept as seed of my seed; her mother's girl. When Constance, my wife, left, Ruthie went with her. But, like all malignancies, she returned in time. Wanted Katy to go live in Taos. That's where they'd . . . *settled*."

"And Katy was drawn to her?"

"Like a moth to a flame. She'd just turned seventeen. The age of Eve. Katy was strong, but not strong enough. Ruthie wouldn't leave her be. She'd moved into a trailer up in Burro Canyon with a couple of apostate boys. Older boys. They were there that night. They were the ones who . . . " He grimaced. "May their black souls never rest."

"Ruthie's trailer mates were Katy's assailants?" Raszer asked, making no effort to conceal his surprise. Endicott offered only a grunt. "So . . . how long did all this—"

"For a summer," said Endicott. "At first, it was just Ruthie, showing up on the porch with her face pierced and her stomach bare, like some sweet sickness Katy couldn't help but succumb to. I chased her away, banished her, but it didn't stop. Next time she showed up, Henry Lee was with her."

"Henry Lee?" Raszer asked.

Endicott passed over the query. "Katy ran out before I could stop her. Came home late. Drunk. I took her before the Overseers that Sunday. They renounced Ruthie and sanctioned Katy. We tried to build a wall around her . . . "

"And that made the forbidden fruit even more tempting," Raszer said.

"Katy never argued, never raised her voice against me. But I knew her faith was gone. Ruthie'd punched holes in it. She came around one night with both boys. Henry Lee, and that . . . that miscreant. It was a Friday in August. I'd gone out to minister to one of our families and left Katy alone. The four of them went off on two motorcycles, got high on cheap wine and pills, and broke into the Kingdom Hall."

The wind from the northeast, the very wind that crests the San Gabriels above Azusa and careens down through boulder-strewn arroyos into the L.A. Basin, had begun to drive the rain onto the deck. Raszer would have cursed but for his new client.

"Would you like to go back inside?" he asked.

"No," said Endicott. "I want to tell the story and be done with it. They desecrated the hall. To describe everything they did would itself be a blasphemy, but I can tell you this: They painted the walls with occult signs. Signs to invoke Satan to enter our sanctuary. No amount of whitewash will ever erase that sacrilege. They polluted that sacred place with every kind of filth and fornication. I can't account for my daughter's part in this, except to say that she was under some kind of sorcery, God help her . . ."

"Were any photographs taken of the walls?" Raszer asked.

His visitor gripped the railing. "The police . . . have them."

"I'll check those out. Kids pick up these signs and symbols from the Internet. They don't necessarily know what they mean, or what effect they can have. Was there anything else? Anything important?"

"Behind the lectern, they wrote some words on the wall. I pray God they were not Katy's epitaph."

"What were the words?"

"Nothing is true. Everything is permitted."

Raszer pursed his lips. After a moment he asked, "What was the upshot?"

"By the time the crime was discovered, Ruthie was gone. Back to Taos, I suppose. Katy confessed—not to me, but to another girl from the congregation—and then it all came out. An assembly of the elders was convened to weigh on Katy's disfellowship. There is no harsher sanction. Disfellowship is living damnation. I recused myself so that I could stand witness for my daughter, because I couldn't accept that the little girl I'd raised was beyond redemption. The Overseers granted me a year to restore her to the fold. On her eighteenth birthday, Katy was taken again into the hall. For a year, we were like . . . like Lazarus and Martha. My Katy returned! And then, and then . . . "

"She backslid," Raszer surmised. "The two boys, the ones you say assaulted Katy at the rave . . . were they prosecuted for their part in the Kingdom Hall vandalism?"

"To my everlasting regret," Endicott replied. "No. The Elders thought it best to handle them through the families, through our own church law. Had we left it to the police, they might have been in a prison cell on that awful night."

"About that night," Raszer said, "the night of Katy's abduction. You said that Ruthie and the boys had gotten Katy into drugs. The whole picture: the Lincoln Continental, the business suits, the style of execution . . . is there any evidence to suggest a drug deal gone bad? That Katy was taken as some kind of . . . payment?"

"If she was, and she is paying off their debt, I'm afraid she's already damned."

"Not if she's been taken beyond the range of her free will, Mr. Endicott. We like to think our souls are sovereign, but I've seen strong people lose themselves in the presence of power, and a girl like Katy, raised not to question authority—"

Raszer stopped midsentence. Something was wrong.

Endicott turned from the rail and stumbled forward, coughing up a throatful of mucus and bile. Raszer offered an arm, but the man charged past, staggering down the steps into the midst of the statuary. He stopped in front of the goddess Cybele.

"Mr. Endicott?" Raszer called out. "Silas?" He descended into the garden. The black sky suddenly dropped a payload of nickel-size hailstones; they ricocheted like bullets off the stone. Endicott stretched his fingers toward the goddess, then withdrew. With her right hand, she offered a carved pomegranate, indistinguishable in size and shape from an apple. In her cupped left palm, Brigit had placed a little black "moon rock" Raszer had once bought for her at the Griffith Observatory. It was the rock that held Endicott's stare. He spun around, his index finger raised, then fell like a tree, knocking Raszer off his feet and pinning him to the wet ground.

After a moment, Raszer gingerly rolled Silas Endicott onto his back. There was no reflex, only the wheezing exhalation of foul breath as his lungs emptied. No pulse, either. To all appearances, the old man had dropped stone dead.

THREE

BRIGIT HADN'T SCREAMED, but the sight of a corpse in her father's garden, especially one as formidable in death as Silas Endicott's, had to have marked her. Raszer watched for signs of delayed effect. As he drove her to LAX the following morning to be returned to her mother's house, to school, to her "normal" life in Connecticut, he decided to face the matter head-on.

"I can still remember seeing my first dead person," he said. "How weird it was. It was my grandpa, my mother's dad. One minute he was there, alive, beside me and somehow *inside* me, too. The next minute he was gone, and there was an emptiness in me. That part of me that was him had died."

"Yeah, but it wasn't like that with Mr. Endicott," she said.

"How do you mean, honey?"

"It was like he was already gone."

"I think I know what you mean," said Raszer. "He was—"

"No," she said. "Not that."

Raszer gave his daughter a sidelong glance. "Not what, muffin?" He knew what she'd meant, because he knew that *she'd* known what *he* meant, and that was the way they had communicated almost from her infancy. He wanted to hear her say it anyway. It was important, he thought, not to use telepathy as a substitute for expression.

"Not that he was sick and all," she replied. "It was more like he was a ghost. Like he actually died a long time ago."

"I think his people would have mentioned that detail when I called them at the Kingdom Hall in Azusa."

"Maybe," she said. "Or maybe they're just used to it."

"You mean, like 'Old Silas is up to his tricks again, haunting the streets of Hollywood . . . searching for his lost Katy'?"

"Something like that, yeah."

She wasn't yet on the plane, and Raszer already missed her. He had to swallow hard. He hated returning Brigit to his ex-wife, hated the sheltered life she was going back to, hated the ache she left behind.

"Well," he said, exiting at Sepulveda for the airport, "it's an intriguing idea. And I don't dismiss the notion that a man's passion can outlive his body. But we did see the paramedics carry him out, didn't we?"

"Yeah, I guess we did," she said, squinting in imitation of her father. "But still—"

"I know. That's what I was trying to say before. Death doesn't make sense. The thing that makes us alive can't just all of a sudden go away, can it?"

"Do you think Mr. Endicott was a good man, Daddy?"

Raszer sighed unconsciously. He was turning onto the Departures ramp. "I think . . . he was as good a man as someone who's been in a box all his life can be. Maybe didn't quite see the whole picture. 'A foolish consistency is the hobgoblin of little minds.'"

"Who said that?" she asked.

"Emerson, I think."

She repeated the sentence soundlessly, then announced, "I don't ever want a hobgoblin in *my* mind, Daddy."

Raszer laughed and reached over to yank her hair as they entered the parking structure. "I don't think you need to worry about that, honey. Anyhow, I do believe that Mr. Endicott loved his daughter, and that's good enough for me."

"Are you going to find her, Daddy?"

"Well, I'm going to see about that this afternoon. I'm going to speak with the other men at his church, and see what they want me to do."

"I hope you do, Daddy."

Before they left the car, Brigit opened his glove compartment and fished around until she found his Swiss Army knife, the one with the corkscrew and the awl and the scissors, and then she snipped off half an inch of hair and gave it to him. It was something she did each time she left, and each time, he put it into his wallet.

"Daddy?"

"Uh-huh?"

"If you'd died when I was little, or if I had . . . would we still be having these talks?"

"I know we would, baby," he said. "You're my cosmic muffin."

✦ ✦ ✦

RASZER WAS DUE at the Kingdom Hall in Azusa at one o'clock, but before that, he had an appointment in Hollywood with one of the women who, along with Monica and a few others located in various parts of the world, formed his psychic shield. His work required such a profound and potentially risky displacement of personality that he felt secure only by letting each of them know where he might be headed—only when they laid their hands on him in affirmation of his true name. Technically, Hildegarde Schoeppe was his shrink, but she was more than that, and he was anxious to get her read on his present state of readiness to take on an assignment. He'd not been feeling especially fit lately.

The drive from LAX back into town was distinguished by just one thing, which occurred only at this time of year or in the rare event of a Santa Ana condition. At a certain point along the northbound Harbor Freeway, if the clouds had lifted and the smog had flown, the San Gabriel Mountains rose up, bushy and wild and capped with the virgin snow that was L.A.'s only natural water source (not counting the current deluge). They were all the more epic for their nearness to a big city, and when they appeared, Raszer's spirit soared up to the ragged summits and returned as clean as freshly laundered white linen. Today, however, he was not to be graced. The downpour had stopped for just long enough to ease his worries about Brigit's flight, but was now back with renewed intensity. He couldn't even make out the Hollywood Hills. And so he exited the 101 at Gower and headed up Beachwood Canyon Drive in a surly mood, more than ready for Hildegarde's ministrations.

Beachwood Canyon was L.A.'s richest redoubt of Hollywoodland history, and maybe its best-kept secret. Other enclaves in the hills had their own cloistered charms, but only Beachwood remained as the mad barons of old Hollywood had designed it. The notorious Madame Blavatsky, nineteenth-century doyenne of the occult arts, had built her Xanadu there, as had Charlie Chaplin, and no less a connoisseur of the transcendent than Aldous Huxley had chosen to end his years in a home beneath the HOLLYWOOD sign, his bloodstream surging with a farewell dose of pharmaceutical LSD.

The whole length of Beachwood Drive was the town at its most alluring, alchemical and absurd. The flats at the bottom, where it spilled onto Franklin Avenue, were still resolutely tawdry, despite the city's recent cleanup campaign. Shopping-cart people and saucer-eyed waifs shared the sidewalk with aged B-movie actresses who, when they ventured out, still wore red lipstick and dressed like vamps. A few blocks up, you saw them as they had been, coming out of stilt-legged apartment buildings with names like the Casbah or La Paloma, late for their auditions: would-be starlets with ironed hair and a willingness to ruin their reputations in order to make them. It was on a cul-de-sac just off Beachwood that Jack Warner was rumored to have kept a "dormitory" for his studio's stable of nubile talent. Nearby were the allegedly haunted barracks in which the blacklisted Hollywood Ten had held their clandestine meetings.

The style of the architecture was equal parts Barcelona, Tangier, and Mitteleuropa, and with the steep ascent, the houses became grander and stranger, though not ostentatious. Raszer's pulse still throbbed with the climb, for this causeway of eager flesh and yearning spirit, leading to nowhere but the never-land of Old Mulholland Drive, was his Hollywood, a place as indecipherable as a code in cuneiform.

Hildegarde leased office space in an ersatz Tudor building adjacent to the Annie Besant Lodge, a tiny, whitewashed chapel dedicated to the memory of old Hollywood's patron theosophist. She claimed that her proximity to the shrine was conducive to the sort of therapy she offered, which was basically Jungian depth psychology with a pinch of mandrake root and eye of newt. She greeted Raszer with a hug and a once-over.

"Good morning, Stephan," she said, a trace of German still evident in the *Good*. "I don't often see you at this time of day. You look . . . foggy."

"It's the rain," he said, taking his familiar chair near the casement window. "I can't seem to wake up."

She carried over an embroidered ottoman, set it down in front of him, and parked herself near enough that they were almost knee to knee. Hildegarde was not one for clinical detachment. She was a handsome woman of about fifty, with ash-blond hair and a Nordic build. She was not Raszer's physical type, which had kept him on the safe side of the doctor-patient divide, but plenty attractive enough to flirt with. Raszer would no more have engaged a male psychoanalyst than he would have hired a male escort.

"You look ready for Valhalla," he said. "Like you spent the night throwing thunderbolts with Thor. Maybe we should forget the session and fly to Cabo."

"I have never known such a sweet-hearted man," she said, nailing him with a pair of piercingly blue eyes, "who takes such great pleasure in being a bad boy."

"It's my upbringing, doc. My mother operated a bordello."

"Right. So, how are we feeling these days? Still in a funk?"

"I'd rather you didn't use that bedside *we* unless you're planning on tucking me in tonight."

"With you, Stephan," she said, "the *we* is more than manner. You are the most incorrigible Gemini on my roster, and I say that as one who isn't big on astrology."

"Yeah, well . . . " he mumbled, and thought for a moment about how he really was feeling. "I had to take Brigit to the airport this morning."

"Ah," she said, and bit her lip in sympathy. "How was it?"

"I got into a scrap with the airport security guy," he said. "The bastard wouldn't let me go to the gate with her."

"Nobody gets to go to the gate anymore, Stephan. You know that. Why did you start a fight you knew you couldn't win?"

He stared out the window. The rain was making tributaries on the roof of the Annie Besant Lodge. "It's the whole scene, I guess. It raises my hackles. The armed guards, the wary ticket agents. It's too much like the first time. Once they take her to the other side, she's not in my life anymore, and I feel like I'm busted all over again."

"But she is in your life. Be glad for that. And listen—" She leaned forward and touched his knee. "If I know anything about the human mind, I know that Brigit no longer carries a conscious awareness of having been forcibly removed from your house. I've been with her. I've analyzed her. I know she doesn't."

"You mean she's sublimated it," he said. "But it's still there."

"Of course it's still there," said Hildegarde. "Her bond with you wouldn't be so strong if her separation from you hadn't been so painful."

"She saw a man drop dead at my house yesterday."

"Oh? Who was he?"

"I think he's my new client," said Raszer.

"Aha," she said. "Well, if you have a dead man for a client, I think you had better tell me about the case."

On the wall behind her was a framed black-and-white photograph of C. G. Jung, the Swiss psychoanalyst and onetime protégé of Freud who'd broken with his mentor over fundamental questions about the roots of madness. Beneath the photograph was a plaque bearing a Latin inscription attributed to him. In translation, it read: SUMMONED OR NOT SUMMONED, GOD IS PRESENT. Raszer glanced at the plaque, then back to Dr. Schoeppe.

"What do you suppose old C. G. would have had to say about a small black rock in the palm of the goddess Cybele?"

"You're being cryptic, Stephan. Explain."

"The dead man came to my house to ask for help finding his daughter, who was apparently abducted from a mountain rave a year ago by three men in a black limo. She was raised as a Jehovah's Witness, but she'd fallen in with a bad crowd—renegade boys from the church. There's a sister from Taos involved—allegedly the catalyst."

"And the girls' mother . . . where is she?"

"Presumably also in Taos. Probably waiting for the saucers to come."

"I love Taos," said Hildegarde.

"Me too," said Raszer. "But it does tend to attract people looking for an exit."

"And the black rock?"

"You've been to my house. Out back, there's a statue of the Phrygian mother goddess, Cybele, that I had shipped from a flea market in Paris. One of her palms is open, like this, and Brigit—scamp that she is—saw fit to put a moon rock in it."

"A moon rock."

"Yeah," said Raszer. "They sold like hotcakes for a while. Supposedly fragments brought back from the moon landing. Probably about as authentic as medieval saints' relics, but from the way old Silas Endicott looked at it just before he keeled over, you'd have thought it came from the seventh circle of hell."

She clapped her hands together and stood up. "Let's take a look," she said, and went to a floor-to-ceiling bookshelf. She pulled out Jung's *Man And His Symbols*, flipped through it, and found nothing. In a lesser-known text, however, she found a cross-reference under *Cybele* and read, "'The *baitylos*, a black meteorite associated with the cults of Cybele and Attis and purportedly found on the summit of Mt. Ida in Pessinus.'" Hildegarde glanced up from the page. "Pessinus . . . that's in Turkey, isn't it?"

"Right. That's where Cybele's cult peaked. Sometime around the seventh century BC, though she had a revival in Rome in the early Christian period. What else?"

"That's about it—not much to go on, is it?" She licked a long-nailed finger and flipped a page. "Hang on . . . here's something. 'By way of both its physical appearance and etymological association with Cybele, also known as Kybele,

Kubaba, and Kube, the sacred stone is thought by some to be mythologically related to the Black Stone in the Ka'ba of Mecca, object of Muslim pilgrimage, and to the Thracian word for *dice*.'"

"That's a twisted trail, all right," said Raszer. "*Kube*. Cube. *Dice*. Islam?

"The Ka'ba was a pagan shrine long before Mohammed consecrated it."

Raszer squinted. "Yeah, you're right about that. Well, any sort of paganism would've given the old man tremors, but what are the odds he knew any of this?"

"I guess that's for you to find out, Stephan," she said. "Maybe the kids his daughter fell in with were into some kind of ceremonial magic. Maybe the sister . . . left something similar behind." She replaced the book, then returned to her seat. "The important question is what all this means for you. What you're going to make of it."

"I dunno. I'm going up to Azusa to see the Elders of the church—the JWs—this afternoon. They work as a family. They may want me to pursue this, or they may not."

"That's not quite what I meant, Stephan," said Hildegarde.

"I know that's not what you meant," said Raszer. "I'm stalling."

"In light of your present state, you may be tempted to see this thing as a chance for personal redemption, dropping out of the blue as it did."

"The sky hasn't been blue for weeks," said Raszer.

"Don't play," she said, crinkling her brow. "The thing is, not everyone who is lost can be found, or wants to be. We do what we must, as best we can, and accept that not all riddles yield to our wits—not all mysteries are fathomable."

Raszer suddenly felt moved to break into song. "*Ya do what you must, and ya do it well*," he chanted nasally. "Now, there's a synchronicity."

"I don't understand," said Hildegarde.

"Buckets of Rain," he explained, nodding to the window. "It's a Dylan tune."

"Ah," she said. "But you do know what I mean."

"Yes, but *human* mysteries—I think—have their roots in some kind of detour, some hidden variable that alters what otherwise would have been a person's route. If you can work your way back to that detour, you can get to the bottom of things."

"Sometimes, yes," she said. "Otherwise, I don't suppose there'd be much use for my profession, either. Just try to give yourself a little slack. You redeemed your lost years the first time you helped someone in trouble. God does not subscribe to the Hollywood dictum that you're only as good as your last picture."

"I'm not so sure about that," said Raszer. "God's a tough critic."

"I think you're speaking of someone closer to home," she said, and banked a glance off the old scars on his wrists.

"Don't accuse me of 'ego inflation,'" he said, unconsciously massaging his right wrist. "I've never bought into the 'I am God' thing."

"No, Stephan," she said. "You've strapped your ego into service of the Grail, which is noble in a medieval sort of way, but it's still very much exposed. You take failure badly, and that stunts your chances of ever putting the cup to your own lips."

"Maybe," said Raszer.

She let him sit in silence while the rain played *rat-tat-tat-tat*. Now he couldn't get the Dylan tune out of his head.

"Tell me something, Hildegarde," he said. "What gives a man a sense of worth?"

"If you're talking about worth in the *world*," she said, "there is no universal. For you, I'd say it's the belief that your actions are *effective* . . . in an almost magical way."

He got up and walked to the window. Once again, the rain was falling hard enough to make sheets. "I had a seven-year streak," he said quietly. "All that time, I felt her breath on my shoulder, her hand guiding my wrist. But now . . . "

Raszer turned to Hildegarde, and the look in his eyes was very much like that of a man in love. "For me, being worthy is knowing that I'm *Her* man."

Hildegarde smiled. "You're speaking of your Lady. Your dark muse. The one who gave you the light. The one who came to you in your dreams when you were a boy."

"How many men have you treated who lost their virginity to a succubus?"

"Only one who's fully functional."

"I pushed her out of my head for almost twenty years," he said. "It scared me that much. Until that day in the hospital. She's the one who brought Brigit back. She's the one who gave me my . . . "

"Your calling. And now you feel she's deserted you."

Raszer didn't answer, and his therapist did not press.

"I'll make you some root tea," she said, standing, and touched his shoulder lightly. "If you're going to face the Elders, you'd best be wide awake."

"Ah," said Raszer. "The famous root tea." He turned back to the window and directed his gaze past the eaves of the Annie Besant Lodge to the wet street, where at that moment a sleek black Lincoln was prowling up Beachwood Drive to where the money lived. *Don't be crazy*, he thought, shaking off a shiver. *It could be any movie star*.

FOUR

"Azusa . . . wow," Raszer said aloud, as he drove past paint-starved little houses displaying Uncle Sam's colors and thought, *I could be in Chattanooga . . . or heading up into the Blue Ridge from Front Royal, Virginia.*

He was not in either of those places, but could be forgiven for having a weird sense of geographical dislocation. Raszer was a scant forty minutes out of Hollywood by way of the eastbound 210 freeway, but no drifter left here without bearings would have recognized the place as California. Azusa is part of the Los Angeles no one knows.

The weather abetted his disorientation. The foothills were ghosted with mist and heavy with new growth. Raszer had spent time in San Gabriel Canyon, had even fished here once with a girlfriend, but the skies had been brilliant blue and the mountains their usual toasted brown. He'd stopped for lunch in Azusa and noticed its Rotary Club retro look, but that was in summer. Now, after three weeks of rain, the little shopping district had the storm-swept air of an Oregon fishing village; the whole town looked as if it were awaiting fulfillment of a biblical prophecy. On every streetlight, posted like yard-sale signs, were handwritten placards bearing the names of the town's war dead. The names were mostly Hispanic: RODRIGUEZ, DOMINGUEZ, ESCOBAR. And when the signs weren't advertising patriotism, they were advertising religion.

Near the intersection of Foothill and Alosta, Raszer pulled up to the curb to consult a weathered sign of the sort once erected at the entrance to all American small towns. Its painted centerpiece read: WELCOME TO AZUSA—GATEWAY TO THE SAN GABRIELS. On the two-by-four crosspiece above it was written an invitation to all comers: WORSHIP AT THE CHURCH OF YOUR CHOICE. On either side, whitewashed pickets hung from rusted chains and pointed the way to the sanctuaries, among them the Kingdom Hall.

Rising to the north, like the last standing wall of Jericho, was the big screen of the abandoned Foothill Drive-In Theater. No Wal-Mart or Costco had yet claimed the real estate occupied by its sprawling lot, still marked off by the posts that had once done double duty as loudspeaker cradles and soft-drink holders. *It's still 1962 here*, Raszer thought. He'd been born in a town that looked like this.

As he'd expected, the Kingdom Hall was nowhere near as majestic as its name, recognizable as a church only by its stark, white-framed exterior and a flight of concrete steps leading to a double-door entrance. It took a few moments for Raszer to apprehend the incompleteness. The roof came to the usual apex, but there was no crucifix. The absence of the cross, with its associations of blood sacrifice and redemption, made the place feel something other than canonically Christian, and in fact, the Witnesses departed boldly from scripture on this score. According to them, Jesus hadn't assumed his heavenly throne until 1914, when the New System of Things was declared. Raszer stepped from the car, crushed out his cigarette, and crossed the wet street.

Entering the unlocked hall's foyer, Raszer found himself in darkness. The door shut behind him with an echo off polished floorboards and hard surfaces, barely visible as gray half forms in the empty meeting room. This was the very space allegedly trashed by Katy Endicott and her pals, and though it wasn't hard to feel for her father's shame, something at Raszer's core registered all the reasons a teenager might feel driven to raise hell here. It was a cold, utterly humorless room. In place of the fragrance of incense was the caustic odor of Pine-Sol. In place of music, there was only the rain.

Yellow light spilled from behind a half-open door in the rear of the hall. Through the crack, Raszer glimpsed an old Frigidaire, the droning of its compressor masking the sound of mingled male voices until he'd drawn very close. Suddenly, the door opened fully, and on its threshold stood a silhouetted figure as short as Silas Endicott had been tall. It registered almost as a child until it spoke as a somewhat tightly wound man.

"Mr. Raszer?" he said. Now the voice seemed almost thrown.

"That's me," Raszer answered. "Am I early?"

"No," said the man. "Please join us. We've just been discussing what little is known of your work."

"Well," said Raszer, stepping into the kitchen, "I'll try to fill in some blanks."

The short man offered his hand and said, "My name is Amos Leach. I'm Presiding Overseer of this congregation." He had a common, gray face, the impression of which was made indelible only by a Reagan-esque cockscomb of reddish hair that came to a widow's peak midway down his forehead. He wore a plaid shirt and dark sans-a-belt trousers. The trousers' vintage was all that recalled Silas Endicott's sartorial antiquarianism. Otherwise, Leach and the other Elders might have been a group of merchants meeting to discuss the pressing need for a stoplight on Main Street.

There were six men seated at the Formica-topped table, one chair at the far end conspicuously empty. Raszer was introduced around and invited to take the folding chair nearest the door, directly in the path of a chilly draft from the Hall.

"This is Jim Bidwell," said Leach, placing his hands on the broad shoulders of the beefy man on Raszer's left. "He'll be taking over Silas's duties as Ministerial Overseer."

"Big shoes to fill," said Jim Bidwell. "Big shoes."

"From what little I saw, Mr. Bidwell," said Raszer, "I'd say you're right about that." He scanned the table. "I'm very sorry for your loss, gentlemen. It must have come as a great shock."

"No," said Leach. "Not in truth. Silas wasn't well. Hadn't been since the, er, desecration two summers ago. I think he died to the world that day." Leach dropped his chin solemnly and the others followed suit, leaving Raszer to ponder his daughter's words. "There is no shame as deep as the shame of a disobedient child."

"Amen to that," said the man on Raszer's right.

"And this," said Leach, following the voice, "is Sam Brown. He's our Ministerial Servant. He runs the office, and he'll be your main contact should we decide to proceed with this, uh, matter."

Sam Brown was a black man in his sixties. He was the only person of color in the group, but it was a small group. As with many evangelical sects, the growth of the Witness flock in recent years was owed in large measure to the blurring of color lines. Raszer sometimes wondered if L.A.'s inevitable armageddon would come down less to a battle between rich and poor than to one between believers and nonbelievers. Amos Leach must have detected just the slightest movement of Raszer's eyebrow, because he felt obliged to say, "We're all servants here, Mr. Raszer. Unlike the world at large, we do not denigrate servitude. Our church is the faithful and discreet slave of the Lord."

"Amen," said Jim Bidwell, and the others nodded their agreement.

Leach took his chair at the end of the table opposite Raszer and laced his stubby fingers together. He cocked his head, thought for a moment, then said, "We thought we ought to ask you, Mr. Raszer . . . are you yourself a Christian?"

"You might do better to ask me," said Raszer, "if I'm a man who can be counted on to keep his faith—and his own counsel."

"And are you?" asked Leach.

"Yes, I am," Raszer affirmed, although something about Amos Leach gave him pause, something off-kilter about the small body and big hair.

"That's good," said Leach. "If we should decide, as a body, to engage your services, we'll need to have your complete discretion. We don't want any headlines."

"You won't get any," said Raszer, having anticipated the concern. "In seven years of work on six continents, with one exception, I haven't generated a single line of copy. I'm not in the Yellow Pages, and whatever's on the Internet is currently being swept clean. I prefer to work very, very quietly, and I don't leave footprints."

"And your fee for finding a missing person?" asked Leach.

"Ordinarily, six thousand a week, plus expenses."

Raszer saw Sam Brown roll his eyes. Jim Bidwell shook his head gravely. Leach looked from man to man, clucked his tongue, and asked, "And how many weeks?"

"Very hard to say," Raszer answered. "Six. Eight. Anyway, I don't waste time."

"I'm afraid Silas didn't leave us that kind of money," Jim Bidwell said.

"Maybe we ought to let the dead bury the dead," said Amos Leach.

"We're the trustees of Silas's legacy," Sam Brown countered. "And we made a—"

Painfully aware of his empty bank account, Raszer adjusted. "I'll drop it to forty-five hundred with a five-week cap. My daughter . . . wants me to find your girl."

"You understand, Mr. Raszer," said Leach, "that we'd expect you to return Katy to her flock . . . spiritually unblemished."

"I don't do reconversions," said Raszer. "Depending on what Katy's been through—and assuming she's alive—she may well want to come back to the fold on her own, and I'll do my level best to correct the effects of any coercion, confinement, or manipulation so that she can make that choice. Despite what you may have read in the press, I'm not for hire as a deprogrammer. Not in the usual sense."

Amos Leach leaned forward, his fingers still knitted. "In *what* sense, then?"

Raszer took note that the Overseer's voice had broken into a higher register.

"Deprogramming, exit counseling—whatever you want to call it—is a little like shock therapy. Effective in the short term, but the problems remain because only the *brain* has been tinkered with. I try to approach my strays as embodied souls who may've wandered off to follow a star but wound up out in the cold. I offer them a coat, and the label on the coat says, '*This is Who I Am, more or less as God made me. This is how I saw the world before anybody told me different.*' Most people are happy to put on the coat once they see how exposed they are. But I won't have it tailor made to fit any particular doctrine or dogma. If I were in that business, Mr. Leach, somebody could just as easily hire me to deprogram your son or daughter."

Sam Brown cleared his throat and broke the tense silence. Amos Leach affected indignation and hammered his entwined fists on the table. "Are you comparing this house of God to a cult, Mr. Raszer?" Midway, his voice broke again.

"No," said Raszer. "I don't use that word much. Belief in a higher purpose gets channeled into all sorts of streams—big and small, clean and polluted. They all go to the sea. The *sea* is what I try to show them." Raszer sat back, and the cold draft hit him.

"What is it, Mr. Leach, that leads you to think Katy Endicott—wherever she may be—might need deprogramming?"

"She left the flock," said Leach. "That speaks for itself, as far as we're concerned."

"You've got an eyewitness who says she was forcibly abducted," said Raszer.

Leach pressed on, as if oblivious to the point. "And those goats up in the canyon she fell in with," Leach replied, "those boys."

"Goats?" Raszer queried.

Jim Bidwell chimed in. "Those who speak against the Witnesses," he said.

"I'm not clear on this," said Raszer. "Those were the same boys who—"

Leach continued his thread: "They were dancing to the Devil's music—"

"Raped her," Raszer finished. "Again, according to your sole eyewitness."

"And there's no doubt in my mind," Leach went on, "that they pawned her off to pay their debt."

Sam Brown spoke up. "I should explain, Mr. Raszer, that we have pondered this matter deeply and come to the conclusion that the, uh, assault on Katy Endicott that night was, if I can put it this way, a kind of send-off. That the boys had already sold her into some sort of white slave ring. Well, that's our theory, anyhow."

"It's not a bad one, Mr. Brown," said Raszer, "as theories go. I want to ask you gentlemen about those boys. Whatever this was, they were also ultimately victims of it. Are their families still members of your congregation?"

Jim Bidwell cleared his throat. "The families—well, they're a bit of a problem right now. Most of them have left us. They stayed on even after two of the boys—the ringleaders—were disfellowshipped a couple years back, but after the killings, they turned around and blamed it on the church."

"So there's a real history here," said Raszer. "Why were they disfellowshipped?"

Amos Leach answered. "Against the command of the Elders," he said, "they enlisted in the Army and went off to fight in Iraq."

Raszer blinked. "And that was enough to get them booted out?"

"We're good citizens," said Leach, "but we believe that there's only one nation worth fighting and dying for, and that is the Theocratic Nation of Christ, which was established in 1914 to prepare our flock for the End Times."

"The world belongs to Satan, Mr. Raszer," said Bidwell. "Just look around. Look at any meeting of the UN General Assembly."

Raszer ignored the political contradictions. He had to stay on point or risk losing them, and he was now far too intrigued to chance that. "And when the boys came back from the war?"

"They were worse than before," said Leach. "That's when the real trouble began. That's when they took that trailer up into the canyon and started luring the other kids there. You see, we've got some protection from Satan's power in our communities. We learned a long time ago how to circle the wagons. But once you venture out into the world, you're at his disposal, and once you've been to Babylon, you carry his disease."

"It wasn't too long after they got back," said Sam Brown, "that Ruthie—she's Katy's older sister by a year—showed up. Her and the oldest boy, Johnny

Horn, they'd been sweethearts before Silas and Connie—that's Silas's wife—split up."

"Okay," said Raszer, "I get it. I'm going to need the names and addresses of all four boys' families—the three who were killed and the witness—and the same for Katy and Ruthie's mother. I'm assuming you've got them."

"We can give you the Strunk family," said Amos Leach. "And we'll give you the last known address for Silas's wife. But the other families, no."

"Then I'll have to get them from the police," said Raszer. "That is, if you want me to take this case."

Leach smiled, and Raszer felt sure he saw his eyes flash briefly. "I'm sure you'll manage to get what you need, Mr. Raszer. And Sam here will assist you in every way."

"Then we have an agreement?" Raszer asked.

"We'll take it under consideration," said Leach. "If you want my opinion, this is good money after bad. Silas's legacy could've been a new Hall. But let's say we have an agreement on principal. We'd sure like to see Katy redeemed."

"I will find her," said Raszer, "if you want me to." Now it was his turn to lace his fingers in symmetry with Amos Leach's. "But at the risk of laming my own horse, let me address Mr. Leach's opinion. Katy Endicott is now of legal age. I can't force her back. She could be anywhere in the world. That means time, and my time isn't cheap, even at a discount. Do you have the resources to see this through?"

"Silas's estate passed to the church on his death," Sam Brown replied, "and there is a codicil to his will requiring that we use as much of it as necessary to find and restore his daughter to the fold. Katy is one of our own. At the time of her disappearance, she had more good years behind her than bad ones. She's still a member of the Little Flock. She belongs *with* us," he said. "In the nation of Jehovah."

Amos Leach looked on, unblinking. "We'll call you," he said.

Raszer's tires were hubcap-deep in runoff by the time he left the Kingdom Hall. There had been another downpour, only now abating. Even the hard rain, however, felt gentler than the steeliness inside the church. Of all six men, only Sam Brown had given off a scent he recognized as anything like his own.

And Amos Leach—something wrong with that picture.

◆ ◆ ◆

THE CALL DID COME, late that afternoon. Despite Sam Brown's assistance with names, addresses, and some background, Raszer was a long way from having what he needed to begin a proper investigation. He needed the families' help, and he would not live fully in the world of the case until he'd seen it through the eyes of the eyewitness, whose name was Emmett Parrish. Still more essential was the perspective of perhaps the most important participant: Ruthie Endicott. Finding her would take some legwork.

Each case had its own landscape of mayhem, and that was where he needed to locate himself, because until Raszer had fashioned a living narrative of the events leading up to the night of the rave, his intuition would not boot up. At his best, he was capable of thought pictures that neared the clarity of lucid dreaming, or even so-called remote viewing. It wasn't like the psychic radar of those who could lay a missing girl's angora sweater against their cheek and conjure a sense of her whereabouts. It was both eerier and more methodical than that. All stories had a fractal nature. They were made of the same tiles, only the design of the mosaic had been changed. Every possible outcome was like a different world; Raszer's trick was to figure out which world this case occupied.

He wanted to get up into the mountains, to the site of Katy's abduction, before the rains closed San Gabriel Canyon Road. He couldn't even begin serious work until he'd stood at the crime scene, but before that, he needed to make a visit to the Azusa Police Department and the detective who had handled the case. Among other things, there was a set of snapshots he very much needed to see: those taken on the morning after Katy Endicott's crew had despoiled the Kingdom Hall.

FIVE

"JOHNNY HORN," said detective Jaime Aquino, laying open a third file folder on his formerly pristine desk. "Also known as Johnny Jihad . . . after he came back from the war, that is." He looked up at Raszer, more as a young father than as a cop, and stubbed his index finger into the morgue photo of a young man of twenty-two: close-cropped blond hair, wide, sensuous mouth, neck broken at the brainstem. "Some boys go to war and never get to know the enemy. Never get close enough to smell him. They go back to their families, their little towns, the farm or the coalmine—maybe have a few bad dreams, but they shake it off. Johnny Horn came back *as* the enemy. From what we know, he came back sure that everything he'd ever been taught was wrong."

Raszer lifted his eyes from the photo. "He had a bad ride over there?"

"I don't know about that," said Aquino. "His unit was in Karbala, not Baghdad. He wasn't wounded. His military records don't say much."

"So, how do you account for his change?"

"I think it started before he left," said Aquino. "Trouble in the family, some minor run-ins. Then him and his buddy—this guy . . . " The detective dropped his finger onto a second morgue shot, one of a mannish boy with a crest of spiked hair, a lip ring, and a dagger tattooed on his left breast, with the inscription SHE MADE ME DO IT. "Henry Lee is—*was*—his name. The two of them enlisted, and the shit came down on them. Johnny was tossed out of his church, tossed out by his family, and then he's in fucking Iraq for two years. He had nothing to come home to, but he came home anyway. Him and Henry. They shipped out together, they came home together."

"And moved into the trailer," Raszer said.

"Right. Up above the Burro Canyon Shooting Park, on the east fork, not far from the state corrections fire camp. It was an abandoned heap from the '60s, wedged up in a gulley. How it got up there, I couldn't tell you. But Johnny took it over and set himself up like some mystic commando. Stenciled a big peacock on the side of it."

"A peacock?" Raszer asked.

"Right. He had guns, he had pills, he had a pirate radio transmitter and a rebuilt generator to power his music, and after a while, he had girls. The boys from town, the slackers and gamers, some from other families the JWs had—what do they call it?—*shunned*, they loved Johnny. Made him a hero. They'd truck up there Saturday afternoon, do some shooting at the range, and then play that hardcore techno shit all night, till it shook the canyons. Drove the Forest Service and the other trailer folks *loco*. They finally confiscated his generator. I guess that's when the kids started looking for other places to dance, if you can call it dancing."

Aquino did a wild-eyed impression of a raver's pogo, as good as a man of thirty-two could muster while seated, wearing a shirt and tie, and with pictures of his young children on the wall. Raszer sensed that the detective, though square, was probably not a bad dancer himself, given the right music.

"Why didn't they move him off the land?" Raszer asked. "I don't get it-firearms, drugs, a state prison facility nearby . . . "

"Well, unfortunately," Aquino replied, "we didn't know the whole story until after the fact. Johnny and his friends fell through a crack. That's federal land up there, but it might as well be no-man's-land. Technically, the Forest Service could have instituted procedures, but it all happened pretty fast, and—believe it or not—Johnny had the folks up there both spooked and sweet-talked. He was smooth. And he had all the weapons cached. He learned that in Babylon. He learned that from the enemy."

"You say he was a good talker, and you called him a 'mystic commando.' What was his rap? What brought the boys up there, aside from pills and girls?"

"Well, again, we got most of this from Emmett. That's Emmett Parrish. He's the boy who got cold feet that night."

"Right," said Raszer, glancing down at the names Sam Brown had given him. "The witness. He was one of Johnny's regulars, too?"

"Yeah. According to Emmett, Johnny was into anarchy. He called his little club WARM, for World Anarchist Reform Movement. Had that painted on the trailer, too. He claimed he had 'brothers' in the Middle East and other places. Might've been bullshit . . . he didn't know which end he was coming from, and he didn't care. He had stuff up there about Aryan Nations, the Red Brigades, Hezbollah, and the Freemasons, for chrissakes. All he knew was that everything was wrong, and that all laws were made to enslave. When you added Henry Lee's magical shit in with it, it was quite a mix."

Switches began to click in Raszer's mind. The first tiles in the mosaic fell into place. "Tell me about Henry. What kind of magic was he into? Silas Endicott called it Satanism. Was it?"

"Not exactly, although what do I know? That's your business, right?"

Raszer cocked his head and waited for the other shoe to drop.

"You're the guy who worked that militia cult up in Shasta, right?" Aquino said.

"How did you know that?" Raszer asked. "I was undercover, I didn't appear in court, and I wasn't in the papers—not that time."

"Cops have their own Internet," Aquino said, grinning. He picked up the telephone and shook the cord, making it dance. "It's called *la vina*."

"Okay," said Raszer, holding up his palms in surrender. "Fair enough. But for the moment, I'm just a PI looking for a missing girl, and I don't know anything. So what was Henry's brew if it wasn't the usual small-town, heavy-metal Satanism?"

"My guess is, it was something else the boys brought back from Karbala," said Aquino, sliding open the top right drawer of his desk. "Along with this."

He held up a palm-size piece of black ore, dimpled with little pits. It might have been basalt, or a small meteorite, but it looked a whole lot like Brigit's moon rock. A lot like the rock that had given Silas Endicott apoplexy and then stopped his heart.

"May I see that?" Raszer asked. It was heavier than he'd expected.

"We found a few of these in the trailer, along with some weird little statues," said Aquino. "It's technically evidence, but I, uh, kept one as a souvenir. Sometimes, when I get bugged that we never solved this case, I take it out and use it as a paperweight." He shrugged. "Like it's gonna talk to me, right?" Detective Aquino's chair creaked as he sat back heavily. "It's just iron ore, but of a type found across northern Iran and eastern Turkey. Possible meteoric origin. I have no idea what it meant to Henry or where he got it from over there. The kids who could tell us are either dead, missing, or out of state."

"You mean Ruthie?" Raszer said, his eyes fixed on the stone. "Katy's sister?"

"Yeah," said Aquino. "Maybe you won't have the same jurisdictional problems we do. All we ever found of Henry's was a book about something called chaos magic. But the best clue, Mr. Raszer—for someone smarter than me—is what we *didn't* find . . . "

Raszer looked up and slowly closed his fingers around the stone.

"The best evidence," Aquino continued, "was on Henry Lee's body."

He spun the file folder 180 degrees, pushed it toward Raszer, and flipped through a few more morgue photos until he came to one detailing the midbody. Henry Lee's uncircumcised penis lay to the left in repose, but beneath it, there was nothing but a badly healed scar.

Raszer moved closer in. "Am I seeing what I think I'm seeing?" he asked.

The cop's eyes met Raszer's. "He had himself neutered. And not by an expert surgeon, either. He must've done it when he was in Iraq, or after, because his predeployment physical was normal. Now, why would a man do that, Mr. Raszer?"

Raszer sat back and pushed his fingers through his damp hair. He had some ideas, but none trumped his own puzzlement. "If it *was* voluntary, I dunno. There are eunuchs all through history, mostly slaves but occasionally saints. A whole range of stuff goes down in the transgender sector, but the cut would have been cleaner. I can imagine a number of reasons it might have been done *to* him, though, especially in Iraq. Maybe he got caught messing with a local girl. Maybe his appetite for rape didn't start with Katy Endicott. Did you get a look at his military record?"

"Nothing but a couple of minor AWOLs and a reprimand for smoking hashish on a weekend leave. No visits to the medic, except for a case of bronchitis." Aquino pulled a magnifying glass out of his drawer and handed it to Raszer. "Take a look at that scar. According to the coroner, the wound was cauterized. See these secondaries—here at the stem, and there? Those are burn scars. Coroner's hunch is, the wound was sealed with the flat side of a red-hot knife. Immediately after the cut. If I was a crazy Arab and I'd caught him doing my sister, I don't think I'd bother with the post-op."

"I see what you mean," said Raszer. "It definitely suggests procedure—either prescribed punishment or self-mutilation."

"What about some weird religious thing, Mr. Raszer? Some kind of cult."

Raszer pulled in a breath as a substitute for the cigarette he wanted.

"You're thinking of Heaven's Gate, the *Star Trek castratis*. I dunno. There is one thing that fits, but I'd like to do some work before I conjecture. I'm still trying to get you guys to take me seriously . . . especially now that I know you're talking about me."

Aquino nodded. "If you come up with something, will you let me know?" he asked. "This is still my case, and there's not a night that it doesn't cost me sleep."

Raszer took out a cigarette and rolled it over his fingers. "I know what that's like," he said. "Like having a ghost in the house. I'm gonna grab a quick smoke. Looking at dead people has that effect on me. Care to join me outside?"

During the break, they talked only of the rain's mixed blessing: a verdant, blossomed spring that would lead inevitably to a summer of tinder-fueled wildfires. Drought or deluge—in California, you were damned either way. By mid-October, the chaparral would have reached its flash point, and flames could tear through a town like Azusa as freely as huge boulders once had in the days before the WPA and Army Corps of Engineers had fortified the San Gabriels with dams and debris basins.

"Well," said Raszer, "I guess you can rest a *little* easier knowing you've got a chain gang up there obliged to fight the fires . . . at the correctional facility."

Aquino held the door as Raszer stepped back inside. "I wonder about that," he said. "I think if things got really hot, they'd just duck the wardens and race the flames into town. I don't like living downwind from either nuclear plants or prison camps."

"I hear you there," said Raszer. "But that's the price we pay for paradise, right?"

Aquino paused just inside the door, out of the desk sergeant's earshot. "Say, let me ask you something: You said some men do that to themselves . . . " He made a slicing motion across his groin. " . . . Cut themselves voluntarily. I hear different things from different people. Can a man still, you know, *be a man* afterwards?"

"I think it depends on the man," said Raszer. "But yeah, physiologically, he can. No sperm cells, of course. The sultans had eunuchs guarding the harems because they didn't want another man's bastard claiming the kingdom. To the degree a man's sex drive comes out of his gonads, it'll cool him down, but the machinery still works."

"I've been wondering," said Aquino, "because in the pictures the kids took—"

"Pictures?" said Raszer, arching his eyebrow. "I'd like to see those."

When they returned to the office, they spoke of the third boy murdered on the night of Katy Endicott's abduction, the third of her alleged would-be rapists. He was a high school dropout named Joseph Strunk, also from a JW family, who'd graffitied his nickname, SKRUNK, across the free walls of a number of buildings in Azusa. Like other aimless teens in this halfway house of a town—neither part of L.A. nor sufficiently distinct from it to give a teenager pride of place—he'd fallen under Johnny Horn's spell, but unlike the others, he'd apparently enlisted full-time in Johnny's WARM. His file didn't offer much else of interest.

Emmett Parrish, the boy whose account had provided the only firsthand evidence of all three crimes—rape, murder, and kidnapping—seemed likewise a cipher, another kid bound for oblivion, in spite of his fateful decision to opt out of the gangbang and hide in the tall pines.

"I take it you've gotten to know Emmett pretty well," said Raszer.

"As well as he will let me know him," Aquino replied. "He was borderline crazy even before all this happened. In and out of clinics and counseling centers from the time he was five. The Witnesses don't make it easy on kids who don't fit in. Church and family are one thing. They come down hard on the parents if the kids act up, and then the parents come down hard on the kids." He whacked the desk for emphasis.

"Like the Old Testament law that says a father's responsible for the sins of his son until he reaches puberty," said Raszer.

"Something like that. I belong to an evangelical Christian church, Mr. Raszer, but as far as I'm concerned, the JWs are a cult. The Parrish kid was damaged goods. We were lucky to get a full statement out of him that night, because after that, he just zombied out. Even if the other three had lived and gone to trial for rape, I'm not sure how effective a witness he would've been against them."

"But you do believe his account . . . " said Raszer.

"I do," Aquino replied, "because it fits with what the rangers found at the crime scene—and because it's too crazy to make up." He drummed his fingers on the desk. "I think that night, Emmett Parrish was too scared to lie."

"And too scared to make out the Lincoln's plates, or provide a good description of the abductors. The men in the limo—"

Aquino shook his head. "When he talks about it, it sounds like a movie. The fog, the black suits, the whole works. But it fits with the way the necks were snapped. The coroner said it was one for the books. Only a strand of nerve tissue left connecting the third and fourth vertebrae. Squeeze a little harder, their heads would have popped off."

"Christ," said Raszer. "What are we dealing with?" He looked hard at the morgue shot of Johnny Horn, trying to glean something—anything—from the grains of silver oxide in the photograph. "What about links between the rave promoters and the abductors? You've been through all that, I guess. No drug burns, paybacks?"

"The rave promoters were two small-time crooks from Irwindale," said Aquino. "They basically used these dances as a methamphetamine market. They were Johnny's connection, and the lead dead-ended at a meth lab in Tijuana. No drug lords, no limos."

"Was the FBI in on this? Or the DEA?"

"FBI, yes. For a while. I'll give you the field agent. You're welcome to him."

Raszer nodded knowingly. "You know, Detective," he said, "there are a lot of square pegs here. For one thing, I thought the whole L.A. rave scene shut down a few years back . . . after those girls drove their Toyota off the Angeles Crest Highway."

"Everything comes to Azusa a few years late, Mr. Raszer—and usually tainted."

"Yeah." Raszer sat back and sighed. "Can I take a look around up there?"

"Be my guest," said Aquino. "It's all still there, but you probably won't find much. Johnny's trailer was stripped down to the insulation, and anything not nailed down at the old Coronado Lodge was taken into evidence. I'll give you the directions." He opened his drawer and handed Raszer a business card. "If the rangers bother you, tell them to call me. And don't forget to buy your Adventure Pass or they'll ticket your Avanti." He glanced at the wall clock. "You better get up there before the light goes."

"You're right," said Raszer. "But, uh, before I do . . . can I get a look at those snapshots?" He nodded to the morgue photos. "I'd like to see what these two boys looked like when they were alive and kicking. And Silas Endicott died before he could give me a picture of his daughter, so I'd better get a look at her."

Aquino swung around to his PC and angled the monitor toward Raszer. There was no reason to close the mini-blinds on his north-facing window; the sky above the mountains was as dark as factory smoke. "The actual pictures are at the courthouse in San Dimas," he said, "but I had them digitized. It's amazing what you can do these days with this software. There's stuff in these pictures you'd never see in the original."

"'To see the world in a grain of sand . . . '"

"What's that?" Aquino asked.

"Nothing," said Raszer. "It's a poem. It just means there's always something hiding in plain sight, sometimes in layers so deep, you have to think it more than see it."

"You're pretty philosophical for a PI," said Aquino, with a smile. "But I guess that's about what I expected. I don't think you'll see much poetry in this freak show." He double-clicked on a .jpg icon and opened up a file that was, at first glance, too murky to register.

"What are we looking at?" Raszer asked.

"Let me bring it up a bit," said Aquino. "This is a little group shot, right after they broke into the hall. Ruthie Endicott set the camera on the, uh, lectern and put the timer on, then ran back into the picture. That's why she's blurred. Too bad these kids couldn't afford a digital camera."

"Give me the chronology," Raszer said, leaning forward. "This is two summers ago, in August, right?"

"August ninth," Aquino affirmed.

"August ninth," Raszer repeated.

Aquino nodded. "August ninth . . . the anniversary of the Manson murders."

Raszer cocked one eyebrow. "Okay. And give me their ages at this time."

Detective Aquino took a pen from the coffee cup on his desk and went down the line, identifying the four children of the apocalypse, one by one.

"This is Henry Lee, twenty, in living color," he began. "He's got his pants on here, but soon you'll see what's left of the family jewels in action."

The defiant crest of orange hair stood high on Lee's head. He was naked to the waist, and the tattoo on his breast was clearly visible. In his left hand was a can of spray paint, and he was grinning for the camera.

Aquino moved his pointer right. "And here we have Johnny Jihad in all his glory. Twenty-two. Notice the T-shirt. You can bet he didn't buy that in downtown Azusa."

Johnny Horn stood almost a full head taller than his compadre Henry Lee. His head was shaved to the scalp, and his blue eyes made the pixels in the digitized image spin like dervishes. Even in sweltering August, he wore a long-sleeved flannel shirt, but it hid neither his steroid-pumped physique nor the Osama bin Laden T-shirt he wore beneath. Judging from his eyes and coiled, predatory bearing, Raszer pegged him as a meth freak. He was formidable, the clear focus of the family portrait.

"They send him off to fight Islamic terrorists," Aquino said, "and he comes back one of them. No wonder we're losing the war."

"You said it yourself, Detective. Some boys eat what they kill." Raszer studied the face and peeled away its onionskin of punk rage. "I doubt the T-shirt says much about his political sentiments, other than *fuck you*. That guy's too amped up on his own revelation to be anybody's sleeper agent. You know, Detective, there's a long history of Christian soldiers marching off to war and coming back transformed by their encounter with the alien. That was partly the story with the Crusades. Maybe Johnny looked through the scope and saw himself. Maybe he saw his father and knew—after he'd pulled the trigger, anyway—that the ordinary life was over for him."

"Well, anyway," said Aquino, "it is now."

To Johnny Horn's left stood Katy Endicott, the only one of the four not looking at the camera. She was looking up at Johnny, but whether with unreserved adoration or *what do we do now, Johnny?* uncertainty wasn't clear. The shadow of his big shoulder fell over her eyes, but the cant of her chin suggested a little of both. Having met her father, another towering figure with a zealot's eyes, another man whose certitude had left her little personal autonomy, it was not difficult for Raszer to read the body language of a devotee. The language said, "Whither thou goest, I will go."

She was petite, presumably from her mother's side, with long brown hair pinned back. She wore—of all things to wear to an orgy of desecration—a simple print dress, hemmed just above the knees. She was a pretty girl, maybe even exceptionally so, but it wasn't the mimetic prettiness of the girls down in *twee* San Marino, much less of the mall queens in Sherman Oaks. Two things distinguished her immediately. Like her father, Katy Endicott was an anachronism. Her slim, delicate form could have been cut from the photograph and pasted into one fifty years older without the slightest temporal dissonance. And there was, in the tilt of her head, the parted lips, and the woozy drape of her forearm, a languor, like that of a young novitiate awaiting her first nocturnal encounter with the Holy Spirit, her body an empty vessel of sacrament.

"She doesn't seem the type, does she?" said Aquino.

"No," said Raszer. "And then again, yes. Something . . . missing."

Aquino blinked. "Well, not like the sister, anyway. That one's a pistol."

And Ruthie was. For a few ticks, Raszer could not remove his eyes from the outline of Katy's face, but once he did, a number of things became clear. The redheaded, nose-ringed, midriff-baring blur that was Ruthie Endicott flashed *alter ego* like a pop-up window. Even out of focus, all that was absent in Katy was aggressively present in Ruthie; all that was formless was flesh. How could a little sister, in this day and age, *not* have wanted to follow her down the rabbit hole? *A sweet sickness*, Silas had called her. To Raszer, she looked like rhubarb pie too good to spoil with vanilla ice cream.

In the subsequent photos, arranged in Detective Aquino's surmise of sequence, Ruthie more than rose to her persona. She lifted her halter top for a low-angle shot that could only have been taken from between her legs, spray-painted the white wall with pentagrams, and sucked on a baby pacifier while being taken from the rear by Henry Lee. Although the grainy photo was not anatomically revealing, Raszer could only assume that Henry—if he had indeed been without testicles at the time of the photo—was one of those geldings who could still get it up.

From the accounts given by Silas and the Overseers, Raszer had taken Johnny and Ruthie to be the former high school sweethearts, but the photos suggested that at least a passing change of partners had occurred. In every shot featuring Katy, it was Johnny Horn her eyes sought out: Johnny defacing bibles, Johnny torching a pile of Watchtower newsletters in the middle of the floor, Johnny spraying NOTHING IS TRUE . . . on the wall behind the lectern—and, in the photo that must have turned the walls of Silas Endicott's heart to paper, shirtless Johnny resting the black rock on Katy's head as she, on her knees, took him in her mouth.

All the sex play and schoolyard Satanism notwithstanding, the most transgressive photo was the last, taken when the quartet's work was done, and again on a timer so that all could be duly credited members of this latter-day Clyde Barrow Gang. This time, the sisters stood side by side, flanked by the boys, with Henry the one to dash into frame at the last second (Raszer could not imagine Johnny hustling for anything but his own call to arms). The wall behind them was black with pentagrams and triple sixes, skater glyphs, and slogans, some of which evidenced surprising wit:

144,000 IDIOTS CAN'T BE WRONG.
HERE GATHER JEHOVAH'S WITLESS.
THERE IS NO GOD BUT CHAOS, AND JOHNNY JIHAD IS HIS PROPHET.
NOTHING IS TRUE. EVERYTHING IS PERMITTED.

Also featured was Aleister Crowley's DO WHAT THOU WILT SHALL BE THE WHOLE OF THE LAW—known and misunderstood by every Luciferian punter and surfer of magickal websites. The psychological basis of most of this stuff was as clear as the sneer on a misfit boy's face or the simmering resentment of a cast-off daughter, and for these and other reasons, Raszer felt sure that most of the handiwork was Ruthie's and Henry's. There was one strikingly original touch, however, that felt like Katy's, and it made Raszer's scalp tingle with precognition.

The sisters had exchanged outfits for the final shot. Ruthie stood doe-eyed and satirically demure in Katy's dress, glance averted and hem raised in a vulgar curtsy. Despite the face jewelry and the butcher-chopped hair, it was the dead-on impression of a near twin. Katy, in Ruthie's low-rise jeans and halter, had slung her hips out, made her eyes up like a dime-store vamp's, and had both arms wrapped around Henry Lee's naked waist. A wardrobe change and a little mascara, and she was Salome. The only thing left of her reticence was a downcast stare and the sweet sweep of her cheekline.

Aquino turned to Raszer. "I'd have a stroke, too, if she was my daughter."

"Well," said Raszer, "I'll grant you that none of these kids look fit for the choir, but whether it's Hollywood or Des Moines, they're all good at playing bad nowadays. It's the new normal. Hell, they do it on the Disney Channel. Would you mind printing me a copy of the first and last pictures—the group shots? And if you've got a more conventional photo of Katy—yearbook, whatever—I could use that, too."

"Sure thing," said Aquino, switching on his printer. "I'll give you the one that's gone out to all the law-enforcement and social-services people."

"The thing is," Raszer continued, "what do we *really* have here? Sex, sedition, and sacrilege. It's not pretty, but you can see how four kids—brought up in a radically conservative sect that tells them all but 144,000 of the chosen are damned—might act out in some pretty transgressive ways, especially when three of them are kicked off the reservation and the fourth—Katy—watches her sister run off to Taos to do all the bad things she can't. A year—almost a year and a half—later, we've got rape, execution-style murder, and kidnapping. What's the connection?"

"Well," Aquino said defensively, "we haven't made it yet. We're just small-town cops, Mr. Raszer. Maybe a sophisticated thinker like yourself—"

"C'mon, Detective," said Raszer. "Azusa's small-town, but you're not. You're a sharp and determined guy. You must have had theories."

"As many as you can shake a stick at," said Aquino. "First we thought drugs, like you said. Johnny and Henry were dealing. Meth, ketamine, PCP . . . they even had tanks of nitrous up there. And there's evidence that Katy continued using even while the Witnesses had her on, uh, probation."

"And could the limo guys've been old-guard drug lords or gangbangers, fighting a turf war over the foothills with this self-made potentate in his mountain stronghold? Azusa's not all that far from Compton. Could Johnny's customer base have grown fast enough to threaten suppliers with enough margin to afford chauffeured Lincolns?"

"Nah. Didn't pan out. But in a related area, he might have been a threat."

"What's that?" Raszer asked.

"Prostitution. One of the girls questioned at the rave gave us the tip. We followed it up, found out Johnny had four or five female disciples, ages seventeen to twenty-one, hooking for him. He'd send them out fishing down in the flats . . . Upland, La Verne, as far east as San Bernardino. The amazing thing was, Mr. Raszer, he had them doing it for the cause. For his 'war chest.' None of these local girls made more than milk money."

"Was Katy Endicott one of the girls?"

"Nobody's gone on record with that," said Aquino. "But it's possible."

"Okay. *Interesting*," said Raszer. "That may explain the JWs' theory that Katy was bartered into some kind of white-slavery ring. But still, putting four or five girls on the street wouldn't ordinarily get you killed. And it's not likely these thugs were interceding to prevent or even avenge a rape. They don't sound like white knights to me."

"Unless . . . "

"Unless what?" Raszer asked.

Aquino's modesty kept his self-satisfaction in check, but just barely. "Unless this particular sex ring was after girls who hadn't been spoiled."

Raszer began to nod slowly. "Virgins," he said. A volley of hail hit the window like a spray of rock salt. "Was she?" he asked.

"At least until that night, she was," Aquino replied. "If we can believe Emmett Parrish. Emmett called her 'the last pure thing.' Of course, we have no way of confirming that."

"*The last pure thing,*" Raszer repeated. "And that night . . . was there evidence of actual penetration? Condoms? Katy's blood or fluids on any of the boys?"

"The short answer is no," said Aquino, handing Raszer a folder containing the photo printouts. "But this is where it gets foggy. And I mean that both ways. All we have is Emmett, and he's back there in the bushes with an obstructed view. Henry and the other boy are holding Katy down on the trunk. Johnny is first up. He's the only one who had a shot, and the only one found with his dick out. Emmett *thinks* he raped her, but the physical evidence suggests otherwise. There was no vaginal fluid, no tissue, no blood, and the only ejaculate we found was all over the trunk. You see, Mr. Raszer, he ejaculated when his neck was snapped, same time as he shit himself."

"Uh-huh," said Raszer.

"That's about it," said Aquino. "As far as we know, Katy may have left intact."

Raszer looked out the window. Fog was coming down, and he had at best a scant two hours of light. Without shifting his gaze from the mountains, he asked, "Are you a fan of alternate histories, Detective?"

"How do you mean?"

"It's a style of fiction," said Raszer. "I guess they'd call it sci-fi at the bookstore. Anyhow, what the writer does is take some historical event and extrapolate what might've happened if just one or two little things had gone differently. Say, Hitler got the bomb before we did, or Linda Kasabian called the cops before the killing started."

"Okay," said Aquino. "I'm with you."

"Well, let's suppose your virgin theory is right. And let's imagine the Lincoln got stuck in the mud and arrived ten minutes late. The gangbang goes on as planned, and it's plain as day to the kidnappers that Katy Endicott has been defiled. What happens?"

"They don't take her. She's damaged goods."

"Right," said Raszer. "And what possibility does that open up?"

"You're suggesting that Johnny Horn was trying to protect her?"

"I'm not sure," said Raszer. "Inoculate her. Lay claim to her. Maybe he sold her out, then had second thoughts. We have to figure that as badly as these kids behaved, they were all raised up in the church—and that gangsters, no matter what period or place, always live in the dark ages. I know it's a stretch, but we're talking alternate history. And what's Katy thinking? She leaves the dance hall without a coat . . . "

"Probably hot and high as a kite. Between the dancing, the dehydration, and the drugs, some of these ravers run temperatures of 106, 108 . . . "

"You're right, Detective," said Raszer, and pointed to the now neatly stacked manila folders. "In the version of history that's in those case files, you're right. But, like Richard Feynman said, reality is a sum over all histories, and *A* doesn't always go to *Z*."

Aquino smiled, a little impatiently. "Well, I don't know Richard Feynman, but I do know perps, and I know that in your alternate history, these guys probably would have killed Katy Endicott, too."

"What I'm afraid of, Detective, is that in almost *any* conceivable history, that may have happened. If Katy's alive, it's because they're making use of her. On that I think we agree. Did you work any other leads?"

"Only one that matters," said Aquino. "But I don't think those crayon pushers in Homeland Security took it seriously. They were too busy making color charts."

"Terrorism?"

"Johnny bragged about the 'friends' he'd made in Iraq. His 'global network.'"

"But they never found any emails? Cell phone records?"

"Not that they shared with us. Maybe you can get something."

"You'll put me in touch with the boys' families?"

"We'll do whatever we can, Mr. Raszer," said Aquino, rising from his chair. He smiled and pointed to the telephone. "And I'll be on that grapevine."

Raszer noticed for the first time that Aquino stood only about five-foot-five. Somehow, the broad shoulders, mustache, and cop body language had made him seem taller. Raszer found most L.A. cops to be more style than substance, but he liked Aquino. He liked that he had kids, and that he saw Katy Endicott as one of them.

Detective Aquino scrawled a set of directions on a Post-it note and handed them to Raszer. "You're a very interesting man, Mr. Raszer. I'm glad to have you on the case. Just be sure you don't get in over your head."

They exchanged tight-lipped smiles. Given even what little he knew of Stephan Raszer's history, Aquino could not have expected his advice to be followed.

✦ ✦ ✦

WITH THE POST-IT stuck to his speedometer, Raszer ascended the steep grade into San Gabriel Canyon via Highway 39. The sky was churning overhead, as if ready to disgorge the Valkyries. At about 2,800 feet, signs informed Raszer that the road was open to the Cold Brook Ranger Station but closed to Crystal Lake, due to snow. That, he figured, ought to be enough pavement to get him to the east fork and, hopefully, to the 3,600-foot elevation of the old Coronado Lodge. The snow line was at four thousand feet, but he was bound to encounter hubcap-deep mud on the fire roads. He glanced down at his feet and cursed. Raszer had ceased being fussy about his Avanti—so long as its rebuilt V-8 growled—but he hated getting his good boots muddy.

Of the passable canyons along the Front Range, San Gabriel was the most dramatic in its sweep. The haunches of the five-thousand-foot peaks that formed its gateway described an almost perfect Delta of Venus, with the pyramidal mass of Mount Baden-Powell rising distantly to fill the cleft. The effect, in fair weather or foul, was to lure a traveler deeper into the breech, and with the mist hanging like a bridal veil and the lower slopes turned Galway green, the place was fit for hobbits. As the river that had carved this epic "V" eons ago came fully into view, surging and slaked by a month of rain, there was also evidence of giants—or at least of the gigantic ambition tapped by the public-works projects of the Roosevelt years. At three thousand feet, the broad span of the old Morris Dam appeared. It wasn't shiny and Olympian like the Hoover Dam, but it was big enough, and somehow more epic with its old-school masonry and parchment patina. It looked like a Cinerama screen erected for the children of Odin.

Beyond the dam lay a sprawling reservoir as flat, green, and waveless as an Amazonian lake, but banked by rugged scree and chaparral, rather than viney jungle. L.A. was a city of reservoirs standing in for lakes and lagoons, of which there were no naturally occurring examples. That the city did not die of thirst—that it survived at all—was owing to the greed of cowboy capitalists and the past largesse of the federal government. The latter had now mostly left the state to fend for itself, and the former hadn't done a thing for the infrastructure in decades. California was crumbling, but here stood mighty Morris Dam, holding back the floodwaters of the San Gabriel River in the name of the common good and the publicly owned Department of Water and Power.

Even after twenty years in California, the term *canyon* felt somehow unsuited to what Raszer saw around him. It evoked images of the stark, infernal fissures of Arizona and Utah; the British word *glen* seemed more fitting for this wooded gash cleaved between the shoulders of the fitfully slumbering beasts rising up on all sides. *Canyon* described a dead place, but these mountains were alive and still forming, spilling their soft earth into the chasm with each tectonic lurch left or right, threatening to close in on the narrow road at each dizzying switchback.

In spite of their immensity, the San Gabriels were fragile and trembling, big mounds of packed soil held fast by spiky yucca, whitethorn, and creosote at lower elevations; scrub oak, sycamore, and walnut further up the slope; and, at and above the snow line, stands of Jeffrey, Coulter, and Lodgepole pine. Woven like pastel threads through the underbrush at all elevations were a hundred varieties of wildflowers.

The mountains extended enormous, furry forepaws of land into the reservoir's mirroring emerald expanse, and from a dozen rocky outcroppings above, waterfalls sprang like ribbons of lace.

For a few minutes, Raszer unhitched both past and future, forgot himself and why he was there, and returned to a place from his dreams, where sweet woodsmoke rose from cottages of stone and fathers lulled daughters to sleep with tender half lies about twilight encounters with the fairy folk. He cleared a mud-slicked bend at a reckless fifty miles per hour, fishtailed briefly, and spotted up ahead the low trestle that spanned the San Gabriel's rapids and led to East Fork Road. Then he remembered.

He pulled briefly off the road. At the start of each of his earlier assignments had been a moment like this, a moment when he could have turned back to the comfort of fantasy; to his books, his music, his women, his Brigit. At this point, it would not be a difficult retreat. He'd taken no money, nor set anything of consequence in motion. He could exit now without leaving even a ripple of his presence, and with his boots clean. He stepped out of the car, lit a cigarette, and stared across the reservoir at the trestle.

In all likelihood, Katy Endicott was as dead as Johnny Horn. He knew the odds and had seen the forgone conclusion etched on Aquino's face. No ransom note, no cat-and-mouse with the press or the cops, no grainy videotape of the victim pleading for her life or even boasting—Patty Hearst style—that she'd thrown in her lot with her captors. And if she were dead, pursuing her ghost would still be costly. There would be more victims—there always were—and always the chance that one of them would be him. And for what purpose? The girl's father was gone, and Raszer's prospective employers did not inspire a great deal of passion for the quest. Moreover, the whole Scotty Darrell debacle had handed Raszer an escape clause from his otherwise unbreakable contract with fate. He could still get a real job.

And so he had to ask himself again: *What is it I'm after? Why should I cross that bridge?* By any standard, it was an ugly case, maybe the ugliest he'd taken since the turn of the millennium. Given the shakiness of his psyche, did he really need this?

The answer, which came with his last drag on the cigarette, was as prefigured as the fractal pattern of the opposing shoreline, and, like most everything about Raszer, it came in shadow and light.

As a dog senses the presence of bad spirits, Raszer sensed that behind events like Katy Endicott's abduction, behind inexplicable acts of abuse great and small, there was often to be found evidence of grander malfeasance. The highway "detours" he'd spoken of to Hildegarde did not just spring up spontaneously—they were erected in the dead of night by an adversary wilier than the Coyote. The odds against the innocent and guileless in this world weren't a matter of "natural selection"—they'd been set by a power whose abiding interest lay in seeing that the game was fixed.

In its service, this power enlisted sociopaths, tyrants, and all those with great amounts to lose if the fix were off. Raszer knew this power couldn't be vanquished; it was part and parcel of the world. But he hoped that by learning its name, he might obtain some leverage over it. The trouble was, the name kept changing. No sooner had he held it on his tongue than it was lost to him, forgotten like a dream that dissipates upon waking.

This was the genius of all conspiracies and cabals: The links they forged through a transient common purpose dissolved as soon as the fatal blow was struck. You could try to pin it on the Bilderbergs or the Trilaterals, you could aim from right or left, but the true GamesMasters were beyond ideology and evasive as eels. And yet—Raszer was convinced—some resonance of their original sin must remain, some trace of the secret name whispered when their knives were first raised. Where there was design, there had to be evidence of its craft. Common felony left evidence that police agencies were quite good at following. But crimes of soul theft and subversion were of a different order, and that, Raszer knew, was why Silas Endicott had sought him out. Whatever entity plotted such skulduggery was beyond human justice, but it could be brought to heel by threat of exposure, and this was often enough to secure release of a captive. Of necessity, Raszer subscribed to the notion that the world was saved one life at a time.

And there was this, too, as much a part of Raszer's raison d'être as his pledge to gather orphans under his coat—the gold at the end of the rainbow. It was taunting him right now: An errant ray of western light had struck an outcropping on the mountainside east of the trestle, illuminating the possibility that just once, as payment for services rendered, he would pursue a stray beyond the edge of the familiar and find himself in another country, one where there was no market in souls, where poets stood taller than plunderers, and young girls were left in peace to blossom like orchids.

In that alterworld would be his house, his daughter, the women and men he loved. It would not look much different, and humans would still be far from gods. But the fix would be off, and there would be no profit in dominion. He crushed out the cigarette, got back into the Avanti, and turned the wheels toward the East Fork Bridge.

SIX

ALMOST AS SOON as he'd crossed the bridge, color had drained from the landscape. It wasn't unusual for California to go monochrome in the absence of sunlight, especially in the hills. It was all pastels and earth tones, shades that bled quickly in gloom. But this was stark, and Raszer had instinctively looked up at the sky to see if some even more ominous front was coming in. It wasn't that. It was just the mined-out look of the San Gabriel's east fork, the sudden feeling of isolation, and the fact that the murky part of the job had begun. He wouldn't see bright colors until he'd found his first lead.

Now, he stood ankle deep in mud, having hiked the ravine up to the location of Johnny Horn's trailer. He'd parked in a gravel lot opposite the access road to the Burro Canyon Shooting Park, from which, even now, he could hear the reverberant pings of gunfire, a *whoop* or two, and the occasional cackle of an automatic weapon. One of the other cars in the lot had a Phish sticker on its bumper. California: sweet land of libertarianism. Where the "don't fuck with me" gun culture meets the hippie ethos.

He hopped a swiftly flowing runoff trench and scrambled over a cluster of boulders just beneath the wooded notch where Johnny's trailer sat on cinder blocks. *Trailer* was a generous description. It was more like a large camper, vintage 1970, and wedged into its spot as tightly and improbably as Aquino had suggested. A road of sorts snaked its way up to the site, with space enough to pull in three or four cars on the triangle of land before the trailer, but it was impassable now, cleaved by the rain into a delta of tributaries. A monsoon season like this one would have killed both Johnny's social life and his business activities.

With its peacock emblazoned broadside blocking the mouth of a wider canyon beyond, the vehicle had an unmistakably defensive stance. The hammering rain and withering sun had chipped and faded the spray enamel, but the image of the big bird still telegraphed warning. It wasn't hard to imagine that the trailer's original owner had been a smuggler or a survivalist, and had positioned it so as to control access to the gulch. Its fortress elevation would have provided advantage over any IRS or ATF agents who came snooping, and maybe this—and memories of Ruby Ridge—was partly why the law had left Johnny alone. Maybe it was also partly why his killers had waited to strike until he'd left the nest. The embankments on either side were so steep that a visitor could not approach without being exposed—another guerrilla trick the boys might have picked up in Iraq.

He took another look at the peacock before heading around back. *Why a peacock?* he mused. *Why not a raptor of some sort?* Something else to ask Hildegarde about.

Whatever its original use had been, the area on the far side of the trailer was a natural dance floor, a massive slab of granite about the size of a small ice rink. Johnny and Henry had made this Party Central, and evidence of revelry remained in the cheap Japanese lanterns strung through the cottonwoods and dangling like sodden orange cocoons over the flat, gray expanse. Even muted color leapt from the monochrome backdrop, and Raszer paid attention. In contrast, the waterlogged mattresses strewn around the perimeter, some folded over or pulled back into the privacy of the brush, were virtually camouflaged by the drabness. Fire pits had become cesspools; in some of them, beer cans still floated and used condoms bobbed like dead, swollen fish against the banks. It was not a shot for the Sierra Club calendar.

The initial survey told only the story Raszer already knew: that Johnny and his pals had, for a time, staged their own postmillennial version of Woodstock in this canyon. The mounts for Johnny's huge loudspeakers remained where he'd placed them, braced with steel strapping halfway up the trunks of twin sycamore trees. A power plug hung impotently above a plywood shell that must have housed his generator. In its vicinity, Raszer could still smell gasoline fumes.

He cast a sidelong glance at the dance floor, the ceremonial ground of Johnny's nihilistic tribe, and, using his peripheral vision like a good shaman, could almost see the Endicott sisters dancing with their shirtless warriors, arms flailing, eyes glazed with amphetamine ice. Despite the evidence of orgiastic sex, the vibe of the place was distinctly unerotic, and the dope Johnny had dealt would not have altered that state. Speed, nitrous, and pet tranquilizer were not the makings of either love-fest or vision quest. They were, however, a recipe for collective paranoia, an all-too-familiar trait of the marginalized groups Raszer had come to know. It began with flight from society and proceeded to isolation and autocracy, then to the mythos of Us versus Them, and finally to guns. Sooner or later, the guns brought on the very cataclysm the great leader had prophesied, for power had to be met with power.

Johnny Horn, along with his minister of propaganda, Henry Lee, had been executed, but not by agents of the state. They had been executed, Raszer sensed, by a state without borders, governed by a constitution without principle. The longer Raszer stood, the more the poison of the place got into him, until he found himself almost unable to move. He realized he'd been stalling; he still needed to investigate the trailer.

Begin, he'd once been taught by a Chumash tracker, with smell. *Close your eyes*. First, there was the pungency of locked-in damp, of mildew, of a hundred yeasty organisms replicating themselves behind the trailer's fake paneling and exposed insulation. That odor dominated and had to be dismissed before the subtler scents revealed themselves. More precisely, it had to be normalized as the ambient smell of the place, then shifted to the background. *Smell with your skin*, the Indian had told him, *not only with your nose*. This was more difficult, but it could be learned and had a basis in both physiology and in the altered consciousness of synesthesia. The lingering effects of Hildegarde's root tea gave him just enough of a boost to get there.

Although the trailer had been stripped of everything absorbent but the rock-wool insulation in its walls, it retained the locker-room odor of men in their natural state. Underlying this, however, were a number of scents that fired off recognition in different parts of Raszer's brain. Gunpowder. Grain alcohol. The alkaline signature of amphetamine sweat. And two distinctive smells that did not seem to quite belong there: the unmistakable aroma of cloves, as from an herbal cigarette, and patchouli oil. For some reason, Raszer immediately tied the cloves to Henry Lee, but he could not account for the patchouli. It was as if some residual trace of the trailer's original inhabitants had imprinted itself there, as if some atomic memory of 1970 was etched on the stale air in this flimsy aluminum time capsule. For a moment, Raszer felt dizzy and put a hand out to steady himself. On occasion, such sensory dislocation led to blackouts, and the blackouts induced fleeting visions, but he was not ready for the kind of visions this place might bring. Recovered, he moved across the floor and picked up one more scent: wintergreen, as in lifesavers or breath mints. Funny, the molecules of scent that remained in a place. He reasoned there must be a wad of chewing gum stuck somewhere.

The police had removed more than half of the wall paneling, and Raszer muttered, "Shit," knowing that these must be the pieces etched or markered with slogans, insignias, and possibly even phone numbers. He could and would get access to the evidence, but it wasn't the same as seeing it in situ. There were discolorations and mounting holes where the double bunks and drop-down dining table had been. These also had been taken away. All that was left in place, aside from electrical fixtures, were the plastic molding strips that ran along the base of the trailer's walls, and the privy: a tiny sink with a foot pump for cold water, and a toilet with one of those foam-rubber seats popular in the '70s, now yellowed and cracked in two dozen places.

Raszer dropped down to his knees, removed a penknife from the pocket of his duster, and ran its blade behind the molding on all four walls, hoping its forward edge would strike something—a folded note, a hidden photograph. As there had been at least three permanent residents, plus the occasional girlfriend or comrade, crashing in this two-bed space, a lot of sleeping had probably been done on the floor, up against these walls. Raszer would have been content with a matchbook, a coin—any talisman once held by any of the principals—but he came up empty. With a grimace, he stood and faced the toilet.

He lifted the seat with the toe of his boot and squatted down. Urine and vomit had hardened on the rim. Good DNA, if anyone cared to check it. He was about to rise, when he noticed that something had been scrawled on the underside of the seat with a blue ballpoint pen. For whom to see? Who writes on the underside of a toilet seat?

The suppositions ticked in: someone on his knees, possibly nauseous, certainly stoned out of his mind, suddenly remembers something he doesn't wish to forget and doesn't want to share. The handwriting was poor, the hand shaky, but it appeared to be a website address and a name, perhaps a contact's. Raszer took out his little Mamiya digital and snapped a bracketed series of exposures. The ink was smeared in four places, but from what he could make out, the inscription read: a—-n-uts.com, and the name Hazid.

He took a small spiral notepad from his inside pocket and wrote out the letters with underlined blanks between them, like the child's game Hangman. This was not the time for crossword puzzles. The game could be played in his moonlight hours, when he kept long vigils reading or learning a new language at his slate-topped bar, abetted by speedballs of espresso and absinthe. At least he had something. He stood up, took one more look around, and left the trailer.

When he stepped out, he saw that the light had changed, marking what must be a break in the clouds, and that the false dawn of evening so characteristic of the mountain West—the last flare of golden light before the sun's candle was extinguished—had settled over the canyon, making the mist slightly luminous. Only a slice of sky was visible from the ravine, so he couldn't see the light's source, but about two hundred yards deeper into Johnny's gulch, where the chaparral grew thick, there stood an old California live oak whose tiny, reflective leaves shimmered as if spotlit. Passing beneath the string of dripping paper lanterns, Raszer proceeded toward the light.

Back in the brush there was more detritus: beer cans, empty half-gallon bottles of Everclear and Jack Daniel's, a girl's abandoned halter top, and a spent nitrous-oxide tank. Fifty yards before the oak tree, the undergrowth gave way to what looked like it had once been a footpath. The San Gabriel Front Range was crisscrossed with such easements, most of them cut like ley lines almost a century ago, when weekend hikes were part of any healthy regimen and the spirit of John Muir loomed large. Beyond the tree, the path—though arched by creosote and mountain sage—appeared to widen. Could this be the passage that Johnny's trailer was meant to seal off?

With the light fading fast, his feet improperly shod, and the Coronado Lodge still to visit, an extended ramble was out of the question, so Raszer set a bend at the base of a rock face a quarter mile ahead as his turnabout. When he reached it, however, there was further enticement. It was a trailhead, marked by a small granite obelisk inscribed with the following:

EAST FORK TRAILHEAD .6 M
BRIDGE TO NOWHERE 2.4 M

Had he another two hours to spare, Raszer would not have hesitated, boots or no boots. How could any investigator of final things pass up something called the Bridge to Nowhere? But he was rewarded, in any event, for his curiosity, because on the rock face that revealed itself as he came around the bend, someone—evidently dangling from a rappel line—had spray-painted these travelers' tips:

EX NIHILO AD NIHILO
SUICIDE IS THE ULTIMATE ACT OF PERSONAL AUTONOMY

From Nothing, To Nothing. If a thousand things about this case were still as muddy as the soles of his boots, one thing, at least, was becoming clear: Johnny Horn and Henry Lee had found in Iraq—if not before that—a symbiosis of action and ideology. With Johnny as heart and Henry as head, they had taken gameboy nihilism, anti-authoritarian resentment, and some novel blend of heavy-metal magick and near-Eastern myth, and captivated a group of small-town kids. On record, their World Anarchist Reform Movement seemed to have made little noise, but maybe—just maybe—they had attracted the notice of some big players who'd initially found them useful, and then—in a classic reversal—declared them just as expendable. But on the key question, the *why* of Katy Endicott's abduction, there was so little to go on that even Aquino's virgin-sex-ring idea had some weight.

At this very early stage of his investigation, Raszer was inclined to stick with what he called identity motives—that Katy was a victim precisely because she *was* what she was: a formerly devoted member of a rigid Christian sect that insisted on unquestioning obedience. He doubted he would have much more than that until he'd spoken to two people: Emmett Parrish and Ruthie Endicott.

The light from the low sun scrolled down the face of the rock, which was in fact the flat side of a boulder more than forty feet high. Other inscriptions materialized from the pink granite like invisible ink—some no more than initials, others in the faded colors and Aquarian luster of Day-Glo paint—until the vast canvas stood as a chronicle of the past half century and a wailing wall reflecting the descent from postwar aspiration to postmodern despair.

As he scanned the surface, Raszer came across one epigram in faint purple that he found especially wistful: THINK LOVELY THOUGHTS—P.P. It made him smile, but the smile faded when he noticed an accompanying arrow pointing toward the bridge and realized that the attribution was to Peter Pan. "Thinking lovely thoughts" was how the Darling children had gained the power of flight, and Raszer couldn't help but wonder if the Bridge to Nowhere was not also a lovers' leap.

As he turned back toward the trailer, a distant smear of color caught his eye. In the far canyon indicated by the path marker and just visible at the outer limits of his sight, rain had begun to fall again, refracting the sunlight into a gentle arc of yellow, blue, and some deeper hue that appeared to span the gorge. Evanescing within the rainbow was a frail structure of stone and steel, somehow less real than the mirage that concealed it.

For those disinclined to believe in "signs" of any sort, Raszer's sense that the bridge had utilized an optical effect in order to reveal itself to him might suggest that a stay at the Betty Ford Center or the Menninger Clinic was in order. But these were people who'd never opened a book to the very passage they were looking for.

He accelerated his pace as he neared Johnny's trailer. It was late, the Coronado was another treacherous two or three miles up the road, and he'd seen all he wanted to see here, at least for today. In truth, he was anxious to leave. If he hadn't brushed his head against the Japanese lantern or turned to see the gold string hanging down, he'd have been on his way. As it was, he had no choice but to stop.

There was something inside the soggy, misshapen paper lantern, a dark shape nestled against its translucent skin. The knotted gold string—about three inches long and resembling the drawstring of a fine jewelry bag—was the cord asking to be pulled, the party favor with the fortune inside. But what might be delivered into his hands, Raszer couldn't guess.

The lantern resisted at first; its wire frame narrowed at the mouth and appeared to have been squeezed even tighter to secure its cache. Once Raszer had widened it, though, the contents slipped out with a speed and heft that made him jump back. What he held at arm's length was a small, wet pouch of midnight blue velvet, embroidered in Persian style with the same gold thread used to make the drawstring. It felt like about eight ounces, but allowing for the water, whatever was inside would weigh in around six. Raszer held it up to the light. The needlework was elegant, the pattern abstract and unrevealing. A dozen possibilities raced through Raszer's mind. *Diamonds? Iraqi jewels pilfered from a mullah's private stash? A sacred artifact from the ancient city of Babylon, or one of the 'weird little statues' Aquino mentioned? Dope? A roll of bills?*

Whatever it was, his impulse was to obey the instruction of both instinct and police procedure and leave the pouch securely tied until it sat on Aquino's desk. Continuing to hold the dripping sack away from his torso, Raszer made his way slowly back down the muddy path to his car and set the evidence on the passenger-side floor mat to drain.

East Fork Road ran almost level with the San Gabriel River and mirrored its every bend. With the rains, the usual trickle had swollen to a bankless torrent of whitewater, with the two-lane road's narrow shoulder acting as an uncertain levee. Other states might have preemptively closed the road, but this was outback California, whose motto could well be "Proceed at your own risk."

Every year, hundreds of teenagers did just that, stopping to hop boulders or pose for hero pictures, and every year, a few of them drowned. Only a mudslide or a blizzard would prompt the Highway Patrol and Forest Service to drag out the barricades, and even this was controversial, for, remarkably, people *lived* up here. They lived in mobile homes long since rendered immobile, in ramshackle cabins propped on the slopes amid stands of Jeffrey pine, and they lived—though not freely—in the confines of State Department of Corrections Fire Camp No. 39.

Since his time was running short, Raszer drove past the paved bridge leading to the fire camp without much regard, except to note that the forested riverbank prison seemed—at least from his distance—not all that unpleasant. He wondered if it took fleecing some grandma of her life savings to rate such easy time.

Beyond the prison compound, the river widened into shallows where ridges and bars of scree and silt diffracted the rushing water into a dozen currents flowing at different rates. Amid these were hip-booted fishermen—not weekend anglers, but weary hunter-gatherers with nicotine-cured skin only a shade or two off from that of their soiled yellow ponchos, and small, mostly Latino children playing on the muddy banks in patent leather shoes and lacy dresses, waiting for Daddy to reel in dinner.

Just ahead, another bridge spanned the San Gabriel, this one leading to what looked like a pioneer village. In the rain and mud and darkening mist, it resembled a prospector's camp removed from time, if somehow entirely in place. Raszer glanced down at the Post-it note on his instrument panel. Aquino's directions were a little unclear about the next turn, so he decided—as much in fascination as out of disorientation—to consult the locals. He crossed the bridge and passed under a large, painted billboard announcing the Follows Camp, est. 1862, then proceeded past a RESIDENTS ONLY sign to a small parking lot adjacent to a raised picnic area and a rustic log structure with a Miller beer sign lit up in its window.

He stepped out and glanced around, suddenly very much aware that the roar of the river blanketed even the cries of the children playing nearby. The settlement buildings came in browns so darkened by damp that the most distant cabin was barely distinct from the clay soil around it. It was both comforting and dismal, as such places can be: comforting because it had the rainy-day smell and smoked patina of an eternal summer camp; dismal because it was evident that for the wary souls who eyed Raszer from its perimeters, this squatters' village was home.

A plaque beside the picnic area informed him that, indeed, the Follows Camp had been established as a gold-mining community and was now open to families on a year-round or seasonal basis. The full-timers, Raszer supposed, must be an intrepid lot by the slack standards of twenty-first-century America. The nearest supermarket was a good thirty minutes away; a trip to the mall would amount to an expedition.

Raszer flinched. Standing beside a picnic table not twelve feet away was an old-timer in stained overalls, with broken, caramel-colored teeth and a yellowish beard that came to a point at his solar plexus. He wore a misshapen brown hat and highwater boots. Raszer sensed that the man had been there in the fog, watching him, from the moment of his arrival, as still as a mule deer in the brush.

"Hello there," Raszer called out.

"Hello there," the bearded statue came back.

"Can you point me to the old Coronado Lodge?" Raszer asked. "With this rain and fog, I'm afraid I may wind up in Palmdale."

"Won't get to Palmdale on this road," the man creaked. "Won't even get to Manker Flats. She's closed above four thousand."

Raszer waited for him to continue, but apparently the man had retained only the last part of his question, and now hung there in suspended animation, rain dripping from his brim. "And the Coronado?" Raszer recapitulated.

"The Coronado?" he exclaimed, in the way that cranks have of making a question a reproach. "Whatcha want up thur? It's a ghost town. Closed since the big washout in '38."

"1938," said Raszer, and looked around at the erosion the rain had caused to the surrounding slopes. "Was it worse than this year?"

"Hell, yes!" his informant barked. "Took out the new road. Up at the Bridge to Nowhere. *That* would've gotten you to Palmdale. That was the plan, anyways."

"I'll be damned," said Raszer. "I didn't know that." And he added, for safety's sake, "But you *can* still get to the Coronado, right?"

The ancient gold-digger, which was surely what he appeared to be, squinted hard and asked, "*Why?*"

Raszer operated on the share-and-share-alike principle. Caginess would get him nowhere with witnesses, and certainly not with locals. "I'm a private detective," he said. "I'm looking for a lost girl . . . and maybe some new ghosts. Can you help me?"

The man cackled. "*God*, I love that Mickey Spillane. Y'ever read 'im?"

"I've run across his stuff," said Raszer. "His guy gets more girls than I do."

Rumpelstiltskin looked him over. "Doubt that," he said. "Unless yer a fairy."

"If I don't get up to the Coronado pretty soon, I may turn into a pumpkin."

The old man chortled and aimed his right arm northeast. "G'wup to just before the Camp Williams trailer park 'n make a sharp right on Glendora Mountain Road. Almost as soon as y'do, there'll be an old fire road on yer left, goin' into Cattle Canyon. It's still got a little pavement at the bottom, 'cause it was the main road to the lodge for the fancy folks, back in the '20s." He twirled an index finger in the air. "Shit . . . bootleggers, movie stars, ladies of the night! Use to be able to get drunk *and* laid up here for a fin. Anyhow, you'll follow that road as far as"—he glanced dismissively at Raszer's Avanti, then just as doubtfully at his shoes—"as far as your wheels will take you. Might have to hoof it a bit. When you can see the snow line, you're there."

Raszer looked down at his mud-caked boots and indicated the little camp store across the lot. "I don't suppose they'd sell me any galoshes over there?"

"Nope," said the old man. "I'll sell ya mine for a sawbuck."

"Thanks," Raszer said, "but I think you'd miss them." He started to get into the car, then paused. "I take it you heard about those boys who got killed up there a year or so ago. The kids who broke into the lodge for that big dance party."

"Heard *about* it!" he exclaimed. "Hell, mister, I live up in the topmost cabin, and those fools with their music had my heart jumpin' from two canyons away."

"Ever hear anything about the men who did the killing?" Raszer asked. "I know the police and the FBI were up here, so y'might know the killers drove a black Lincoln."

"No, sir. Keep to myself."

"Uh-huh," said Raszer, then paused, because the man's jaw was still moving.

"But when ya get up there," he said, "sniff around the old buggy sheds out back the place. There's an old squatter named J.Z. A fella I used to dig with. He used to make his crib in the sheds. Could be he saw something. If he's still alive. You never know."

Raszer gave his new friend a nod. "Thanks," he said. He fished out his keys and set one muddy boot in the car. "Say," he added, "is there still gold in these mountains?"

"Sure, yeah," said the man. "But I lost my nose for it."

"About that squatter," said Raszer. "Did you tell the police or the feds?"

The man chuckled. "They never bothered to ask."

Almost as soon as he'd closed the door, Raszer became aware of a sweet, heavy scent with a faintly putrid undertone. The little velvet sack, sitting right in the path of the heat vent, had begun to exude aromatic traces of myrrh, musk, and patchouli.

By the time Raszer had hiked his last yard, it was nearly dusk. There was barely enough light to reflect yellow from the police tape still draped on the Coronado's barricaded doors and between two trees up the road—the spot, evidently, where the killing had been done. It was colder than he'd expected. The snow line was indeed close. A harsh, wet wind scooped out the canyon, and the uppermost branches of a few of the taller pines on the property were flocked with ice. Raszer felt an ache in his chest.

It was an ache he knew well, equal parts loneliness, dread, and perverse exhilaration. It was a feeling, he was certain, that had been known to every scout or tracker who'd ever gone ahead of the war party or the wagons. It was accompanied by an awareness of the heartbeat behind his left ear and the hollowness in his stomach.

Aquino had neglected to mention—although it probably went without saying—that the police had boarded and padlocked the Coronado's once stylishly rustic buildings. The main lodge had a stonework portico fit for a Bentley, and eight-foot doors of solid oak. The huge logs of which the lodge was made had claimed a small forest of old-growth trees, but now looked as sad and sunken as the walls of an abandoned outhouse. Three long, one-story outbuildings of knotty pine had accommodated the resort's guests in comfortable, if not exactly luxurious, fashion. All but one of them looked to have been badly damaged by fire. The dance hall, angled forty-five degrees from the lodge and connected to it by a covered stone walkway, was a scaled-down version of a vintage Jazz Age pavilion, built to hold a big band and a couple hundred ginned-up swingers. Though its roof had partially collapsed and its walls had succumbed to dry rot and termites, Raszer saw instantly why Johnny Horn had seized it for his last rave.

He circumnavigated the hall, looking for a way in. It would be bad form to break the police tape or jimmy the locks, but he wasn't about to leave without going in. In the rear of the building, at shoulder level, was a small casement window that presumably opened into a dressing room or toilet. Raszer spent five minutes trying to force it, then gave up and broke the pane without compunction. It was a small marvel, he rationalized, that it had remained unbroken for this long.

He dropped down inside with a *krruunch* that informed him the foundation was no more solid than the roof. He was indeed in the ladies' room, where fragments of an art deco mosaic, and the corroded remains of a makeup mirror, were scattered on the floor and walls. The door was off its hinges, and Raszer stepped out into the ballroom. A gaping hole in the arched roof provided a bit more light.

An empty dance hall is as empty as empty gets. A quick scan confirmed that it was little more than a shell, and that the police had scoured it. Nonetheless, he wanted to cover every warped square foot of its hardwood floor, to stand where Katy had stood, breathe the air that she had inhaled. He regarded this as an empirical exercise, rather than a mystical one, but that was because mysticism was ingrained in his method. If, for one moment, he could feel the morphic resonance of her past presence, he might better sense it when she was truly within his grasp.

From the same deep pocket that held his penknife, he removed a small, high-powered flashlight and swept its beam across the floor as he walked. There was no debris, no matchbooks or cigarette butts, but the hall's very emptiness seemed to reflect the fevered breath of the dancers and the jackhammer rhythm of Johnny's music, driving his acolytes to a place where nothing was true and everything was permitted. Raszer recalled reading that as the rave scene in England had degenerated from ecstatic community to paranoid dystopia, the ravers had talked of "obliviating," of entering a state of "bewilderness."

Ecstasy and oblivion were, of course, two sides of the same coin, the difference being that for a Zen monk, nothingness was a glass at least half-full, where for the nihilist, it was well below half-empty. He wondered where Katy's glass had stood.

The thought of music caused him to pause and regard the raised bandstand. On the night of the rave, there would have been no trombone section, no torch singer, just a solitary DJ with two turntables and a microphone. There was a single item on the bandstand: a common folding table, the type used in cafeterias. Raszer beelined for it, narrowly skirting an open gash in the floor. He vaulted up onto the stage and approached the table. No piece of furniture could possibly have held less promise: no hidden drawers, no deep cracks in its Plasticine surface. And yet Raszer had a feeling. He remembered something he'd once seen at a club. It was in his mind's eye now, and the question was whether it would manifest itself for him.

He squatted, took out his penknife again, and ran its point along the hairline gap between the particleboard underside of the table and its aluminum base. DJs—or MCs in club argot—leapfrogged from gig to gig on the strength of their last mix, and if someone staggered up and shouted, "How do I hire you?" there wasn't time for talk or free hands to write a number. They kept business cards at the ready, wedged into any available cranny for fast access. There was only one such crevice on this table.

What Raszer had seen in his mind's eye was a train of business cards, lined up in the crack under the table's edge, easy to grab between needle drops, but all he needed was one, and one was what he found when the knife edge suddenly stopped. With great care, he extracted it.

MC HAKIM
-TRANCEMASTER-
213/666-0230

A good DJ kept his hands on the platters and his eyes on the dance floor, monitoring the vital signs of every ass, searching every face for hints of ennui, gauging his command of the crowd. "God is a DJ, and this is his church," went one famous "callout hook." The DJ saw the whole and its parts, and he was especially on the alert for walkouts. MC Hakim, whoever he was, might have seen Katy Endicott leave the building. He might recall the pretty girl with the '40s movie-star hair and doe eyes, and whether her expression as she left had suggested delirium or coercion, lassitude or terror. Raszer slipped the card into his pocket and went back out through the window.

Starting at the front doors, Raszer took the walk that Katy and her four male companions had taken, through a stand of pines to the road, and up the slope to where the yellow police tape marked the killing ground. It took less than three minutes, but by the time Katy would have reached the parked Dodge convertible, her teeth would have been chattering. *Whose car? Were there, as Silas suggested, drugs in the trunk? Had that been the lure to get Katy outside?* There was nothing at the site to evidence the horror that had occurred, no *X* to mark the spot. Only the slack yellow tape, flapping in the icy downdraft, and the hiss of the pine needles. Something stirred in the underbrush—a deer, or maybe an opossum—and the hair on Raszer's neck bristled.

In the daylight, he might have lingered awhile to hear whatever tales the place could tell, but Raszer was not immune to being spooked, and decided that he needed to be home at his bar with a glass of good, dry Portuguese red and a fire in the hearth. Still, he remained just a little longer because this was the point of departure, not only for Katy Endicott and the souls of her ill-chosen friends, but for him as well.

A hundred yards off to the northeast, up a narrow and badly rutted service road, were the "buggy sheds" that the old prospector had mentioned.

Raszer would very much have liked to save the sheds for another day. He was clearly going to be spending a lot of time in Azusa, and poking some more around the local mountains might reveal something about the alliances and enemies Johnny Horn and Henry Lee had made during their reign. Furthermore, he felt cold and uneasy.

What would not let him retreat was his thirst to find out if his chance detour into the Follows Camp and the appearance out of the fog of a yellow-bearded prophet were the sort of augurs a man disregards at great cost. The old guy had advised him to check out the buggy sheds for a squatter named J.Z., and he'd seemed to know more than he let on. The day's yield had been good so far. Why not gamble another round?

With gravity and fear dragging on his heels, Raszer trudged up the service road.

The first of the formerly red-painted sheds was an automotive tool shop, with everything from ancient fan belts to leather steering wheels in a state of desiccated preservation. Up on blocks and left to die was the chassis of a very old Ford, as old, Raszer guessed, as the structure that housed it. There was no evidence that anyone had adopted the place as a home. It smelled only of old grease.

In the second shed, he found another automobile carcass, as well as a genuine buggy, its luggage trough littered with what appeared to be the pieces of a disassembled still.

But again, no J.Z.

The third building was set apart from the others and had the slightly more residential look of a caretaker's shed. The door, peeling old paint the color of dried blood, was warped tight but unlocked, and when Raszer finally succeeded in forcing it open, the outrush of feral odor knocked him back, affirming he'd hit pay dirt. He stepped in, propping the door open with a brick, and flicked on his flashlight.

It wasn't the smell of death, animal or human. He'd have recognized that and felt another kind of uneasiness. This was the organic odor of a living presence, the smell of armies of bacteria camped on unwashed flesh, and that brought a different discomfort, because he was therefore invading someone's home. He swept the beam around and saw that there was an old stove, long unused, a chest of drawers, and, in the far corner behind a wall of fruit crates, a man-size nest of dried grasses partly covered by an oil-stained army blanket.

"Hello?" he called out.

Nothing.

"J.Z.?" Still nothing. Confident that he was alone for the moment, Raszer crept warily over to the makeshift bed. He picked up a corner of the blanket and dropped it immediately. The smell was overpowering, and there seemed to be nothing else here. He moved on to the chest.

The drawers were empty. Not so much as a moldy sock. J.Z., Raszer guessed, wore every article of clothing he owned. But laid across the top of the chest was a discolored lace table runner, quite possibly from the Coronado's original linen closet. Placed with an almost fetishistic neatness on the cloth were a variety of small found treasures, things that a child or a magpie might collect: a comb, a key, a shard of mirror glass, assorted junk jewelry, and an assortment of coins. Some of the coins were new, some at least as old as the Coronado; all but one were from American mints, and that one exception drew Raszer's eye, because the words on the coin were in Arabic.

He held the flashlight close. It was about the size of a half-dollar and hexagonal in shape, though its sharp angles were worn soft. The barely recognizable face of a woman was on the head. Raszer had seen pictures of its kind in studies of the medieval Levant. It appeared to be some kind of dirham of ancient mintage. The date contained three numerals, of which only the first—a 5—was legible, followed by the Arabic letters AH, putting it in the eleventh century AD, based on the Muslim calendar.

Moreover, it had been somebody's lucky coin. A tiny hole was drilled near its top edge, big enough to pass a chain or a string through, and its dead center was cratered—nearly pierced—by what must have been a meteoric impact. Whoever had been fortunate enough to wear this charm around his neck had stopped a bullet.

The walls of the shed trembled, and Raszer stepped back into a semicrouch. The wind was coming down fiercely. It could have been that. For a moment, there was only the scraping of branches on the roof, but then he heard a snort, followed by shallow, wheezy breath. Whatever it was stood directly opposite him, on the other side of the thin wall. Raszer glanced at the open door and considered a dash into the open.

"J.Z.?" he called out again, almost hopefully.

There was a quarter-size knothole in the wall. The wind was whistling through it. Raszer leaned in gingerly, keeping one hand on the dresser for balance, and brought his eye to the hole. He blinked and froze.

A jaundiced, bloodshot eye blinked back at him.

A surge of adrenaline hit all his limbs at once. He moved back, turned, and made straight for the door with deliberate speed. No sooner had he crossed the threshold than his inner ear registered a sickening *ccrraack* and the oceanic rush of blood to his brain.

The last thing he saw before consciousness fizzled out was the wine glass waiting on his bar. It would keep waiting.

"Fuck," he groaned, and hit the cold, wet ground.

SEVEN

Raszer kicked and pawed within his unconscious mind, like a man trying to break out of a bag. Sentience began to seep back in, and with it, profound discomfort. Wet, cold, pain, and an almost supernaturally foul odor. Short-term memory returned very slowly, but he was aware of a ringing at the base of his skull that was both the echo of the blow he'd suffered and the lingering effect of Hildegarde's tea, which contained trace elements of ayahuasca, a harmine hallucinogen derived from a rainforest vine. The microdose in the brew, combined with other roots and herbs, was just enough to sharpen his perceptions appreciably, but that included the perception of pain.

His struggle had its root in the waking world. He opened his eyes to see his left ankle—the site of a years-old sprain that sometimes still caused him to limp—bound and tied to a railroad stake that had been hammered deep in the ground. His hands were free, but there was nothing to grab but fistfuls of mud. He felt the urge to retch. Along with the noxious odor came the smell of gasoline.

A small fire of damp kindling smoked and sizzled on his left, and arranged around the fire were not only his wallet, pocketknife, and flashlight, but the trophies of his day's good hunting: the DJ's business card and, most disturbingly, the embroidered velvet sack. The sonofabitch had broken into his car. Only now did Raszer regain consciousness fully enough to regard his captor, who sat cross-legged and humming gutturally while rocking a two-gallon can of gasoline on his lap, like some mutant infant. At his side was the two-by-four he'd used to knock Raszer cold.

J.Z.—for presumably this was the giant whose beanstalk castle Raszer had trespassed upon—did not at first seem to notice Raszer's glare. He was the apotheosis of every homeless man who'd ever haunted a kid's nightmares, and he smelled like a herd of goats in rut. He looked at first to be a sizable man, but that might only have been the mound of clothing he wore, added to with each new discovery of someone's lost sweater or windbreaker. Underneath it all, there might be a frame wasted to nothing but will. He was a white man, but his face was black as tarnish on silver. There was so much organic material on him that he appeared to grow right out of the soil.

The tuneless humming, which came straight from J.Z.'s larynx to his cracked, parted lips, did not encourage Raszer to feel that he was the captive of a rational man, but it did take the edge off his visual ferociousness. If it gave J.Z. a childlike aspect, however, it wasn't innocence; he seemed to know exactly what he was doing. As he became aware of Raszer's glance, the hum caught in his throat, and he stared back with slit yellow eyes that, in reflecting the sporadic licks of flame, were almost lupine.

Raszer slowly sat up, keeping his hands still.

"J.Z.?" he inquired.

"Ay-*ah*," the man said, his lips moving only enough to distinguish the simple phonemes. It was the way people spoke with the most excruciating of toothaches.

"An old friend of yours . . . " Raszer winced and squeezed his eyes shut as a bolt of pain arced over the top of his skull. " . . . The old fellow at the Follows Camp . . . told me to look you up. My name is Raszer. I'm a private investigator, but maybe you know that from my wallet. I'm looking for a girl who was kidnapped here over a year ago."

"Wray-*ah*," J.Z. repeated, for it was indeed Raszer's name he had tried to articulate. The *R* had been throated almost in the French way.

Raszer lifted his foot from the ground and shook the rope, then winced again. The ankle was inflamed. "Why . . . did you tie me up?"

The encrusted smile line at the left corner of J.Z.'s mouth creased just slightly. He spanked one rag-bandaged index finger against the other in the naughty-boy sign language we all learn as children. His hands were wrapped tightly with strips of what might once have been white sheets. Only the blackened fingertips were visible.

"Because I was in your house," said Raszer. "I'm sorry about that. I'm a snoop. A prospector, like you. But I didn't take anything." He glanced down at the items laid beside the fire. "I guess you can see that." Finally, Raszer felt secure enough to use his hands, and pointed at J.Z.'s booty. "Those are my things. May I have them back?"

The old squatter made a snarling sound and shook the gasoline can menacingly. A few drops fell on MC Hakim's business card. "*Ma*-hing-ow," he growled.

"Your things now . . . " Raszer repeated. "Well, maybe by the law of thieves. But your friend told me you were an honorable man—that you might be able to tell me something about that night. When the kids came. When the black Lincoln came."

The fire popped and flared. As if ricocheting, a twig snapped in the woods, and the old man started. His mouth dropped open, his bushy chin reflexively working up and down like a marionette's. At once, Raszer saw the reason for his stunted speech.

Only half a tongue remained in the squatter's mouth, and the stump had been badly self-stitched with what looked like coarse twine, loose ends hanging limply. Even a fleeting glimpse told Raszer that it was badly infected, probably beyond painful.

"Jesus, old fella," said Raszer, in as even a tone as he could muster. "You ought to let a doctor look at that."

J.Z. shut his trap tightly and kept staring off into the woods. His expression was both wounded and frightened.

Raszer scooted himself as close to the fire as he dared. He sensed that with the slightest provocation, the gasoline can would be upended and the whole trove would go up in flames. "Who did that to you?" he asked gently. "Was it the men who came to take the girl? The men in the black car?"

The squatter gave his head a sideways jerk, ostensibly a no. Then Raszer saw that in doing so, J.Z. had shifted his line of sight and was now glaring from beneath heavy, hooded brows in the general direction of the fluttering yellow police tape.

"Over there's where they took her, right?" said Raszer. "And killed those boys. Were you here that night?"

With a touch of silent-movie melodramatics, the hermit pivoted his head like a gun turret and aimed his phosphorescent eyes at Raszer, who suddenly realized that J.Z. had not yet decided whether he was friend or foe. Because the squatter was generically human, because he possessed the faculty of understanding, Raszer had made the mistake of assuming a kinship. But J.Z. was not kin. He was a wounded animal just self-reflective enough to be both paranoid and willful, and he was not holding a gasoline can for show. He was a man who had survived this long only through the cruelest kind of barter. Evidently, he had bartered his tongue for his life.

Now, the stock in trade was Raszer's life for his belongings.

He lifted the can slowly and doused the items with gas, then picked up the first of them—the little high-tech flashlight—and held it over the fire.

"What is it you want, J.Z.?" Raszer asked.

The squatter's upper lip curled, as close to a grin as he could manage.

"You can have it," Raszer said, indicating the flashlight. "It's yours."

J.Z. pocketed the light. Raszer knew instantly he'd given it up too easily, and when the squatter next took the penknife in hand, he protested: "No. I bought that in Amsterdam. That's pearl inlay and solid-gold hardware. Worth at least $200."

Getting into his game, J.Z. held the knife close enough to the fire to raise a lick when the gasoline vaporized. He lowered it another inch before Raszer bid.

"All right, partner," he said. "It's yours." He pointed to the DJ's business card. "In exchange for that little piece of cardboard. There are three boys dead, a young girl missing, and it looks to me like you've lost the better part of your tongue. The number on that card may help me find the men responsible. What've you got to lose?"

J.Z. mulled it over, suspecting a trick. At his age, in his mental state, he probably suspected life of being a trick. After weighing the trade, the old man slipped the knife into his boot, then picked up the gasoline-soaked card and handed it to Raszer.

"*Errhh*," he said, and his breath stank like chèvre left in the August sun.

J.Z. had an uncanny sense of value, or perhaps he'd peeked, because he saved the velvet sack for last. With surprising dexterity for a man whose fingers were practically mummified, he untied the drawstring. J.Z.'s own bouquet easily overpowered the exotic scent. He set the sack in his palm, and made to empty its contents into the fire.

"Okay, you old bastard—"

J.Z. cackled and tipped the sack further. His jackal eyes flashed.

"Once a gold-digger, always a gold-digger," said Raszer, his heart in his throat. "Whaddaya want for that bag and what's in it?"

The squatter's lips parted in anticipated relish. If he'd had a tongue, he would have licked them. He curled his fingers around the neck of the velvet sack and drew it close to his breast. In unmistakable semaphore, and with an almost dapper air, he uncurled one finger to point at Raszer's torso, then yanked his own frayed and filthy lapels, and finally aimed the finger squarely at Raszer's coat.

"Oh, no," said Raszer, broadly waving off the proposal. "Not my duster. It's vintage. Passed down four generations. You'd have to kill me first."

Raszer's claim was not entirely fallacious, but J.Z. sniffed out the overstatement and dangled the velvet sack over the fire, lightly holding the gold cord between the tips of his thumb and forefinger. He let it twist there, flames singing its royal blue velvet to brown, slow roasting whatever was inside.

"Shit," said Raszer, angrily peeling off the garment. "You're better at liar's poker than I am. Give me the sack and my wallet, and you can have my fucking coat."

J.Z. started humming again. Stupidly, Raszer made a grab for the sack, but with his free hand, the old man scooped up his two-by-four club and brandished it while wagging his mutilated tongue from side to side. The sight of it, the stench, and the throbbing in his head made Raszer want to vomit.

"Or," he said, "you can smash my skull in, old man. But then you'd be a murderer, and you'd have to deal with detective Jaime Aquino of the Azusa police, who knows where I am and is expecting me at six o'clock."

It was an empty threat, and Raszer suspected the squatter knew it. By the time the police arrived, he could have dumped Raszer's body in any number of culverts or stream beds known only to him, and by dawn, the coyotes would have finished him off.

J.Z. withdrew the sack from the fire and set it on the wet ground, where it steamed and sizzled softly. He tossed Raszer his wallet, then held out his hand for the coat, twitching his fingers in a *gimme* gesture. Raszer fished his keys from the garment's deep pocket and held them to his chest.

"I want one more thing, J.Z.," he said with a smile.

The squatter growled and narrowed his eyes.

"I want that old coin you've got on your bureau," said Raszer. "The five-sided one with the hole in it. Tell you what: You leave me tied up while you go inside, and to be sure I don't untie myself and make a run for it, you take my car keys as security."

He slipped his finger through the key ring and held the keys out at arm's length. J.Z. rose to a squat, farted, and spat into the fire. Then he snatched the keys and lumbered off, as only an old man wearing forty pounds of wet, filthy, ill-fitting clothing can lumber. In less than thirty seconds, he was back with the coin and they made the trade.

"Fair exchange," said Raszer. "Fair exchange. Now be a gent and untie me."

J.Z. pushed one arm into Raszer's coat, then the other, and turned the collar up. It was a snug fit, but it seemed to satisfy him. "*Hnng*," he grunted. He squatted down and untied the first two of three miner's knots binding Raszer's ankle. He paused, grinned widely enough to reveal red, diseased gums, and, before undoing the last knot, scooped up the open velvet sack and tossed it carelessly onto Raszer's lap.

Raszer glanced down. The sack had upended, disgorging its contents onto his groin. He squinted in the dying firelight, then howled in protest and leapt to his feet as the last knot was undone. The old man cackled and pranced about in his new coat.

EIGHT

RASZER STRODE INTO Aquino's office and set the blue velvet sack, its contents restored, on his desk. The cop gave it a once-over and then looked up at Raszer, not without fraternal concern.

"You don't look so good, Mr. Raszer," he said, and sniffed. "You don't smell so good, either. What happened to that nice coat of yours?"

"I traded it," Raszer said, indicating the sack. "For that."

Raszer felt no better than he looked. He was still chilled to the bone, having limped back down the Cattle Canyon road wet, aching, and with nothing but a T-shirt to cover his torso, then descended Highway 39 with his windows fully open in order to dispel the lingering odor of J.Z.'s visit to his car and the Egyptian-mortuary aroma of the sack. He'd made the stop only to get the sack into evidence and out of his possession.

Detective Aquino fingered the sack warily, then turned it with the tip of his pencil, observing its embroidery.

"Looks like we missed something up there," he said, without affect.

"A few things," Raszer said. "It happens when the locals and the feds are working the same turf. Something always slips through that big jurisdictional crack."

"I guess that leaves room for the freelancers," said the cop. He toyed with the drawstring like a kitten. "It's not gonna jump out at me, is it?" he asked.

"Not now," said Raszer, and pulled out a chair. "I found it tucked into one of those Japanese lanterns Johnny had hanging around the back of his trailer. The cord was dangling down. In plain view, but . . . well, the light had to hit it right."

"Uh-huh," said Aquino. "So what the hell's in there? A tarantula?"

"Nope," said Raszer. "I wish. If I'm not mistaken, Detective, it's Henry Lee's testicles, gift wrapped and embalmed in oils by whoever did the job."

"*Madre de Dios*," Aquino said, crossing himself.

"You said it."

Aquino drew open the sack and poked gingerly at the contents with the eraser end of the pencil. "Man," he said, pushing the sack aside, "what a stink. I'm giving this to the lab guys. If it is what it looks like, it's a new one for me."

He punched a comm line and barked a name into the speakerphone. A moment later, a young duty officer came in. "Jimmy," Aquino said, handing over the sack, "bag this and get it to the lab. Mark it for the Endicott-Coronado case. I wanna know if those are human testicles inside, and I wanna check them against Henry Lee's DNA." The officer took the bag between two fingers. "Don't peek," said Aquino, and smiled.

"So, what else did you come across up there?" he asked, regarding Raszer with thinly concealed chagrin. Absently, he parked the pencil on his lower lip and began to chew the eraser.

"I found the calling card of the DJ who did Johnny's rave."

"No kidding," Aquino said. "Are you going to share the wealth?"

"After I've talked to him," Raszer replied.

"Anything else?"

"Yeah," said Raszer, wiping mud from his brow. "There was. I flushed out an old squatter who lives in one of the outbuildings at the Coronado. Had to take a lump on the head for his company. But it's possible he may have seen something. Somebody cut his tongue out."

Aquino leaned forward, now engaged enough to pocket his wounded pride. "Testicles, tongues . . . I pray God we don't find Katy Endicott's head somewhere. Any connection, Mr. Raszer?"

"I don't know. The old man is so far gone, I can't be certain he didn't do it to himself. He appeared to have done his own stitches. But somebody put the fear of God in him. Either Johnny and his boys or the killers. In any case, he's not talking."

Aquino chuckled darkly. "I guess not. I don't suppose you got anything out of him, then . . . other than a whack on the head."

Raszer bounced an unformed sentence about the Syrian coin on the tip of his tongue, then swallowed it. A connection between the coin and Katy's kidnappers was a wild hunch, at best, but giving voice to it would likely bring the feds and the whole counterterrorism establishment stumbling back into the case with their own agendas, and whatever tightrope Katy Endicott was walking might snap.

"No," he said. "But things don't generally fall together this way unless there's an attractor at the center. My read on him is that he saw the murders happen."

Aquino nodded for a bit too long, and Raszer knew he was being mapped.

"I've heard mixed reports about you, Mr. Raszer," said the cop. "Some guys aren't sure which end you're playing. Especially after that gameboy case . . . "

"Scotty Darrell," said Raszer, knowing what was coming.

"Right. Where you could probably have prevented a shooting if you'd showed your hand to the police."

"Or caused a suicide. Sometimes you're damned either way."

"I know that," said Aquino. "Listen, I'm no Joe Friday. I play off intuition, too. I prefer Tony Hillerman's stuff to police procedurals. But I have to ask you, because my chief is going to ask me . . . you're not one of those 'psychic detectives,' are you?"

Raszer lowered his eyes and smiled to himself.

"I guess you're going to have to decide that for yourself, Detective Aquino," he replied. "I don't put it on my business card, if that's what you mean. I use the eyes I was given." He pushed back the chair and stood up. "It's been a long day. I need a bath and a drink. I'll call you tomorrow. I'd like to see the evidence taken from the trailer and the lodge. And I'd like to speak to the Parrish boy as soon as possible."

Aquino got up. "All right, Mr. Raszer. *Buenas noches*. And, uh, thanks for bringing in the cojones." He paused. "It's a funny thing. I was *up there*. I checked those Japanese lanterns. Forensics covered the site. It just doesn't make sense that we wouldn't have found that bag."

"I don't need to tell you," said Raszer. "You have to be *looking* for it. *Buenas noches*, Detective."

✦ ✦ ✦

RASZER LIT A CIGARETTE and rolled down his windows. The fetid odor of the old squatter, not to mention the smell of perfumed morbidity, remained in the upholstery and in his nostrils. They were both very hard smells to lose, but the tobacco helped.

Was it possible that the little sack *hadn't* been there when Aquino and his CSIs had scoured the scene? Was it possible that a survivor of that night's horror had sought to dump an unwanted legacy? Or was it a plant, a lure, an invitation? Raszer parked the thought and left it. It was nearly seven o'clock. There were other will-o'-the-wisps to chase before he lost them, and instructions to relay to Monica before she checked out for the day. He speed-dialed his private office number from the hands-free car phone.

"Yeah, Raszer," she answered. "Don't you know a girl gets lonely?"

"Sorry, Moneypenny," he said. "I've been wrestling bears."

"Right. Don't call me Moneypenny. It's patronizing. Besides, she was old."

"Yeah, but she had a great ass."

"S'you survived Azusa? No mountain men with banjos tried to sodomize you?"

"You don't know how close you are. I've got a two-inch gash in my skull, my bad ankle's back, and I had to swap my grandfather's duster for a piece of evidence."

"Aw, Raszer . . . I feel your pain. What can I do?"

"Are you good for an hour of OT?"

"It's not like I've got Clive Owen lined up for tonight."

"You're too good for him anyway. Okay. I want you to pull everything you can from the library on castration as a ritual or religious sacrament, particularly as it relates to Sumerian goddess cults or Islamic heresies that might still be active in some crypto form. Plot an epicenter at Karbala in Iraq. That's old Babylon. Link me to anything on the web that's not junk, and set up a hypertext. We've already got a Cybele connection by way of the moon rocks. Let's find out how far south her cult got."

"Can I ask where this is coming from?"

"One of the murdered boys, a kid named Henry Lee, was gelded. He had a knife tattooed on his chest with the words 'She Made Me Do It.' He did a stint in Karbala and came home a sorcerer. And I found his balls in a velvet bag with Islamic stitching."

There was silence on the other end of the line.

"What a difference a day makes," she said. "Okay. Ritual castration. What else?"

"You remember that breakdown we did of the book of Revelation?"

"How could I forget?" she replied. "That was your first big case. I learned everything I know about computers and the Apocalypse doing that."

"Pull it up from the archives. I'd like you to do a text search for any references to the 144,000 who go to heaven in the Rapture. It's a central tenet of the Witnesses' belief system. I remember something, but I need to confirm it."

Nearly six years earlier, Monica and Raszer had deconstructed and indexed the text of the The Revelation of St. John the Divine, the final chapter in the New Testament and the master script for every end-time scenario envisaged by Western man over the last two millennia. The prophecies of John of Patmos had dogged Western civilization like a bad dream, and Raszer hadn't been able to think of a better way to orient himself to the mindset of fanatics than to do his own cybernetic midrash on Revelation. You could reject any man's interpretation, but you couldn't dismiss the power of the vision any more than you could turn away from a wreck on the highway.

"All right, Raszer," said Monica. "It'll be on your laptop. On the bar."

"Have I told you lately that you're a goddess?"

"Just yesterday, but I got my period today, so it helps."

"Speaking of the bar, would you mind opening a bottle for me?"

"Done."

"And, uh, would you pour me a scalding bath? I'm cold, I'm filthy, and I need to go out tonight and see a DJ—assuming I can track him down."

"A bath! Oh, now you're pushing it," she said. "The goddess can be wrathful when pressed into servitude."

"I've learned today that we must all be faithful slaves."

"Will you rub my feet tomorrow?"

"Deal."

"See ya."

"See ya."

Raszer ended the call, tossed his cigarette out the window, and smiled. When all other graces in the world were gone, there would still be Monica.

✦ ✦ ✦

HE PULLED INTO his driveway at eight fifty-six, the Friday freeway traffic having stretched a fifty-minute journey to nearly twice that long. There were people going home to little plots in the Antelope Valley and dusty retreats in Canyon Country who wouldn't see dinner until almost ten. These were the wages of survival in the world's biggest suburb. In the rain-scrubbed northeastern sky, a few stars had come out amid the patchy clouds. The hint of desert on the breeze suggested that the clouds would be out to sea by morning, and that the storm season was over. It came to him—for no apparent reason—that it would be Easter in less than two weeks, and he thought of Brigit.

As always, Monica had armed the security system before leaving, and, as often happened when the day's work had taken him far afield in mind and body, he had to reboot his memory for the code. It was the date of his father's birth, a date he'd never committed to memory in the deepest sense.

He stepped into the office and was comforted by the trace of Monica's scent and the multicolored array of standby lights pulsing gently from the bank of computer and communications equipment. Raszer sometimes had the vaguely alien sense of coming home to a particularly well-appointed replica of his "real" home, like an FBI safe house furnished by a decorator who'd made a study of his past life. It was his, all right, but it was missing something. Once he'd set his things down on the bar, the feeling faded.

The wine had been opened, and his MacBook slumbered nearby, awaiting his keystroke to unveil the Revelations file. A stack of books with pages marked by three-by-five-inch index cards sat on the black slate, just outside the pool of light cast by the overhead lamp, next to a fresh yellow legal pad. Some of them his fingers knew from repeated reference; others, like the M.J. Vermaseren tome *Cybele and Attis: The Myth and the Cult*, he'd purchased years before and never cracked. The fact that Monica could assemble the material so quickly was testament to the weeks on end they'd spent cataloging it in the early days. With rare exceptions, all new stories were old myths modulated by the wave of time and historical novelty. Once you saw this, certain puzzles were solved.

Before heading to the bath, he poured himself a glass of wine and admired the spidery legs it left on the sides of the glass. He drank, then set MC Hakim's business card on the bar and punched in the number. It rang forever before finally bumping over to an answering machine whose tape had been recycled one time too many.

"Listen up, party people," announced a male voice with a north country English accent. "Tonight's TAZ is Tantra on Sunset. Trendy and tiny, but oh so Silver Lake. Trippy chillout and global trance is the mix, so leave the agro vibes at home and bring your desiring machines and your kama suitors, babies. The *puja* begins at midnight."

In spite of the slang and its insinuation of pagan pleasures, there was something weary in the voice, something as worn as the oxide coating on the tape.

Raszer pictured a British expat in his late thirties—maybe even forties—who'd been around in the heyday of the rave movement and was now playing out his line to a diminishing clientele. He knew the venue, an Indian restaurant on East Sunset that converted to a club at the witching hour. The dance floor was barely twenty feet in diameter, and these days, there would likely be as many nodders as dancers. In the neohipster demimonde, cool blue cyberfunk had long since replaced the pink soda-pop fizz of the anthemic Ibiza sound.

The answering machine's beep came after a small eternity, sounding more like a bleat. Unsure that he was being recorded, Raszer began his message tentatively.

"Hello, Hakim," he said. "My name is Stephan Raszer. I'm a private inves—"

There came a drowsy "hello," for which Raszer was totally unprepared.

"This is Hakim," said the voice from the recording. "You're a what?"

Raszer reintroduced himself and offered only the barest hint of his purpose. He informed the DJ that he would be there around twelve thirty, and Hakim agreed to a quick chat during his break. "Never met a real PI," he said wryly. "Might be a kick."

Raszer hung up, peeled off his T-shirt, and finished the wine. The chill was still on him, as was the scent of the squatter. Beside the legal pad, he set the spiral notepad with the partial web address he'd copied from the toilet seat: a—-n-uts.com. Hazid. A shiver ran from the lump on his head to his tailbone. He decided it might be a good mental exercise to try to fill in the blanks while he soaked in the bath, so he carried the notebook into the master bathroom. A candle was burning, and the water was still hot.

✦ ◆ ✦

THE LAPTOP'S SCREEN came up with a file icon flashing against the Moorish desktop pattern. Raszer cinched his bath robe, slipped onto the barstool, and opened the file to a hypertext version of Revelation 14, with underlined passages linking him to pages of exegesis by scholars and theologians from the fifth century on. The passage Monica had highlighted in red was from verses 1–4:

> AND I looked, and lo, a Lamb stood on the mount Sion, and with him an hundred forty *and* four thousand, having his Father's name written in their foreheads. And they sung as it were a new song before the

> throne, and before the four beasts, and the Elders: and no man could learn that song but the hundred *and* forty *and* four thousand, which were redeemed from the earth. These are they which were not defiled with women; for they are virgins.

Raszer clicked on the hyperlinked word virgins, and was taken to a display of related passages from Revelations, as well as a quote attributed to Jesus in Matthew 19:12—the same chapter containing the admonition on marriage that figures into every Christian church wedding: "What God hath joined, let no man put asunder."

Hearing his pronouncement against divorce, the Pharisees had protested to Jesus—in so many words—"If we're not free to dump our wives, maybe it's not such a great idea to get married in the first place," to which Jesus replied in cryptic agreement:

> All men cannot receive this saying, save *they* to whom it is given. There are some eunuchs, which were so born from their mother's womb: and there are some eunuchs which were made eunuchs of men: and there be eunuchs *which have made themselves eunuchs* for the kingdom of heavens' sake. He that is able to receive *it*, let him receive *it*.

Raszer read the passage repeatedly and with increasing speed, until its archaic syntax morphed into a kind of nonverbal vernacular, a direct feed from page to brain. It was a technique for reading sacred texts he'd been introduced to when first undertaking his study, and now he did it automatically. The fact was that unless you read the original Greek or Hebrew, Sanskrit or Arabic, everything was filtered through the translator's biases, and even in the maiden tongue, most scripture and sutra were secondhand news and at least twice removed from meaning. The real meaning was esoteric. As Jesus had said time and again in the Gnostic Gospels: "He who has ears, let him hear." If this was not the case in the matter of eunuchs, it was surely true of an even stranger quote Monica had pulled in from the Gospel of Saint Thomas:

> When you make the male and the female be one and the same, so that the male might not be male nor the female be female—then you will enter the Kingdom.

In just two degrees, Raszer's separate queries about the identity of the Jehovah's Witnesses' "Little Flock" of 144,000 and the history of sacramental castration had been drawn together in a way that put a new spin on Aquino's virgin-sex-ring theory. Suppose virginity—of one sort or another—*was* a factor, but suppose it wasn't about the lust of middle-aged men for young girls. Suppose it was about devotion. Or control.

Raszer left the thought there, reminding himself only of what he'd already learned on so many previous cases: Given half a chance, predators would always use the tools of religion to augment their power over prey. It was the same story with every clique that deserved the pejorative *cult*, whether it was Manson's Family or Jim Jones's Peoples Temple or L. Ron Hubbard's Church of Scientology. There was always an agenda, and if it wasn't about personal power, it was about power on a broader scale.

The castration material was more extensive and more eye opening than he'd expected, and there would be a few nights' work in digesting it. Several items, however, jumped out of Monica's hastily assembled list of bullet points:

- The earliest evidence of ritual castration was found in Sumerian texts from the temple of the goddess Inanna at Uruk, in present-day Iraq. A sample quote from high priestess Enheduanna, dated 2300 BC: "Inanna turns a man into a woman and a woman into a man."

- The priests of the cult of Phrygian mother-goddess Cybele, instituted around the time of King Midas (725–675 BC) and fashionable in Rome of AD 295–390, were known as the *Galli*, and *castrated themselves* in imitation of her divine son/lover Attis, who had done so in penance for his betrayal. According to myth, the birthday of Attis was December 25. Unlike other pre-Christian mother-son cults, the cult of Cybele and Attis was a cult of *abstinence*.

- Origen, the great scholar and theologian of the early Christian church, also "made a eunuch of himself" for the kingdom of heaven's sake.

- In the mid-18th century, an ecstatic Christian sect known as the *Skoptzy* or *Skoptji* arose in the Oryel region of Russia, with ritual self-castration as its badge of membership. The sect attracted military officers, merchants, and the nobles of St. Petersburg, and by 1874 counted 5,444 members (incl. 1,465 women) and tens of thousands of sympathizers. The Skoptzy claimed that they were following Christ in Matthew 19:12, but that *their mission would not be complete until their numbers had reached the 144,000 of Revelation 14:3-4.*

- Just as *castratis* had guarded the harems of the caliphate, the Holy Ka'ba of Islam and its *black meteorite* are to this day secured by an elite guard of eunuchs.

Raszer poured himself another glass of wine and lit a cigarette. The business about the gelded priests of Cybele he'd vaguely recalled, and it had been on his mind since seeing the morgue photo of a neutered Henry Lee laid beside the black *baitylos* rock on Aquino's desk. But Raszer hadn't been able to make the connection to Iraq until seeing that the Sumerian Inanna had also demanded the family jewels. And the gospel passages with their bizarre echo in the Russian sect seemed to suggest a trail of cognitive cookie crumbs that led right to the door of the Witnesses by way of their belief in the special status of the 144,000.

Could a cult of sexual negation born at the dawn of history have survived, like a viral spore, into the twenty-first century? Monica's accompanying web links seemed to hint that it could have, because there were sites—many related to the transgender community—with names like Alt.eunuchs.com and Men Without Balls. He who has ears, let him hear. Sex and gender had *always* been big issues in religion.

Raszer pushed back from the bar, paced, put out his cigarette, and then pulled on a gray turtleneck he'd retrieved from his closet. At this stage, he had to beware of red herrings. They were always present where the occult was concerned, because the occult, by its very nature, concealed the truth by way of an elaborate shell game. The unwise player could easily be drawn off the bead. Nothing yet made the case for substantive linkage of Henry Lee's emasculation, Johnny Horn's reactive brand of anarchy, the Witnesses' literal reading of scripture, and Katy Endicott's abduction.

Except for one thing: The faceless men who had come for Katy had not, despite Emmett Parrish's confused testimony, simply materialized from the fog. They had been drawn there, like sharks to blood in the water. They were the "outside agency," unaccounted for by any other factor. They were Katy's detour, and one of them—Raszer was all but certain—had in the death struggle with three strong, young men lost his lucky coin: the Syrian dirham with the bullet crater. If the man and the coin were companions, then Katy might be outside the bounds of U.S. law. Raszer set the coin on the legal pad and drew the lamp over. He retrieved his loupe from beneath the bar and took a closer look at the badly worn face. Now he was certain it was a woman, and she appeared to wear a crown. Could a Syrian goddess have demanded—as Cybele and Inanna did—the ultimate pledge of fidelity from her male devotees?

He'd left the Avanti's windows down to air out, but it still smelled of funk and balm, so he opened the garage, kick-started his old BSA 450, and tore down into Hollywood, heading east on Sunset toward Silver Lake. The night was cool, but the wind in his hair felt like a baptism. By the time he'd crossed Hyperion Avenue, his mind had cleared of the day's fog, and he was ready to be sociable.

It was Saturday night, after all.

NINE

At Club Tantra, Raszer was greeted by a pretty but instantly forgettable blond in a silk blouse who took his $20 cover and aimed him toward the strobe-lit dance floor. The restaurant's tables had cleared, but for a few stragglers lingering over their vindaloo, and the action—such as it was—revolved around the lanky DJ with a lantern jaw and hands as large and agile as any Raszer had seen. His long, dusty brown hair was chopped bluntly in a style that was defiantly retro and cool at the same time; the gray in the sideburns and the deep creases in his leathery face spoke of long years of late nights, but his blue eyes twinkled. Despite the Middle Eastern moniker, he was, as his accent had suggested, as British as the queen. Raszer liked him immediately, and liked him even more when he spun a dance mix of Kula Shaker's pop-raga "Govinda" and mashed it with a trippy M83 track. He took a small table at the dance floor's edge and ordered a Bombay gin and tonic in honor of the empire.

The restaurant smelled of garam masala and mint, but not much of dancers' sweat. There were perhaps thirty-five bodies in the room—mostly small, mixed parties of people in their late twenties—and only five were currently on the dance floor. The odd number owed to the fact that one of the dancers was working solo. She wore purple sandals with three-inch heels, and looked to be twenty-five and ageless at the same time. Her waist-length black hair reflected blue highlights, and if she wasn't either Tunisian or Egyptian, the movement of her hips in perfect measure with the strobe's pulsed flashes suggested she'd picked up her tricks in the *rai* clubs of North Africa or at private recitals for a Berber warlord. She was going to be a distraction—women who danced well always were. Raszer half hoped she was the DJ's woman, and there did seem to be something between them, because every so often, the sullen arc of her mouth yielded him up a smile.

After finishing half his drink, Raszer took out his own business card, along with MC Hakim's, and cut across an empty quadrant of the dance floor to the

DJ stand. There were a few more dancers out now, as Hakim was into a propulsive trance mix and another batch of drinks had made the rounds. The exotic woman's eyes were on Raszer all the way, like breath on his neck. It wasn't an entirely pleasant feeling, but it wasn't unpleasant, either. He laid the cards side by side on the stand, gave Hakim a nod and a little smile, and improvised some sign language for *talk*.

When break came, the DJ put on a CD of ambient jazz with a Coltrane-ish soprano sax blowing Middle Eastern riffs, strolled over to the black-haired woman's table to exchange what looked like small talk, and then crossed the dance floor to Raszer. His walk was easy and unhurried. He ordered a ginger ale from the waitress, calling her "luv," and then offered his hand.

"Harry Wolfe," he said. "It's a pleasure."

"Stephan Raszer. The same. Still good for that quick chat?"

"Why not, mate? All I'd do otherwise is smoke and flirt with the barmaid."

Raszer gestured to a chair, and the DJ folded himself into it.

"Just out of curiosity," said Raszer. "How'd you come by Hakim?"

"It came with the gig," he answered. "My first big date, back in '84, the promoter told me he couldn't put me on the bill without a handle. I was carrying around a book back then by this guy Hakim Bey, so I lifted his name and it stuck."

"Hakim Bey," Raszer repeated. "The guru of punk. The poetic anarchist."

"Right," said Wolfe. "Big influence on the early rave scene. When it was tribal. When it was good. The whole TAZ thing."

"TAZ?"

"Temporary Autonomous Zone," said Wolfe. "A moveable utopia. That's what we were after in the Orbital days." He chuckled. "The halcyon days."

"I remember," said Raszer. "We didn't get it over here the way you did in the U.K., and the Ecstasy was probably never as good, but I did my share—"

Wolfe made a movie frame with his thumbs and fingers. "Cut to twenty years later, and now you're a . . . " He held Raszer's business card at arm's length. " . . . 'Specialist in Missing Persons.'" He dropped the arm languidly to his side. "Who's missing?"

"Katy Endicott," Raszer said, and took from his jacket the photo duplicate Aquino had printed for him. He unfolded it on the small table. "Since the night of that illegal rave up in San Gabriel Canyon a little over a year ago. I believe you MC'd it."

Harry Wolfe kept his poker face and stole a glance at the photo—the group shot. "All raves were illegal, mate. The good'uns, anyway. But I wouldn't call what happened up there a rave. The truth is, the vibes from that scene were so bad, I haven't taken an outback gig since. I stick to small clubs in the city these days."

His ginger ale arrived, and he sipped it quietly, taking Raszer in.

"Did the cops ever question you about that night?" Raszer asked, then laid his finger on the photo. "Or about whether you'd seen her leave the dance hall?"

"The cops, hardly," Wolfe replied. "But the fucking FBI was all over me. Some wanker with the face of a Pekinese and all kinds of wild theories about sleeper cells and suicide bombers." He jabbed his finger at the photos of Johnny and Henry. "One thing those fuckers were not is 'sleepers.' They did everything loud, as far as I could tell from what little contact I had with 'em. That's probably what got them killed."

"They did have guns," said Raszer. "Apparently, lots of them."

Wolfe laughed out loud. "So does everyone in this bloody country," he said.

"Did Johnny Horn . . . personally hire you for the party?"

"The sleazeball promoters hired me," Wolfe said. "But I had to deal with Johnny about the details . . . the music. He wanted all this agro shit. And Henry, his strange little friend with the *cock-a-doodle-doo* hairdo, wanted these incantations. Rage and magic, man—a bad mix. I knew something was going to go down. I should've taken a pass."

As compelling as the DJ's narrative was, Raszer found his attention ineluctably drawn to the dark woman sitting on the opposite side of the dance floor. She'd been eyeing him with a combination of innocent animal curiosity and predatory aim from the moment Harry Wolfe had joined him. Raszer shook it off and tried to refocus, but the DJ was drinking ginger ale, not gin, and the exchange did not get past him. He took a look over his shoulder, then offered his assessment.

"I think somebody wants to be on your dance card, Mr. Raszer."

"I figured she was your private dancer, Harry."

"She's nobody's but her own," said Wolfe. "We had a thing, but quite frankly, she needed a brother more than a boyfriend." He laughed wryly. "Now I just take care of her. Pay the rent on her flat." He rolled his eyes to the ceiling. "Upstairs."

"Who is she?"

"She is the perfumed garden, mate," said Wolfe, and smiled over the rim of his glass. "Layla Faj-Ta'wil. Somebody should write a song about *her*."

"Is she Egyptian?" Raszer asked. "Israeli?"

"Syrian," said Wolfe. "Crossed with Persian. *Meow*." He leaned in conspiratorially. The slur in his speech would have been easier to buy if he'd been holding a real drink. "You want to know about Johnny Horn, talk to Layla."

Raszer went along with the *entre nous* routine and propped an elbow on the table. "How's that?" he asked.

"She was Johnny's squeeze for a bit. I don't think the arrangement was made in heaven. It was more she was on loan to him."

"On loan from who?" Raszer asked, and hailed the waitress for what he'd already decided would be his last drink.

"On that subject," said Wolfe, pushing back his chair, "you'll have to query her. All I can tell you is that night—after the bodies were found and the whole thing went to hell—she came home with me and didn't let go of me for a week. I don't think she wanted to go back to her keepers."

"Were they also Johnny's killers?"

Wolfe shrugged and stood up from the table. "There's only so much you can get from a woman of her culture," he said. "Whether she wears a burka or a slit skirt. They have their own version of *taqiyya*, if you know what that means."

"Concealment," said Raszer. "Although it's usually to keep the enemies of the faith from knowing what you're up to. Do you trust her?"

"Beauty of that sort can't be trusted. But we connect."

"That's worth a lot."

"Well, there you go," said Wolfe, and offered his hand. "And here I go. Back to the platters. It's a pleasure, Mr. Raszer."

Raszer gripped MC Hakim's oversize hand. "Same here. You've got my card. Call me anytime you feel like talking . . . and don't be surprised if I call you."

"I hope you find your missing girl, Mr. Raszer. I wish I could tell you I knew what happened that night, but I don't." He finished his ginger ale and set the glass down on the table. "But do give Layla a spin, won't you? I'll play something dreamy. She's a lonely girl . . . and the way she smells alone is worth the price of a dance."

Raszer smiled noncommittally and sat back down.

Harry Wolfe began to walk away and then turned. "Funny thing I just remembered," he said. "Back in the day, when everybody was luv'd up on X and we thought we were making a revolution in our heads, the pirate-radio DJs in the U.K. used to call the raves a 'collective disappearance.' As if we'd all go to the chosen potter's field and dance our bodies away until there was nothing but spirit, and then . . . *whoosh!* We'd all find ourselves someplace far better. Maybe that's where your Katy is."

"I doubt it," said Raszer. "But it's a nice thought—unless you mean *dead*."

Harry Wolfe cocked his head and turned, taking a detour en route to his station to exchange a few words with Layla. Raszer began to feel like the apex of a triangle.

As MC Hakim resumed spinning and intoned, "Let's go to Goa, party people," into his microphone, Raszer allowed himself an extended glance at the exotic animal seated across the strobe-lit dance floor. To no real surprise, she was waiting for his eyes. Raszer didn't flinch, except internally. Her beauty was of the bruising sort, and he couldn't help but feel that, somehow, she was being proffered by the DJ. Maybe it was a tender sort of pimping. Maybe she *was* a "lonely girl" who came downstairs to dance and mate under the protective eye of her platter-spinning patron. Or maybe he was trying to get a monkey off his back and onto Raszer's. In any case, the transparency of the setup did not seem sufficient reason to forgo a dance, or to wave off an encounter that might yield such potent information. It was clear from the DJ's rap that Layla Faj-Ta'wil might be, in some sense, a direct link to Katy Endicott's abductors.

While Raszer's mind mapped out a rationalization for crossing the dance floor, his body was already there. She sat with her chin languidly propped on her palm, bejeweled fingers curling back around the fine line of her cheek, dusk-colored nails tapping softly on the cheekbone. Left leg was crossed over right, the drape of her gauzy skirt falling to the side, and the open toe of her spiked sandal aimed in his direction. Her hair was parted on the side, pinned back from one eye and falling over the other, and at the part it went midnight blue. Something disturbingly erotic occurred when Eastern women adopted Western dress and body language. Something that implied the most recondite of secrets. And that was the crux of it, after all—the secrets.

Layla rose from her chair after four bars of Massive Attack's "Teardrop," artfully meshed with some gris-gris, trip-hop version of "Sympathy for the Devil."

She rose weightlessly and came to where she'd danced before, her body moving like kelp in a gentle current. She did not grant Raszer even a sidelong glance, and it made him feel momentarily invisible, as if to exist, he had to join her. Slowly, he stood up, strode onto the dance floor, and didn't whisper, "Would you like a partner?" until he'd curled his fingers gently around her waist.

Layla turned fluidly, the silk fabric slipping beneath his fingers like oiled glass, the muscles in her belly tightening just slightly. Her only assent was to allow his hands to remain on her hips.

Raszer saw MC Hakim smiling softly, eyes half-closed, nodding off to the hypnotic rhythm. Enjoying his work. The rolling motion of his head and shoulders mirrored Layla's own swell. Her lips curled at the corners, watching him watch her.

Raszer smiled. "I'd like to know you," he said. "There's a Moroccan place up the strip that serves fresh mint tea. Can I treat?"

Her eyes narrowed. "You want . . . to *know* me?" she repeated, as if hearing the word for the first time.

Raszer nodded, and while he sunk into her blue-black eyes, thinking to himself that he'd moved her with the notion that a man might want to do something other than fuck her, her right hand fluttered down his thigh, and suddenly all nobler intentions fled and he wanted only to be inside. Her right hip pressed his left, and with the skill of a thief, she slipped two fingers into a tiny pocket in the folds of her skirt and curled them around a silver-plated atomizer the size of a lipstick case.

Moving with him, seeming to find the off-beats between the strobe light's pulses where she would become momentarily invisible, she lifted the hand that had rested on his right shoulder and brought it to his cheek. It was cool against his flushed skin. The other hand, with the atomizer curled in its ring finger, ran up the inside of his thigh to just below his groin. She looked into his eyes and said: "Then you will know me, *ragoli*."

Her hand left his thigh and rode firmly over the stiffening ridge in his trousers. Thus diverted, he didn't see her bring the nozzle of her little silver atomizer to just below his left nostril. *Psst. Psst.* He cocked an ear, thinking she'd whispered something, then felt his center of balance lurch forward and went up on his toes, with only her body to break his momentum. He was numbly aware of her hands against the small of his back as he dropped his head onto her shoulder, crushing his nose against her perfumed neck.

He could walk, but without feeling the floor. He could see, but only as through a prism. The strobe's pulses slowed to a throb, and in the spaces between, there was only blackness. Harry Wolfe appeared and disappeared like a coin trick, spinning platters that emitted a low rumble but seemed to be utterly stationary, and when Raszer looked to him, slack-jawed, for aid, he saw the DJ smile, lift one hand from the turntable, and wave bye-bye, as if to a small child. Oddly, the hand was detached from the wrist.

The sense most completely disabled was Raszer's hearing. What he did hear was very much like what someone deafened by mortar fire would hear: the soft, *shussing* decay of sound, but none of its initial attack. For this reason, he was not aware they had entered a stairwell until they began to climb. With every other step, she incanted, "Okay," alternating with, "*Goood.*"

"*Okay . . . goood . . . okay . . . goood . . . okay . . . good. Kwaeyyees.*"

But counting was beyond him. Self-awareness was beyond him. He had no body, and if he did, it was a sealed box and he was trapped inside. Only echoes of sensation remained, and if his circuits did fleetingly crackle back on, it was only to stream fear to his blunted extremities. When they reached her door, he went down like a rag doll.

Sszzzzt. There was light, and the smell of sulfur from a kitchen match. Raszer's eyes opened; his pupils contracted brutally, sending pain to the rear of his skull. In the match light, he recognized her face, a thing of frightening beauty. She held a little silver spoon, the kind given to newborn babies as a keepsake. Layla had taken off her dress and wrapped herself loosely in a robe of deep purple silk. In the pulsing candlelight, the arc of her breasts and her round belly flickered like magic lantern projections, but his desire to touch her remained, for the moment, as dead as the feeling in his limbs.

She had lit the match to heat the underside of the spoon, and its contents began to sizzle softly and release a narrow plume of fragrant smoke. She brought the spoon to his nostrils, but Raszer kept his eyes on her, just as hers were on him, dropping them just long enough to see that what was vaporizing in the well of the spoon was a resinous little black ball, now partially dissolved.

Almost at once, Raszer was infused with a contentment so unbounded and complete that he heard himself sigh, and only then knew that his senses had been restored. Beginning with his groin, feeling streamed back into his limbs like rivulets of warm oil. Layla had unpinned her blue-black hair, and it half-curtained her face. The other half reflected amber, and he realized there must be another source of illumination.

In sequence, he took note of the candle burning on a rough-hewn dining table eight feet away, of the four posts of the bed he'd been laid on, of the pillow behind his head, and of the fact that he had been stripped down to his shorts and was bound to the bed with two lengths of nylon climber's rope in a very distinctive manner. Each rope looped around an upper thigh, biting gently into his groin, and was then firmly tied to diagonally opposing bedposts, putting his midsection more or less at the crosspoint of a large X. His arms and legs were free, but even had he been inclined to try, he could not have shifted his center far enough to untie the knots. He completed his survey and returned his eyes to her. The spoon was back under his nose. It would have been pointless to hold his breath. He drew in the vapor and became aware of her cool hand on his belly and her long fingernails just inside the elastic band of his shorts.

He glanced from side to side at the ropes binding his wrists. "What are your intentions, Layla?"

"I intend to play with you," she said.

"What'd you dope me with downstairs?"

"Just a little Special K," she replied. "I do not have patience for seductions."

"Ketamine?" he said. "Bad girl. You could have stopped my heart, and then how much fun would I be to play with?"

"No, Mr. Raszer," she said. "I know my drugs. Now be quiet, or you will find yourself having no fun at all." Her nails bit into his groin, just below the scrotum.

"I think I understand," said Raszer. "Was it your handiwork that made Henry Lee a capon?" She didn't answer. It might have been the opium, or it might have been some vague faith in the goodwill of the DJ spinning records downstairs, but Raszer chose to believe this girl would not cause him harm—at least, not the irreparable kind.

Layla slipped the robe off and began to touch her breasts as a man might want to. She traced the nipples, then moistened her finger with her tongue, slipped the finger between her legs and proceeded to prime herself for the main event.

"Why don't you untie me, Layla . . . and let me do that?"

She smiled cruelly. "No," she said. "Enough talking." She swung her leg over his knees, drew his shorts firmly down to the ropes, and added, "It is fucking time."

"I see it is," said Raszer. "Next time, skip the pig tranquilizer and go straight to the opium. You won't have to work so hard on me."

Layla took firm hold of his wrists and brought her mouth down to his lazily stiffening cock. As she did, she took brief note of the old scars and looked up at him.

"I told you," she said, and flicked her tongue out. "I know my drugs. It will take longer, but it will last longer, too." She took him fully into her mouth, then pulled back roughly. "I will make you hard. I will make you so hard you can stab my heart."

By the time they had finished, the music downstairs had stopped. When the blood finally left his brain and surged into his groin with orgasm, Raszer briefly lost consciousness. That had never happened before. He guessed it was the ketamine cocktail, or maybe the ropes against pressure points. Either way, he must have been out for a few minutes, because when he came around, Layla was smoking a clove cigarette and Harry Wolfe was standing over the bed with a grin on his rubbery British face. Raszer looked down and was happy to see that the girl had had the decency to pull up his shorts.

"How was he?" Wolfe asked her, though his eyes remained on Raszer.

"Not bad," Layla answered, and exhaled a long, straight plume of smoke. "He seemed to like . . . being tied up." She was still naked, but unabashed.

"Ah-yeah," said Harry. "We all long to serve la Belle Dame Sans Merci."

"And you, Hakim," said Raszer, sitting up with some difficulty. He was still bound like a steer. "How do you serve? Directing customers upstairs?"

"Oh, no," the DJ replied. "You were a special case." He drew over a chair, sat down, and propped his legs on the bedstead. "You see, Mr. Raszer, we're going to ask a favor of you, and we thought it was only right to offer you some hospitality first. Layla has taught me a great deal about hospitality. It's the Arab way."

"I appreciate that," said Raszer. "But, in that case, how about taking the ropes off? I'd like to get my cigarettes."

"Not just yet," said Wolfe, and scooped Raszer's trousers off the floor. "I'll get them for you." He fished out the American Spirits and lit one for Raszer, then sat back and sighed. "Things have cooled down a bit since that night. The cops have stopped coming around, and so—for the moment—have Layla's old friends. The boys are dead and the girl is gone, and for some bloody reason, ev'rybody seems okay with that. It may not be right, but it's okay with us, too, because—believe me—there were a few months there when I didn't ever think I'd make it through the night. My crime was to play a gig and let a frightened lady come home with me, but in the beginning, you'd have thought I'd captured fucking Helen of Troy. I found daggers pinned to my door, had to replace my DJ rig twice, and I even started drinking again."

"I got angry, then bloody paranoid, but I never, ever told the law that Layla was involved with these guys, because you see, Stephan, *the girl asked me to protect her*, and after a while, I made it my vocation. Stupid, maybe, but I'm my father's son and he was a stubborn wanker. Anyhow, finally, things got quiet. Your investigation is going to end all that."

The emotion in his voice was raw and real, and by Raszer's reckoning, Harry Wolfe was probably as close to sincere as anyone living in Los Angeles got nowadays. He glanced at Layla, curious to see if she was visibly moved by her knight's testimony. Her face wore a kind of sullen gravity, which he accepted as being close enough to gratitude for the moment. Still, there were kinks in the story, not the least of which was that he'd been doped, tied up, and ravished by the tender damsel Harry Wolfe had sworn to protect. One look at the well-developed musculature in her legs and upper arms suggested that Layla Faj-Ta'wil was far from helpless.

There were a dozen questions about the nature of their relationship, but Raszer put them off in favor of a more pressing line of inquiry.

"Which guys?" he asked Wolfe.

"What?"

"You said you didn't tell the police that Layla had been tied up with 'these guys.' I need to be clear—are we talking about the same guys who, according to the eyewitness, killed the three boys and kidnapped Katy Endicott? The guys in the Lincoln?"

"Yes," said Layla, exhaling a lazy plume of clove smoke.

"Mind you," Harry broke in, "we were in the dance hall. There were no witnesses, other than—"

"That poor, crazy boy, Emmett . . . " She'd finished his sentence. Perfectly.

"Who came wild-eyed and howling into the hall afterwards," said Harry.

"But it was *them*," said Layla, shaking her finger. "I know it," she spat, taking hold of the black tuft of hair between her legs, "like I know *this*."

"*Them*," said Raszer. "The same men who, ah, introduced you to Johnny?"

"*Traded* her to Johnny," said Harry.

"Traded you," said Raszer, his eyes still on Layla. "For what?"

"For the girl," Layla replied sulkily. "What did you think?"

"They traded *you*," said Raszer, "for Katy Endicott."

"Yes," she replied, shooting Wolfe a quick glance.

"And then killed their trading partners," said Raszer, catching the look. "Nice."

She crushed out her cigarette and crossed her arms over her breasts. "And the main reason they haven't killed me is that they have what they want. Still, I have not left this building in over a year. I sleep here, I dance downstairs. Harry brings me groceries, things I need. They are not fools. They only take you when you are in the open—when no one is looking. When you go outside with no coat on."

"Who the hell are they?" asked Raszer.

"They are . . . " She turned to Harry for the right word.

"Operatives," said Wolfe.

"Operatives for who? For what? A sex and drug cartel, or something else?" Raszer shifted his glance from Harry to Layla, then back to Harry again.

Harry shrugged. "Don't ask, don't tell. It's when you know who they are and what they're about that they have to hurt you. And that's the sad story of Johnny Horn and his posse. I happen not to want it to be my story. Johnny wanted in. Johnny—"

"Johnny had no clue," said Layla, with what seemed like both contempt and pity and maybe—just maybe—some remorse. "I can tell you this much, and no more." She dropped one bare knee onto the bed and leaned forward, her body within his reach, her breath in his nostrils. She smelled of black opium, Turkish tobacco and sex, rendered aromatic by a fourth scent. Something new. An oil—anise or peppermint? Raszer found himself aroused again.

"The drugs and the sex," she continued, in a soft, dusky tone. "These are used as weapons. Tools. Just as good as gold or daggers when you wish to bring down a man, or a state." She shook the curtain of hair from her eye and crept in closer. "Look how much damage one girl on her knees did to an American president." She put her finger under his chin. "Think how much harm I could do to you if I chose to."

"I don't doubt it, Layla," Raszer said. "Even as sweet-natured as you are."

She drew back a little and said, "But I will not. Because I like you."

"From what I gather," Harry said with a caustic laugh, "and I don't care to gather much—these chaps never lose a match. The only way you win is to walk away. Far, far away. That's where the favor comes in. Might turn out to be a favor for you as well, mate."

"And is granting the favor the condition of my release?"

"Nah," said Harry. "We're gonna let you go. We just wanted a captive audience." He leaned forward. "Granting the favor is the condition of your survival, because if you put these guys onto us, you can bet we'll put them right back onto you."

"Then untie me and let me get dressed," said Raszer. "If I'm going to be bartered with, I'd like to have my pants on."

Harry raised an eyebrow toward Layla and then nodded. "All right, then," he said. "It's not as if we haven't frisked you."

Raszer's captors each took a side of the bed and untied the knots, and as Raszer stepped into his trousers, he asked, "If you went to so much trouble to keep all this from the police and the FBI, why are you telling me? You could have sent me walking without either the workout—nice as it was—or the information."

"I Googled you after you called," said Harry. "You're quite a character."

"Christ," said Raszer. "This is getting really irritating."

"Cops have a way of creating blowback," Harry continued. "The FBI is worse. *You* can't afford blowback, because it'll blow your cover. And unlike cops, PIs only whore themselves for information."

"I suppose I should take that as a compliment," said Raszer.

"Indeed you should, mate. As for why I served you up to Layla . . . well, what can I say?" Harry Wolfe chuckled. "She was hungry." He gave Layla a wink, and she ran her nails over his shoulder, the first sign of affection Raszer had seen between them.

"Okay," said Raszer, pulling on his sweater. "What is it you need?"

"My dad has a little fishing cottage in the Lake district of England," said Harry. "Far from the madding crowd. We can be safe there. *Layla* can be safe . . . if we can get there. But Layla's here illegally and, due to her past associations, is probably on a dozen watch lists. I've overstayed my visa, and my British passport's been revoked because I once brought a suitcase full of Ecstasy through Heathrow. We're stuck, you see."

"In a stateless limbo," said Raszer. "We'll all live there one day."

"A no-go zone," said Harry. "That's what my namesake, Hakim Bey, calls it. We're invisible . . . until we show up at the airport. But if we can get down to Costa Rica, I have friends from the old days who'll arrange transport to the U.K. We can get in by way of the Hebrides. Once I'm home, I'm home."

Raszer lit another cigarette and looked the pair over. "I have a hard time," he said, "picturing the two of you in a fishing cottage."

"Look closer," said Harry, "and you'll see the sword over our heads. Layla and I have made mistakes, and sooner or later they'll catch up. But we're not such bad people, not so undeserving of a little happiness. A fishing cottage will suit us fine." He rested his big left hand on the small of Layla's back. "Isn't that right, my little cat?"

"I will go," she said quietly, "where Harry goes."

"Besides," said Harry, "I miss my da."

"So you want me to arrange a flight to Costa Rica?" Raszer asked.

"Plane, boat . . . " said Harry. "Doesn't matter."

"And what in return, aside from eternal gratitude and good karma?"

"The best for last," said Harry. "Once arrangements are confirmed."

"We can tell you where they have probably taken the girl," said Layla.

"Well, that seems fair," said Raszer, stepping into his shoes.

He picked up his cigarettes and offered his hand in farewell, but Harry Wolfe had something else to say, and just when Raszer had begun to acclimate himself to one skewed reality, they hit him with another.

"Listen, er . . . " said Harry. "I've got to pack up and get across town to feed my dogs. Would you mind, Stephan, staying with Layla tonight? It would be—"

Raszer squinted.

Layla simply lowered her black lashes and smiled.

"I can pay you," said Harry. "For your trouble."

Raszer shook his head. "It won't be any trouble." He sat back down on the bed and flopped against the pillow. "Not any more than it already has been."

"Good, then," said Harry, and gave Layla's hair a playful yank.

And with that, the DJ was gone, and Raszer found himself alone again with a beautiful woman who might, depending on her inclination, be either lamb or wolf.

She stepped out of her shoes and climbed into bed.

◆ ◆ ◆

RASZER AWOKE BEFORE dawn with a buzzing in his head. A pinprick of indigo light moved on the ceiling when he shifted his head. It took him a moment to realize that its source was his eye. With the light came a sharpening of sense. The breath of the sleeping woman beside him carried a scent he now distinctly recognized as wintergreen.

TEN

"ARGONAUTS.COM," said Monica, swiveling to face Raszer as he came in.

"*What?*"

"You left your little notepad in the bathroom," she said. "With the fill-in-the-blanks quiz." She blew the bangs out of her eyes and leaned back. "It's that website for alternate reality gamers, remember? We found it when we were on the Scotty Darrell case. Who's Hazid?"

"I dunno," he mumbled, and closed the door behind him. "It was inscribed on the toilet seat in Johnny Horn's trailer. Along with the other letters. Nice work. You *are* a woman who takes initiative." He leaned against the wall of her cubicle and rubbed his eyes. "Jesus. Could Johnny and Henry have been into this stuff, too?"

"You mean The Gauntlet, or just the role-playing thing?" she asked.

"I dunno what I mean," he said. "I think I need a shower and a nap."

She looked him over and wrinkled her brow.

"Where have *you* been?" she said. "You look like you spent the night in a cathouse. And your eyes are totally bloodshot."

"You're the one who told me I should get laid."

"Judging by the way you look, you got more than that. Who was she?" Monica chewed on her pencil and waited for the answer.

"How badly do you want to know?"

"Badly," she said. "Another dancer?"

Raszer plucked a daisy from her desktop vase and leaned over to park it behind her ear. She looked as fresh and squeaky-clean as he did grotty and disreputable. "In this case, your curiosity is justified. She was the former consort of Johnny Horn, allegedly provided to him courtesy of the men who killed him and kidnapped Katy Endicott, and now being sheltered by the DJ who did the rave at the Coronado."

Her jaw dropped. "Holy shit, Raszer," she said. "You got a triple play!"

"Maybe," he said. "But I have a weird feeling about this girl. She has a little too much to hide."

"Well, I need to hear all of it . . . " She wrinkled her nose. "After your shower."

He stumbled a little on his way through the office, and she giggled.

"She really worked you over good," Monica said.

"Yeah," Raszer said. "Just like a Waring blender." Monica blinked. "Warrren Zevon," he explained, then peeled off his sweater and held it to his nose, remembering. "About that website. Were there any secret drawers? Members-only stuff?"

"It's all password protected. I searched for *Hazid*, but nothing came back."

"Just for kicks, try using all the variations on Scotty Darrell's name as a log-in." He thought for a moment. "And using *Hazid* as a password. Fast work on the castration thing, by the way, and the Revelations scan. Did you see the connections between that Russian sect and the Witnesses?"

"A hundred forty-four thousand of them," she replied.

"And every one a 'virgin.' I wonder—could we be looking at something where being born again means being 'virginized,' giving up gender distinctions? Stay on it, would you?"

"You're not thinking Katy's abduction was an inside job, are you?" she asked. "Like she was chosen by some high council of the Watchtower Bible and Tract Society?"

He propped his elbows on her partition. "It seems completely far-fetched," he said, "but I'm not discounting that the Witnesses could be involved on some esoteric level. Not Silas. Not her father. But one of the other Elders struck me as a little 'off,' psychosexually speaking: the senior Overseer, Amos Leach. Just a feeling."

"You know, Raszer . . . hold on . . . " She made a flurry of keystrokes, then turned to pull a file from the cabinet behind her. "There've been a bunch of pedophile claims made against the church over the last few years by ex-members. One or two prosecutions, I think."

"Check it out."

"By the way," she said. "You'll have to make that nap a short one. Your Detective Aquino called. You're scheduled to interview the Parrish boy and his mother at two this afternoon. After that, he'll take you to the evidence locker."

"Great," said Raszer. "I'll sleep when I'm dead."

"Who said that? Hunter Thompson?"

"No, that's Warren Zevon, too," Raszer explained. "And he is dead. Sadly."

"Yeah," said Monica, eyeing his bare torso. "Now get out of here before you begin to distract me."

"One more thing."

"Uh-huh?"

"When you have a minute, update our list of freelance pilots operating out of New Orleans or South Florida. The real cowboys. Ex-CIA and the like—the guys who can thread the needle."

"Planning a trip?"

"Not me," he replied. "I'll explain. Right now, I need to soak my head."

Under the scalding hot shower, the buzzing in Raszer's head returned. He steadied himself against the turquoise tiles that lined the inside wall of the bath. Sunlight spilled through the little window above, and he squeezed his eyes shut in an effort to attenuate the pain it caused him. His pupils were fully dilated.

The buzzing was a low-voltage hum, like that heard and felt in the vicinity of a power transformer. He'd become aware of it during an earlier investigation, the one that had taken the life of his partner, April, and now he seemed to be stuck with it. At low volume, it came across as continuous and of a single frequency, but when it got loud, he was able to make out discrete but very rapid pulses, and sometimes other frequencies. Its nature was electronic, of that there was no doubt, and he'd been concerned enough to have himself scanned for brain clots and tumors. It wasn't until he'd related the buzz to the activity in his left eye that he'd finally made some peace with it. Raszer was slow to come to such things. As acutely in tune with the external environment as he was, he had a blind spot with regard to events in his own body.

Years before, while Raszer was earning his PI license via a stint with the LAPD Missing Persons Unit, a young FBI agent assigned to an interstate child-abduction case had noticed Raszer's uncanny ability to map out routes that, more often than not, turned out to be the ones fugitives took, and had given Raszer a battery of tests designed to reveal "remote viewing" abilities. Raszer's scores were only slightly above the average. He was not clairvoyant.

It was something else.

With no native talent for either mathematics or chess, he was nonetheless able to "see" probabilities collapsing into events in time and in varying potential realities, and could adjust his forecasted outcomes as the factors influencing them changed. This odd faculty was at its most keen when the flaw in his eye was "active." The knack seemed to apply only to human beings, and particularly to human beings in the exercise of their desire. He could not have employed it at the craps table, except possibly to psych out the croupier.

Now he wasn't sure what the buzzing signified, except that it had started when Layla Faj-Ta'wil had laid her head on his chest at 5:00 AM and said, "If I could make a different world, you would be my pretty man and I would be your woman."

✦ ◆ ✦

AQUINO WAS WAITING in front of the Parrish house, a run-down bungalow on the south end of Azusa. The house had the look of a long-absent father, and Aquino had the look of a man on his way to someplace else. He shook Raszer's hand and grunted.

"The mother doesn't like me," he said, gesturing over his shoulder. "I don't think she likes anybody much. You'll see why when you talk to the kid . . . if you can talk to him."

"What's the history here?" Raszer asked. Storm clouds were still parked along the high peaks of the back range, but on the L.A. Basin side, the sky was clear blue.

"The boy's father was 'disfellowshipped' by the JWs a couple years back, after he had a fling with the church secretary. Apparently, he didn't repent properly, and so the wife and son were ordered to 'shun' him. Tough on a marriage, I would think. After six months of that, the guy split, and Mrs. Parrish—Grace is her name—blamed the breakup on the Elders. Made such a stink that they disfellowshipped her, too, along with the boy, who was already running with Johnny Horn." Aquino spat on the ground. "Like I mentioned before, the kid's had mental problems from early on. Asperger's syndrome, they call it."

"Hmm," said Raszer. "That's interesting."

"Why?"

"I dunno yet," Raszer answered. "Could be a link."

"Like a 'walking autism,' I'm told by the experts," said Aquino. "At least, he *was* walking until he saw his buddies killed. Now he mainly sits in his room in his underwear with the shades pulled, says nothing. The mother waits on him like he's some invalid. Be prepared. It's weird in there, and the kid doesn't seem to bathe."

Raszer cast a glance toward the ramshackle front porch.

"Has he been treated?" he asked. "Is he on meds?"

"He saw shrinks while the investigation was in process," said Aquino, "but now, I don't think so. I've urged the mother to get him help, but old habits die hard with the JWs—even ex-JWs. They don't like psychiatrists. I'll tell you, Mr. Raszer, they are the most closed-in people I've ever seen. Germs grow in closed places."

Raszer nodded. "You ever come across any of these allegations of child abuse or pedophilia involving Witness families?"

"Not personally," Aquino replied, "but I'm aware of them. The problem is, it all stays inside. Under church law, you can't accuse a man without two witnesses, and where's the second witness to an act of sexual abuse?" He pulled his car keys from his pocket. "Anyhow, Grace is waiting for you inside. I told her you're a nice guy. When you're done, come over to the station and I'll take you over to Evidence."

"Thanks, Detective," said Raszer. "Any word from the Horns or the Lees?"

"They're even less anxious to talk than this one. But I'm trying. If all else fails, we'll pay them a cold call."

Grace Parrish was a fragile, tubercular-looking woman with long hair braided down to her midback. She might have been pretty once. In spite of the strain, her skin was still unlined, except around her mouth, which seemed frozen in the clench of someone suppressing tears. Raszer made her out to be about thirty-eight, which meant she'd borne her only son young and then quit. There was probably a story in that.

She led Raszer into a sparsely furnished living room where all the seat cushions were vinyl covered. In the corner was a La-Z-Boy recliner that must have been her husband's; Raszer could still see the impression of his body in the imitation leather. On the white walls, Raszer counted the grimy stencils of half a dozen removed picture frames, probably family photos, possibly of church-related occasions. Mrs. Parrish sat down to an unfinished cup of tea, the Lipton's tag still hanging over the chipped rim, and motioned Raszer to a faded yellow armchair.

"Thank you, Mrs. Parrish," he said, "for letting me stop by. I'm sure Detective Aquino told you I'm investigating Katy Endicott's disappearance."

She took a sip of tea and held the cup just beneath her chin. "You're working for *them*." Her gray eyes had been aimed into the cup until she'd said the word *them*.

"You mean the Kingdom Hall," said Raszer. "No, to be accurate, I'm working for a father who lost a daughter. The church . . . has agreed to lend its assistance."

"Ha!" she blurted, and set the teacup down hard. She coughed, and continued. "The only thing they want is to get their property back."

"What do you mean by that?"

"I mean nothing," she said. "Absolutely nothing."

Her voice had the ragged quality of someone continually swallowing back stomach acid, but there was a sweetness and docility in it, too, Raszer thought. She must once have been a good parishioner, a "wise and faithful slave."

"I sense there's not much love lost between you and the Elders," he said.

"Why should there be?" she said. "They drove both my husband and my son away. They just couldn't keep their fingers out of it. None of it."

"You mean your personal life?"

"I mean everything," she said, and now Raszer could taste the bile in her throat. "My kids, my home, my kitchen . . . my bedroom. What to read, what to watch, what to think. It's like an infes . . . an infes . . . " She swallowed. "An infestation. You don't see it until it's gone, and you're left with nothing."

"What about your faith?" Raszer asked.

"What about it?"

"Do you still have that, or did they drive that away, too?"

"That's a funny question for a private detective to ask," she said.

"Why don't you and I begin here by admitting that we don't know anything about each other, so we have everything to learn? I'm not here to grill you, Mrs. Parrish. I'm here to try and understand what happened to your son, so that I can understand what might've happened to Katy Endicott."

"The only thing I have faith in, Mr. . . . *Razor*, is it?"

"Yeah. *R-a-s-z-e-r*. But you said it right."

" . . . Is that things can't get any worse."

"Well, your son is alive," Raszer said softly. "Are you at all close to the other families? The Horns or the Lees or . . . what was the other boy's name?"

"Strunk," she said, almost in a whisper. "Joey Strunk. He was Emmett's friend. He had dinner at my table at least once a week . . . till all this craziness happened. I talk to his mom, poor thing. The others, no. You see, Mr. Raszer, once the Witnesses shun you, you stay shunned. They made us invisible. The Horns and the Lees, they never stood up for us. Never even stood up for their own children—until it was too late."

"So through all of this," Raszer said, "you never had contact with the church."

"We're *apostates*," she said, and wiped two fingers across her brow. "Like we've got triple sixes on our foreheads." Grace Parrish paused to take a sip of cold tea. "At least I've got my memories of a time before the Witnesses, and sometimes I can grope my way down the hallway by those. That boy in there . . . "

She turned to stare at the closed bedroom door behind her left shoulder. A big black *X* had been spray-painted on it.

"My son," she said. "He doesn't know how to live in the world. He doesn't have any memories, except for seeing his father leave and his friends killed. The one time he stepped outside the church, all hell came down—just like they said it would. He blames me. He shuns *me*. If they'd have him back, if I'd *let them* have him back, he'd probably run . . . " She tightened her lips until the blood had been squeezed out, and then released the words: " . . . right back into their arms."

Grace dropped her head into her hand and began to weep. Raszer leaned forward, wanting to go to her side but not wanting to violate the sanctuary of her grief.

"I'm sorry," he said, and his voice had absorbed some of her anger. "Truly sorry it's gone this way. Sorry that religion is ever about control. It isn't supposed to be like that, Mrs. Parrish. It's supposed to be about comfort. And wisdom."

She wiped her eyes with the back of her hand and waited for her focus to return so that she could register him clearly.

Raszer allowed himself to be examined, let himself go passive on the inside. He let her look as long and hard as she wanted to, and waited for her to speak.

"You want to understand what happened to Katy Endicott?" she said. "I'll tell you one thing, mister. I don't know if she's alive or dead. I don't know if she's whoring herself or chanting 'Hare Krishna.' All I know is that she never could've gone where she went if her father hadn't paved the way. You take a person's choices away, and you might as well be a rapist. Silas Endicott was no better than those boys."

"Did you know him well?"

Her mouth, the most expressive part of her face, was dismissive. "He was the pastoral overseer. The enforcer. He was the one who came to the house that day to tell us my husband had been disfellowshipped. But he wasn't the worst of them."

"Amos Leach," said Raszer.

She stared and said nothing, but that was affirmation enough.

"May I speak with Emmett?" Raszer asked.

"You can try," she said. Some of the tightness had left her voice.

"I'm not a therapist, or a deprogrammer, or, God knows, a priest," he said. "I'm a tracker, mostly. But my *work* is with people—often young people—who've been . . . isolated. Stripped of choice. Sometimes spiritually defrauded."

"You mean cults?"

"If you mean that in the sense of control, yes."

She stood up and smoothed her dress, then walked to the bedroom door and knocked softly. When no answer came, she leaned in, her hand on the knob.

"Emmett?" she called. "Emmett, there's a gentleman here to see you."

Raszer approached and stood at her side.

"I'm going to open the door now, Emmett," she said. "I'm going to let Mr. Raszer come in." She turned the doorknob slowly. "He's looking for Katy Endicott."

The room was unnaturally dark, even for the abode of a recluse, and it took Raszer a few moments to make out the small, slack figure on the far side of the unmade bed, sitting against the wall in his white briefs. His long hair was knotted and unwashed, of indefinable color. His bony arms were hitched around his knees.

"Hi, Emmett," said Raszer. "May I come in?"

The boy didn't stir, but in the faint light from the hall, Raszer saw his eyes shift.

"My name's Stephan," he said. "I think maybe you can help me."

The smell of the room was close, human, but not as fetid as Aquino had led him to believe it would be. There was even a vague sweetness, and Raszer noticed candles placed on various surfaces. The bedsheets smelled of semen, but a boy's, not a man's.

"I'm gonna have a seat on the bed here," said Raszer. "If that's all right."

He thought he saw the boy shrug his shoulders. Or maybe not.

"I don't know if your mom told you. I'm a private investigator. I look for missing people. Right now, I'm looking for Katy Endicott."

Emmett was as still as a spider in the corner of a web and, except for periodic blinks, might have been almost undetectable in the darkness. He could have been hiding, or he could have been getting ready to pounce.

"Anything you can tell me about the night she was taken—and the men who took her—would be a big help. And just so we're square, I don't share secrets. I don't have to. I don't go after the bad guys, I just try to get back what they've stolen."

✦ ◆ ✦

DURING THE TEN MINUTES of intervening silence, Raszer glanced about the room. There was nothing to evidence a young man's presence: no trophies, no Xbox, no pinup girls or rap stars or Lakers posters. The only thing on the walls was a single black stripe at a height of about forty inches, spray-painted from corner to corner and running just over the top of Emmett Parrish's head. It seemed to Raszer to define a safety zone of some sort, and if so, he was out of it—either threatened or threatening.

"You've got a good idea there," he said, slipping off the bed and onto the floor, about five feet away from the boy. He took off his jacket and pulled his black T-shirt over his head. "It's cooler down here on the floor. A lot cooler without clothes. Don't take it wrong if I join you. It's just . . . well, we could be here for a while."

Emmett didn't flinch as Raszer tossed his jacket and T-shirt on the bed, and made only the faintest grunt when he unsnapped his jeans and stripped down to his shorts.

"You're a briefs man, huh?" said Raszer, indicating the boy's underwear. "I used to be. Even used to wear those bikini ones for a while. Now, I find most women prefer boxers. I dunno, maybe they're less obvious."

Emmett shot a sidelong glance at Raszer's shorts. His eyes seemed to widen when he saw that they were a green-gold paisley print. Raszer scooted a few inches closer. Without warning, the boy put a hand inside his own underwear and began to play with himself, like a squid threatening to release his ink of invisibility.

"I have this superstition," Raszer said, "that every time you fake it, you get one less for real. You go ahead, though, if you've got the urge."

Emmett paused for a moment, leaving his hand where it was.

"I met someone who knows you," said Raszer. "A very pretty Middle Eastern girl by the name of Layla. I gather she was Johnny Horn's girl for a while."

The boy's wide mouth gaped just slightly.

"I gather also that before she was Johnny's, she belonged to the men you saw take Katy. And that there was some kind of . . . arrangement."

The breath whistled out over Emmett's dry lips.

"But you didn't tell the police about her."

Emmett shifted left to reclaim his distance from Raszer.

"That puzzles me, because she would have been their strongest lead to the kidnappers. To the men who killed your friends. Without her, all we've got are four phantoms in a black Lincoln who almost come off like heroes, by your account."

"No," Emmett said, from the back of his throat.

"No, what?" asked Raszer.

"Wasn't like that," said Emmett.

"What was it like?"

"Fucked up," said Emmett. For a few moments, he locked onto Raszer's right eye like a homing signal, then shuddered and said, "Oh, shit."

"What is it, Emmett?"

"You'll get inside me, won't you?"

"No," said Raszer. "I can't do that, and I wouldn't if I could. But I think it might be a good idea for you to come outside for a while. It must be pretty scary in there."

"I feel naked."

"You are naked, Emmett, but so am I."

"You can see me?"

"Yes, I can, Emmett. You're real as rain."

Once again, the boy locked on, eye to eye with his visitor, and this time, he passed something across the space between them. Raszer felt a muscle twitch.

"God is great," said Emmett, without inflection. "God is good."

"Yes."

"But God went away, and the Devil owns the world."

"It seems that way sometimes," said Raszer. "It must have that night."

"To whom shall we go?" said Emmett, parroting a Witness pitch line.

"John, chapter six, verse sixty-eight," said Raszer. "Good question. I think you can only answer it as a negative: not to the Devil."

"What if the Devil pretends to be God?"

"That's the puzzle, isn't it?" said Raszer. "But in a way, you solved it. God took a powder. In the meantime, anyone who says he speaks for God is probably a liar." Raszer felt a current move across his scalp. A static charge built up in the still, stale air, and he felt, more than heard, a *snap*. "God speaks through the ear of the heart."

"Henry Lee saw the Devil," said Emmett. "So did Johnny. In Babylon."

"He's playing both sides against the middle over there."

"Johnny said like you did. He said the only way to beat the Devil was to doubt everything people said. Nothing is true—"

"Everything is permitted," said Raszer. "Except for one thing."

"What?"

"Playing God. What did you see that night, Emmett?"

"It was really dark," the boy said.

"Yes, and foggy, too," said Raszer. "But you saw the car come."

"I was in the woods. In the trees."

Emmett still had a hand on his genitals, but now more like a frightened child, or a man facing death.

"You were hiding."

"Yes . . . no. Henry showed me how to be invisible. Henry said there had to be a witness."

"A witness to what, Emmett?"

"When he called forth the servitor from the sigil. When the magic happened."

Raszer's lower half became aware of a cold draft coming from under the bed, but in this very awareness, he realized that this part of himself was detached from whatever part was in contact with Emmett Parrish.

"What kind of magic was Henry making?"

Emmett glanced up at the black stripe that ran just over the crown of his head, then looked at Raszer. "Can I tell you?" he asked. "You won't say anything?"

"I won't say anything, Emmett. People wouldn't understand."

"To protect Katy," said Emmett. "Henry said that the s-servitor—the magical Thought-Form—would make it so the men wouldn't take her away. He had everything prepared. He said they just had to do the sex thing, like in his book."

"You told the police it was rape."

"Like you said, people wouldn't understand. It was pretend. But it was real. It was a kind of . . . *acting*."

"Was Katy acting, too?"

"No. Henry said that would mess it up. He said she had to think it was real. But they got her all fucked up on GABA so she wouldn't freak out."

"GABA. GHB, right?" said Raszer. "The stuff you mix up in a bottle?"

"Yeah. It fucks you up good. Makes you all lovey. Then you pass out."

"So Johnny and Henry—and your friend Joseph—they knew the men were coming? And they thought they could use magic to trump them? To protect Katy, kind of like"—Raszer tapped his knuckles on the black stripe—"like this protects you."

"Henry did. But Henry said that when you make a servitor, if . . . if something goes wrong or if you don't finish the ritual, it can go against you. It's s'posed to go away when the magic is done, b-but if something happens . . ." His cheek twitched.

"The entity you've created," said Raszer, "can take on a life of its own, right?"

"How did you know that?" said Emmett.

"They don't make PIs like they used to," said Raszer. "I'm not going to find Katy Endicott by tracking credit card receipts."

"You know chaos magick?" asked Emmett, and suddenly he seemed very young and—despite the lines of experience already carved into his pale face—very, very innocent. "'Cause this thing . . . it won't go away. Can you make it go away?"

"I can't make any promises," said Raszer. "And you'd have to *act* . . . just like Henry said. Act as if we together have power over the servitor."

"I could try."

"All right," said Raszer. The cold was creeping up his limbs, a cold that did not make any sense in a sealed, stuffy room. "Would it be okay with you if I took hold of your wrist?"

"I guess," said Emmett, in a small, distant voice.

As soon as Raszer touched the boy, he knew where the cold came from. It came from the woods just below the snow line, and carried the scent of cedar and fear. It was the cold you felt when you were lost and alone in winter without a coat. A big V-8 purred in the background; the smell of its exhaust filled the room. The car door opened and the dome light shone on black leather.

This was the place where Emmett's mind still lived. He'd brought it home.

"We need to do something first," Raszer said. "We need to remember before we forget. There's a girl out there as scared as you are, only she doesn't have anyone to hold on to. I need to know where these men came from, and what Johnny owed them."

Emmett shook his head. "They never told me," he said. "Or Joe. It was something they got into over there." He glanced down at Raszer's hand, at where it gripped him. He saw the old scars on Raszer's wrist.

They were an offering to the boy. A psychic kinship.

"In Iraq," Raszer said, after a beat. "In Babylon."

"I guess. All Johnny ever said was that the men came when you went beyond the perimeter. When the game got real. They weren't good or evil—they were something else—and you only had one choice after they came. You had to serve them until you knew enough to be their master."

"*When the game got real*," Raszer repeated to himself.

"And then you'd win. You could make a new world. That's what Johnny wanted. He said this world was going to end soon, and chaos would rule."

"Pretty heady stuff for a boy from Azusa, California," said Raszer.

"Johnny always said that Jesus was a yahoo, too."

"And what would Johnny's new world be like?"

"Perfect freedom," said Emmett. "Or p-perfect slavery."

Raszer moved closer, wanting to lend some of his own ebbing body heat, and this time Emmett didn't recoil. His lips were a dull purple, and his teeth were chattering. Moreover, he'd made his inner coldness manifest in the room. Quite a trick.

"And Katy . . . did she know these men?"

"No," Emmett replied. "Only from Johnny talking about how they were his *t-ticket* to paradise. Katy was like an angel. Katy was—"

"—the last pure thing?"

Emmett nodded. "Until Layla. Katy wanted to be like her . . . wanted Johnny to want her like that, and Johnny said she could. She *would* be, if she f-followed the plan."

"The plan—*right*. So she didn't struggle . . . didn't scream when she saw him killed?"

Raszer pressed his thumb lightly into the papery skin on Emmett's wrist. The pulse was reasonably strong, but it was ticking at barely more than a beat per two seconds. Without taking his eyes off the boy, Raszer reached over with his free hand and pulled his jacket down from the bed, then draped it around Emmett's frail shoulders.

"She didn't . . . I don't think she saw what they did. Like I said, she was way fucked up. We all were. I wish I was *more*. It was dark, and there was the fog, and it all happened way too fast. Johnny and the rest, they were just . . . they just went down like birds. Like there was life and then there was . . . there was . . . *nothing*, except this . . . this thing that Henry made. This *entity*. This thing in the woods with yellow eyes, howling and screaming, pressing me down. *Oh, God*. Oh, God, the *smell*. I puked so bad . . . and then I just ran. I ran all the way back inside."

Raszer pushed up to a squat and slipped his hands beneath Emmett's armpits, talking the whole time, keeping his eyes on the boy's wildly dilated pupils. "I was up there yesterday, Emmett. In those woods. On that road . . . "

Using only the rock climber's strength stored in his legs, for his arms had no leverage, Raszer began very gingerly to slide Emmett Parrish's body up the wall, crushing him to his chest as they cleared the black stripe. "I think I had a run-in with your 'entity,'" he said. "The smell is the giveaway. Got a good whack on the head from him, too. An old squatter. Believe me, he's as flesh and blood as you are."

"Are you *s-s-sure*?"

"I'm sure," said Raszer. "He was probably just as freaked out as you, too."

"You mean . . . somebody else saw what happened?"

"Uh-huh. Lost his tongue for it, evidently. There was a second witness, Emmett."

Emmett suddenly realized that he was standing, his head well clear of the protective barrier. His knees gave out in Raszer's embrace.

"Oh, shit. Oh, shit," he whimpered. "I can't—"

"Yes, you can," said Raszer. "It's okay. It's cool. Tell me something, Emmett: When you were little and there were monsters in the room, who cleared 'em out?"

"M-my f-father," the boy stammered.

"Well, I'm a father, too. I've got a license to sweep out servitors."

For the first time, Emmett Parrish smiled, then giggled, and after that, he cried.

"There's something I don't understand, though," said Raszer. "If Johnny had this whole deal set up, and Katy was ready to go along . . . why did he and Henry switch the game plan at the last minute and try to double-cross these guys with a sex-magic spell?"

"It was Henry's idea. I think he thought he could defeat them 'cause he had something of theirs. Something he won in the game. The sigil."

"The sigil?"

"The black rock."

"What about Johnny? Was he in on Henry's plan?"

"I dunno about Johnny. I don't know anything. I just went along."

"Who does know?" Raszer pressed. "Who's still alive, that is."

"Layla would know," said Emmett darkly. "And maybe Ruthie."

"Katy's sister," Raszer affirmed. "How would Ruthie know? She was back in Taos, wasn't she, when all this happened?"

"Her and Henry had this connection. He called her his mystic sister. He must've emailed or texted her ten times a day." Emmett's body temperature had at last begun to rise, and his jaw relaxed a little, but Raszer did not let go. "Henry said you could use the web for magic, too. He said he could change the quantum flux. He swore that him and Ruthie even had sex on the Net, and that it was better than physical."

"Would Ruthie also know how Henry lost his testicles? Do you know?"

Emmett flicked a strand of hair from his pocked face and turned aside, suddenly conscious of his near nakedness, and Raszer's.

"All I know's he said they had more power off his body than on it."

Raszer processed this. "Emmett . . . were Henry's testicles a sigil, too?"

"I think so. That night, when he made me invisible, he gave me this blue velvet bag to keep. With his . . . his things in it."

"Did you hide that bag in one of Johnny's Chinese lanterns, Emmett? Up there behind the trailer? Emmett? *Emmett*?"

A thin column of light from the cracked bedroom door bisected Emmett's face, and he squinted hard. Standing in the crack was his mother. Raszer turned his head and saw Grace Parrish's face shift from surprise to relief, then alarm, and finally puzzlement, like cloud shadows scudding over an uncertain landscape, giving it form.

"Excuse us for a minute, Mrs. Parrish," said Raszer, "while we get our street clothes on." He returned his eyes to the boy. "I believe we'll be right out." He nodded to Grace and noticed that the woman's jaw had gone slightly slack at the sight of his paisley shorts, and at the intimacy with which he held her son. "Not to worry," he said. "It's an old sweat-lodge technique. Sometimes bare skin makes for a better connection."

"I'm not worried, Mister Raszer," she said, stepping back. "I just can't believe nobody's tried it before."

She closed the door gently, and, without further words, the men went about the small ritual of getting dressed. All of Emmett's T-shirts were clean. When they had finished, Emmett left his room for the first time in months, his fingers gripping Raszer's wrist until he had been safely planted on the sofa.

✦ ◆ ✦

LAYLA STEPPED FROM the shower, tucked the towel around her torso, and listened. She did this habitually, because if anyone had entered the flat during her shower, she was certain his presence would reveal itself to her acutely sensitive ears. Today, the vigilance was unwarranted, because Harry had come with her staples: goat's milk, candy, and a new pair of shoes, and was waiting for her in the bedroom. Harry adored her still. He would die before letting anyone enter her bath. She counted on that.

She stood at the foggy mirror and began to comb out her thick, lustrous-black hair, making three parts in the form of a Y and applying a scented oil to her exposed scalp. She lifted the comb, then stopped and listened again. It wasn't a sound, but the absence of sound that had caught her notice. When Harry was there, he laid on the bed, noisily turning the pages of her fashion magazines, or chatting on the cell phone, or both. He did it to reassure her. Human noises were comforting, he'd told her. Now there was no sound coming from the bedroom but for the faintest gurgling, like that of a coffee maker in its final cycle. She listened as a bird listens, intently focused but disengaged from self. All ears.

"Harry?" she called through the door, and, immediately upon saying it, felt the muscles in her belly tighten. By the time she said it a second time, the tone was markedly different.

"Harry!"

There was no reply, but with her ear to the door, she could hear the gurgling, draining sound a little more clearly. Then she heard what sounded like breath, and the soft rattling and shifting of hangers in her closet. She squatted down and peered through the old keyhole. She could see nothing in the background but her walk-in closet, its doors closed, and nothing in the foreground but Harry's right boot, parked just where it ought to be at the foot of her bed, toe up. The boot trembled once, then again, and listed to the side, motionless.

Layla put her lips to the keyhole. Her voice was low and strong now. "*Harry?*"

Layla had a gun, but it was in her closet. She waited, counted, and breathed, and when the waiting was over, she flipped the deadbolt and very slowly opened the door. The scream that should have come from her throat stayed pinned down in her breast, where she'd put it long before. From years and miles away, she heard the bell and knew it was for her.

She strode deliberately to the night table and scooped up Raszer's business card from where he'd left it. The scream stayed inside even when she stepped barefoot into the warm pool of blood at the bedside. Then she turned to the bed, took the cell phone from Harry Wolfe's right hand, and, wiping the bloody keypad on her towel, backed into the bathroom, leaving footprints. As she did, she counted the daggers embedded in Harry's flesh. If the message was what she thought it was, there would be:

One, two, three, four, five, six, seven . . .

Once inside, she locked the door and sat down on the toilet, trembling in spite of herself. She couldn't be absolutely certain there weren't knives raised over her. When she had composed herself, she punched in the number on the business card.

ELEVEN

"THIS IS HENRY LEE's little black book," said Detective Aquino, unzipping the evidence bag and removing a well-worn paperback. "It's all Greek to me."

"Well, Latin, anyway," said Raszer, accepting the book. "But you probably know that. *Liber Null—The Book of Nothing*, or of no value, at least not to the uninitiated. I've got a copy in my library."

"I guess I'm not surprised," said Aquino. "It's a book of magic spells?"

"More like magical *practice*," Raszer answered, flipping to the title page, and an inscription: *Henry—Good luck on the left-hand path. Do nothing is the law. Cheers, H.*

"Hmm," Raszer mumbled, and turned to Aquino. "Any idea who H. is? *Cheers* would suggest a Brit."

"I thought the same thing," Aquino repled. "Of course, we couldn't ask Henry. When I pressed Emmett on it, he said it was probably a British soldier Henry met in Iraq. But I got the feeling he was making it up. So what's the book for? Not pulling rabbits out of hats, I guess . . . "

"No," said Raszer. "Not unless a rabbit is what you're after. It's for achieving results. You might even call it pragmatic sorcery. The left-hand path is the path of power through intuitive self-knowledge. The magician uses his active imagination to harness the chaos at the heart of the universe. From that, he makes his own gods."

"You lost me there, amigo. Exactly how does he do that?"

Raszer lit a cigarette and sat down on an oversize trunk. They were in a warehouse space in San Dimas shared by regional police departments, an elephant's graveyard of evidence collected from ten thousand crime scenes: an archive of sin. On Raszer's left were two nitrous oxide tanks, found at the trailer in Burro Canyon, and the fragments of a backyard methamphetamine lab. On his left was a box containing an assortment of Henry's black rocks and fat little Mesopotamian goddess statuettes.

"Back in the '70s," Raszer began, "a British magician by the name of Peter Carroll, who'd been—until then—an adept of Aleister Crowley, decided that ceremonial magic had gotten too highfalutin—too full of silk robes and mumbo-jumbo. He was a bright, serious guy, as far as it goes, and he'd noticed all the bizarre stuff happening in science: chaos theory, black holes, quantum entanglement, you know . . . "

"No, I don't, actually . . . but go on."

"Well, to Carroll and his friends, all the old Egyptian magic, with its determinism, its invocation of dead gods, and its elitism, just didn't jibe with a science that said the universe came down to quarks and uncertainty. Old-school magic was for horny old men in smoking jackets. Carroll wanted rituals that were effective, so he threw the religion out of magic and focused on screwing with the universe itself."

"Screwing with the universe," said Aquino drily. "Okay. You still haven't told me how it works. How you make a god."

"Maybe you should read the book," said Raszer. "I'm not saying I'm a believer, but, like all magical insight, it has an angle of truth. Put it this way: modern physics says, in a way, that everything is everything. The universe in a nutshell . . . "

"I did try to read *that* book."

"If the universe is enfolded in every stitch of space time, then God's in the stitches, too. Which means God's in you and me . . . in the fabric, not a separate thing. And if chaos is bubbling under it all, then *some* force has to evoke order—things, people, events—from the chaos. Carroll says basically that this force is imagination, the same kind a method actor uses to create a character. You go into your temple—if you're Henry Lee, maybe that's a trailer—you set your goal: You want Susie to love you, or you want a better job, or whatever. Then you work yourself into a state of gnosis—"

"What's that?"

"Let's just say it's a kind of mainline to the divine, without any interference from the mind. It's living inside the truth."

"How do you get there? Yoga? Meditation? Magic mushrooms?"

"All or none of the above. For chaos magicians, it's whatever works. Sex can do the trick, if it's done right . . . even focused masturbation. Self-inflicted pain. Anything that takes you beyond ego. Then you say to yourself, *I believe in Isis, or I believe in Cthulhu, or I believe in Mary Worth . . .* "

"It doesn't matter what you believe in?"

"Doesn't matter, as long as you believe for the duration of the ritual."

Raszer held the cigarette in his teeth and reached behind him on his left into the box containing Henry's icons. He fished out the largest and most worn of the black rocks.

"Then you summon your servitor—your god-form—into a sigil, like this rock or a statue, and you go to work. How you do the work is what the book's about. How successful *Henry* was is hard to say, but he sure had an effect on Emmett Parrish."

"I'd like to hear about that," said Aquino. "Did he stick to his story?"

"I—"

Raszer's cell phone bleeped, sparing him any dissembling. "It's Raszer," he answered, bouncing Henry's rock on his palm. It was surprisingly heavy for its size, polished from handling, and had a distinctive navel-like dimple. And there was something else, something he couldn't quantify—an emission, a kind of heat.

The voice on the other end was all contained panic. Remarkably contained, considering its message. Raszer glanced at Aquino, shook his head, and rolled his eyes apologetically toward heaven. He put the phone to his chest.

"It's, uh, my girlfriend," he said, and winced. "Will you give me a minute?"

Aquino grunted knowingly, and gave a nod. Raszer stood, and with a thief's sleight of hand dropped the rock into his jacket pocket. As he walked across the concrete warehouse floor, Aquino's eyes tracked him. As practiced as Raszer's own method acting was, it couldn't disguise the draining of the blood from his face.

"All right, Layla," said Raszer softly, when he had gained fifty feet of distance. "Take a breath and start again. I'm here. I'm listening."

"Harry's dead," she said. "It's them. He's in my apartment."

The words were all in her throat, their pitch flattened by fear or numbness.

"Harry's in your apartment?"

"Yes. On the bed. No, I mean the killer—"

"Where are you now?"

"In the bathroom."

"Is it locked?"

"Yes, but that won't—"

"Okay. I want you to listen and do exactly as I say, all right?"

"All right."

"Even hired assassins—especially hired assassins—try to avoid collateral damage. If you stay where you are, he will probably leave. I'm going to call the police, and then I'm coming straight to you, okay?"

"Yes."

"Now, when we're done, I want you to put down the phone, walk over to the toilet, and take the lid off the tank in back. That's probably the heaviest thing in the bathroom. It will knock even the biggest man cold. Stand behind the door, up against the wall, and raise the lid above your head. If he manages to get in, bring it down hard and take his weapon. I'm on my way. It's going to be okay."

Raszer flipped the phone shut and stood for a moment with his back to Aquino. There were advantages, not to say honor, in telling the truth, but the truth would take time, and a small-town cop might create variables whose impact he couldn't predict. He turned around and raised his hands in the air in a gesture of defeat.

"I've got trouble, Detective," he called out. "Gotta go. I'll call you from the car."

Aquino smiled grimly. "Don't cut me out, Raszer," he shouted. "You could find yourself very alone up here. And, uh—" He aimed a finger at Raszer's left pocket. "You'll return that piece of evidence when you're through examining it, right?"

"Right," said Raszer. "Thanks. I'll call you." He turned and strode deliberately to the exit, all the while hearing Harry's words in his head: *A fishing cottage will suit us fine.*

As soon as he'd cleared the door, Raszer speed-dialed #9. It was a direct-dial to the BlackBerry carried by Lieutenant Borges of LAPD Homicide, promoted to that division only two years earlier from the Missing Persons Unit that Raszer himself had briefly served. Borges wasn't the top cop, but he was the one man on the force who took Raszer at face value and could be counted on not to go procedural on him if the game called for different rules. He was a tall, crater-faced Argentinean with his own sense of the surreal, and he was as familiar with L.A.'s alter-reality as an international port of mayhem and occulted enterprise as he was with its potholed streets.

Nothing could save Harry Wolfe, and nothing short of light-speed would have gotten Raszer there fast enough, so he drove with due speed by the fastest route he knew, down the 2 freeway's roller-coaster grade to the 5 North and off at Glendale Boulevard. When he arrived at the scene, he found Sunset barricaded between Hyperion and Maltman, and traffic snarled beyond hope of getting within a block of the building. He parked in a red zone adjacent to the Silver Lake Spanking Parlor, jumped out, and sprinted onto Sunset and past the barricades with his PI card held high.

"Stephan Raszer," he called out to the beat cops. "Borges wants me. Can you radio ahead?"

His legs turned to molten lead. Up ahead, he counted six squad cars with lights flashing and a paramedic van with its stretcher out. Beyond the second set of barricades stood a KTLA news van, and pulling in beside it was the local Fox affiliate. All the street noise played second fiddle to the weirdly phase-shifted beating of three helicopters—two police choppers and a news unit—in the cloudless blue sky overhead.

Not again, he thought, slowing his pace. *Please don't let her be dead.* Because if she were dead, it could only be the result of his having intruded on her haven, breaking the fragile membrane of security that playing possum afforded her. Impractical as it was, Raszer sought to never leave tracks, to leave a scene as he had found it, to not let his zeal for the quest be the cause of pain to any but his adversaries. It was of a piece with his thirst for anonymity, his resentment of guys who peed all over their turf, his almost Asian desire for lightness of being. In practice, such nonintrusion was a quantum impossibility, no more realistic than expecting an electron to disregard the presence of an observer and a battery of measuring equipment. Still, he hoped.

He spotted Borges in the midst of a huddle, a head taller than anyone else, and better dressed. All eyes were on the top floor and roof of Layla's four-story building. At the moment, there was nothing to see there, but when Raszer surveyed the same elevation on the opposite side of the street, he saw the police sharpshooters lined up like tin soldiers. Harry Wolfe's killer had not left the building.

"Luis!" he called out to Borges, fifteen feet short of the huddle. "Lieutenant . . . "

Borges stepped away from his men and approached Raszer with a slow nod and a tight smile, combing his fingers through a crop of thick hair the color of tarnished silver. He offered his hand; Raszer grasped it warmly.

"What have we got?" Raszer asked.

"We've got a corpse, a killer, and a hostage," he replied.

"The girl's alive, then," said Raszer, scanning the building's facade up to its flat, recessed roof.

"So far."

Raszer squinted, his eyes still on the building. "Where are they?"

"On the roof, we think," said Borges. "There's access from the fourth floor, but there's also a tunnel canopy extending from the door, and they haven't come out from under it yet. Ten minutes ago, he was on four, and told us he had a hostage and a gun, and that he'd kill her unless we landed a chartered helicopter on the roof and took him to Death Valley." Borges grunted. "Strange, eh, compadre? Most of 'em want to go someplace nice—Cuba or Cancun or the Bahamas. This one wants to go to hell."

"He wants to get lost," said Raszer. "Have you gotten a look at him?"

"No."

"How about the voice? American? Middle Eastern? Any accent?"

"American," Borges replied. "Young. Scared. Maybe New England."

This was not what Raszer had expected to hear. *New England*? Borges placed a hand on Raszer's shoulder and walked him out of both hearing and camera range.

"Now, why don't *you* tell *me* what we've got in there?" he whispered. "You mentioned these folks contacted you for a border hop. Said they were scared about some kind of cartel coming down on them. Looks like they had reason to be."

"Yeah, but there's more to it, Lieutenant."

"There always is with you, Raszer."

"It's connected somehow to those rave murders up in San Gabriel Canyon last winter. And the abduction that night of a Jehovah's Witness girl I've been hired to track." Raszer inclined his head to the building. "They were there. At the rave. The dead man was the DJ, and the girl . . . well, she took up with him. She's Syrian. She'd promised me a lead on the abductors. Then she wanted to get as far away as possible."

"And you promised her and her boyfriend a ride," said Borges. "*Tsk, tsk.*"

"I said I'd look into it. I liked them. They seemed . . . caught in the middle. Not clean, but not filthy, either. I think I may have complicated things."

"It wouldn't be the first time, would it?"

"I do my best, Luis."

"I know you do, but this is L.A. Your best or my best is always outdone by somebody else's worst."

Suddenly, the phalanx of marksmen above hunkered into position, and the cops on the street moved out of their huddles. The news crews scrambled, racking their zoom lenses to telephoto. All attention went to the roof as the killer's voice was heard.

"Five minutes!" he shouted. "You've got five minutes to bring me my helicopter before I take her head off!" And then he added tentatively, "And I mean it."

Borges motioned to the cop on his right for a bullhorn, and spoke into it without stridency. The sound of the device was harsh enough. "Stay cool. It's been dispatched. Don't hurt the girl. If you hurt the girl, we'll take you out. Do you understand?"

There was no response, but the voice rang in Raszer's ears and sent currents into his stomach. It was more a boy's voice than a man's. And something else. He turned to Borges. "He doesn't sound like a pro, does he?"

"No," said Borges. "He doesn't. Not what you thought, eh?" He dropped the bullhorn to his side. "Come with me. Let's see if we can give him his close-up."

Nearby, under a makeshift awning, was a police A/V crew with a direct feed from the TV camera in one of the choppers above. Borges radioed the pilot.

"Come around and bring it down about a hundred feet," he said. "Easy. Just enough to make him feel the wind. See if you can get me his face."

The pilot complied, and Raszer watched with Borges as the small figures on the rooftop, once again withdrawn beneath the canopy, began to fill more and more of the monitor screen. The image was overlaid with sighting brackets and crosshairs, and these would also appear in the video scopes of the marksmen on the opposing roof. Both Layla and her captor were in shadow, but Layla's form and face were unmistakable. She wore a saffron-colored bathrobe and, as far as evident from this distance, nothing else. All that could be said about the assassin was that he stood behind her, was a few inches shorter, had a gun under her chin, and appeared to be wearing a billowing white robe with a bright, blood-red sash. Nothing more was visible until the chopper's blades drew near enough to lift the border of the green-striped canopy and, for an instant, reveal a smooth, unlined face with a distinctive beauty mark just above the lip.

Raszer froze, his eyes glued to the monitor.

"Luis," he said to Borges. "I know this boy."

Borges turned halfway, one eyebrow hiked way up.

"Is there a hostage negotiator on-site?" Raszer asked.

"On the way," Borges replied, waiting.

"Can I borrow your bullhorn?"

"Do you know what you're doing?" the lieutenant asked.

"I'd better," said Raszer.

The two men locked eyes, Raszer nodded, and Borges warily handed him the bullhorn.

"Scotty Darrell!" Raszer called out. Immediately, on the monitor, they both saw the boy's head jerk. After a few seconds, the words came, and Raszer knew they would be transformative and final, one way or the other.

"Well played, Scotty," he called. "I could use a man like you. A man with a keen mind and a steady heart."

Borges looked at him cockeyed, but did not move to take the bullhorn. The other cops on the ground jerked their heads in the direction of the A/V station, and out of the corner of his eye, Raszer saw one reflexively put his hand on the grip of his service revolver. Borges saw it, too, and put his palm up. The chopper hovered in place, bobbing slightly, and the image on the monitor went briefly out of focus.

"Scotty Darrell!" Raszer repeated. "Nod your head if you can hear me."

On the screen, they watched Scotty swivel and poke his head into the light, keeping the gun lodged beneath Layla's jaw. He surveyed the roof quizzically, then raised his eyes toward the hovering helicopter, connecting with the camera. Layla's eyes flashed in the brilliant blue reflected from the sky. She had recognized Raszer's voice.

Raszer turned to Borges. "Do you have a PA channel to that chopper?" Borges nodded.

"Can you make my voice come from up there, too?"

"What do you have in mind, friend?" he asked guardedly. He trusted Raszer's instincts, but only so far. If he let a freelancer take control of an active crime scene and it backfired, they would have his badge. He knew, however, who and what Scotty Darrell was, and was a step ahead of Raszer's reply.

"To make the choice for him," said Raszer. "To keep him in the game."

Borges aimed a finger at the audio console and gave its operator a nod.

"Open the mic," he ordered. "And kick up the volume." He turned back to Raszer. "Make it good, my friend, or I'll be chasing coyotes in Nogales and you'll be out of business."

Once Raszer saw that the audio man had complied and pushed up the volume fader, he brought the bullhorn back to his lips. He had to lick them. His mouth was bone dry, and got drier with each beat of his pulse.

"Remember, Scotty," he said. His voice boomed out over the rooftops of East Sunset. "One more level to go. Number nine. Are you game? Are you ready to ride the big snake?"

The chopper camera zoomed in on the boy's anxious face, now half-lit, and the snout of Layla's gun slipped briefly from its pocket of flesh. She flinched. Raszer's eyes were on the monitor. He prayed the girl wouldn't do anything rash, then decided not to leave it to God.

"Stay put, Layla," he commanded. "Scotty's with us. He knows the rules."

From the left, an unmarked squad arrived, disgorging the hostage negotiator and a team from downtown. Raszer lowered the bullhorn and pivoted to face Borges nose to nose. He made his bid, knowing it was the last for both Scotty and himself. He had disconcerted the boy, made him question his mission, and if he did not follow through, the sharpshooters would find reason to take him down.

"Let me go up there, Luis," he said. "Alone."

"No way, amigo," said Borges. "I'm already way off the map."

"Look at me, Luis," said Raszer. "Look *with* me. Remember what happened in Barstow. Remember Las Cruces. *Fuck* . . . remember Waco. What happens when the big guns move in? This is about more than one perp, more than one murder. This kid is the skeleton key to a hundred doors. If he dies—and he will, by his own hand or yours—they all stay locked. Let me go up. Give me fifteen minutes to get the gun."

"And if I wind up with your blood on my hands, too?" Borges replied. "How will I sleep at night?"

"The same way I do, Luis," said Raszer. "By knowing that the Devil will think twice before playing you for a fool."

Borges ran his hand through his hair, took one glance at the approaching hostage team and one look over his right shoulder at the men whose allegiance he would forfeit if he failed, and then picked up his radio.

"All stations! I'm sending a man up! Cover the roof and the roof egress and take the suspect out only—I repeat, *only*—if there is clear intent to harm." He hesitated, then added, "And I don't want a hundred bullet holes. Stick with the firing order. If Chopper One gets it done, everybody else hold fire." Then he switched off the radio and muttered, "*Madre de Dios*, Raszer. Go."

When he'd reached the fourth-floor landing, Raszer paused to catch his breath, resting the bullhorn on the bannister. Directly ahead of him was a short set of steps leading to the roof exit. To his left and down the hall, the door of Layla's apartment stood menacingly open and unattended. Per Scotty's demands, the cops had cleared out of the building. In the corridor's ceiling, just outside the flat, a skylight sent a cone of sunlight to the threadbare carpeting nine feet below. The sunlight animated the dust motes into a dervish dance, and for an instant less than time, the motes aggregated themselves into the upright form of Harry Wolfe, arms extended, legs splayed, seven silver-handled knives sunken into his major arteries: biceps, heart, throat, solar plexus, two in the groin. Like an image projected by a camera obscura. Raszer rubbed his eyes, shook it off, and approached the steps.

Poor Harry, he thought. *He'll never see that cottage.*

Before putting the bullhorn to his lips, he rapped on the door three times and called out. When there was no answer, he switched on the device.

"Maimonides!" he called, using the name of Scotty's Internet avatar, the name he had learned from The Gauntlet's puppet masters. "I'm here to take you home. I am unarmed. I am alone. I am coming through the door. Stay beneath the awning."

Raszer pressed his ear to the door. There was some shuffling against the gravelly surface of the roof, then: "Wh-who are you? Who sent you?"

Raszer anchored his back against the door, hand on the knob, and rested his head. *Who sent me*? Giving the right answer—if there was a right answer—would be like choosing which wire to clip on an improvised explosive device. The Gamesmasters wouldn't do. Fraters Vanitas and Ludibrium probably wouldn't do. He closed his eyes for a count of three breaths, listening only to the rumble of the old air-conditioning compressor on the roof. In the lens at the apex of the triangle whose base points were his closed eyes, he saw the daggers that Layla had said were embedded in Harry's flesh; he saw Layla's eyelashes dip in invitation to dance; he saw the old Syrian coin sitting on the squatter's bureau, felt its chain being snapped by clawing fingers, saw the spray-painted words "Nothing is true. All is permitted." He saw Johnny Horn's trailer and smelled the wintergreen.

"I'm your next guide, Maimonides," he said. "I was sent by Hazid."

Raszer turned the knob and pushed gently. He couldn't allow Scotty time to reflect. The knob rotated, but the door was jammed or blocked. In that moment's reprieve, he realized that although he and Scotty had never met face to face and Scotty probably didn't read the newspapers, he could not gamble that the boy hadn't seen his picture on the Internet. Further, L.A.'s ubiquitous news choppers would soon start buzzing the roof and broadcast his face. He tore off his linen shirt and wrapped it around his head, leaving only a pale blue tank top on his torso. He reached into his pocket and found his sapphire-lensed sunglasses. An instant later, he heard something heavy being dragged, and the door was freed.

Scotty backed Layla to the far end of the arched canopy. He looked more frightened than the girl. The boy gave Raszer's dress and fair features a once-over, probably thinking that his Imam ought to come garbed in something a bit less makeshift.

"Hello, Scotty," said Raszer, holding his palms up. "I've wanted to meet you. For a few minutes, gametime is suspended. The clock has been stopped, and you're getting a chance to opt out. After those minutes are up, play will resume, and those men on the roof and"—he indicated the hovering chopper—"up there will kill you. I can bring you out safely and be your guide through the next level, but first we have to send a signal. We need to step into the light, and you need to let the girl come to me. Then you'll drop the gun and kick it over to me. Do you understand?"

The boy blew a long strand of sand-colored hair away from his mouth, exposing the beauty mark once again. Raszer recalled that Scotty's mother, the former ballet dancer, had an identical mark.

"This isn't part of the plan," the boy said. "I should wait for the helicopter. I should complete my mission."

"That was your *last* move, Maimonides. This is a new one. Did you forget how to riff?"

Raszer knew that every second was putting Borges farther out on the limb. Neither did Layla Faj-Ta'wil look like she had a great reservoir of patience.

"I'm going to step out first," said Raszer. "I'm going to put my hands at my sides so they can see I'm not afraid. I'll circle back over to the center of the roof, just beyond that skylight. You stay under the canopy, release the girl, and then kick me the gun."

Raszer did not wait for assent, but backed out into the hard blue light, lifting the bullhorn once more to his mouth. "We're okay here, Lieutenant," he said, and his voice echoed down from the chopper above, causing a shriek of feedback. "Turn off the top speaker," he called. "He's giving me the girl."

But Scotty did not give Raszer the girl. Instead, once Raszer had reached the far side of the skylight, Scotty nudged her out from under the awning, still holding her neck in a vice grip and keeping the gun under her chin.

Shit, Raszer thought. *What is this*?

"I want diplomatic immunity," said Scotty, walking Layla forward. "I want the—the Syrian ambassador. I want *you*—" Thoughtlessly, like the gamer he still was, Scotty punctuated the word *you* by taking the gun from beneath Layla's jaw and pointing it at Raszer. At the same time, the chopper dipped and another blast of feedback screamed from its speaker. Scotty flinched, and Layla needed only that lapse to snap the gun from his hand, step back into his center of gravity and, with just one hand on his forearm, execute a flip that sent him flying three feet into the air.

It happened faster than the response time of an LAPD sharpshooter, but that wasn't the oddest thing. Just before Scotty crashed through the skylight, he spread his arms, opening the folds of his nylon caftan to catch the updraft, and appeared to hover in midair for a second or two. Then it was all shattering glass and brutal impact, and Scotty was down.

Three bullets zinged across the rooftop. Raszer leapt across the shattered skylight and took Layla down. *Idiots*, he thought. He heard the lieutenant's voice from below: "Hold your fire, goddamnit! Raszer? Are you all right up there?"

Raszer depressed the bullhorn's talk button. "We're good. Nobody shot . . . yet. I've got the girl. Suspect went through the skylight. He's in the building. *Unarmed*."

When the message had been delivered and the air was still, Raszer looked at Layla, who lay beneath him, smoldering on the tar and gravel roof, the saffron robe hiked up around her naked hips. "Why did you do that?" he asked her.

"Do what?" she said.

"Flip him," Raszer replied. "Why'd you flip him?"

"He was getting nervous," she answered tartly. "Nervous men with guns annoy me." Her belly rose and fell with her breath like a bird's, and as she exhaled, he became aware again of the wintergreen scent that he'd caught a trace of the night before.

"I'll try to remember that," he said, and smoothed the robe down to cover her midsection. He sat back and held his hand out. "May I have the gun, please?"

She scooted herself a few inches away. "It's my gun," she protested.

Her finger was on the trigger. A shadow of consternation passed over her face. For a moment, Raszer was not sure she wasn't going to shoot him. Then he realized that her eyes were on a spot three feet to his right. Henry's black rock had been dislodged from his pocket in the melee and lay on the roof, its dimple reflecting the L.A. sky.

"Where did you get that?" she asked.

"It's on loan from a friend," he answered. He rose to his knees and peered into the jagged hole left in the skylight, down through the column of sunlight and whirling dust. There were shards of glass on the carpet, but no Scotty. He turned back to Layla.

"I think I'd better—" His cell phone bleeped and he fished it out of his pocket.

"We've got him," said Borges. "He tried to fly out the second-floor window."

"He tried to what?" Raszer called back. "Is he hurt?" He quickly retrieved the rock and dropped it back in his pocket.

"No, amazingly. My men are talking him downtown. I think you'd better—"

"Can you meet me in room 411?" said Raszer. "I need for you and me to see the victim before anything changes. I'm bringing the girl down." He hesitated. "Borges?"

"Yeah?"

"Sorry to put you on the spot."

"All's well that ends well," said Borges. "I'll see you in 411."

✦ ◆ ✦

HARRY WOLFE'S EYES were open. Strangely enough, his mouth was closed and his features were not contorted, almost as if the killer had taken the time to compose his victim's flesh in death. The bedspread was saturated with blood, staining its mustard-hued cotton a muddy brown. Light from the hall glinted off the silver-handled daggers like the flames of sacramental tapers. A police photographer took a round of digital pictures before Borges motioned him off to the side. In an alcove, a pair from the CSI unit pulled on plastic gloves and awaited Borges's clearance, while behind him, the aging Asian medical examiner slipped in almost unnoticed. Borges wrapped his fingers around the bedstead, sniffed the air, and turned to Raszer.

"What do you smell in here?" he asked.

"Blood, urine, and incense," Raszer replied.

"Nothing else?"

Raszer cocked his head. "I smell a death and a woman, but we knew that."

"I smell sex," said Borges. "Recent sex. C'mon, amigo, you've got a nose for it." He inhaled deeply, his wide nostrils flaring. "It's all over everything. Do you suppose they were screwing before she went in to take her shower?"

"It didn't occur to me to ask," said Raszer.

He was glad Layla wasn't present to hear him finesse the matter of their congress. She was down on the street, being examined by the paramedics and attended to by two female officers, who'd brought her something to wear from her closet. At Layla's bidding, it was a yellow dress with matching shoes and scarf. Evidently, she wanted to look good for her trip downtown.

"Frankly, Raszer, the girl doesn't seem all that broken up," said Borges, his eyes on Harry's corpse.

"She's hard to read," said Raszer. "But I know what you mean."

"How long were you here last night?"

"Long enough to get their story," Raszer replied.

"And that they were scared of these . . . 'operatives.' These men she'd been running with who are tied up in your murder-kidnapping." Borges grunted and lowered his head. "So, let me get this: She's living here unmolested for a year, you pay her a visit, and the next day, her boyfriend's dead and she's a hostage."

"I can't deny the chain of causation," Raszer said. "I violated their sanctuary, opened the wound. I just can't figure how—"

"How the bad guys got wise so fast?"

"Right."

"A dozen ways. Maybe they had the room bugged. Maybe the girl is dirty. If what you say is true, I can see why they might want to get their merchandise back. But why him?" Borges nodded toward Harry. "Why kill the DJ?"

"I don't know. It fits a certain kind of ancient gangster MO. A pure terror killing. A warning for all concerned to keep their heads down."

"You think maybe he was playing both sides?"

"Not at the moment, I don't," said Raszer. "He seemed square to me. But like you said, I'd only just met them. Maybe they were both working an angle."

"We're going to have to grill her."

"Right."

Borges extended his arm and traced the cruciform pattern constellated by the knives. "You know fanatics, Raszer. Give me your take. Hired killers don't usually leave their weapons behind . . . especially not that kind of cutlery. Those look like they belong in a museum. Who still kills this way, outside of Palermo?"

"Only devotees of the art. Based on a little knowledge and a lot of conjecture, I'll say the hardware is Syrian. My knife instructor used to drill me on this stuff. These are reproductions of a tenth- or eleventh-century design, but good ones. They'd have left them only if they were scared off—unlikely—or if leaving them has a ritual purpose."

"You say *they*," Borges observed. "You don't think your boy was up to the task?"

"I can't see it. Can't put it together. Not by himself. For one thing, the physical strength needed to drive steel through muscle and into the mattress. For another—"

"No struggle," said Borges. "The bed isn't even rumpled."

"Right. It's almost as if one chloroformed him while a couple others did the wet work. The boy's duty may have been standing guard. He may be a patsy. He's obviously had his head scrambled, but this kind of work takes a special breed of apostle."

"Not being sentimental about your little lost sheep, are you?"

"Always a possibility."

"So, who dresses in white caftans with red sashes? Some new Islamist group?"

"Nothing new about it. Have you ever heard of the cult of the Assassins?"

"I might have," said Borges. "Refresh my memory."

"A radical Shiite sect—the Ismailis—spawned a splinter group called the Nizaris, formed in the eleventh century by a talented upstart named Hassan-i-Sabbah, who preached a kind of mystical terrorism and held a mountaintop fort in Persia. His group became known as the Hashshashin. They also had a Syrian branch, with a headman known as the Old Man of the Mountain. This was all during the *last* crusade the West made against Islam. Now we're over there—"

"Everything old is new again," said Borges dryly. "*Hashshashin*. Anything to do with hashish?"

"So they say," Raszer replied. "Used as an inducement, and allegedly as part of a mind-control program. It's where we get the word *assassin*. Their MO was planting sleeper agents—*fidais*—among their enemies and killing up close on prearranged cue . . . with daggers. In the '50s, the CIA even based its own assassination manual on their technique. The *fidais* were almost always killed, but it didn't matter . . . they'd been promised paradise and a harem of black-eyed virgins. They were the first suicide bombers."

"Jesus," Borges whispered. "It sounds just like—"

"I know," said Raszer. "The feds will go nuts with this. They'll have the threat level up to purple. I'll tell you what I think. It's not unusual for gangsters or cultists with nonpolitical agendas to borrow the name, legacy, or methods of some powerful military order for their own purposes. In this case, what I have so far points to a criminal syndicate more interested in international drug and sex traffic than in jihad."

"As I recall, the FBI was pretty sure that your boy Scotty had gone the way of that other kid—I forget his name now—the 'American Taliban.'"

"That kid," said Raszer. "Lindh is his name. As mixed up as he was, he actually spent time in an Al Qaeda training camp. Scotty was playing a fucking game."

"What's the difference if it ends up this way? Anyway, I'll have to brief our counterterrorism unit, and that will probably flag both the FBI and the NCTC."

"That's all right," said Raszer. "There's a field agent I've been wanting to meet."

"Well, you're in it now, so you'll stay in until they chase you out. We'll interrogate the boy together. You seem to speak his language: *Hazid sent me.* Ha! Liked the turban, too."

Raszer winced. "How'd you hear that bit?"

"That audio system works both ways." Borges grinned and draped an arm around Raszer's shoulder. "I had you on mic the whole time. Seems to me you speak the girl's language, too. She didn't look all that bothered to have you between her legs."

"You had to be there, Luis," said Raszer.

"I'll bet," said Borges, and turned to wave in the medical examiner and the CSI team. "All right, folks. Let's go to work. I want every hair—pubic or otherwise—in the room. And toxins—check for evidence of a knockout drug. This bed is way too neat."

"One thought," said Raszer, who was calculating the odds that a strand of his own hair—pubic or otherwise—might be found on the sheets.

"Let's hear it."

"The historical Assassins used poison-tipped daggers. Guaranteed to kill even if they missed their mark." Raszer aimed his finger at the knife rooted in Harry Wolfe's heart. "If that one was the first blow, and it delivered the medicine, he wouldn't have moved a muscle afterwards."

"A paralytic?" Borges asked.

"Something like that," said Raszer, who'd had some experience with them.

"We'll have the lab check it. You still carry those little needles around?"

"Only when I expect to use them."

"Still no gun? Not even after what you've been through?"

"Not if I can help it."

During the exchange of words, Raszer's eyes had locked on Harry Wolfe's serenely closed mouth. It bothered him. There was artifice there.

"Doctor Cho," he said to the ME, who'd just removed Harry's boots.

"Would you mind taking a look inside the decedent's mouth?"

The examiner looked to Borges for approval and received a nod.

Cho shuffled to the head of the bed and inserted a forefinger from each of his gloved hands between Harry's lips, finding the teeth, gently releasing the jaw. The dead man's mouth fell open. Raszer moved in closer. At first glance, it looked like the petals of a crimson rose. The examiner removed a small, wadded rag, saturated with blood, and stepped back. "Oh, my, my, my," he said, shaking his gray head.

Poor Harry Wolfe had lost his tongue.

Lieutenant Borges shook his head. "Jesus. It's just like Nogales. They'd sneak up on you while you sleep and pinch your nose, and when you'd open your mouth to breathe, they'd grab hold of your tongue and—*ssssst*—one slice."

"It seems to be a trademark," said Raszer. "Let's talk in the car."

At the threshold, Raszer turned and said, "Motherfuckers. Why'd they have to make him suffer?" He shook his head. "I hope to God he was dead already."

Harry Wolfe, aka MC Hakim, knight-protector of Layla Faj-Ta'wil, lay still on his bier, his soul on its way to Avalon—or some place far from the the Lake District, at any rate. Finding Katy Endicott alive had just become a decidedly longer shot.

"I need to make a call," said Raszer, as they emerged into the lacerating sunlight. "Two calls, actually."

The first was to Detective Aquino, to whom he owed an update.

The second was to his daughter. Whenever evil showed its face, Raszer felt the need to check on Brigit, and the feeling was never without its measure of remorse.

TWELVE

THE INTERROGATION ROOM was one of five in the sub-basement: small, stark, and one of the last public places in L.A. where smoking was still permitted. Scotty was seated at the far end of the shiny white table, his wrists cuffed and his ankles in irons, back against the wall. At the moment, he seemed far more interested in who might be on the other side of the two-way mirror than in the men gathered to hear his tale.

Raszer sat on Scotty's left, the wrinkled linen shirt restored to his back. Borges was on the right, his tie still squared, his suit jacket on. Hovering over the table, his breath on Raszer's shoulder, was Bernard Djapper of the FBI, deputy to the special agent in charge of the L.A. field office, the man whom Harry Wolfe had described as having the face of a Pekinese. He was pear-shaped and baggy-fleshed, but groomed and tailored like a London banker, as if to compensate for nature's sloppiness. He wore a pin-striped vest with a watch pocket, from which he occasionally drew and pointed what appeared to be a solid-gold toothpick. He was agitated, and paced the room like a D.A. working the jury box. Everything about his bearing said *by the book*, yet his dress and affectation made him something of an eccentric.

Lending a very different presence to the proceedings was the man from National Counterterrorism, Douglas Picot. Had this been Sioux City, or even Sacramento, the NCTC might not have had a deputy on hand, but L.A. was a state unto itself. His carefully chosen and perfectly enunciated words issued from the round mouth and outcurled lips of a child rooted in the oral stage, and his fingers were as smooth and small as a porcelain doll's. Somehow, he'd survived the regime change in Washington. His "expertise," Raszer learned, was profiling sleepers in local Muslim communities.

They were midcourse on the first round, and Scotty Darrell had not yet asked for an attorney, or to call his parents, or even to use the toilet. From the moment of his capture, he had emptied out. He was not especially nervous now. He wasn't rude or recalcitrant or surly. He wasn't anything, really.

Deprived of his game identity by Raszer's *outing*, he wasn't yet able to relocate any element of his former self. He was either the perfect assassin or the perfect fool.

After a full minute of silence, punctuated by the second hand of an old IBM wall clock, Raszer said: "On the roof, you asked for the Syrian ambassador. Why?"

Scotty cocked his head. "Does anyone hear a ticking sound?"

"Were you bluffing, Maimonides?" asked Raszer.

"It's Ishmael," Scotty answered.

"Ishmael the son of Abraham and Hagar, Ishmael the Seventh Imam, or Ishmael the narrator of *Moby Dick*?" Raszer asked.

"Or the Ishmael who blew away those kids at Virginia Tech?" said Djapper.

Scotty said nothing.

"Screw this!" Djapper spat. "We have him on video shooting a tram driver and holding a gun to a hostage's head. There's blood on his hands, and when the lab matches it to the dead man's, he'll be put away. In the meantime, let's either get busy or hand him over to the truth squad. You heard him. A clock is ticking." He stared bullets into the back of Raszer's head. "Why is this guy here, anyway, Lieutenant?"

Raszer remained still and lifted his eyes to Borges for intercession. He strongly suspected that Scotty was still "playing" in some way and would shut down unless someone played along. It was all in the eyes, which were sheeted over with a kind of psychic sugar glaze. They were the eyes of a person occupying an internal landscape. For Scotty, it might be this room and the people in it that were a virtual reality.

Borges spoke up, gently motioning Agent Djapper back into his corner.

"I understand that the FBI has a role to play in this case, Agent Djapper," he said softly. "But it's my interrogation. I'd like to hear the suspect answer the question."

Raszer offered Djapper a chair. "Why don't you have a seat, Special Agent? Take a load off. We need to help Scotty make the right move."

"Are you an assassin, Ishmael?" he continued.

"If you want me to be," said Scotty.

"What do *you* want to be?" Raszer asked.

"Someone who knows something—*anything*—for certain," Scotty replied.

"An honest answer. And a good one. I may have a new assignment for you, Ishmael. You pulled off the last one. Killing Harry Wolfe . . . "

Scotty's eyes gave the slightest flicker of dissent.

"You did complete your mission, didn't you?"

Scotty mumbled something that sounded like a no, and lowered his head.

"I think," said Picot with a snort, "it's time to take this in a new direction."

Raszer held up a hand. "Just one more; then he's all yours."

"The men who really put those knives into Harry Wolfe . . . who do *they* serve? Who gave them their mission?"

Scotty smiled the faintest of smiles.

"You know, don't you?" he said to Raszer, then assayed the other men in the room, one by one. "*They* know. They think *he* serves *them*, but he serves no one. The Old Man is Lord over the All and the Nothing."

"The Old Man." Raszer nodded, but did not ask for the answer he guessed he was already supposed to know.

Douglas Picot cleared his throat. "You actually seem to know a lot of things for certain, Scotty. If you're as close to the 'Old Man' as you say, then you ought to know his name."

"No one gets close."

Picot leaned forward.

"You're right. No one gets close. So, how do we know he's real?"

The faint smile returned.

"I'll tell you what I think," Picot continued, drumming the table with his doll fingers. "I think this is all a fairy tale. An elaborate cover story. A new spin from our old enemies. How did you get here, *Ishmael*?"

"I don't remember," said Scotty, with the look of a man trying to gauge the authenticity of a videotape in which he appeared but did not seem to be quite himself.

"Would it jog your memory if we shipped you back? It can be arranged. You wanted the Syrian ambassador—we'll give you better. Of course, you might never come home. Not in one piece."

Borges's voice broke the silence. "Whose dried blood is on your hands, Scotty? It *is* Harry Wolfe's blood, isn't it?"

Scotty regarded his hands curiously and said nothing. Borges nodded to Raszer.

"Why did Harry Wolfe have to die?" asked Raszer. "I can't guide you on unless I know where you were coming from." He felt the weight of the other men's impatience. Even Borges would be forced to pull up his rope soon.

"Who is Hazid?" Scotty replied, and laid his shackled hands on the table.

Raszer held the boy's eyes and slowly drew in a breath. Here was the pass-key, and Raszer knew that Scotty would not offer the door a second time. The name Hazid had to have something to do with the "initiation" to this most deadly level of gaming. If Scotty himself hadn't scrawled the name on the underside of Johnny Horn's toilet seat, then some other would-be initiate had. The air pressure in the room seemed to increase, as on a rapidly descending airplane, and Scotty was in the cockpit. Raszer chose omission as the lesser sin and ignored the question. Maybe—just maybe—Scotty would read it as complicity and let him in.

"We're at a border crossing, Scotty," Raszer said. "You have no passport. You have only me to take you across. Turn back, and I can't help you. Go forward, the game will be different, but at least you'll be in it. What does a pilgrim ask of a new guide?"

Raszer waited. It was another gamble. He was banking on the supposition that, in a pinch, Scotty would obey the rules of the game. They were all he had now.

"How—" Scotty cleared his throat and swallowed. "How can I serve?"

Raszer reached into his pocket and unfolded the printout of Katy Endicott's picture. He laid it on the table. "By telling me if you've seen this girl."

Scotty stared at the picture, at first blankly. Then the look came back—the look of someone recalling a parallel existence, but now the frosting in his eyes had melted.

"I saw her in the Garden," he said, his voice thick. "I saw her in paradise."

"Where is this garden?" Borges asked.

"Nowhere," Scotty answered.

"How did you get there?" Raszer continued. "You were playing the game, and then—"

"They came for me. In winter." He gripped himself. "I was cold."

The boy began to cry softly, and when Raszer put a hand on his shoulder, the tears escalated to sobs. He clenched his fists and raised his hands to his face in shame.

"What is it, Scotty?" Raszer asked. "What's happening?"

"I peed my pants," Scotty answered, pounding his forehead.

"And before *I do*," said Lieutenant Borges. "We're all gonna take a break."

✦ ✦ ✦

RASZER TOOK THE ELEVATOR to the plaza level for a smoke, and Borges found him seated on a stone bench beneath a solitary palm with a piece of garden gravel in his hand. The late-afternoon winds were beginning to whip the spiky fronds of the palm tree overhead. He'd scrawled the name Hazid on the pavement at his feet.

"What's it about, Raszer?" he asked. "Is it a person or a thing?"

"I don't know. I'm not sure it's not a red herring. I took a chance up on the roof based on something I saw in Azusa. He may've just picked up on that." Raszer tossed away the rock. "I'm thinking it may be some kind of key. But Christ, Luis, it doesn't even make sense that these two cases are related. How does life get that weird?"

Borges smiled broadly and took a seat. "It just does, my friend. I was raised on the *pampas* in Argentina, where the gauchos used to make room at the campfire for the ghosts of the men they'd killed that day. Before I came here. I worked the Tex–Mex and Arizona borders, where nobody even knows what country they're in."

"I guess you've been out there." Raszer paused. "By the way, thanks for giving me some rope with Scotty."

"Just enough to dangle yourself over the cliff, amigo."

"That's all I'll ever ask," said Raszer.

"Anyway, I had to. Otherwise, giving you the bullhorn wouldn't have made sense to the brass. I have to at least *look* like I do things for good reason."

Raszer laughed softly and rubbed out the letters *H-A-Z-I-D* with the toe of his boot. "All things considered, they're going pretty easy on him, don't you think?"

"It's only the beginning," Borges replied. "And you and I are still in the room."

"I don't know . . . I almost get the feeling—"

"What?" Borges pressed.

"Nothing. Just a thought. An unformed thought. Probably smoke."

They began to stroll back across the sprawling city hall plaza. The sun was already low in a pastel sky, and their shadows preceded them by a good ten feet.

"It's crazy. This kid I've been tracking for over a year suddenly parachutes into a case involving an abducted Jehovah's Witness girl, two murdered Iraq vets, and some kind of trafficking ring using medieval terrorist techniques . . . where's the link?"

"You're the link, for one thing," said Borges. "We both know everything's just a jumble of possibilities until somebody draws them together. Like dropping a magnet into a bowl full of ball bearings. I've had cases where nothing—I mean *nothing*—happened until I went out and drew fire. Until I baited the trap with my own scent."

"You're right," said Raszer, remembering what he knew but so often forgot in the course of events. "There has to be an *attractor*."

"Another thing. You've got kids out there playing this game. Who knows what kind of connections they've made on the Net? Who knows how many Ishmaels there are? That's a world beyond our jurisdiction. Anytime you're near a border, you've got predators. If I didn't know that before, I learned it cold in Nogales. The wolves wait there, between the known and the unknown."

"A no-go zone," Raszer said, half to himself. "You've given me an idea, Luis."

"You think maybe the kid—Scotty—was snatched, like your girl? That these guys wait for the lamb that strays from the herd?"

"He said 'they came for him in winter.'"

"You said you thought somebody had messed with his brain . . . "

"He's been rewired, Luis. It's like somebody's commandeered this game at its highest levels, when the players are way out there. I'm not sure if Scotty knew whether what was happening to him in there was real or 'virtual.' To tell you the honest truth, on this case, I'm not so sure myself."

They had arrived at the revolving door, and Borges turned to him. "Tell me a little more about this crazy game. As many times as I've read the accounts, I still don't really get how it moves from the Internet to the real world."

"It starts out like any game of make-believe. The thrill of danger without the physical risk. The target is college kids, or anyone from age seventeen to thirty in an institutional setting. You find your way to the main website and pick a character, only it's a philosopher or a saint instead of an action hero. You learn to act as he would act, think as he would think. Then the Inquisition comes after you. Things start to get real. You get threatening text messages and think you're being followed. It becomes what they call a 'chaotic fiction.' There've even been cases where mock torture chambers were set up in dorm rooms. You get a credit card you didn't apply for, then an email saying you've run up ten grand in charges but they'll let it slide if you confess. Your GPA suddenly drops to 2.0, and the dean is on the phone to your parents."

"They can do that?"

"They're hackers. As good as they get. It's a massive Kafka-esque freakout, but the thing is, it's exciting as hell. Because *you* are at the center of it. Somebody cares enough to give you nightmares. The only people you can trust are the Masters. Anyhow, there are hundreds of variations, but finally, the only way to escape your persecutors is to leave the Web, give up your 'real' identity, and slip into the false one. You go on the lam, all the while following the instructions you pick up at Internet cafés. Very glamorous, and very scary. You make yourself a servant of chance, and chance remakes you. You forget who you were."

"Unbelievable," said Borges. "How can anybody forget who they are?"

"You remember the Dungeons & Dragons thing, don't you?"

"The kid who died hunting a monster in the high school ventilation ducts?"

"Something like that," said Raszer. "But the thing is, the monster had become real to him. When I was about ten, me and my friends invented a Halloween story about a man in a white trenchcoat who was snatching kids from swing sets. We did it to scare the seven-year-olds, but we wound up scaring ourselves. All of a sudden, parents wouldn't let their children outside anymore. Then the cops started questioning men getting off the commuter trains in their Burberry raincoats. One day, they arrested the father of one of my buddies in the movie theater balcony—groping a sixteen year-old boy. He was wearing a white trenchcoat. That's a 'chaotic fiction.'"

Borges rubbed his long chin. "You know how to get in touch with Scotty's parents, right?"

"Yeah. I'd like to call them, if it's okay."

"Sure. But give me the number. I'm going to need them out here on a morning plane. I'm calling it a day on the interrogation. It's late. I need to get the kid processed, get his clothes and the blood evidence to the lab, get the med guys to take a look at him. And I'm hoping our G-men will decide to go play in someone else's yard for a while."

"Not much chance of that, now that they've got the scent," said Raszer. "The NCTC guy's already made his Al Qaeda connection, and that mouser from the FBI—"

"Piece of advice: If you want to stay off the leash on your abduction case, you might want to make yourself scarce here for a day or two. Otherwise, you're gonna have feds spitting down your neck all the way to the 'Ninth Circle' . . . or wherever it is you have to go to find your girl. *¿Comprende?*"

"*Sí, comprendo*," Raszer replied. "But at some point, I have to finish what I've started with Scotty. That's my covenant. Will you keep me briefed?"

Borges nodded. "You do the same," he said. "In the meantime, there's the Syrian girl. She's told my partners absolutely nothing worth squat."

"Is she a suspect?"

"Not at the moment, but she's a piece of work. I could hold her as a material witness, but right now I'm more interested in watching her next move. I'm letting her go as soon as we get her statement, but I'd like you to keep an eye on her for me. Take her home. Better yet, take her to a motel. I doubt she'll want to go home."

A gust of wind from the northeast swept across the plaza, taking them both by surprise. Raszer shivered as it passed over his shoulders.

"She'll come out the Temple Street doors in about twenty minutes. You can pull into the alley that's kitty-corner, where the squads park, and watch for her. I'll tell her you're her ride."

"Thanks, Luis. And thanks for the trust."

"If you can't trust a man who died and came back, who can you trust?"

THIRTEEN

TWENTY MINUTES CAME and went while Raszer waited in the alley, across the street and a hundred yards south of the building's main entrance. Four lanes of coursing rush-hour traffic separated him from the revolving door through which Layla would exit. A couple of women had already come out, neither wearing a yellow dress. The door and the broad steps leading up to it were within shouting distance, but Temple Street ran one way southeast, and he'd have to circle the block to get to her. He might have waited curbside, but at this time of day, that would have put him in a traffic lane. He was concerned she wouldn't see him, and had just about decided to walk over when there was a knock on his passenger-side window. He rolled it down.

"Nice car," said Agent Djapper. "I haven't seen one of these in years. Is this the original leather?"

"Yes, it is," said Raszer. "I bought it at an estate sale. An old guy from Mar Vista who never took it out of the garage. I don't treat it quite so delicately."

Djapper ran his large hand over the doorpost. "I think I'd have repainted it," he said. "Cream yellow's a little soft for a guy's car."

"I like to think of my cars as girlfriends," Raszer came back. "I'm not sure I'd feel the same about a guy color. Anyway, it was a gift from the old fellow to his wife. The story was, he bought it for her on the day she left him, and it never clocked a mile. When there's a story connected to something, I leave the color alone."

"Hmm," Djapper grunted, and leaned farther in, resting his arms on the door. "Listen," he said, "I didn't mean to cramp your style in there. Some of that was for show. I didn't know about your connection with Borges. You worked MP with him?"

All the while, Raszer had kept one eye trained on the revolving door, but here was what seemed to be an olive branch, maybe even a prelude to an offer of help.

"Just long enough to get my license," Raszer said. "But I learned a lot. He's a very sharp cop."

"Yeah, well, listen . . . he says you've got a gift. And, frankly, we could use one on this case. It's been stone cold since Katy Endicott disappeared. As clean as a mob hit. Now, I don't know what connection this Darrell kid has to the Coronado, or exactly where you fit in, but—"

"Hold on a minute," said Raszer, putting his palm up. There was an after-image in his brain, a black blur. He'd let his focus drift for a moment, but in that tick, a sleek form had passed in front of the alley, headed southeast. A black limo, the least unusual sight in L.A., on the edge of his vision. But what was it that had raised his pulse?

"So, anyhow," Djapper continued. "I was hoping we could—"

"Hold that thought," said Raszer, a little more firmly, his hand still raised. He closed his eyes. The smear of an image would remain on his visual cortex for only an instant longer. What? *What*?

"Oh," said Djapper, fingering the leather upholstery. "Yeah. Borges's guys told me about this. You're having one of those visions, or whatever. Those things you—"

Blue license plates. Blue plates with few numbers. Diplomatic plates.

"I gotta go, Agent Djapper," Raszer said, as calmly as he could. "Do you have a card? I'll call you." He glanced across the street and saw a flash of yellow refracted through the spinning door, cursed, and dropped the gearshift into first. He gunned the engine, holding the clutch just below the break point. Djapper lazily peeled a business card from his billfold and held it out to Raszer. His upper lip drew back from his teeth in what was supposed to be a grin but looked instead like a lapdog's snarl.

"In a hurry?" he asked.

"Yeah," said Raszer, snatching the card and nearly taking the man's arm off as he tore out of the alley. "I am." He wasn't sure that Djapper had heard the last part.

But for the constant stream of traffic, Raszer would have cut a wide arc across the one-way street and swung around to the curb. For an instant, he remained perpendicular, straddling two lanes, horns blaring, weighing the risk of plunging into the face of the stampede. Layla had now exited the building and stood on the top step, scanning the busy street, her yellow scarf waving like a racing flag on the stiff breeze. Raszer made his move, carving a reckless diagonal across four southbound lanes and maneuvering himself into the right turn lane as quickly as he could. The limo, if it was bound for Layla, already had a good half block on him.

Chrissake, Raszer, he told himself. *It's probably an airport limo*. The plates might've been livery plates, the driver some out-of-work actor hoping to pick up a mogul and schmooze him all the way to the Palisades. They wouldn't risk snatching Layla in broad daylight, here in the midst of the law enforcement sector, in snarled traffic, with motorcycle cops and helicopters deployable on a moment's notice. And yet Raszer had a physical certainty, trickling like a cold stream of mercury down the back of his throat, that this was precisely what they intended to do.

Los Angeles was not New York, not a fortress island whose bridges and tunnels could be blockaded, whose teeming sidewalks would furnish a thousand witnesses. In spite of the all-seeking sun, or maybe because of it, it was a city of shadows, and a long black car could slip into any one of them.

He raced around the long block, onto Main, then First, then Broadway, hugging the curb, never leaving second gear, laying on the Avanti's reedy, bi-pitched horn. But even so, the circuit could not be made in less than three minutes, and by the time he made the right turn back onto Temple, there was no more yellow dress at the top of the stairs. He pulled over to the curb, threw on his emergency flashers, and leapt out of the car, sprinting to the top of the steps to survey the congested street.

Amid the Infinitis and Lexuses and the odd, cratered Nissan belching burned oil, Raszer spotted no less than four limos. Two of them were Town Cars, but neither bore the distinctive blue plates. Traffic was piling up behind the flashing Avanti, causing cacophonous havoc in the two right lanes. Turning on his heel, he pushed through the revolving doors without much hope, calling her name into the reverberant lobby with its marble steps and drab oil paintings of past mayors and DA's. Nothing. Raszer exited the building and shot a glance across the street. Agent Djapper had left. That got him thinking, until something way off in the distance caught his eye.

Raszer took the long steps two at a time and scrambled into his car, all the while trying to keep what he'd seen in focus. Nearly a block and a half down Temple, highlighted only because a ray of the setting sun had nicked the corner of a skyscraper's glass facade and been diffracted down to the busy street: the tail of a yellow silk scarf, caught in the rolled-up window of a black Town

Car and flapping at thirty miles per hour. *Goddamnit!* Raszer hammered the steering wheel as he squealed away from the curb, boxed in on all sides. He cursed because it was all so obvious now. Of course these people could not allow Layla Faj-Ta'wil to provide testimony, and probably the only reason they hadn't killed her was that they wanted her back in their employ—if indeed she had ever left it.

A couple of blocks ahead, Temple Street crossed Alameda and narrowed as it entered a residential section of Little Tokyo. A left turn would take them north into Chinatown, a right would steer them into South Central, but Raszer guessed that the driver would avoid broad thoroughfares and instead jog south onto First Street and head across the river into East L.A., where things got confusing and there were a thousand places to duck out of sight. At least, that's what *he* would do. Racing to catch up, Raszer weaved roughly in and out of traffic, hearing the engine whine in protest as the tachometer hit 6,000 rpm.

He got close enough to see the Lincoln make the first right turn, but after that, it was all intuition, because the car had disappeared from sight. At the junction of Alameda and First, Raszer waited at the light, gunning the engine and switching his left turn signal on and off. Indecision was excruciatingly unpleasant for him. His mind skittered over the possibilities.

A double-back into the city and a quick trip to LAX?

No, they wouldn't risk passport control just yet.

A detour to the westside diplomatic sector?

No, the license plates had to be a ruse. These men were not agents of any state, though states might well have reason to fear or protect them.

A stop at some faceless safehouse in the barrio, where they could conduct their own interrogation of the prisoner?

The third possibility seemed the least unlikely, and so Raszer made the left and crossed over into East L.A., where the buildings were smaller and humbler and English was a decidedly second language. The Los Angeles River, printed as an undulating blue band on city maps, had long been nothing but a concrete-walled drainage channel, coursing with runoff only during the rainy season. A good four feet of water was left from the most recent downpour; the rest had been washed to sea, along with the leavings of a city with no public trash pickup. In spite of fencing and locked gates, the river had remained—as rivers do—stubbornly in the public domain. Poor children picnicked on its steep cement banks and played perilously close to its retaining walls; their elders breached the fences to dump in things they didn't need but couldn't afford to have hauled away: sofas, TV sets, and the occasional corpse. The ocean claimed them all.

Boyle Heights was the central city's most vibrant Latino district, and home to its best Mexican food. The air was soon filled with the smell of newly griddled tortillas, and Raszer became aware that he was ferociously hungry. As he cruised north on Sotto Street, looking left and right down the residential side streets with their parched but well-tended squares of lawn, his hope of finding Layla began slowly to lose out to his appetite.

A plaintive trumpet solo drew his ear left to Mariachi Square, the hub of the neighborhood. There, the best of the local musicians displayed their skills in a ceaseless competition for wedding and birthday gigs. A dozen versions of "Santa Lucia" vied and congealed into a sound collage of Latin brass and string. Young girls danced in frilly whites and black patent leather as old women nodded their heads in time.

Raszer pulled up to the light and rolled down his window. On the nearest corner of the square, a man was grilling flour tortillas and spooning in carne asada.

The aroma drifted into the car, displacing all others, and Raszer closed his eyes for just a moment. When he opened them, the light had turned green, and the thought of food temporarily fled. On the far side of the wide intersection, on a gravel lot advertised as ESTEVEZ FLEET SERVICE, sat the black Town Car, distinguishable from dozens of other Lincolns, Caddies, and pimped-out stretch Hummers only by the yellow scarf whose tail hung limply from its right rear window. Raszer rolled across the six-way intersection, growing more aware with each yard that he had no weapon, no backup, and no law enforcement authority.

It was a situation peculiar to his trade. He had to make the best of it. He also had to ask for help when he needed it.

He flipped open his phone as he pulled alongside the lot and began to punch in Borges's pager number. Two young mestizo men, armed with whisk brooms and minivacs, appeared at the Lincoln's rear doors and revealed it to be empty. Raszer turned into the lot, drove up to within six feet of the Lincoln's bumper, and turned off the ignition.

"*Buenos tardes*," he called out to the cleaning men, for the dusk had come down. "Hello." He walked toward them at a measured pace with both palms open.

One of them, dark-skinned and wiry, ducked out of the backseat at the sound of Raszer's voice and froze. From the look in his eyes, he might have been just one night over the border. He shot a nervous glance at the office kiosk in the center of the lot, from which there protruded the massive paunch of an older man, wearing a gray suit and a bolo.

"*Con permiso*," Raszer said, directing his words to the less antsy of the two. "*Una pregunta*." He indicated the Lincoln. "*La limusina. Donde esta—*"

"They're not going to understand you, amigo," called the fat man with the bolo, who had the look of an owner, or at least the owner's man. "They barely understand me. They're Indians. Good workers, though." The man extended his meaty hand, the engraved silver-and-turquoise buckle on his size 44 belt preceding him like a hood ornament. "Diego Estevez," he said. "I run this lot. And a few others."

"Stephen Raszer." He displayed his license. "I'm a private investigator." Raszer noticed that Estevez had a glass eye that skewed right, but the other one was squarely on the ID.

Estevez grunted. "I guess it's real. I wouldn't really know. You have an interest in this automobile?"

"In the men who just got out of it," Raszer replied. "Regular customers?"

"No," said Estevez. "First-timers, in fact."

"Is that so?" said Raszer. "How long did they have it?"

On the boss's nod, the mestizos had gone back to work.

"Two days," Estevez answered. "Guess they wanted to impress somebody. That's most of my business. Company functions. Conventions. Out-of-town big shots. Or sometimes," he chuckled wetly, "somebody just wants to get laid."

"Two days, you say?" Raszer aimed a finger at the blue license plates. "What's with the diplo plates?" he asked. "Do you have contracts with the consulates?"

"Take a look around," said Estevez. He pointed out a white stretch with the same plates, and three more Town Cars similarly outfitted. "And take a closer look. They're just livery plates made to look like diplomatics. They cost me thirty bucks extra per car, but I mark up the rental a hundred. Some customers want them. Adds to the prestige, you know. They figure they can double-park without getting a ticket."

Raszer smiled and hiked up an eyebrow. "Are they legal?"

"Sure, they're legal. Everything's legal in Los Angeles." He pronounced *Angeles* with a hard *g*. "Until it isn't."

Raszer scanned the lot and turned back to Estevez. "Your customers got out of here in a hurry. Five minutes ago, I was on their tail."

"They were all paid up. All I ask is the cars come back with a full tank and no new dents. What they do with them or in them is their business."

"Even kidnapping, Mr. Estevez?"

Estevez lowered his head, and the glass eye rolled toward the sky. "Look, Mister Raszer. I get lots of turnover. I don't run background checks. They're bad for business."

"But I'll bet you do take a driver's license and credit info."

"Not to give out to any Columbo who comes cruising by."

"I'll tell you what," said Raszer. He took a $100 bill out of his wallet. "You don't want LAPD Homicide and the FBI poking around here. I'll pay for a day's rental if you—"

"Homicide?"

"That's right," said Raszer. "You might want to have your employees check for blood on the seats. And that yellow scarf—"

The fat man waved off his money and began to walk away.

"I don't need your business, Mr. Raszer. And I can handle the police."

"How many lots like this do you have, Mr. Estevez?" Raszer called out.

Estevez turned halfway, giving Raszer his good eye. "Five," he said. "Two in the city, two in the Inland Empire, and one in Palm Desert. Why?"

"And how many undocumented workers do you employ?"

Estevez lumbered a few steps back in Raszer's direction. "You come to Boyle Heights making threats, Mr. Raszer, and you might not make it back to Beverly Hills."

"I don't live in Beverly Hills, Mr. Estevez. And I don't make threats, only promises. I'm looking for a missing girl who could be your own daughter. Think about that."

Estevez nodded toward the yellow tassels dangling from the rear window. "The lady with the scarf?"

"Not her," said Raszer. "But she *is* a material witness in a murder investigation."

The big man reached over and snatched Raszer's $100.

"I'll let you take a look at the rental contract," he said. "And then I want you to leave. You're upsetting my employees."

Estevez led Raszer to the kiosk and stepped up into it with effort. There was no room inside for a second person. He flipped through a sheaf of carbons on a clipboard and handed it to Raszer, who scanned it quickly, then looked up.

"Where's the top copy?" he asked. "I can barely make this out."

"The customer gets that. Once I'm paid, I don't care much about the details."

The limo had been rented to a "Mr. A. Bacus," whose company was listed as Southeastern Supply Corp. in Sofia, Bulgaria. There was no street address, no phone, and under "Driver's License," it said simply, "Honduras."

The contract was marked "paid," and Estevez had added "cash" in a scrawl.

Raszer looked up. "Jesus. You let a $60,000 car go on this?"

"They left a deposit," Estevez said, smiling.

"How did they leave here?"

"In another Lincoln," said Estevez. "Just like the one they came in."

Raszer squinted. "One of yours?"

"No. They were picked up. All four of them. And the woman, too."

"The woman," said Raszer. "How did she look?"

"Good," said the fat man, and licked his lips.

"You know what I mean, Mr. Estevez. Did she look frightened?"

"She didn't look happy, but she didn't look kidnapped, either."

"Right," said Raszer, and handed back the clipboard. "First-timers, you said?" Estevez nodded. "And none of your lots ever rented a limo to Southeastern Supply Corp. before this?" Estevez shook his head. "Well, then," said Raszer. "I'll be on my way. If you don't mind, I'm going to take the lady's yellow scarf with me. *Hasta luego*."

"What are you going to do, mister? Follow her scent like a dog?" Estevez chortled, the phlegm shaking in his throat like a snake's rattle.

"Maybe," said Raszer, pulling Layla's scarf free of the window.

"Shouldn't be too tough to sniff her out," said Estevez with a grin. "I couldn't help but notice when she got out of the backseat . . . she wasn't wearing any panties."

Raszer got back into his car, hung the scarf around his neck, and drove straight back across the broad intersection to the tortilla stand. He hadn't stopped thinking about food since his first whiff.

As he stood watching the old man drizzle sauce on his taco, Raszer considered how starkly the events of the past eight hours had altered his own gameboard. What's more, the stakes had been raised again: another homicide, another captive, and now the prospective involvement of the federal counterterrorism sector. Whatever tale Scotty Darrell did have to tell was probably not the one they wanted to hear or, in any event, made public. Far more convenient to label him an "enemy combatant" and ship him off to some Eurasian gulag, where our side could reshape the wet clay of his mind as effectively as the bad guys had.

A vague, backlit outline of the beast was beginning to emerge: some massive, transnational human-trafficking operation that snatched errant souls and then sent them—retooled—back out into society to do its bidding.

But to what larger purpose?

Raszer didn't sniff a conventional Islamist agenda, though there were superficial resemblances to that family of zealots spawned by the Islamic Brotherhood. The modus operandi of the Takfiri sect, the hardcore of the hardcore of Islamist extremists, appeared to be in play. These were the men who drank beer at barbecues and patronized lap dancers, whose children might go to school with yours, whose backyards might border yours, but who could toss it all aside on a single whispered command, climb into the cockpit of a DC-10, and steer it straight into oblivion.

Al Takfir Wal-Hijira—Anathema and Exile—practiced the most confounding form of Oriental subterfuge, the art of *taqiyya*, the absolute concealment of one's true belief and purpose, even to the point of denying one's God. A thousand years before Al Qaeda had found this practice useful in breaching Western defenses, the Order of the Assassins and its mythical chief, the Old Man of the Mountain, had embraced it.

Raszer hadn't yet had the time to brief Monica. Without her in the loop, he felt like the sole carrier of both a lethal virus and its antidote. He decided he'd call her as soon as he had eaten. Food was paramount. Food, and a moment's rest in the purple twilight of Mariachi Square, where the children in white still danced and a man with a big guitar played "Malaguena." Life and joy abided here, and music summoned better angels, no matter how sinister the backdrop. This, he had to remind himself of. He found a bench, maneuvered the soft, dripping taco into position, and opened his mouth. Then the cell phone burped.

He set the taco down on the bench in its wet wrapping of wax tissue.

"Borges?" he answered, without looking at the display.

"Daddy?" replied his daughter.

"Oh, hey, baby. Yeah, it's me." He recalled that he had left Brigit a message before leaving the crime scene in Silver Lake. "I wanted to make sure you settled back in out there. How are you?"

"I'm okay," she said. "It's always a little weird coming from you to Mommy. You guys are so totally different. Are you okay? You sound funny."

"Yeah, muffin, I'm all right. I'm on a case, that's all."

"That missing girl? Katy?"

"Right. Only it's gotten a little more mysterious than that."

"It always does with you, Daddy. You'll probably wind up in some place with snake charmers and magic lamps."

Raszer paused, smiled to himself. "Have you been dreaming again?"

"Yeah," she said softly. "You were with a girl. Not Katy, though."

"Do you still have that big map of the world on your bedroom wall?"

"Uh-huh. With blue tacks in every place you've been."

"And colored yarn stretched between them, right?"

"Yep," she said.

"Let your eyes go lazy and tell me if the yarn makes any kind of design."

She thought for a moment. "It's kind of like a bicycle wheel. Or a spider's web. 'Cause everything always connects back to L.A."

"So, draw out the next spoke in the wheel, in your mind. Where does it go?"

"I dunno, exactly. One of those weird countries with *-stan* at the end of it?"

"Your radar's pretty sharp, kiddo. I don't know where I'll wind up, but that part of the world sounds like as good a bet as any. Wanna help me?"

"Sure."

"How do you think bad people get good people to do bad things?"

"Umm." The receiver went quiet as she thought. "Maybe by scaring them. Or by switching bad and good around so you can't tell the difference."

"Like how?"

"Well, one time this girl Jordan asked me to lie for her. I said lying was wrong, and she was like, 'No, lying is okay when the person you're lying to is a liar.' It kinda made sense, and for a few days, I was all upside-down about it. Then one day my friend Kirsten came up to me and said, 'Why did you tell that lie? Now I'm in trouble.' My one little lie grew into this big lie, and then I remembered why it was wrong."

"And why is that, baby?"

"'Cause if you see the world through a lie, it's not the real world. And pretty soon, you don't know what's true anymore. You start to believe in the fake."

Raszer smiled and parked the cell phone against his shoulder. With his hands free, he reached carefully for the dripping taco. He had it within three inches of his lips again when a call-waiting signal bleeped in his ear.

"Hang on a sec, honey," he said, setting the taco back on the bench. "I've got another call. It may be the police."

"Okay, Daddy."

He pressed the RECEIVE button, leaving a greasy imprint, and answered, "Raszer."

"Raszer . . . it's Detective Aquino. Up in Azusa."

"Oh, Detective . . . good. Did you get my message? I wanted to tell—"

"Right," said Aquino. "I saw it on the news. How fast can you get up here?"

Raszer's mouth went dry. "Is it Emmett?"

"No. I need an ID. Can you meet me at the Malthus Mortuary on Foothill?"

"Who's dead?" said Raszer. "Hang on . . . I've got my daughter on the other line."

"I'll see you there," said Aquino, and clicked off, leaving Raszer in the dark.

"Brigit, honey," he said, knowing how oddly disconnected he must sound to her. "I guess I've gotta go."

"What's wrong, Daddy?" she asked. "Now you sound even weirder."

"Everything's okay, sweetheart," he said, though he knew she would not be reassured until she heard his voice in the familiar register again. "It's just work."

"Be careful, Daddy," she said. "Please."

"I will," he said. "I promise. Bye, baby."

He flipped the phone shut and muttered, "Damn," under his breath. He hated leaving her with worries, and hated mortuaries almost as much. *Whose corpse could it be*? He took one last look at the taco. Its corner had drooped over the edge of the bench, leaking chile verde sauce onto the ground. His mouth watered. He reached for it, hoping for one bite before leaving. The phone rang again. "Damn!" he repeated.

"Raszer, it's Borges," said the Lieutenant. "I got your page. Sorry for the delay. I've got federal agents crawling all over me. Have you got the girl?"

"I'm the one who's sorry, Luis," Raszer replied. "They got to her first."

"Who got to her?"

"The bad guys. In the limo. I don't know how, but they caught her just as she was leaving the building. I couldn't get around the block fast enough. Goddamn one-way street. I tailed them as far as a fleet-service lot in Boyle Heights, but they had a second car waiting. She's gone . . . at least for now."

Raszer left his dinner on the bench and made for his car, stomach rumbling.

"This doesn't sound right," said Borges. "She had to be in on it. How else could they get the timing so right?"

Raszer pulled open the car door, dropped into the worn leather bucket, and started the car. "Right . . . or else they had an inside man."

"What's that mystic eye of yours tell you, Raszer? Is she square?"

Raszer threaded his way up Cesar Chavez Avenue and ramped onto the I-5 North, headed for the Pasadena Freeway. "I wouldn't call her square."

"What about the fleet service. Did you get anything on the car?"

"Not on the pickup car," said Raszer. "Except that it was another Lincoln. But on the drop-off, yeah. It had phony diplomatic plates and was rented by something called Southeastern Supply Corp., Sofia, Bulgaria. Renter was an 'A. Bacus.' Honduran license. You're going to want to talk to the fleet manager, Estevez. Greasy character."

"Estevez," Borges repeated. "I know him. Everybody in Boyle Heights knows him. *Greasy* doesn't begin to describe what he's into. Spell the name of the renter . . . "

"What?"

"A. Bacus," said Borges. "Spell it out."

"A-b-a-c-u-s."

"Abacus," said Borges.

"Christ," said Raszer. "I need to get my blood sugar back up."

He shot through the tunnel and onto Highway 2 North, going eighty-five.

"And some sleep," Borges said. "I'm gonna need your help with Scotty. We may not have him long. The feds want custody. They're already singing 'national security.' You know, when they put the FBI and the CIA under the same tent, I thought it was a good idea. It just turned out to be a better way to keep us all out of the circus."

"I phoned Scotty's parents," said Raszer. "Did you hear from them?"

"Yeah. They'll be here tomorrow. The mother . . . she was pretty upset, no?"

"Oh, yeah," said Raszer. "How do you make sense of shit like this? Listen . . . " Raszer took a cigarette from his pack and parked it between his lips. "If you get some time with Scotty before they take him away, see if you can find out any more about how these guys got to him. He was out there playing this crazy game, with no compass, no direction home. He was looking for God—"

"And found the Devil instead," said Borges.

"Right," said Raszer. "Or the Devil found him."

Raszer flipped off the phone and tossed it on the passenger seat. He lit the cigarette and sped east on the Foothill Freeway. As he searched his mental photo files, he realized—with a perverse sense of relief—there was probably only one body anonymous enough to require his identification.

FOURTEEN

"THAT'S HIM," RASZER SAID with a nod. "The old-timer up at the Follows Camp said his name was *J.Z.* J.Z. what, I couldn't tell you."

"John Zimmerman," said Detective Aquino. "We actually found an old unemployment comp stub in his underwear—which he obviously hadn't changed for a while. It was his only ID. He probably kept it in case he forgot who he was. He must've been living up there, in that shed, for almost forty years. How does a man—"

"I don't know," said Raszer, scrolling his eyes across the old squatter's pale, wasted form. The skin stretched over his rib cage was so thin that there hardly seemed to be blood in it. "Jesus, there wasn't much of him, was there, under all those rags?"

"Ninety-one pounds naked," said Aquino. "The clothes on his back weighed almost as much. He had to have been living off his own muscle tissue. When there wasn't any more to metabolize, he just stopped living." The detective cocked his chin in the direction of a tall, lab-coated man in the corner whose hair was styled in a monk's tonsure. "Isn't that right, Isadore?"

"Yes," said the man. "His stomach was empty. He was consuming himself."

Raszer peered into the shadows. He hadn't even noticed the mortician on entering, but now he was impossible to miss. He gave a nod.

"Isadore handles all my autopsies," said Aquino. "He does better bodywork than all the guys in L.A., only the funeral trade pays better than the county."

"I guess he's a good man to know, then," said Raszer. "Where'd you find him?"

"Isadore?"

"No," Raszer said with a chuckle, then indicated the corpse.

"In the shed. About three o'clock this afternoon. God, what a smell. I got to thinking—after you ran off—about that little blue sack you brought me last night. That if the old guy was a scavenger, he might have picked up something the killers left behind. Or been able to give me something, anything, to corroborate Emmett's story."

Raszer aimed an index finger at J.Z.'s thin blue line of a mouth. The upper lip had already molded itself against the toothless gums behind. "He wasn't about to say much. Our killers made sure of that."

"Yeah," Aquino said under his breath. "Mostly I just wanted to see for myself. I don't know how we missed him the first time. We went through those sheds."

"He probably cleared out when he saw you coming. Or maybe the killers scared him into the woods. I'd find a cave to hide in if somebody cut out my tongue." Raszer considered his next words. "The man who was killed today in Silver Lake—he was the DJ at the rave that night. I found one of his business cards up at the Coronado . . . "

"You're finding all sorts of things we missed," said Aquino, rubbing the black stubble on his chin. "Maybe you are a 'psychic detective.'"

"I got lucky," Raszer said. "I pick a thread and follow it. Sometimes it gets pretty tangled, but eventually—"

"You find your way."

"Right. But anyhow, that's not my point."

"What's your point?"

"The DJ . . . they cut out his tongue, too. Just for show."

"So you think it's some kind of autograph?"

"Maybe," said Raszer. "From what I've been able to learn, these guys practice their own version of omerta. That's probably how they manage to blend in—to come and go without a trace. What I picture is four guys who look like chauffeurs. Mannequins. Identical black suits. Identical haircuts. And they go from one rented Lincoln Town Car to another, never saying a word more than is absolutely necessary." He shot a glance at the body, then one at the mortician, and then asked Aquino, "Can we get out of here?"

"Sure," said the cop. "Let's do that. Have you eaten?"

"Only my own muscle tissue," said Raszer.

At that moment, Aquino's young deputy strode in holding a dry cleaner's garment bag. His heels clicked on the tiled floor. The echo made the place feel colder.

"Just in time," said Aquino, taking the bag and discharging the deputy. "The old guy was wearing this when he died. Looked pretty stylish for a vagrant. I thought you might like to have it back."

"My duster?" said Raszer.

"Didn't think you'd see it again, did you?" Aquino replied, handing Raszer the garment bag. "We had it cleaned for you. Super rush job. The smell should be out of it."

"Let's hope," said Raszer.

"We're going to drop in unexpectedly on the Lee family. Henry's mom. Sometimes that's best. Then I'll take you over to the Falls for a steak, and you can tell me all about what happened in the city today."

"I'll tell you whatever I can, Detective. A steak buys a lot from a hungry man."

⬩◆⬩

AQUINO MADE A U-TURN on the dark side street and grunted. "I always miss this turn at night. The Lees are on the one street that doesn't have streetlights. I think they like it that way. As you're about to see, they don't welcome visitors."

"Are they still welcome down at the Kingdom Hall?" Raszer asked.

"Even more since that night," Aquino replied. "It was like the church threw a tent over the house. Silas Endicott kept them in the flock. Paid regular visits. My guess is, he kept hoping he'd learn something about how Katy went so wrong."

"Because Henry and Katy were close?"

"Because Henry and *Ruthie*—Katy's sister—were close. And two summers ago, Katy decided she wanted to be Ruthie. I don't think Silas could make sense of that. He'd given up on Ruthie; she was her mother's girl. But Katy, she was *his*."

Aquino turned onto a cul-de-sac that backed up to the San Gabriel's runoff basin and a chain-link fence bearing an ancient sign from the Department of Water & Power that read: TRESPASSERS WILL BE VIOLATED.

"I thought Ruthie was Johnny Horn's girl," Raszer said. "High school sweethearts and all that."

"She was," said Aquino, turning off the ignition, "until Katy came into the mix that summer. After that, Ruthie took up with Henry." He gave Raszer a nod. "But I have a feeling you know that."

The Lees' was the last house on the left. Their driveway was loose gravel poured over rutted earth, and they had no garage, just a sagging carport sheltering an old Ford van. The lawn had gone to seed and was as patchy as a worn carpet. The house itself, a small California ranch, was dark but for the flickering of a TV.

"According to Emmett Parrish and a few of the townie girls we talked to in the course of the investigation, Henry stayed in touch with Ruthie after she went back to Taos. Emailed her almost every day from an Internet café on Foothill."

"Did you ever get a look at those emails?" he asked.

"The server was clean," Aquino replied. "We subpoenaed the café's backup drives, scoured them, nothing. I don't know how he did it, but he wiped his footprints."

"Maybe he learned that in Iraq, too," said Raszer, half to himself.

"How do you mean?"

"Just thinking out loud," said Raszer. "And you never questioned Ruthie?"

"No. She wasn't a suspect or a witness. And she was in New Mexico."

"What about the FBI?" Raszer asked. "They weren't limited by the state line."

"If they did talk to her," Aquino replied, "they didn't share it with us." Aquino gave the aluminum door three unambiguous knocks. He turned back to Raszer. "Don't expect tea and cookies."

"Okay," said Raszer. "Is there a Mr. Lee?"

"He works the docks down in Long Beach. Night shift. It's just Alice and a six-year-old. But the kid should be in bed." Aquino knocked again. A casement window squeaked open, and a woman's voice called out, as raw as the March wind.

"It's almost nine o' clock, Officer," she said. "You've got no business—"

"It's *Detective*, Mrs. Lee," replied Aquino. "And I do have business. I need to introduce you to Mr. Raszer. He's a private investigator your church hired to find Katy Endicott. It was the last thing Silas did before he died."

"Introduce me?" she exclaimed. "I'm a woman alone with a young child to care for, and you come here after dark to *introduce* me? No, sir, Officer. You can bring your friend back here in daylight, or Sheriff Maca can have my complaint."

"You're not as friendly in the daylight, Alice," said Aquino. "C'mon, give us—"

"I'm sorry, Mrs. Lee," Raszer broke in, stepping off the stoop. "Stephan Raszer. It's my fault. The case is moving very quickly. There was a homicide and a hostage situation in the city today. Maybe you heard about it on the news—the police arrested a young man who may have been involved with your son's killers—and Katy's kidnappers. I need your help."

Detective Aquino parked his hands on his hips and observed.

After a few seconds of silence, Alice Lee replied, "I only have one son, Mr. Raszer, and he's here inside with me now. The other one was dead to me long before those men killed him. The other one died in Babylon."

Raszer drew a breath of mountain air that still tasted of the day's smog. "You mean to say Henry wasn't the same boy after Iraq . . . is that right, ma'am?"

There was no reply, but Raszer heard a small voice call out, "Mommy?"

"It's okay, sweetheart," Alice Lee whispered. "Just some men to see your daddy."

Raszer sat down on the stoop and took out a cigarette. "How old is your little guy?" he asked.

"Just turned six," she answered. "God willing, he'll see thirty without a war."

"What's his name?"

"Ezra," she replied. "And it's past his bedtime."

"I think you're right, Mrs. Lee," said Raszer softly. "I think something happened to Henry, and Johnny, in Iraq. I'd like to un—"

"I'm a patriot," said Alice, not able to conceal the quaver in her voice. "But that war is Satan's curse on this country. Now let the dead rest, Mr. Raszer."

Raszer flipped open his Zippo and spun the spark wheel. He let the flame burn for a few seconds so that she could see his face from her window, then lit his cigarette. "I will, Mrs. Lee," he said. "But I'm hoping that Katy Endicott is alive."

"Alice—" Aquino said, but Raszer gestured silence.

"Maybe she is, and maybe she isn't," said Mrs. Lee. "I pray God for Silas's sake she is, but I've got my doubts. Anyhow, whatever you want to know about Henry, you can ask that hell-bent sister of hers. She knew him a lot better than I did. She knows the whole sad story. Now kindly leave us alone. There's been enough trouble on this house, and I don't like the neighbors seeing the police on my doorstep."

Raszer stood up and shook off a shiver. "If you want to talk—"

"I won't," said Alice Lee, and with that, the window closed with a *ccrraack*.

The Falls Steakhouse was a bar & grill built in the late 1940s, when people still called them that. A weathered wood-frame building, it stood at the north edge of town, right at the gaping mouth of the canyon. Its white clapboard had long since yellowed, and its neon sign's dark letters would never light up again. It was the sort of place frequented by old couples who remembered the fox-trot, and cops who knew they could get a decent T-bone and a full pour for the price of a blind eye to its lapsed liquor license. It was a place to be drunk and sad and listen to Julie London on the jukebox. The booths were dark and musty, and Raszer and Aquino had the whole row to themselves.

Raszer pushed away his plate, leaving the home fries and overcooked broccoli untouched, while Aquino nursed his third Cherry Coke. Had the detective ordered a cocktail, Raszer would have joined him, but he never drank when his dinner partner was cold sober, especially when the dinner partner was a cop.

"You didn't like your meal?" Aquino asked, eyeing the plate.

"The steak was good," Raszer lied.

"Not exactly Morton's, is it?"

"No, but the atmosphere's better," said Raszer. "Right down to the bullet holes in the bathroom wall."

"This used to be a mob spot," said Aquino. "Back in the days when the Hollywood money still drove up through the canyon to the resorts on Angeles Crest. They'd stop here to get oiled. And if a guy didn't have an escort for the weekend, he could find one here. All kinds of disreputable types."

Raszer indicated the two highway patrolmen seated at a distant table. "Does that explain why it's so popular with cops?"

"I guess like attracts like," said Aquino with a smile. He cleared his throat. "I feel for your friend Borges," he said, and let it hang.

"How's that?" Raszer asked, after a beat.

"You know . . . one day he's king of the roost and thinks he pretty much knows the score. The next day he's got feds crawling all over his turf and doesn't have a clue."

"Is that how it happened up here? After the murders?"

Aquino drained his Cherry Coke and held out the glass for another. "That guy Djapper and his team moved in within twenty-four hours," he said. "Even took my office until they'd set up HQ at the ranger station. They used Katy's abduction as a pretext. Somehow, they knew from the beginning she'd been taken out of state. Where the lead came from, I dunno. After that, they muddied up the trail for me real fast."

Raszer sat back and scowled. "The papers played the story as if the JWs wanted the investigation kept within the family. One piece in the *Times* even hinted at some kind of inside scandal tied to these church sex-abuse allegations that are flying around. It struck me as wrong that a triple homicide would get so little media—now, even more so. Do you think it was the Bureau that kept the lid on?"

Aquino wiped his moustache and leaned forward. "Let's just say that the feds wanted it contained because they were onto something bigger. And they had accomplices at the Kingdom Hall."

"Even Silas Endicott?" Raszer asked.

"Even Silas," Aquino replied. "Until he came to see you. I think something was stealing his sleep. Maybe the same thing that steals mine."

Raszer heard the overlush string prelude to an old Al Martino ballad swell up, and watched a corseted woman of seventy with a tar-black beehive and eyeliner drawn out to her temples back away from the jukebox in three-inch heels.

"Man," he said. "I didn't think they built them like that anymore."

Aquino turned discreetly to look. "That's Agnes, " he said. "The owner. Until 1975, she was Jimmy Fioricelli's girl. Those bullet holes above the urinal . . . the bullets went through him first. I think the mob gave her the restaurant to keep her happy, but she never plastered over the holes. I figure she wanted to make sure that every time one of Jimmy's killers took a piss, the thought would cross his mind that he could be next. The cops were there *that* night, too, dining on rare steak while they carried Jimmy out."

"It's never clean, is it?"

Aquino shook his head.

"What's costing you sleep, Detective?"

"A lotta things. But mostly, something that hit me one day, after my last run-in with the FBI. These people, the ones who had those boys killed and took Katy Endicott, they're in the woodwork like dry rot. And more and more, I think whoever is calling their tune might be right up at the rooftop, where the rot is worst. Sure, we've still got cops and generals, and some guy we call the president, but they're window dressing. The real work is being done by private contractors, and they've got a different agenda. That's what's killing my sleep. I can't take anything straight anymore. I don't trust my chief, I don't trust that guy Amos Leach, I don't even trust the woman who shares my bed. And I sure don't trust that tight-ass Bernard Djapper."

"I don't like him either," said Raszer. "But he seems to be warming up to me."

Aquino chuckled for the first time.

"Tell me about this Syrian girl," he said. "And her boyfriend, the DJ."

Raszer picked his words carefully. "I'm not altogether sure he was her boyfriend. But they did have a mutual interest in staying alive, and that makes for a pretty strong bond." He gave a small sigh. "You know, Detective, one thing doesn't add up. You seem like a solid cop, the kind of guy who wouldn't be put off a scent easily. How could you not've checked out the DJ? Those guys are like owls—they see everything. You must've known about him . . . and the girl. From Emmett, if nothing else."

"We did," said Aquino, and a flush rose into his cheeks. "And we would have found them. We would have asked for LAPD assistance. Except for one thing."

"What's that?"

"Djapper told us they'd both left the country, and that the Bureau was on it."

"Sonofabitch," said Raszer. "One of them—either the DJ or the girl—was an informant. And if it was the girl—"

It came back in stuttering images: how Djapper had suddenly appeared at Raszer's car, anxious to make small talk, as he was waiting for Layla to come out.

"What are you thinking?"

"Something I don't want to think: that Harry Wolfe wouldn't be dead if they hadn't let him be. And that my crazy kid Scotty is the perfect patsy."

"Now you're thinking like a cop. Now you know why I don't sleep." Aquino hailed the waitress for coffee. "So maybe the Syrian girl works both sides and the feds figure she can lead them to the end of the rainbow . . . but I don't get your kid. How do you figure that someone you were hired to track from Vermont over a year ago showed up on cue in this case? To tell you the truth, that makes me wonder a little about you."

Now, Raszer finally leaned forward.

"I can't account for it," he said. "Except by the logic you use when you say that these people are in the woodwork. The kind of logic that gets you locked away for a long time. If Silas Endicott came to me to find his daughter, it was in some weird way a consequence of my involvement in Scotty's case. The connection is that there's someone out there grabbing kids when they're in that limbo between adolescence and adulthood, and using all avenues of approach: the Internet, the military, the fundamentalist churches . . . anywhere kids are in a passive, acquiescent state of mind. They lure them like the Pied Piper off to this 'Garden'—wherever that is—do whatever it is they do, and then shoot them back into the world like time-release viruses. Whether Katy Endicott is being programmed as a sleeper agent or a sex slave, I couldn't tell you, but it all serves someone's agenda. What I want to know is whose."

"Yeah," Aquino whispered, and at last sat back and relaxed. "Thanks for sharing. I wouldn't want to start mistrusting you. I'm just beginning to like you."

"Don't trust anyone but yourself and God," said Raszer. "And keep an eye on God. She makes a lot of wardrobe changes."

Aquino lifted his brows. The jukebox flipped from one Italian crooner to another. Perry Como was singing "Catch a Falling Star." The place was stuck in 1959. "When you see Ruthie Endicott," Aquino continued, "and I know you will, be sure and ask her if she's had a visit from our friend Agent Djapper. It's none of my business, really, but I'd like to know."

⬩ ◆ ⬩

FROM THE AVANTI, Raszer phoned Monica and asked her to come in an hour early the next morning to make his travel arrangements. He cursed when she told him he'd made the evening news in his makeshift turban. In the end, he thought, there was no way to avoid celebrity in Hollywood.

The last stop on Raszer's long road home was the Kingdom Hall, where—if he had his days straight—the weekly meeting of the Theocratic Ministry School ought to be just letting out. He hoped to get a few words, and a check, from Amos Leach. He wasn't at all in the mood for it, but it had to be done, and he wanted a second chance to size up Leach. There'd been something unnatural about the man, something not right: clothes a bit too loose on his frame, head and hair easily a size too large for the body. Then there was the voice—the voice of a ventriloquist's dummy. The fundamentalist sects were rife with odd, sexually conflicted characters who'd sought refuge from their own shadows in Christian rectitude, but Raszer had never met anyone quite like Leach. He didn't seriously suspect the man to have been complicit in Katy's abduction, but he wanted to be sure Leach hadn't made him a pawn in some larger game.

He spotted the stark, white building in the overspill of a streetlamp and adjudged that the assembly, if it had occurred, was long over. The curbs were empty, as was what he could see of the rear parking lot. The lights in the kitchen, however, were burning, and it stood to reason that if anyone was keeping late hours, it would be Amos and the Elders. Raszer dimmed his headlights and rolled up against the curb. For a few moments after he turned off the engine, he sat and listened to the frogs spawned by the heavy winter rains. Then another kind of croak made itself heard.

It was Leach's voice, all right, issuing from an open kitchen window. He was engaged in what sounded like heated argument—more precisely, bickering—with another man whose own vocal timbre was too low to identify from this distance. Raszer opened and closed the car door quietly and crept up the driveway to a place just beneath the high window. He wasn't able to see, but he could hear.

"You're threatening me, Sam," Leach shrilled. "You oughtn't threaten a brother, least of all one who backed you all the way to Bethany."

"I'm not threatening you, Amos," replied a low, even voice that Raszer now recognized as that of Sam Brown, the ministerial servant. "I'm counseling you, as you've counseled me, but you don't seem to be listening."

"Listening to what?" Leach shot back. "Innuendo? Some fairy tale from eight years ago? Didn't you learn anything from that McMartin business? *Children lie*, Sam."

"The mother stood against you before the assembly, Amos. She said there was a second witness. I think we both know who that is. At the least, it's my duty to inform the district Overseer, maybe even Circuit. I know what they'll say: There's been enough bleeding; close the wound. I just wish you'd make it easy on us."

Raszer squatted down and rested his back against the stucco. The night was quiet and cool, almost sepulchral, but apparently, noise and heat surrounded Amos Leach. The boy's mother? Which boy? A second witness? To what?

"Make it easy on you," Leach mocked. "*Make it easy* . . . You mean resign my position as an Elder. It's not going to happen, Sam. I've been chosen to lead."

"Amos—"

"You don't get it, do you, Sam? I guess maybe you wouldn't, growing up . . . disadvantaged. There's rules for the flock and there's rules for the shepherds. Men like you and me—spiritual leaders—we're not gonna go out and rob a convenience store. They're not gonna find us in the gutter with a needle in our arm, or catch us plotting against the government. We're accountable. And in return, we get—"

"Yes, Amos," said Sam Brown gravely. "We *are* accountable. That's why—"

In the midst of the tomblike darkness, Raszer's cell phone beeped. He'd forgotten to silence its ringer, forgotten that it was in his pocket. *Idiot*, he thought, as he fumbled for it, scampering back down the driveway toward his car: his sanctuary, if he could reach it before Leach apprehended him, before the doors of the Kingdom Hall flew open and his first paying job in a year hissed away with the curse on Leach's lips. He dove into the front seat, scrunched down, and pressed the phone to his ear.

"Hello?" he whispered harshly.

No reply.

"Hello? *Who is this*?" he repeated.

The hall's doors opened, spilling light on the stoop and the sidewalk. Sam Brown stepped out and surveyed the driveway, then the street. When he'd gone back inside, Raszer slid himself up against the worn-smooth leather of the seat back.

In his rearview mirror, a dark, inchoate form materialized, barely in motion, but Raszer was too busy finding his breath, fumbling for his keys, to take it into his field of conscious vision. He turned the ignition key and let the engine warm.

He waited a few moments and then eased away from the curb, making the first available left to get back to Azusa Avenue. He'd just lowered his window and lit a cigarette when the high beams blinded him. There was a Lincoln on his tail.

His first conscious reaction was willful disbelief. *No way*. Men in black limos didn't come after him; he went after them. And until now, the Lincoln had seemed almost chimerical, a thing imagined as much as seen. *Get on the freeway and go home to a fire and a good rioja. Yes*. But in his mind's chronology, Raszer had already registered fear. Deep and primal, beyond rationalization, it had traveled up his brain stem from his gut, and he'd known decisively that home and hearth would never truly be safe zones again. What he felt was the certainty of prey that a predator had found his lair.

Twice the big Lincoln rammed his rear bumper, and indignation as much as anything else made him drop the Avanti into second gear and floor the accelerator, blowing through the red light at Foothill Boulevard with his horn blaring.

The westbound freeway entrance was a hundred yards up on the right, and Raszer hugged the shoulder and sped up as he entered the overpass, knowing that he could take the ramp at sixty while the Lincoln would almost certainly have to slow down. He heard the V-8 surge and saw the headlight fill his right side mirror as the bulky Lincoln rode up improbably on his right, its rear bumper throwing sparks off the inside wall of the viaduct. Its angle of attack was designed to force him away from the approach and onto a straightaway into the industrial south end of town, a far better place to do murder.

Raszer again felt the Lincoln's front bumper hard on his rear. "Goddamnit!" he howled, as he lost control of the back half of his car. He punched the accelerator and steered right, hoping to fishtail around the limo and come back at the ramp from the other side. All that accomplished was to put the limo's bumper foursquare onto his right flank, bulldozing him down both lanes as effortlessly as if he were new-fallen snow. In another two seconds, he'd most likely roll; Raszer used up one of them to squint through the glare of the Lincoln's headlights and the heavily tinted windshield.

What he saw informed him of how to use the remaining second.

The face of the driver was utterly impassive. Not so much as a clenched jaw marred its fearsome serenity. In fact, the lips were just slightly parted in anticipation of the kill. From what scant information Raszer could gather in the blink of an eye, the face had no marked characteristics, no obvious ethnic stamp—but then, of course, Raszer was constructing a physiognomy from little more than an eye socket and the line of a mouth.

It was enough to tell him that his death would mean little to this man and would never be recognized as murder. He would be just one of two or three dozen accidental calamities visited upon L.A. that night.

He accelerated forward—the only way he could go—and hurtled over the curb, shaving steel from the Avanti's oil pan and spinning up mud from the saturated earth. As soon as he'd cleared the Lincoln's bumper, he spun the wheels hard left and shimmied back onto the pavement ten feet behind the limo. Its brake lights glowed an unnatural red, and its rear tires were obscured in small clouds of vaporized rubber.

Just to the left was the eastbound ramp to the 210 freeway, bound for San Bernardino and the desert beyond, headed anywhere but to the solace of home. Raszer shot onto it, narrowly avoiding a broadside with a hearse bearing the stencil of the Malthus Mortuary. For nearly five minutes, he purred along at ninety-seven in the carpool lane with nothing in his mirror, crossing the double yellow to make for the I-15 South, from which he could connect to Interstate 10 going back into L.A.

He'd just reached for his phone to page Lieutenant Borges when he spotted the Lincoln again, bearing down from the right, making at least 103. Raszer made up his mind to cobble the best from a very bad situation. The local news didn't cover L.A.'s notorious high-speed chases at night, but the highway patrol might; failing that, he would lead the Lincoln back onto Borges's turf, if its driver would be led. He nudged the speedometer to 105, and with a less than steady thumb punched in the rest of Borges's number.

In spite of its horsepower and the recklessness of its driver, the Lincoln could do no better than keep up with the Avanti's rebuilt engine. At 5,000 rpms, it made a sound that limousines rarely make, and each time it crept up on Raszer's bumper, he shot forward by four car lengths. In fact, he could have lost it, but then he would also have lost the opportunity for apprehension. He scanned the freeway. L.A.'s deserted downtown glimmered ahead like a mirage. There wasn't a squad car in sight. He might as well have been on the Autobahn, for all the undermanned LAPD cared about speed limits. He wondered why he hadn't yet seen the snout of a gun protrude from the limo, then realized that his pursuers might have a greater purpose in mind: to follow him home. He reconsidered his gambit.

The junction of the I-10 and the Hollywood Freeway offered a last chance for evasion. The 101 ramp came up quick and could be overshot, especially by something as unwieldy as a Lincoln. If Raszer made as if he were continuing west on the 10 and then veered onto the 101 at the last instant, he might shake his tail. They'd been within six car lengths of his bumper for nearly thirty minutes, and he was enjoying neither the steady trickle of sweat running down the bridge of his nose nor the knifing pains at the base of his skull. Borges hadn't returned his page, the highway patrol hadn't appeared like the cavalry on his flanks, his gas gauge was on E, and he couldn't reach his cigarettes. Time to make a choice.

Raszer surprised even himself by politely putting on his turn signal and ramping onto the 101 North at an even speed. The municipal district was in sight, offering some measure of sanctuary. The arteries were thickening with traffic, and not even jaded Angelenos could fail to note that a yellow Avanti with its entire right side cratered was being chased by a Lincoln with a badly dented grill. He went back to plan one.

If the police would not come to Raszer, he would come to the police. Borges was bound to have a man or two stationed at the crime scene in Silver Lake. The place where the killers had last struck might be the one sure place to elude or entrap them.

If they let him get that far.

Raszer had begun to maneuver right for the Echo Park exit when the air around his ears was buffeted by the full-bore pulse of the Lincoln's engine. It came up on his left without warning, and a pea would not have fallen through the gap between its door handle and his. The rear window slipped down about six inches in what seemed altered time, and Raszer felt his insides retract. From the window emerged a man's hand: a large hand with five long, fine digits, one adorned with a silver ring set with a single ruby. Held between the thumb and forefinger was a sixth digit, equally long and fine but feminine in provenance, severed at the knuckle from its owner and still tipped with the dusky purple nail that identified it as Layla Faj-Ta'wil's.

Aiming the finger like a dart, the assailant shot it through Raszer's open window and onto his lap.

Raszer swerved and went metal to metal with the Lincoln for an instant, sending it into a skid across one lane of traffic. He wrenched the steering wheel right and shot down the Echo Park exit ramp while the Lincoln flew ahead, remaining visible just long enough for Raszer to see its brake lights glow. You didn't back up on the Hollywood Freeway. He began to wonder if going home wasn't the more prudent course, and then realized with a pang that home might not be any safer.

After ten minutes of threading his wounded vehicle through the side streets of L.A.'s most unnavigable district, he arrived at Sunset and Hyperion, two blocks east of Layla's apartment. All evidence suggested he'd lost the Lincoln, and it seemed unlikely that it would show up here on its own. Since that had been the whole point of the detour, he was no longer sure why he'd come. The cell phone beeped: Borges, answering his page.

"Raszer," he said. "*¿Que pasa?*"

"Jesus, Luis," said Raszer. "I paged you twenty minutes ago."

"*Lo siento*," Borges replied, "but you're not my only guy. I was with the chief. The feds are moving Scotty to a secure facility in Arizona. Some Air Force base. If you want a last word on this, get down to the Federal Building at 9:00 AM. Room 626."

"Moving Scotty . . . as a detainee or as a material witness?"

"Both, I think," Borges answered. "I'll tell you what Djapper told me. They think Al Qaeda—or some offshoot of an offshoot of it—has gotten inside this crazy game your kid was into. They think there's some big human-trafficking operation going on, so now they've got DOJ and even State Department people questioning him."

"I think they're onto something," said Raszer. "But it isn't about Al Qaeda. That's the standard bullshit. This is something new—or maybe something very old. And moreover, it's Shia, not Sunni. Haven't these idiots figured out the difference yet? I'm gonna take a different route, though. I need to get my stray back."

Raszer pulled up to the curb in front of the Tantra. The club was closed, but the police tape stretched across the front of Layla's building hadn't otherwise affected pedestrian traffic on the busy strip. "Meanwhile, the killers just rode my bumper all the way down from Azusa . . . which means they followed me there, too. I lost them at the Silver Lake exit from the northbound 101 and came straight to the crime scene. Don't ask me why, but I had the notion I could draw them here."

Borges cleared his throat. "Are you sure it was them?"

"Oh, yeah. I'm sure. They turned my car into scrap metal and tossed the Syrian girl's ring finger through my window. I'm assuming you took her prints, so getting a match shouldn't present a problem."

"Can you ID any of the men?"

"The windows were tinted like Ray-Bans, but I did make the driver. It's a face I won't forget, Luis."

"Good. We'll do a sketch. When you were up in Azusa, did you leave your car for any length of time?"

"Yeah," said Raszer. "I had dinner. You think they stuck a tracer on me?"

"Check the underside of your gas tank," said Borges. "And feel around inside the rear bumper and wheel wells. The state-of-the-art transmitter's about the size of a quarter and not much thicker. If you find it, hand it over to the officer just inside the building. Give me a description of the car, and we'll go after it. I'm sending men over there, but I doubt your friends are going to show up in that part of town."

"No," said Raszer, "I don't suppose they will. Do you want me to stay put until your guys get here?"

There was a pause. "No," said Borges. "I want you to go home."

"Home? My fondest hope is that these guys don't know where I live yet."

"They know where you live, Raszer. And they've got business with you. I'm going to put three of my best men on your house. You can sleep tight."

"Sure, Lieutenant," said Raszer. "Like a baby, right?"

"Right. And give that finger to the officer on-site, too. If you can find something to wrap it up in, uh, it might be appreciated."

"Right," said Raszer. "I'll see what I've got. Until recently, I had a little velvet jewelry bag that would have been just perfect."

FIFTEEN

RASZER STOOD NUMBLY in the driveway and mourned his battered car. It was worse than he'd imagined. On one level, the cratered metal was a map of grace. Had they hit him on the driver's side, he might have looked worse than the Avanti. But at the moment, this gave him no consolation. He loved the car, and it had been cruelly violated. As much as it pained him, he couldn't stop examining and reexamining each and every gash, like a jilted lover obsessing over the details of his betrayal.

Finally, the descending chill of night—a chill that no one who lives in L.A. is ever really dressed for—drove him inside, but even then, he stood silently at the front window and continued to stare at the torpedoed hulk of his car. After a short while, the emptiness of the dark house at his back made him realize that part of the reason he'd lingered outside was an unreadiness to be inside and alone. There was nowhere to run if his assailants did come to finish their "business" with him.

He thought about Harry Wolfe, and about the bloody stump the killers had left in his mouth. Raszer didn't want to die in bed, much less pinned to the mattress. He hadn't found a transmitter on his car, but that didn't mean they couldn't find him. He wondered how long it would take for Borges's men to assume stakeout positions. These were the times when he wished he owned a gun. At all other times, he was glad he didn't. It would offer temptations he did not want to court.

He found his way to the bar in the dark. He hadn't turned on the recessed lighting, or the floor lamps whose familiar spill patterns made him feel welcome. In the darkness, he felt like an intruder in his own home, but he didn't want to swim about in front of lighted windows like a big fish in an aquarium. It was only the third or fourth time in ten years that such caution seemed warranted. Raszer didn't use letterhead stationery or hand out flyers, and he billed from a

P.O. box. He wasn't listed in the Yellow Pages. He and Monica had kept everything except their command of cyberspace deliberately old school, and for the most part, it had meant that he could take his meals in peace, invite a woman to spend the night, and let his daughter play in the garden. He wondered now if his home would ever be safe for Brigit again.

The thought of losing his house hit him with the same kind of animal panic as the thought of giving up cigarettes, and he knew that, sooner or later, both fig leaves would have to fall. You finally had to face the world the way Adam and Eve had faced the wrathful god whose footfalls had shaken Eden: naked. It wasn't a pleasant prospect, and as he straddled his stool at the slate-topped bar, he took refuge in a glass of port and a Cuban cigar. It was too late in the evening for red wine.

Raszer's bar was a study in anachronism and a key to his psyche. At his right was a rotary phone whose number was known to only two dozen people in the world. It was a safe line that he used mainly for outgoing calls, but when it rang, he answered. To the left of that was a tricked-out MacBook Pro that was networked to his front office, the security system, and a matrix of international police and nongovernmental agencies, some of which tracked missing persons, others the emergence of new religious and pseudo religious movements worldwide. It was when the two phenomena conjoined that Raszer received a bulletin.

Directly in front of him was a bookstand on which his current reading was opened: an 1826 edition of the Koran he'd purchased from an antiquarian bookshop in Hampstead, with the Arabic on the left and an English exegesis on the facing page. Overhead was a lensed halogen track lamp whose beam encompassed the dimensions of the bookstand, and no more. On Raszer's left was a cedar inbox in which Monica placed the day's research and any important messages, and farther to the left were his ashtray, his wine glass, and a candle.

He set the cigar in the ashtray and fished through his inbox. Clipped together were three documents: a printout of the Argonauts.com homepage, a page of related links for "Advanced Immersion Reality Field Gamers," on which Monica had circled the sub-link gtlt7+, and the login page on which she'd entered the name *sdarrell* and the password *Hazid*. In a dialogue box below appeared the reply: "Gaming privileges for sdarrell have been suspended." A fourth page lay by itself, highlighted in yellow. It was the most intriguing of all.

She had given *sraszer* as a user ID and once again entered *Hazid* as the password. The reply was:

> hello sraszer. welcome to altgtlt8. to verify your status as gauntlet L7 we will need your poe, present locus, and ema of your GM. you will receive a response within 24 hrs. remain in position and do not reply to this message. allah be praised.

✦ ◆ ✦

RASZER FELT SUDDENLY that others were present, that the darkness held dozens of germinal forms, waiting to be invoked into being. They could be summoned with as little as an email, and all they needed was a locus and a poe, which was Gauntlet argot for *point of entry*, the place (in time and space) from which a player had entered the game. In Raszer's case, it was right here, right now. *Hazid* was the rail switcher, the detour to a different kind of game.

One small but significant detail in the altgtlt8 posting caught his eye. Despite the near universal use of lowercase letters in Internet communication, Raszer could not imagine an Islamic fundamentalist spelling the name of Allah with a small *a*. Behind one mask was another, and another, and even the wearer had probably forgotten his true face.

He got up from the stool and walked into the kitchen, wanting something he'd forgotten by the time he got there. It was dark, and the big cast iron stove creaked and pinged with the heat of its pilot lights. He checked to see that the door leading to his rear deck was securely locked. Outside in the canyon, the northeast wind was whipping up an L.A. sirocco, and even the coyotes were quiet. It was going to be a long night. He returned to the bar, then decided he'd better sleep while he could.

> *The desert wind tugged at the big tent's moorings. A lantern swung, casting oversize lunar shadows on silk. Raszer sat with Harry Wolfe on a sand floor laid with carpets. They were close enough to whisper, but what passed between them was instantly consumed by the wind's howl. The flap opened slightly, revealing a black sky pinpricked by starlight. For an instant, a face appeared, not unfamiliar. Like Scotty's, but darker. Harry motioned Raszer closer and whisperered, "Everything is permitted."*
>
> *"Why?" Raszer asked, unable to hear his own voice.*
>
> *"At the bottom of the well," said Harry, "there is no water."*

A second face appeared at the tent's opening and filled Raszer with fear. It was the face of the man who had been driving the limo. The flap closed again; Raszer's mouth was dry.

He fumbled for the glass of water on his nightstand, knocking it over. Someone expelled a scented breath, not in the tent, but nearer. Wintergreen?

The lantern's ellipse swept to and fro over brightly colored carpets: red, saffron, deepest eggplant. Piles of desert provisions, and among them the curled form of a young woman. Raszer called her name.

"Ruthie . . . "

The girl stirred, and the central tent pole—a shaft carved from the trunk of a date palm—creaked like a ship's mast. Ruthie Endicott lifted her head. Raszer smiled, then glanced back at the front flap. This time it was only the wind. When he returned his eyes to Ruthie, she had become an old man or, rather, a man of middle age made old by the desert, a diet of sweet dates, and the absence of dentists in this foreign place. Or was it an old woman?

"Have you heard the tale of the two birds?" asked the old man-woman.

"Ruthie?" Raszer repeated, troubled and talking in his sleep.

"It's me," came a voice unsettlingly close.

Something slipped into Raszer's pillow with the sound of a soft tearing. Something cold, hard, and close. Two fingers pinched his nostrils shut. He gasped and tried to scream, but his mouth had filled with warm blood. No sound came but that of a drowning man.

✦ ◆ ✦

RASZER'S DOORBELL RANG at 3:40 AM. He thought it was in the dream, but then remembered that dream doorbells are different. The first thing he did after he'd opened his eyes was to feel for his tongue. Then he tried to get control of his hearbeat. When he turned on the light, he saw that a nine-inch knife was embedded in his pillow.

Sweat broke out on his forehead. He withdrew the knife and swung his legs over the edge of the bed, waiting to move until his eyes had adjusted to the darkness. Then he staggered barefoot to the front door, arm cocked, the knife held at the height of his left ear. The hardwoood floor was cold, and a presence hung still in the air. His heart was in his throat. Someone had been in his house, and might yet be.

There was a cop at the door, one of Borges's men.

"Mr. Raszer?"

"Yes," Raszer answered, his ear against the door, his feet spread for flight.

"Are you all right?"

"As far as it goes, yeah," Raszer answered. He punched in the code to disarm the alarm system.

"My partner saw something on your deck," said the cop. "Do you mind if we check around back?"

Raszer unlatched the door. "You might be a couple of minutes late," he said. "The guy was in my house." He stepped out onto the stoop, naked to the waist in his drawstring sweats, and displayed the knife. "He left this in my pillow."

"Jesus," said the cop, a man in his forties with long sideburns and thinning, slicked-back hair. "Not exactly the tooth fairy, was he?"

"No," said Raszer. "But if they keep leaving these trophies around"—he nodded at the knife—"it's going to cost them a lot of quarters."

"Maybe we should take a look inside," said the cop.

"I'd apppreciate if you did," said Raszer. "Is Lieutenant Borges reachable?"

"Not at this hour," replied the cop, then whistled for his partner. "Not even Borges. Any idea how the guy got in?"

"None," said Raszer. "There are three doors, all triple-locked and alarmed. This one, the slider on the rear deck, and the library. I haven't checked the others yet."

"So what, then?" the cop said drily. "The guy came down the chimney?"

"You tell me," said Raszer. "You're the one on stakeout."

The man's partner, a squat fellow of about thirty, puffed up the steps and introduced himself to Raszer. The wind whipped through Raszer's big cedar tree, depositing needles on the stoop. "Wicked night, huh?" said the younger cop.

"Oh, yeah," Raszer replied, and held the door. "You guys want some coffee?"

"That'd be nice," said the older cop, admiring the array of equipment in Raszer's front office. "Can you switch on the lights for us?"

"Sure," said Raszer. "I'll make a pot. I think I'm done sleeping. You guys have a look around. Take your time, and don't forget to look under the beds."

Raszer heated some water on the stove, then transferred it to the carafe of his Cona, a blown-glass percolator that looked like it belonged in an alchemist's lab or an art museum. He lit an alchohol burner beneath the carafe and spooned a couple of ounces of a Guatemalan grind into the top compartment. Then he lit a cigarette, sat at the bar, and waited while the men searched. Despite the timing of their arrival, he hadn't for a second doubted their credentials. Nobody but cops and plumbers could manage to look both so ordinary and so on top of their game, and L.A. cops were as perfectly cast as if a Hollywood agent had pulled them out of a cattle call.

The LAPD had a dirty reputation, but if anyone's men were clean, Borges's were.

The tall one wandered back into the living room, put his hands on his hips, and surveyed the surroundings. "Nice layout," he said. "You wouldn't know from the street there was this kind of space in here."

"I knocked down a few walls," Raszer said. "And dropped the living room sixteen inches. I don't like running into things."

"Who's your general contractor?"

"Venezuelan guy," said Raszer. "I'll give you his card. So what'd you find?"

"You're right," said the cop. "The doors are all secure. But the bathroom window's wide open."

Raszer stared for a beat and then said, "Shit," remembering that he'd opened it after his shower in the early hours of the long day.

The second cop entered heavily from the other end of the house's sole hallway. "Those fancy alarm systems don't do much good if—"

"Yeah, but hold on," Raszer said. "It's a heat sensor. How do you figure—"

"They all have blind spots," he said. "Shit, I've busted perps who could slip through them like centipedes."

"Maybe the guy was cold-blooded," the tall one said with a chuckle. "Anyhow, he's gone now."

"That's a relief," said Raszer. "I think I owe you guys. The doorbell probably scared him off. Otherwise, that knife might be in my chest."

"Or it could be he just wanted to let you know he was around," said the plump one. "Pros don't kill unless they've been paid to." He sniffed the vapors rising from the Cona. "This coffee ready yet?"

Raszer took a glance. "Give it another three minutes or so," he said. "It's worth the wait."

"In that case," the first cop told him, "we're gonna check the canyon. Your guy didn't leave by way of the street. My guess is, he's waiting it out in the chaparral."

"Have at it," said Raszer, getting up from the stool. "I'll keep the coffee hot."

There was no would-be killer hiding in the brush like a Western movie outlaw. Raszer hadn't really expected there would be. He was beginning to feel the sensory shift that always occurred when his missions were in full play. He was beginning to accept the presence of daemons. They came with the territory, and with the orientation essential to its navigation.

It was only as the dawn broke that the chill left his shoulders and the memory of his dream and its aftermath began to fade. By the time the first ray broke over the canyon, he was uncertain of where the dreamline had crossed into reality. He washed and shaved, and dressed for his trip downtown for one more pass at Scotty Darrell.

Lieutenant Borges was there to meet him at the building entrance and hustled him inside. "I hear you had a visitor last night," Borges said.

"It seems that way," said Raszer. "Thanks for your guys. Am I on time?"

"Yes and no," Borges replied. "They scrapped the group interrogation. They're taking him into federal custody. That guy Picot, from National Counterterrorism, seems to be calling the shots. I'd make a stink, but the chief's already told me to let it ride. Scotty's folks are here. I thought you'd want to see them."

"I do," said Raszer. "How are they?"

"Shell-shocked."

"Yeah. There's something really wrong here."

"What else is new?" said Borges. "The strange thing is that the feds don't seem all that curious about your four goons in a rented limo . . . although Agent Djapper did ask to sit in on your statement."

"That's fine," said Raszer. "I'm off to Taos to see Katy's sister, and I wouldn't mind having a fed on my tail. If we start going in circles, I may end up following him."

Borges pressed the elevator's DOWN button. "Following him where?"

"To wherever he thinks I'm going. The game Scotty was playing—we know that's how he got sidetracked. But I may have found the channel they used to get to him. The players' only contact with the GamesMasters once they're in the game is via emails from Internet cafés. That's how they get instructions: go to this address, board this bus, and so on. In the actual game, the moves are plotted randomly. But these guys have hacked in and altered the game so the player thinks he's got a sort of immunity from consequence. Virtual terrorism. Everything is permitted."

"You mean he thinks he's still playing?" Borges interjected. "Even when somebody dies?"

They stepped into the elevator and Borges pressed SB3. Going down.

"Right," Raszer said. "They may even have convinced him he's in some pupa state between Earth and heaven. That's the genius of the con: They've taken the precepts of the game—to put yourself at God's disposal—and spun it to their purposes; they've put themselves in God's place. And when you consider how many people are playing these alternate reality games—not just college kids, but secretaries, salesmen, soldiers—it's potentially huge. A mass conversion that would make the Reverend Moon turn green with envy. Think of it, Luis: These days, if you're under thirty, you spend half your time in a metalife. The feds are right. It is a human-trafficking operation, but it's about more than sex or debt bondage or terrorism. The traffic is in minds."

The doors opened to the sub-basement. It was ten degrees colder.

"For what purpose, Raszer?" Borges asked. "If you're right . . . "

"I think it's about turning the world on its head. Flipping the poles. Up is down. Wrong is right. The Syrian girl gave me a clue. She reminded me of how easy it was to paralyze the United States government with a blowjob and a stained dress."

"You're getting conspiratorial on me again."

"Sometimes conspiracy's just a matter of giving possibilities a nudge. In the end, every blowjob's part of a bigger picture. Every stained dress tells a story."

Borges paused in the wide, echoing hallway. The recycled air was perfumed with Mr. Clean. "Do your girlfriends call you paranoid, Raszer?" he asked.

"A few have," Raszer answered. "A few have also justified my paranoia."

A door swung open twenty feet down the hall and banged against the stopper. Two men in suits came out. One of them was Douglas Picot. Behind them, a pair of federal marshalls escorted Scotty Darrell, not yet used to his leg irons. He stumbled as they crossed the threshold. Agent Djapper brought up the rear.

"Here come the real paranoids," Raszer said.

"Goddamnit," Borges muttered. "Why did they have to bring him to his parents in chains? These guys don't have a pisspot's worth of class."

Scotty looked pale, stringy, and scared. Seeing his parents' faces must finally have clued him in to the fact that the gauntlet he was now running was all too real. He stood accused of a robbery (the convenience store), a shooting (the tram driver at Universal City), and a murder (Harry Wolfe), among other things. And yet, if Raszer was right about the sort of programming he'd been subjected to, Scotty hadn't understood until very recently that these were real crimes attributable to a real person. His ontological referents—his sense of *what was* and *what was real*—had been messed with. What elegant evil it was: as if his captors had fitted both his consciousness and his conscience with a drop-down screen that flashed: *Pay no attention to that twinge in your gut—it's only a memory of life.*

Scotty glanced up and saw Raszer coming, and his eyes lit briefly with hope, dimming again only when Raszer's own face failed to affirm it.

"Well, Mr. Raszer," said Picot, "we meet again. No rooftop escapades today?"

"Not before noon," Raszer replied. "Where are you taking Scotty?"

"That's classified," said Picot.

"Of course it is," Raszer shot back.

"You'll have to step aside," Agent Djapper broke in. "We're—"

"Not quite so fast," Borges countered. "I need a paper trail on this handover. Have you finished processing—"

"Every last form," said Djapper. "It's all in order."

"I think you're making a mistake," Raszer said, ignoring Djapper and stepping into Picot's path. "Give me a half hour, and I may be able to spare the taxpayers some money and you a lawsuit."

"That won't be possible," Picot said unctuously, through the little hole in his face that served as a mouth. "But we appreciate the offer."

"Can I assume you have a federal judge in your corner?" Raszer came back.

"Are you presenting yourself as Scotty's attorney, Mr. Raszer?"

"No, but someone ought to. Has he seen one?"

Djapper piped in, right in Raszer's face. His breath smelled of tooth rot beneath the mint. "Mr. Darrell is an unlawful combatant."

"That's funny," said Raszer. "He looks like a scared kid to me."

"Even mass murderers cry for their mothers, Mr. Raszer," said Picot. "And there are twelve-year-olds out there who can build an IED. It's best not to think too deeply about this. In case you hadn't noticed, we're at war. It's a battle between one kind of human—and another." In contrast with Bernard Djapper, whose prickliness came as quickly to the skin as the sweat that dampened his dusting of baby powder, Picot seemed to have no internal heat. He was the sort of Dorian Gray whose age would always be forty-four on the outside. "Now, if you'll excuse—"

"Can I ask you something, Picot?" Raszer said, quietly intense.

Picot nodded stiffly.

"Are you comfortable in your skin? Do you like the role you're playing?"

For just an instant, the question appeared to create a hairline fracture from the top of Picot's skull to the toes of his tasseled slip-ons. Then he quickly reconstituted himself and offered the weakest of smiles.

"Scotty," Raszer said, locking his eyes on the boy. "I'm going to try and get you some help. In the meantime, tell these men the truth. Not the truth you've been taught recently but the truth your body remembers. Where is the Garden, Scotty? The girl I showed you yesterday . . . where do I find her?"

Scotty's reply was a non sequitur. "Do you think I'll be home for Thanksgiving?" he asked, his expression revealing nothing.

Waiting until he was sure the boy had no more to say, Raszer nodded. "I hope so," he said.

And Scotty was taken away, the echo of his leg irons making the long hallway sound like the hold of a slave ship. *Bruised, railroaded, and mindfucked*, Raszer thought, *but not stupid*. "Will I be home for Thanksgiving?" Scotty had said.

For Turkey.

Borges led Raszer into the big room Scotty and his federal guard had just exited. Seated at the far end of a conference table, their postures as stiff as if waiting for someone to say, "At ease," were Scotty's parents. His mother was as regally long-necked and sculpted as Raszer remembered her to be, but her eyes were rimmed with red, and the cavernous space made her small form seem doll-like. Even so, her tensile strength registered—a dancer is always a dancer. Scotty's father was twice her size, but similarly bony. His eyeglasses were askew, and it looked like he'd last combed his long gray hair three times zones away. Raszer doubted either of them had slept since getting the call.

"Mr. and Mrs. Darrell," Borges said softly as they entered. "I'm sure you remember Stephan Raszer."

Scotty's mother looked up. Her eyes briefly flashed anger, then softened to pleading. "How . . . " she asked, " . . . how could you have let him stay out there for so long?"

"I wish I could answer that, Mrs. Darrell," Raszer said. "All I can say is that I'm sorry it's come to this, and that I'll find the people who used your son this way. That wasn't Scotty on the roof yesterday. And I'm convinced he's innocent of the murder."

Scotty's father sat forward slightly. "What are you saying, Mr. Raszer? That he's been framed, or that we should prepare to mount an insanity defense?"

"That he's not in possession of his will, Mr. Darrell. Or his identity. He was acting as his game avatar. That's what he's been taught to do. And if this is what I think it is, your son is only one of many. Soon enough, others will begin showing up."

A muscle in Mrs. Darrell's cheek twitched. Otherwise, she was stone still.

"Look at it this way," said Raszer. "When the Marines send a boy into Fallujah, they give him moral immunity. So he kills anything that moves. Is he insane? Not according to the Marines. But if he did the same thing in a high school cafeteria . . . "

"I see your point," said Scotty's father. "Situational insanity."

Raszer nodded. "Still, something in Scotty's makeup drew him deeper into the game to begin with. If I knew what it was, I might have better luck drawing him out."

"Is it really all about this ridiculous game?" Mr. Darrell asked. "One day he's quoting Thomas Aquinas, the next he's practicing jihad? How can this—"

Raszer pulled out a chair opposite Scotty's mother. "The Gauntlet is a bunch of brainy college kids exploring the limits of free will. Trying to find out where God steps out of the burning bush to say, 'Thou shalt not.' But at the higher levels, where Scotty was playing, you're in a moral limbo. You have to be pretty centered to resist the friendly stranger who offers you a ticket to heaven. How do you know you haven't, in fact, won the game?"

Mrs. Darrell nodded silently and folded her arms, suddenly chilled.

"Ever since they started hauling in every potential shoe bomber in sight," Raszer went on, "the shrinks who work for federal grant money have been gathering pages and pages of data on what makes a would-be 'terrorist' tick. A lot of it's useless, but two things are consistent enough to look right."

"What are they?" Mr. Darrell asked.

"Humiliation is one. A pattern of humiliation. Uusally it's tribal, or racial, or colonial, but it can also be personal."

Mrs. Darrell seemed to falter briefly, then asked, "And the second thing, Mr. Raszer?"

"What they call a 'predisposition to suicide,'" said Raszer. "In other words, these kids don't have to be persuaded to die, because they're soul-dead already. What keeps them hanging on, living with Mother or suffering the nagging wife, is that they don't want to die for nothing. What they need is the opposite of a raison d'être. I had hoped to find out what your son's was."

"His reason not to exist?" asked Mrs. Darrell. "What are you saying?"

"Scotty tried killing himself when he was only thirteen," said his father. "He wasn't smart enough to know that a vial of his mother's Xanax wouldn't do the trick."

"I remember you telling me that," said Raszer.

"So," Borges interjected, "you don't buy the government's line that the boy's a convert to Islam, or the Islamist cause?"

"No," Raszer responded. "Maybe to an Islamic myth . . . or to some ideal of insurrection. But Scotty doesn't strike me as the least bit dogma driven. I think he's seen heaven and wants to go back. I know a few good psychiatrists who work with federal prisoners and can do expert-witness duty. If I can convince Special Agent Djapper that one of them might be able to get the information he's after, we may have a chance."

"Who took him away?" asked Mrs. Darrell. "Who are these people?"

"That's what I intend to find out, Mrs. Darrell," Raszer replied. "Because, as I said, Scotty isn't their only victim. There's a young woman—"

"Well, if it helps," said Scotty's father, "we're dropping that lawsuit. Whatever else happened, you found our son alive, and we're grateful."

"That means a lot," said Raszer. "More than you know."

✦ ◆ ✦

RASZER GAVE HIS STATEMENT to the police with Agent Djapper in attendance. His description of the limo and its driver was good enough to yield an APB and a strikingly accurate computer composite of the man's face. He bought Djapper coffee and waffles at the Original Pantry, a downtown greasy spoon so ordinary it was chic, and told him just enough about his travel plans to ensure that the FBI wouldn't be far behind him. Then he headed home in his battered Avanti to set up his itinerary and mission protocol with Monica.

In fact, he knew she'd be two steps ahead of him, and that was exactly where he wanted her to be.

SIXTEEN

"YOU'VE GOT AN eleven-forty to Albuquerque," Monica told him, "and a Jeep to get you to Taos. But I have no idea where you want to sleep."

"Any motor inn along the Paseo. I'm on the budget plan. Speaking of . . . did we get paid yet?"

"I've sent a courier," she replied. "Thank God for that Sam Brown guy. The other one—Leach—he seems a little slithery. Imagine that: a snake in the revival tent."

"I think he's in trouble. I overheard something last night. Fragments—but I think he may have a history with one or more of the boys. It was Sam Brown reading him the riot act. I got an inkling that Katy Endicott might be tied up in it somehow."

"Yuck," Monica said. "When are we gonna wise up and give the priesthood back to women?"

"Not soon enough," said Raszer. "Anyhow, let's get down to business."

"Well, we'll have the check in the bank before you leave, and the second payment invoiced, and now that the Darrells have dropped the lawsuit, we can tap your dwindling reserves. But you're right—you *are* on a budget. How far off the map are you headed this time, and what sort of resources are you going to need? You've been even more cryptic than usual about your travel plans, Raszer."

"To tell you the truth, I don't have my bearings yet. But let me tell you what I do have, and you tell me if it looks like a web any spider you know would spin."

Monica watched as he took a cigarette from the floppy front pocket of his cotton shirt: silver-gray, short-sleeved, open to the breastbone, nicely wrinkled. The kind she liked best on him. She liked him very much, in fact, but was careful not to let him take her affection for granted.

"Pull down the map, would you?" he asked, and remained cantilevered against her desk as she stood and smoothed her skirt, as was her habit. His eyes went distant as she pulled a classroom-size political map of the world down over the scheduling board that spanned most of the office's north wall, but he missed neither her practiced movement nor the fit of the knit fabric against her backside. The truth was that he considered her essential. The truth was that he often heard himself speaking from her lips. Raszer thought that knowing another human being that well was possibly the sexiest thing on earth, especially when sex wasn't part of the package.

Odds and ends from his last assignment remained in place on the map's dry-erase, magnetic surface: Scotty Darrell's coordinates, as well as those of a handful of other advanced Gauntlet players whose paths of pilgrimage he'd managed to get from the GamesMasters before their disappearance. Many of the players had left the North American continent. Some had gone south, into the Latin countries. Others had inevitably tracked west to the great deserts of the Southwest, the American Canaan. But a number of currents seemed to converge on the ancient nexus: on ports like Alexandria, Haifa, Tripoli, Tarsus, and farther inland, even to the frontiers of that black farce of a war that had filled the rivers of Babylon with enough blood to ensure a bad harvest for six generations.

To Iraq, where Johnny Horn and Henry Lee had gotten their call.

"Do you want me to clear it?" Monica asked.

"No. Leave everything for now." Raszer leaned forward, intent on the criss-crossing trajectories. "So here's what we've got so far, working backwards from today: We've got an American college boy with a remapped mind in federal custody for an alleged act of terrorism committed while wearing the garb of an eleventh-century radical Shiite cult, which operated from bases in Syria and Persia and murdered its political enemies with Syrian daggers at close range. He claims to have been in the service of someone he calls the Old Man, and the feds—at least this guy from counterterrorism—seem to know who he's talking about."

"He just *happens* to be the same boy I tracked down the rabbit hole of an alternate reality game based in the thesis that absolutely everything is open to question except the existence of God. And now he's implicated in both the murder of the British DJ who MC'd the rave from which Katy Endicott was abducted and at which Katy's boyfriends, Johnny Horn and Henry Lee, were killed, *and* the attempted kidnapping of Layla Faj-Ta'wil—a Syrian woman and onetime consort of same Johnny Horn—who was hiding out with the DJ and may have a history with our killers as some kind of sexual terrorist—"

"Or at least, that was your firsthand assessment of her skills," Monica teased, taking shorthand with her right and moving magnetic game pieces with her left.

"Not just mine," said Raszer. "Harry Wolfe, aka MC Hakim, deceased, affirmed it, and Layla herself alluded to sexual espionage. That's how she got involved with Johnny. I think it's possible she never left the payroll."

"Whose payroll, exactly?"

"That's what we need to know. If I'm anywhere close, there's quite a history."

"So give me a lesson, Professor."

He got up to join her at the map. "The MO in Harry Wolfe's death is straight out of eleventh- and twelfth-century accounts of the Nizari branch of the Ismailis, otherwise known as the Assassins. Its founding father was Hassan-i-Sabbah, the original Old Man, a brilliant theoretician and strategist, and a kind of holy anarchist. 'Nothing is true; everything is permitted' were purportedly his dying words, the same words Henry Lee scrawled on the walls of the Kingdom Hall."

"Selective murder for the purpose of terror was his strategy—maximum impact for minimal effort. And he didn't necessarily have to take out the king. A second fiddle did just fine with far less risk. If our group has modeled itself on the Assassins—if something with the reach and resources of a multinational but some kind of quasireligious, maybe even anarchoreligious, agenda is recruiting smart but malleable kids and persuading them they're in God's hands—think of the trouble they could make. Especially if their operatives think they're in virtual reality with a license to kill."

"What kind of 'persuasion' would that take, Raszer? You've told me yourself you don't really believe in brainwashing."

"I don't," he said. "I agree with Goedel that the mind isn't ultimately programmable. But I do believe it can be led through a series of deceptions to conclude that it's found a new truth on its own, even if that truth is that *there is no truth*. Zen masters use trickery, too, but for good purpose: to get your consciousness unstuck. The original Hassan may have done the same to prevent Islam from becoming rigid. Legend was that he'd built a garden so much like

Eden that his hashish-drugged acolytes would wake up there convinced they'd drunk the nectar of heaven and died to the flesh. After that, getting them to do suicide missions wasn't difficult. Think of that power in the hands of a criminal syndicate. What if someone has rebuilt Hassan's garden?"

"Go back," she said. "Go back to Layla and Katy and the trade, and why Johnny, Henry, and Harry Wolfe had to die. Tell me why they were a threat, and then tell me if we have anything you can drop in an evidence bag."

"I will," he said, "but first stick one of those red pieces on Turkey."

"Okay," she said. "But why?"

"Because when I saw Scotty this morning, I asked him where the Garden was, where he'd seen Katy Endicott. You know what he said?"

"What?"

"He asked me if he'd be home for Thanksgiving."

"And . . . "

Raszer aimed a finger at Turkey. "That was his answer. I'm going to assume he gave me credit for being able to take a hint."

"It's a stretch, Raszer," she said, but moved the marker there anyway.

"Not really," said Raszer. "Not if you'd seen what I saw in his eyes. And besides, it sort of adds up."

"What adds up, Raszer? Bring me in. You've been out doing, uh, fieldwork while I've been stuck here researching eunuchs. What have you got?"

"For starters, I've got an eleventh-century Syrian coin from the scene of Katy's abduction. Hold on a sec." Raszer strode out of the office; when he returned, he pressed the coin into her palm. "That was worn around somebody's neck, probably yanked off during the struggle. It stopped a bullet. Could it have been Johnny's or Henry's? Doubtful. The year of its mint matches the peak of the Nizari sect's power. It likely belonged to one of the killers. By the way, see if we can find out whose face that is on the head. A local goddess, I'm guessing."

"Okay. You've got a Syrian coin, Syrian daggers, and a Syrian woman, all of which you connect to these medieval Assassins, but how does that get you to Turkey?"

"All right," he said, and approached the map slowly. "I'll give you a link: opium." He stroked the sandpaper stubble on his chin. "Actually, I just made that up, but there may be something to it. The nexus of deep politics has always been dope, sex, and economic power.

"Wherever this group is operating, it has to be in a corridor that sees traffic in illegal commodities and unorthodox ideas. Turkey borders Syria, Iran, and Iraq in the southeast. Those borderlands were Assassin turf back in the day, and this mountainous sector, running from the easternmost prong of Syria, skirting across the top of Iraq and straight into Iran, has always been ungovernable, a no-go zone that's now a hornet's nest, thanks to the mess we made of the Kurdish problem. It's what the Balkans were to World War I, and it may yet be Armageddon.

"Now, from what we know of their MO, this group looks to be nominally Shiite, but the Syrian Alawites are too shrewd to give them sanctuary; same for the Iranians and the Kurdish tribal leaders in northern Iraq. No one would embrace them openly. Where would they set up shop? Unlike Syria, Iran, and Iraq, Turkey isn't in a state of war with the U.S.—not yet, at least. Trade—trade in opium, arms, and people—is wide open. Eastern Turkey is on the Silk Road for human trafficking. It's the Wild West without Wyatt Earp."

Monica blinked. "Did you just ad-lib that whole thing, Raszer?"

"I've been kicking it around a little," he replied.

"I'd hate to see them cut out your tongue. It does such nice work."

"And there's another missing piece of the puzzle: Henry Lee's testicles. I'm hoping Ruthie Endicott can help me there, if Henry had something to say about it in all those emails he sent her. Castration ties in with a number of our other threads. The old cult of the Phrygian mother goddess, Cybele, with its eunuch-priests; Turkey, again; and the black rocks that were found in Henry Lee's collection, with the same mineral makeup as the *baitylos*—Cybele's sacred meteorite.

"Can we get those from pagan Turkey to Islamic Iraq, where Johnny and Henry made their connection? Sure, because Cybele is also Kuba, which relates to Ka'ba and another black meteorite—the Ka'ba Stone, the Al-Hajar—the one pilgrims on the hajj kiss on their circuits around the shrine. In pre-Islamic times, the Ka'ba was consecrated to the *unsas*, the Daughters of God of the Satanic verses, who had origins in Sumeria . . . which is Iraq, where the first accounts of ritual castration are found."

"It's always a big loop, isn't it, Raszer? Always spokes on the same wheel."

"And there's always a woman at the center of it," he said.

"In this case," she picked up, "a ball buster. We've got a Jehovah's Witness tie-in, too. The business about 'eunuchs for the kingdom of heaven,' and the

144,000 virgins who make up the Little Flock. What if Henry Lee somehow conflated stuff he'd learned from the church with something new he picked up in Iraq? What if his castration was voluntary? And Katy . . . Katy . . . Katy is a virgin."

"Right," said Raszer, the cigarette dangling from his lips. "I wonder . . . "

"You wonder what?"

"Okay, let me work this through: According to Aquino and his CSI team, Katy was never raped. She would've lost her market value. That was the implication of Emmett's story: that Johnny and Henry staged the rape to make her worthless to the bad guys, and that Johnny backed out of the trade. But it was too late. The limo pulled up and the killers preempted the gangbang, and that was the motive for murder—to preserve Katy's value. Settle a score. Eliminate witnesses . . . except that they missed Emmett and let Layla slip. But they carried Katy away with her virginity intact."

"To this 'Garden,' right? Where Scotty Darrell says he saw her, and which you think is in Turkey? The Garden . . . which is what? Some sort of exotic sex park for rich sheikhs willing to pay big bucks to deflower an American virgin?"

"That could be its cover and cash source," said Raszer. "This does have the smell of an HT racket, at least on the surface, and, for reasons obscure to me, virgins have always fetched a good price."

"Why 'obscure to you,' Raszer? Pray tell . . . "

"I prefer experience. Even as a kid, I liked Mrs. Robinson better than Elaine."

"Mmm. That explains why your ex-wife couldn't resist college boys."

"Or valet parking attendants," Raszer added. "Anyhow, sex tourism doesn't explain Scotty Darrell, or his reference to the Old Man's being 'lord over the all and the nothing.' It doesn't explain ritual murder. It doesn't explain why they would go after Jehovah's Witness kids, or how—if we can speculate—Amos Leach might be tied into all this. And frankly, it doesn't explain why LAPD headquarters is crawling with counterterrorism people. I think they're using these girls as ploys . . . to entrap, compromise, induce." He paused to stub out the cigarette. "Where else have we heard about beautiful young virgins in a garden?"

Monica glanced at the map, bit her lip, and replied, "9/11. The thing about the hijackers each being promised seventy black-eyed virgins."

"Right. The *houris*. The cup bearers in the Islamic martyr's paradise. Offering all the goodies that pious Muslims can't have in life. A garden flowing with rivers of milk, honey, and sex. That's what Hassan-i-Sabbah tried to simulate in medieval Persia."

"*Houris*?" she asked. "That wouldn't happen to be the origin of *whore*, would it?"

"Let's check it out," said Raszer. "Linguistics is the key to almost everything, and sacred prostitution has a long history."

"But you don't think this is an Al Qaeda sort of thing . . . "

"Meaning what?" Raszer asked. "An Islamist terror network? Maybe on the surface. Recruiting alienated, gullible young men from the border. Persuading them everything they've ever been told is wrong. It's the way all secret societies work: hook them with status; draw them in with privileged knowledge; lock them in with fear. But this doesn't feel overtly political or sectarian. They're not claiming responsibility like Hamas. This feels like Islamic Scientology. They're most likely after *influence*."

"What kind of influence? Like the kind superlobbyists have?"

"That and more. What the original Assassins seem to have wanted was 'special status.' They claimed direct spiritual lineage from Muhammad. They were fanatics in a fanatical time, but they rarely killed Christians. In fact, they made political alliances with the Christians." Raszer paused, then repeated it: "Alliances with the Christians. Alliances with . . . "

"'The enemy of my enemy'?" Monica said softly.

"'A battle between one kind of human and another,'" he whispered.

"Come again?"

"Something Douglas Picot let slip."

"How're you going to connect all this into something I can put on an itinerary?"

"I don't know yet. The solution to a mystery is never an isolated piece of evidence, but accumulated implications that ultimately become unavoidable conclusions."

"And now you want to go to Taos . . . to accumulate more implications."

"I need to hang with someone who knows Katy well. All the others are dead."

"Let's get you properly equipped," she said. "I may not see you for a while."

"I'll need approach shoes, desert boots, my kits, and that GPS phone Geotech has been begging us to try. Maps. And—" He paused. "I guess I should have the implant."

“Right. And if you’re going to be tramping around the Near East, you’ll need to see Dr. Cutter before you go. I’ll find out what shots are current for that area.” She smiled. “But first you see Dr. Monica.” She unlocked a cabinet and took out a device that looked a bit like a popgun. “Loosen your pants and show me some cheek. Time to put the bug in your ass. I won’t lose you this time.”

“Wipe that grin off your face,” he said, exposing just enough flesh to allow access for the tracer implant. “I’m about to give you some bad news.”

SEVENTEEN

RUTHIE ENDICOTT had heard all the talk. Taos, New Mexico was magical. Taos was holy. People saw Jesus here, and statues bled. Taos got inside people's heads and made them drunk with visions of psychedelic sugarplums. It had even gotten to her mother, Constance. She was a "hearer," one of the 2 to 3 percent of the local population who lived with a distant diesel engine known as the Taos Hum rumbling in her head. For relief, she'd gone from medicinal teas to tequila and then, when the hangovers had only made it worse, to a steady diet of OxyContin. It made her difficult to live with, and so Ruthie spent most days in town and slept where she could find an empty sofa or a bedmate she could buy off with oral sex.

For a twenty-two-year-old whose body art mapped a trail of flight from her evangelical roots and who lived in a more or less permanently altered state, Ruthie was pretty rationalistic. She dismissed the Taos Hum as being "what was there when noise wasn't." To her mother, she'd say, "Whaddayou expect? It's so damn quiet up here, you can hear yourself sweat," and to another hearer, "Those mountains move, right? You gotta figure they make some kind of racket."

Ruthie's common sense did not innoculate her entirely against the Taos mindfuck. She dreamed night after night that she was being swallowed up by the Rio Grande Gorge, the titanic gash that cut through the planet about twelve miles west of town. It didn't seem to matter what drugs she took—the dream came. It had started a year ago when Angel, her mother's hombre, had told her of a local myth about the fate of unrepentant souls. She'd figured he knew what he was talking about because Angel himself was a *penitente*, a member of a secret and exclusive order of men from old Spanish families whose blood went back to the conquest, community leaders who every Easter weekend reenacted the crucifixion of Christ so realistically that women and kids were allowed to witness only from a distant ridge, in case they tried to stop it.

This year, Angel had been selected by lot to play the part of Jesus, which meant that he would be scourged, mocked, and forced to bear his cross up the rocky path to Calvary. He'd told Ruthie and her mother that this was a great honor, to suffer as Christ had, and that they would be privileged to nurse him through recovery. Ruthie intended to make herself scarce. As far as she could see, her mother had left one religious fanatic for another, and this one a Catholic, which meant that he could behave badly on Saturday night and still be graced on Sunday morning. Her father would've seen through that. Silas knew you were either graced or not, and Ruthie knew which side of that line she was on.

For her, Taos was an exile. She believed she was dying on this seven-thousand-foot altar, where even the mountain streams were said to run with the blood of Christ. She'd rejected her father's gray-bearded hanging judge God, only to face a far stranger one: a God who raised the red dust from the streets and spun it into helixes of lavender, pink, and rusty gold. Ruthie blamed the altitude, the Indians, and the old hippies who ran the restaurants and shops and had probably spiked the drinking water.

Over and through all of this, Ruthie heard a bomb ticking. One way or another, she wanted out. Any ticket would do.

✦ ✦ ✦

THE ALTERCATION WITH Monica had come at the conclusion of the pre-trip briefing, when Raszer informed her that she was to take her work home, as it wasn't safe for her to remain alone in his house. He wouldn't see her hurt, and he wouldn't see her used to compromise his mission. His mind was made up.

"No way, Raszer," she said. "All my files are here. Our whole operation."

"That's what external drives are for. We're going to have to become as mobile as a carnival. I've lost my anonymity. It had to happen sooner or later."

"There isn't enough time to turn this around, Raszer," she protested. "I'm not set up. I'm not wired. I don't even have a landline at home. I live in a studio apartment."

"You can do 80 percent of it from a laptop, and I'll have the guys at Intelletech set you up. I don't have a choice. If you're here alone, you're hostage bait."

"Then get me a bodyguard," she said. "Maybe that big Dane from Aegis. No one would get past his pectorals."

"You'd like that, wouldn't you?" he said. "Just you and Erik the Red, eating pastry."

"I confess I have a thing for big lugs . . . and pastry."

"A big man just makes a broader target," said Raszer. "And if they drop him, they've got you *and* access to this office. Nope. I'm locking up the house and double-encrypting everything. I want this place as useless as an empty missile solo."

"Raszer, I won't—"

The phone rang. She answered without breaking her glare, then handed him the phone. "It's the FBI," she said. "For you." Monica crossed her arms and put the toe of her high-rise sneaker forward, a signal that the matter wasn't settled.

"Agent Djapper," said Raszer. "How are you?"

"Can we meet before you leave?" Djapper's tone was more than a little furtive.

"What did you have in mind?" Raszer replied.

"There's a Starbucks at Highland and Franklin."

"I guess you know where I live, too," Raszer said with resignation. "Anyhow, I have a better place, a little less public. The Bourgeois Pig, at Franklin and Cheremoya."

"The *what*?"

"Next to the Daily Planet bookstore. Across from the Scientology celebrity center. You know, the big chateau. The Pig is the only café in L.A. with any atmosphere."

"I'm not big on atmosphere," Djapper said pointedly. "But if the coffee's good—"

"How about three o'clock?" Raszer asked.

"See you there," Djapper said, and hung up.

Raszer gave the phone back to Monica. "I've got a meeting," he said. "And you need to get me on Dr. Cutter's list. We'll discuss this, uh, other business later."

⬩◆⬩

RASZER'S SECURITY WORRIES were not lessened by what Agent Djapper had to tell him over coffee.

"We're going to put a couple of men on your house," said the FBI man, spooning up the topping from his double decaf mocha. "And I'm going to offer you some advice."

"What's that?" asked Raszer.

"If you like being alive, walk away." Djapper dropped a dollop of whipped cream into his coffee and began to stir. "This whole mess falls into a jurisdictional crack between what we can do, what local can do, and what Langley can do. If you insist on crawling into it, we can't help you. In fact, we might just have to plaster over the hole and leave you in there. We'd know a lot more, but ever since the NSA flap, everybody's dainty about the Internet, which is where this thing lives, an area my boss calls virtual conspiracy: stuff that gets plotted in alternate reality games but hasn't happened—*may not* happen—in the real world. It turns the whole idea of probable cause on its head."

"The new frontier," Raszer said, tossing back his espresso. "It's why an amateur like me can make a living."

"You may think you know what's going on here, Raszer, but—"

Raszer shook his head. "I don't even pretend to know. But I'll bet you do."

"No," said Djapper. "Not entirely. But, unlike you, I know enough to know what I don't want to know. I can tell you this: This game your boy Scotty was into, it spread like cancer. It metastasized and went global, and somewhere along the line, it became terrorism. You see, the wrong people began to take notice of it, saw there was profit in it. Just like the way the mob took over the heroin trade."

"Nothing of value stays independent, does it?" Raszer said. "Who's Hazid?"

Djapper didn't miss a beat. "Hazid might as well be the Wizard of Oz."

"And the crew in the limo? They're not munchkins—the dents on my car attest to that. You've sure got probable cause there. Is that another crack you won't crawl into?"

"This may sting a little bit, Raszer," Djapper replied, "but no one except you and that crazy kid in Azusa have seen this 'black limo' or the phantoms riding in it, and an abundance of evidence suggests you're both certifiable paranoids."

"Bullshit. Whose script are you reading from? Douglas Picot's?"

Djapper ran a paper napkin over his lips. "I'm offering advice that could save you and your family a lot of grief. If you're not interested—"

Rasze's tone was stiff. "What do you mean by 'my family,' Bernard?"

"Oh." Djapper shrugged. "I just assumed that you . . . that they'd rather see you alive." The agent leaned in and scooped a chocolate biscotti off the plate. "Let me tell you why I think the Coronado case went cold: maybe because the 'victims' were guys you don't want in your neighborhood anyway. Like Scotty Darrell. Maybe because there are certain curtains you open up and then realize you should close. They might look like a crime, but they're actually a work in progress."

An ink-haired girl with the pallor of a corpse strolled by, jangling face jewelry. An aspiring screenwriter at a nearby table looked up from his laptop as she passed, then hammered out a few words, folding the girl neatly into his scenario. The girl vanished into the daytime blackness of a billiard room with purple walls.

"I would've preferred Starbuck's," Djapper snorted. "I really stick out here."

Raszer smiled, keeping silent his thought, which was that Bernard Djapper would stick out anyplace but his mother's living room.

"Nah," Raszer said. "The worst that'll happen is that one of these writers will spot your designer suit and pitch you his movie." He paused. "I hear what you're saying, and it's not the first time I've heard it. But you know I'm going to go after the girl. So let's help each other. Where is she?"

"No place you can get to," Djapper replied. "No place you could even drop a Delta Force team into. You'd have to be invited. Our best spies aren't even that smooth anymore. They're technicians, too straight to bend themselves around corners. But you, Raszer, now . . . " Djapper widened his eyes. "You're not straight, are you?"

"I guess it would take bent to know bent," Raszer replied. "But let's be straight about two things: I need to find Katy Endicott, and if you help me, I'll try to do it without stepping on toes."

"I doubt that would be possible."

"In any case, I'm going to find her."

Djapper wiped his mouth again, and the gesture read as a write-off. "I'll give you two things. Ruthie Endicott is one. She's got something, and she knows that sooner or later she'll have to come out with it, because otherwise she's facing a bleak future."

"Explain. Has she broken federal law?"

Djapper snorted. He leaned right into Raszer's face and spoke emphatically, his gravity undercut by the muffin crumb that remained affixed to his upper lip. "She's dangling at the end of a long chain that involves interstate drug smuggling, human trafficking, industrial espionage, and blackmail—all stuff her boyfriends were into. The fact is, she should be in jail, and would be . . . except that we need her loose as bait."

"You have hard evidence that she was involved in criminal activity?"

"Circumstantial, but solid. Henry Lee had the mouth, but she had the fingers."

"What? Pushing dope to Azusa High School? Running teenage prostitutes?"

"Oh, Mr. Raszer . . . "

"And all this can somehow be connected to a mountaintop redoubt somewhere in the Middle East? To Scotty Darrell, and Layla Faj-Ta'wil? And maybe even back to you and whoever's party you don't want to bust? And you call *me* paranoid?" Raszer shook his head. "What is she, then, some kind of 'asset'? Are you playing her?"

Djapper laughed. "No. That would require some trust. She's a Taos tramp. She's off the circuit, but that doesn't mean she can't be plugged back in. Her boys came back from Iraq with a mission. She signed on. They're dead, and somehow she's still alive."

"These people kill to protect the chain. Maybe she's not really a link."

"Well, you start pulling on that chain, you're bound to find out."

"I have to pull it. It's my nature."

"It's your funeral."

"I don't get you. You asked to meet. Part of you seems to want to help me."

"That's true. Part of me does."

"On the other hand, you seem to be telling me that if I pursue this case, I'll be stepping into some Operation Mongoose sort of minefield. You seem to be suggesting that the people you're tiptoeing around have some common interest with the people who kidnapped Katy Endicott."

"I never said that."

"Never said what?"

"That the Bureau—"

"What about the NCTC? What about Picot?"

Djapper turned to look at the purple-haired girl.

"If I can say so, Agent, you seem a little torn."

Djapper kept his eyes on the girl, flicked the crumb from his lip, and spoke almost as if in soliloquy. "That question you asked Picot in the hallway . . . about the role he was playing."

"Yeah?"

"Nothing," said the FBI man, wiping his hands. "I just thought that maybe . . . maybe you'd be someone . . . I'd like to know."

Raszer was momentarily quieted.

"Well, I'm . . . flattered. And I rarely turn down an offer of friendship."

"I'll tell you about these people: They lame you, they let you live, and they put you in debt bondage. It all comes down to what they can hold over a person's head."

With that, Djapper pushed back from the table and stood up.

When they hit the bright sidewalk, he offered Raszer a stick from a half-empty pack of Wrigley's gum. The flavor was wintergreen.

"Your regular brand?" he asked Djapper.

"Kills the coffee breath."

"Yeah," said Raszer, taking out a cigarette. "But it'll rot your teeth."

"Ha," said Djapper, and then again, less jovially, "Ha."

✦ ✦ ✦

RASZER BOARDED A DC-10 in the bright coastal haze of an April morning. Ahead of him in line was a little rich girl clutching an oversize plush bunny, a reminder that it was nearly Easter, and that he needed to make a contribution to Brigit's collection of eggs, the wooden ones the old babushkas in the Ukraine hand-paint with gnarled fingers. He'd gotten her started when she was three, and now she scoured flea markets for them.

Special Agent Djapper was a hidden variable. It seemed clear he was caught in the crosscurrents he'd hinted about. What else was new? The feds had been playing footsy with organized crime for nearly a century, and at any given time, half the investigatory agencies of the U.S. government were plumbing rackets from inside the sewer pipes. It was a matter of pride for them to think they could work both sides. Maybe the only way for Djapper to get free of the current was to pull someone else in.

Djapper had made good on his promise to put an FBI surveillance team on Raszer's house, and as this gesture had unsettled Raszer as much as it reassured him, Monica had won her battle and remained in place, with her $2,000-a-week Danish bodyguard.

✦ ✦ ✦

The Jeep Monica had reserved for Raszer was a ragtop red Wrangler, and he promptly unhooded it for the drive from Albuquerque to Taos. Like a coyote, he wanted to sniff his way into town, making the perfume of creosote, piñon, and mineral dust part of his own scent, exchanging its atoms with his own. He wanted to feel as if he'd ridden the wind into Taos like a hawk, so that once he got down into the maze, he might retain that perspective. There were three questions he wanted to ask Ruthie Endicott, and seeing the answers for what they were might require an aerial view.

The first one was a formality, but it had to be asked. Had she received any form of communication from either Katy or her abductors, whether by proxy, ransom note, threat, or direct contact, since the night of the abduction?

The second question was operational and, once again, had to be asked. Had Ruthie's mother at any time engaged the services of another private investigator?

The third question was the one that *mattered.* It broke down into three parts: Did Ruthie have any knowledge of how Johnny Horn and Henry Lee had entered their killers' employ? Had she ever seen or met any of these men? Did she still have the emails she'd received from Henry over the year preceding his death?

If Ruthie had kept the emails, they were presumably not accessible to the FBI, or Djapper would have gotten his hands on them already. If she could be persuaded to give Raszer that access, he'd need to rely less on Djapper's dubious patronage.

As he ascended the grade from Santa Fe toward his destination, he watched the cloud shadows creep up the slopes of the Sangre de Cristos like blood spreading on rough linen, defying gravity, staining the pink rock and pine in shades of royal purple and midnight blue. In the shaman art of the Chimayo Valley, the mountains were always defined by the shadows that fell on them. The color of the shadows changed throughout the day, but was always some variant of blue. The mesas surrounding Albuquerque were muted, striated pastels—baked colors—and Santa Fe's red clay glowed at sundown. But Taos was blue, and blue is the color of the mystic, the color of blood seen through the bridal veil of skin. It never surprised Raszer that places of spiritual pilgrimage had become what they were. It wasn't the churches or temples or New Age dude ranches built on their soil; it was the genius of the places themselves.

No one had to tell this to the Pueblo Indians, of course. They were the longest-standing residents of Taos, still harvesting the sky in a settlement north of town with no indoor plumbing, content to live and dance and perform all bodily functions in the sight of their god. People came to Taos for visions. Even agnostic painters came for vision and called it the "quality of light."

Whatever anyone chose to call it, the place had it, and Raszer conceded that as much as he was here to grill Ruthie Endicott, he was here for an epiphany.

He'd taken the main highway north from Santa Fe and then detoured into the Chimayo Hills just past the turnoff for Los Alamos, where six decades earlier J. Robert Oppenheimer had midwifed the atom bomb and declared, "I am become Shiva, destroyer of worlds." The old coach road that was now Highway 76 cut through high country occupied by ten generations of weavers, and was still the route of choice for art hounds.

But Raszer wasn't buying art today. He was making a pilgrimage of his own, to a place pilgrims had come at Eastertime for nearly two centuries, an adobe chapel known as the Santuario de Chimayo, where, it was said, the soil healed and visitors were encouraged to sift it through their fingers and cake it on their wounds. It was ritual, yes, superstition, probably, but Raszer, who undertook each rescue mission with the awareness that he might not come home, was not beyond either of these. If the soil of Chimayo healed, so much the better. He'd need all the psychic armor he could carry.

The Santuario's builder had cut a well in the chapel floor, through which visitors could touch the soil below. It was dark inside, even in mid-afternoon, and as Raszer stepped in, he was only vaguely aware of another presence: a girl—more precisely, a young woman—lying prone before the hole in the floor, face to the ground, arms spread in apparent supplication. Her hair was black—or seemed so—and fell around her head. She wore a simple sundress, pale blue, and its skirts had ridden to the top of her brown thighs in the effort to position herself. Suddenly, she thrust her hands down into the soil, then rose to her knees, scrubbing her face with the red soil.

Only then did she see Raszer, who was instantly pierced by the whiteness of the eyes behind the mask of dirt. She fled like a fox.

There it was. Taos. Penitential and erotic. The Spanish legacy, the El Greco languor, and the shaman-sense that things weren't as they seemed. No wonder D. H. Lawrence had asked that his ashes be brought here.

Raszer went to the well and dropped to a squat, inhaling the girl's afterscent along with the mineral cologne from below. The trace lingered, but her image became less distinct with each second. It was hard to know for certain if he'd seen what he'd seen: hard in the reborn stillness and darkness of the place; hard after ten years in the liminal zones; hard when hers was the same face and form he saw in oblique reflections from shop windows, and in his dreams. Seeing her now was, in any event, a good sign.

Nothing was retrieved by the eyes without first having been cast by the mind on the tabula rasa of mean existence. Scent was a more accurate gauge of reality than sight, which was probably why animals survived by it.

✦ ◆ ✦

HIGHWAY 68 INTO TAOS was like all access roads to all places of pilgrimage. The camp followers of sprawl—fast-food outlets, insurance offices, beauty salons, liquor stores—had found their way there and planted flimsy foundations. Not even timeless Taos could keep Burger King off the Paseo del Pueblo Sur. Even so, the steep boulevard leading to the old village promised haven from commerce, if only because there was nothing beyond but the mountains and the Rio Grande.

Raszer dropped his bags at the Adobe & Pines Inn, the most indigenous of the more modestly priced places on the strip. It was a low-slung, tile-roofed hacienda of 1832 vintage, surrounded by orchards and fronted by an eighty-foot grand portal. The beds were as sturdy as galleons, the decor tastefully rustic, the breakfast advertised as home-cooked. Raszer took an approving look around, then headed into town.

Special Agent Djapper had given Raszer the last known address for Constance and Ruthie Endicott, estranged wife and elder daughter of the late Silas. It was a tiny, wind-blasted cracker box of a house on farm property along the Camino del Medio, probably built to shelter a ranch hand's family and now rented by the month. The screen door was half off its hinges, the porch sagged with dry rot, and the place was clearly unoccupied, but through a pane glazed over with red dust, Raszer spotted an empty half pint of Cuervo and a cat curled on a stained pillow. He figured that the cat probably came with the house, the Cuervo with Ruthie.

He stepped off the porch, feeling temporarily adrift. He'd purposely not warned Ruthie of his coming, for fear she'd bolt, and because both Djapper and the Elders of the church had assured him that mother and daughter were still in Taos. But people did blow in and out of this town like tumbleweed, didn't they? And where would Ruthie have blown? The wind rippled across a swath of columbine and carried the delicate fragrance to his nostrils. Spring in the high country. He thought of the girl in the church, of the dress she wore, and he determined to start from scratch, beginning with the local phone book, then the local Witnesses, and then the local taverns.

After two hours of leaving calling cards, Raszer circled back to Taos Plaza, dead center, as in all old Spanish towns. He parked himself on the steps of the bandstand and surveyed the tiled plaza and the little shops that bordered it. The locals were inside the shops, the tourists squinting through the glass at turquoise and silver and glazed pottery—squinting because the storefronts all mirrored the low sun. There were barely two hours of daylight left, and Raszer was no closer to finding Ruthie. In the window of a New Age trinket store, he spotted the reflection of a crew of townie kids headed off in a huddle. They had just about vanished when he saw a fringed pant leg rounding a bend into a narrow lane off the northwest corner of the plaza.

At the end of the lane, wedged into a cul-de-sac, was the Alley Cantina. The door was open, and a Ryan Adams song slapped off the surrounding adobe. The kids had gone inside, as the air was turning cool, and Raszer followed them into the dim, moderately crowded barroom. It smelled of hops and tortillas, and he realized he had a taste for both after the drive. He found a stool, ordered a Carta Blanca, and finished a basket of nachos before taking Ruthie's picture out and calling the bartender over. It wasn't difficult to command his attention; Raszer was easily fifteen years older than the next-oldest person in the room. Beyond that, he had a $20 bill on the bar.

"Ever seen this girl?" he asked. "The hair might be different. Look at the eyes and the mouth. And the attitude."

"Uh-*huh*," the bartender grunted, drying his hands with a towel.

Raszer held a beat, hoping for some elaboration on the grunt.

"Does that mean you've seen her?" he asked. "Her name's Ruthie."

"Is she in trouble?" the bartender asked with a grin. "Wouldn't surprise me, with that mouth. You a cop?"

"Nope," said Raszer. "Private investigator. It's actually her little sister I'm looking for. She was abducted over a year ago in L.A. I just want to talk to Ruthie."

"Right, well . . . I'm not positive, but she looks familiar. Cat's eyes. See those even in the dark. Lemme call Sage over. She's half Tiwa. Knows everybody." The bartender summoned a heavy, brown-skinned young woman who smelled of her namesake and had been drinking in the corner. She came slowly, gravity weighing on her limbs. The Tiwa were the Indians of the Taos Pueblo, but this girl—Raszer guessed—was an outcast.

Raszer introduced himself and refreshed her 7 and 7.

"Know this pistol, Sage?" the bartender asked her. "Isn't she the one—"

"The one who rode off on Bobby T's Indian last Saturday," Sage affirmed. "Hell, you oughta know her. Your drink orders double when she comes in. All the boys scrambling to get 'er lubricated." The Tiwa girl turned to Raszer. "Are you a bounty hunter, mister, or a Hollywood casting agent?"

"He's a private eye," answered the bartender. "But he is from Hollyweird."

"She done somethin' wrong?" asked Sage. "I sure hope you haul her ass off somewhere. Us local girls got enough competition."

"Not that I know of," said Raszer. "But I will try to sideline her for a few days."

Sage smiled and tipped her glass to Raszer's. "She 'n her mom live out by the tin works on outbound Highway 64. There's a trailer park called Reynaldo's. Not too trashy. The mother's got a man. It's his trailer. He's a holy roller."

"You wouldn't happen to know his name?" Raszer asked. "There could be a lot of trailers out there."

"Sure I do," said Sage. "For a refill."

Raszer nodded to the bartender.

"It's Angel," she said. "*Ong-hell.* Angel Davidos."

"Thanks," said Raszer, handing the girl her drink. "You've been a help."

EIGHTEEN

THE WIND COMES UP with sunset in the mountain Southwest, and for at least a few minutes, modern man walks in the same spirit world as his ancestors. Raszer felt it rising on his back, finding the dampness in his shirt, in the furrows that ran along his spine. It was as if the massive red ball of the sun was displacing an ocean of air as it sank between the peaks. It was also a harbinger of night's coming, and of the wolves. The turnoff to Reynaldo's RV Park was as advertised, just north of the Taos Tin Works, through a broken gate that led to a graded dirt road over an empty pasture and past a stand of cottonwoods. On the far side of the grove, across a little stream, a wooden fence bounded a few acres of flat, rocky land that was home to a transitory community of about three hundred souls. There were campers up on cinder blocks that looked to be there for keeps, forty-year-old trailers with hulls as encrusted as ships in dry dock, and a few late models of the Winnebago type. The turf occupied by long-term residents had a sunken-in look and an accretion of mostly out-used junk that was probably kept in place to mark the imaginary property lines.

Having Angel Davidos's name was no help. There was no directory at the front gate, and no landlord on-site. So Raszer began at an outside corner and wandered up and down the ill-defined paths between the trailers, the streets of this makeshift neighborhood. The residents, many of them Hispanic or of mixed race, seemed to be either in the act of preparing the evening meal or out in meager yards, enjoying the sunset and cocktail hour. The smell of beer and marijuana smoke hung in the air like a net suspended from the trees, and griddle smoke drifted from tiny, louvered kitchen windows. There could, Raszer thought, be worse ways and far worse places to live.

Some of the owners had buttressed the front steps of their homes with narrow wooden decks constructed from plywood and two-by-fours, just wide enough to accommodate a couple of beach chairs and a barbecue. A few had flower boxes, American flags, and a coat of paint, enough to create the semblance of a front porch. On one of them, painted pale yellow and located at the far end of a diagonal thoroughfare running from corner to corner in the lot, Raszer spotted a girl in a blue dress, waiting.

There was no question she was waiting. Her elbows were propped on the railing, and her chin was in her palm. Her feet were bare, and the skirts of her sundress billowed around her legs like lace curtains in a storm. Raszer approached from fifty yards' distance with the sun at his back and his shadow thrown long in front of him. At one point, he instinctively lifted his arm in greeting, and she did the same. He doubted immediately that what he saw was what it appeared to be.

He doubted it because the hair spilling messily around her heart-shaped face was long and auburn, like Katy's. Her oval mouth was a natural dark pink, like Katy's. The tilt of the head and the sweet little smile seemed to be Katy's, too, based on the photos.

The blue dress belonged to the girl in the Santuario de Chimayo.

Up to a point, Raszer enjoyed having his mind fucked. It was part of the learning curve, always instructive, and visions no longer unsettled him. In fact, he chased after them. But this was different. The girl on the deck was not the girl from the Santuario de Chimayo, yet she seemed to *know* of her. She was not Katy Endicott, either—not unless things were really upside down—but she seemed to want to suggest that possibility. The impression was more than mimicry. It was closer to channeling.

Why? Nothing about the vision on the yellow deck said "Ruthie" except for the feline eyes and the guile. As Raszer drew closer, she toyed with him, shuffling personae like playing cards, all of them some variation on the theme of bruised innocence. Finally, she leaned into the railing and just let the wind blow back her hair.

"Lookin' for a showdown, cowboy?" she asked, when he was within thirty feet.

"Nope. Looking for a girl."

"You don't look like you'd need to look hard," she replied.

"You'd be surprised," he said, moving closer. "Were you expecting me?"

"I was expecting somebody," she answered. "But not you. Fat, sweaty, and bald, I guess. Like most private dicks really look."

"And wearing wingtips and a worsted-wool suit in summer, right?"

"Somethin' like that. Or maybe that guy with the glass eye."

"The bartender from the Cantina call you? Or was it the Indian girl?"

He stood beneath her now. Her face was in the shadow of her hair, but her eyes, which on closer inspection were emerald green, had him fixed.

"Neither one," she answered. "Matter of fact, it was Lupe down at the police station. Ex–sister-in-law of my mother's hombre. Those people stay close."

"I guess so," he said. "Nice to have friends in high places."

"She's only a dispatcher, but Lupe knows what's what." She cocked her head, exposing one side of her face to the low sun. There were pale freckles on either side of her nose. "But thanks for cluing me in. Pays to know who'll sell you out for a drink."

"What'd you do with your hair? I'd have figured you for a natural redhead."

"Wasn't any more natural than this," she said, pulling at a strand. "I forget what color my real hair is."

"Well, it's red, according to your California driver's license."

"Which one?"

Raszer laughed. "Mind if I have a cigarette?"

"Not if you give me one."

He shook one from the pack and held it up for her to withdraw. He lit it, carefully navigating between the hanging curtains of hair, and she touched her palm to the back of his hand to steady the lighter. A learned gesture—movies, probably. Then he lit his own and stepped back to exhale the smoke—also a learned gesture.

"You and your sister," he said, "you were pretty good at trading identities, right? From the looks of it, you decided that the world needed Katy more than Ruthie."

"That ain't exactly rocket science," she said, blowing smoke toward the foothills. "Katy's a *good* girl. The world likes them, but they don't get to party much. You sure she didn't take *my* place?"

Raszer squinted. "I guess that's a possibility, isn't it?" He took a step in and wrapped his hands around the lower railing. "But I don't think so, Ruthie. You've got the same bone structure—amazingly so—but the eyes are all your own."

She scooped up a handful of skirt and squatted down to his level, placing her hand next to his on the one-by-four railing. She had a tangy smell, like citrus and musk. It occurred to him that she might be wearing a wig, a notable extravagance for a girl of modest means.

"So, who hired you?" she asked. "My father?"

"Yes," Raszer replied. "It was the last thing he did, Ruthie."

"The last thing he did before what?"

"Oh, God . . . you didn't get word up here?"

She shook her head and gently bit her lip.

"Your father died, Ruthie. A stroke. He collapsed in my backyard after telling me the story. I'm really sorry to be the one—"

She tossed the cigarette into the dust and stood back up. "Someone had to," she said. "Don't be sorry. He's with his Little Flock up in heaven, and we're still down here in hell."

"That may be," said Raszer. "But I am sorry for your loss. No matter how you get along with your old man, he's the one charged with protecting you. When he's gone, you're on your own."

"Nobody ever 'protected' me but me," she corrected him.

"Not even Henry?" Raszer asked.

Ruthie looked away.

"What are you doin' here, anyway, mister?" she said, bitter. "I don't know anything. I told the FBI that already."

"You know a whole lot more than I do, Ruthie. Three boys are dead who didn't have to be. A fourth one's half-crazy and won't come out of his bedroom. A fifth is probably on his way to Gitmo. And there are two corpses in the L.A. morgue with their tongues torn out. All because the men who abducted your sister are still at large. Anything—I mean *anything*—you can tell me about Johnny Horn and Henry Lee will help."

She looked at him sideways. "Yeah, well, I don't wanna talk here. My mother'll be home soon. Shit, I'll have to tell her about Silas. What'd you say your name was?"

"I didn't." He offered his hand. "Stephan Raszer."

She took his hand, then gave it the slightest squeeze. "The La Fonda has a private bar with good margaritas. It's dark in there. You know where it is?"

"I know it well," said Raszer. "Good choice."

"About eight okay?"

"Perfect," said Raszer. "I'll see you there."

"Maybe," she said. "Or maybe I'll send a friend."

✦ ✦ ✦

RASZER SMOKED A CIGARETTE on the plaza and admired the Hotel La Fonda's glazed brown-sugar facade. The massive oak joists—a ton each—that supported the second story thrust forth from the adobe walls and framed the night sky. The light spilling from the gently arched doors was white gold. He'd been here once at Christmas, years before, when the luminarias lined the rooftop and the grand portal, and Taos powder covered the ground like jewel dust. Children in serapes had sung carols in voices as sweet as mountain water, and no one had moved an inch until the song was done. The La Fonda was what an inn should be, what the Holy Family should've been afforded. If at all possible, Raszer wanted his wake to be held in this place.

Ditching the cigarette, he walked in, following his nose into the hotel bar, where a group of local artisans was holding a salon around the hearth and the barstools had been commandeered by fur-collared ski bunnies from L.A., smelling of Angel perfume. He spotted his table, a deuce in the far corner, half-cloistered by a Spanish dressing panel and overlooked by an ornately framed reproduction of one of D. H. Lawrence's "forbidden paintings": a lithe young man urinating on dandelions.

He ordered a brandy and soda to take the chill off his shoulders, and settled back to wait. He didn't know what to expect. He wasn't even sure Ruthie would come. She'd already shown him that she could be as much a trick of the light as anything else here, in the town where C. G. Jung had come to learn that synchronicity was a fancy name for what the Pueblo shamans experienced when the scorpion's tail traced their name in the dust.

The local artists were trading stories around the kiva. A tall man in an embroidered blouse—a potter, judging from the red clay under his fingernails—told of the day a pregnant coyote had walked into his studio, her swollen teats brushing the plank floor. She'd emptied the cat's milk bowl, then sat on her haunches to watch him work for nearly an hour before wandering back onto the road. That evening, on his way home, the man testified, he'd found her body on the highway, skull crushed, and had carried her to his garden, where he buried her and her unborn pups. The potter, a single man, told his friends that never had he grieved for anyone as he had for that coyote.

"Am I the girl you're looking for?" someone said, stirring Raszer from his reverie. Her hands were on his table. Same hands, apparently, but not quite the same girl.

Raszer gave her a once-over. "I dunno," he said. "I guess you're one of them."

Ruthie's hair was jet black and pixie-cut. Her lips were as red as a wound, and she wore a spandex bodysuit the color of old wine. As she dropped into the chair, the scent came off her, good and strong, and Raszer recognized one of its components: patchouli. Just a trace. The patchouli he'd sniffed in Johnny Horn's trailer.

"What're you drinkin'?" she asked.

"Brandy," he said. "House brand. Like one?"

"No way," she said, after sniffing it. "But I will have a martini. I feel like impairing my judgment."

"Gin or vodka? Dry or wet? Olive or twist?"

"Gin. Dry. Six olives."

"I hear experience talking," Raszer observed. "How old are you now, Ruthie?"

"Twenty-three on Valentine's Day," she answered. "But age has nothin' to do with it. My mom's forty-four and doesn't know shit. I could've told her tequila ain't the thing to make hallucinations go away. I don't even know if she knows what a blowjob is."

"Happy birthday," Raszer said, and ordered her drink. "What kind of hallucinations?"

"She hears the Hum," said Ruthie, throwing a spider's leg over the table.

"The Taos Hum?" Raszer asked.

"So she says," the girl replied. "And Angel—that's her hombre—he believes her. Says she's hearing the hoofbeats of the Four Horsemen of the Apocalypse."

"That's a new one," Raszer said, and handed her her martini, six olives clustered on a swizzle stick. "Angel doesn't subscribe to the New Age theories, I guess."

"New Age! Ha! Angel's as *Old Age* as they come. He's *medieval*. He beats himself with a yucca stalk and wears cactus-thorn vests, and he's all excited that he's gonna play Jesus on Good Friday. He's more like my father than my father, except that he fucks my mother. I wish I'd been raised a Catholic. Lots more fun."

"I think I've heard about this," said Raszer, watching her drain the gin from her glass. "The Brotherhood of Light, or something like that, right? They reenact the crucifixion and do penance for the community."

"Whatever," said Ruthie. "Personally, I think they get off on it."

"In a way, maybe," said Raszer, still searching the face to find the girl behind the mask. "What we get off on is whatever takes us out of ourselves. The medieval flagellants believed that the spirit could escape through the lacerations in the flesh; that they were breaking the body down to its essence."

"You're a little weird for a dick. What gets *you* off?"

Raszer took a swallow of his drink and sat back. "Finding people."

Ruthie examined his hands. She did it sidelong, but he noticed anyway.

"Are you married?" she asked.

"Nope. Only to my work. Tell me about Johnny Horn."

"What about him? I lost it to him when I was fifteen. We stayed stoned through high school. Then he got into meth, paintball games, and Henry Lee. He went to Iraq and came back with big muscles, some new friends, and this whole 'warrior' thing. We started up again because it turned me on at first, but it turned Katy on even more. I think she had the hots for him even back when she was doing her daddy's-girl thing."

"Tell me about Johnny's new friends."

Ruthie drained her martini and popped the last two olives into her mouth. She held up the empty glass and pinged it like a service bell with the long, scarlet nail on her index finger. Then she gave Raszer a practiced little smile.

"Christ," he said. "If I bought enough rounds in this town, I could probably find out who killed Cock Robin."

"Hey," she replied, "I told ya I needed to get impaired. You think I'm gonna come across without a little persuasion? Like you said, mister, people are dead."

"Fair enough," said Raszer, and summoned the waiter. "But two's the limit on those things. Otherwise, you won't be coming across anything but a toilet bowl."

Once she had her drink and another six olives, Ruthie made herself comfortable. She shimmied her butt from side to side in the overstuffed chair until she'd found the sweet spot, threw her leg over the arm, and reclined languorously, stirring the martini like a moll in a gangster's penthouse.

"Who are you when you're not being somebody else?" Raszer asked.

"Somebody else," she answered, and Raszer knew that Ruthie Endicott was one of those small-town girls who are bigger than their origins from birth, the sort of girls they'd once made movie stars out of. "Ya see, mister, when you grow up in a Witness family, you're only allowed to be what you aren't. So, after a while, you just go with it."

"Is that the way your mom is, too?"

"Worse. She doesn't have a personality, except for what a man gives her. Only reason she had the gumption to leave Silas was 'cause he caught her in the bible closet with the neighbor. She's kinda empty. Maybe that's why she hears the Hum. It vibrates in all that empty space."

"Does she work?"

"She works the front desk at the Fechin Inn."

"Nice place."

"Yeah. I'll never stay there, that's for sure."

"Did you ever meet the guys Johnny and Henry hooked up with?"

"In Babylon?" she said.

"Yeah. In Babylon."

"Not the big guys. They never came around. A voice on a cell phone, that's all. A message on a website that disappears the next day. But one day, that summer we trashed the Kingdom Hall . . . guess you heard about that, right? That was Henry's trip. Baptize the place with sex, blood, and magic so that nobody'd ever be able to do what they'd done to him when he was little without stirrin' up this, uh, *spirit thing* he'd created. I dunno. Henry was crazy, but if anybody could do that . . . "

"Create a thought-form . . . an egregore," Raszer said.

"Right. You did your homework, mister. Anyhow, one day that summer, this big limo pulled up the dirt road to Johnny's trailer, back up in San Gabriel Canyon. I lived up there then, at least as much as I did at home. This tall guy in a dark suit got out 'n whistled for Johnny. He coulda been any L.A. limo driver, any race but white. Hell, I couldn't tell. Nowadays, everyone in L.A. looks either Arab or Mexican."

"Just the one guy that day?"

"Yeah. Anyhow, Johnny kinda sashays down there 'cause he doesn't like to come to anybody's call . . . not since he got back from Babylon. And Henry goes with him. Henry was Johnny's magical shield. Ever since what happened over there, they're thick as thieves. Got so Johnny and I couldn't even fuck without Henry hangin' around, doin' his voodoo on us, so eventually we just included him. That's when I found out that Henry and me had this . . . connection. We didn't even have to be in the same room, and we could get off just thinkin' about each other. It was wild. Mystical, kind of."

Raszer decided that he also needed another drink. She had a full wind, and now that she was going, she might go on for a while. "And what happened at the limo?"

"The guy popped the trunk and the three of 'em walked around back to look at whatever was inside. I couldn't see from where I was. Dope, I figured. I saw Henry's face go a little weird, and then Johnny said, 'Yeah, I can move this.' I could see Henry shaking his head, which is what made me think it was some kind of weapons. But Johnny blew him off, because Johnny was the shit and he wanted to do whatever these guys wanted him to do, 'cause he wanted to move up in the organization."

"But Henry wasn't so hot on the idea."

"He was at first," she said. "When they first got back from Iraq, they were both all fired up on go-pills and this gnarly root that they used to chew on all the time, and spouting off about how they'd had this beautiful mindfuck over there and realized that all the moral laws the world goes by are bullshit and don't apply to the knowers of truth, and that the only thing that matters is pure anarchy, because God is chaos and you have to embrace the chaos—and that it's a state of mind, like being really awake for the first time in your life, and this state of mind has a name and the name is *kee-ya-mee* . . . and there was this glowing peacock who was Lucifer—"

"*Qiyami*," Raszer said quietly.

"That's right," Ruthie said. "That's what they called it. Wouldn't begin to know how to spell it."

She popped another olive into her mouth and sucked out the pimiento. The waiter strolled by, and she promptly bottomed up the rest of her drink and handed him the glass with a nod and a wink.

"I gave you a two-drink limit," said Raszer.

"Yeah, you did," she replied. "But he doesn't know that."

"So what made Henry have a change of heart?"

"Henry figured everything by magic. His black stones, and whatever his thought-forms told him, which of course was just him talkin' back at himself. Henry used to say he loved me. He said I was the pussy his girl-self had. But who he really loved was Johnny. Not in a fag way. Henry wanted Johnny to be a holy warrior, a master. They had these big dreams about goin' back to the Middle East and being anarchist mercenaries, but it was like some stupid game. Johnny wasn't ever gonna be master of anything except a trailer in Azusa. I know that now. Anyhow, Henry's magic told him things were fucked up. And then there was other stuff that went down . . . "

Her voice trailed off, as if down a long tunnel, and her head hung limp for a moment. The gin was getting to her. She might be hard-boiled, but she was also a tiny thing, probably not more than a hundred pounds. Raszer let the "other stuff" go for the time being and seized on something else.

"You said Johnny and Henry's trip was like a game. Could it have been?"

"Could have been what?" She was slurring a bit, and knew it, and tried to cover it up.

"A game. Like World of Warcraft or Dungeons & Dragons. Could they have gotten into some weird role-playing thing when they were in Iraq with all the other gameboys?"

"*Whoa.* I'll have to think about that one. It seemed pretty real to me. They ran meth, they ran girls—these little sluts from Duarte and Upland who worked the truck stops in San Bernardino—and at the end, they ran guns to Compton. It just kept gettin' heavier. These guys were testing them, setting them up for something big."

"Like what?"

She shrugged her shoulders. She wasn't telling yet. Instead, she said, "So, have you decided yet if you wanna fuck me or not?"

"Excuse me for a minute," said Raszer, pushing back. "Nature calls."

She shrugged again and waved him a little bye-bye.

When he returned from the men's room, Ruthie's head was on the table. He wasn't particularly surprised. He'd had a feeling about the third martini. He made apologies to the waiter for what looked a little less than chivalrous, paid the check, and eased her up from the table, folding her arm gently around his neck. The bar's matronly hostess cocked an eyebrow on their way out. Raszer pressed a $5 bill into her palm and said, "My daughter . . . has to learn to pace herself."

Outside, the downdraft from the mountains was stiff and the stars glowed like coals. Raszer's Jeep was parked on the far side of the plaza, and even a scant hundred pounds dead drunk is no waltz. To passersby, he thought, it must have looked like he was dragging a corpse.

When they got to the car, he opened the passenger door with his little finger, scooped Ruthie up, and poured her into the seat. He had the key in the ignition when it hit him that he hadn't put the top back up and the night was cool, so he stepped back out and buttoned it up. On a Jeep Wrangler, this was a noisy, manual operation, but Ruthie didn't stir or make a sound the whole time. Only after he'd finished and started the car did it occur to him that for the same reasons he'd felt the need to snow the hostess, he could not take Ruthie Endicott home to her mother in this condition.

"Ruthie," he said, to his conscience as much as to the limp form beside him. Her head had already found the console, and her forearm was draped over the parking brake. "I'm gonna let you sleep this off for a while and get some coffee into you before I take you home, all right? Okay with you?"

There was no response, not that he'd expected one.

"Ruthie?" he said, lifting her arm from the brake.

"*Mmm.*" It had the tone of an assent, so he put the gearshift into drive and negotiated the one-way streets back onto the Paseo. In five minutes, they were at the inn; fortunately, no one was lounging on the grand portal. He steered her through the blue-framed door of his room and rolled her onto her belly on the brass bed with its patchwork spread. She looked even smaller there. Small but formidable, with strength in the arch of the spine and the shoulders. He noticed in the soft light from the bedside lamp that her cheeks were rouged and the black hair had red highlights. She'd evidently designed to play vamp for their first formal encounter. He decided, for the moment, against the intimacy of removing her shoes. He lit a cigarette, brewed a pot of the in-room coffee, and sat down in the stretched-hide armchair with the local paper and the briefing book Monica had prepared for him.

It was a leather binder with a snap strap and eight years of hard duty, stuffed just thick enough to be held firmly between thumb and fingers. There were pockets for his maps, photos, and travel documents, and dividers marking off the main areas of research: human trafficking and debt bondage, especially for the sex trade and especially through the Eurasian corridor; a history of Shia splinter groups and crypto-pagan sects in Iraq, Iran, Syria, and Turkey; a selection of bulletins from Interpol's I-24/7 network, detailing recent instances of political and industrial terrorism and assassination not specifically linked to any of the known organizations; a primer on MMORGs and ARGs, multiplayer reality games that had gone global with the explosion of the Internet across all borders. And there was more—packed in with Monica's characteristic thoroughness—including lists of translators, outfitters, doctors, and hired guns available from Istanbul to Damascus.

Most important, there were the beginnings of the two research threads Raszer had asked Monica to follow after his meeting with Special Agent

Djapper. The first he'd begun himself with a call to a mathematician in Santa Cruz whose hobby was graphing the co-occurrence of seemingly random and unrelated events on the world stage: the hunt for what chaos theory called *strange attractors*.

On the same day, at the same moment in time, a parliament might be dissolved, blue-chip stock might tumble, and the wife of a minor official in a third-world country might be kidnapped. What linked these disparate events could be the collapse of a currency or a phase of the moon or nothing at all—it wasn't always logical.

Raszer, wondering if the phantoms he was chasing might be exerting such tidal forces, had given the mathematician two coordinates: the date and time Scotty Darrell had shot a tram driver at Universal City, and the date and time of Katy Endicott's abduction. The second thread was less theoretical. Given Djapper's tip that to enter the nest of these neo-Assassins, "you'd have to be invited," Raszer had asked Monica to research which agencies, NGOs, and religious groups had had luck forging ties to the renegade Shiite factions pocketed across the Middle East, from Mosul to the Bosporus. If Katy's abductors did have an Islamist agenda, he was sure it wasn't orthodox.

Raszer had begun to think about just how he was going to get in, and in what suit of clothes. It spooked him to know so little about his adversary. That meant that any stranger could be his killer. It meant being very stingy with his trust.

Slipped into the binder's rear pocket was the yearbook photo of Katy that Aquino had given him. The silent movie sweetheart was even more in evidence at this age—in the lazy eyes, the plump cheeks, the old-fashioned perm. It seemed almost as if Silas Endicott had made his youngest daughter over as Mary Pickford. *Yes*. That was what the eyes invited. *Make me over.* For some men, a girl like this would be a collectible.

Raszer studied the photo of Katy, then glanced up at her would-be evil twin, supine on the bed, and then felt a small shudder of understanding.

A cone from the big sugar pine out front dropped on the roof above his head. If he'd not recognized the sound, it might have gotten him to his feet. As it was, he found himself too agitated to go back to his homework. He set the binder down and walked over to the small, rough-hewn bookshelf beside the bed, not expecting to find much. Motel bookshelves always seemed to be for show, containing nothing but a few dog-eared mysteries. He squatted down in front of the shelf, not two feet from where Ruthie lay. She hadn't stirred. Not even a drunk's little snore. Her fragrance came to him: citrus and musk. *Oranges*? Oranges and damp fur, and that trace of patchouli. But sweet and pungent, too, like a hard marmalade. Dark and concealed, like a fruit cellar.

On the lower shelf, parked between the Bible and Grisham, was a slim, small volume of poetry by the thirteenth-century Persian mystic Jalaluddin Rumi, once little known beyond his turf. Now, he was a staple on the yoga circuit, but no less a poet for it:

The tongue has one customer:

The ear.

He flipped through the pages. They smelled of wood shavings and red wine.

If anyone asks what "spirit" is like,

Or what God's fragrance is like,

Lean your head toward him or her

Keep your face there close—and say:

Like this.

He heard her breathing, and when she turned her face his way, the scent came again. He moved a little closer, sniffing, ears pricked, a bear on its haunches. It was in her hair. In that blood-black bob, and who knew if that was the real Ruthie, or if there was a prison cut beneath, ash blond or purple or orange. He set the book down, keeping a hand on the shelf, and brought his nose to the strand that lay across her eye and cheek. Her right eye opened under the veil of hair, but she didn't move a muscle.

There were two knocks on the blue door, rapid-fire. Soft, but urgent. Then footfalls on the wood planks outside. Raszer pivoted, still in a squat, then dropped one knee to the floor. He held his palm to Ruthie as a signal to stay put, keeping one eye on the door and the other on the big, latticed window to his left.

The boughs of the sugar pine were swaying, brushing the window. *Tap, tap, tap*. The wind had picked up, and a second cone hit the roof, sobering Ruthie up more effectively than motel coffee. She lifted her head, pushing the hair from her eye.

"It's just a pine cone," he said quietly. "Not to worry. I'll go see what this is about. But just in case . . . why don't you hit the deck for a minute."

"If you say so," she said, obliging. "I hope you're not gonna get me killed."

"Not if I can help it," Raszer said. He went to the bedpost, remaining in a crouch.

A brown satchel that resembled a saddlebag hung over the post, and from its rear pocket he slipped a seven-inch knife with a black pearl handle and a steel blade bearing the stamp of its Swedish maker. He nested it in the back of his jeans and went to the door.

"You're gonna defend me with a Boy Scout knife?" Ruthie asked from behind the bed.

With his right shoulder levered against the door, he began slowly to turn the knob. "Who's there?" he asked, for the hell of it. There was at least a chance that the inn's manager or a disoriented guest had knocked, or even that the winds had blown some debris against the door. Nature had a funny way of teasing its human overlords.

No one answered.

He gave his neck muscles a stretch and shook the stiffness out of his shoulders before cracking the door. The aroma of pinesap entered his nostrils, and blown dust stung his eyes. Pinesap and something else. Wild fennel? Or wintergreen? He realized his hair was on end and that fear had crept in under the wind, but he also knew that these collisions of scent and shiver were at the heart of crime and passion.

As he stepped out onto the planks, keeping his hand on the doorknob, Raszer wondered what an assassin might use to cover the odor of bloodlust. Something sweet? No, sweetness was a lousy cover-up. Something clean. Fresh. Something to remind him of a loving mother whose breath had smelled of betel or mint.

The Inn's grand portal sprawled to darkness in both directions. A sloping tile roof admitted little moonlight, so, at either end, details went to gray. Nobody was out, but three rooms down, the hollowed-out sound of country radio issued from an open window. Raszer told himself it was too early for this level of apprehension. Five people knew he'd come to Taos: Borges, Aquino, Monica, his daughter, and Djapper. Of the five, the last was the dodgiest, but it would take more than dodgy to tip off foreign assassins. It would take treason.

In a deeper sense, though, suspicion was always apt, especially around shape-shifting women. Ruthie, too, knew he'd come to Taos. The back of his neck bristled as he stepped off the deck and felt soil beneath his feet. Then he heard gravel spitting at the end of the Inn's long, wooded entrance road, and pivoted to see the taillights of a big, black car pulling onto the Paseo del Sur.

They were here, they knew he was here, and they almost certainly knew whom he was with. The mystery was what they'd come to deliver. It would have been easy enough to kill him at this stage, but it also would have been messy. Killers exhibited an odd kind of patience. They waited until you were almost in their skin.

Raszer dropped to a squat and examined the faint bootprints in the dry dust. His visitor had walked lightly. The prints would be clearer in the morning with the low sun. He stood and padded softly along the access road, the scent of his predator fading with each step. No scent hung around for long in the Southwest, except when the air was dead still. The desert might be the natal ground of religions, but it was also the ally of malefactors. If the Devil had a home, it was in shifting sands and windblown dust.

When a cloud crossed the moon and snuffed his light, Raszer turned back toward the inn. Except for the scent and the current running up his brain stem, it all might have been illusion. Not even the taillights were a definitive ID. Except for the scent, and a plain white envelope tucked beneath the mat at the door of his room, he might eventually have found repose that night.

He stooped to pick it up.

Inside was a folded sheet of paper bearing a computer printout of a digital photograph. The photograph was of Monica, leaving his house after locking up for the night. Just a little feint to throw off his balance and let him know that Djapper's FBI men weren't the only ones watching over her. Just enough to ruin his evening.

Raszer reentered the room and latched the door. Ruthie was nowhere in sight, and that notched his pulse up a few beats until he saw that the bathroom door was closed. He poured himself a cup of coffee. He sat on the edge of the bed, took a gulp, and enjoyed it not in the least. *Blecchh*. Even high-grade motel coffee was still motel coffee. After a couple of minutes, his recently comatose guest emerged, flushed and distinctly content.

"So, what was all that about?" she asked, zipping up her bodysuit. "I got a little amped up. Had to discharge my battery."

"Do you always have an erotic response to fear?" he asked, and took another bitter sip. "Or was it something I said?"

"Somethin' you did, maybe," she replied. "Sniffin' around me like a big dog. Shit, I guess you answered my question, all right."

"What question?" he said, knowing full well what she meant.

"The one I asked you back at the bar, Sherlock. Whaddaya think?"

"Oh, that one," said Raszer. "You should never ask a man that question. You might not get the answer you want to hear."

"Oh, yeah? And what do I wanna hear?"

"If you're asking the question, then what you want to hear is yes."

"Well, I guess you know everything, don't you?" She waited for a second, then sat beside him. "So who was outside?"

He lied, sort of. "Nobody. But I think we should get you home. You ready?"

In reply, she kicked her shoes off, pulled down the quilt, and rolled into bed.

"Don't think I better go home tonight," she said. "I feel like a snooze. *Home*. Ha! Not like anybody's waitin' up, 'cept maybe Angel, with his prayer beads and his whip."

"Friday's his big day, right?" said Raszer, laying the quilt over her.

"Yeah, right. Good Friday. Never could figure out what's so good about it. Neither could my f . . . neither could Silas."

"Where do they do it? The crucifixion?"

"Out in the foothills east of Arroyo Seco. They've got a *morada*—a chapel—out there, and all the stations of the cross marked out. It's a weird scene. Sad, too."

"I'd like to see it," said Raszer. "Any chance?"

"Could be arranged," she said. "If you're that into it." She plumped up the pillow and settled in. "You know what I'd like right now?"

"I'm afraid to ask."

"Somethin' to eat. Is there a candy-bar machine around here?"

"No, but there is a breakfast kitchen off the main salon. It's not do-it-yourself, but I could probably scrounge you a muffin if it's not locked."

"That'd be just dandy," she said, and smiled sweetly.

"I'll see what I can do," he said. "You owe me one."

It took Raszer a minute to locate the kitchen lights, and another to locate the pantry, and all he could scavenge was a roll and a banana. Faintly, he heard a car start up, and thought nothing of it. When he got back to the room, Ruthie was gone and so was the Jeep. *I borrowed your car*, read the hastily scrawled note. *Come to the porch of the Taos Inn at 7 tomorrow night. There's somebody I want you to meet.*

Raszer stood for a moment with the roll, the banana, and Ruthie's note in his hands, taking stock of the altered circumstances and wondering how concerned—and how pissed off—he ought to be. Then he set them all down and began to undress, tossing articles of clothing one by one over the rocking chair near the hearth. On foraging through his duffel bag to retrieve his toothbrush, he noticed that its contents were unsettled. A moment later, he affirmed that the Jeep wasn't the only thing Ruthie had borrowed. Henry Lee's black rock—the one he'd pilfered from the evidence room in San Dimas—was missing. He didn't at first see any particular reason for alarm. It didn't surprise him that she'd gone through his things. She was the type and, despite the kittenish behavior, was probably still suspicious of his motives and mission.

In fact, Raszer made Ruthie as the kind of girl whose sexuality was never entirely without design. Besides that, she'd been Henry's girl, and might have felt she could claim the rock as a keepsake. In any case, an act of petty theft clearly wouldn't trouble her conscience. He'd have to keep an eye on her, and he'd have to get the rock back.

He fell into bed, exhausted. As an afterthought, he retrieved the Rumi anthology from the lamp table. Halfway through the third poem, he fell into a sound sleep. There wasn't much point in troubling himself at this hour. He'd worry when the sun came up.

NINETEEN

MONICA BLEW A KISS to the FBI men on her way up Whitley Terrace, and they returned the favor. They were parked in a red zone about four houses down from Raszer's, and they'd been to Starbuck's. Both men held the signature cup. Like all things in America, the look of FBI men had changed, even in the relatively brief time she'd had dealings with them. They were less burly, less square-shouldered, less white. But the suits, the rock-hewn faces, and the sunglasses remained, as if the Bureau's idea of blending in hadn't really changed since 1955. There was something comforting in that.

Lars, her Danish bodyguard, was waiting on the front stoop. He sat beneath some sort of Scandinavian porta-shelter resembling a beach cabana on a sling chair that looked as if it might collapse at any moment under his mass. It was fog season, and the nights were cool and damp, but by noon the bleached sun would burn through. He'd been there all night and would remain there through the day, with a short break for lunch and a couple of forays into the surrounding area to check for trespassers. Lars claimed never to sleep, or, at any rate, to be able to sleep with his eyes open. He spun a good yarn about his mother's ancestors being Selkies, the fantastical seal people of North Sea legend. But Monica felt sure she'd caught him dozing during the long afternoon hours when the sun was warm. As with the FBI men, his assumption of the cloak of masculinity comforted her, even if it was only bluster.

So far, neither Djapper's men nor the great Dane had been given cause to demonstrate their prowess, and the first day had passed with the guys in the car and the guy on the stoop eyeing each other warily, which in Monica's opinion was what men did when they had no real work to do. But this morning, Raszer had emailed her a scanned copy of the photograph, and it didn't appear to have been shot with an especially long lens. He was worried, and now he had her spooked. As she mounted the steps, picture in hand, she took a breath and prepared to grill the walrus.

"Morning, Lars," she chirped. "Sleep well?"

"Ha!" he answered, standing up and habitually flexing his pectorals. "You know me better, Miss Lord. I sleep like a fish."

"So you say. Well, could you try being a shark during the day?" She handed him the printout. "Somebody took my picture yesterday. Too close for comfort."

Lars knitted his brow. "Hmm," he grunted. "It was when you leave. I was to checking out the canyon. Damn." He glared at the plain black sedan down the street.

"They're federal agents, Lars," she protested. "They're not gonna send my boss a threat. Somebody took this from right across the street."

"Maybe," said Lars. "But I talk to them anyway. Okay if I keep this?"

"Sure," said Monica, but her eyes were on the mail slot, from which a plain white envelope protruded. She stooped to withdraw it. "Now, what do you suppose this is?"

Lars shook his head and shrugged. "I see nobody all the night, Miss Lord. I don't move. Not even to use bathroom. You see—" He reached behind him and grabbed what seemed to be a kind of high-tech bedpan, shaped to be worn inside the trousers. From the sloshing sound it made when he held it up, she gauged it had gotten good use. "I have Stadium Buddy. Holds a full liter. Good for the long watch."

"Well, somebody was up here, Lars," she said, tearing open the envelope and unfolding another photo print, this one of Raszer carrying what looked like a very unconscious girl across the threshold of his motel room. This, she reasoned, must be the infamous Ruthie. "I don't like this, Lars. I think we'd better both go talk to the FBI."

Lars narrowed his eyes. "Tonight," he said, "I will wearing night-vision goggles and set up listening post. No one will come close, even."

He smiled in a way that was probably meant to be endearing, so she handed him the crumpled white bakery bag she'd been holding in her left hand.

"For you, Lars," she said. "Prune Danish. Your favorite, right?"

"Every good day begins with prunes," he said, opening the bag, and offered her one. "You like to sharing?"

"I'm doing yogurt and berries," Monica replied. "Same effect, less carbs."

The men in the black sedan, Agents Strokh and Jiminez, likewise hadn't spotted the furtive photographer, but guessed that the picture had been taken from either beside or inside the house directly across from Raszer's. "We don't have wraparound or x-ray vision, miss," Strokh said.

"Yeah, well," Monica said, "what's to keep them from bashing in the side door, then? Maybe one of you should get out and take a walk once in a while. Sheesh. Where do cops get the idea that a stakeout is like a night at the drive-in?"

"We'll do our very best, miss," Jiminez replied with training-school civility.

"Will you let Agent Djapper know that we're being stalked on both ends?"

"Yes, ma'am. We will," said Strokh.

Unsettled, Monica booted up the office and made herself a cup of jasmine tea. She passed up the berries for now and regained her composure by going methodically through the morning routine: Interpol's I-24/7 site, the State Department's human-trafficking bulletins, Homeland Security's unreliable threat assessments, the somewhat more reliable wire services, and the LAPD's overnight arrest reports, all of which she and Raszer had obtained hard-won access to.

In addition, she checked out the weather, travel alerts, disease outbreaks, and exchange rates for every country her boss might conceivably step into. Finally, she went through email from thirteen different servers, six of them as encrypted and snoop-proof as current technology allowed.

The first set of graphs from the chaos mathematician in Santa Cruz had come through. Depending on how one read the tea leaves, they might or might not be revelatory. On the day Scotty Darrell had wounded a driver at Universal Studios, the price of the company's stock had dropped rather dramatically—before the shooting had occurred. Disney and the corporate owners of the Six Flags chain had also taken hits in the ripple effect that followed. Up to that point, big entertainment-sector stocks had largely weathered the economic shitstorm that had battered the country in recent years.

Also on that day, and perhaps only whimsically related, the L.A. City Council had banned lap dancing, and the French parliament had passed an ordinance requiring Muslim girls to remove their veils in French public schools. There were other simultaneities, some absurdly far-flung, including an IAEA announcement that a significant quantity of enriched uranium had been reported missing from the Ukraine.

She emailed the mathematician her thanks and simultaneously began to download two large files, one from the BBC and one from a Swiss blog–cum–pirate news service known as Charlie Hebdo. Both reports dealt with the strange-bedfellow relationships that American Christian evangelicals had cultivated with Zionists, on the one hand, and with the sworn Islamist enemies of Israel on the other.

The dalliance between the Christian Right and the Israeli Right had been well reported, but the kinship between crusade and jihad was murkier, not to say counterintuitive. Understanding it required investigating at least as far back as the Soviet invasion of Afghanistan, when American evangelicals had found common ground with the likes of the Taliban in their opposition to godless communism, and employing the sort of tactical thinking that is common in criminal organizations but foreign to most people.

What seized Monica's attention was a mention of a conference held in Damascus in 2002 by a group calling itself the International Interfaith Council. According to the report, the IIC was a creation of the Chalcedon Foundation. The stated goal of the conference was ecumenical outreach, but given its timing in the wake of 9/11—Monica was thinking like a chaos theorist now—the secret agenda might have been grander and more alarming.

Some of the organizations represented at the conference were unfamiliar, but she recognized its principal American sponsor. The Chalcedon Foundation was the fountainhead of Christian Dominionism, the doctrine that held that Old Testament law ought to be the final word on Earth in these end times preceding the Second Coming. God's law trumped man's law, which meant that government should, if necessary, become an instrument of divine rule.

Theonomy, they called it, but there were other names. Western co-sponsors of the conference included the Christian Broadcasting Network, the Unification Church, and the American Enterprise Institute, and among the attendees—cloaked in the guise of something called the Admiralty Group—was what might have been a deputation from the Church of Scientology. If this weren't spooky enough, the Swiss report went further. It alleged that on May 3, 2002, the last day of the conference, a private jet had landed in Damascus and disgorged a passenger registered as Morton Lutz, otherwise known as then assistant under secretary of state Douglas Picot.

On the Muslim side of the table were arrayed clerics and sheikhs of all stripes, from the ultra-orthodox Shiite mullahs of Iran to Sunnis whose strident Wahabism would not have displeased Osama bin Laden. There were renegades from schismatic sects like the Nusayris, and militant pan-Islamists affiliated with Hezbollah and the SSNP. There was no mention of the Ismailis, the radical branch of Shi'ism that had spawned the Assassins and inspired the MO of the organization with which Stephan Raszer was now playing hide-and-seek.

But the mix was weird enough. Televangelists, Christian reconstructionists, neocons, and midlevel American diplomats had broken bread with Islamists in the heart of a country the United States had then been rattling sabers with.

Monica was about to digest the Swiss blogger's theory about why the "moderate" Sunnis, who in all but a few countries still constituted the Muslim ruling class, had been underrepresented at the conference, when there came a sudden gust of wind, an aroma of sage, and the sound of pages rustling from around the corner in Raszer's library. Monica's throat tightened. She knew immediately that the French doors leading to Raszer's herb garden had blown—or been pushed—open.

"Lars!" she managed to croak out. He was on the other side of the front door, or should have been, and it panicked her further when he didn't answer. She rolled slowly back from her workstation, stood, and entered the short hallway connecting the office with the library. For good measure, she called out. "The gun is loaded, so don't make me jump."

She did not, of course, have a gun. She didn't have even her pepper spray.

On the bookstand Raszer kept by the door, the pages of the Qur'an lifted one by one, fanned by the steady northeastern breeze. The door was wide open. The sunlight reflected from the vellum made her squint.

"Lars?" Monica called out again.

She stepped out into the little garden, where the ma huang shared root space with moonlight sage and mint. She was alone, and the outside gate remained locked. She stood for a few moments, watching the wind make waves over the plant tops, and then something came to her, the sort of thing that only crazy people think. The sort of thought you don't give breath to, because breath marries wind and wind carries thoughts into the world of real things.

She shuddered, wishing she had a lover's ear to whisper it into, and a lover's arms for sanctuary from its implications. *It's coming down*, she said to herself, *a bigger lie than has ever been told, a bigger scam than has ever been worked.*

"Miss Lord?" Lars called out from behind her. She spun around, mouth open to cry out. "I thought I hear something in back," he explained. "But everything's quiet."

"Yes," she replied, composing herself. "It is for now."

◆ ◆ ◆

RASZER SPENT THE MORNING hunting for Easter eggs. He'd been remiss. By the Christian calendar (at least, in the world west of Rome), it was Maundy Thursday, tomorrow was Good Friday, and Sunday was Easter. Brigit would have her egg only if he found it today. He might've finessed it by telling her that he was headed into the Byzantine world and observing Easter later this year, but she'd have seen right through it. No, he had to find the egg, and it had to be right, because she would measure his devotion by it.

Easier said than done.

The boutiques of Taos had iguanas, dancing shamans, and coyotes, but eggs seemed to have no place in Southwestern iconography. Strange . . . it wasn't as if birds didn't lay on the mesa as they laid on the steppes, or that the egg was any less a symbol of regeneration. Maybe here, regeneration was symbolized more aptly by the snake shedding its skin.

He stopped at the newsstand on the plaza to inquire about books by local authors on the subject of the *penitentes*, and was directed to the historical society, where he found what the curator assured him was the only reliable account, a slim volume called *Brothers of Light*, by Alice Corbin Henderson. In a glass case of Pueblo artifacts dressed up and priced as objets d'art, he saw what he wanted for Brigit. A petrified snake egg encased in a geode with crystals as blue as the shadows on the Sangre de Cristo slopes. It wasn't Russian, and it wasn't painted, but he closed his eyes and saw her placing it proudly on her bedroom shelf. When he opened them, he found he had to wipe the right eye dry. Until that moment, he hadn't seen how worried he was, how heavily it weighed on him that this assignment might leave his daughter fatherless.

Just across the way, partially masked by a pine grove, was the Fechin Inn, the most beautiful hotel in Taos. Beautiful not in the Mediterranean way, but like a fine, handmade chair, labored over and loved and rubbed and oiled until it looked more like wood than the trees from which it was made. He had some time before hunger got the best of him, and wasn't due to brief Monica until two, so he crunched across the fallen pine needles and pushed open the art deco glass doors, wondering if he would know Constance Endicott when he saw her.

She was smaller than he'd imagined, though it shouldn't have surprised him. Both of her daughters were the size of those 40's film stars who looked so grand on the screen but stood barely taller than children. He'd pictured her being closer to the stature of her late husband, Silas, who'd been a veritable oak. But this made sense, too: a china doll, its features all in miniature, like a human banzai tree whose limbs had been kept trimmed to the length of perfect, preadolescent beauty, so as not to intimidate the menfolk. She stood behind the registration counter, a large oil painting of Taos in snow on the wall at her back, and watched him walk up.

"Good afternoon," she said. "Checking in?"

"No, actually. Wish I was. I—"

She was lovely, like her daughters, but it was a loveliness more lined and bleached than her forty years should have shown. It wasn't the overbaked-clay look that some desert Caucasians have, but the grayed porcelain of an antique left in the attic. All the fervor was in the eyes and chin, and there Raszer found the only clue to how she'd ended up in a trailer in Taos with a penitential Catholic named Angel Davidos. Ruthie's leonine fierceness was nowhere in evidence, as it had been in Silas, who, oddly enough, had dismissed Ruthie as "her mother's daughter." Freud had been right: We hate most what resembles the incorrigible qualities in ourselves.

"I just wanted to check your rates," Raszer said. "Maybe see a room. I'm planning a special occasion. Would you mind showing me—"

"I don't think that will be a problem," she replied, and turned to a young Latina in a print vest. "Lourdes, would you cover the desk while I show Mr. . . . "

"Rose."

" . . . Mr. Rose one of the rooms?"

The girl nodded and stepped to the front.

"So . . . " said Mrs. Endicott, coming around to Raszer's side. "A single? Double? A suite? You said a special occasion . . . "

"Yes. Yes, a kind of reunion, I guess. Let's see a suite. Why not?"

"Our suites are very nice," she said, and led him through a native garden fragrant with cactus flowers, and then up a short flight of stairs. "A reunion," she repeated. "Family? An old fl . . . *friend*?"

"Someone who was lost and now is found," Raszer answered. "Someone I'd like to welcome home properly."

She paused at the top of the stairs and turned halfway, her face in shadow.

"Oh, I see," she said softly. "Well, I'm sure that she . . . or he . . . will love it here. Everyone does."

"She . . . actually," said Raszer. "And I'm sure you're right. Have you lived in Taos long? Or are you a newcomer, like me?"

"Not long," said Constance, taking out her passkey. "But it feels like home."

"Yes, it does. It's beautiful and rugged and spiritual all at the same time."

She pushed open the door of room 233, and sandalwood wafted into the hall.

Raszer stepped in. A fire was laid in the hearth, and fresh fruit and a bottle of wine were on the table. The mountains made a living mural on the west wall.

"It's perfect," said Raszer. "And probably costs it, right?"

"Two sixty-five a night," she said. "It's our best. We do have less—"

"That's all right. Like I said, a homecoming." He wandered over to the window. "I'm thinking," he said without turning, "of bringing my family here to live, but I worry a little about the isolation. Do you have children?"

She cleared her throat and jingled the keys. "I have two grown daughters, but only one is with me. I can't say that she—"

Raszer turned. "Grown daughters? I wouldn't have guessed—"

She smiled modestly and took a step backward, out of the sunlight. It occurred to Raszer that Constance Endicott might never have been flirted with. Married and pregnant at seventeen, and now nursing the wounds of a Latin flagellant—when had she had the time and the opportunity? She pressed her fingers to her temple and shuddered slightly.

"Are you okay?" Raszer asked, taking a step toward her.

"Yes," she said. "It's just a sinus headache. The altitude. I'm still not used to it."

"I know what you mean. The altitude, the dry air. And then, on top of that, you have to deal with that rumbling that goes on all the time . . . "

She trained one eye on him, and for an instant, it seemed to offer him something. Raszer gave back what he could. All he wanted was for her not to feel crazy. *Too bad*, he mused, *that I can't turn on this thing in my eye at will. Wouldn't it be nice to be able to validate somebody's psychic intimations with a look?*

He couldn't have known that, for Constance Endicott, that was more or less exactly what had happened.

✦ ✦ ✦

THE DAY TURNED WARM for about two hours after noon. Raszer thought about lunch, then considered an hour or so of bouldering in the rugged foothills Ruthie had identified as the site of the Good Friday ritual. Getting heart, lungs, and mind in shape for the austerity of the Middle East had been another part of his rationale for spending three to four days in Taos.

But the sun was high and he was feeling oddly spent, almost as if the signs of premature aging Ruthie's mother had evinced had made him feel his own age more keenly. And lurking somewhere beneath this fatigue was the awareness that he was a target, and that venturing alone into the wilderness might be foolhardy. So he returned to the inn to call Monica.

Out front, he found his Jeep waiting. The keys were dangling from the ignition, pinning a note that said: *Remember: Meet me at the Taos Inn at cocktail hour. We're going to see a friend.* He went inside to make the call.

"Everything quiet at home?" he asked her.

"Everything except my nerves," Monica replied.

"I told you we should've locked the place up."

"You know damn well I couldn't have tracked you as effectively from my place. Besides, with a 260-pound Norseman and the FBI on-site, how much safer could a girl be? If they'd put SWATs on the neighbors' rooftops, we could probably nail these guys the next time they come around."

"Maybe," said Raszer. "And maybe not. How's Lars?"

"I think he has some issues with the FBI. He practically accused the two agents of taking my picture, and he stands out there with his chest out, like he's daring them to come closer. I wonder if he had a run-in with the feds at some stage of his career."

"Maybe it's an alpha-male thing," said Raszer. "He *is* a Viking. And with you being an athletic blond, you've got the Brunhilde thing going. I can almost picture you with a breastplate."

"Yeah. Anyhow, I'm glad he's here. How's Ruthie? Has she come across?"

"Little bits at a time. The Johnny-Henry dynamic is clearer. And there's an unnamed someone she wants me to meet tonight. About what happened in Iraq, I think. She stole my car, but then she brought it back. She seems to be her own woman."

"Just don't sleep with her."

"I have no plans to sleep with her, But, you know, if women would stop looking for affirmation through sex, that advice would be a lot easier to follow."

Monica had no retort, and when she resumed, she chose a new subject. She told Raszer about the first set of chaos graphs, and the odd fact that Universal Studios had taken a beating on Wall Street *before* its tour had suffered Scotty's assault.

"And you're thinking somebody triggered a little foreshock in the market," Raszer said. "A little panic wave whose real purpose might be somewhere else?"

"I'm not sure I took it that far," she replied, "but basically, yeah."

"Hmm."

Then she told him about the conference in Damascus.

"Well, now," Raszer said, after a pause. "That's pretty interesting. And you say no major news organization covered it?"

"They weren't invited," Monica replied. "It sounds more like a meeting of the families. This renegade BBC reporter—the same guy who stirred up so much trouble a few years ago by claiming that Al Qaeda was a trumped-up Western bogeyman—he got the scoop, and then the Swiss blogger ran with it and did an exposé."

"So let me understand: We've got a secret meeting organized by Christian theocrats and attended by Islamic theocrats and an assortment of faith peddlers, all of them with an authoritarian bent and connections in Washington, which is represented in the person of Douglas Picot. A meeting of the faithful, to seek common ground in the strife-torn Middle East. And there's not a Jew in sight."

"That's about it, Raszer," Monica said. "No Jews, no Catholics, no mainline Protestants, and, if I'm reading this right, they pretty much excluded the three-quarters of the Muslim world who consider themselves moderate. So . . . what do you make of it?"

He lit a smoke and stepped out onto the portal, then spied a hammock strung between two pine trees twenty yards distant and took the phone there. It was exposed, but it was also in plain sight of every room at the inn, and therefore as safe as any place he was likely to perch.

"Let's begin with what *isn't* hidden. Hardcore evangelicals and hardcore Shiites both see themselves as alienated from the mainstream. Marginalized by the modern world. They're Abrahamic in their outlook. The Sharia is basically Old Testament law: clean, severe, unambiguous. Both are distinct minorities within their traditions, but minorities with muscles and weight. The Nusayris run Syria with only about eleven percent of the population; fundamentalists controlled Congress with less than that. So much for the surface.

Beneath that it gets weird, like it always does with Puritans—especially when they get a whiff of power. I picked up something a long time ago from guys like Adler and Reich: When a group's been on the outs for too long, its way back in is usually some kind of fascism, using the state as a spiritual bludgeon."

"Okay," Monica said. "I get all that. But what were they brokering so soon after 9/11? What was going on in the private suites and the sheikhs' tents? That's what I want to know. And *why* was the State Department there?"

"I think the answer depends on whether they saw what was coming. If you'd known in 2002 that this whole thing was going to degenerate into global sectarian war and cripple the ruling parties on both sides, then you might have wanted to move into position to grab the spoils, negotiate the peace, even before the war was over."

"What kind of peace, Raszer? What would the terms be?"

"You want the paranoid answer?" he asked.

"It's usually the closest to the truth, isn't it?"

"Let me think about it before I speak it."

"Do you want me to keep digging?" Monica asked.

"Oh, yeah. And see if you can find out if the Jehovah's Witnesses sent a rep."

"Raszer?"

"Yeah?"

"How about we have the professor run a chaos graph on the conference dates?"

"Good idea."

"Raszer?"

"Uh-huh."

"What if nothing is true? What if these people who call themselves fundamentalists aren't Christians at all? What if they're something else altogether?"

"Ah," he said softly. "Now you're standing in my shoes."

She swallowed hard. "And how do you know what's genuine and what's fake?"

"You don't always."

"Does anybody know the truth?"

"Those who know don't say. And those who say don't know."

✦ ◆ ✦

For a few minutes after Raszer signed off, he sat in the hammock with his feet on the ground, feeling dizzy. He realized he hadn't eaten. An aching melancholy, something like loneliness, came over him with the change of light in the west. He knew what she was going through. It was one thing to say this stuff, and another to feel it deep inside.

He then did something that he never, ever did when there were killers in the tall grass. He laid back, watched the sun play hide-and-seek with the pine boughs, and slept. He dreamed of eggs. Eggs in pale yellow and speckled blue, gilded eggs and eggs bejeweled with rubies, ostrich eggs and serpents' eggs, all rolling down an expansive grassy steppe that sloped dramatically to the desert floor far below, where a man in a white robe with a red sash waited.

Raszer might have slept the day away, if not for the trace of wintergreen that drifted through the pines at about four o' clock. He'd never especially liked the smell, and now he was beginning to hate it.

TWENTY

"THANKS FOR BRINGING my car back . . . undented," said Raszer, tossing his keys onto the pale green table. "At least you're an honorable thief."

"I only steal what I need," Ruthie said. "I'm a practical girl."

"And you stole Henry's sigil to do some practical magic?"

"What in hell's a sigil?" she asked.

The previous night's prewar Berlin hairstyle was gone, and Ruthie now displayed a sunset-red townie cut, cropped and blunt cut. It was closer to the look he'd expected, except that her round cat's face was scrubbed clean and free of makeup. She wore an army green T-shirt and baggy cargo pants and made Raszer think of those bright-eyed, barely legal Alabama girls they'd sent over to serve in the slaughterhouse in Babylon. The sexuality remained but was now more androgynous. Was this, too, intentional?

"Don't be coy, Ruthie. You knew Henry's MO. He'd summon his 'thought form' down into the rock and then do some voodoo. I'm just wondering why *that* rock."

"Well, since you know so much, you oughta know that it can be any rock, or statue, or whatever, but a power object is best. Somethin' with some history. And that rock—the one with the big dimple in it—if what he said was true, it's got *some* history."

"Tell me."

"If I tell you, I'll have to kill you," she said, and the corners of her mouth curled.

"Do I have time for a drink?" Raszer asked, pulling out a chair. The Taos Inn's broad porch was about half-full with locals and a few off-season tourists and the wooden floor creaked drily as the waitress approached.

"Sure," said Ruthie. "We got all night." And then she added, "At least, until it's time to see my friend Shams. Order one for me while you're at it."

"Sure," said Raszer. "How about a Virgin Mary?"

"Very funny," she said. "I'll have a Dos Equis."

Raszer ordered two of them and turned to Ruthie. So, Shams must be his mystery contact for the evening. Interesting name. The sun dropped into the V between two distant peaks, and gilded the Taos Inn with a diffracted ray. Raszer sat back. He decided to let the matter of the black rock go for now. "Tell me about Shams," he said. "He or she?"

"He's a he," Ruthie answered. "But I think he's seen it from both sides."

"How so?"

"He told me that he lived as a woman for a year, wearing a burka and sucking off the soldiers who came over the border between Iraq and Turkey. He said he wanted to understand Muslim women and the 'mystique of the veil.' I guess he does now. Funny thing is, he said it wasn't all that unusual over there, men dressing up as women. The soldiers didn't seem to care. A mouth is a mouth, right?"

"So what's his story?" Raszer asked. "Was he in the fight over there? Did he know the boys, Johnny and Henry?"

"He didn't know 'em, but he could've," Ruthie said. "He was based in Karbala at first. Then in Mosul. He enlisted right at the beginning. First in line. Not because he was gung-ho or anything. I think maybe he thought it'd be a good way to die. He was, like, thirty or something. Shit, I dunno how old the guy is. I just know he's the shit. After three fuckin' tours, he still wasn't dead, so he figured maybe he was immortal. He signed up with Blackwater and went back. He said he had to finish the game."

"The game?"

"Right. Then he saw what they were doin' over there. That's when he went native."

"What game? The Gauntlet?"

"Shams knows about all the games. I think he's even invented a few. And he knows these people."

"Katy's abductors . . . "

"Yeah," she said, grabbing the cold beer from the waitress's tray. "Them."

Raszer waited for his beer to be delivered. The sun had now dropped fully into the breach, and the alpenglow rendered the mountains luminescent.

"How does he know them? From the game?"

"He'll tell you the story," said Ruthie. "One day he just walked away from his post. Lived like an Arab, in Turkey, Syria . . . even Iran, I think. Converted to Islam and learned all sort of weird shit. I guess they must've pulled him in the same way they did Johnny and Henry. Except Shams got free of 'em. They don't scare him. The fucker lives in a yurt up by Red River. He knows all this survival shit. Like I said, he's deep."

Raszer picked up the tabletop candle and lit it with his Zippo. He studied her eyes for a moment in the underlight. Until now, he hadn't been able to gauge Ruthie's intelligence, and knew even less about Katy. Judged solely by their actions, neither one seemed more than natively bright, but he saw now that Ruthie had a plan for him.

"When do we go see him?" he asked.

"After you feed me," she replied. "Can I order a burrito?"

"Order whatever you like," he said. "Has your mother or father ever hired anyone else to find Katy? PIs, ex-FBI men, bounty hunters . . . "

"Not as far as I know," she answered. "My mom couldn't afford it, and my old man . . . well, for a while, he was gonna go lookin' himself, but I guess he gave that up."

"Where would he have looked?"

"I dunno . . . Asian sex clubs, maybe. Maybe that's why he never went."

"And where do *you* think she is?"

"Who the fuck knows?" Ruthie said. "She doesn't send me postcards. But Shams says he knows, so I figure it must be over there."

"In Turkey?"

"Ask Shams," she said, and took a look around to see who was within earshot. "See, *I am* scared of these guys. They like to cut off parts of you." The waitress checked in. Ruthie ordered a burrito with extra cheese, Raszer a bowl of *albóndigas*.

"I'm betting you have a pretty good idea where she is, too," said Raszer. "Because Henry must've known, and the two of you stayed close."

"Henry had visions. 'Flash frames,' he called 'em. Things he saw in his scrying stones. But he'd never been there . . . to El Mariah, or whatever they called it." She reached down into an oversize Navaho-weave handbag she'd set beside her chair, and drew out a plain tan envelope stuffed with documents. "Here," she said. "Check it yourself. This is what you came for, right?"

Raszer accepted the folder, opened it, and saw immediately that it contained printed copies of the email correspondence between Ruthie and Henry. He nodded. "This, yes," he said, then reached across the table, gently touched her head, and indicated her heart. "And what's in here . . . and there." He sat back. "So, why do I rate?"

The food arrived and was set before them. The waitress paused for approval.

"'Cause you didn't fuck me when you could've," said Ruthie. The waitress cleared her throat and backed away. "And because you went to see my mother."

"She knew who I was?"

"No. She told me some guy came by about a homecoming, and *I knew*."

"How did you manage to keep these from the FBI?" Raszer asked.

"Simple. I hid them." Ruthie forked into her burrito.

"Yeah, but the original data. Hell, the feds can decrypt email with a keystroke."

"Henry and Johnny used a pirate server. They might've been hicks, but they weren't dumb. They picked up a lot from the insurgents in Iraq. The FBI is old school. Wherever they are, guys like Henry are three steps ahead. Those files are long gone, and they used the hard drives to make IEDs."

Raszer set the folder aside. "So nobody's ever seen these?"

"That's right," Ruthie said. "That FBI asshole . . . he never got close. These are Henry's last will and testament. These are his love letters to me."

✦ ◆ ✦

AT NINE THIRTY, they navigated a switchback on their way up the Front Range and sent a coyote scampering into the chaparral. It was dark on the mountainside; the lights of Taos, far below, did not send up much spill. There were other predators in that darkness. It occurred to Raszer that the dark had never been the friend of social man. Social man loved fire, gaslight, even neon. It was the sociopath who found allies in the lampless night.

On the other hand, you could love the dark and not love what it concealed. Once, on a conditioning trek through Goblin Valley, Utah, Raszer had awakened in his tent to a holy vacuum, soundless except for the gentlest of *tip-tap-tip-tap-tip-tap-tip-taps*. He'd switched on his flashlight to find his sleeping bag swarming with little scorpions. That's what the darkness held.

Never, ever forget it, he told himself. "How much further?" he asked.

"About four miles, and then another mile up a dirt road," Ruthie answered. "Almost to the ski valley. Shams gets snow in October sometimes. Least he says so."

"Well, since we've got a ways, why don't you tell me—from your memory of Henry's letters—how he and Johnny first hooked up with these guys."

She said nothing at first. They made another switchback, and Raszer lit her a cigarette. It was a small gesture, but it would mean something passing from his lips to hers.

"They were in some little village south of An Najaf, supposedly a nest of bad guys. They'd been there all day, goin' from house to house, herding the families out on the streets to search for weapons, and they hadn't found nothin' except a bunch of scared kids and women. The men were mostly farmers and boys too young to fight. Henry said it was just like what his uncle said about Vietnam: that you didn't know which old hag might be packing heat in her laundry basket, or which kid might be running information to the enemy, even though prob'ly none of 'em were. There were about eleven of 'em, all young guys from the boonies, and one girl from Alabama.

"Around sundown, one of the soldiers freaked 'n shot a kid—a boy who'd snuck up behind him, wantin' to trade his mom's jewelry for American candy bars. Blew his little head off right in front of his house. They tried to make it right with the family, but Henry knew they should get the fuck outta there. There was blood and brains on the ground, and the kid's mother just laid down in it and screamed all night until finally they shot her, too.

"Anyhow, they made camp in the middle of town, and just before dawn, the villagers attacked with knives and hatchets and whatever they had. Just crazed, that's all, 'cause of the kid. And Henry 'n Johnny's unit started blasting away, killing anything that moved. Killing the women and the kids and the old men. Then all of a sudden the insurgents—I guess they were Sunnis there, I can never remember which—came down outta the hills, started raining shit down on them.

"Three or four of their guys—Johnny and Henry's guys—went down right away. Another guy had his arm shot off. Henry said the fucker just sat down in the dirt and kept tryin' to stick it back on. The Alabama girl, she musta looked at those dead kids and thought, *What the hell am I doin' here instead of gettin' married to the town dentist*? 'cause she turned around and shot the CO, and then she took it in the chest."

"Anyhow, now they're down to, like, four or five, and Johnny just goes apeshit, picks up one of the bodies for a shield 'n just wails on these wogs, killing, like, ten of 'em, screaming the whole time, 'Not me, motherfuckers! Not me!' And there's smoke everywhere and they can't see shit. They can't see shit except each other, Johnny and Henry. It's just the two of them. They're all that's left, and outta the smoke come the insurgents, walkin' real slow and wearing rags on their heads and scarves so they can't smell the death, and it gets real quiet and the boys know it's all over. Henry says that's when he died. He said he was never the same after. And the insurgents—the Sunnis or whatever—make a circle, and the guns go up and they try to make Johnny and Henry get on their knees but they won't do it. And then there's machine gun fire from every direction, and the Iraqis just drop where they are. Just like that.

"Next thing, they hear this weird flute that sounds like a sparrow hawk, and when the smoke clears, there's this guy, this fuckin' sheikh dressed in black from head to toe, and six more mean motherfuckers with Uzis. Henry said they looked more like Indiana bikers than Arabs. And the sheikh starts laughin' and says to Johnny in English, 'We need to talk.' And they take them to this camp in a . . . a *wadi,* Henry called it, and feed them roasted lamb and hashish, and that's where the deal went down." Ruthie stubbed out the cigarette and pointed with her right hand. "That's your turn, by the way. Up past that big tree."

Raszer made the turn in silence and heard the Jeep's tires bite into loose dirt and rocks. The headlight beams came to a vanishing point thirty yards ahead, and then there was nothing but black. He'd never seen that before. No reflection. He stopped the car.

"So what was the deal?" he asked her.

"The deal was, there's only one army, there's only one fight. There's only one insurgency that matters. We're it. You two guys are warriors, but you'd be dead warriors if we hadn't just saved your asses. Now you play on our side."

"And I take it they accepted . . . " said Raszer.

"They took a blood oath," said Ruthie. "They got shitfaced on hash, they got laid, and they woke up in the desert two hundred yards from their base. Johnny said it was destiny. Henry wasn't so sure. But I don't really think they had much choice."

"And they served out their tours?"

"Yeah. They didn't hear from these guys until they were back in the States."

"And Henry left Iraq with his testicles?"

"Drive," she said. "I've told you enough for now."

Raszer put the gearshift into first. "Direct me," he said. "I can't see a thing."

◆ ◆ ◆

A BUILD-IT-YOURSELF YURT could be purchased on the Internet. On the granola circuit, they had attained a certain multicultural cachet. The yurt occupied by the man who called himself Shams had not come from a kit, but appeared—based on what the glow from its central fire revealed—to have been constructed from raw materials in the manner of an Uzbek or Kazakh original. The basic architecture was universal: a circular, wooden frame with a skin of felt or canvas, a single door, and a conical roof with an aperture at the peak to let smoke out and light in. After that, it was a matter of style. Some yurts had raised floors, some were furnished like teahouses. Shams' was right off the Mongolian steppes, and so—at least, it seemed at first—was Shams himself.

He was hanging by his feet from one of two heavy crossbeams that quartered the circle and braced the yurt's six-foot walls just below its circus-tent roof. Hanging, as in dangling, his head about eight inches from the floor, his arms folded across his chest. It was difficult to get a fix on his face, given the dim light, the quantity of blood that had rushed into it, a full beard, and a knitted Mongolian shepherd's cap with a pointed top and large earflaps fastened at the chin.

"How do, Shams?" said Ruthie.

"Hi, precious," he replied, in a voice as reedy as a *duduk*. The white markings in his beard gave the impression that there were eyes both above and below his mouth.

"You got time for visitors?" she asked.

"I've got all the time in the world," said Shams.

He reached up effortlessly, grabbed the beam, and untied the thongs binding him. Then he did a short flip, landing upright, all five-feet-four of him. Raszer stepped into the firelight. The hearth was vented by an aluminum hood that tapered to a chimney. It gave off enough heat to make the yurt's interior sweat. Hanging over the fire was an iron kettle in which something with a powerfully alkaline odor simmered.

"I guess I'm the one responsible for the impromptu visit," Raszer said, offering his hand.

"And you would be?" asked Shams, pulling off his sheepskin glove.

"Stephan Raszer. I'm looking for Ruthie's sister."

"Ray-zer. Raaay-zor," said Shams, feeling the name on his tongue as he took Raszer's hand. "Interesting name."

"We have that in common. I only know of one other Shams. Shams of Tabriz, the spiritual mentor of Jalaluddin Rumi . . . and one of the few guys to survive the Mongol assault on the Ismaili citadel of Alamut. The Assassin fortress."

"Praise Allah!" said Shams, with a twinkle in his eye. "*I am remembered! My name is known to someone.*" He bent back and threw a lusty "Ha!" toward the hole in the roof. "That's the cry of the exile when he reaches Na-Koja-Abad. Do you know it?"

"I have a feeling I should," said Raszer. "I may be going there."

Shams waggled his finger. "Not so fast, brother," he cautioned, then swept his arm over a wooden floor covered with Turkish carpets and an assortment of pillows. "Sit," he said. "Sit."

From the moment Shams gripped his hand, Raszer took him as a man entirely self-created. He might've been raised in Fresno or Cedar Rapids as Arnold Schmidt, but somewhere along the way, he'd become Shams. And if on the street, someone were to walk up and say, "Hey! Aren't you Arnold Schmidt? I went to high school with you," they'd be wrong. You could call it a con, but Shams didn't strike Raszer as a flim-flam man. No wonder Ruthie called him "the shit"; he was the transformed identity she probably wished for herself, the role you play when you've played out all the others.

Their host sat first, and they joined him in a half-moon of cushions around the fire. "Shams I am," he said. "Shams the sham. Shams the shaman." The hearth, which sat on three stumpy cast iron legs, was a circle within the greater circle of the yurt. It resembled the votaries found in ancient tombs, a big cast iron dish hammered out over some Hephaestian forge. The kettle hung about eight inches above the coals by a hook at the end of a winched steel cable. Steam rose into the chimney along with smoke.

"What's cooking?" Raszer couldn't help but ask. It didn't smell like stew.

"Broth," Shams replied. "Mushroom broth. Ready to sip in two minutes."

Raszer smiled. "Those aren't morels in there. I smell heavy metal."

"A connoisseur of fungi, are you? Well these aren't psychotropic . . . not exactly. . . but they will cure warts and whooping cough, restore lost hair, and give you a hard-on that lasts through any dark night of the soul."

"You don't say," Raszer said. "Satisfaction guaranteed?"

"Or your manna back!" answered Shams. "So, what's your duty, friend? Are you after wisdom or just information? 'Cause if you want information, you can Google it."

Raszer considered his reply.

"A little of both," said Raszer. "I try to get people out of trouble when they want to be gotten out. Have you played The Gauntlet?"

"Most assuredly, man. I played it for two years. Even wrote a piece of it when it went persistent. The Gauntlet's the king of the IRGs. Or was, until the FBI opened the curtains. Now all that's out there are the weekenders and the guys who played their line all the way out to the ninth level. It was like living inside the web, man. You just jumped from link to link and never knew where you'd wind up. A God game."

"Like I said," Ruthie told Raszer, "he knows." She curled up tight and laid her head on Shams' thigh, and with his tea-stained fingers he began to stroke her hair.

"You started playing when you were in-country, right?" Raszer asked.

"On my second tour, yeah. But I didn't jump the wires until my discharge."

"Jump the wires?"

"When you leave the Internet and go walking. Though it ain't like you leave 'virtual reality' and enter the 'real world.' It's more like you take virtual reality with you."

"Were any of the other soldiers into it?"

"Most definitely, *rafiq*. Especially the guys working intel. It played like a Eurail pass to the Middle East. It works in the Muslim world. Muslims understand submission to God. It was too heady for most of those Mississippi boys, but not for the codebreakers."

"I lost a kid to it," said Raszer. "Somebody I was hired to bring home. I studied the game, but from the outside. The designers did their homework: Aquinas, Erigena, Averroes, the *I Ching* . . . all of that. But at some stage of play—way the fuck out there when the player's been stripped of everything that binds him to his old self—it starts looking like a proving ground for sociopaths. My kid got sidetracked. Now he's in federal custody. An 'enemy combatant.' An accused assassin. And that ties into Katy—"

Shams pushed up to his knees and scooped himself a cup of the steaming broth, then sat back on his heels. "Indeed. You see there, that's what the GamesMasters didn't think through. They *were* fuckin' seminarians, after all.

All spirit, no psyche. They didn't consider the predatory instinct: that if you put all these innocents out there on the road to Damascus, sooner or later some buzzard is gonna pick 'em off. I can still quote from the book of play: *Do not resist the entreaties of your guide, for God may appear in the guise of the corrupt or malign, just as his opposite may appear beneficent. It is not for you to discern the difference. It is for you to ask only, 'How can I serve?' In doing this, you will always find favor with God.*"

"Sounds like good advice for rising in the Mafia," Raszer observed.

"Right," Shams continued. "At the lower levels of play, the worst that can happen is you wind up working for some sleazebag and getting your nose rubbed in shit, which is a kind of inoculation if you think about it. I ran whores for this evil fucker in Dubai, and believe me, I never wanna see the inside of a whorehouse again. Seeing evil makes you not want to be it. Plus, for the first six levels, you're still wired in to the game, to the other players. You're swappin' war stories in chatrooms, gettin' texted and instant-messaged in the middle of the night, sent to porn websites where a pop-up window gives you your next set of directions, even going to parties where half the guests are actors. You've got a safety net, and you can call for a DX if you get scared.

"But once they give you Extreme Unction, you lose your bearings unless you're really together. Take this, for example: *You're in the seventh circle of play. You've jumped the wires and you're offline, man.* No email, no text messages, no nothin'. The pay phone rings on an empty street. How the fuck do they know you're there? A recorded voice says, *Your next guide is a deceiver and a criminal. Query him about the holiest place he has ever been and the wisest person still residing there. Offer to carry a message or gift to that person on behalf of your guide, and request a letter of introduction. Upon meeting, ask, 'What is expected of me?' Play out your line until you begin to feel the snake.* This is where the men separate from the boys, 'cause you don't know where the fuck you are, man."

"So you toss three coins and read the *I Ching*?"

"That works," Shams replied. "However you do it, you have to stop trusting your own instincts—which are basically faulty—and start trusting the snake's. Because the snake doesn't think—it knows. God is in the *I Ching*. He's also in the Big Mac wrapper blowin' down that empty street. Will you recognize Him? That depends on something beyond instinct or intuition or intelligence: it depends on *knowing*."

"So who gets through the eye of the needle?" Raszer asked. "Who wins?"

Shams took two rough ceramic mugs from beneath the tripod and filled them with the black broth. He handed one to Ruthie and one to Raszer. The liquid was viscous and filmy and fermented. It smelled as old as the Mesozoic era.

"You haven't told me about the side effects yet," said Raszer.

"Put it this way," said Shams. "I'll make a whole lot more sense. Trust. Drink."

So Raszer, knowing that the price of knowledge was often at least a bellyache, drank, and at first felt only a warm throbbing in his solar plexus and an immediate cold in his extremities. Ruthie smiled, drained her cup, and laid back again.

"I made it through," said Shams. "I saw the place where everything turns inside out. Na-Koja-Abad. The landscape inverts, brother, and you're standing outside yourself, looking in. Then I got sick, truly sick—some kind of Turkish flu—and had to come back.

"But here's what I came back with; here's how the players get it wrong, how your kid wound up in federal custody and Ruthie's friends wound up dead. Every river forks, man. Everything in the universe is a fuckin' dichotomy. Nothing is one. If there ever was a One, it existed just long enough to blow the seeds off the dandelion, and all that's left is a trace of breath. Monotheism is bullshit. But they don't tell us that.

"So you're out there, your feet covered with blisters and your tongue swollen from thirst, but you don't care 'cause you've got the world inside you; you're going to God. You're on the fuckin' yellow brick road and you can see the Emerald City. And then you come to a fork. And at the fork, there's a sign that points left and right. The left arrow says PATH OF ALL, and the right one says PATH OF NOTHING, and you say, *What the fuck*?

"One last riddle to solve? *Bullshit*, you say. *You can't fool me. I know God is both all and nothing. I know God is One.* But you can't just fuckin' stand there—you have to make a choice—so you drop to your knees and pray for gnosis. You call on God, and God rises up from the rocks like a grinnin' harvest moon and his light shines down on *both roads*.

"So you smile and you're about to toss a coin, figuring it's all good, when the man in the black robe appears on the right fork and says, 'Welcome home, pilgrim.' Maybe he offers you water; maybe he's set it up so he saves your life. You look up to God for guidance but God just shines on. Because, *rafiq*, God doesn't make choices. *We do*. The Almighty doesn't care if we kill or steal. *We do*. God didn't make the rules. *We did*. So we have to choose the road that allows us to rule ourselves in God's name."

In the silence that followed, Raszer noticed that his fingertips had grown numb. The interior of the yurt seemed larger and the distance between its inhabitants greater, as if space itself had expanded. *Cures warts, my ass*, he thought. The brew was both psychoactive and mildly toxic, like all shamanic cocktails. Smoke and steam poured through the yurt's aperture, where the wind took it and exposed clear black sky and the three stars on Orion's belt. Raszer felt faintly nauseous and laid back on a cushion to regain his equilibrium. The stars were rushing away, and the fire was not enough to warm him.

Go with it, he reminded himself, as he always had to.

"Does anybody ever choose the other road?" asked Ruthie, from a distance.

"Sure, they do, sweetheart," answered Shams. "But only if they've been oriented to it. Only if they know that in this world, there really is a choice."

"What about you, Shams?" Raszer asked. "What was your choice?"

"Like I said, man, I got sick. I turned back. I don't flatter myself, though."

"And the players who take the left fork . . . what happens to them?"

"They transcend the game, man. They become a sort of Gauntlet VFW. They call themselves the Fedeli d'Amore. They guard the path, offer the pilgrims comfort. But they don't tell you what to do, and once you've passed, you're on your own."

"You said you came down with a *Turkish* flu," said Raszer. "Does that mean—"

"There's more than one path in more than one country," said Shams, "but I'm betting the Urfa route through southern Turkey's the one you want. There's a pilgrims' hostel in Harran—south of Sanliurfa, where Abraham lived and Jesus preached. That's the part of Turkey that's more Syrian than Turkish and more Kurdish than Syrian. The trekkers have passed through there for years. It used to be run by the Franciscans. Now it's all Gauntlet vets—the Fedeli. If anybody's got a treasure map, they do. They run it like a wilderness outfitter—but that's just the front. You gotta ask the right questions."

"Such as?" Raszer queried.

"What is expected of me?" Shams replied. "Or try this ditty: *Do you know the way to El Mirai*?" He sang it à la Dionne Warwick.

"El Mirai?"

"I'm guessing that's where you'll find her. I can't say more."

"Why's that?" Raszer asked.

"Words fail here, brother. Action speaks. But if you want to get in the game . . . "

"Right," said Raszer. "I think I understand. But tell me this . . . "

Raszer was now fully supine, as were Shams and Ruthie. Splayed out around the hearth. The broth had leveled them. The effect, it seemed to Raszer, was a little like that of *Salvia divinorum*: mind receptive, reeling; body in a state of near paralysis.

" . . . The man on the right fork," Raszer continued, more aware of his tongue than usual. "What does he offer?"

"Perfect order in exchange for perfect chaos," said Shams, chuckling darkly.

"And what's the price of his goods?"

"I'll tell you what the fuckin' price is," said Ruthie, up on an elbow. "Something nobody should ever have to pay. One day, just before I got my ass hauled back to Taos for good, Henry asks me to take a walk in the canyon, back there behind Johnny's trailer. By this time, me 'n Henry had been together for a while and, far as I know, Johnny was doin' some mindfuck on my kid sister while he banged that bitch-whore Layla. Henry'd been sick for a few days. Just disappeared somewhere, but it wasn't the first time, so I let it go. But now he's actin' even weirder than usual and walkin' like a cripple, so I ask him what's wrong.

"He says he wants to tell me, but he's afraid I'll reject him. I told him I'd never do that. So he says these goons came to him and Johnny after they found out that Johnny raked a little extra for himself on that gun deal. They're like, 'How can we trust you guys for the big jobs? If you can cheat us, you can cheat the Old Man. It happens again, we'll put ferrets up your ass and let them eat their way out through your intestines.'

"So now they want a show of loyalty. Something precious, they say, 'so we can assure the Old Man you're *fid-ah-ee*.' *Fidai*—that's what they called themselves. Johnny says whaddayou want, and they say they want *me* to be one of their export whores. Johnny turns to Henry and Henry says, 'Fuck no' and Johnny says, 'No fuckin' way.' They put Johnny against the wall, and they're all methed up, 'n they say, '*Okay,* rafiq, *we'll take your eye, then. No one reaches El Mirai without sacrifice.*' And they put a knife to Johnny's eye and they're gonna do it . . . except that Henry yells, 'No. I'll give you what you want. Make me a servant of the master. Make me a virgin.'

"And they heated the knife with a blowtorch and tied him down on the rocks behind the trailer and did it right there. They castrated him and burned the wound shut and gave him his balls in a velvet sack. Henry loved me that much, he loved Johnny that much, and Johnny saw it go down and it tore him up for weeks, and that was when he decided they wouldn't get what they *really* wanted: my virgin sister. But they did, didn't they?"

"Christ," Raszer muttered.

"Harsh," said Shams. "That boy didn't need balls. He had heart."

"So Aquino was wrong," Raszer thought out loud. "It didn't happen in Iraq. It happened here." He rolled onto his side and looked at Ruthie through the smoke. "What did Henry mean, 'Make me a servant of the master'?"

"Some of the Witness honchos—the top guys, the anointed ones—they have themselves fixed. They call it becoming a servant of the master. It's a big secret, like everything else about the JWs. Henry used to talk about doing it. He said it'd free his mind. That church got inside him more than he knew—it gets inside of everybody."

"Some men make eunuchs of themselves," said Raszer, quoting scripture.

"What's that?" said Ruthie.

"I guess this accounts for Amos Leach," Raszer mused.

"That creep," Ruthie spat. "He screwed up Henry good. Emmett Parrish, too. Henry never squealed, but the theocratic council finally had Amos fixed to stop it."

Raszer turned toward his host's shadowed face. "Something here doesn't square, Shams. These assassins . . . the 'Old Man' . . . your guy in the black robe. From the MO, you'd think we were looking at a revival of the old Ismaili cult. But the Ismailis weren't thugs. Even the crusaders praised their integrity. The Templars adopted parts of their doctrine. When they struck, they killed, and always for strategic purpose. They didn't torture, they didn't recruit outside the faith, and they didn't kidnap kids."

"Just because it calls itself a duck," said Shams quietly, "doesn't mean it is, right? You gotta listen for the quack. The 'Christian Coalition' isn't really so Christian, is it?

"Like I said, every river forks. Whatever's left of the true Ismailis, they're in India, or burrowed in with the Sufis or the Druze or the Yezidis. But there's always the diseased offshoot that gets left behind for dead in the wasteland. One day, a little rain falls, and the shoot digs roots and buds. Often as not, my brother, it's the bastard who claims the crown . . . and the family name."

"So we're dealing with an Islamic fraud," said Raszer.

"We're dealing with the right fork," said Shams, rising to a squat. "Be it Islamic or Christian or whatever. But you need to think on this before you jump in. Let that brew seep in." He moved to the fire and took a bundle of sage and local herbs, tied with hemp, from a sack hanging from the tripod.

"Drift for a while," he whispered. "Drift . . . " Shams waved the little sachet over the coals until it caught fire, then blew it to hot ash, sending the aromatic smoke in their direction. "*La ilaha illa Allah . . . La ilaha illa Allah . . .* " he chanted, his voice growing more distant with each recitation of the Shahadah. He stood and walked the perimeter of the yurt on his tiptoes, fanning the sage. To the right . . . to the left . . . to the right . . . to the left.

Very soon, he was seen no more.

"Ruthie?" Raszer heard himself say. Had he said it in a dream? He saw the prone form of a woman against a red background and geometrical designs, but could not seem to bring her into focus. There was smoke in the air. Or was it just the narcotic fog of sleep? The wind made assault after assault on the yurt's felt walls, but what yields will not fall.

I am safe in here, he thought.

He looked down at his body and it was small, tapered. The air around him was grainy. His jaw was sore.

At the clucking of a hen, he looked right, and there was Shams, three feet in the air, the Mongolian shepherd's cap pulled down over his eyes. A dog growled, and there again was Shams, spread-eagled against the vaulting canvas roof, his arms in cruciform, his eyes rolled back to the whites.

A small bell rang, and Shams sat against the upright on the opposite side of the yurt, tossing a pomegranate in the air. Raszer felt sure that Shams was in all three places at once, but because he could not see all three places at once, his certitude turned to anxiety. His eyes began to burn, then his lungs, and a moment later, he realized that the yurt was on fire.

"Ruthie!" he called again, much louder. "Shams!"

A clawlike hand gripped his shoulder. Raszer wheeled around and staggered. "Shams?" The round head was hairless on top without its cap. Shams pushed him to the floor and said, "Down, brother, down. The Devil's at play."

Ruthie fumbled with the yurt's door, in a panic made clumsy by sleep and sorcery. Shams reached up and grabbed her by the hair, pulling her into their huddle on the floor. "Don't you dare, precious," he said. "Don't let in what's out there." He motioned toward the heavens. The fire was burning from the roof down. He sniffed and scowled. "Must be ethyl alcohol," he said. "Nothing else would light up that canvas. Mother*fuckers!*"

"You got a gun, Shams?" Raszer asked.

"Keep a .22 under the floor," Shams replied, "for the occasional rabbit stew. But I've got better. Follow the leader."

Like a salamander, he slithered across the floor without lifting his belly more than an inch, rolled back the corners of six carpets one by one, released a catch, and slid open a three-foot square hatch. It opened so quietly, Raszer thought, that it must be on greased bearings. Shams turned, hailed them over, and then, laying a finger aside his nose like Clement C. Moore's Saint Nick, disappeared down the hole headfirst.

The crawl space beneath the yurt's plank floor was far larger than was to be expected, as Shams had scooped out a ton of earth, right down to bedrock, and fortified the crumbling clay walls with one-by-six planks. A ten-year-old could have stood upright, and Shams wasn't a great deal bigger than that. He'd installed ceramic drains for the rainy season and cut peepholes into the platform, offering a wraparound view at ground level. Most critically, he'd created an emergency exit, and Raszer now saw why nearly sixty degrees of the yurt's shell was flush with the concave rock face outside.

"The Army taught you well," he whispered to Shams.

"Hell," said Shams. "The Army taught me shit. I learned this from the Bedouin. They're always squirreling stuff away. There's a glacier split in the rock, a tunnel that runs about forty feet in and then opens into a crevasse. If we're quick, we can get up on top before they know we've left the building." He grabbed his .22 from where it sat propped against the wall and turned to Ruthie. "Your new friend brings a lot of heat, princess." He tore off the burlap curtain covering the tunnel and motioned her in. "Ladies first. We'll be right behind."

No sooner had she slipped in than there were boots hammering the floor above. Two sets of boots, as far as Raszer could tell: one heavier, one lighter. Shams urged him into the tunnel, but Raszer signaled a moment's pause. Just ten inches from his nose there was an eighth-of-an-inch gap between two of Shams' floorboards, a place the rugs didn't quite cover. Through it, he could see that the fire had now burned halfway down the cylindrical walls of the yurt. The arsonists did not speak, but Raszer could see dark forms moving about in the dull glow above. He caught a bit of a torso, and the stock of an automatic weapon, then a tantalizing glimpse of a stocking-covered face.

One of them squatted down and ran his fingers over the floorboards, obscuring Raszer's view.

They hadn't yet discovered the trap door. Only a matter of seconds. He felt Shams tug at his sleeve. *Just give me one look*, Raszer thought. The shape of a chin, the outline of a nose: anything I can log into memory. Acrid smoke entered his lungs and he suppressed a cough. The fingers retreated, leaving his view unobstructed for just long enough to see the veiled eye of the assassin coming down to the crack, and for a few moments, they were eyeball to eyeball and equally blind. Then he received communion, from the intruder's mouth to his.

Wintergreen.

The scent of the aromatic oil overpowered most—but not all—others. The mouth held a tongue and the tongue held its own bouquet, and the bouquet recalled flavors he'd had in his own mouth only days before. At that instant, scent congealed into certainty. The Syrian girl had become his pursuer. He hadn't wanted to believe it, had hoped that she could be turned and might lead him to the center of the maze. He put his hand to the crack, pivoted, and followed Shams into the tunnel.

On top of the rock, thirty feet above, they hunkered down and watched the arsonists creep away from the smoldering yurt and disappear over a ridge. Raszer kept the rifle's sight trained on their backs. When they were gone, Shams turned to Raszer and said, "You sure you want to run The Gauntlet, man?"

Raszer nodded. "Forgone conclusion, I'm afraid," he said.

"I'll make arrangements, then. You just follow them. Allah be praised."

TWENTY-ONE

"HE TOOK THAT pretty well," said Raszer, then let the scalding coffee poach his lips for a second. "I wouldn't be so cool if somebody'd just burned down my house."

"Maybe that's why he lives in yurts," Ruthie offered. "Shams doesn't like to get attached. He'll hole up in town for a couple days and then build another one."

It was two in the morning, and cold. They were parked in a gravel lot outside an all-night Internet café called Nocturno, out on the north edge of town, beyond the Pueblo. Its proprietor was a lanky Tiwa half-breed called Lon who seemed to know Shams pretty well, and its denizens were a motley collection of local insomniacs. Shams had asked to be taken there so that he could "put out some code" and "call in the 82nd Airborne," both of which Raszer took as cryptic references to whatever it was that would pave his own way into The Gauntlet as a player on the Urfa route.

When Raszer had queried him on it, Shams had replied, "Don't ask, don't tell. That much, the Army *did* teach me."

Today was Good Friday, the beginning of the Easter vigil. One way or another, Raszer intended to be on a plane by Saturday morning. The fact that he didn't yet have tickets purchased or a specific route mapped out was peculiar to his way of doing things: He could move only as quickly as his knowledge allowed, and knowledge had a way of trickling in like a slowly thawing creek.

He knew now that he was bound for southeastern Turkey, possibly by way of Istanbul, possibly via Athens. Monica had various contingency plans in place, reservations held, outfitters and guide services contacted, but all of it might have to go by the boards, depending on what Shams came back with.

"Well," said Raszer, "I expect he'll be here for a while. I should make a report. Although I'd hate to see the cops go rushing out after these guys with guns blazing."

"Wouldn't you like to see them dead?" Ruthie asked.

"Not yet," said Raszer. "Sometimes the man on your tail ends up being your guide. If you eliminate him, you've got no scent."

"Do you think they wanted to kill us . . . or just scare you off?"

"I think," Raszer said, "they wanted to terrorize us. The word *does* mean something. They won't want to kill me until they figure out what I know, and who I might've told. What do you want to do, Ruthie? You look like you need sleep."

"*Want* to and *have* to are two diff'rent things," she replied. "I *want* to go to the Alley Cantina and do about six tequila shooters. I *have* to go home and help Angel prepare for his big day as Jesus. I promised my mother. They come for him before sunrise. You know the story: Judas and the kiss and all that. We have to witness, my mother 'n me. We have to pray with him. It sucks, but it's the least I can do for her. We're the two Marys, the mother and the whore. Shit. I'm really not down for this."

"Okay," said Raszer, turning on the ignition. "I'll take you home, and then I'll swing back here to see if Shams needs a lift. Where will he sleep?"

"Prob'ly at the Pueblo. At Lon's place. Shams is one of those people who finds a bed wherever he is. That's how he made it for three years over there."

Raszer aimed a finger at the dusty front window of the Internet café. "Is this where you picked up your emails from Henry?" he asked.

"Yeah."

"Does the FBI know that?"

"Yeah, but like I said, it didn't get them anywhere."

"Hmm," said Raszer. "That was then, this is now. Anyway, why don't you run in there and tell Shams I'm taking you home? And tell him he can crash in my room at the inn if he needs a place."

Ruthie hopped out of the Jeep and strode into the café. Raszer blinked, because he saw an afterimage of her movement trailing through the night air. The effect of Shams' brew was still with him. *Oh, yes, time can be slowed.* He watched as she made small talk with Lon, poured herself a cup of black coffee, and flirted with the local boys. She seemed in no hurry, but neither was Raszer. Finally, she approached Shams and jingled the bell on the tassel of his cap. He put an arm around her waist and with his free hand scribbled out a note. He handed it to her and said something that made her frown. She stepped back and shook her head, then leaned in to hug him.

A minute later, she was back in the Jeep, handing Raszer the note.

"Bad news?" Raszer asked.

Ruthie stared stiffly out through the windshield.

"He said there's no way I can come with you," she said in monotone.

"He's right," said Raszer. "Nobody's paying *you* to risk losing your tongue."

"It's *my* little sister they took. And *my* man they murdered."

"And all that would just get in the way," Raszer said softly.

She lit one of his cigarettes and shook out the match. "Whether you knew it or not, mister, when you came through Taos, you came to pick me up. Now take me home, would you?"

"Sure," said Raszer, dropping the gearshift into reverse. Before backing out, he paused to open the note from Shams.

Be on the bridge over the Rio Grande gorge at sunrise on Easter Sunday. Don't ask. Just trust the Game. Remember—Harran. The Fedeli d'Amore. El Mirai. Tell them Shams sent you.

Raszer gazed through the dust-flocked window of Nocturno at the elfin survivor seated at a lamplit terminal in the rear, typing in his "code" with two stubby fingers. When Shams looked up, Raszer nodded, and Shams returned the nod. The look in his eyes said, *Vaya con Dios*; it gave Raszer a pang. After that, Shams continued hammering away at the keyboard, sending out signals to the 82nd Airborne.

✦ ✦ ✦

"ALL RIGHT, RUTHIE," said Raszer, pulling to a stop in front of the trailer park's gate. The sun was still moribund. She had only a few hours to sleep, and so did he. "You've been delivered. Be a comfort to Angel. It can't be easy going on the cross. And thanks for everything you've given me. I *will* bring your sister home."

"You haven't seen the last of me," she said.

Raszer held her stare for a moment, and then said: "No. I don't expect I have."

"My old man was wrong about most things, but he was right about one of 'em: If I'd let Katy be—if I'd never shown her my side of the street—she'd still be safe in Azusa. She'd still be in the Little Flock. Bound for heaven."

"Don't damn yourself too quickly."

"Oh, I'm damned, all right," Ruthie replied. "That's already settled. But I plan on makin' the most of it."

"Why do you think Emmett Parrish called Katy 'the last pure thing'?"

"For one thing 'cause he was nuts about her. For another, 'cause she was. Even when she was bad she was good. Hell, she might be the only thing *worth* rescuing."

Raszer reached across her lap and opened the door for her. "You'd better get in there," he said. "It'll be sunrise before you know it." He paused. "I'm going to do some climbing in those foothills in a few hours. What are the chances I could get within observing distance of the ceremony?"

"You could," she said, "if you know where it's at. They keep it a secret until they leave the *morada*. That's the little adobe chapel at the end of Pima Road. The procession goes there. We—the women, that is—stay outside while they beat themselves bloody. Then the *hermano mayor*—the top dog—he whispers something to one of the old women. We walk alongside the men for a while; then we break off 'n hike for, like, ten fuckin' miles into the mountains till we get to a place—usually a cliff or bluff or something—that overlooks the hill, Calvary, where it all goes down."

"You know, Ruthie," Raszer said. "I've got a feeling about you."

"Yeah? What's that?"

"I've got a feeling that you know in your soul that whatever it is that makes people believe that much—enough to beat themselves, enough to lose a piece of themselves for you—it's not just mumbo-jumbo. It's passion. You just forgot how to believe, because believing meant swallowing your father's creed or your mother's passivity, and you didn't like the taste of either one."

"Well, I dunno," she said, and hopped down from the front seat. She closed the door softly, then leaned back in for just a moment. "But I'm starting to believe you."

"Good," Raszer said. "Now go inside the trailer and fetch me Henry's rock."

⬩◆⬩

WHEN RASZER STOPPED BY Nocturno on his way back to the inn, Shams was gone, and Lon, the owner, claimed not to know where.

"He does that," Lon said. "Just goes. Sometimes I think he's fucking with my head. Shams is only half flesh and bone, you know. The rest of it, he left over there in the desert. Tonight he said he was going out to smoke a bowl. Never came back."

"Ruthie said he might be crashing at your place tonight," said Raszer. "Any chance he'll show up there?"

"You never know with Shams," said Lon. "But my door's always open."

"Well, anyhow," said Raszer, scribbling down the name of the inn. "If he comes back, would you give him this and tell him he can reach me there?"

Lon, who had the immovable, stone-set face typical of his people, glanced at the note.

"You're the PI, right? The tracker. Looking for Ruthie's sister."

"That's me," said Raszer.

"My father was a tracker," said the Indian. "Piece of advice?"

Raszer nodded. "Always."

"Out in the world, the scent of prey is everywhere. It smells like fear. But the scent of a predator, that's different. The scent of a predator is no scent at all, unless it's somethin' to cover up the blood in his mouth."

"Thanks for the tip," said Raszer. He indicated the computers. "And for these."

Lon chuckled. "I hope you have better luck than that FBI guy."

⬩ ◆ ⬩

AFTER THREE HOURS of sleep at the inn, Raszer was in the front range of the Sangre de Cristo Mountains, free-climbing the face of a thirty-foot boulder. The sun was still low in the eastern sky, resting lollipop orange on the hills above Chimayo, and the air was cool and electric. He'd brought a pack with his rock shoes and the essential climbing gear—harness, rope, carabiners, cams, and stoppers—but the sight of the boulder with its fissures etched by the morning sun made him abandon everything but the shoes and go with feet and fingers.

Now, at twenty feet, he'd run out of cracks.

Stupid, he thought, looking down at where the skin of the rock curved away and left empty space. *All I need to do is turn my ankle again and screw things up right.*

Raszer had begun two of his last three jobs limping. People like Hildegarde, his analyst, kidded him that it was to remind him of his mortality, to keep him from leaping thoughtlessly into the flames. He'd dragged his bad ankle across the Australian outback and into the deserts of Morocco, and it had, arguably, slowed him down just enough to keep him alive. Still, he had no desire to take it into Turkey, and the prospect instilled enough caution to make him reconsider the rock face four inches from his nose.

He turned his cheek into the stone, breathed, and allowed the climber's panic to run its course. The rock came into sharp focus, he found a divet with his left toe, and he powered up the remaining ten feet to the top.

For the next four hours, he did more of the same, ascending roughly a hundred feet into the front range with each climb. He found, without much surprise, his flesh willing but his spirit weak. This disparity, he supposed, would color the whole assignment. He was doing it partly on his own dime, for a dead client and a furtive group of Elders whose reasons for wanting their stray back were dubious at best. He knew less about his destination than he had on any prior job.

The risks to life and limb seemed substantial, and he had a bad feeling about the project. The overriding factors were pride and desire, desire that had now been fanned by Shams' description of a place where—as he'd put it—the world turned inside out. Desire to reveal a bit more of the holy iceberg.

Raszer worked himself gradually west throughout the morning, toward the cow path that eventually became Pima Road, location of the *morada*, the starting point of the Good Friday rites of the *hermanos penitentes*. On some stark ridge north of there, there would be a crucifixion, and Raszer wanted to see it. He'd brought his binoculars and enough water to stave off the effects of the midday sun, and hoped to find a perch overlooking Calvary. He didn't truly expect darkness at noon. But such ceremonies surely sent a kind of semaphore to God, and Raszer's vocational curiosity demanded that whenever such a signal was sent, he be there to see if God answered.

At eleven fourteen, he came over a ridge and saw the procession leaving the *morada*, with the women at a safe distance. Their numbers were smaller than Ruthie had suggested. Sign of the times. Some were stripped down to shorts made of a rough fabric, and flogged themselves as they marched while singing a hymn that was as raw and spiky as the chaparral they traversed. The words were unintelligible, but the tune had the keen edges and plaintive leaps of a Moorish dirge.

Above it all was the screech of the tin flute, playing an accompaniment that was less complement than commentary. The flute, Raszer supposed, stood in for the sounds of women mourning the death of a god. Other men, younger, wore blue jeans and T-shirts: the more recent initiates who hadn't yet earned the privilege of pain. Four of them carried the upright post of the cross, and Angel—as Jesus—bore the crosspiece on his shoulders. When he stumbled—as he did twice on his way up the steep path—his knees came crashing to the rocks, and he was beaten by the men portraying centurions until he staggered to his feet. It was theater, but it was theater that sought the purest catharsis. If it had a color, the color was purple.

Raszer picked out Ruthie with his binoculars, but it was yet another version of her, this one with long black hair to match that of the young Latinas in her company. How many wigs she had, and how she paid for them, were questions for which Raszer conceded he might never get answers. Why she had them was becoming easier to guess. Ruthie was trying to find a me she liked better than the one she'd been born with.

There were nineteen women, all walking a rough trail through yucca and creosote. Ruthie walked with her spine straight in spite of the steep incline, and had an arm wrapped around her mother's waist. She looked as proud and pious as the other women. Almost exemplary. The loose, gauzy skirt she wore draped her lower half in a way that was both devotional and provocative. She was the Magdalene, complete with earthenware jar of balm. Raszer found this Ruthie the most intriguing one yet.

The women arrived at the overlook and took their places along the rocky wall like soldiers on a parapet, while the men descended into the canyon, singing their grim *alabados*, marking time with the stroke of stalk against torn skin. From a distance too great to see blood or feel empathy, their procession was as fiercely erotic as an El Greco canvas, but eroticism is what distance from violence allows.

Raszer saw Ruthie brace her left arm on a boulder and lean hard into the canyon, shading her eyes from the midday glare of the sun. She turned abruptly to her mother and shouted something urgently. Then she pivoted about and, for a few moments, scanned the massive slope behind her. Raszer knew she was looking for him. One by one, the older women fell to their knees and crossed themselves, followed by the younger ones. Only Ruthie remained standing, and suddenly she bolted, following the men down into the arroyo.

Raszer began to run, too, and his heart was again in his throat. He swung wide of the women, to the side of the overlook opposite Ruthie, where a steep trail spilled rock debris down the walls of the canyon. The far side of the chasm rose in steppes, one of them a small butte of soft stone, pink as flesh. On the butte, a stake had been erected, and on the stake hung a naked man, his bearded chin fallen to his chest, his bald head crisscrossed with lacerations. Ruthie raced ahead of the men, who had slowed their pace to gape at the sight. When she was within thirty feet, she began to scream.

"Shaaaaaams! Shaaaaams!"

Raszer scrambled down the nearly vertical rockfall, tumbling twice and tearing open the skin on his wrist and elbow. He raced the perimeter of the butte to the only clear path up, the path that Ruthie had taken, and the closer he got, the more wind was pulled from his lungs.

Ruthie tried frantically to shinny and claw her way up, to reach her friend's feet, as if she imagined she might pull the nail from his flesh and set him free. By the time Raszer reached her side, her hands and bare feet were full of splinters, but she would not stop climbing, and she would not stop screaming.

They had crucified him on a *stauros*, a single, massive upright at least fourteen feet high, and Ruthie must have known they'd done it for her sake. This was the way the Witnesses claimed it had been done to Jesus. There was no true cross, only this profane axle joining heaven and hell. Shams' arms had been extended above his head, his wrists bound to the stake, and the rope looped around his neck so that when he tired, strangulation would follow. A single spike had been driven through his feet. The high sun and the wind's hot breath had already dried the river of blood that had coursed down his thighs from the wound left when they'd cut off his genitals.

Raszer pulled Ruthie down into his arms and collapsed to the pink dust, crushing her into a fetal ball, rolling her to and fro. When the screaming stopped, she began to moan, and he moaned with her. He said nothing. Nothing would have done.

The *hermanos* slowly gathered round, hands clasped in front, eyes down. Angel had been relieved of his cross and came forward, falling to his knees, still carrying a whisper of the song on his breath. He looked up, then at Raszer and Ruthie, and reached his hand forward to touch her trembling shoulder.

Raszer nodded to Angel and said quietly, "Her friend. A good friend." Then, just as quietly, he cursed. Nothing ever changed. Herod and Pilate still ran the show.

"*¿Porque, amigo?*" Angel asked. "*¿Porque?*"

"*No se*," Raszer said. "*No se.*"

After a few minutes, Ruthie's mother arrived and knelt at Ruthie's side, and Raszer gingerly handed the girl over.

"Who did this?" asked Constance Endicott, her throat tight with fear.

Raszer thought he had better not answer. Instead, he stumbled to his feet, opened his pack, and hammered a piton into the stake at a height of about three feet. He took a step up and pounded in another one, and that brought his shoulders to the level of Shams' head. He took the rope from around his neck, and as Shams' jaw slackened slightly, Raszer noticed that a small paper scroll had been inserted into his mouth. Upon removal, it appeared to be a plain white business envelope, sealed with an extravagant amount of old-fashioned, red sealing wax.

On closer inspection, Raszer discovered embedded in the glob of wax the severed front half of Shams' tongue.

A cloud passed over the sun, and the butte fell into shadow. Over the crest of the front range was the faintest purple penumbra: an approaching spring cloudburst. As the ropes binding his wrists fell away, Shams' arms dropped, but slowly, like a bird folding its wings. With the envelope in his hand and Shams' torso laid over his right shoulder, Raszer carefully descended and laid the corpse on the soft rock. He stripped off his topshirt and laid it over Shams' midsection, covering the wound. He did not want anyone but the coroner to see that the killers—in the fashion of barbarians from time immemorial—had stuffed the severed organs into the hole.

As if they had been rehearsing it for centuries, the women set about tending to the body. From the top of the butte, there was an unimpeded view of Pima Road and two other fire roads ascending the range from the southeast. Dust rose in small cyclones from all three roads, and from the dust emerged three long black cars.

Raszer registered each car, then dropped his gaze and carefully peeled open the envelope, working his fingers around Shams' tongue. The note was written in Arabic, and it took Raszer three or four readings before he had it.

The man who plays at both sides in the same game

defeats only himself. This is the end to which all

duplicity leads. Fear the name with two faces.

It was a warning, of course—but one he wouldn't heed. Raszer took one more look at Shams and realized that he no longer felt for him the thing known as pity—only a kind of kinship.

So be it.

That meant he was ready for them. The protagonists of ancient myth sometimes seemed absent of feelings. He thought it more likely that they allowed themselves to feel only what they could afford to feel.

TWENTY-TWO

WHEN IT WAS ALL OVER, when all procedures had been attended to, all reports filed, and the body of Shams of Taos lay still and cold in the mortuary, Raszer returned to his room to pack his bag. The day had turned overcast and gusty, and as it dropped into evening, cold enough to light a small fire in the kiva. He wanted a drink—the only outward sign that he was unsettled—but denied himself that anesthesia, knowing he had one more New Mexican night to get through on his wits before departure.

Departure for where, exactly, and by what mode of travel were undetermined. He'd counted on one last dispatch from Shams. All he had was a direction to show up before sunrise at the Rio Grande Gorge—like being told to go to the Sonoran desert and wait for the saucers. It was so murky that he could not even bring himself to brief Monica. She'd immediately suspect a set-up and make him question his instinct, which was that he should be there, no matter what.

The local cops were out chasing banshees in black limos, and had by now undoubtedly called in the state police and the FBI. Raszer wasn't expecting any arrests. The killers weren't out cruising old Route 66, waiting to be caught in the snares of an APB. It was beginning to seem as if they could materialize anywhere at any time. As if their black wings were beating the still air in a dead space between two worlds.

Shams' death, like Harry Wolfe's, was on him. It had already begun to merge with the larger stain on his soul, the one that spread like red wine on a tablecloth—a disease of his psychic skin. He was going to have a lot to answer for when he faced his maker, but the more pressing question was what he'd have to show. Was the world safer for these deaths? Were the spiritual predators and soul thieves any less likely to prey? It wouldn't do to agonize. That was what they wanted.

The Devil's goal was to make sure that you thought of no one else but him. Jealous, like a lover. Soul by soul, the ancient, protective magic was being snuffed out in the world by the ardor of evil.

It was impossible to know what sort of information they might have extracted from Shams under torture, but Raszer guessed they had gotten an earful of artful bullshit and nothing more. Shams had been a soldier long before and long after his tours of duty. And, as the old Indian had said, he'd left his body behind. The thing to do now was to follow his ghost, and that meant following his directions.

Finding Ruthie, and finding an ally in Shams, had briefly reignited Raszer's passion for the mission. That fire, and its warmth, were gone now. Ruthie had gone back to the trailer with her mother, pale and voiceless, too shaken to say goodbye. He reminded himself as he stuffed the last article into his pack that the surest sign that the endgame had commenced was that comfort had fled. A certain chill made itself felt, and a loss of equilibrium that he felt in his gut and associated with going too high on the swing set as a child. Colors bled from the world. It was the sensory experience of an animal.

All of his provisions went into a collapsible mountain pack with a light aluminum frame. It could be carried like a duffel or worn like a trekker's backpack. He carried three full changes of clothing and the standard survival gear for an extended pack-in to a wilderness area. Along with these, Raszer had his climbing kit; his combat knife; the gunmetal case containing his paralytic darts; a store of antibiotics and disinfectants; ephedra for staving off sleep and keeping his head clear; a selection of garden-grown herbs for teas, unguents, and purgatives; and numerous sources of instant protein. The only electronics he carried—aside from the tracer chip—was a wireless device dubbed the Ionophone, custom-designed by a spyware company in Copenhagen. It served as cell phone, web terminal, camera, GPS mapper, and general lifeline. This, however, would be left behind at some point, because what oriented him also exposed him.

Raszer dropped off the Jeep at the Enterprise lot in Taos, leaving the keys and a note on the front seat, and hired an all-night taxi service to take him to the Rio Grande Gorge. It didn't take the look on the driver's face to tell Raszer it was an odd destination: Who but a suicide plotter heads to a four-hundred-foot gorge in the last bleak hour of night? Raszer had set off for stranger places, but never with so little orientation.

It was predawn when he pulled his pack from the taxi. They were on the bridge that spanned the gorge, and the dark gave no hint of the vastness of the place. Only the wind, roaring down the great gash of the Continental Divide, informed him that he was in the midst of something biblically large. The wind masked even the rumble of rushing water five hundred feet below. It tore at the skirts of his duster and lifted his close-cropped hair. It filled his ears with the seashell sound of a limitless ocean and chilled him to the bone. He was on top of the world, on a suspension bridge, and he was alone with the alone.

This is it, Raszer, he said to himself, and laughed darkly. *This is what you live for*. It occurred to him that he might actually be some sort of exotic idiot. Who the hell lives for the frisson of holy terror?

The feeling was on him as soon as the taxi's taillights had vanished. Vertigo, body and soul. Exacerbated by the darkness and the ever-shifting wind. He couldn't find his center, and he dropped to his knees, fearing that otherwise he might get sucked over the rail. It was low here, a perfect place for jumpers. The desert West was proceed-at-your-own-risk country. It swallowed up victims without offering so much as a burp.

In his mind's eye, Raszer saw Shams on the stake and instinctively reached for his own groin. *My cross will come*, he thought. *I won't come out whole*. He crouched, clutching his belly like a World War I grunt on the Marne with a bayonet wound in his gut. He heard Ruthie screaming in the back of his head and took another hit. *Not so tough, are you, Raszer? Not so intrepid. The world at its blackest is a shade too black for you. Evil takes great pains to keep up with the times, while good recedes into a paradisiacal past. Can't go back. Can only go on to the end, and hope that the end is also a better beginning. C'mon*, he whispered to the wind. *Amaze me. Show me something I haven't seen before.*

The wind began to have a pulse, the cyclical throb of a truck engine laboring to turn over after weeks of subzero. He saw the pulse as well as felt it: As first light broke over the eastern foothills, he perceived the wind and the mineral grit it carried as incandescent and wavelike, as if the giant trough of the Rio Grande Gorge had filled with a primeval ocean of dust and he was about to drown. Wave after wave hit him, and it was all he could do to pull himself upright to the rail. The pulse grew more rapid, ricocheting off the canyon walls, deafening, and then suddenly the surging stopped. A curtain of sunlit dust hung across the gorge like a veil, and through it he saw a moving form: a black, avian form coming toward him with its talons extended.

The skin of the helicopter was as black and sleek as a licorice jellybean, its hull as broad as a small gunship. It was clearly of military origin, but had been stripped of any sort of emblem or identifying mark. It was a transport chopper, but hardly utilitarian in design. It had the look of an exotic prototype, probably commissioned by the Pentagon for a few hundred million and then pawned off on the private sector. It was also a right-wing paranoid's nightmare, down to the dreadlocked pilot with the toffee skin and oversize sunglasses, who set the ship down on the bridge so gently that the resulting *thump* felt like a giant cat's paw.

The passenger side of the bubble slipped open silently; the pilot turned and spread his lips to flash a wide, brilliant smile.

Raszer lifted his pack and walked slowly toward the chopper, one fingertip skimming the railing. The giant propeller thrummed its oscillating, dragonfly tremolo, beating the still air into sun-gilded froth. The pilot kept on beaming. Was it a welcoming smile or a *we got you, fucker* smile? No way to tell, not even with his antennae up. No frame of reference for something this bizarre. Here was the black chariot, comin' for to carry him home.

Inside his skull, the land around him unrolled, its features flattening into shapes on a gameboard. And it hit him that from this moment on, he *was* in the game, and that this was the only way to gauge things. In the game, he would, of course, step into the black helicopter.

Shams had made it so.

It was written.

It was a game but not a game. Just the sort of cognitive displacement the architects of alternate reality gaming had aimed for. A mindfuck. And the only way to play it was to leave himself behind. If he thought about what else he might be leaving—if he thought about his daughter, or Monica, or Ruthie—he would not be able to play. And so he put them all off the gameboard and proceeded alone.

The pilot rose to help Raszer stow the heavy pack in the rear. Then he took his seat, motioned for Raszer to buckle up, and prepared to ascend. He wore a white cotton shirt and shorts, and sandals. He looked like Ziggy Marley at twenty-four. How he'd come to fly a bird like this was anybody's guess. There was no sign of a weapon, but the instrument panel gave evidence of military application. After a few minutes, the radio crackled into life, but the pilot squelched the signal and moved instead to slip in a John Coltrane CD. They flew straight up the gorge, skirting the pink canyon walls, riding so low that the runners occasionally sliced through the crest of the Rio Grande's waves.

In a manner of speaking, they had already entered another country.

They were headed north into Colorado. A private airfield was Raszer's guess, but who knew? He didn't ask the pilot; he offered only the opinion that Coltrane's modal soprano sax and flying went well together.

"Nothin' like the 'Trane to put ya head up in the air," the pilot agreed. It occurred to Raszer that the pilot might be good and stoned, an impression reinforced by the faint perfume of hashish in the cabin.

Raszer recalled The Gauntlet's initiatory greeting, and inquired of his pilot whether he knew of anyone who could make use of "a keen mind and a steady heart."

"Matter of fact, now," the pilot replied, grinning, "I do."

When the southern Rockies appeared, they were like a levee of stone scooped into place by giant hands, a massive dike to hold back the inland sea. There was snow on the peaks, but not much. It had been dry again this year. After another twenty minutes or so, the pilot turned to Raszer and said, "Almost home."

Raszer looked at the pilot and asked simply, "Will I be with friends?"

The pilot lowered his glasses. "Unless I'm mistaken," he replied. "You're not here to make friends." He grinned. "But you might find some along the way."

"Did you know Shams?"

"Ev'rybody who was in Babylon knew Shams," the pilot answered. "Or knew about him. Nobody ever went native like Shams. Shit, you could put me down naked with my ancestors' people in Ghana, and I couldn't go as native as that motherfucker. Some guys just got to see it from the other side. He hated what we were doin' over there, but there wasn't anybody you'd rather be next to when the bullets flew."

"I would've guessed that," said Raszer.

"Hang on," said the pilot. "I'm takin' you down."

Raszer took one look outside the bubble and felt his pulse rise. In the space of their brief conversation, the chopper had descended dramatically, and the serrated edges of at least a dozen peaks were within shaving distance of the runners. How that had happened, he couldn't guess. "Down where?" Raszer asked, seeing only steep runs caked with hard, perennial snow. "Are we going to slalom into the airfield?"

The pilot pointed ahead. "Over that humpy ridge," he said. "An old Army strip."

Scattered hangars and Quonset huts came into view in a flat-bottomed valley between two peaks. The base was small, but the landing strip was long enough for a jet. Beyond and far below, Raszer could just make out Interstate 25 and a settlement.

"Where are we?" Raszer asked. "We can't be that far over the state line."

"Closest town on the map is Trinidad," said the pilot, pointing to the same settlement. "But I can't say I've ever been there."

"Trinidad, Colorado," Raszer said under his breath. He drew from the well of his brain an obscure factoid he'd come across in Monica's research on castration: The town of Trinidad had earned some notoriety in the 1960s as the home base of the doctor who'd pioneered transgender surgery, and for a time after that, its sleepy Main Street had become a mecca for those seeking alteration, and a halfway house for those altered. That was before the business moved to places like Copenhagen. It was undoubtedly coincidental, but coincidence was never just a random shuffle; it was a clustering of potentialities around a single set of certainties.

A helipad marked with a red *X* was adjacent to one of the larger hangars. There wasn't another soul in sight, but as the chopper dropped delicately to the pad, two men in blue mechanics' suits emerged from the hangar and stood clear of the propeller's reach, waiting to escort the new arrival.

"First leg of many," said the pilot, and grinned again. Almost as soon as Raszer had hopped out and pulled his pack down, the helicopter lifted off again.

"Take me to your leader," Raszer said to the men, one of whom took his pack. The other smirked and gestured for Raszer to accompany him. A door with peeling red paint and a grimy little window led into the largest of the hangars. The door was common enough, but the scene inside was anything but.

First, there was the aircraft: a corporate jet without a corporate logo. Like the helicopter, it hadn't a single identifying mark. From the size of the fuel tank, Raszer gauged it to be good for domestic runs of a few thousand miles at most. It wasn't going to get him all the way to Turkey, but it was impressive nonetheless: sleek, low, and blacked out. A small team of mechanics and a pilot were readying the plane, all wearing the same navy blue jumpsuits, none paying notice when he came in the door. And there was a send-off party of sorts, a delegation assembled, he presumed, to see him off: a gentleman rancher in flannel and denim, a technician in a lab coat, a graying Asian fellow with a doctor's bag, and three men in suits, one of whom stood a head taller than the others and had a bearing that only the best old-school Yankee breeding could buy.

Standing in the hard cone of light spilling from a suspended work lamp, Raszer found himself feeling—once the escorts had left his side—as if he'd just been beamed down from another galaxy.

The tall man came forward.

"Welcome," he said. "You follow directions very well, Mr. Raszer."

Raszer looked the man over. He was perhaps sixty-two, with hair the shade of smoke combed fastidiously back from a high forehead, and piercing blue eyes. In the fine lines of his face, Raszer could almost trace his path from Exeter to Harvard Yard and into the corridors of power. Everything about him said *directorate of operations*.

Raszer swept his arm across the hangar to the mechanics, the pilot, the jet. "Is this a federal operation?" he asked. "If so, I may be in the wrong terminal."

"Not the kind that comes under congressional oversight," said the man.

"How about the kind that comes under Douglas Picot's purview?" Raszer asked.

"Oh, no," the man replied. "Picot would have every man in this room facing sedition charges."

Raszer held. The man had him pinned in the light, such that he couldn't escape it without stepping sideways or backward. "Was Shams one of yours?"

The tall man gave a bare nod.

"Recruited in Iraq? In pretty deep, then, I guess . . . "

"As deep as it gets," the man said.

"How deep is that?"

"So deep he didn't know he was in," the man from Langley replied.

"Ah," said Raszer. "Then I suppose he died for your sins."

The CIA man nodded toward a card table in the corner, next to an old Coke machine that dispensed eight-ounce bottles. "Let's get acquainted, shall we, while your coach is prepared. My name is Philby Greenstreet."

"That can't be right," said Raszer. "Unless some GamesMaster dreamed you up."

The tall man chuckled without turning as he strode toward the lightless corner, then fished in the pockets of his wool trousers for change.

"Coca-Cola?" he asked Raszer. "I've always loved these little bottles. You can almost imagine that it's still a drug."

"And a cheap drug, at that," said Raszer, as Greenstreet dropped a dime into the machine. "No, thanks. But I would like something to get this bad taste out of my mouth. You wouldn't have a stick of wintergreen gum, would you? Someone's been leaving the scent all over Taos, and now I've got a yen for it. There's even a certain FBI agent—"

Greenstreet glanced briefly at Raszer, then pushed the bottle cap off his Coke with the nail on his right thumb as effortlessly as if he'd been flicking lint.

"You've got a good nose, Mr. Raszer," he said. "*Oleum Gaultheriae.* Oil of wintergreen. Chemically, methyl salicylate. Masks the breath and overpowers other odors—even the odor of internal decay. Suppresses sexual excitement very effectively. A remarkably small dosage is absolutely lethal. Its use goes back at least 150 years. It's a cheap poison pill for men who want to keep their minds on their work and never, ever want to be caught alive. That would describe your adversaries, but I doubt very much that it describes your FBI agent. What makes you think he's on your tail?"

Raszer half smiled. "Maybe he's got nothing better to do. You're either very well informed or very fast on your feet, Mr. Greenstreet. "

The CIA man took a sip of his Coca-Cola and smiled. "Such pleasure for one thin dime," he said. "Very few real bargains left in this world, Mr. Raszer." He eyed the jet. "I'd venture to say that you're about to receive another one of them."

"So that's yours?" Raszer said. "The agency's?"

"God, no," said Greenstreet. "Not even black ops would touch this mission. The jet is on loan from a philanthropist who happens to be a great fan of The Gauntlet. In fact, he owes his wealth to the game. In a sense, he's never stopped playing. You might say he's your next 'guide.' I hear you're working for well below your usual fee, so I'm sure you'll appreciate his munificence."

"I rarely look a gift horse in the mouth," said Raszer. "But you worry me a little, Mr. Greenstreet. How do I know *you're* any more trustworthy than Picot?"

"You don't," Greenstreet replied. "Except that you evidently trusted Shams' instructions, and wound up here." He motioned for Raszer to take a seat at the card table, then set down his bottle and pulled out his own chair. "Some of us," he continued, "share more with you than you might imagine." He paused. "We also share a keen interest in the place and the man you are soon—hopefully—going to meet."

"You mean Na-Koja-Abad," said Raszer, recalling Shams' citation. "And the Old Man."

"Na-Koja-Abad," repeated the CIA man. "Curious name, eh? 'Nowhere-Land.' Does it exist only in the world of The Gauntlet? Or is it a real place—like Tora Bora—with coordinates a GPS device, or a tracker like yourself, can identify?"

"You don't know?" Raszer asked incredulously.

"*Na-Koja-Abad* is a Sufi term for the middle world between form and substance. A numinous state of mind, or more precisely, a state of half-being. It was appropriated by advanced Gauntlet players to describe the mystical experience of those who make it all the way to the Ninth Circle on what they call the Urfa route. You won't find it in a CIA brief. But as you've already deduced, the Old Man's people have taken over the game, and it appears they have a bait-and-switch operation going. Na-Koja-Abad is promised, but something else is delivered: *El Mirai*—the mountain stronghold of these thugs you've been playing cat 'n mouse with."

"So El Mirai is real. A physical place. Even though it means '*The Mirage*'?"

Greenstreet hesitated, then gave an inscrutable reply. "For all intents, yes. But—"

"—its locus is on the border of Na-Koja-Abad. Nowhere-Land."

"Now you're getting the swing of it."

"Evil on the perimeter of the holy."

"If you were the Devil," said Greenstreet, "wouldn't you build your hot dog stand near the entrance to paradise?" He took a swig of Coca-Cola. "They're designing a whole new kind of terrorist up there. The design isn't perfected yet, but when it is, we'll have an army of Takfiris, as diverse in appearance and ethnicity as a United Colors of Benetton ad. They won't fit anyone's 'profile.'"

"Something like that, I figured," said Raszer. "But what's the objective? I'm guessing it isn't the restoration of the caliphate."

"The details will have to wait," Greenstreet replied, "for your safety and ours. But I can give you a sense of what you're up against."

He leaned in and placed his hand on the table, not two inches from Raszer's own wrist. It was a surprisingly intimate gesture for a man of Greenstreet's type.

"Let me ask you this: As a child, did you ever find yourself wishing for the storm to end all storms? The one that would shut the whole world down?"

"The snow day that lasts forever," said Raszer. "Sure, it probably crossed my mind once or twice. And I always liked disaster movies."

"Me, too," said Greenstreet. "There's an apocalyptic urge in the human psyche. The desire for a clean slate. On the whole, it's not unhealthy. It makes revolutions possible. But there's a reactionary gene that often accompanies it. Some revolutionaries grow up to become Robespierres. Absolutists. Fundamentalists. I almost did. I worshipped my parents when I was a boy, thought they could do no wrong, and that every moral lesson they taught, they also exemplified.

"When I got a little older and could see my father's infidelity and my mother's alcoholism, I hated them for it, hated them for revealing that the world wasn't a tidy place. I resolved to clean it up, to cut out the rot. Eventually, I came to my senses. But suppose I hadn't. Suppose my black-and-white view of the world had hardened until I couldn't see shades, much less color. Until I believed that only a holy fire could sterilize the planet and restore God's dominion. Suppose my goal was—through ten thousand small acts of terror—to bring society to a point of maximum entropy. To a condition that demands intervention . . . and a new kind of state."

"It's not exactly breaking news that there are people at both the western and eastern poles who value order over freedom. But—"

"The news would be that they'd joined forces, and employed a third force to foment the chaos. When you swallow fundamentalism whole, you ultimately conclude the world is unsalvageable. The end—restoring purity—justifies any means."

Raszer lit a cigarette and sat back. "I'm getting the outlines, but I'm still not sure I see how a Scotty Darrell or a Katy Endicott would serve the cause. Why not use pros instead of college kids?"

"Because the Scotty Darrells and Katy Endicotts don't need fake passports. Because we'd never see them coming. Think of it: ten thousand Ishmaels just as wired into an alternate reality as Scotty. A post office rampage here, a campus massacre there; an amusement-park ride runs amok, a security guard is shot, the BlackBerry wireless network crashes. Housing values crater and the Tokyo market dives. All basins of chaotic attraction, all portents of the End Times. And with each incident, the End Timers cry, '*We told you so!*'

"A kind of spiritual vertigo kicks in once you accept apocalypse, and vertigo isn't only a fear of falling—it's an inclination to fall. Isn't that what 'Bring it on' really means? And in every high school cafeteria, at every community college, in every miserable army unit assigned to police a prison, there's some lonely, disaffected kid who grows more certain every day that the world is irredeemable and he may as well go out in a blaze of glory. What if someone devised a way to exploit that disaffection by means of a virtual reality? Wouldn't *that* account for Scotty Darrell?"

"Jesus . . . this is really happening. How many of him are out there?"

"We don't know. There were seven degrees of initiation for the original Nizari Assassins, and the first required a keen understanding of what makes for the best recruits. Each recruit brought in at least two more, until the growth of the cult became exponential. We're catching this early, but if the public had any idea how many Iraq war vets are listed as MIA, how many milk-carton kids and runaways had been sucked into this—if we don't find out where this operation lives and pull open the curtains on it—in three years' time, the U.S., Europe, and Israel will face an epidemic of terror. Not from Al Qaeda, but from our own children."

"You know," said Raszer, "I got pulled into this because a Jehovah's Witness girl had been abducted. Along the way, there've been hints that certain Elders of the sect may not have had clean hands. This . . . network of fundamentalists you spoke of . . . are they pimping out their own kids for the cause?"

"Hardcore fundamentalists are often supralapsarians—people who believe the elect can do no wrong. They're guaranteed heaven, so there's nothing to lose."

"Are there people in our government aiding and abetting this?"

Greenstreet gave him a loaded look.

"Christ," said Raszer. "We really have gone off the deep end. What about the Islamic establishment, the saner clerics and mullahs? Do they accept the Old Man and his group? I mean, where the hell did he get his charter?"

"I'm afraid he got his charter—in part—from us. In Afghanistan, in the '80s, when we made our bed with the Mujahedin in the fight against the Soviets. That's where the seeds of this theocratic alliance were sown, the root of the rot. He was one of the warlords our money and guns found their way to, but unlike Massoud and Hekmatyar, we never acknowledged him. He was an unidentified asset. Later on, when we still thought we could control him, his men trained with Blackwater, and Blackwater—as you may know—was midwifed by a consortium of Christian Dominionist groups. We know what happened there. What did Nietzsche say? If you gaze into the abyss for long enough, the abyss begins to gaze right back at you."

Raszer blinked slowly.

"You'll connect the dots on the other side, and you'll let me know what to call it. He's learned from the founding fathers of Islamism—Sayyid Qutb, Abu Faraj al-Libbi, and Ayman al-Zawahiri—but he's also gone to school on us. In 1953—at roughly the same time Qutb was setting up *al Takfir wal-Hijra*, the CIA circulated a top-secret manual entitled "A Study of Assassination" to its operatives in Guatemala and Iran, where we were busy orchestrating regime changes. The manual and the techniques it described were based on a study of the original Assassin cult, and included a primer on how to assimilate oneself to an alien culture. Just like Mohamed Atta did. I'll wager that manual sits on his bookshelf, right alongside *The Protocols of the Elders of Zion*."

"Who exactly do you speak for? This can't be the company line."

"You've heard the expression 'The right hand doesn't know what the left hand is doing'?" Greenstreet replied. "Superficially, we spies may all walk and talk alike, but we practice our own version of *taqiyya*. Dig deeper, and you'll see that the intelligence community is full of heretics—heretics who've bothered to read the Constitution."

"The loyal opposition," said Raszer.

"Some of us would like to be able to recognize this country ten years from now."

"Right. Tell me this. Do we know for certain that the Old Man of the Mountains is real, not some myth created by this cabal to throw guys like you off the scent?"

"We think he's real, but the truth is that every account we have is hearsay. He's left footprints. There's evidence of arms dealing on a massive scale—mostly old Soviet-bloc weaponry, bought cheaply by traffickers and resold at a huge mark-up to the U.S., among others. Hell, by 2008, how sure could we be that bin Laden was real? Is the Old Man real? Well, you are going to let us know."

"Why should I succeed where you haven't?"

"The poor man passes where the king's way is blocked. You have only one modest item on your agenda: to get your girl out. That gives you credibility.

Plus, you speak passable Arabic, a little Farsi, and French. Most important, you speak *his* language."

"Right. And if I'm busted, I'm on my own?"

"Of course. But without the escort we're offering, you don't really stand a chance of getting within a hundred miles of your target."

"Escort?"

"You'll be briefed on the other side."

"Do I have a choice here?" Raszer asked.

"Time is running out on us, my friend. It may comfort the voters to think that a new man in the White House means a new history, but history doesn't change with a single election. Plots begun under previous regimes have momentum. Think about the Bay of Pigs. Wars begin and end long before and after their little ticks on the timeline. America is a stage trick. Elvis's cloak is still on the stage, but Elvis has left the building. We're on the road to Armageddon, and that suits the End Timers just fine. Now, you can ignore this and play out your little part, or you can be part of something bigger."

Raszer allowed himself to examine the man who'd called himself Greenstreet. Fat chance his name was Greenstreet, let alone *Philby Greenstreet*. On the other hand, it was almost too preposterous *not* to be true. His face spoke of the steel-core integrity of old spies, the sort who considered Ike and JFK the last presidents worth speaking of and still made yearly donations to the Harvard alumni fund.

"Something bigger . . . " Raszer repeated.

"Worth mortgaging a piece of your soul for, Mr. Raszer?"

"Worth more than *my* soul," Raszer answered. "If what you say is true. The question is whether it's worth risking Katy Endicott's soul. You see, in the end, that's all I can allow to count. I've had to keep it simple for myself. My job is to get her out."

"Saving the world one soul at a time?" Greenstreet ventured.

"Maybe paying my debt one soul at a time."

"What debt is that?"

"Do you believe in grace, Mr. Greenstreet?"

"In my own fashion. Why?"

"Years back, I made a fatal mess of my life—some old ghosts I couldn't shake. The truth is, I'd already been counted out and was just waiting for the bell. I didn't realize that every punch I'd taken had also bloodied the people around me. Then I nearly lost my daughter, the one thing that had any real value. That's when I learned to pray . . . and learned that God doesn't sit around waiting for the phone to ring. God has to be summoned from a bottomless pit inside your heart. My prayers were answered, but grace doesn't come free. I made a deal. Her life for my promise to return lost sheep to pasture. A kind of indentured servitude, I guess."

"So, it's true, then," Greenstreet observed. "You *do* have a calling."

"Like I said: a debt. Now, I have three questions for you, Philby. The first is, this vast conspiracy you've described . . . even for a professional paranoid like me, it's hard to swallow. How do you pull off a coup like that without the support of the generals? And how would you sustain it if the military lined up against you?"

"The generals? The military? Think, Mr. Raszer. The Iraq war rendered the military irrelevant, emasculated it. It's a shadow of what it was before. After all, that was the rationale for privatization, wasn't it? Why do you need the military when you've created a private army and a worldwide network of arms merchants to drive it?"

"Okay, let's say you're right. And let's say you get me in there. What possible difference can one man make?"

"The difference a candle always makes when lit against the darkness. To our knowledge, no Westerner we know of has ever gotten close to the Old Man, except as his captive, so you'd be a viral agent. His mystique lies in occultation. How does the song go? *Got to be good-looking 'cause he's so hard to see.* Neither he nor the plot he's furthering can survive open curtains. His power flows from his command of The Gauntlet; it subsists only so long as conditions of the game support it."

"In the early days, that power was mostly virtual. Its force lay in its potential: the absolute allegiance of the Old Man's followers—the players who'd come to him seeking a truth beyond all other truths. Now, he's begun to muddy the line between the virtual and the manifest by dispatching his acolytes to commit real acts of terror in the real world. But when you move pawns to attack, they also become vulnerable.

"We understand that you've had considerable experience with role playing, Mr. Raszer. You've infiltrated more than a dozen highly secretive organizations under assumed identities. This is the role of a lifetime. You'll travel with a small escort of veteran players who know the territory and can get you past hot zones, but you'll enter the fortress alone as a French-Canadian Catholic monk. Your 'avatar,' if you like."

"And what do I have to offer in trade for Katy Endicott?"

"You are authorized to offer the exchange of one of the Old Man's captured operatives for her release."

"Which operative?" Raszer asked. "It's not Layla Faj-Ta'wil, is it?"

"No," Greenstreet replied. "Your bargaining chip is Scotty Darrell."

"So, you guys have him?"

"We will shortly. We're waiting on one variable."

"That's good, I guess. But your idea is a nonstarter. I won't put Scotty back in there, Why would he have that much value in trade, anyway? Mother birds generally don't take the babies back once they've fallen out of the nest."

"True, but Scotty has a mission, and the Old Man wants it accomplished."

"What's the mission?"

"All we know is that it's programmed to set off a chain reaction, the likes of which you can't imagine. We suspect there may be close to two hundred sleeper agents across the globe whose own missions will be triggered by Scotty's. At that point, the game will become horribly real. It's even possible your girl has an assignment in hand already. They're preparing to dispatch their young assassins as we speak. "

"Jesus," said Raszer. "Suppose this lunacy works according to plan. Suppose all these human time bombs go off and we're all terrorized enough to believe that only the muscle of an authoritarian state can restore order. We get a Christian theocracy in the West and an Islamic theocracy in the East. What does the Old Man want out of it?"

"What he really wants is the subject of a great deal of conjecture. Power, guns, land—certainly. Control over the global sex and opium markets—quite possibly. He knows these appetites will abide even under a repressive regime. In the beginning, everyone behaves, recites the Commandments—or the Sharia—but soon enough, the rulers begin to indulge their vices, and it's back to business.

"'Business' will be quite good, as it always is under fascism. Eventually, the whole thing collapses from internal rot, like Rome did. Then you have a new dark age. And *that*—in my opinion—is what the Old Man's really after. There's evidence that in the inner circles of his cult, among the elite corps of soldiers, a pre-Islamic religion of Syrian derivation is practiced. A religion demanding absolute and incontrovertible celibacy, if you know what I mean."

"Now it begins to add up," said Raszer. "All right. This escort you say I'll have to El Mirai—do they know they're working for you? For the CIA?"

"They know they've received their commission from Philby Greenstreet," he answered with a smile. "But, in short, no. They are stateless people, transnationals. Their services have been engaged by an NGO that is in fact a front for a mirror CIA station that exists only in the virtual topography of The Gauntlet. Its existence is nothing more than artful illusion. Vapor. But if we prevail, it will be actualized and eventually will replace the existing order. Many kings begin as pretenders, you see, but if they pretend ardently enough, they eventually claim the throne."

"'Only in the topography of The Gauntlet?' What the hell does that mean?"

"You must bear in mind, Mr. Raszer, that you are now through the looking glass. You're heading into the gap between form and substance, and there'll be times when you simply don't know what's real. All creation begins as virtual, as quantum potential. The Gauntlet is a game of becoming, and its players—the serious ones, at any rate—seek to ride the wave of becoming without looking back or forward. It's a balancing act. Do you think you can pull it off?"

"I don't know. But I've been waiting all my life to try."

"That's my boy," Greenstreet said.

"One little detail concerns me."

"What's that?"

"These people have been on my ass for a week. They know where I live. They know what I look like, they probably know I'm coming, and somehow I doubt that a French accent and a monk's outfit are going to fool them."

"Maybe not," said Greenstreet. "But without a cover, you have no recourse to deception. You are, as we say, creating a 'legend.' You'll receive instruction on the other side. You'll have to use all your craft to stay alive until you've reached your destination. But once you're there, you *will be* your avatar. You'll be in the game, and whether you survive or not will depend on how well you play it. You see, they'll be playing, too."

Raszer took a moment to digest.

"Are you ready, Mr. Raszer?"

"Why not?"

"Come along, then. You'll need a couple of inoculations if you're going into eastern Turkey."

"I've had them," Raszer said. "I've got the papers to prove it."

"You haven't had this one. There's a particularly virulent new strain of H5N1 in the mountains west of Hakkâri. Believe me, you don't want it."

"Avian flu? All right," said Raszer. "Just don't put the needle in my ass."

"We'll try to find a place that's not so hard," Greenstreet said.

Almost before the spike entered muscle, Raszer knew he'd been doped. "This may leave you a little drowsy," the Asian medic had said. Within seconds, the hangar began to spin, shapes and colors at its outer limits rushing off in a centrifugal blur. He was hauled up from the chair and guided to the jet, the pilot at one elbow and the medic at the other. He turned just before being ducked into the dimly lit cabin and looked around for the CIA man, wearing an expression that plainly said, *Why the mickey? I would have gone quietly*. But the lanky old spook was at first nowhere to be seen, and Raszer's mind began to riff. Other figures began to materialize and supplant the anonymous figures in the send-off crew. They emerged like wraiths from the corrugated tin walls of the hangar, as if through theatrical curtains the color of mercury, concealing a world waiting in the wings of his imagination.

Among those making the curtain call were Lieutenant Borges of the LAPD and Detective Jaime Aquino, though not separately: They were one body, one form. Ruthie and her mother showed, and likewise kept slipping in and out of phase: now one woman, then two, then none at all. Emmett Parrish was there. And Silas Endicott came in the person of the old squatter from the Coronado Lodge, wearing Raszer's duster and making sparks as he walked. For a couple of seconds, Raszer actually tried to impose some rational order on the visions, and then it hit him that if he truly was off to see the wizard, the residents of Oz might have the look of familiars.

And then, for the duration of a sneeze, his mind seemed to clear. Through the red door on the far side of the hangar came a scowling Amos Leach, his hair piled high, wearing an orange print sundress, followed closely by none other than special agent Bernard Djapper. Raszer's throat closed in panic, but not even a surge from his adrenal glands could offset the effects of the dope. Before his mind could verify what his eyes had seen, Philby Greenstreet leaned into the cabin, gave his shoulder a squeeze, and whispered, "Bon voyage. Let's hope for better times."

From time to time during the long flight, little pieces of consciousness flared, and Raszer would become aware of the engine's muffled hum or the soft lighting in his fiberglass cocoon of uncertain metamorphosis. At one point, he thought he noticed that the fabric of the seats and the pattern of the wallpaper were a matching design of Chinese characters and *I Ching* hexagrams.

Later, he saw only the uniform color of potter's clay. Except for those few, vague sensory impressions, he slept the dreamless sleep of suspended animation, an Argonaut cryonically preserved for his voyage to an alternate cosmos. As for the pilot, he never said a word.

The fleeting vision of Leach and Djapper, Raszer could not, or would not, retain. In fact, he found a gap where his short-term memory should have been, like the erasure of a tape or the redaction of paragraphs from a classified document. As with a dream on waking, the harder he tried to retrieve it, the further it receded.

He had no way of knowing the direction of travel, but some internal compass gave him a vague sense of going northwest over the Siberian peninsula, rather than the usual geosynchronous polar route. Still, the lack of certainty troubled him. He'd forgotten about the little fragment of nanocircuitry in the left cheek of his ass, forgotten for the time being that Monica could probably plot his coordinates to within a few degrees. In the gray of predawn, in some cold, bleak, and unvegetated part of the world, he was removed from the jet by the pilot and a man in a balaclava, and deposited in the cargo hold of an old military transport, an aircraft that—like the helicopter and the jet—bore no mark of nationality or corporate identity.

He saw these things as if watching himself in a video. He was in a world beyond nations and logos. He was running The Gauntlet, and the luxurious part of the trip was over. The rattle and roar of the transport plane upset his stomach and shook a little of the pixie dust from his brain, and after a very long while, a few of his baseline neural circuits began to hum intermittently.

He was descending.

TWENTY-THREE

"IS THAT HIM?" a man speaking Arabic asked. "He is not what I expected."

"What did you expect?" said another man, also in Arabic, but of the American Foreign Service variety.

"*Je ne sais pas*," declared the first man, slipping seamlessly into French, then to English. "I expected a soldier, but he looks like a guilty saint. Or perhaps a thief."

"Either will serve us better than a soldier, Rashid. A soldier would only get shot at." After a pause, the second man said, "Wake him up."

"But he is awake," said the first man. "At least, his eyes are open."

Raszer wasn't awake in any sense he'd known outside the womb. The words spoken not six feet from where he lay, in languages he knew reasonably well, had traveled over his cortex like sounds in deep water. Like the chatter of dolphins, he knew there was meaning there, but what it was lay beyond any conscious decryption. Beside that, his larynx was paralyzed, as in those dreams you can't dispel by screaming. An oxygen mask was suddenly clapped over his face, and at the same time, he received an electric shock that ran from the tip of his tailbone to the top of his head.

The jolt tripled his pulse rate, and he began to gulp down air hungrily. In less than a minute, he was fully awake, and a minute after that, he was sitting up on the cot.

"Jesus," he said. "What was that?"

"Don't try to gather up your thoughts too quickly," said the American, a round, fortyish man with an olive complexion and dark, wet eyes. "You may drop them."

Raszer pressed his fingers against his eyelids, shook the fog from his head, and looked around. He was in a small room, empty but for the army cot, a writing table, and an old-fashioned washbasin. It had the stark, scrubbed look of an infirmary examination room. A single shuttered window let through the tiniest bit of pink morning light, and an overhead fan spun noisily on worn bearings. The floor was of worn cedar planks, dimpled by bootheels, and the walls were administrative tan. If someone had said, "1908," he wouldn't have blinked.

His pack and personal articles were parked against the wall near the door that led to a larger office. He spotted a GLOCK automatic pistol beside a tumbler of water on a rolltop desk, and above the desk hung a cheaply framed watercolor depicting an azure lake surrounded by mountains and a crusader castle that appeared to grow out of the rock. On the floor beside the desk was a hookah. There must have been an unshuttered window, because a column of light, whirling with dust motes, bisected the room and screened Raszer's view of whatever was beyond it.

"Where am I?" Raszer inquired.

"You're on land fought over by Greeks and Hittites and Urartians and Persians and even the French," said the American. "Trade routes and ports, the casus belli of the ancient world. Now it's oil, tribe, and religion. Not much progress to show for twenty-five hundred years, eh? In any case, still apparently worth fighting for. Right, Rashid?"

"If the oil has not all turned to blood," said the smaller, darker man, a Kurd who wore khakis and a loose white cotton blouse that set off his vividly red headdress.

"Specifically," the American continued, "you're in Iskenderun, Turkey, formerly Alexandretta. The French got it in the carve-up after the First World War, and they still *parlent français* in the cafes. Everywhere else, you'll hear Arabic or some variety of Turkic. There also happens to be an American air base nearby."

"It's easy to get lost between cultures in the Hatay," said the man called Rashid. "Syria is only a few kilometers away, and it would be closer if she had her way."

"Lost is right," said the American. "That brings us to you, Mr. Raszer. I understand you're here to find a girl, and we can help you. But a woman as the object of a quest is always more than a woman, right? Do you know what the stakes are?"

"You'll have to let the sap drain from my skull. How long have I been out?"

"A while." The American extended his hand. "Philby Greenstreet," he said. "My people had it changed from Greenblatt three generations ago, but that doesn't seem to have fooled anyone."

Raszer shook the hand and kept his game face, but felt a cold flush he associated with taking psychotropics in the wrong setting.

"Why," he asked, "do I feel like I've fallen down the rabbit hole?"

"Because you did," replied his host. "You came out on the other side of the world."

"Then I guess the only thing to ask," Raszer said, following the rules of the game, "is whether you can make use of a keen mind and a steady heart."

"You bet we can," the man replied. He gestured toward his companion. "This is my partner, Rashid al-Khidr. We pretty much run this I-double-R office."

"I-double-R?" Raszer repeated.

"International Refugee Relief. We do our part to put a Band-Aid on the collateral damage from the wars: displaced families, orphans, visa and sanctuary applications."

"Human trafficking?" asked Raszer.

"That too. When we have the resources."

"Right. I have a hazy recollection of being told about you. Very hazy. You're the 'mirror,' right? Should I expect to meet any more Philbys along the way?"

"You never know," said Greenstreet Number Two. "Not to worry; things will come back to you when you need them—kind of like a foreign language. You were given some of the geopolitical picture on the other side. In Islamic parlance, the *zahir*: the outer reality. Important for keeping your bearings. But you won't master the game without *batin*: the inner meaning. That's what we're for."

"Let's stick with *zahir* for a minute," Raszer said. "Tell me where it is I'm going."

"That's not strictly a matter of geography," Greenstreet answered. "On the map, you'll be going across the Mesopotamian flood plain of southeastern Anatolia. Ethnographically speaking, it's the land of the Dimili Kurds. Mostly Alevi Shiites, which is to say, not really orthodox Muslims at all. The whole region's a war zone these days, but it's a picnic compared with your destination. You're headed into some of the roughest, most lawless terrain on the planet: the Hâkkari highlands, where Turkey, Iran, and Iraq meet. A piece of turf claimed equally by the three nations and the Kurds, and currently held—feudally speaking—by the Old Man.

"On the way there, time moves in reverse. You'll see the world Alexander saw. You're going across the country of the Sin-worshippers, the fire jumpers, the sword swallowers, dervishes, and the devotees of the Peacock Angel."

"When do I meet the lotus eaters?" Raszer asked.

"If it lives and spouts heresy," said Greenstreet, "it's out there. The whole stretch, from Gaziantep to the Iranian border, is a world apart. Like I said, nominally Shia, but Islam around here is as much a matter of brand loyalty as shared belief. You'll cross the Tigris and enter the oldest continually inhabited settlements on Earth. En route, you'll pass by some of the best-kept secrets in civilization. And just when you think maybe you've reached the source of it all in the high country near Hâkkari, everything drops into nothing, like some huge cataract falling straight to hell, and no satellite can map it, and no drone can fly over it, and that, Mr. Raszer, is where your girl is. Literally, in the middle of fucking nowhere."

"Well, let's go, then," said Raszer, slipping woozily off the table. "What's the mode of travel? And what sort of souvenir do you want me to bring back for you?"

"Other than your skin, just an account. We'd like to know how these people turn bored college kids and pissed-off hayseeds into sleeper agents and saboteurs. Ishmaels, they call themselves. Or Isma'ils, after the son of the sixth imam, Jafar. Isma'il."

"I'm aware of the mythos. It's all lifted from the Nizari Assassins, right?"

"That's all subterfuge. We know you know cults, Mr. Raszer, but believe me, this isn't Jonestown. It's deeper, wider, and much, much slicker than that. This guy's the angel of the bottomless pit. His only religion is . . . " He turned to the Kurd. "Rashid?"

"*Nothing,*" said al-Khidr. "*Nihil.* He tells the Sunnis he's their man and the Shia he's theirs, and collects tribute from the Kurds by telling them he's playing both for their benefit. His elite soldiers secretly pledge fealty to an iteration of the Syrian-Nabataean goddess Atargatis—but his own beliefs are more subtle. If indeed he has a God, it is the apotheosis of the nunc: the crack between spirit and substance, where all ceases to be. The blackness at the bottom of a well. Negation."

"Atargatis," Raszer repeated. "Syrian. Negation. *Ex nihilo, ad nihilo.* Shit."

"They're oblivion seekers," Greenstreet said. "A professor at Harvard once told me that there are really only two belief systems in the world, coiled around each other in the human psyche. A dyad, he called it. He said that philosophical truth consists in believing both at the same time, and that dismissing one in favor of the other leads to totalitarianism. One is the conviction that this is truly the best of all possible worlds, and the other is that it's the worst. Great drama is all about the conflict. *To be, or not to be*. The truth gets lost in translation, of course, but that's how you'll slip through."

"I just hope I come out with my tongue," said Raszer. "And my testicles."

"I hope so, too. You're referring to their taste for dismemberment. Doctrinally, that comes from their pledge to this goddess, the one Rashid mentioned. In her heyday, her devotees gelded themselves. At least, that's the line he feeds his troops."

Raszer strode over to his pack, squatted, and fished until he came up with the Syrian coin he'd traded his duster for. He held up its face. "This goddess?" he asked.

His host took the coin, eyed it, and nodded. "That looks like her." Glancing at his watch, Greenstreet said, "Let's get a bite, shall we? Do you like your food spicy?"

"I'd like anything that'll burn this fog from my brain."

Greenstreet went to the desk, parked the handgun behind his belt buckle, and slipped on a sport coat. On the adjacent wall was pinned a large map of Turkey and the bordering countries, dotted with dozens of colored tacks marking out routes traveled by refugees and the traffickers who exploited them. Raszer retrieved his cigarettes and Zippo and walked over to the map.

"May I ask your expert opinion, Mr. . . . Mr. Greenstreet?"

"Sure," said his host. "You can ask."

"Is there something . . . anything . . . that connects Katy Endicott with the rest of the Old Man's milk carton kids? Some common quality he sends his scouts out to look for?"

"I can't say for sure," Greenstreet replied, "never having seen them all in one place. But I'll give you a semi-educated guess."

"That's good enough for me."

"Remember the Manson girls? Squeaky, Sadie, and the rest. Your turf, right?"

"I suppose you could say that," Raszer replied.

"Well . . . that rare combination of physical appeal, native intelligence . . . and malleability. Add in antisocial tendencies, some daddy issues, and stir. How's that?"

"And the reason these abductions aren't causing more of a public outcry . . . "

"They will. Once we shine a light on 'em. But, for now, these are mostly the kids that nobody misses a whole lot. Someone did miss your Katy. That's why you're here."

Raszer nodded, and returned his eyes to the map.

"Which of those routes am I taking?" he asked.

"You and Rashid will be flown to Gaziantep. You'll take a *dolmus* to a safe house just outside of Urfa. In the morning, you'll be called for by a young man named Dante and bused to Harran—one of the weirdest places in the world, for my money. From that point on, we don't know you, and you'll be in the care of the Fedeli d'Amore."

"I guess Shams knew whereof he spoke. The Fedeli—"

Greenstreet held up his palm, then tapped the face of his watch. This portion of the briefing was over. "Let's walk," he said, "and eat. Rashid will cover the rest."

As soon as they stepped outside, Raszer smelled the Mediterranean. There were other scents, too, of olive and citrus rind and fig, but the primeval tang of that most ancient of seas overpowered them. Farther down this great fishhook of coastline lay Beirut, Haifa, Gaza, and, at the barb, the once great city of Alexandria.

They walked three abreast up the steep, narrow street toward the old quarter, casting long shadows. Raszer struck a match on stone and lit a cigarette. Little was said, because too much needed saying. After a few minutes, Greenstreet gestured and said, "Here we are. The Saray. Best restaurant in Iskenderun. And the best view."

A dozen small tables spilled onto the street from the canopied double doors of the restaurant, each one with fresh flowers and a million-dollar panorama of the curving coastline and the turquoise sea. Greenstreet took the most isolated table and gestured for Raszer to sit. He did so gratefully, because his legs had suddenly turned to soft clay. The entire setting—the solid, cloudless sky that merged seamlessly with the water, the whitewashed buildings, the cobblestone street—began to evanesce, then flicker back into register like a silent-movie image. He was accustomed to arriving in a foreign country and feeling oddly out of whack, as if he'd been teleported and hadn't yet fully reconstituted, but this state was profoundly unsettling. In a word, trippy.

Greenstreet must have seen the uneasiness cross Raszer's face, because he smiled and said merely, "You'll get used to it."

Used to exactly what, Raszer had to wonder, for of all the strange places he'd toured his mind to, this was perhaps the strangest. A question passed over his lips without any forethought. "How close is the world to disaster, Mr. Greenstreet?"

Greenstreet shot a glance at the Kurd, then said, "At any given time in history, Armageddon waits, just on the other side of the curtain. It could take the form of a comet, plague, climatic shift, or barrage of dirty bombs going off in major cities, and all it needs is a little encouragement. In the years leading up to 9/11 and the months and years that followed, that encouragement was given. The most reactionary elements in Christian and Islamic fundamentalist circles lay down together, blessed by the agencies of state in which they'd entrenched themselves, and conceived a beast."

He summoned the waiter. "Let's take a meal together and hope for better times."

At four forty-eight in the afternoon on that April day, after they had nourished themselves with generous helpings of flatbread slathered with *cevizli biber*—a paste of walnuts, chilies, and cracked wheat—and washed it down with cold beer, Raszer glanced at his watch, then at the lengthening purple shadows of their three seated forms, angling sharply away from the table and merging in the middle of the street. His eyes traveled up a minaret to the place from which the muezzin would cry at eventide, then down the steep hill to the sea, and finally back to the middle of the street.

At that point, he saw that there were just two shadows, his own and that of the red-turbaned Kurd named Rashid al-Khidr. He returned his gaze to the table and confirmed that, indeed, the chair formerly occupied by the man who'd called himself Greenstreet was empty. Moreover, it was pushed in snugly against the table as if it had never been occupied at all.

"Where'd Philby disappear to?" Raszer asked, his tongue slowed by the beer.

"Sorry?" Rashid replied.

"Mr. Greenstreet," Raszer repeated. "Men's room? Or is he getting the bill?"

"I think you must be confused, my friend," the Kurd said. "Perhaps the travel, or the time shift. You came to us from Mr. Greenstreet, but Mr. Greenstreet is not here."

"Now, wait a second," Raszer insisted. "I know the CIA is good with smoke and mirrors, but I can still hear his last words. He said, 'Let's hope for better times,' right?"

"Indeed, indeed. You were telling me of your conversation in the airplane hangar, and of how you came to be delivered to us, and of the vision you had just before the hatch was closed. It will not be the last such vision, I am sure."

A number of improbabilities passed through Raszer's mind, each one more outlandish than the one before, and each one in conflict with his bodily experience. It was a credit to the spiritual training he'd undergone that he accepted fairly quickly that he wasn't going to get an explanation—or anything like the quotidian truth—from the man seated opposite him, and that he might never see the second Mr. Greenstreet again.

"All right," said Raszer, and downed the remainder of his beer. "So be it. If he's gone, then he must have told me all he could. But give me a second to recalibrate. You and I are getting on a private plane for Gaziantep, right?"

"Yes," replied al-Khidr. "Just as I told you. In fact—"

"Just as *you* told me?"

Rashid checked his watch. "It should by now be fueled and ready. Shall we go collect your things and be on our way?"

"Why not?" Raszer pushed back from the table. "I'll take care of the check."

"It's taken care of," said the Kurd. "Everything is taken care of."

TWENTY-FOUR

THE CESSNA'S ENGINE DRONED. Rashid had said little so far; the pilot had said nothing at all. This had been all right with Raszer, who was still far from clear-headed; he took the opportunity to rest his head against the thick pane of glass. He dozed with one eye closed and the other fixed emptily on the weirdly unfolding landscape below.

After a minute, he felt Rashid's eyes on him. "The Bektash Sufis," said the Kurd, "say that creation is continual. Now you see it, now you don't."

"So do the Australian aboriginals," said Raszer, without moving his head. But his words were lost in the rumble of the engines.

✦ ◆ ✦

AFTER THE LANDING and a brief rest in Gaziantep, they boarded the *dolmus*. It was evening by the time they reached the small city of Sanliurfa—'Glorious' Urfa—so named by Atatürk for its stiff resistance to the French occupiers nearly a century before. In another epoch, it had been Alexander's Edessa, and before that, if three thousand years of legend carried any historical weight, the Ur of the prophet Abraham, father of the People of the Book.

And Urfa—Rashid had told him on the bus—was believed by many pious Muslims to have been the historical site of the Garden of Eden.

Paradise or not, the massive dams and aqueducts erected on the Euphrates plain by the Southeastern Anatolia Project had restored some verdancy to the arid land. As far as the eye could see were fields of olive and pistachio and glacial wrinkles of earth with new growth. En route, they'd passed no less than three dams, the largest of them at what had been the Hittite city of Carchemish. All around them was soil reclaimed from desert by governmental largesse. Only after the stop at Birecik did the surroundings return to their naturally barren state, and within thirty minutes, the windows had accumulated a coating of rust-colored silt.

The twilight sky over the town of Urfa seemed a different shade from what Raszer had seen through the windows of the *dolmus,* a different shade from anything he'd seen before. It was magenta at the horizon and deepest purple at the zenith, and the shadows in the old medina were of the same hue.

The pilgrim cities of Islam came brazenly alive at night, as if Allah had retired with the sun, allowing his unruly children to turn the streets into carnival midways. And at the center of Urfa's hubbub, in the oldest part of the old city, was a colonnaded mosque of great age. Through the columns, Raszer spied a sprawling rectangular pool, its waters roiling and flecked gold by thousands of enormous, teeming carp. There were so many fish that the surface appeared a living organism.

"The fish are sacred," Rashid explained. "They were once consecrated to Atargatis, that same Syrian goddess we spoke of in Iskenderun. Now they belong to the prophet Abraham. The legend is that when Nimrod threw Abraham from the tower, Allah turned the burning pyre below to a pond full of carp."

⬥ ◆ ⬥

AFTER DARK, THEY DINED on a tiled terrace in the rear of the safe house, watched over by an armed guard and tended to by a cook. They were served *lahmacun*, a local dish of spicy minced lamb on wafer-thin bread, and Rashid had even managed to obtain a bottle of Minervois. But Raszer, who usually savored food under even the worst of circumstances, had no taste for it tonight. He was troubled by what the events of the past twenty-four hours signaled regarding the reliability of his mental processes.

He was used to labyrinths, but how would he find his bearings in the mirror image of a labyrinth?

"I have a very strange feeling," he told Rashid. "Clinically speaking, I'm not sure it's a lot different from paranoid schizophrenia, and that worries me."

"Describe it to me," said the Kurd. "I may be able to help."

"That may be a little tricky. I feel as if I'm in a borrowed body. As if my own body never left that slab in your office back in Iskenderun. Maybe never left the hangar in Colorado Springs. Maybe never left the bridge over the Rio Grande."

"And what would it mean if that were truly the case?"

"You really want me to say? All right. It would mean that my consciousness is occupying a kind of shadow person. It would mean that the Gauntlet I'm running is in a separate reality. I won't say *virtual reality*, because that would imply a simulation." Raszer's gaze shifted inward, and he spoke half to himself. "I wonder if this is how Scotty felt."

"How else would you expect to feel, Mr. Raszer? You have experienced a profound dislocation, and you have advanced very quickly to a high level of the game."

"How?" asked Raszer. "By what mechanism?"

"To begin with, things formerly hidden have been revealed to you. Things that alter the shape of the world. There is no psychotropic more potent than knowledge. What is it that the Gnostic Gospel says of the seeker? 'When he finds, he will be troubled, and then astonished. And in astonishment, he will rule the world.'"

"I doubt I'm destined to rule, Rashid, but up to a point, I can navigate that world. I'm stuck on a couple of details. For one, if what I'm sensing is genuine, it would most likely mean that you don't exist in any way the world would recognize as real. Has the CIA been messing around with stuff like counterfactuals and quantum detours?"

"I could not say if I exist in a world separate from yours, Mr. Raszer, because as a resident of that world, I would not know that it was separate. It would simply be my world, you see. You would be a visitor. All I can say is that you should honor your intuition, and conduct yourself accordingly."

"I was afraid you'd say that."

"You probably know that the CIA's most important work on remote viewing was done at the Stanford Research Institute in the '60s. After that—after funding for the project was discontinued—work continued under the cover of various black operations. I do not know how far they got. Perhaps our meeting is evidence that they got very far indeed. Let me ask you, Mr. Raszer: Do you believe in the transmigration of souls?"

"The short answer is yes. But I wouldn't have thought it could be induced."

"But why not?" Rashid countered. "How else does the shaman enter the body of the man possessed by demons? Not everyone is capable of such slipping in and out of body, of course, but you would seem to be an ideal candidate. Is this not, in a sense, how you have rescued your lost ones in the past?"

"Never thought of it that way, but—"

"So if your government, or certain forces within your government, wished to put a man inside the fortress of these assassins—a man whose presence might, shall we say, introduce certain variables—would they not turn to someone like yourself?"

"I'm a candidate, all right. Maybe the Manchurian kind. Maybe *I'm* the assassin—" Raszer shook his head. "What happens to the old me if they kill the new one?"

"There are no guarantees," said Rashid. "But let me say this from my own heart. Should that happen, my belief is that your soul, which is also your Rabb—your Lord—will find its way home. You see, in a spiritually developed individual, ascent and descent are continual processes. God descends to you and you ascend to Him. In this very moment, you are flickering like cinema between being and nonbeing. What we call reality is merely 'persistence of vision.' You will learn to walk with one foot in the occulted world and one in the revealed; one in *fana* and one in *baqa*. And you will receive tutelage in this matter from those you will visit next: the Fedeli d'Amore."

"I'll do my best to walk that line. But just the same, I'm going to leave you something to post to my daughter if I don't make it back from the other side."

"Of course."

"What time does this fellow Dante come to fetch me?"

"He will come in the crack between night and dawn."

"When else, right? I'll leave the letter here on the table."

"I envy you, Mr. Raszer. You are going to meet some quite remarkable people. In the land you'll be traveling across—the land of the Alevis, the Yarsanis, the Yezidis, and the Bektash—if you scratch a Muslim, you will find a member of the Cult of Angels: the Yazdani. A faith older than Islam, older even than Judaism. Its survival relies upon deception. Across this landscape, many of its greatest prophets have been crucified. Crucified not by Romans or Crusaders, but by fellow Muslims. Before you reach your destination, God willing, you'll encounter the green man, Khezr, the great trickster. Flowers spring up in his footsteps, and streams alter their course. Him, you may follow without hesitation." Rashid scooped the last morsel off his plate and popped it into his mouth. "And now, I must get some rest—and you also."

"Right. But first, when am I briefed on this identity I'm supposed to assume? This priest, and how he talks his way into El Mirai."

"You will practice a subterfuge," said Rashid, with a little laugh. "You are good at that, are you not? His name is *Frère* Gilles Deleuze. The Fedeli will see to your transformation. It's quite right to say that you have left Stephan Raszer behind."

"And why should the Old Man—the self-proclaimed Lord of Time—do business with a humble friar? If what you say is true, he has powerful friends."

"Because—along with Scotty Darrell—you have something else that he very much wants."

"What's that? I'd like an ace in the hole, because I'm not keen on trading one hostage for another, and even with a silver bullet, I wouldn't kill the king for you."

The Kurd leaned in close, and his gaze bore into the pale blue iris of Raszer's left eye. "This eye of yours," he said, aiming his finger. "It sometimes sees past disguise, yes? Perhaps even beyond the curtain of death?"

"It goes a little haywire every so often. Makes things much more complicated."

"While you wait tonight for the arrival of your escort, contemplate why pilgrims to Mecca circle the Ka'ba seven times and kiss the black stone set in its eastern corner . . . and why they have been doing so since long before Mohammed came."

"That's all you're going to give me? An Islamic koan?"

"Goodnight, Mr. Raszer. *Bonne nuit, Frère Deleuze.*"

✦ ✦ ✦

RASZER REMAINED ON the terrace for an hour after Rashid had gone. When he'd finished the last of the wine, he made his way up to the bedroom designated as his. He lay down, then got up and smoked a cigarette, then lay down and got up again. He couldn't seem to shake the feedback loop that the phrase "since long before Mohammed came" had triggered in his brain.

It had to do with the strange tale Ruthie Endicott had spun when she'd returned Henry Lee's black rock to him on the night before Shams' murder. It was a story his research had at least partly prepared him for, but its implications were explosive. Henry had filched the talisman from right under the nose of the mysterious Black Sheikh after seeing it used to conjure a bit of chaos magick in the tent outside Najaf—the tent where he and Johnny had sworn fealty to the Old Man.

But it wasn't only the stone's magical potency that Henry had risked losing his head for. It was what the sheikh had revealed about its origins. If true, the two-pound chunk of meteoric rock was more than a relic. It was a key to the germination of Islam in something that didn't resemble Islam at all. Something that would shake every mosque from here to Amsterdam and make much of the Islamist cause look like one enormous act of masculine overcompensation.

He decided to check in with Monica, who was surely beside herself by now. It had been forty-eight hours.

The Ionophone, which had at least a dozen features he'd never use, was fancier gear than he liked to carry, but it did have one utility of great value, though to access it he had to open a small plate on the backside and use a jeweler's screwdriver to adjust a tiny set screw. This effectively disabled the phone's GPS capability by scrambling the outgoing signal, a form of data encryption.

"What the hell, Raszer?" Monica said. "I lost you over the Bering Strait, then I picked you up again over the Caucasus. I had you as far as the Euphrates, and now you're off the grid again. That $2,000 transmitter in your ass doesn't seem to be working as advertised. How did you get there? None of the commercial flights—"

He explained as best he could.

"I don't like this," she said flatly.

"I'm not crazy about it either, but there you have it. I could have wandered around southeastern Turkey for weeks and not gotten this close to Katy Endicott."

"Yeah, but at what price? You've made yourself part of someone else's agenda."

"How else do we ever really get what we want?"

"What can I do?" Monica asked. "I feel useless."

"For one thing, you can call in a favor with our guy at the DIA, and pinpoint American and Turkish troop deployments *and* Kurdish separatist hot zones along the Turkey–Iraq border. I want to steer clear of combat as best I can."

"That's not going to be easy where you are."

"I know. Kurdistan isn't even a real country, and it's in a state of war with three of them. Only in the New Age can you make war on a virtual nation."

"Men make war on their nightmares. Always have. What else?"

"Go back into those threads you started on pre-Islamic cults. Let's see if we can get an inkling of where that black stone in the Ka'ba is supposed to have come from."

"The one that looks like a vulva?" she asked.

"Right. According to Islamic legend, it was given to Abraham by the angel Gabriel. There are feminist scholars—and others—who say it's a meteorite used in pre-Islamic worship and later co-opted. There's a connection with the Satanic Verses. Go into the related etymology: Kubaba, Kybele, and Koran. Qur'an. I remember something about Mohammed's tribe being the Quraysh, devotees of Q're. Kore . . . the same one worshipped at Eleusis? Does that make the Koran the word of Kore? And see if you can tie in a Syrian or Nabataean goddess named Atargatis. That's whose head is on the coin I found, and reportedly she's the mascot for the Old Man's fedayeen, his most loyal soldiers.

"There's something really ancient at work here," Raszer continued. "We need to look again at how any of this could possibly relate to the deep history of the Witnesses, to Henry Lee, to castration—to the whole idea of becoming a 'virgin.'"

"Are you going to tell me why the stone in the Ka'ba has anything to do with you . . . or Katy Endicott? It's in Mecca. You're in Turkey."

"Because I'm betting it can be used to work some very powerful magic, and because—as crazy as this sounds—it's just possible that I have a piece of it, or at least what someone thinks is a piece of it."

"The rock you lifted from the evidence room?"

"And that—according to Ruthie—Henry Lee stole from the Black Sheikh."

"Jesus. Well, it makes sense they'd want it back. But I still don't—"

"Look at it this way. Suppose what you discovered about that conference in Damascus is really the nightmare it seems to be: a movement of Christian and Islamic fanatics and their proxies in government to trigger a series of catastrophes that would usher in a rigidly masculinist theocracy, east and west. How much mojo would that movement have if it were revealed that the foundations of Islam lie in the worship of a castrating goddess? How much juice would Pat Robertson have as a eunuch?"

"Before I met you, Raszer, the world was a much simpler place."

"Sorry, sweetheart."

"And whose side is this 'Old Man' on?"

"Neither. And both. He's a broker. A profiteer. And probably a sorcerer."

"Okay," she said. "I'm on it. And when will I hear—"

"As soon as I'm settled with the Fedeli d'Amore, who seem to be the same guys Shams referred to as running a hostel near old Harran. But I don't know what to expect. Not after being briefed by two CIA men who are both named Philby Greenstreet."

"Philby Greenstreet?" Monica repeated.

"That's right."

"Two spooks with the same name?"

"Yeah."

"Expect double the fun, then. Or twice the trouble."

TWENTY-FIVE

RASZER AWOKE AT 4:44 AM and, for a few plummeting moments, had absolutely no idea where he was. A sharp, pinging noise pricked his ears, and he realized he'd been stirred by the sound of someone throwing pebbles at the French window. He swung out of bed, stretched the deathlike sleep of long travel from his limbs, and went to the window, half expecting to see a street urchin straight out of Dickens.

Dante was not a boy, but he wasn't quite a man, either. Twenty-two, twenty-three at most, shaggy haired, round faced, and as saucer-eyed pretty as a Renoir child. He had wound up and was getting ready to hurl the next pebble when he noticed that Raszer had stepped through the window and onto the narrow balcony.

The first light of a false dawn had begun to filter into the old city, painting everything in a watercolor wash of palest blue. Even Dante's fair skin looked bluish.

"Frère Deleuze?" the boy called up. There was a soft Scottish burr in his accent.

"*C'est moi,*" Raszer answered. "But English is my second language."

"That's good," Dante said. "Because my French is crappy."

"Did they tell you why I'm here?"

"To find a missing girl, right?"

"I need to get to El Mirai. Can you help me?"

"If anyone can," replied the young man. "Are you ready to go? The Harran *dolmus* leaves the *otogar* in forty-five minutes. At Harran, my crew will come for us in the pickup. It's a thirty-minute ride to Suayb, and another twenty to Sogmatar. We'd better get going. Big party tonight."

"I'll be right down," said Raszer. "But I didn't bring my party dress."

Quietly and quickly, he repacked his things, then took a minute to compose a note of thanks to Rashid al-Khidr, the latest of his guides on this, the strangest of his journeys. He couldn't be sure that he would ever see the man again. He slipped the note under Rashid's door and padded down the stairs into the cool of the new day.

◆ ◆ ◆

THE SUN BROKE over the distant hills as they were entering the outskirts of Harran and sat like a half-exposed pewter dish for what seemed a long time. By the time they reached the old town center, it had risen fully, and the honeyed light it cast on the ancient beehive huts made them look like marzipan. The huts—dozens of them—were constructed of mud brick, without even the most rudimentary frame, and were entirely uniform in design. Like desert igloos, they had been built straight up from the soil to their pointed tops, and seemed so much a part of the landscape that it surprised Raszer to see human forms emerge from them. Harran had been continuously occupied for six thousand years. The huts were not quite that old, but they might as well have been. The settlement had the look of Afghanistan in Appalachia: rugged people with skin like tarnished brass instruments, and children who seemed far too young for them, playing amid detritus: rusted bicycles, ironing boards, and the odd piece of exercise gear.

"Is this home?" Raszer asked his guide.

"Used to be," answered Dante. "Used to run the outfitting business out of two of the beehives, side by side. But we outgrew them. Needed elbow room." He paused.

"Abraham lived here," Dante continued. "Before he was called to Canaan. The Greeks came through. So did the Romans and the Mongols. They all let it be. It's a godly place. And the people are good-hearted. But we didn't quite fit in. You probably wouldn't either."

"What do you know about me?" Raszer asked. "Besides the fact that my cover is a French-Canadian monk."

"That you're a private eye."

"And who'd you hear that from? Rashid? Or Philby Greenstreet?"

"Neither. We heard it from Shams."

Raszer recalled Shams' late-night emailing from the cyber café in Taos.

"So you know—you knew—Shams. Did he live here for a while, too?"

"He passed through. Stayed for a bit. He was righteous folk. A real baba."

"A baba?"

"A guide. A gate. Comes from *bdb*. A portal to gnosis."

"Yes, he was that. Do you know . . . what happened? Back in Taos."

"Word got through. We held a vigil. But Shams will abide. It isn't the first time he's died. Won't be the last. That was just a meat puppet they killed in Taos. Bastards. They're big on display, big on the horror show, they are."

"Who are they trying to scare?" Raszer asked.

"Right now, you."

The *dolmus* pulled under a makeshift carport next to a filling station and squealed to a stop. Dante gestured to a waiting Toyota pickup. "There's our ride."

"How many of you are there?" Raszer asked.

"You'll see soon enough. Let's grab your gear and go. We're staked out in Suayb, about twenty kilometers north of here. We've gone, uh, underground."

✦ ✦ ✦

THE DRIVER, who introduced himself as Chrétien, wore a red bandana over silky hair as long and unkempt as Dante's. He was taller, a few years older, and had the look of a natural leader, but Raszer saw no overt acknowledgment of rank. Chrétien, despite his name, was not French, but spoke English with the elongated vowels of a Dutchman. He was shirtless and skinny and baked the color of bread crusts by the sun, and he goosed the speedometer to sixty on roads that weren't meant for more than forty.

He glanced at Raszer's pack, then at his boots, and nodded what seemed to be his approval. "When they said you were from L.A.," said Chrétien, "I thought you might show up wearing Gucci loafers. Are you equipped to pack in for a week?"

"I may need a few more things," Raszer replied, "depending on what sort of country we're going to be crossing. I was told you guys could help me with that."

"As long as you don't ask for porters and a five-star chef."

"Not everyone from L.A.'s a slave to luxury," said Raszer. "Although I'll admit I could use a massage and a hot bath."

"Well, there's a *hamam* outside of town if you like it rough. They'll scrub the scales right off your hide."

"Maybe when this is finished," Raszer said. "Speaking of porters, though, can you steer me toward a couple of reliable guides, guys who can keep me clear of combat zones? I'm told I need to get to Hâkkari."

Chrétien shot Dante a grin and kept it on for Raszer. "Will we do?" he asked.

"You'll more than do," said Raszer. "If you're up for it."

"The question is, are you? Ever been that deep into eastern Turkey?"

"I've never been deep into Turkey at all. But I take it you have."

"The twelve of us, we've all played the Urfa route to Hâkkari and the crossroads. But only Dante and I have seen what happens if you take the wrong fork."

"And lived to tell the tale," Dante added.

"And lived to tell the tale," Chrétien repeated, and punctuated it with a fist pump. "Dante was in debt bondage to that motherfucker for nearly two years."

"I got out when he sent me to blow up a resort hotel in Mersin. People would have died. That's where I drew the line. That's where I started to rewrite the rules. Bad things happen when you ask the wrong people how you can serve them."

"Doesn't that sort of moral judgment violate the rules of The Gauntlet?" Raszer asked. "Aren't you supposed to rely on God and the puppet masters to pull you out?"

"The way we came to see it," Chrétien replied. "The way the Fedeli see it, God makes the rules until you've played long enough to know that God's the eye of the heart. That's the epiphany. God sees us with the same eye that we see God. The whole point of The Gauntlet is to become your avatar, to leave your old shell at the side of the road and take on the spiritual body. Then you can be a baba for other pilgrims."

"And what happens to your old shell?"

"Wind drift. Carrion. Buzzards peck at it. Sun bakes it. Bullets rip through it. Doesn't matter. You're dead to it. That much, the Old Man has right. He just has fucking everything else wrong."

"So you—you and Dante—were in service to the Old Man. Did you meet him?"

"Never stood closer than twenty-five meters. He won't allow it. But the guy has presence, I will tell you that. From any distance, you know he's there. You'll see it when you get there . . . if you're able to get in. He's got those kids under some heavy rain. He's shown them the black gnosis, and when you see that, all the curtains come down and you don't know there's any light out there. Your girl, she's in a dark place."

"I was told she was in a garden—"

"It's a garden, all right, but it's a garden of ignorance. Like fucking Disney World on DMT. A garden ruled over by a very jealous god. You know what he calls himself?"

"The Lord of Time?"

"When he's not calling himself Melek Ta'us. The Peacock Angel."

"Melek Ta'us," said Raszer. "That's Lucifer, right? In the Yezidi sect. The angel who wouldn't bow to the demiurge."

"Yeah, but the Yezidi wise men—you'll meet some of them on our way—they're not buying it. They know it's a scam. The people in the villages around there, they buy it. And the fighters and tribesmen—enough of them—swallow it, too."

"Totally," Dante added. "That's how he got forty warlords and ten thousand tribal Kurds and Persians to pay him tribute."

"And my lost girl—Katy—how does she serve him?" Raszer asked.

"You've heard the stories. The Old Man took those Marco Polo legends about Hassan-i-Sabah building a paradise on Earth for his assassins and built a theme park for nihilists." He paused, sobered. "And the girls—American. Uzbeki. Azerbaijani. And especially Iraqi girls, blown out of their homes by the war. They pour across the border into Syria with nothing but the clothes on their backs and nowhere to turn but the sex trade. The Old Man's agents scoop them up and put them to work. And the Syrians look the other way because the Old Man is helping to solve their refugee problem."

"So," Raszer said softly, "it *is* a trafficking operation."

"Yeah," Dante replied. "Girls. Opium. Guns. But it's a shitload more than that."

"His belief system sounds like a real mixed bag. Yezidi dualism. Ismaili antinomianism. Postmodern nihilism."

"All and none of the above," said Chrétien. "This guy's a warlord for the new age. He pulls threads from a dozen different local traditions and knits them into a Persian rug of lies. There's only one thing the Old Man *really* believes in."

"What's that?"

"Annihilation," answered Dante.

"Tell me something else," said Raszer. "The Fedeli d'Amore—"

"All will be told," said Chrétien, "in the right set and setting." He pulled the truck to a halt in front of what looked like a fallen house of cards built from two-ton slabs of white granite.

Raszer got out and turned a circle. The impression was of limitless whiteness. It was a vista drained of all primary color but for the hard blue of the arching sky. In the distant hills, there were patches of state-irrigated land, but few and far between, like pieces of a quilt that would never be finished. In the foreground, masked by the uniform color of the soil, were dozens of outcroppings—carved blocks of bleached stone eight to ten feet high, fallen in upon themselves and concealing chambers beneath. Raszer realized he must be standing in an ancient graveyard, final resting place of chieftains and kings, and that below him must lie a vast underground mausoleum.

"Who's buried here?"

"It goes back at least to the Hittites," said Chrétien. "Maybe farther. But the herders and peasants moved in centuries ago and have squatted ever since. No one bothers them, and so far, no one bothers us. It's sacred ground. There are hundreds of underground chambers, cool in the summer, warm in the winter. All you have to do is keep to your own turf and respect everyone else's. And you can't beat the rent."

"And the outfitting business keeps you going?"

"Mostly, yeah," Chrétien answered. "At least a hundred trekkers come through here every season, headed to Nemrut Dagi or other places on the pilgrim's map. And then there are The Gauntlet players. They can't pay, but we put them on the road anyway. Pro bono."

"And we fix things," added Dante. "The people from the villages, they're crazy about junk electronics: portable TV's, cell phones, MP3 players . . . anything that runs on batteries. But they're not much good with soldering irons and integrated circuits."

"And you are?"

"We've got some world-class geeks in our band of merry men. Guys who might be running companies in Silicon Valley if they hadn't taken up The Gauntlet."

Raszer turned to Dante. "Want to show me around?" he asked.

"Sure," the boy said. "Follow me down. The others should be making it back from their morning rounds pretty soon."

Now that the sun had reached full morning, Raszer gauged the outside temperature at around eighty-two, but as soon as they stepped over the threshold of the burial chamber, it plummeted ten degrees, and grew cooler still as they penetrated the vault. A narrow entrance passage broadened after about ten feet, and he felt, more than saw, the chamber expand on all sides, for his eyes had not yet adjusted to the darkness.

It was as quiet as any place of the dead ought to be, yet the air was pregnant with echoes. Every footfall, every click of the tongue, left two, three mimetic replicas behind. This led to a host of odd sensations, and only increased Raszer's feeling of displacement. Whoever had built the tomb had made room for a lot of tenants, because it was clear from the multiple air currents in the crypt that it continued for hundreds of subterranean yards, maybe farther.

Raszer's nose picked up damp canvas, sweet Turkish tobacco, kerosene, and fresh mint, and through the soles of his boots he felt the floor change from stone to thin carpet. Dante took his elbow and led him to sit on the rug beside a hookah and a pile of blankets. Gradually, his pupils dilated, and before long he realized that there were more than just the three of them.

A shaft of sunlight penetrated the entry passage and spilled onto what Raszer now saw was a very faded Persian rug. Directly across from him sat a young woman flanked protectively by two boys Dante's age. She wasn't classically beautiful, except at the forehead. The face was long and bony, the eyes deep set beneath heavy brows, a generous mouth pierced by a silver ring. But the more he looked at her and she at him, the more impressed he was. She was formidable.

"Will you take some mint tea?" she asked.

"Yes, please," said Raszer.

"Father Deleuze," said Chrétien, "this is Francesca. She's the only mother we've got. She speaks sixteen languages, including all the major Kurdish dialects. And we're all madly in love with her. The dude on her left is Mikhail. And this is Jean."

"Glad to meet you all," said Raszer. "And now that I have, it begs a question. None of you look more than twenty-five, but for you to have been here when Shams was doing his tour, you'd have to have begun playing when—"

"If you try to count years," said Chrétien, "you'll make yourself crazy. There's a little trick you learn when you get to the Ninth Circle of Gauntlet play.

It's called stopping time. Time—chronological time—flows over normal people like a river because they're not in synch with the flux, with the now, the immediate. They fight the river, and the river leaves the sediment of years on them. They get left behind, and they get old. But if you're in synch with the river, you don't collect sediment. You just float."

Raszer's eye widened. "Are you saying you'll never grow up, as long as you stay in play?"

"Think of it," said Chrétien, "as being like an astronaut in suspended animation on a ship approaching an even horizon at something near the speed of light. We'll get older, but slowly. If we return to the world, though, it catches up with us."

"Now that," said Raszer, "is quite a trick. Maybe the greatest trick of all."

"No. There's better. Dante, why don't you begin with our blessing?"

Dante extended his hand to Chrétien, who in turn linked his with Raszer's, and then, like fog creeping in from seven separate passages leading off this central chamber, the rest of the group materialized, until twelve of them—thirteen, counting Raszer—were joined in a circle, hand to hand.

Dante recited:

To every heart which the sweet pain doth move,
And unto which these words may now be brought
For true interpretation and kind thought,
Be greeting in our Lord's name, which is Love.

"I know that," Raszer said. "From somewhere . . . "

"The original Dante's message to the original Fedeli d'Amore," said Francesca.

"It was his bid for membership in their secret society," added the present-day Dante. "And it worked."

"We welcome to our number," announced Chrétien, "Father Gilles Deleuze of Taize, who wishes to be escorted to Na-Koja-Abad, the eighth climate. In the shadow of Na-Koja-Abad, in the place called El Mirai, he hopes to find the one who goes by the world-name of Katy Endicott, and deliver her safely into our care. We pledge to him our protection, insofar as it is in our power to grant it, and ask now that the Green Man, al Khezr, guide us beyond the crossroads. In the name of the creator, Khawandagar, and of the uncreated, Haq, let it be so."

"Let it be so," chanted the group.

"We ask also that our actions take place in the eternally created present, that there be no thought of past or future, and that we be guided only by the truth as first shown to us by our beloved baba. The world begins now."

"The world begins now," they all repeated.

"And from *alam-al-mithal*, the middle world, we call a servitor, spirit of Shams of Taos."

"For every beginning, there is an end," said Francesca, initiating a litany.

"For every lord, a vassal," said Dante.

"For every angel, a devil," followed Mikhail.

"For every life, a death," said Jean.

"For every height, an equal depth," said the fifth.

"For every joy, an equal sorrow."

"For every kindness, an equal cruelty," said the seventh.

"For every pleasure, an equal pain."

"For every good, an equal evil."

"For every truth, an equal lie."

"For every soul in the other world, a soul embodied."

"For every heaven, an abyss," said Francesca, closing the circle.

"So taught our baba," said Chrétien. "Peace be unto him."

"Peace be unto him," they all said.

"Woof!" came an echo.

At some point during the recitation, a new member had joined the circle, its presence evidenced only by a soft panting. The dog, which Raszer guessed to be some kind of Irish wolfhound, had appeared to Francesca's right and was now resting its muzzle on her skirts.

"Father Deleuze," she announced, "we would like you to meet our baba, Shaykh Adi, master and protector of our circle."

"Shaykh Adi . . . " Raszer repeated.

"He returned from the Eighth Climate to be our guide and guardian."

"The hardest kind of evil for people to see," said Dante, "is the evil that looks like good. But Shaykh Adi sniffs that shit right out. He finds the snake under the rock."

"He chose the form of a dog because the dog is sacred to our faith. You see," she said, rising from the circle and indicating the crypt wall. "Here he is."

Painted in natural pigments that might have been millennia old were a series of figures, among them was clearly a canine holding a wriggling snake in its jaws.

"In the native religions of the Kurdish people," Francesca explained, "dogs symbolize harmony and unity; snakes stand for discord and separation. Not in a dualistic way, but as counterbalancing forces. You can't have one without the other."

Nearby was an elegant symbol from whose north pole seven gently arching ribs flowed like lines of longitude, passing through an array of seven beads at the equator and rejoining at the south end of the axis, where they formed a vortex leading back up the circle by way of a vulvalike ellipse at the center.

"And that," Raszer said, indicating the symbol. "Tell me about that."

"At the top," Francesca replied, "is the Haq, the pearl of the godhead, and emanating from that is Khawandagar, the creator. The seven arcs are the seven avatars of each of the world's ages. They're our guides through all incarnations until we reach full humanity. Jesus was one of them; so was the Prophet, and Isaac, and Ali. We can flow back to the source through these, or we can, if our hearts are strong enough and the Khezr is willing to guide us, take a shortcut through the center—"

"And then what happens?"

"We learn to live simultaneously in two worlds," she replied. "Our physical bodies remain in the world of *zahir*. But our subtle bodies pass through the eye of the heart"—she placed her finger in the center of the ellipsis—"and merge with the world of forms. We put on the psychic skin of our avatars, and evil can't touch us—"

"Because you've shed your own skin?" Raszer asked.

"You've got it," said Chrétien. "But it's a real trick to maintain that state. The subtle body flickers on and off like a strobe . . . sometimes even like a dying bulb. Sometimes you lose it altogether, and you're stuck back in the world, washing dishes and swatting mosquitoes."

"And that can get dangerous," said Dante. "Because when you walk the middle path, you can just as easily fall toward evil as good."

"So we try to straddle," said Chrétien.

"And you're straddling now?" asked Raszer.

"Can't you feel it?"

Shaykh Adi gave a soft but emphatic bark, and his eyes glowed. The dog seemed to know. The dog, Raszer could persuade himself, did seem to be in two worlds.

Francesca smiled at his recognition. "The Kurds who live between here and Hâkkari practice the oldest organized religion in the world. Organized, meaning it has a cosmology and shared ritual. It influenced the Essenes and early Christianity. It shaped the Romans when they came here as conquerors and turned them on to Mithras, who is one of its avatars. It nearly absorbed Shia Islam in the Middle Ages, and still colors it. It sent the crusaders back to southern France, singing troubadour songs to the Lady—who is our lady, the lady of the Fedeli. It branched off into Baha'i in the nineteenth century. And it's the bedrock of the Bektash Sufis, who roam all over these lands. The Cult of the Angels, they call it. It's the face behind the veil."

"And what about the other cult?" asked Raszer. "The cult of the Old Man."

"If you go back far enough," said Chrétien, "it's a graft from the same tree. But so were Cain and Abel. The original Ismaili Assassins—back in the eleventh and twelfth centuries—they were Gnostics, mystical terrorists. Omar Khayyám was down with them. So was Shams of Tabriz. And the Templars carried their wisdom back to Europe. On seventeen Ramazan—the eighth of August in 1164, Hassan II, the son of Hassan-i-Sabbah, declared the Qiyamat, the great resurrection. The chains of worldly law were broken, and every man and woman was freed to live in the spirit as the vassal of his or her own lord. Like the '60s, only without the bad acid. Nothing is true, all is permitted.

"But that was meant to apply to life in the resurrection body—the body without organs. The lords of this world misread the message . . . used it as a cover for lawlessness and greed. That's the problem with the world—the rulers can't read poetry."

"So," said Raszer, "the Old Man appropriates the belief system of the Nizaris, offers his followers a paradise on Earth, and rents his services out to Islamist and Christian fanatics alike, knowing that he'll wind up in the catbird's seat if he can mediate their common agenda. Is that about the size of it?"

"There's a war on for the soul of the world," said Francesca.

"Look at where we are now," said Chrétien, picking up Francesca's thread. "American troops and missile launchers all along the Iraqi border with Syria, Turkey, and Iran. The Yanks have lost the Kurds—if they ever really had them—because they reneged on their promises in order to placate Turkey. And they've catalyzed a regional war. Syria's one big arms bazaar and a conduit for human traffic. Israel's pincered between two conflicting Palestinian states. Everybody's locked into conflict, with no way out. The world is in a preapocalyptic state."

"Seems that way," said Raszer. "Since you're the crew that's going to take me across this battlefield, I guess I should ask: Who are your friends and, more important, who are your enemies?"

"You'd be better to ask who *isn't* our enemy," Francesca replied. "We're a threat to everyone from emperors to schoolteachers. Right now, we're a particular threat to the Old Man's recruitment effort, because pilgrims pass through here on their way to him."

"As far as friends go," said Chrétien, "we can count on the Yazdani spiritual leaders—the genuine ones—and the Bektash Sufis . . . when we can find them. And the Kurdish tribesmen . . . if they aren't under the Old Man's boot."

"Those are good friends to have in this neighborhood," said Raszer. "And if we need muscle . . . to get Katy safely out of the country?"

Dante answered. "Hired guns aren't hard to find here."

"How large is the Old Man's posse?" Raszer asked. "Hundreds? Thousands?"

"At least three thousand at El Mirai," said Chrétien. "And more scattered around the globe."

"Jesus. All from The Gauntlet?"

"No. Only his assassins-in-training. The others are captured, like your girl, or put into debt bondage—only he gets a little help in that regard. There are field agents—church pimps, to put it plainly—planted within theocratic ministries on both sides who single out the most alienated, most antisocial, most hopeless of their flock."

An image of Amos Leach flickered onto Raszer's mental screen.

"And," added Chrétien, "he's got mercenaries at his disposal—both local tribesmen and professionals."

"I guess I should have figured that," said Raszer. "When do we leave?"

"Soon," replied Chrétien. "But first, we dance. And make you over."

"Right . . . Dante mentioned a party. What's the occasion?"

Dante grinned. "Ever hear of the Ayini Jam?"

"The spring equinox festival?"

The boys looked at each other. Dante answered. "It's going on all over Kurd country. Peaks two nights from now. That's when the candles get blown out."

Raszer cocked an eyebrow.

"And," concluded Francesca, "you'll never be afraid of the dark again."

TWENTY-SIX

MONICA DRAGGED HER latest files into the folder named Ka'ba on her computer's desktop. As was to be expected with web-based research, some of the material was dubious, some seemingly authoritative. A piece by a goddess scholar named Rufus Camphausen even came with pictures of the rarely photographed black stone, secured in the corner of the shrine by an oval-shaped silver band and looking—Monica had to admit—like a vagina. What a twist. The same puritanical Muslim men who wouldn't allow their wives to leave the house unaccompanied, lining up to kiss the cunt of a pre-Islamic goddess. It was four o'clock in the afternoon, and she decided it was time for tea.

Four monitors were arrayed at her workstation, each one with multiple windows open, each of them displaying information related to Raszer's current assignment. Monica scanned them to be sure she'd saved anything newly written or discovered, then rose from the console, empty cup in hand. As she began making her way to the kitchen, the room grew suddenly dimmer. The effect was like that of a partial eclipse, but there were no acts of God scheduled for today that she knew of. The floor lamps in Raszer's sunken living room had dulled to a sort of burnt umber, and she saw ahead that the light over his slate-topped bar was flickering.

"Shit," she said out loud, and turned in alarm toward the office. "It's a brownout."

She hurried back toward her station, intent on backing up and shutting down before there was a power spike—a constant hazard in L.A. She got to the threshold just in time to see the first of the viral worms crawling across the monitor screen on the left. It was computer language, but not one she recognized. The characters now gobbling up her research were none that had origins on her keyboard in any configuration she knew. They streamed in from the upper right-hand corner of the screens, leaving gibberish in their wake. Her throat tightened, constricting her windpipe.

She set her cup down, rushed to the console, and began frantically—and, she knew in her heart, pointlessly—trying to hold off the invading armies. In all their years in this office, they had contracted only one virus, and that had been in the days when there was little to lose.

Within a matter of seconds, everything on her hard drive was gone.

"Fuck! Fuck! Fuck!" she screamed.

Then, with the empty screens and a ripple of breeze through the open garden doors, the terror came. It spread over her skin like a frost, leaving her fingertips numb and cold. "Lars?" she called through the window. He ought to be just outside. He ought to answer right away.

But he didn't.

She willed her legs to carry her to the front door, and peered through the pane to his post on the balcony. The chair was empty; his makeshift beach cabana had fallen over. Pulling a breath into her lungs, she opened the door and stepped out. "Lars?" she called again, feeling the name catch in her throat. Two houses down, where the green sedan belonging to the FBI surveillance team ought to have been, was an empty space at the curb.

"Shit," Monica whispered. Empty hard drives, empty chair, empty parking space. The next thing to be emptied, she reasoned, would be her veins. Her impulse was to start walking and keep walking—right down the middle of the street—until she'd reached Hollywood and the safety of numbers.

But she didn't want to get into her car. They might have fucked with it. She didn't want to go back into the house. Monica understood in that moment of paralysis the difference between even dedicated amateurs like her and professional soldiers and spies. Stress training enabled them to make good decisions in situations like this one. They were taught, fundamentally, how to stay alive, because that meant being able to carry out the mission. All she had was her native wit and a loyalty to Raszer that went beyond all rational explanation.

But she was also stubborn, and it was her stubbornness that impelled her back into the office to shut down the system, retrieve their two external hard drives, and lock the place up. She did all this on autopilot because, as far as she could tell, her brain was not working. Finally, she got into the car, tossed the drives on the passenger seat, and turned the ignition with her eyes shut tight.

The Toyota started without a bang, the brakes seemed to work all right, and she was so relieved that she failed to notice as she turned onto Whitley Drive that a white delivery van had pulled away from the curb behind her. After ten minutes' driving, her pulse at last left her throat, and she opened the glove compartment to retrieve the security cigarette she kept there for bad dates, hormonal days, and moments like these.

◆ ◆ ◆

SPECIAL AGENT BERNARD DJAPPER dried his hands, adjusted his bow tie in the mirror, and prepared to leave the airport bathroom. Behind him, the stall door opened quietly and the young man slipped out. Djapper felt reasonably calm—all things considered—but he knew that soon enough, the tension would rise back into his jaw. He dreaded that feeling, because he knew it meant he was not resolute.

The thing was not to show it. Whatever transitory passions had, in the previous minutes, rippled the perfectly composed landscape of his exterior must now be patted as neatly back into place as his cowlick. He'd spent considerable time and effort making himself an exemplary model. An exemplary model of *what*, precisely, he could no longer remember. Some paragon of responsible masculinity once glimpsed in an old movie or a children's book. Someone always addressed as Mister, or Sir, or Father. Not too many years ago, there had briefly been a woman in his life (the corner of his mouth twitched at the memory of her). Before leaving, she'd told him that he worked so hard at being "normal" that he'd made himself anything but. *Bitch.*

Something he glimpsed as he stooped to pick up his briefcase disturbed him, and he turned back to the mirror. An unruly eyebrow hair. He removed from his briefcase a small leather grooming kit, took out a pair of tweezers, and plucked it out.

A smile flickered across his face, an acknowledgment of the vanity of his vanity. He knew that the pride he took in his appearance had no basis in beauty. But his ordinariness served to disguise the extraordinarily complicated man beneath, and it was from this deception that his pride flowed. If F. Scott Fitzgerald had been right to say that the mark of intelligence was the ability to hold two conflicting ideas in the mind at the same time, then Djapper might be a genius, for he could hold two minds in his mind at the same time. He was, in his own estimation, an expert liar.

Nobody knew the real Bernard Henry Djapper.

Very little had ever come "naturally" to Djapper; he'd worked hard for everything he had. Some men, he thought, hadn't earned their grace—the private detective, for instance. Even he, Bernard Djapper, had been seduced, and he'd nearly given away the store. After years of painstaking self-containment, he'd nearly spilled it all. Like that grade-school guilt flush that made you want to confess that you'd put the tack on Teacher's chair, even when you hadn't. Djapper hated himself for it, and hated the detective. How nice to think that men could make themselves over. How nice to think that a man could choose his "role." Some men had destinies. The possibility of friendship—of a connection—had almost detoured Djapper from his. Never again.

The enemy was forever equating what was "natural" with what was good. But nature was corrupt and corrupting. Likewise, natural history—if allowed to run its course—would weaken human purpose. History sometimes had to be redirected, even radically, if only to prevent entropy and rot. No prospect was as exciting to him as being a shaper of history, and no history could be more thrilling than the one being shaped right now. It was the first thing he'd ever felt willing to die for.

Every so often, things would reach a point of confusion, and Djapper would begin to lose himself in his deception, become so enamored of its craft, that he forgot why he was doing it. At such times, it was necessary to remind himself of what he really wanted: He wanted things to be clean. Uncomplicated. If someone had suggested to him that this presented a paradox—that a man preferring black and white could live in shades of gray—he would have answered, "No, I'm not a paradox. I'm a patriot."

He left the bathroom and made his way out of the Tom Bradley International Terminal. His cargo had been shipped and, when it arrived at that distant port, would introduce viral agents into Stephan Raszer's game, as surely as one monkey could infect an entire zoo. These agents would compel countermeasures on Raszer's part, but nothing would kill the contagion. There is no antibody for the unexpected. It wasn't that Djapper desired to see the PI dead; it wasn't about desire at all. Raszer was simply in the way of the particular history Djapper and his colleagues were trying to effect. He looked forward to assuring them that the obstacle had been eliminated.

There was one more chore to do before he could assure them that everything was back in place. From LAX, Djapper headed northeast on the I-5 toward downtown Los Angeles, where a team of private security contractors in Douglas Picot's charge were now preparing to convey Scotty Darrell to Edwards Air Force Base, on the wind-raked desert flats east of Mojave, California. From there, the plan had been to rendition Darrell into hands less bound by law and convention. In U.S. custody, he could only cause trouble. As an enemy combatant, he was effectively disposed of.

But Agent Djapper had been informed that there was more mischief afoot. The fabric had begun to fray even before the election, and now, with less than two years left before the end date, there were seams showing everywhere. If the boy boarded the plane, it would be the beginning of the unraveling of everything. If he boarded the plane, he was going to Greenstreet.

He could not be permitted to get there.

The traffic was good, and after twenty minutes, he pulled into the underground garage. At the last instant, he veered into the lane for valet parking. *What the hell*, he thought. *You only live once*. He pulled up and stepped out, nodding stiffly to the attendant who held the door for him, then breezed through the security doors on just a single flash of his badge. It was true what they said: Act powerful, and people assume you are. If he'd self-parked, they'd have run his credentials, maybe patted him down.

The basement corridor Scotty was due to be brought down was long, wide, and dim, and broken up by alcoves leading to file rooms and unused offices. In any case, it was a Sunday, and not even the most dedicated civil servants were working. It led directly to the parking garage; halfway down, there was an emergency exit to the alley off Hill Street, an exit Djapper meant to use. He parked himself in the alcove nearest the exit and dropped briefly into a squat. For some reason, he thought it would be appropriate to pray, but he really had no experience with it. He mumbled a few words about fortitude and then stood back up. The gun felt good against his ribs. He wanted to put his hand on the grip, but knew that if he did so, his palm would soon begin to sweat and make his hold less than sure at the critical moment.

He heard footsteps.

As he put his hand on the grip, he told himself that he was more than a Jack Ruby. Ruby had slithered from beneath a rock and struck to prevent a great unmasking of deep power. This was different. Wasn't Djapper, like Picot and the others, an idealist? The world they wanted was one in which the choices were clear, where ideas and cultures in stark opposition were allowed to face off. As it had been in the '50s, with the Reds. How was the right side ever to win if history continued to blur the distinctions?

With regard to his own fate, he was realistic. They'd told him he'd do two years at most. But they'd told Ruby that, too, and he'd died in his prison cell.

The party turned the corner much sooner than he would have estimated based on sound. The echo of jangling chains off linoleum and high-gloss institutional paint had created an illusion of distance. Djapper was surprised to feel his mouth go dry on first seeing the boy. He'd played this through so many times. Scotty, shackled, had a DynCorp man at each elbow and two more behind. At the rear were three NSA agents and Douglas Picot. For all the speed with which they'd reached the main corridor, they now moved as if through water.

A slowing of time occurs on the cusp of violent events, like a rallentando just before the big finish in a symphony. Djapper had experienced this phenomenon before drug raids, and once when thwarting an assassination. The ether through which time flows suddenly attains a higher viscosity. When he stepped from the alcove, his gun drawn, there was an instant of cessation within which he was able to perceive the shape of things with absolute clarity. He could see the secret thoughts concealed by each guarded expression and suddenly knew that behind any conspiratorial act are as many differing agendas as there are conspirators. In any case, he'd passed the point of retreat.

He took another step and aimed for Scotty's heart.

While the others seemed barely to register him at first, Scotty turned instantly, and so did the course of events. The boy wore an expression Djapper had seen before on the faces of the condemned. He smiled, and Djapper realized he'd been trumped, and that Scotty would be the one to make history today. He felt a rush of vertigo as two of the DynCorp men broke from the posse. They pinned his arms against the wall and hammered the gun loose. Scotty dropped his chin to his chest and mumbled something that might have been a prayer. Three seconds later, the explosion came.

In his last moments of consciousness, Djapper witnessed the carnage from the vantage of the ceiling, nine feet above the killing floor. He'd heard of such things happening at the instant of passage from life to death, but didn't know whether he was being afforded the perspective because he was having an out-of-body experience or because his head, blown from his torso, was tracing an arc over the scene with still-seeing eyes. All members of the escort were dead, and the Darrell boy was in a hundred little pieces.

With a terrible *thump*, the curtains dropped and it was dark.

✦ ◆ ✦

"How the hell did he get a bomb?" Raszer asked, on a static-ridden connection between a hillock in Sogmatar and Lt. Borges in Los Angeles.

"Obviously, they had someone on the inside," Borges replied.

"Obviously, but who?"

"Scotty saw a lawyer his parents brought in, and an outside doctor checked him over at the lawyer's insistence."

"Not likely it was either of them," said Raszer.

"Not likely, but at this stage we can't dismiss anyone. Jesus, what a mess. You see these things on the news, but close up, you can't imagine the damage."

"How about you, amigo? Are you okay?"

"Christ. This is going to push the mother off the deep end."

"It makes a shitty job even shittier, Luis, that's for sure. I feel like I've outlived my usefulness."

"Not to me," said Borges. "Know what my grandmother used to say?"

"No. What?"

"You walk through graveyards, don't be surprised if the dead follow you home."

"I'd better go, Lieutenant," Raszer said. "Will you let me know what develops?"

"I will," said Borges. "You be careful. And if you find yourself without any cards to play, come home. I wouldn't advise bluffing with these people."

"Thanks, Luis. You be careful, too." Borges clicked off, and Monica was back on the line. "Monica," he said. "I think I may need some protection."

"Let me see what I can find over there. How many men?"

"Maybe three, four. To station along the approach to this . . . fortress."

"What do you want me to do about our files? Should I try and retrieve the data?"

"No. Not now. We'll rebuild everything when I get home. For all purposes, we're closing up shop."

TWENTY-SEVEN

THE MOON WAS FULL, and bright enough to make bobbing shadows on the pale rock. People were dancing wildly, arms in the air. The empty whiteness of the rising land was even more apparent by night, when it glowed as if absorbing ultraviolet from the stars. There was music—of *saz* and spiked fiddle and frame drums hammered in furious counter-rhythm—and vocalizing in blue moans and ecstatic shouts.

The temple ruins at Sogmatar were a second-century watchtower built of blocks quarried from the same white stone that formed the low, surrounding hills. But the place was older than that. It was at the northernmost reach of Mesopotamia, an outpost of the Babylonian moon god, Sin, and his orgiastic Sabian cult, but long before that, a shrine of Venus in one of her guises. There were Syriac inscriptions on the rock, and a crescent moon carved on the tower. From here, on the Anatolian massif, the Tigris on its southeastern course passed through the first cities and had carried away the blood of the first wars. Down that red river—maybe not far—some white-knuckled Carolina kid clutched his rifle as he felt the breath of ancient gods on his neck.

This place now served as the ceremonial ground of the band of brothers into whose hands Raszer had been delivered. It was about twelve miles north of the Fedelis' Suayb retreat. They had traveled here in a small fleet of old Land Cruisers, and later been joined by a ragtag collection of visitors, local twenty-somethings of both sexes who had evidently trekked in from neighboring villages. Altogether, there were about thirty bodies dancing a dithyramb beneath the moon, firelight strobing their brown flesh. They were grouped tightly atop a flat expanse of rock. Shouts went up and the huddle broke as the dancers drew back to reveal what was in their midst.

On a seat once occupied by a priest of the moon god, Stephan Raszer sat cross-legged, his freshly shaven head reflecting moonglow. Francesca held a straight razor in her hand and appeared pleased with her work. She looked to

Chrétien for assent. Nodding approval, he approached Raszer and regarded the transformation. "Not bad," he said. "It's amazing what changing just a couple of features will do."

Someone brought Raszer a tarnished mirror. At first, it startled him not to recognize his own face. He realized he hadn't looked in a mirror since leaving Taos, and wondered if it was possible that the disembodied feeling he'd had over the last twenty-four hours might be linked to a change in his appearance greater than what the girl could have accomplished with a razor, a brush, and a pair of tweezers. Could his inner state somehow have been externalized? No, he concluded quickly. Too crazy. And yet. His scalp was hairless, and his eyebrows had been thinned and dyed with henna, and these cosmetic strokes had changed everything.

"Wow," he whispered. "That's some makeover."

"It's all about directing attention," Francesca said. "For example, you haven't stopped looking at my lip ring since you got here, so you probably haven't noticed my chin. A shaved head alters the shape of a face. Different eyebrows make different eyes. But you're not finished yet. We need something to draw attention away from your mouth. That mouth gives you away." She smiled. "I'll bet the girls like that mouth. It's full of bad intentions."

"What do you have in mind?" Raszer asked, now aware of her dimpled chin.

"Well, there is one little touch that would do it, but it would involve some scarification."

"Scarification?" Raszer repeated.

She ran a fingernail gently down his left cheek, stopping just short of his mouth. "If we make a cut along this line, it will be the first thing people register. It will be the thing they remember. But we'd have to let it scar, and then you'd be stuck with it."

"Kind of a souvenir." He paused. "To remember you by, Francesca. If you think it will make the critical difference, go ahead."

In truth, the only thing that concerned him was that it would frighten Brigit.

"We can't use the razor, though," said Chrétien. "Too clean a cut. If it's going to scar over right, we need some rough edges. A piece of flint, maybe."

Raszer slipped off the stool and surveyed the site. There were other shrines on other rises in the land—he counted four within sight—each one reflecting the silver from above, but this one seemed to be the hub. He'd read about the

Sabian moon worshippers. Their rites were wild and had survived here well into the Muslim era. The new priests of Allah had for a time coexisted with the old priests of Sin, or Marilaha, or the most ancient: Bel. *Bel.* Be'el. Betyl. Beth-El. Ba'al. Baal. Baetyl. Sacred rock. There were thousands of chips of all sizes scattered in the vicinity. He picked up one about the size of his palm from beside the fire and handed it to Francesca. "Let's do it," he said, and sat down before her.

The dancers had moved back and slowed to a willowy sway, quiet now. "I'll have to be fairly brutal about this," Francesca said, examining the stone for its sharpest edge, "if it's to look like a wound."

"I understand," said Raszer. "I'll try not to hit back."

A smile crossed her lips, and without preface, she leaned in and kissed him full on the mouth, her jeweled lips parting just enough for him to feel her tongue against his teeth and taste the silver in her ring. Then she took a step back and struck the blow while he was still dizzy from the kiss. Blood ran into his mouth and he felt the night air in the cut, but he was surprised by how little pain there was. She held the towel against his cheek to staunch the flow, then took his hand and moved it into place.

"Press firmly," she said. "Until your pulse slows. We'll have to cauterize it to keep it from getting infected." She raised her eyes to Dante, who then went to the fire and probed through the white-hot ash with a stick, looking for a suitable stone. Raszer lifted the cotton towel from his face and tossed it to the boy to use as a mitt.

"I want you to lie down," said Francesca. "Over there." She indicated a slab of stone, half-buried in the alkaline soil, and led him to it, then motioned for him to lie down. All the while, she kept hold of his fingers.

"I'm not a virgin, you know," said Raszer. "In case that matters to Venus."

"Venus will have to take you as you are." She placed her free hand on his forehead. "Dante," she called. "If it's hot enough, bring it over."

Dante folded the towel over twice and removed from the fire a smooth stone the size of a child's fist. From the corner of his eye, Raszer saw Chrétien signal the musicians, and they began to play an incantory rondo that had a bit of the blues in it. The dancers started swaying again, but with a certain restraint. The other members of the Fedeli were mixed in with the locals, some of them having paired up for the dance with village girls who wrapped around them like vines.

The dancers stirred, and two in the front parted to let through Shaykh Adi, the Fedelis' canine *dai*, who came panting to the altar. The dog nuzzled Francesca and then lapped wetly at Raszer's open wound.

"The baba's blessing," said Francesca.

An instant later she pressed the stone to Raszer's cheek and he heard the hiss of his own skin being seared. The *saz* played a lick, and Francesca stroked his newly shaven head. The dancers drew nearer, the smell of flesh was in his nostrils, and for a moment, Raszer's mind's eye left his body and raced out over the Sumerian plain.

He heard his name called, but he did not answer to it. For now, it belonged to another.

TWENTY-EIGHT

THE TOYOTA LURCHED over a steep embankment and came to a stop, its engine surging twice before dying. They were atop a mesalike land formation just above the old traders' road, a passage that had been there in one form or another since the days of Marco Polo. Francesca cranked the ignition, and the engine protested with a deep and ominous whine. A second attempt, and it turned over.

"She's getting old," Francesca said. "She's gone 118,000 miles on the same set of valves. All the dust here wears them down. But she'll make it to Hakkâri."

Raszer nodded, less than reassured. There were four of them in the Land Cruiser, with a second vehicle hitched behind. Francesca took turns at the wheel with Dante, and Raszer shared the backseat with the dog, Shaykh Adi, who'd taken to laying his perpetually drippy muzzle on Raszer's thigh, the loose flaps of his cheeks spreading like a skirt and leaving an expanding wet spot on Raszer's khakis. He'd have preferred Francesca's head in his lap, but could hardly say no to a holy man. Given the dog's exalted status, his affection might be a form of grace.

The Land Cruiser's luggage area was loaded to the ceiling with gear. There were boots, climbing slippers, heavy woolens, axes of half a dozen sizes and weights, and three hundred meters of nylon climbing rope, along with the other essential hardware of the craft. It seemed like overkill to Raszer, who liked to travel light.

They had left Suayb before dawn and had been on—or off—the road for close to eight hours. It was now approaching high noon, and even at 4,400 feet, it was getting hot. They were traveling high roads, some roughly paved and some not much more than cattle paths, skirting the Turkish–Syrian border and dodging north as necessary to avoid battlegrounds in the ever-metastasizing war.

The virus of conflict that had traveled up the Tigris by way of the American invasion had now spawned opportunistic infections from the Hindu Kush to the Caucasus. Closest at hand was the bloody game of tit for tat between the Turkish army and Kurdish separatist forces, in which U.S. troops had been given the impossible role of referee but were slowly and surely being drawn into the fight. Anti-aircraft fire issued from the floor of the valley below, and there were bright flashes of light in the hard blue sky, followed by concussions that shook the mountains like the bass on a hip-hop track. Based on what could be seen at this height, a battle analyst would have had a hard time drawing conclusions about the alignment of forces, much less putting points on the scoreboard.

There seemed to be both Turkish and U.S. aircraft in evidence, dropping payloads on whatever and whomever was unfortunate enough to be wedged between the two steep mountain ranges. From time to time, a fearsome-looking eggbeater would swoop into the breach and pepper the foothills with fire, but it was hard to identify its target. The official story was that the Turks were raining hell on the Kurds and the PKK's stingers were hitting back, while the Americans were bombing the middle ground, ostensibly in an effort to enforce a cease-fire and—at all costs—prevent Syria from throwing in with Turkey against the Kurds and rupturing the NATO alliance in the process.

But everyone knew that things had gone far beyond that. If someone wound up dropping a nuclear weapon on Mosul, it would be the first time in history that a state had been destroyed before it had even raised its first flag. Because the borders were where they were, it would also be an act of war against Iraq, and against both U.S. and Iranian interests, and that would be the beginning of the end—the twenty-first century's Sarajevo.

It would have, Raszer thought, a symmetry worthy of some grim bard's epic poem: the nations of the world, spoiling for apocalypse in the land that had first given rise to the notion of civilization. If what Philby Greenstreet had told him was true, the end of civilization was precisely what those cheering on the End Times wanted, for only then could the self-anointed prophets of an avenging God reclaim dominion over Earth.

Francesca released the catch on the Land Cruiser's hood, and Dante got out to have a look. Raszer, itching for a smoke, joined him on the overlook and gestured to the fireworks in the valley.

"Is this a preview of what we'll be passing through?" he asked.

"Sad to say, yeah," Dante replied, checking the fuel injectors. "There will be some quieter stretches away from the border, and after we cross the Buzul

Dagi into the Old Man's autonomous region, it's a no-go zone. Until then, we'll see a lot of this."

"How the hell are we going to avoid checkpoints?"

"Have faith, *rafiq*. You're not our first pilgrim."

"I might be the first to have a price on his head."

Dante reseated the injector cable and lowered the hood. "Not even," he said, and gave Francesca a thumbs-up. "We all do."

⬩◆⬩

AT SIX O'CLOCK, after ten hours of hard driving that had gained them barely three hundred miles, they came to a small village in the Mardin Daglari range, tucked into a transverse valley about sixty miles north of the border and an equal distance south of Batman, the closest town of any size. This village could not have been home to more than three or four hundred people, yet it had the look of a destination. Its cobblestone main street was lined with brightly painted dwellings and shops bunched on a precipitous slope, slipped into place like colored beads on a string. In the angled light of late afternoon, the place gave rise to a deep sense of dislocation in Raszer.

"Does it have a name?" he asked Francesca. "This village."

"No," she replied. "That's one of its charms. According to the stories, the villagers figured out centuries ago that if you didn't name your town, it didn't get on the map, and if it wasn't on the map, no one came looking for it. It was an enclave of Nestorian Christians fifteen centuries ago. Now it's a kind of refuge for renegades of all stripes. And we are welcome here."

"Nestorians," Raszer repeated, lifting Adi's muzzle gently from his thigh.

"They rejected the notion that *God* suffered on the cross," Francesca said, "or that Mary was literally the mother of God. Jesus was an avatar, not a god."

Francesca signaled for the group to follow her down the oddly empty street. "The Nestorians made too much sense, so they condemned them as heretics."

They were joined by the dog, who came straight to Raszer's side. "Weird time, the fifth century," he said. "This whole part of the world consumed by the issue of what Jesus was: Arians claiming he was wholly physical, and Docetists and Monophysites claiming he was wholly spiritual, and the Church frantically trying to hold the middle by insisting he was both. You have to give them credit for taking their religion seriously, but they all sort of missed the forest for the trees, didn't they?"

"Which forest?" asked Dante, catching up.

"Well, as far as I've been able to tell, Jesus never claimed he was the only one with keys to the kingdom. He said he was one with the Father, but if anyone had asked, I think he'd have said it was pretty much the same for all of us."

"Every man both lord and vassal," said Dante. "That's what Ibn Arabi says."

"Where is everybody?" Raszer asked. Not a shop seemed to be open, nor was there evidence of life behind the dwellings' fancifully painted shutters.

"They're all getting ready for the Jam," answered Francesca. "The Jamkhana. The festival. It's the big finish of the Naruz celebration. New Year's. Tomorrow, there'll be one hell of a rave."

"It's a shame we'll miss it," said Raszer.

Francesca came to a stop in front of an absurdly narrow one-story building with a blue door, wedged between two somewhat larger stone structures. "We won't miss it," she corrected. "Not for the world. We'll be staying here two nights."

"That's news to me," said Raszer. "I'd love nothing better than to take in the local color, but we have miles to go—"

"Trust us," said Francesca. "Those miles will go much faster after you've been adjusted."

"Adjusted to what?"

"This village is a crossover, Stephan. A *pardivari*. A sort of bridge."

"Okay. So it's like getting used to the altitude before going for the summit," Raszer said.

"Right," Dante answered, pushing in the door and holding it for his companions. "And the crossing begins here." They filed in, the wolfhound bringing up the rear.

Raszer's first adjustment was to the darkness of the little tavern, which appeared at first no larger than a generous cupboard. It was a minor masterpiece of spatial planning, as the proprietor—a gaunt figure with a luxuriant moustache—had somehow found room for an eight-foot bar of rough cedar and four stools. All the booze must have been stowed beneath the bar, as there was space behind it only for the rib-thin owner and a large, tarnished mirror that gave the place what little depth it had. An oil lamp cast a faint glow on the man's face. The rest of the room receded into blackness.

Francesca greeted the proprietor in what Raszer took to be Kurdish. It was a language he knew nothing of, and had had no time to crack. She motioned for them to sit, but Raszer remained standing. His eyes were drawn to the stranger in the mirror—the stranger that was his transformed self—and to the glints of gold floating behind its aged surface. The proprietor smiled and nodded to each of them in turn, then uncorked a tall bottle and set four glasses on the bar. He poured from it a clear, thick liquid.

Raszer lifted the glass to his nose and sniffed. Anise. Herbs. And a lot of alcohol.

"Ouzo?" he asked Francesca.

"The local version: raki. If you don't want to melt your intestines, stick with Altibas or Tekirdag grade. This is Ismet's own family's Tekirdag, and it's got a few extras."

In practiced fashion, Ismet, the bartender, topped off each of the four glasses with water poured from a clay pitcher, then stepped back an inch and tipped his head.

"We drink," said Dante.

"We drink," echoed Francesca.

As he swallowed, Raszer felt fire pour down his gullet.

A chuckle, soft as the padding of an animal in damp underbrush, came from a table in the rear of the tavern, an area that was only now becoming visible, and dimly at that. Raszer turned. The man at the table was twice its width, and his robes draped the chair. He wore a fezlike cap of black felt and wool on his head, and his enormous fingers were wrapped around a little glass.

"We're not the only ones here for cocktail hour," Raszer told Francesca.

"That's Baba Hexreb," she replied. "Local wise man. It's him we came for . . . and Ismet's raki. When the stars are aligned, the combination is awesome."

"Will you introduce me?"

"Of course," Francesca said, nodding to the bar. "Bring your glass."

Before they had risen from their stools, Baba Hexreb cleared his throat and began to tell a story, peppering his throaty English with Arabic.

"A Bektashi was in a mosque one day, listening to the *hodja* give a sermon. He was about to nod off from boredom, when the *hodja* began talking about the beautiful virgins that awaited the faithful in heaven. When he heard the word *heaven*, the Bektashi came to himself and asked the *hodja* excitedly, '*Hodja efendi, will wine and raki be served to the faithful in heaven also?*' The *hodja* became furious and shouted back, 'You pagan, what do you think heaven is . . . a tavern?!' The Bektashi smiled and replied, 'Ha! And what do *you* think heaven is, *efendi* . . . a whorehouse?!'"

"I've got one for you, Father," said Raszer, drawing out a chair. "A Bektashi approached the *hodja* after prayers. 'Tell me, learned one,' he asked, 'if you set both a bowl of water and a bowl of wine in front of your donkey, which will he drink?' The *hodja* replied without hesitation: 'The water, of course, because my donkey is a pious servant of Allah.'"

"'Well,' the Bektashi said, 'you are correct on one count: He will drink the water—but not because he is pious. He will drink the water because he is an ass.'"

Baba Hexreb chuckled and lifted his glass to Raszer, saying, "Sit, sit, my friends. It is the eve of the festival, and for now, we have Ismet's place to ourselves. Tomorrow, we will not have room to stand." He took a drink, then leaned forward and laid his forefinger on Raszer's wrist. "And who, my friend, are you . . . who dresses as a servant of Christ and speaks as an intimate of the Sufis?"

"It wouldn't surprise me to hear that Christ had found hospitality here," said Raszer. "If he were here today, he might dress as a Bektashi like yourself—"

"*Sshhhtt!*" said Hexreb, putting a thick finger to his lips, the corners of his mouth curling around it in a grin. "Don't give me away. There are still witch-hunters about."

"Apologies," Raszer offered, indicating the holy man's black cap. "Your *taj* gave you away."

The baba rolled his coal black eyes warily upward, as if expecting to find a perching bird on his head. He removed it quickly and hid it in the folds of his lap, looked from side to side, and then shrugged. "A *taj* is just a *taj*. Perhaps I am only an imposter. What is the English word? A *sham*."

"I doubt that," said Raszer. "But I expect to find a few where I'm going."

"And where is that, Father?"

Francesca leaned in. "This is Frère Deleuze, Baba. Or, at least, we have made him so. We are taking him to El Mirai. He is here to bargain for the release of an American girl who has been enslaved there. We've come here to seek your blessing."

Hexreb gave Raszer a second inspection. "I don't know how well you bargain," he said, "but your guise is convincing enough. Take it from one who knows deception."

"Is the Bektashi order still outlawed here?" Raszer asked.

"Officially, yes, but we abide. Our *tariqah*—our spiritual path—has always annoyed officialdom, whether it be Ottoman, secularist, or Islamist."

"Because you hold that Allah is in the heart, and not in the law . . . "

"Because we tweak their noses with truth," said the baba.

The dog, which had until then remained on guard at the door, came to Hexreb, its claws clicking rhythmically on the rough plank floor. It sat to await his acknowledgment, which he gave quickly and respectfully.

"Hello, *dedebaba*," he said in Arabic. "Welcome back. And how is life as a dog, the most blessed of lower creatures?" Adi gave his beefy hand a lick. "Ah, I see. Yes, I will convey this most important of precepts. Thank you for reminding me."

Baba Hexreb summoned the proprietor to bring the bottle of raki, then folded his hands on the table. Together, they made a mass of flesh the size of an ox's heart. It seemed to Raszer that the size of the man was a factor of his accumulated goodness, and that if he grew wise enough, he might become a giant. For all the weight he carried on his frame, his face showed not the slightest strain. He replaced the *taj* on his bald head and spoke.

"Shaykh Adi reminds me of something too easily forgotten by humans, who are not as adept as dogs at sniffing out malice. We are inclined to believe—because the ascetics have taught us so—that to enter the world of spirit is to escape evil, as if the Devil dwelt only in flesh. We think if we leave our prison of bones, we can soar freely over the ocean that has kept us from the sublime. But evil does not stop at the water's edge. Like the serpent, it simply swims across, our soul's own shadow on the waters. True, the essence of *marifah*—real knowledge—is distilled in spirit, and this is why we seek that far shore. But woe to him who fails to grasp that the Devil has demons to match God's angels. This is *haqiqah*—reality. Has there ever been a thing acquired by virtue that evil does not wish to have by theft?"

"Granting all this, Baba," Raszer inquired, "why hasn't the world already gone to the Devil?"

The holy man chuckled. "Look around, Father. Would you not say it has?"

"I take your point . . . but as long as people like yourself—and my friends here—are around, I have to believe that the better angels have a chance."

"Indeed," Hexreb affirmed. "Because even bad men were once children. Even the worst of us carries the seed of Allah in his heart, and sometimes waters it."

"And the man I am going to see . . . is Allah to be found in his heart?"

"If indeed he is a man, yes. We have the most to fear if he is merely a thought, enshrined in an idol, for these thoughts—unleavened by the human heart—are the most dangerous of creations. And there are men in whom the seed finally shrivels and blows dry, men in whom the soil has gone to dust. In these men, Shaytan may turn the mirror of the soul on his own face and deceive the man into thinking he sees the face of God."

He paused and turned his ear to the door. "Listen. Do you hear how the wind rises outside with the coming of night and seeks every chink in Ismet's door? If you step outside now—in twilight—you may encounter evil disguised as townsman or beggar. The same holds true for the hours before dawn, and for the places of the world without history or tribe. A man may be on his way home, when Shaytan will put his leg in the path. Having tripped you, he will offer to help you up. This is where it begins.

"We have but one task—on this, I know my young friends will agree—and that is to become fully human. The Ismailis of old—the Nizaris—were not wrong to say that resurrection must be our own doing. They were not wrong to think . . . may I say this in Arabic?"

"Of course," said Raszer. "I'll try to follow."

" . . . That we are swaddled in ignorance from birth. We are taught to trust in the perception of teachers, princes, and mullahs whose own vision is clouded by lies and laws. But the world is both more terrifying and more wonderful than what they describe. There are many—often the most pious—who reach manhood convinced of their righteousness, when in truth their souls have long since been seized by the Devil. Their errors are passed on like infection, generation after generation. And so Hassan-i-Sabbah taught that we all must allow the *dai*—the teacher—to strip us down until nothing remains but the original self, and then teach us to see anew. For only the man who has stood against Shaytan in the soul's clothing can claim truth. This, however, requires great trust in the teacher. We have handed him our naked soul; what if, rather than tenderly wrapping us in his cloak, he should decide to ravish us? To shape our will to his own design and employ it as he wishes? The one you go to see is such a fiend."

"Can he be persuaded to let at least one child go?" Raszer asked.

"I doubt that he can be persuaded by reason," the baba replied, returning to English, "though perhaps you can turn his own unreason against him. It will be a bit like steering a ship without the stars, Father. You will be able to use only the lights of his world to find your way, and as those lights are false, all illumination must come from within you. Good luck, Father . . . may the breath of Allah be at your back."

Baba Hexreb finished the last of his raki and set the little glass down gently. He could easily have crushed it to powder in his palm. He rose, stooping to stroke Shaykh Adi's head and accept one last lick, and then made his way out of the tavern, moving lightly for a man of his size. He left no wake, but Raszer felt a great vacuum in his absence, and a great longing to follow. The tavern suddenly seemed twice as large.

Ismet came to their side and spoke to Francesca.

"He'll take us to our quarters for the night," she translated.

Raszer looked around for a door or stairwell in the still-murky light. "Our quarters?" he thought aloud. "Are they curled up in another dimension?"

"In a way," Francesca replied, and gave a nod toward the back of the room.

There was, in fact, a doorway at the rear of the tavern, draped with a curtain and leading through a pantry that opened on a brick patio partially covered by a wooden trellis, lathed in intricate Islamic design and wound through with flowering vine. The accommodations had the look of a makeshift field hospital: six metal-framed cots side by side on the bricks, separated by small night tables of unpainted wood. An embroidered blanket served to curtain off two more cots at the far end, which Raszer presumed were for female guests. There was clean, sweet-smelling straw on the brick and indigo-glazed pitchers of water on every nightstand. Beyond the patio, the white hills rolled away like breakers in the early moonlight, jeweled with the flickering firelight from nearby shepherds' dwellings. It was a good spot.

"Ismet will bring us some dinner," said Francesca. "Technically, we should be fasting before the festival with the rest of the town, but we're—"

"I'm not averse to fasting," said Raszer, "if it's the custom."

"It's your choice," said Francesca. "But no one will fault you for eating. We have a slog ahead of us, and in two days you're going to be burning through your protein."

"Well, right now I'm going to step out front for a smoke . . . get the sense of this place before I settle in."

"Stay close," Francesca counseled. "We're safe in the village, but these hills get pretty rough at night, and the night before a Jamkhana is one of those twilight times the baba talked about. The evil is real. Would you like Dante to come?"

"Thanks, but no. Just need some time in my own head."

Raszer was unsettled, and troubled by something the baba had said. He was afraid when it came down to it, he might not have the stuff to "stand against Shaytan in the soul's clothing." In the end, the one thing Raszer believed a man could not be was a spiritual coward. And so, from time to time, he felt the need to tempt the Devil.

The street descended steeply into a canyon, its carefully laid stones giving way first to a rutted dirt road and then to a precipitous footpath. A ball would have rolled a mile or more before stopping, and on the last hundred yards of cobblestone, Raszer had to lean back on his heels to avoid toppling over. The surrounding hills, scrubby, bleached, and wild, were laced with boundary walls and dotted with small stone houses. He saw only one other human being on his way down, a woman who stepped outside her front door to retrieve a bucket and regarded him as if he were taboo. Maybe he was. Maybe local custom was to stay indoors on the night before a festival, for the same reasons people in old Europe had known not to venture out on All Hallows' Eve. He lit a cigarette. For a long time, it had been his way of whistling past the graveyard. Now that he was old enough to feel mortality's pull, he saw the perversity: The very thing he used to keep the fear of death at bay would probably kill him.

It was chilly, and he was glad he'd worn his coat. The days would grow hot as they moved deeper into the land and the season, but the nights would remain wintry for another month. He came across a flock of sheep without a shepherd by the roadside. The animals made no sound to acknowledge his passing; in fact there was no sound other than the whisper of wind in the brush. By the time he'd reached the floor of the canyon, there was also very little light except for the dim glow of retiring dusk. He turned before going on to make sure he could still see the tiny lights of the village. The path began to ascend again, taking him behind a long, low ridge. The wind poured over it like surf and filled his ears, and in its roar he began to hear other things.

At first, they were things the wind was *like*: waves, trains, furnaces, and flames. Soon he was able to make out voices, mostly low and monotonal. He reminded himself that this in itself was no cause to question his wits. Alone in the evening of desert in a strange land with a head full of raki and thoughts of final things, he would have been crazier *not* to hear things on the wind. The voices didn't alarm him, even when they began to articulate regular phrases and separate into strands of pitch. What did alarm him was that after fifteen minutes on foot, he emerged from behind the ridge and could no longer see the village. What's more, he'd lost the road. There was nothing under his feet but a steep, unbroken pasture offering not a single landmark. He methodically paced out the vicinity.

For fifty yards in all four directions, there was no sign of road or path.

He made sure to return to his starting point after each reconnaissance, so as to maintain his orientation. It was no use. He'd lost all sense of which direction he'd come from. It was as if he were at the axis of a compass and the land was turning around him. There were familiar sensations: the tightening of the throat and the sudden void in the pit of his stomach; the stiffening of limbs. Things that all trekkers—even tourists—experience when they've lost their way. Soon, however, the panic escalated, because he became convinced that although he had no idea where he was, his adversaries did.

On the face of it, he told himself, this was nonsense. He dropped to a squat in the dry grass, took a long breath, and then began methodically to plot his location by the stars. He knew that he'd walked southeast from the village and couldn't have gone more than a mile. He knew they'd entered the village by a narrow but crudely paved road from the south, and that therefore if he walked due west by about two-thirds of a mile, he should close the triangle and come to the road.

But then the voices came with new urgency, and a mist rose and threw gauze over the stars. The brush crackled ten feet to his right. He heard some distant perturbation of the night air and suddenly, from the crest of a hill dead ahead, there came a wheel of fire, rolling straight toward him. As he moved aside to let it pass, he identified it as a tractor tire someone had doused with gasoline and torched. The shudder subsided. *Effective*, he thought, *but a pretty low-rent scare tactic for global terrorists. More likely, local hooligans getting a jump on festival day*. He'd just about settled his heartbeat when he felt a finger on his shoulder.

He went into an immediate crouch, then spun on the balls of his feet in all directions. The physical response had to precede the mental, or he was screwed. But despite his readiness to face an assailant, he didn't really expect one to be there. The tap had had the weightlessness of something reaching in from the other world.

"Okay," he said aloud. "Come out, come out, wherever you are . . . "

There was neither sound nor touch, but from the wind arose an incomparable sweetness. It was the scent of an Easter morning, of everything good that had ever been promised to him, and all it seemed to ask was that he follow.

"I'm not all that easy," he said. "Give me a face to go with the perfume."

Then, suddenly, it was gone. The chill air rushed back in to fill the void, and he saw that full night had come down and he was truly lost. Through the mist, he managed again to find the bright stars in Orion and began to make his way westward. After five minutes, he checked the heavens for his bearings and froze. The mist had cleared, but revealed a new sky of constellations he didn't recognize. Orion was gone; so was Ursa Minor. Everything had shifted, as if the earth had tilted into the southern hemisphere.

Jesus, he thought with a shudder. *Can the Devil do that*? The scent came again, and this time he followed.

"Lead on," he said to the phantom. "You don't even have to blow in my ear."

He followed because he was lost and because at the moment, being anywhere had more appeal than being nowhere. Beside that, he still possessed the hustler's confidence that he could scheme his way out of hell if he had to. And he followed because he trusted his nose, and his nose told him that no scent that fine could issue from evil. With evil, there was always a whiff of decay, wasn't there?

He followed the scent as if riding a boat's wake across a sea of grass and stone. For seconds, it would be lost to him, and then he'd pick it up again, ahead or off to the right or even behind him. All the while, to keep himself company and to keep panic at bay, he conducted a conversation with the thin air or whatever it might conceal.

"Animal, vegetable, or mineral?" he asked.

"Bigger than a breadbox?"

"Christ, how did it get so cold? Did you have anything to do with that?"

"Show me the way to go home," he sang. "I'm tired and I wanna go to bed."

"*Watch your step*," whispered the wind, and he felt the breath against his eardrum before stumbling over a rocky outcropping and falling on his face.

"Fuck," he said. The hard earth was like a serrated blade against the gash in his cheek. He pushed himself up and rolled into a sitting position.

"What a show-off," he said, flicking the soil from his wound. "I'm onto you. You're just *me* in some twisted, noncorporeal way, right?"

The grass trembled, and the sweet scent returned. “Or are you?” he said. “Tell you one thing: I couldn’t wear that cologne in a men’s locker room and get away with it. If you’re the Devil, you’re a little fey, aren’t you?”

Raszer knew well that these things didn’t just happen willy-nilly—supernatural experiences, visitations, whatever you chose to call them. Various agencies had to coalesce. You could label them outside forces or a message from the captain of your soul, but they were real enough, and once you’d opened yourself to them, they came often and sometimes in series. The difficulty was in distinguishing the genuine (which were the upshot of true extrasensory perception) from the false alarms and counterfeits. The counterfeits were the work of Satan as Raszer knew him.

Satan was anything that threw you off the true scent.

There was a band of loose rock under his feet. Unnatural, like gravel. The air rippled with the flapping of enormous wings as a buzzard flew past, low and close. He took a step and stopped to let his heart slow. There was pavement beneath his feet. He squatted down and touched it. Asphalt. Still warm from the day’s heat. There were footfalls on the road. Light. Rapid. A boy of about nine came running out of nowhere. He spoke in breathless Arabic, casting anxious looks in the direction he’d come from, to Raszer’s right and the northwest.

“They come,” he said. “The men. They come.”

“What men?” Raszer called out in the boy’s tongue.

The kid neither replied nor broke stride, so Raszer caught up and ran along. He couldn’t be sure that the boy did not suspect him of being one of the very people he feared.

“What men are these, my friend?” he asked again.

The boy slowed his pace just a bit and regarded him warily.

“They take the children,” he answered, and then took off like a shot.

Raszer trotted to a stop in the middle of the road, bent to catch his breath, and watched the kid fold himself into the darkening mist. He caught the glint off a puddle of motor oil near the shoulder and looked to the west to see one, then two, then three sets of headlights turn from a crossroad onto the main highway.

Even at a mile, he could tell that the beams were too widely spaced for the subcompact Toyotas and Nissans people drove in this part of the world. Once the faint red of the taillights became visible, he marked off the length of the vehicles and knew he must be looking at three big, low-slung automobiles, now heading straight for where he stood.

To no surprise, his nocturnal spirit guide had vanished, and he was left utterly exposed and with no better than fifteen seconds to make himself scarce. On either side of the highway was empty white scrubland, sloping so gently away that a man would easily be found in the crosshairs of a night-vision scope. It would be impossible to put himself out of range in the time remaining, and nothing out there to provide him with cover. He'd just decided his best option was to crawl into the scrub and lie flat when he glanced to the east and saw another set of headlights break over a hill, half a mile away in the opposite direction.

All of a sudden, it was rush hour.

The lights of this new vehicle were considerably higher and much more closely spaced, suggesting a small truck or some other commercial transport. That seemed a far safer bet than what Raszer feared was coming at him from the west. Some rough and hasty triangulation told him that the opposing headlights were roughly equidistant, so he opted to go belly down in the dust until the truck was within fifty yards, and then try to flag it down. In truth, he really didn't have any choice.

By the time he was settled in the dirt, the vehicles had covered another third of a mile. Only when he felt certain that the element of surprise would compel the driver on his left to stop, rather than swerve, did he rise to a sprinter's crouch. He'd been granted a small window of grace by the caravan approaching from his right, for it seemed to be moving at the stately pace of a motorcade and was still a quarter mile away. He could only assume that the leisurely speed allowed the drivers to scan the countryside for prey.

By the time he launched himself back onto the pavement, he had already identified the vehicle of his hoped-for salvation as a *dolmus*, one of the little buses that move the Turkish citizenry from village to remote village in the absence of a good rail line. *Surely it will stop*, he told himself, as he began to wave his arms with an authoritative urgency. The fog had begun to roll onto the road again, and although it provided a measure of cover, there was also the risk that the driver wouldn't see him in time. Raszer glanced quickly over his shoulder. The motorcade had sped up. He waved his arms more insistently. From the look on the bus driver's face as he ground to a halt on the center line, Raszer surmised that he probably wouldn't have stopped, except to avoid running him down. Once he had, Raszer wasted no time leaping on.

"Is there a village nearby?" he asked in rushed Arabic. "I'm lost."

The driver blinked. It was not his native language. It took a moment for him to compute the response. "There is only one village on this road. There we go."

"Good," Raszer said, and smiled. "Allah is merciful." He watched the movement of the caravan past the driver's-side window. The cars rolled out of the mist one by one. On identifying the first, he felt momentarily silly. Far from being sinister, it was a lumbering grocery truck, probably the thing that had held up the traffic. "I will pay when we get there," he assured the driver. "Let's go."

The second set of headlights brought nothing more dangerous than a vintage Mercedes—a rarity in these parts, to be sure, but hardly the Fourth Horseman. The driver dropped the bus into gear but kept his foot on the brake, as if wondering for a moment if he shouldn't eject this anxious stranger. The third set of headlights flared on the windshield, and Raszer heard Turkish pop music playing faintly from a car radio. The lights passed slowly and faded like a wink, but the music continued to issue from a stationary source. The bus driver turned to his window, and Raszer's pulse hammered his larynx.

The third vehicle had stopped beside them, long and sleek and so black that it stood out even against the half-hearted night. He waited for the tinted window to be lowered, part of him wanting to see the face behind it, and part of him poised to leap from the bus and scramble into the brush for whatever advantage distance and darkness might provide. Time skipped in place like the second hand on a broken watch. The window remained up, but Raszer knew that the eyes on the other side could see him in the green glow of the dome light. The question was what they saw. Was it Stephan Raszer or Father Deleuze? Attempted flight would point only to the former. The limo's idle had dropped to a soft growl.

The bus driver turned away from the window and lifted his foot from the brake.

"Bless you," Raszer whispered as the little vehicle began to accelerate.

It wasn't until they'd covered half a mile and he was sure that the black limo wasn't going to pursue them that Raszer turned to survey the cabin for a seat and saw her. She was four rows back, right on the threshold of invisibility, her features lit only by the dull glow from the instrument panel. The pumpkin-colored hair—or wig, in this case—was pinned up, its tail sprouting like a flame from the top of her head. Her lips were parted and the lipstick matched the hair.

Her green eyes were wide and staring. Raszer recognized the sleeping boy beside her as Mikhail from the Fedeli d'Amore compound. He must, he thought, be her escort.

"Hello, Ruthie," he said. "Fancy meeting you here."

He watched her watching him, reconstructing his face: restoring the hair to his shaven head, the natural color to his dyed eyebrows, the flesh to his disfigured cheek.

Then she raised her hand tentatively above the seat back and gave a little wave.

TWENTY-NINE

THE AIR CRACKLED the minute they set eyes on each other. Francesca and Ruthie were opposites, and not the kind that attract. Francesca was self-possessed and strong spined, and had the spiritual fierceness of a woman who has seen the world to be a deeply fucked-up place and steels herself each day to fight off its many evils and cultivate its few precious goods. Ruthie Endicott was also fierce, but in a feral, reactive way. She had also seen the world's blemishes and seemed to feel she was one of them. She'd determined to be the antagonist, rather than the protagonist, in the story of her life. Both women were willful, utterly authentic and dead certain of their sexuality, and that's probably where the trouble began.

"How did she find us?" Francesca whispered, after taking Raszer aside.

"Well, it would appear that Mikhail brought her here."

"Yes," she said, with some impatience, "but how did she find Mikhail?"

"I'm still trying to figure that. She says . . . that Shams told her long ago where to find the Fedeli. That's possible, though getting here this quickly couldn't have been easy. She says she borrowed the money from her mother's boyfriend. That's also possible. A stretch, but possible. She says she wants to be the one to bring her sister home. I don't think that's going to happen, but I'll have to do some—"

"She'll put us all at risk." said Francesca. "I can smell it."

"She'll alter the equation, that's for sure."

Raszer knew instantly that he'd come across as a shade too flip. Francesca's long, fine nose thinned, and her dark brows shifted in preparation for a display of Mediterranean temper.

"You go out—foolishly—without letting any of us know. You are gone for three hours—"

"Three hours?" He shot her a doubting look. "How is that possible?"

"Three hours," she affirmed, pointing at her wristwatch. "And you come back . . . with her. What are we supposed to think?"

"I don't know," Raszer said. "I think I need to sleep on it. Which bunk is mine?"

Francesca indicated the cot Ruthie had already passed out on.

"She saw your pack underneath." said Francesca. "She has a sharp eye, and a better nose, and she has already made her claim." She paused. "Sleep well, Father."

"I intend to honor my vows."

"We'll see. Men of God should never deny themselves the true chapel. I doubt those vows will hold up tomorrow."

"What, exactly, is going to happen tomorrow?" he asked her.

"It is the first full moon of spring and the last night of the Jam in this town. You might call it an explosion of love . . . and we will need every drop of it for what is ahead. Restore yourself, Father, first with sleep and then with laughter. It may be a long time before we laugh again. And who knows how long before you have a woman?"

She turned away and he reached for her, taking gentle hold of her upper arm. She glanced at his hand, then raised her eyes to him. He nodded toward the tavern in front, now closed but unlocked. She followed without resistance. When it was dark, he spoke softly: "Listen. I don't know what the hell happened out there. You can spend your life reading the lives of the saints and still not be prepared when something holy comes your way. I only know that it probably had to happen, and that she probably has to be here. She told me . . . she has dues to pay."

"What does that mean?"

"Maybe that she got her sister into this mess and now feels like she has to be part of getting her out. Maybe to honor her friend Shams. Or maybe it's just that everyone looks for redemption in their own fashion. There was a car out on the highway. An American limo . . . pretty rare here, I would think. And a village boy, running away, saying something about men who take the children. Could they have tracked Mikhail?"

"It might be the same men . . . or different men," she said. "The wars have stirred up an army of orphans, ready to follow anyone with a smile and a stick of candy. Half the village girls will have whored themselves before they are sixteen.

Many will end up in debt bondage. Wars make some men rich. Limousines are not as rare as you think."

"So you don't think we need to get the hell out of here . . . like, tonight?"

"I will think it over," Francesca answered. "But I think we are safest here. Turkey is crawling with predators right now, but they rarely enter the villages. Especially not this village. They wait on the outskirts. At the moment, we are better off here than on the road. When the festival is finished, yes . . . by that time we must be invisible." She touched her thumb and forefinger to his eyelids and said, "Now . . . to bed."

✦ ◆ ✦

THE MUSIC BEGAN just after dawn with simple dance rhythms beaten out on frame drums by the village women. The drums looked like oversize tambourines without the jangles and were played with the heel of the hand. Raszer had awakened to the sound and lay still, tapping the rhythms on the frame of his cot in imitation. They seemed to be in mixed meters of three and four, but he sometimes lost the downbeat.

His impulse had been to rise immediately and go to the street, not to miss a moment of whatever timeless ceremony was about to begin. His body, however, had been made a prisoner of Ruthie's limbs. The mattress was barely three feet wide, and she had entwined herself in him. As soon as he was fully awake, he realized he had just two choices: to disengage or accept. Raszer got up.

He'd slept fully dressed. Now he pulled on his boots without bothering to lace them and stumbled into the tavern to find Ismet smoking at the bar, a carafe of what Raszer hoped was coffee at his elbow. The front door was open; the drums echoed off the cobblestones. Raszer lifted a hand in greeting, then turned and quietly closed the door that led to the sleeping quarters. Shaykh Adi slipped through at the last second and joined him at the bar.

Ismet filled a demitasse with coffee as thick and black as pitch. He pushed over a little bowl of rock sugar and without a word, dropped two large chunks into Raszer's cup. This was Turkey. It was presumed he wanted it sweet. Raszer lit a cigarette, gave the dog a scratch on the head, and took the coffee down in a single gulp. His teeth ached like ice on a new filling. On the next cup, he'd forgo the sugar.

Normally, he'd have tapped the bartender for all he knew about the day's festival and the general lay of the land, but he didn't speak Kurdish and he'd already discovered he wasn't going to get far with Arabic. He decided to try English, just so he didn't have to sit there mutely, exchanging awkward smiles and nods.

"Big party," he said, gesturing toward the street.

Ismet returned a mostly toothless smile and poured him more coffee. When he went for the sugar, Raszer lightly touched his leathered knuckles to ward him off.

"Not much of a sweet tooth," Raszer said, touching a finger to his teeth.

Ismet mimicked, tapping his empty gums, shrugged, and said something that probably meant, *Yeah . . . you see where it got me.*

"I feel like an American asshole, coming here without boning up on your language." Raszer stubbed out his cigarette.

"*Asssh*hole," Ismet repeated, and grinned. He took one of Raszer's smokes for good measure and lit it with both pleasure and a sense of entitlement. After exhaling blue smoke over Raszer's head, he nodded in the direction of the open door.

"*Mum sondii,*" he said.

"Come again?"

"*Mum sondii.*" Ismet retrieved a nearly exhausted candle from the end of the bar.

"Candle," said Raszer, touching it.

The proprietor filled his cheeks with air and blew.

"Candle . . . blown . . . out."

Ismet nodded.

"Tonight?" Raszer asked.

"Yes. Tonight," said his host, and turned a little circle with his hands in the air.

For a few minutes, they sat in companionable silence. Then Raszer stood, gestured to the street, and offered Ismet another of his cigarettes before heading outside.

At this stage of the day, the parade was mostly grandmothers and children wearing boldly dyed prints of indigo, tangerine, saffron, and cinnabar. Some of the children carried handmade pinwheels in matching colors. A few old men stood nearby looking on, their skin like sun-dried fruit. The sixteen-to-sixty age group was entirely unrepresented, probably sleeping in, in preparation for a long night.

With the rising sun, the hillside village turned first pink, then lavender, and was finally bathed in a glow like the skin of a blood orange. The elders acknowledged Raszer politely as they passed, some even granting little bows. Only later did it occur to him that the presence of Shaykh Adi at his heels was probably what had elicited such gestures. He knew from his studies that the Alevi people believed in the transmigration of souls, but it surprised him that they identified a saint in canine form so quickly.

After a while, he went back inside. It was best, he thought, to wait for the others to wake before doing any serious exploring.

He and the group held a council at suppertime. They'd had an afternoon of sun, music, and bittersweet local ale, and refrained from discussing the business ahead of them. Ruthie's arrival had introduced too much uncertainty, so, for the time being, they simply allowed the pageantry to wash over them. The five of them—plus the dog—took an outside table at the village's only sit-down restaurant, a little kebab place with waiters in yellow turbans who took turns sitting in with the band when they weren't handling orders. The stone patio was set back from the street and wedged between the restaurant and a tobacconist's shop. The sun was dropping, and in less than an hour it would be cool, but for now the day's warmth remained on their skin. It had been a day of strolling, sampling meat pastries, learning the local dance steps, and observing what, to all appearances, was a typical spring festival with pagan roots, but offering no hint of the evening's promised revelry. Throughout the afternoon, the two women had kept each other in their sights.

The drinking did not begin in earnest until the unmarried young men began to materialize at around three o'clock. This was probably out of consideration for the children, who, along with their grandparents, began to disappear as the sun dropped.

Raszer had taken Ruthie aside at lunchtime, but she'd seemed preoccupied and not in the mood for explanations.

"Why, Ruthie?" he asked. "And just as important, *how*?"

"I can't not be here," she mumbled behind red-tinted sunglasses.

"Because you feel responsible for what happened to Katy."

"Don't shrink me, okay?" she replied, turning away. "Can't people ever just do something because it feels right?"

"Sure," he said. "Some people can."

She glared at him. "But not me, right?"

"Sure, people act on noble impulses. But this can't have been all that impulsive. Things get complicated when you travel to a war zone. How'd you pull it off so fast?"

"Shams and me," she said, "we were gonna come here and look for Katy. Had it planned for a long time. Then you came along . . . and he died, so I adjusted the plan."

"Who paid for the ticket? I'm not sure I believe—"

"You think because I live in a fucking trailer that I don't have resources?"

"I have no doubt you're resourceful. But you have to admit—"

"Look, mister." She sighed and gave him a square-on look. "Can I tell you something?"

"I'm listening."

"Henry left me some cash, money he skimmed from the gun and dope deals him and Johnny were doing for these dicks. Nobody knew about it."

Raszer calculated the odds that there might be even a drop of truth in her statement. He doubted it, but didn't argue.

"Money would explain a few things. Not all of them."

"You don't look so bad bald," she said. "And with that slash on your face, it makes you look kind of holy and nasty at the same time."

"That's good," he said. "Maybe you won't fuck with me as much."

"So, what's the story with the Italian bitch? I don't think she likes me."

"You ought to be able to figure that one out. And if you expect to hang around, you'd better follow her lead. She's tougher than you are."

"Are you fucking her?"

"I'm a priest."

"Since when did that make a difference?"

✦ ◆ ✦

AT 7:07 PM BY RASZER'S WRISTWATCH, things suddenly got unnaturally quiet and Raszer heard a distant *mey* flute, accompanied by something that sounded a bit like castanets. The tune was haunting, infectious, a string of notes repeated again and again and commanding attention. On the patio, a few of the young men began to tap out the rhythm on their tables and exchange knowing glances. The women—some veiled but most in colorful headscarves—whispered and giggled with one another. One of them boldly removed her scarf and shook out her chestnut hair. None of the others followed suit, but most began to sway gently in time.

When the sound of the flute floated close enough to tickle their eardrums, it was joined by drums of a deeper tenor, and soon after, the *saz* player in the restaurant band began to pick out the tune. Dante leaned over to Raszer and said, "It's beginning. Watch the street."

"The holy men and dervishes will come first," said Francesca. "To bless the feast and remind us that it is a *zikr*, a remembrance of our origins."

"What is this?" asked Ruthie.

"Nothing you've seen in Azusa," said Raszer. "Not even in Taos."

Ruthie returned a blank look. Francesca smiled privately and began to sway in time.

Now the waiters emerged in a procession, carrying silver trays crowded with small glasses containing an amber-colored liquid. After all the patrons had been served, all but one set down their trays and joined the *saz* player at the bandstand. The remaining waiter went to the gates of the patio and stood patiently with a full tray. When the first of the red-sashed dervishes twirled into view, he stepped into the street and began to distribute the communal elixir to the vanguard of holy men. Not only did each manage to claim and hold on to his glass without ceasing to whirl, they all then extended their arms and poured the concoction into their mouths without spilling a drop. On that signal, the bandleader raised his own glass and directed all to drink. The liquor was deeply herbal, and Raszer registered it as even more potent than Ismet's raki.

"Wow," he said, his eyes watering. "Can I take some of this home with me?"

"You'd never get it past the airport dogs," said Dante.

Francesca nodded. "Not the male ones, at least," she said cryptically.

Raszer had a thought, but kept it to himself.

There was a small explosion as the vanguard of spinning fakirs collectively cried out, hurled their glasses to the bricks, and then danced barefoot in the shards. Not one of them flinched, faltered, or let out a cry of pain.

"That's the one I want to learn," said Dante, looking on.

Raszer nodded and felt the flush of the liquid amber spread into his limbs. It seemed to induce a cathartic reaction, because he could sense the glass underfoot.

Next in the procession came a breathing mass that soon revealed itself as a train of men and women in interlocking human circles, alternately revolving and meshing ceaselessly, like the gears of some elaborate machine. Though Raszer had seen nothing quite like it, he had heard of such things. Ancient ring dances like this one had been humanity's original expression of group identity. Within each grouping, the dancers linked arms and chanted the flute's melody. Collectively, the circles interconnected like a child's paper chain, one turning through the next, and at first the mechanism remained an illusion. After a minute, however, Raszer saw that there were breaks in each ring through which the others wove. Once he'd seen this trick, the next move became apparent: With every full turn, each circle would "give up" one participant to the next circle, gradually seeding the links in the chain with members of the other sex, until, when they'd reached the point of gender balance, they began to shed their opposites and restore themselves to homogeneity—although with an entirely new makeup of individuals. In this way, the circles were continuously refreshed and their members redistributed, so that in a roughly seven-minute cycle, every man had been linked once to every woman. The front circle was constantly replenished from the rear. The mathematics of it were pretty impressive.

"It's brilliant, isn't it?" said Francesca.

"It's a giant sorting machine," Raszer observed.

The waiter delivered a second round. Table by table, the restaurant's patrons rose to join the dance.

"It's electrical," said Dante. "The dancers who get passed are like free electrons in a circuit. When it gets going fast, the whole thing starts to hum like a transformer."

"All dance is ultimately about survival," said Francesca. She turned to Raszer, clinked his glass, and drank. He did likewise. "And now," she announced, to him and to the table, "it's our turn."

It seemed to Raszer that she had sent him some code. The prospect of ending the evening in her embrace was far from unappealing. But the story of this night wasn't theirs to tell. The dance would tell it, and the dance did not seem to play favorites.

All ecstasy worth the name flows from repetition at increasingly higher spiritual voltages. For three hours, the dance wound its way through the hamlet without letting up. At the end of those hours, there was little left of Raszer as he knew himself. The whole thing was a quantum blur, and so was he. The night had dropped, the troupe of musicians had grown to the size of an orchestra, and the air was rich with a sweet, earthy fragrance that might or might not have included opium smoke as a component, along with human oils and the vapors of the liquor. As the drums grew deeper, louder, and greater in number, they overwhelmed all but the shrillest of the wind instruments. Over the course of his revolutions, Raszer came to know the face, the breath, the laugh, and the kiss of just about every soul in the village, save for the elders and children who'd retreated behind their doors. The dance was designed to shrink the circles by twos over time: from twelve to ten to eight to six to four, and with each diminution to increase by inverse proportion the amount of time the participants spent linked in sweat and sinew.

The couples who left immediately joined other similarly reduced circles, such that their size remained constant, giving up one couple at a time until, finally, there were only pairs. The sorting ensured that no woman would end up dancing with the one who'd brought her. When it got down to dyads, they locked arms and spun themselves into a centrifugal cloud until, by and by, one of the parade marshals—the holy men—would tap someone on the shoulder. This, he inferred, indicated a kind of temporary betrothal: a license to be licentious.

It was hard to tell if the system could be gamed by personal choice. Raszer was pretty sure it wasn't meant to be, but on the other hand, the lords of the dance would probably have had to allow some room for human caprice in their calculations. And so, it was with both surprise and a certain sense of symmetry that Raszer found himself in his last circle of six with two fleshy village women, two tall men of indeterminate age, and Ruthie Endicott.

A trio of drummers drew near, heads bobbing, eyes rolled back to the whites. Ruthie shot sidelong glances to the older women who flanked her, then leveled a woozy gaze at Raszer. He couldn't say how high she was by now. He knew that he was flying. One of the village women momentarily broke the chain to lift her skirts just above the knee. The second woman went her one better and took the silky fabric provocatively to midthigh, then flashed Raszer a wink.

Ruthie was not to be outdone. With hand on haunch, she began to knead the cotton smock she'd borrowed for the evening—hardly more than a brightly dyed sack—gathering the fabric into pleats that drew the hem first to her knee, then to her thighs, and finally to her swaying hips, permitting Raszer and his rivals a glimpse of what was, after all, to be the final ground of the dance. The gesture had the power of a claim. The village women unlocked themselves from the circle and dragged the two tall men away by the shirttails.

They stood in semidarkness at the entrance to a cul-de-sac, encircled by drums whose rhythm still recalled the original tune from hours ago. The drummers were faceless, perhaps even veiled. It seemed that their function was not only to exhort the dancers, but also to give musical sanction to each act of consummation.

It was Ruthie who found their beat. Perfectly. With each orbit of her hips, she backed a few inches further into the cul-de-sac. Had Raszer wanted to retreat or delay, he would first have had to break through the tightening circle of drummers at his back, but he had no wish to retreat. The three-hour ceremony had succeeded in suspending time, and with it, all sense of causation. Now there was only a single moment of wanting, and what he wanted was this girl.

A few yards deeper into the cul-de-sac was what appeared to be an abandoned donkey cart, its bed sloped at a forty-five-degree angle between two rough-hewn wooden wheels, anchored by its heavy, rusted hasp. A single kerosene lamp, its glow reduced by a soot-blackened enclosure, hung from a post overhead. The youngest of the drummers set down his instrument, shinnied up the post, and snuffed it out. In the seconds that followed, the village—already dark—grew darker still, as all lamps were extinguished, all candles blown out.

Raszer peeled off the sweat-dampened black hoodie he'd worn as a buffer against the night's chill, and laid it over the unfinished cedar slats of the bed. Then he placed one hand on Ruthie's right elbow and the other on the back of her neck and lowered her gently into place, letting her brace her bare feet against him. He slipped his hand under her knee to part her legs, then caressed her center until she cried out. He kissed her, swallowing her tongue and holding it with his breath until he was inside her, and when he had released it, her lips curled into a smile.

She breathed into his mouth the words "Now you're in real trouble, mister." And he was.

This would change everything. Sex always did.

THIRTY

THE PALE SUN ROSE over the front range like a blob of mercury, gradually displacing the lid of dawn. They had been on the road to Hakkâri for three hours. Raszer had taken shotgun position so that he and Francesca could map out the approach to the neo-Assassin fortress, which, by her estimate, they would reach in three days, weather permitting—the first by car and the second two on foot. The distance was not excessive, but the terrain was exceedingly rough, and the primitive routes riddled with Turkish army roadblocks and PKK flashpoints.

Ruthie leaned forward and laid her elbows on the seat back. "Did we do it last night?" she asked Raszer, eyes bloodshot behind her red bug glasses.

This drew a gesture from Francesca that Raszer knew well: a biting of lip, a lowering of eyes, a turning away to stare out the window at the passing whiteness. Like tea leaves, it required interpretation. It might have registered disdain for Ruthie's ignorance of the nature of the ceremony they'd joined in, it might have signaled disapproval of Raszer's lapse in judgment, or it might have been something else.

There'd been an hour's worth of strenuous argument that morning over whether Ruthie should be sent back to Suayb with Mikhail, who had finally boarded the 7:00 AM *dolmus* alone.

The principal reasons for their eventual decision to allow her onboard—with Francesca dissenting—were arguable, and Raszer knew it. The first was a sense that she was a loose cannon, more controllable nailed down to deck than rolling free. The second line of reasoning, Raszer thought more compelling: If Katy Endicott, after more than a year of captivity in a cloud-blanketed mountaintop fastness, was in the classic cultic mindstate, she might not want to come back to the world without some sign of what it held for her. Ruthie was a bright, shiny lure. She had been for Katy before, and she had been for Raszer only last night. Ruthie Endicott was a human chaotic attractor.

There were other reasons Raszer kept to himself. The first was that he suspected she knew more than she let on, and that he might eventually get it out of her. The second had to do with the kinship born of lovemaking. He wanted to see her home.

"Once we get to Daglica," said Francesca, aiming a finger at a point roughly forty miles east of Hakkâri on Raszer's survey map, "we'll leave the cars and pack in. The high passes are snowed in until late May, and even if they weren't, anyone stupid enough to drive into the Buzul Dagi right now would lose his car to the PKK or the Turks . . . maybe even the Americans. The days will be hot and the nights will be cold, and everyone will have to carry his weight." Raszer watched Francesca's glance shift to the rearview mirror. It was ostensibly to affirm that Dante was still on their tail in the second Cruiser—recently unhitched for the mountain roads—but her eyes dropped and remained fixed on the middle of the backseat.

"If you're worried about me carrying my weight," said Ruthie, "don't be."

"Experienced hikers die in those mountains. What experience do *you* have?"

"Plenty," said Ruthie, and sat back hard.

"Right," Francesca replied tightly. "All the wrong kind."

"This is bullshit," Ruthie spat.

"Enough," Raszer said, raising his voice. "Things change. You try to play that to your advantage." He leveled his eyes at Ruthie. "Ruthie, if you don't want to be sent to Istanbul on the next bus, you'll jump to every word she says. She will keep your head attached to your body."

He aimed a finger out the side window.

"I don't know if you noticed," he went on, "but ever since we started climbing into these foothills, there've been vultures in the sky." Raszer turned back to Francesca. "Now, you were saying . . . "

⬥ ◆ ⬥

BY MIDAFTERNOON, the windows were caked with dust the color of camel hair. The dust found its way into everything and had an adhesive consistency that reminded Raszer of metal filings clumped by a magnet. The mountains here were no one's idea of pretty, but against the preternaturally blue sky, they did have a stark mineral magnificence—God's own quarry, set aside for the making of

Adam and his dusty kind. There were flashes of places Raszer had been before—the Golan Heights, or even certain stretches along the California–Nevada border—but nothing in his experience quite compared to the emptiness.

Abandoned to warriors and brigands, the space offered little evidence of any permanent settlement—an occasional shepherd's hut, perched way up in some cleavage of earth, a stone well, but nothing that resembled community or commerce. There were the skeletal remains of bomb-gutted military transports overturned on the roadside, wheels stripped, canvas in wind-whipped tatters, and empty crates and trunks of ordnance, but so far, no soldiers. Francesca assured him that this would not remain the case, that the mountains they were headed into were the heart of the Kurdish war. She added that if the fighters weren't on the road, that meant only that they were in the hills, sighting down at them.

At four o'clock, as they began to mount a steep grade, Francesca slowed and pulled onto the shoulder. Once Dante had drawn up behind, he hopped out, taking a pair of binoculars up the rock.

"The last time we were through this pass," she said, "there was a Turkish army checkpoint on the other side. If it's still there, we may have to double back and take the long way around."

Raszer ran his hands over his brown friar's robe, the mainstay of his disguise. "Will this getup help or hurt?" he asked her.

"It probably won't hurt," said Francesca. "There are still Christian missions in these mountains. And they used to let us bring European trekkers through here in spring and fall. Things have changed, though." She climbed out of the car. "I'm going to pee," she said. Shaykh Adi followed her into the gully, presumably to do the same.

Raszer gave Ruthie a nod. "Go now if you need to. If we get stuck at the checkpoint, you may not be able to get out for a while."

"So did we?" she asked again, and smiled.

"If you're not sure," he said, returning the smile, "then I'm going to say no."

She gave him her middle finger, and he got out to have a cigarette.

Within sixty seconds, there was a fine coating of dust on his shaven pate. In another sixty, the grit was in his teeth. The wind here was abrasive enough to polish a diamond. He left the car and hiked a couple hundred feet into the scree to collect his thoughts. Francesca came up out of the ravine and stopped a few yards short of him, her hands on her hips. For a moment, she made as if to speak, but didn't.

Raszer crushed out the cigarette and turned to see Dante rockhopping down the incline like a goat, the binoculars in his hand. He arrived out of breath.

"What's it look like?" asked Raszer.

"There's still a checkpoint," the boy answered, "but it's PKK. That's good for us. If the Kurds control this pass, then they probably control the whole sector."

"Safe passage?"

"Well . . . safer. We've been using Kurdish guides on our treks for years, sometimes even sharing campsites with PKK units way up in the hills. We're closer to Baha'i and they're closer to Alevi Marxists—but it's the same root: Yezidi. "

"These mountain Kurds are Yezidi?"

"Most of 'em. Or some variation. In five years, this spot'll either be the northern frontier of a Kurdish state or the site of an Armenian-style genocide."

"Let's go," Francesca called, heading down the slope. "We've got to make another hundred miles before we stop for the night."

They piled back in, Raszer keeping his shotgun seat. Francesca pawed through her belt pack and handed Raszer the Canadian passport and visa that the authors of his present journey had prepared for him.

"Compliments of Philby Greenstreet," she said.

Raszer examined it. It was a first-rate job.

With a groan and a rattling of valves, the Toyota crested the seven-thousand-foot pass. Along with the engine's cacophony was another soundprint: a high-pitched whine accompanied by a throbbing drone, punctuated by two sonic booms.

"Stop the car for a sec," said Raszer. "And let me use your binoculars."

Three miles down the narrow and precipitous road, he could make out the checkpoint clearly. He couldn't tell how heavily guarded it was, but the nearby barracks suggested a small garrison. He lifted his gaze to the sapphire sky and saw the vapor trails, then followed them to the tiny, birdlike shapes at their head and put the field glasses to his eyes. "Shit," he said, then got back in the car.

"Those are American fighters," he told them. "A flyover. Wonder whose side they're on today."

"I hope they don't mistake us for a convoy," was all Francesca said.

A scant minute later, there came another rumble, throatier, rougher, and closer. After that, multiple drones of various pitches. More planes. Francesca dropped the Toyota into second and braked.

"It's a squadron," she said. "Can't tell whose . . . probably Turkish, from the sound of the engines."

"With the Americans as their escorts," said Raszer.

The mountains shook, releasing a cascade of rock, and in the valley below, the earth erupted in flame, smoke, and soil as if heaving up a dozen small volcanoes. When the dust cleared, what had been a Kurdish outpost was no more.

"Jesus," Ruthie hissed, perching forward to peer over Raszer's shoulder. "That could have been us."

It took almost ten seconds for the road to stop trembling.

Raszer turned to Francesca, who had stopped the car. "Is there another road?"

"Not one we can get on soon. We'll have to make it at least to the Zap River gorge near Uludere before we have an alternate. The road splits just past there, and there's a low route that runs along the river. Unfortunately, it's popular with pirates."

"Pirates?" Ruthie queried.

"Thieves and human traffickers," explained Francesca, and added, "They especially like American girls. They fetch a good price in Bahrain."

"Well, we'll see how it looks when we get there," said Raszer. From his duffel he pulled out a plain white T-shirt. "Give me a sec," he said. He hopped out, tore the shirt down the middle, and tied it to the antenna. "Let's go," he said. "Slowly. If there's anyone alive down there, we're liable to get shot at coming this soon after."

From two hundred yards away, they could see that the road had been cratered and was entirely impassable. There was nothing left of any of the standing structures but rubble and ash. The sole sign of life lay ahead of them in what remained of the road. A soldier had been thrown by the blast and had landed a good hundred feet from what had once been the gate. Both arms and one leg were gone, and the remaining leg was folded grotesquely behind him, as if he'd been a toy, dropped by a careless child. The limbless torso arched and dropped spasmodically, a mortally injured bug pumping out its last reflexive heartbeats. Francesca stopped ten feet short.

"Oh my God! Oh my God!" Ruthie burst out, just short of hysterical.

Gripping the wheel, Francesca drew a breath and turned to Raszer. "We'll have to go around. We should have enough ground clearance. The land is pretty flat here, but . . . there may be mines." They blinked at each other. She nodded toward the body in the road, her jaw tight. "What do you want to do?"

Raszer thought for a tick before replying. "What I would want done."

Francesca nodded, and Raszer stepped out. She was close behind him. He dropped to a squat beside the soldier, the hem of his priest's garment wicking up the young guard's blood from the road. He was not more than twenty, and twitching uncontrollably. Raszer made the sign of the cross, then took his thumb and forefinger and laid them gently on the soldier's eyelids. "Let's get you home," he said. He slipped the soldier's pistol from his belt and put the barrel to the young man's fire-blackened forehead. *He must be cold*, Raszer thought, his own hand shaking. Then he fired.

Francesca, beside him now, wore an expression he couldn't decipher, and it shook him. He kept the gun, retrieved a box of cartridges from the soldier's pouch, and said, "Let's go."

They returned to the cars and talked soberly as a group about the course they would take to avoid tripping land mines. Reasoning mines would lie on the perimeter rather than close in, they opted for a route that took them directly through the ruins, even if that meant driving the Land Cruisers over smoldering piles of wood and heaps of fallen brick that might conceal their own perils. Francesca eyed the pistol warily as Raszer got back in.

"I know," said Raszer. "I don't like them either. Do you want me to drive?" She shook her head.

They rolled through the fallen outpost at a deliberate pace. Too fast would have been foolhardy, and too slow would have invited fire from any possible survivors. There was a fifty-foot span of open scrub on the southeast boundary of the compound to be crossed before they could return to solid pavement, and it presented the greatest hazard.

It was the only place Francesca hesitated.

Raszer thought they ought to hug the road as closely as possible, but he kept his own counsel and let the driver drive. The killing of the young soldier was in his blood like venom. He knew he'd done what the moment's truth called for, but he couldn't shake the doubt. The bombs had taken the soldier's limbs, but Raszer had taken his life. Would he have done the same on a Jerusalem street in the aftermath of a suicide bombing? No. Different rules applied. Under those rules, he'd have stayed at the man's side until the stretchers came, and then walked away clean, knowing full well that too much blood had already been lost, and that even if by some chance the soldier did survive, he'd curse his rescuer. Human choice is about what is exigent, and exigencies are different in a war zone. Raszer knew all this, but it didn't stop the ache.

Suddenly, the front wheels hit pavement, and two seconds later they were clear. Dante's vehicle, however, had slipped into a rut carved by the bombs, and his rear wheels were stuck and spinning.

"Fuck. I'll go back and give him a push," Raszer said, opening his door.

"No," Francesca said firmly. "No. He'll get himself out. Stay where you are."

He knew she was right, but he could see that her teeth were on edge. As a leader, she'd had to calculate the incalculable: the awful preferability of losing one, rather than two or more. "But if he keeps spinning his tires, he'll dig up whatever's down there.""He'll get himself out," she said. "I know he will."

Raszer watched the car through the dust-caked rear window and realized that his impulse had been partly penitential, and penitential heroism is usually suicide.

"Thatta boy," he whispered, as Dante's tires finally bit into earth.

"Easy, now," Francesca urged.

"He's out!" Ruthie cheered, as the Cruiser lurched forward.

"Now just follow my tracks, Dante," said Francesca. "Follow my tracks."

"Hoo-wah!" Ruthie shouted when Dante was safely across the shoulder.

And though the specter of bombs and blood hung in the air like smoke, the earlier fractiousness faded and they began, at last, to feel like one.

For the next forty minutes, they kept the speed moderate and traveled without incident, although the road was pocked with bomb craters every few miles, as well as with other evidence of the combat that had torn the mountains for nearly two decades. On the high, flinty ridges, Raszer glimpsed the remains of Nestorian churches; higher still were what appeared to be much older ruins, windswept citadels of the Assyrian culture that had once commanded all within reach of the Tigris. It was as rugged as the Hindu Kush and just as unconquerable. How the Turks thought they'd ever keep it from the indigenous Kurds was beyond his imagining, but they were still trying, almost a century after the meddlesome West had carelessly drawn its borders.

No one, he thought—not even the legions of an empire—keeps land like this from its tribal stewards. But nations and jealous husbands are forever trying to hold on to what can't be kept, and now—against all logic—Turkey had the help of its NATO ally.

They entered the Zap Gorge in high afternoon, and the granite sepulchre of earth closed around them, leaving only a narrow river of sky eight thousand feet above to mirror the ancient current below. Dante informed Raszer that there was a village thirty miles away, near the Uludere junction, where they could rest and find food and provisions. They knew the Fedeli there, he said, as it had been a frequent base camp for their trekking forays into the local mountains. It would be a safe stop. "As long," Dante added, "as it hasn't been bombed."

Just short of their destination, they came around a bend and encountered a fruit stand commandeered as a checkpoint by a detachment of the *pesh merga*, the provisional army of a nascent Kurdistan. With them were half a dozen Kurdish irregulars, the fierce hill fighters who were the guerilla vanguard in this oldest of wars. American involvement had accomplished what a half century of Turkish and Iraqi bullying had not: It had unified the squabbling factions of the independence movement, bringing the Marxist PKK into the same camp with the nationalist PDK and PUK. The hill fighters were turbaned and brown like old gold; but for their new Russian rifles, they might have stepped from the pages of Kipling. Several were in animated conversation with a formidable-looking young commander, who broke the huddle to step into the road and order Francesca to halt. A saber scar ran from his left ear to his upper lip, his thick hair was crow black, and his eyes were startlingly blue.

"Let me talk to them," she said. "I think we'll be all right."

The commander fingered the white T-shirt dangling from the Land Cruiser's antenna, while the other soldiers filed out from the fruit stand and surrounded the cars, rifles at the ready. As he watched Francesca's approach, he seemed to Raszer to take the measure of her stride more than that of her gender, and in this there was a measure of respect not seen in the West. Raszer could hear only fragments of the exchange, but its tone was not as forbidding as the fighter's appearance. Francesca displayed a series of documents, explaining them in language the soldier seemed to understand. Then she pointed back up the road, and Raszer knew she must be relating news of the bombing.

Through the windshield, Raszer saw Francesca step back. She indicated the road ahead and asked a question that caused all of the soldiers to prick up their ears and step away. A minute later, she was back in the driver's seat and exhaled a sigh of relief.

"I'm impressed," said Raszer. "What was the magic word?"

"Philby Greenstreet," she answered. "And a 100-euro bill."

"That name travels well." Raszer said. "How did you explain us?"

"Pilgrims. Trekking to the old Chaldean monastery on Buzul Dagi. I said you and Ruthie were a French-Canadian priest and a fallen woman on a penitential trek."

"Not that far from the truth," said Raszer.

"Kiss my ass," said Ruthie. "Can't fall if you never stood up."

And for the first time on the trip, they all shared a laugh.

"Anyway," Francesca picked up, "we're clear as far as Ispiria and the pack-in point. Once we're on foot, it'll be riskier. There are Turkish commando units in these mountains, and mercenaries. He told me the Americans can't have a ground presence yet because they're still officially neutral, so they contract the dirty work out to mercenaries. That way, they can claim they're still supporting the Iraqi Kurds while opposing the Turkish Kurds in the name of NATO. Even though it's the same army. What a shitty business . . . and all over an area the size of Belgium."

Raszer looked around. "And about as developed as the moon. No farming, no cities, and, from what I've heard, not much oil either . . . except down Kirkuk way."

"No," said Francesca, starting off. "It's mostly unarable, extreme . . . but it's also one of the world's great land bridges. This was once the kingdom of Urartu. The prophets walked down into Mesopotamia from these mountains. Noah's flood covered these peaks all the way to Ararat. In so many ways, this is where it began. Worth holding on to, don't you think?"

"A sacred well is worth more than the water that's in it," said Raszer. "People always spill blood and treasure over land like this. Bet the Old Man understands that."

"You can be sure he does," Francesca replied. "If this place becomes the prize in a full-out war involving Turkey, Iraq, Iran, and the Kurds, with the U.S. playing arbitrageur, who do you think will collect the fee?"

"How much land does he control?"

"It's not insubstantial, but it's not about size. He controls four key passes and has some of the Iranian Kurdish warlords—wild, renegade bastards—in a kind of thrall."

"So I've heard."

"But it's more than that," said Francesca. "It's influence. He's like a tumor with tentacles reaching into Washington, Moscow, Beijing, and Riyadh. He's got something on all of them, because they've all used him to do things they couldn't admit to."

Ruthie was staring out the window, uncharacteristically silent. "What do you say, Ruthie?" Raszer asked her. "Does all this square with what Henry told you about the Old Man?"

"Henry didn't tell me all that much," she answered. "Except that the most powerful people in the world don't have titles or wear crowns, 'n that he was one of 'em."

Raszer turned back to watch the gorge narrow into midafternoon blackness, the vaulting rock above having caused its own total eclipse. He heard his stomach growl. "I suppose I should've asked before," he said. "Why aren't you armed, Francesca?"

"There's a long tradition in this region of giving protection to pilgrims. If you carry arms, you forgo protection." She acknowledged his rumbling belly. "Forty miles the other side of this gorge," she said, "is Ispiria. That's where we'll leave the cars and gather the rest of our provisions. And sleep. And eat. I can hear that you're hungry."

✦ ◆ ✦

Ispiria was at the eastern mouth of the gorge, on a summit reached after a long climb out of darkness into the burnt-gold and diminishing sunlight. It was not a village, as such, but a reconstituted Assyrian Christian abbey, now used as a combination outpost and field hospital for the Kurdish fighters and their families. In the court surrounding its ancient fountain, a Kurdish wedding was in progress. The sudden explosion of raucous sound and color was an elixir after the starkness of the road.

Francesca and Shaykh Adi hopped out and were greeted warmly by a man who was possibly the oldest living creature Raszer had ever laid eyes on. His *kaffiyeh* was crimson, his *jellaba* was white silk, and his eyes—like the young Kurdish commander's—were the color of the pigment ground from lapis lazuli. After all of them had been introduced and toasted by the wedding party, they were shown to a colonnaded quadrangle of patchy grass in the shadow of the church's domed roof, where they could lay their bedrolls and recuperate before what Raszer was told would be a full meal.

Dante pulled the Land Cruisers into the side-by-side stalls of an unused stable annex and barred the doors. The keys were entrusted to a young monk.

Behind the main structure, the abbey's property extended to the mountainside and was bordered by the colonnade. Their billet was just to the near side of this. Ruthie collapsed almost immediately, while Francesca and Dante retired to a shaded corner for what appeared to be their afternoon devotions. Raszer dropped his gear and headed immediately back to the wedding, the holy dog at his heels. He was intrigued by the old villager, captivated by the backhills twang of the music—a kind of Anatolian hillbilly sound—and at this moment felt the need for a crowd, even if he was a stranger in the midst of it.

He found a vacant place on the fountain's rim that the late-afternoon sun still warmed. Within twenty minutes, he guessed, the last of the light would be swallowed up by the gorge they'd just emerged from. He picked out the bride, a lovely copper-skinned girl of probably not more than sixteen, in a blossoming green skirt with a white underdress. Like all the women and most of the men, she took delight in dancing. The smiles were unforced, the sensuality unabashed.

Someone shouted behind him, and Raszer reflexively turned his head. The low-angle sunlight had swathed the white peaks to the northeast, painting the rock like gold leaf. What impressed him—made him shield his eyes, in fact—was the mirrorlike intensity with which the mountain reflected the light. Its crown suddenly burst into refracted flame, as if concealing a supernova. There were more cries, and a disparate chorus of *ahhhs*, as the wedding party stopped to observe the spectacle. Raszer stood, turned, and followed the villagers to a rise in the street. The old man in the crimson headdress came to his side, holding the hands of two children. He offered both Raszer and Shaykh Adi a nod. "English?" he asked, with a heavy accent.

"*Français*," Raszer replied.

"Ah, *comment allez-vous*?" the man asked. "You are a long way from home."

"*Très bien, merci.*" Raszer pointed to the mountaintop. "*C'est sublime.*"

The sense of the miraculous was redoubled by what happened next. The sun dropped a notch farther and the beam directed at the summit was suddenly as focused as that of a laser. By his own poor scientific reckoning, some kind of interference pattern was being created by the cross-hatching of direct and reflected light, and in the heart of the blaze there appeared the form of a city unlike any he'd ever seen or imagined. Like a dreamer's Constantinople formed of white gold and sheathed in ice, it shot spire upon spire into the darkening sky, fingers reaching for the face of God.

"*Qu'est-ce que c'est?*" Raszer asked the patriarch. The dog whined softly.

"Na-Koja-Abad," the man answered. "Home."

"How many days' journey?" Raszer asked, for he was still—despite his heart's own semaphore—trying to fix the place in the coordinates of a measurable world.

"A life's journey," answered the man with a chuckle. "For some, more."

He asked if Raszer knew Arabic, and Raszer nodded.

"This then you must remember: *Wahdat-ul-wujood*. All in God and God in all." The elder rubbed his chin. "You are a man of light seeking the light," he added, studying Raszer's face. "Carry what you have seen here. It is the only truth. There is no death where this vision lives. Allah be praised."

"Yes," said Raszer. "Allah be praised." He paused. "This vision . . . this place—does it have anything to do with El Mirai, the citadel of the one they call the Old Man?"

The man put his finger to his lips and shook his head. "One mimics the other, and for some, that is enough. But they are as far apart as diamond and glass." As an afterthought, he whispered, "Old Man—ha! I am the only old man here!"

When Raszer looked up again at the mountain, the city was gone.

THIRTY-ONE

A MILE ON FOOT INTO THE Baskale Valley, they came across a vast field of yellow tulips, their stems bent so that the cups were overturned and facing the earth.

"*Ters lale*," said Francesca. "Crying tulips. The Bektashi say that they bow in submission to Allah. And weep for the children of Ali."

"They grow in this bowl because it collects the rain and the warmth of the sun," said Dante. "But once we climb out of this valley, you won't see anything but the toughest wildflowers. And on the far side of Güzeldere Pass, it's a desert."

Their provisions had been supplemented by stock from a storage locker the Fedeli kept in Ispiria for the treks they led in late spring and early fall. They now had nylon rope and climbing hardware and supplies for sudden mountain storms, though Francesca's forecast was that the weather would remain dry and might even turn hot. If they sustained a brisk pace, Raszer estimated they'd make their destination by the morning of the third day. The plan was to then make a base camp at the foot of the citadel, and for Raszer to ascend to El Mirai alone the next morning.

For the first part of the journey, they were on paths well worn by trekkers before them. The grades were steep, the stones sharp underfoot, and though the air remained dry and relatively cool, the sun was merciless. A layer of sweat formed every few minutes, then was blown dry by the next ferocious updraft. Dehydration was a real risk, and so—Raszer was told—were human and animal predators.

All through the nineteenth century, intrepid Englishmen had risked these mountains for the archaeological treasures of ancient Urartu and Assyria, and many had had their throats slit by nomadic brigands. The treaties of spirit and flesh the Fedeli had made over seven years of leading trekking parties through the highlands of the Kurdish homeland offered some degree of protection, but only where the thieves were bound by tribe. Danger might come from renegades and mercenaries of any stripe. The greatest measure of safety came not from their alliances or from any makeshift diplomatic immunity, but from the inhospitality of the land itself. It seemed empty of life.

They made camp on a butte that rose like a river lock from the valley floor and overlooked the next day's stark journey into nothingness. They broke a full two hours before sunset because they'd made excellent time, because Francesca was concerned about dehydration, and because travel late in the day invited thieves. They pitched two tents, bootleg versions of Red Cross originals, which offered some degree of inoculation—one for the men, and one for the women. Between them, they dug a fire pit and channels to drain any sudden mountain cloudbursts. Then they scrambled down the runneled sides of the butte to collect fuel from the dry brush and fallen walnut trees that clung improbably to the loose rock. By five o'clock they had a good fire, and by six thirty, Francesca had stuffed five eggplants with walnuts and dried chilies for roasting, and, with grudging assistance from Ruthie, had made flatbread from flour and water.

They ate only what they could consume entirely. Their only intoxicants were fear and the hyperawareness it induced, a kind of feral vision. All sensation was enhanced because all the usual insulation was gone. The partial antidote for this animal edginess was—as it had always been—to huddle close and swap stories. And so it was that Raszer persuaded his two guides to tell him how the Fedeli had come to be.

Francesca had been on The Gauntlet for a little better than a year, after having abandoned her graduate studies at the University of Bologna. Her thesis work on semiotics, never completed, had dealt with sexual signifiers in the visions of the saints. She was one of few women who'd embraced the game's gamble, and it had finally led her to the international resort areas of southwestern Turkey.

"I was waitressing at a café in Bodrum. Waiting . . . and *waiting*. You do a lot of that in The Gauntlet. Day after day, I looked for my next guide. Finally, I realized I'd been looking right at him for weeks. There was a little man who came in every morning for espresso. Bald, plump, totally ordinary. One day, for a laugh, I asked him if he could make use of a keen mind and a steady heart. He was a trader, and I became his assistant. Three months later, I was in the back of a truck full of girls—mostly Kazakh and Ukrainian—being transported through the Caucasus to the Old Man's harem. All of us doped up. The truck stopped in a mountain pass. There was a melee. Shouting in Farsi and Kurdish. I thought for sure we were going to be gang-raped and left in a ditch with our throats cut. In a certain way—terrified as I was—I didn't care. I was over. Finished. Then the flap opened and let in this hard blue light, and standing with the sun at their backs were Chrétien and Dante and four Kurds with AK-47s."

After a pause to refuel the fire, Raszer turned to Dante.

"What about you, Dante? How'd you and Chrétien hook up?"

"I'd only been on the circuit six months from a POE in Glasgow. But I was fast. I'd been a gamer practically from the cradle. Got started with the MMORGs when I was a wee bugger, 'n got so good at it that me dad took me to California when I was eleven to see if the big game developers wanted to pick my agile little mind."

"Anyway, I found m'self in Berlin and heard through the chatroom that an *anarkunst* cell had formed around this crazy Dutch engineering student in Sarajevo. Anarchist art. Six or seven guys who plotted victimless terrorism, blowing up statues and symbols of the new world order and such. I thought, *That sounds cool.*

"We pulled a few off, and then things got hot and we had to split. Passage was arranged through Hazid. That's the crossover, mate. We all thought Hazid was just a moniker for the GamesMasters—a synecdoche, if you know what I mean—but it's the feckin' wormhole to El Mirai. It's where the Old Man gets you. A small plane to Albania and then trucks to Aleppo. This mercenary pronounced himself our new guide and said he was taking us to the Lord of Time, the mother of all poetic terrorists. I thought he was talking about bin Laden, and at the time, I thought, *Why not*?

"We drove the Black Sea coast and down through the Caucasus into the Iranian borderlands and finally to Hakkâri. When we got to the crossroads, we were starved and hallucinating. They took us up this long, steep path. We kept catchin' glimpses of this unbelievable castle, built right into the cliff, and every time we stopped to rest we passed around a pipe of hashish laced with opium. By the time we got to the gates, we had to be carried in on litters. We were stone out of it. We woke up in the Garden. We were fed and treated like kings. We had more women in a week than most men have in a life. It was a dream, paradise. *Aye*—a sham paradise.

"One morning, after a night of screwing and cocktails of opium, E, and GABA, I woke up in total darkness. I mean, *total.* Imagine that: openin' your eyes and seein' nothin'. The air was stale and still and I couldn't move me legs . . . 'cause I was in a feckin' box. A coffin. I started to scream, and I screamed until I screamed out the contents of my mind. Finally, the lid was opened and this sheikh in black robes told me I was dead, and now my Qiyami could begin. My resurrection.

"They took me and Chrétien and trained us for six months in the art of *taqiyya* and the guilt-free kill. We learned how to get in close enough to smell the pee in our targets' trousers and still get away clean. And we learned how to be invisible, how to be so inside the game that we could work at the feckin' FBI for twenty years and nobody'd be the wiser. We couldn't be killed, ya see, because we were already gone.

"But one day—out in the courtyard during exercises—Chrétien told me he'd seen the flaw in the whole scheme. 'The crack in the world where the light gets in,' he called it."

"What was it?" Raszer asked.

"The night before, he'd been doin' this new girl in the Garden. In the middle of it, she started callin' him by a name nobody'd called him since he was a kid. 'Please, Nilfi . . . please, Nilfi.' That's what she said. Only, he was hearin' it like from a very long way away, through another pair of ears. His given name was Nils, but his friends and family called him Nilfi when he was little. He looked at the girl, and went, 'Oh my fucking God!' 'cause he realized that some missing part of him knew her from before, and that if he felt something like that, he couldn't be dead. He was in a borrowed self. So the motherfuckers had lied to us. Ergo, nothing they'd told him was true, and everything we could do to escape was permitted."

"How did you get out?"

"We decided to be the perfect *fidais* until the time was right—until they judged us ready for an assignment. Months went by. Finally, it came. Our target was a Yarsani chieftain in the neighboring valley who'd refused to pay tribute to the Old Man. We snuck into his camp with a trading party, but instead of killing him, we became his pupils. He taught us piracy and he taught us about the Bab—the prophet of the Baha'i faith. We started intercepting the Old Man's cargo shipments. That's how we met Francesca: She was part of the cargo. We brought 'er back with us, and for a while the three of us ran guns to the Kurds in Hakkâri. Then we formed the Fedeli. It was Francesca's idea—a good one. To fight bad faith with good faith."

"Yes, it was," said Raszer, and gave the dark-eyed girl a nod through the woodsmoke. "So none of you ever came face to face with the great Lord of Time . . . "

"Only the ninth level *fidai* ever see him. And even they can only look at him in a mirror . . . so they say, anyway."

"Good way to maintain mystique," Raszer commented. "Or a fraud."

"They also say," added Dante, "that to get to him, you have to pass through as many doors as there are rooms in heaven, and that ordinary men are old by the time they reach his threshold. But he can travel the same distance in the blink of an eye."

"Keep in mind," said Francesca, "that none of this is 'real' in the way that a market stall in Istanbul is real."

Raszer sighed. "Right. It reminds me of how you can make the moon disappear from the sky by putting a hand over one eye."

Ruthie, who might have been expected to snort in the face of all the obscurity, was again silent. Raszer's gaze settled on her and stayed until she felt it.

"You killed that guy," she said. "That soldier. He couldn't fight you. You shot a guy with no arms or legs to fight you off with."

"Chill, Ruthie," said Dante. "He was seconds away from an agonizing death. We couldn't leave him and we couldn't take him. What would you have done?"

She ignored him. "How's it feel to blow someone's brains out, mister?"

Something was going on. It was as if she were looking for a good reason to hate him.

"It feels . . . " Raszer replied slowly, "like a fist closing around your heart, Ruthie. Because in the end, a human soul isn't private ground, really; it's common ground. So when you kill someone, it's like ripping them out of the same soil your own roots are in. And you feel that. If you're human, you feel it. Does that answer your question?"

A dog howled from a canyon that might have been miles away, and was answered by one nearer. There were drums after that, rumbling like thunder, and finally, voices on the wind, raised in sung lamentation.

"What are we hearing?" Raszer asked, his ear turned into the current.

"Kurdish hill fighters," said Francesca. "They must have a camp up in those peaks. When one of their men is killed, they keep vigil through the night. They dance and sing. They want their enemy to know that nothing can kill their thirst for freedom."

"I'd like to have them on my side in a fight. If you'll all excuse me, I think I'll turn in."

⬩◆⬩

THE SCREAM CAME FIRST inside Raszer's dream, but within some fraction of a second pierced the membrane of sleep and brought him to his knees. There was an instant when he thought it might be an animal, so alien was the sound of a full-grown woman's shriek. It was Ruthie. He fumbled for the pistol and rolled through the tent flap. The temperature had dropped fifteen degrees, and the chill conspired with her second scream to stiffen the hair on his neck. Dante and Shaykh Adi, who had been taking their turn at sentry duty, were now racing down from the crest of the butte, the dog leaping in and out of the flashlight beam.

"Slow down!" Raszer said in an urgent whisper. "Keep it quiet and circle around to the right side of the tent. Back me up. Do you have your knife?" Dante nodded mutely. "Good." Raszer dropped to one knee and addressed the animal, already bristling with instinctive alarm. "And you . . . " He stroked its back firmly. "Be cool."

It occurred to Raszer as he padded toward the tent, the dog at his side, that if there were indeed another human being in there, he probably would have stifled Ruthie's second scream. The thought that he might be about to corner some nonhuman predator was, in a way, more unsettling. These mountains had once been home to tigers, and there were many varieties of wildcat still in the region. He'd had experience with men, but little with animals.

A flashlight had been turned on in the women's tent. He saw Ruthie's stiff-backed silhouette against the canvas. There were no other forms. Francesca must still be flat. *Stay that way*, Raszer said to himself. *Stay that way*. He wondered if it could be a scorpion, a big spider. Or something more fantastic—a djinn. A servitor.

There wasn't a third scream. Some signal from Ruthie's brain stem must have told her to play dead. The silhouette was as motionless as a mannequin and all the weirder for that. Raszer crept up to the flap and took hold of the hem, then turned to order Shaykh Adi to sit and stay well back from the tent. For whatever it might be worth, he delivered the instruction in Arabic. He knew that whatever kind of creature might squat behind the flap needed to be given a clear exit route. Hearing neither movement nor the rapid breathing of an animal, and smelling nothing but the mineral wind, he began to wonder if she'd merely spooked herself, but he called out anyway: "I have a gun aimed at your head. Back away from the girl. Drop your weapon and crawl out of the tent, or your brains will be on the canvas."

He heard a tiny voice, at first unrecognizable. It came only from the throat.

"Stephan . . . it's . . . it's a . . . "

It was Francesca.

" . . . Ss . . . ss . . . "

"Oh, fuck," he said under his breath, and drew back the flap gingerly. Coiled at the foot of Ruthie's sleeping bag was a mature puff adder, its jeweled skin glistening. If it struck, she would likely die; they could not get her to an antidote in time.

"Okay, Ruthie," he said softly. "That's good. Keep still. Shallow breaths. Very slowly, slip your hands inside the sleeping bag . . . " He opened the flap as far as it would go and laid its corner on the damp canvas of the tent's roof. For the moment, it held. He set the pistol on the ground and checked to see that his knife was still in its ankle sheath. "If your sleeping bag is like mine, it has both outside and inside zipper pulls. See if you can feel for it with your right hand. Easy. Don't let him see any movement. When you've got hold of it . . . blink." She did as she was told. A few seconds later, her eyelids came down. "All right, good. Now unzip it as far as you can go without moving your upper body."

He watched her forearm sink into the bag and stop just above the elbow.

Shit.

"That's not enough," he said. "Go a few more inches; let your right shoulder follow your arm . . . like a nice, easy stretch . . . Keep your left shoulder and your head still. That's it. Just a couple more. Easy."

He took a breath. "Okay. Good. Now breathe. Pull the air into your lungs, steady and slow . . . a little at a time, like a balloon."

Raszer dropped to a squat, unsnapped the straps of his ankle sheath, and slipped out the seven-inch blade, setting it on the ground just outside the door. He heard Shaykh Adi growling and turned to see the fur along the dog's spine standing erect.

"Easy, old man," he said.

He pivoted back to Ruthie. "Hold that breath in," he said in a soft monotone. "Now bring both hands back to where your knees are. Palms up. Fingers straight and together."

She blinked once.

"Good. When I say, 'Now,' you throw that sleeping bag over the snake as completely as you can. Don't stop to check your work. Roll right across the tent to the farthest corner, where Francesca is. And then don't make a move."

The adder had taken all this in without comment. Only a reptile could have maintained such composure. Any mammal would have turned at least once to observe the threat from its rear.

Raszer inched closer, "*Now!*" he said.

She did as instructed—albeit stiffly—but almost immediately the snake sensed its entrapment and began to move. A bad situation, but Raszer was in it now, so he threw himself on top of the sleeping bag and felt frantically for the snake's bulk beneath the fabric. The sensation of taut, sinuous movement under his belly made him shudder. This was a formidable creature.

Once he had both hands around its middle, he began instantly to feel for the head, for he knew he had to have a grip on it before attempting to take the snake outside. He felt a narrowing and finally a slight yielding at the glands and clamped down. The sleeping bag's slippery nylon lining gave him dubious grip, but there was no time to waste, so he pushed back from the balls of his feet and shot out backward through the flap, bringing the bag and its flailing contents with him.

"The knife, Dante!" he shouted. "Give me the knife!" He rolled over on top of the writhing serpent, only barely able to maintain a hold on its gullet. He felt the knife's leather grip slap against the palm of his right hand.

"I need light," he called to Dante, who was momentarily rooted in a paralysis he couldn't free himself from. "Light!" Raszer shouted again, the snake's tail whipping, its entire body convulsing in the effort to break his grip.

An agonizing instant later, the light flicked on and Dante held the beam shakily on the edge of the bag, where only the tongue could be seen, still flicking maniacally in and out of the nylon cocoon.

"Thanks," Raszer said, then glanced at Dante. "Are you all right?"

"I will be," came the answer. Dante dropped to his knees. "I'll grab hold of the tail and try to stop him wriggling. When you cut, cut high . . . just below the skull. If you hit the right notch, the knife will go through like butter."

Raszer flattened out his body and squeezed hard. He'd have to slip his hand down to expose the head and access the soft spot. That would mean momentarily loosening his grip. The spill from the flashlight caught the gold glint in Shaykh Adi's eyes. The dog had moved in close and was watching the snake's tail whip. His growl was feral, his attention rapt.

Raszer rested the knife's edge alongside his knuckle and used the blade to lever his hand out of the way. He found the notch behind the skull and put all his weight into the slice. The reptile's reaction was electric: As soon as it felt the blade's bite, it summoned all its strength into its midsection and writhed violently, shaking its head free in one massive convulsion. Raszer felt the head slide from his palm and his life slip into thin air.

He sprung back and waited for the attack.

But it didn't come. In the instant of the adder's escape from Raszer's grip, Shaykh Adi's powerful canine jaws had found its tender neck and clamped down hard.

Dante swung around and turned the flashlight on him. The dog had carried the writhing animal to the remains of the fire and was now shaking all four feet of it violently over the still-warm coals. The snake arched and recoiled and whipped helplessly for a while and then, finally, went limp. Adi held it in his jaws for a few moments longer to be sure, then flung it onto the coals. A conclusive hiss rose from the embers.

Dante came to Raszer's side. "I'm sorry," he said. "I was slow on the uptake."

"Don't beat yourself up," Raszer replied. "Snakes scare the best of us." He gave Dante's shoulder a squeeze, but his confidence in the boy's reflexes was shaken and Dante must have felt it.

"God, I hate those motherfuckers," said Ruthie, emerging cautiously from the tent with a blanket wrapped about her shoulders. She cast a glance at the fire, then a wary look at Dante. "Are there a lot of them around here?"

"The adders are rare in high country," he said. "You find 'em mostly on the Syrian plain and down through Arabia. But there're plenty of others. And tomorrow, we'll pass through the Valley of Serpents in the late afternoon. The valley's a natural heat-reflecting dish, and the brown snakes slither down from the rocks at sunset to keep warm through the night. We just have to make it through before the sun goes down."

"Goddamn right we will," said Ruthie, shivering.

Francesca approached and stood next to Raszer. "You okay?" she asked.

"Yeah. Fine, thanks."

"Hmm," she said. "You have steady nerves."

"Just faking it," he said.

"Is there really a difference?"

"Maybe not," he said.

Francesca whistled Adi to her side. "It'll be sunrise in three hours. We'd better try to get some sleep."

"Yeah, right," said Ruthie, rolling her eyes. "I don't exactly have Lara Croft in my tent to protect me."

"Ha!" Francesca shot back. "And who are you? You could have brought thieves from every direction with your howling."

Ruthie made a move toward Francesca, and Raszer caught hold of her elbow.

"All right," said Raszer. "Here's what we'll do. Shaykh Adi will finish the night with the two of you. He's the hero, anyway. And I'll take the next watch."

"Agreed," said Francesca. "But check on us, will you?"

"Of course," said Raszer. "Make sure your flap is zipped tight." He stooped to pick up the semiautomatic pistol from the rocky ground. "And try to get along."

There was, however, a problem with Raszer's plan. Shaykh Adi, who until now had tolerated Ruthie, suddenly decided he didn't like her at all. She entered the tent, and when Francesca then commanded the dog to follow, Adi refused.

"Maybe he still senses the snake," Raszer said. "I don't think animals figure time the way we do. It's all still happening for him."

"He senses something," said Francesca softly. "But no. I've seen Adi kill at least a half dozen snakes, and he usually sticks to me like glue afterward."

"You go in first, then call him," Raszer suggested.

This strategy succeeded, but not for long. Raszer had just settled into his vigil atop the rise when he heard Adi begin to whimper, then whine, and finally howl. With a curse, Raszer fumbled his way out of the tent and met Francesca and Adi halfway.

"It's not going to work, Stephan," she said. "Something's wrong."

Ruthie emerged halfway from the tent and shook the hair from her eyes. She eyed Raszer. "How 'bout her and the dog sleep with Dante and you sleep in here? What's with the separate tents, anyway? We're not fuckin' Muslims."

Francesca parked her hands on her hips and waited for Raszer's reply.

Raszer scratched his two-day growth of beard and ran a hand over his polished scalp. Alone with Ruthie was not a place he wanted to be right now. He knew himself too well. A curious and unsettling thing: The more reason he found to mistrust her, the more he found himself inflamed by her.

"Here's the deal," he said. "I'll sleep in your tent. With *both* of you. And I'm bringing the gun in case either one of you disturbs my beauty rest."

An hour later, as he finally drifted off, he thought to himself that a man could probably do worse than to wrestle a snake before bed.

THIRTY-TWO

THE COASTAL FOG OF SPRING, rendered milky by the morning sun's straight-on rays, reached all the way to the front stoop of Monica's Silver Lake duplex. This was her least favorite time of year. It felt nothing like the Aprils she'd known as a child in southern Ohio. It lacked the kiln-baked clarity of L.A. summer and the stormy drama of what passed for winter. The best thing about it was the jasmine.

She could smell the bloom as she sat down on the stoop with her tea to read the *International Herald Tribune*. There was more trouble for the Kurds in the very part of the world Raszer had entered. An article just below the fold all but made it official that the Americans were providing stealth backing to Turkey in the increasingly savage battle to deny its largest minority population a homeland. Some alleged that the Syrians were arming the Kurds, and the Russians were said to be behind the Syrians.

Raszer hadn't phoned Monica in forty-eight hours, and she hated that. She knew he was in mountainous backcountry where even satellite communication must be spotty, and she could get only intermittent and questionable fixes on his location by way of the implant. He'd told her that he would leave the phone behind when he reached his destination, but based on his last report, he was still a night short of that.

Her bodyguard had vanished: paid off, shipped back to Denmark, or dead, and the clear message was that the same fate awaited any others. So, she was to remain here under house arrest, exposed and unprotected, and cut off from the technology that might enable her to pull Raszer out of a fix.

She heard her phone ring. She hoped it would be him, but suspected it wasn't. It was the wrong time of day. When she got to the phone, she saw that the button lit up was his public contact number, the one he wrote on his business cards for people he cared to share it with.

"Hello," she said. "Stephan Raszer's line."

A woman spoke. Soft-voiced, tired. "Is Mr. Raszer in?" she asked.

"No," she replied. "He's on assignment right now. Who's calling?"

"But this is his number, right?"

"Yes. Who's calling, please?"

"My name is Constance Endicott."

"Hello." Monica entered the caller ID number into a small terminal beside the phone and received confirmation that the call indeed came from Taos, New Mexico. "How can I help you, Mrs. Endicott?"

"You know who I am?"

"Yes, of course: Katy's mother. We . . . Mr. Raszer is—"

"Is Ruthie with him?"

God, how she hated these moments. *Think, Monica, think. Truth or dodge?*

"That seems very unlikely. Why do you ask?"

"I haven't seen her for four days. A terrible thing happened when Mr. Raszer was here. Maybe you know. A friend of Ruthie's was . . . killed. She was devastated. Then something else happened—I don't know what—that frightened her. She got very angry. The next thing I knew, she was gone."

"Let me see what I can find out," Monica said gently.

"There's something else."

"Yes?"

"I received something from Katy. A letter. Well, not a letter, really, although it did come in an envelope. It's a note on a torn piece of muslin. I can't imagine when she wrote it . . . or who mailed it for her. But it is her handwriting—the note, not the envelope. The envelope has nothing but my name and 'Taos, New Mexico.' It's a wonder it got here. The postmark is from Hamburg, Germany, and the date is August 9 of last year."

"What does the note say, Mrs. Endicott?"

"I'm afraid it doesn't make much sense. She must have written it very fast, poor lamb. It looks like 'N.C.D.C. 12-24.' Then it says, 'I love you. Katy.'"

The last words were swallowed hard.

"I think you should take some hope from this."

"What's your name?"

"Monica."

"Thank you, Monica. Bless you. I hope you're right."

Monica set the phone back in its cradle and felt suddenly overcome. She dropped into the nearest chair and let her head fall to her knees. Had she eaten anything today? She couldn't remember. Then the shudder came, seeming to begin at her very center—in her womb—and moving up her body until it escaped as a sob.

Through the nearly expressionless voice of the mother, she'd glimpsed the daughter, and what she'd seen had made her wonder if Raszer would ever get Katy out. Men devised the most insidious traps for women, baiting them with protection that really wasn't protection at all. Sooner or later, Prince Charming became a prison guard.

✦ ◆ ✦

MORNINGS IN EL MIRAI were mostly a state of mind. Evenings, too, for that matter. In the Garden, it was always the same hazy, languid afternoon. The sun never set. The natural light refracted through the massive crystal dome was replaced seamlessly at dusk by artificial sunlight, maintaining the Garden's moist warmth and extravagant foliage. Morning was whenever Katy woke from opium slumber, and night came when the man-boys had spent themselves in her and curled at her feet.

Every two weeks (or so Katy gauged, because all time was relative there), the men and women would file into separate groups and be taken out to the great court for exercises. To counter the soporific effects of the opium and awaken the mass mind, they were roused with stiff doses of MDMA, delivered in honeyed goat's milk. As one, they mirrored the precise, tai chi–like movements of their instructors for what had at first felt like endless hours but now felt like relief. As she let go of herself, Katy found it easier to be part of the group. They were led through a series of martial routines, some involving knives. Once, she had cut herself, and the blood had surprised her. She felt bloodless.

These outings and her own bodily cycles were the only way to measure time. In the beginning, she tried to use them to keep count of her days of captivity, but soon she lost track. She began to doubt that there was really another life outside, much less one she still desired to return to.

Then, little by little, Katy began to forget herself.

There remained certain markers, if she chose to pay attention. Food was delivered at what seemed to be regular intervals, although it was mostly for the new arrivals, who had not yet lost their taste for meat. Once you had been in the garden for a while, it began to feel unnatural (and like far too great an effort) to take nourishment from anything other than the ripe fruit always within reach. There were offerings of quince, persimmon, kumquat, and peach; plump berries of a dozen kinds that perfumed the breath and stained the hands and lips, and made the simple white smock she wore over her bare flesh look as if it had been dyed for an Indian bazaar; dates that sugared the tongue like marzipan; and figs so engorged with jammy pulp that they split on the branch and infused the air with the scent of a sweet rot. Katy had ceased to have interest in sustenance beyond this, and the opium.

For a while, her body registered time in the attentions paid to her flesh, the spaces between visits from a familiar boy. But soon there were so many familiar boys, and no part of her they had not visited. The hashish kept their appetites keen, and the opium enabled them to fuck her endlessly, until she was in a state as perpetually swollen as the figs, a sweet soreness made endurable by the opium. The opium made everything okay. In dreams, her father sometimes came to her with eyes of flame, but she woke laughing, not shamed, because the opium vapor blurred the world's edges. Even so, there was a nausea she couldn't shake, a feeling of displacement, her stomach left at the top of the roller coaster. And so she begged for more drugs, and when she begged, they took more from her, until the only happiness came with emptiness.

In recent days, there had been a new kind of forgetting. At least twice, she had awakened and been unable to remember her name. The boys had often talked of how their training had made them forget who they'd been before. For them, forgetting was a matter of mind; for Katy, it was a matter of body. Her body no longer contained a sensing self she recognized. Soon, she anticipated, there would be nothing left of herself at all. It was as this new, nameless person began to emerge that she learned they had something special planned for her.

They told her she was favored, and gave her another name.

They gave her a retinue of attendants, and the ripest fruit.

Katy didn't remember writing a note on the fabric she'd torn from her smock, but she did remember the boy's face. Some secret memory trace held Scotty, as it held all kindnesses shown to her in an unkind life. There was a second face she remembered. She saw it when she closed her eyes, and, in the absence of mirrors in the garden, had decided that it should be—must be—her own future face. It was the face of a girl like her, but one who was wicked and wise. As Ruthie, she could exist here. As Katy, she was already dead.

⬩◆⬩

THE VALLEY OF SERPENTS was one of the oddest natural formations Raszer had ever found himself in. Less a valley than an enormous V of black flint, it looked like a runoff channel cleaved by a corps of giants. Its sides were steep and slick, and everything that skittered down them wound up accumulating in the center until it was carried away by the winter rains. Francesca told him that in November, the cleft often filled to a depth of forty feet and was as thick with mountain vipers as a pot of boiling spaghetti.

They identified three varieties of snake in the first mile, the nastiest of which was known as Wagner's viper. There were hundreds of these, in shades of orange and umber and rust. Most seemed to be in the process of slithering back up the slippery banks, which gave the enormous wings of featureless rock the appearance of an exotic, trembling butterfly.

The serpents still in the shadowed cleft were sluggish from the early morning's cool. Francesca and Dante had brought with them long, forked branches of walnut they'd whittled to precision and now swept across the rocky path like dousing rods, scooping up the somnolent reptiles and flinging them as high up onto the banks as they could. For the first fifteen minutes, Ruthie covered her head each time a snake was hoisted, but after a while, even she got used to the routine. They sang verse after verse of a Sufi drinking song as they proceeded, their voices producing a cascade of echoes.

By the sun, they were in the cleft for only ninety minutes, but it felt like hours. When they began their ascent to what Francesca told Raszer would be the last and highest of the passes before the alpine terrain gave way to high desert, they were already nerve-tired and damp with the sweat of apprehension. No one wanted to look back, but at four thousand feet, approaching the leading edge of a glacier, they finally stopped to review their accomplishment.

"Fuck," said Ruthie. "Do we have to come back the same way?"

"Best not to think about it now," said Francesca. "Let's just get there."

"We're working on a chopper, Ruthie," he said. "I doubt your sister will be in any shape for hiking. The challenge will be flying through here without getting shot at."

"The best would be a Red Cross helicopter," said Francesca, "or something made up to look like one."

"I'll see what I can do," said Raszer. "How much farther to the pass?"

"We're going to try to make it by noon," she answered. "Then we'll eat. Let's get going. There may be snow."

"Just one party after another," Ruthie said. "Snakebite, then frostbite."

At eight thousand feet, the ragged edge of the glacier spilled across the path in a tongue of ice a mile wide, slowing their pace by half. After another five hundred feet of ascent, the air began to thin out and their steps grew even more labored.

They stopped to share the last half liter of water, the last they'd have before reaching a glacial stream that Francesca had told them would parallel the path on their descent. A few hundred yards farther, and they entered the clouds, and for some time had only the rhythmic *tap-tap-tap* of the snake sticks fore and aft to keep them in line. It was a wholly alien experience to be guided by sound, rather than sight—the experience of the blind. The first impulse was to freeze; after all, who could know what precipice might lie ten feet ahead?

Dante did know, of course, and could have walked it blind and deaf. Once Raszer had relaxed into that sureness, the attenuation of his sight and the consequent sharpening of his hearing became almost pleasant. Along with the rarefaction of the air, the touch of dizziness caused by altitude, and the muffling of footsteps inside the cloud came a kind of altered state. They passed beneath a ledge, and the sun was momentarily lost. Raszer imagined himself without sight, and wondered what meanings beauty might have in the absence of vision. Then, suddenly, he felt a sharp, searing pain in his left eye, as if it had been pierced through.

He staggered to a halt and bent over. Had he walked into something?

"Everyone all right?" Francesca called out.

"Think so," said Raszer, feeling his eye and finding it undamaged. "Just a headache, I guess. Blood vessels, maybe. Altitude, probably."

"The altitude, aye," Dante echoed. "We'll be headed down soon."

They came out from under the ledge, and the vapor was instantly suffused with a white light that made it seem incandescent. A rush of icy air followed. Ruthie called out from inside the cloud.

"Tell me there's something on either side o' this path, dude . . . "

"Just follow the sticks," Dante counseled. "Keep 'em lined up in the space between your ears, and you'll be fine. Hold on to Adi's tail if you want."

"So you're saying there's nothing there, right? How long is the drop?"

"You don't want to know," said Francesca. "Be quiet and listen."

"Shit."

They walked that way for another five minutes. Suddenly, there was a ferocious updraft, and the cloud bank was dispersed almost instantly. It was impossible not to feel a surge of carnival vertigo on seeing that they were 9,200 feet above sea level, with a sheer drop on either side of a path not more than four feet wide.

"Beautiful," said Raszer.

"It's savage, isn't it?" said Dante. "And look." He raised his arm and pointed to the northeast. "There's where we're going."

"You won't see it again until morning," Francesca said softly. "The angle is just right here, but after we drop a hundred feet, it will disappear."

"Jesus," whispered Raszer, finally registering the massive battlements and towering minarets rising from the desert peaks some twelve miles distant, as the crow flew. Indeed, it was not the ephemeral city he'd glimpsed from Ispiria, although if the light were just right, a man could be fooled. "That's it?" he asked. "El Mirai?"

"That's it," said Dante. "It sits a mile above a southern branch of the Silk Road in territory claimed by three countries—four, if you count Kurdistan—but occupied by none of 'em. It's a no-go zone, and it has been for at least a thousand years. It's no' even on a map. Even Marco Polo had to find his way there by trusting a blind man."

As Francesca had predicted, the fortress soon vanished from sight, and as she had promised, a stream of cold, clear glacier melt furnished water a mile on. They stopped for a lunch of dates and flatbread, and by midafternoon they were on the lee side of the mountains, where the look of the land was dramatically different. The three o'clock sun burned unfiltered through a sky that was almost violet, and the rocks were the color of rust. Patches of meadow were visible far below, but they were the golden brown of Assyria and not the green of the irrigated west. At five o'clock, they made camp for their last night in the familiar world.

After everyone else had crashed, Raszer stirred the embers of the fire, lit a cigarette, and retrieved the gunmetal ionophone from his pack. He'd used it on only one prior job, and had to meditate for a few minutes on how to reprogram the thing to disguise his location. It registered the latitude, longitude, and altitude precisely enough to guide a missile, and as soon as he made a call, anyone spiked into Monica's line would know exactly where he was.

He disabled the autolocate function and set his coordinates at the offset he and Monica had agreed on, which put him—according to the readout—in the Alps somewhere east of Grenoble. Why not?

She picked up after four rings. It must be five in the morning.

"How's the skiing?" she asked, registering his decoy location.

"Good at nine thousand feet," he said. "How are you?"

"I'd be better if I heard from you more often."

"As often as necessary, partner," he said. "No more than that."

"Yeah, yeah. How close are you?"

"Within sight."

"You made good time. Listen, I have more on that black stone—"

"Good. Tell me in a sec. First: Sometime tomorrow afternoon, we'll make the lodge. I'll send you the specs as soon as I'm there, and then you can let our friends know. There's a village south of the base—the only one in the vicinity. That's where I'll bring her. I'd like to chopper out. Do we have a pilot and a couple of freelancers?"

"We will by tomorrow. I'm cross-checking references and verifying credentials."

"Good girl."

"It isn't going to be cheap, Raszer."

"It's never cheap to salvage a career."

"And you'll never be rich. Not the way you go at it."

"Who needs money when they've got Monica?"

"Let's get married," she said.

"Book the church."

"How's Ruthie behaving?"

"Better than I expected. But I still can't connect the dots. Any luck tracing her ticket purchase?"

"Yeah. She paid cash. She had all her docs. She was ready. And . . . her mother called yesterday. She suspects Ruthie's with you. Should I tell her?"

Raszer thought for a moment. "Yes. Tell her she's fine. See if *she* knows where the money came from. Was that why she called? To find out where she was?"

Monica told him about the cryptic note with the dated postmark.

"You're breaking up . . . did you say, 'AC/DC'?"

"No . . . *N, C* . . . " The line went haywire with static.

"Monica? Monica? *Shit.*" He'd lost her. He tried a number of times before conceding that he wasn't going to get her back tonight.

⬩◆⬩

FRANCESCA AND DANTE were up before dawn, and camp was broken by sunrise. The two Fedeli, attended by Shaykh Adi, offered fifteen minutes of prayer to the big red ball in the sky. Raszer joined them for the closing devotions, while Ruthie stood at a distance, wrapped in a blanket and shivering.

The prayer was simple and eloquent. It invoked a number of avatars, including Sahak (the prophet Isaac), Nusayr (who was Jesus, the Nazarene), and Mirza Husayn Ali (the founder of Baha'i faith), and asserted that light can be summoned even from darkness. It ended with a call to Khezr, the wandering green man of the ponds and rivers, to guide them on the remaining journey.

They descended nearly two thousand feet in just over three hours. It was hard on the knees, and Raszer felt his bad ankle protest. The weakness had plagued him for a decade now, and at this stage of his life, he acknowledged that he'd probably never shake it.

Half a mile ahead, the path widened and rose slightly toward two natural pillars of tawny rock that were joined by an arch at the top and formed a towering dolmen, a mineral portal to the promised land of Na-Koja-Abad.

"Wait'll you see this," said Dante.

"Tell me it's a Club Med with an open bar," said Raszer.

"Kind of, yeah," Dante said with a grin. "But it's off-season."

The topographical dish did not reveal itself until they had passed through the pillars, but when it did, it summoned awe. Spanning the field of vision and extending all the way to the next ridge was a rippling field of green, budding stems, hundreds of thousands of them, each just short of a meter in height. The flowers hadn't blossomed yet, but the large, wineglass-shaped buds were the powdery aquamarine of a Cretan mural. Raszer guessed the field to be not less than twenty square miles.

"Jesus," he whispered. "Poppies?"

"The largest field of opium poppies in the known world," said Dante. "And it belongs to no one because it's claimed by everyone. The tribal councils work out the division every spring, but always with the understanding that the field belongs to Allah and he's the final arbiter. The Americans won't touch it because it would blow up in their face, but I bet they get their cut. And for the past twenty years—probably as payment for services rendered in Afghanistan and other places—the Old Man has been able to claim the entire eastern half. That's his base. That's where the juice comes from.

"The Kurdish marksmen watch over the southwestern quadrant, the Turks and the Iranians squabble over the northwestern part and occasionally shoot at each other, and in the east, there are mercenaries in the employ of El Mirai."

"And we're going to walk through the middle?" asked Raszer.

"It's the only way to go," said Dante. He pointed downward to the cut that bisected the center. "Any other route would raise suspicion, make it look like we have something to hide. We're just a trekking party taking two clients on a pilgrimage, right?"

"Right," said Raszer. "And you've done this before?"

"Absolutely," Dante answered. He unstrapped his backpack, took out a tightly rolled Red Cross flag, and, after shaking out the wrinkles, tied it to his snake stick and let the stiff breeze take it. "First off, the mountains beyond the eastern ridge of the dish are popular with climbers. Second, the crossroads at the base of El Mirai have become mythical. You wouldn't believe how many people will pay good money, risk the snakes and the sharpshooters, just to know that they really exist. The cautious ones'll settle for a glimpse from the hills, just to say they've been there. The serious trekkers, they want to experience the topographical inversion for themselves."

"Shams talked about that," said Ruthie. "I never knew what the hell he meant."

"Some huge shift in perspective, right?" said Raszer. "Is it . . . magnetic?"

"Not magnetic," Dante replied emphatically. "It's metanoia. Turns your head."

"The idea goes back at least to Ibn Arabi," said Francesca. "It happens about a mile before the crossroads . . . if everything is right. When you cross into Na-Koja-Abad, Nowhere-Land. It can't be put into words. Best I've heard it described is that you stop seeing inside out and start seeing outside in. The same landscape, but not the same, because the vanishing point is . . . inside your head, or your heart, or wherever active imagination is. I know, words are lame, but—"

"Active imagination . . . " Raszer repeated.

"Yes," said Francesca. "But not like imagining you're a princess or a dragon slayer. This is when you realize that the world you see outside is just a projection of the world God sees inside. It's plugging right into God's imagination."

"It sounds like tripping," said Ruthie.

"Yeah, but . . . no," said Dante. "You don't ever come down from this trip."

"It's the object of The Gauntlet, right?" Raszer asked. "No reference points. Like Mach space. Everything flips and you're inside the game—just you and God."

"And up is down and right is left and everything is permitted," added Dante. "And if you can come back from that and still be on the path, nothing will ever knock you off it again."

Raszer thought for a moment. "So how did someone like Scotty Darrell get so far off the track? He must've passed through here, too, right?"

"Yeah," Dante replied. "But you have to know where you wanna go before you go there. Have to have your bearings. Scotty didn't . . . and he had a bad trip." He hoisted the pack onto his shoulders. "Let's go," he said. "And don't touch the flowers unless you want to get your fingers shot off."

✦ ◆ ✦

THE BUDS WERE STILL too new to have come under the knife. When they were ripe, their various tenders would descend from the ridges, blades in hand, and score the delicate, blue-green pods to release the sweet resin inside. That resin would become the salve for the world's ravages, from toothache to childbirth to cancer to despair about the very thought of life. In differing formulations—heroin, morphine, laudanum, hydro-codone—it wrapped its users in a chemical cocoon designed to make everything okay.

They kept their eyes forward en route through the field, joining their voices in a Sufi couplet that Francesca began to recite as soon as they were amid the budding stems. She had advised them all to keep to their private thoughts and resist the temptation to scan the surrounding hills for sharpshooters, lest they provoke suspicion.

"What if we fall asleep?" Ruthie had asked.

"We won't," replied Francesca.

"Dorothy did," Ruthie countered.

"Dorothy was dreaming already," said Raszer.

"Oh, yeah," said Ruthie. "I always forget that."

When the sun-warmed breeze from the south whistled over the field, the fat buds became a percussion ensemble, tapping against one another en masse and creating a distinct set of pitches—like a thousand bamboo wind chimes set in motion. Despite the field's hypnotic effect—which extended to its absolute quiet when the wind ceased—Raszer couldn't help but feel that they were under the gun from every angle. What a brash thing to do, trespassing the king's opium field in broad daylight. Yet he understood what his guides were about and didn't question it. It was as fools that Grail seekers had always approached the castle, stepping across the jaws of dragons.

When at last they reached the far side and ascended once again into the foothills, Raszer felt a certain relief, despite the clear fact that they were now in the Old Man's kingdom and the most dangerous leg of the journey had just begun.

The next stretch was the most physically demanding. The sun was merciless, and sources of fresh water almost nonexistent. One by one, the aridity of the place got to each of them, striking Ruthie first with dizziness and a racing heart. Francesca was least affected. She had a light, bony frame and a Mediterranean constitution, and probably could have done well shouldering jugs of wine up and down the mountains of Sicily.

"Once the sun is at our backs, the going will get easier," said Dante.

"If we don't die first," said Ruthie.

"What's our ETA?" asked Raszer.

"About five," Francesca replied. "If all goes well at the crossroads."

To conserve energy and moisture, they talked little for the next four hours. Even when they stopped at one o'clock to eat the last of their sheep's cheese and flatbread, they let the wind and the harsh cawing of the scavenging birds do the talking for them. They had now achieved the familiarity that allows for silence.

In the emptiness, Raszer discovered that the poison of despair that had accumulated in his organs over the last hard year in Los Angeles hadn't been fully purged; his spiritual autoimmunity remained weak. Evil, like all pathogens, was opportunistic. It waited for the chink, the fraying, the crack. It could wait a lifetime for one soul. Raszer had a sick feeling that the man inside the fortress had been waiting for his.

The scavenging birds that circled overhead only added to the sense that he was walking into a death trap. To the Assyrian priests, the birds had been known as monk vultures for their bald heads and cowls of plumage. They were enormous, some with wingspans of nearly eight feet. *You can't have me*, Raszer called from inside, but they got to him. Vultures know it's only a matter of waiting.

⬩◆⬩

THEY SAW NO ONE, nothing with a beating heart, for almost three hours. The surrounding crags might indeed have been climbing destinations, but the canyons below looked like every ancient world depiction of hell Raszer had ever seen. Gehanna. Sodom. The Pit. They'd entered the first world, the first place to claim a culture, and all around them was evidence that this culture had gone to dust.

They struggled up one last, long grade—more than three miles at a forty-five-degree angle—before the land leveled out to a high plateau and they spotted, at what appeared to be about five hundred yards ahead, a grove of walnut trees, the ground beneath them carpeted in deep green vegetation. Just ahead of the trees, the path widened into a narrow dirt road that ran right through the arbor.

"There's a wee tributary," said Dante. "Dry in summer, but now there should still be snowmelt. If we're lucky, we'll find a drink."

"And cool off a bit," added Francesca.

"And rest," Ruthie moaned. "My feet have blisters on top of blisters."

"Those trees definitely look inviting," said Raszer.

"Well, keep your eyes on them," cautioned Francesca. "This is where—for some people—it begins to happen. Perspective may start to shift. Reference points change."

Almost as soon as she'd said those words, Raszer began to notice that there was in fact something slightly wrong with the picture. Though surrounded by sawtooth peaks, the area was almost perfectly flat—a natural arena. In the midst of the barrenness, the anomalous grove of trees and the little green park they sheltered looked as if Magritte had conceived them. What rendered the scene most surreal was the fact that there appeared to be nothing beyond the trees. When he looked at them, he looked straight into them, and neither sky nor mountains beyond were visible through their leaves. In the intervening space, atoms of blue fell from the heavens like glitter and reflected the blinding sunlight. Shaykh Adi bounded ahead and seemed swallowed up by the sparkle. He barked twice and then briefly disappeared from sight before rematerializing much farther ahead than seemed possible in the short time that had elapsed.

"Did you see that?" Raszer exclaimed. "How did he do that?"

Dante laughed. "It's no ordinary place."

"And he is no ordinary dog," added Francesca.

"What the fuck're you all talking about?" Ruthie asked.

"Just keep your eye on Adi," Dante replied.

Now, a second strange thing occurred. Shaykh Adi kept trotting toward the trees—that is, his four legs appeared to be in locomotion—but did not seem to be bringing him any closer. His size didn't change relative to the grove, but remained exactly the same, as if he were trotting on a treadmill. Nor did the trees loom any larger or come into focus, despite the fact that the group had closed another hundred yards; their leaves and branches remained a vivid but impressionistic blur, like a photo taken with a very long lens.

Raszer felt himself draw back suddenly.

"What is it?" asked Francesca.

"That was weird," he said. "For a second there, I thought I was looking at a movie screen. Everything went kind of flat." He pivoted around, surveying the mountains and the path behind them. "Okay . . . now I'm back in it, only I can't seem to find myself."

He paused. "I mean . . . I can't find . . . where I'm looking from."

"Can I have whatever drugs he's taking?" Ruthie said.

"Just watch the trees and the dog at the same time," he said. "You'll see what I mean. It's like one of those Magic Eye puzzles you have to look at in a certain way." He turned to Dante. "How far are those trees? I would've said a third of a mile five minutes ago, but they don't look any closer—"

"Wow," Ruthie said suddenly, shielding her eyes. "It's really blue here. How the hell did it get so blue?"

"Feels like we're in the sky, right?" said Dante. "Or like the sky is in us."

Raszer stopped. "Now what . . . or who . . . is that?"

A small figure had emerged from the grove and stood in the middle of the road, the color of its form only a shade off from that of the trees. Shaykh Adi evanesced from the dazzling blue again, all four legs in accelerated motion, and now did seem to be closing the distance to the mysterious personage. The old dog was running.

"He sees a friend," said Francesca.

"Is it a mirage?" asked Raszer.

"Not unless Adi sees the same mirage you do," said Dante. "Which is unlikely."

Raszer began to walk again, then stumbled and stopped, extending his arms for balance. "Whoa! Shit!" he called out.

"What?" Ruthie asked. "What's goin' on?"

"Something's off with my equilibrium," he answered. "I was moving forward, but it felt for a second like I was going backward." He cocked an eyebrow in Francesca's direction. "Is this it?" he asked. "Is this what you meant by a shift in perspective?"

"It's the beginning of it," she affirmed. "It will take some getting used to. When I was in university, I took a class about the language of cinema. One day we studied this thing they called the Hitchcock zoom. It was a camera effect he used a lot. He'd pull the camera back while he was zooming the lens in. It made people sick to their stomachs, totally threw them. Do you know the effect?"

"Yeah. That's not a bad analogy," Raszer said, feeling his way forward. "Only this effect is happening behind my eyes, not in front of them." He looked ahead; the small figure had assumed the proportions of a man. Or a woman—he couldn't be sure. It was of small stature and seemed to have a lot of hair. Maybe a beard. The impression of camouflage grew stronger; the person's color was nearly indistinguishable from the color of the foliage.

"Now tell me that isn't someone we need to worry about," Raszer said.

"Adi doesn't think so," Francesca replied.

"Whoever he is," said Dante, "he's king of the grove."

Raszer felt a tingle up his spine.

"Do we have to kill him to get past?"

"Who is both turtle and hare?" Dante asked. "And shows pilgrims the way in darkest night?"

The figure began to move toward them, and at the same time, Ruthie broke into a sprint. From the cloud of dust she left behind, Raszer heard her shout, "Shams!"

He looked at each of his companions in turn.

"There are more things in heaven and earth . . . " said Francesca.

"Khezr can assume any form he wants to," said Dante.

"So can the Devil," Francesca cautioned. "Go slowly."

Ruthie called out once more and opened her arms, but she now seemed to be stuck in temporal quicksand, just as Adi had been minutes before. If not for its unsettling weirdness, it might have been funny: the cartoon character locked in a digital loop. Raszer slowed his pace and kept watch—he didn't want to miss a millisecond. Steadily, the green figure that might or might not be some evocation of Shams of Taos—a magical servitor summoned by their morning prayer—approached Ruthie and passed right through her.

Or, rather, Ruthie passed through him.

She dropped to her knees in the dust and began to sob. The man walked a few steps farther, close enough that Raszer was able to gauge his height and bearing as indeed being like Shams'.

Then he vanished. Just like that.

Raszer increased his pace, wanting to get to Ruthie. His three guides were a few steps behind. It was only the sense and scent of a presence on his immediate right that made him turn, and when he did, he shouted in alarm.

"Say, *rafiq*," Shams incarnate said calmly. "How goes the journey?"

"Jesus," said Raszer, and looked to make sure the others could see what he saw.

"Hardly," said Shams. "But now I know what the poor fucker went through. Do you always bring trouble when you travel?"

"Not intentionally. God, I—"

"Don't mention it, Padre. The hurt's gone. I'm fuckin' free. *Moksha*. Liberation. Not that I don't miss the carnality sometimes. But there are compensations. Like finding out who I've been all along."

The rest of the party caught up, and Shaykh Adi returned and began to lick Shams' hand. They walked five abreast toward Ruthie, who remained on her knees and watched their approach wide-eyed, like some tree creature from the dark green grove that opened beyond her like a cave entrance.

"Speaking of trouble," said Shams, with a nod toward Ruthie, "you'll want to keep a close watch on that one."

"I knew it," Francesca said, not able to conceal a look of vindication.

"Then you know more than she does," Shams said. "Ruthie doesn't know if she's bad or good, damned or saved, ugly or beautiful. She just survives. She's pure that way, but you gotta be wary. Somewhere in there, though, there's a soul worth saving."

"You feel like telling me how to go about that?" Raszer asked.

"No," said the phantom Shams, "because I might be wrong." He glanced down at his evanescing form. "I'll be gone soon. As you can see, I'm starting to pixilate. So listen up: Don't go by way of the crossroads. You won't make it through without more blood. There's a detour a half mile short of it . . . take you around the north side of the citadel. Go straight up the cliff. Make a big entrance. Just you, *rafiq*. Only you."

Raszer nodded, mute. Shams' legs had already become memory traces.

"A few more things," he said, as if from a dust cloud. "First off, tell Ruthie I sent my salutation, and that her man Henry's okay with where he is. Second, that little chunk o' rock in your pack—worth its weight in diamonds. And the Kurd with the big scar and the blue eyes—him, too. If you run across him again . . . "

"Wait!" Raszer cried out.

But the apparition walked on, turning only to say, "You'll see me a second time . . . if you're lucky!"

Then he vanished like a puff of smoke. In his path, a trail of violets sprang up.

Raszer turned to Dante, who simply nodded; then he made for where Ruthie knelt in the road. He wanted to deliver Shams' message before it left him. Six feet away, he suddenly grabbed his head and stumbled, dropping to his knees.

"Christ," he said. "Where am I?"

Francesca came to his side and asked, "What do you see?"

Raszer put his hands out and felt about for something solid, like a man playing Blind Man's Bluff. He felt for her, too, and it maddened him that he could not place her.

"I see everything," he replied, "but it's all . . . flipped. No. That's not right . . . It's . . . " He wiped his eyes and realized he was dripping with sweat.

"You're no' going to be able to describe it," said Dante, who had joined him. "Nobody ever has. But I know what it looks like."

"Is it happening to you, too?"

"Yeah, but we've adapted." He chuckled. "We've been this way a few times. You learn how to fold it in. One illusion laid on another."

"So, which one do I pay attention to?" Raszer asked.

"Well, if you can figure out how to watch both at the same time, you might begin to see what's real."

"That," said Raszer, "is going to be one hell of a trick."

"We're going to get you on your feet," said Francesca, "and bring you into the trees. It's cool in there, and there's water." They took hold of him under the shoulders and pulled him up. "This is going to feel strange. Just take one step at a time."

They guided him into the grove, and Stephan Raszer managed—somehow without retching—to take in the oddest sensation of his natural life. No psychotropic drug had ever come close. It would beggar any artist's descriptive powers, though it occurred to him that it might have been what M. C. Escher was getting at. With Francesca, Dante, and Ruthie all offering support, he picked up his feet and moved them as he'd been instructed. But they failed him, because he was moving at once toward and away from the grove, as if into the vertex of some impossibly angled mirror. How was he to reconcile these perspectives? On a macroscopic scale, it was as if the galaxies said to be hurtling outward from the primeval big bang were simultaneously contracting to their point of origin.

They stepped into the grove and laid Raszer on a bed of startlingly green moss that bordered the little stream. That the moss was luminous was somehow the least of his surprises. He saw Ruthie remove herself to a distant tree and fold like a doll.

There were birds in the grove, ample shade, and water so sweet and clear that it seemed a soul could be suckled on it. Raszer supposed the place was a kind of oasis, fed by the stream when it swelled, though that could not account for its unnatural serenity. He relished every minute of rest, because he knew they could not stay long. His profoundly altered perception would have to be accommodated, and quickly, as a man abruptly dropped on the moon would have to learn to walk again. He tried to remember the last time he'd thought he might be losing his mind—there'd been more than one occasion—and how he'd gotten through it. Not so much by holding off the madness as by accepting it as another mode of being, like having a cold or being in love.

He felt warmth in his hand and realized Francesca was holding it. Then he put a question to anyone who might have an answer: "How long before this tapers off?"

"About halfway between here and our base camp, you should start to get your land legs back," Francesca responded. "But it's not going to go away completely. At least, let's hope not. It would be a shame to lose a new sense after coming so far to get it." She squeezed his hand. "What do you feel right now?"

He considered her question, and then something began to happen. The effort of answering caused something to well up in him. He looked at his companions in turn, doing his best to register them with his crazy double vision, seeing them—against all good sense—as existing both outside *and* inside him. He became aware of the pulse in his left eye and a needling sensation in the iris.

"I feel," he said, "like someone here knows me. Has known me. Forever."

"Na-Koja-Abad," someone whispered. Was it Dante?

"Of course I know you, Stephan," said Francesca. "How could I not?"

He didn't ask her to explain herself, nor did he attempt to articulate the other thing he felt, which was that these people had in an instant become his only world—the sum of all his worlds. He would die to protect them from harm. There was a brief pain in his left iris as the stream of light broke through and hit the leaves above undiffused. Francesca was the first to see it. She leaned in.

"How do you do that?" she asked.

"It's the hole in my dike," Raszer said.

"Or the crack that the light gets through," said Dante, recalling his story.

"Have you always had it?"

"No. It came with a loss."

"Someone died?"

"Yeah."

"Someone you loved?"

"You could say that."

"And after that, your life was different . . . "

Raszer took a glance around at the fantastical grove. "Definitely," he answered. A pause. "I think seeing Shams like that set it off. Some kind of resonance."

She peered into Raszer's eye and tracked the thread of indigo light that issued from it up to its terminus on the leaves above. A small voice rippled across the grove.

Ruthie, cooling her feet in the stream, called out, "I saw it before. On the night of the big jam. When we were—"

She hesitated, seeing Francesca raise her head, then continued, "So you're sayin' that was real back there? If that's true, where'd he come from . . . and where'd he go?"

"Not a mirage," said Raszer. "More like what Henry used to talk about."

"What did Shams say?" Ruthie asked warily.

"He said to tell you that Henry's okay with where he is."

Ruthie smirked reflexively, but couldn't hold it. Despite herself, she was moved.

"He also warned us away from the crossroads. He said we wouldn't make it through. He suggested we detour around to the north side of the citadel and go straight up the cliff. Can it be done?"

"It can be done," Dante replied, "with a full kit. We're carrying less than that. You'd have to free-climb a good part of it. Are you in shape for that?"

"I guess we'll find out," said Raszer.

THIRTY-THREE

FROM THE COVER OF massive boulders five hundred feet above, they observed the fabled crossroads. It didn't conform to the mental image Raszer had been carrying.

That image—with him since Taos—was more like that mythical Mississippi Delta junction where young guitarist Robert Johnson had pawned his soul to the Devil for the gift of the blues. With date palms and dromedaries. But this place was as far from the Mississippi as you could get. This place was Nowhere-Land, the event horizon of a black hole into which he would soon cast flesh and fate. The roads that intersected here were rutted old camel tracks amid bleak, haunted mountains.

Yet it was hardly deserted.

There was no sign of the Mephistophelian Black Sheikh of whom both Henry Lee and Shams had spoken, but they had plenty of company. On the near side of the dusty crossing, a mixed company of uniformed *pesh merga* and irregular Kurdish hill fighters, rifles in hand, had taken position. Facing them down from the far side were an equal number of gunmen, of various races but mostly white, wearing black T-shirts and cargo pants. They cradled assault rifles with sniper scopes in their thick arms and wore pistols in thigh holsters. Some had shaved heads; others had heavy-metal manes tied back from long faces bearing chin beards and goatees.

The only one wearing anything like a uniform was the apparent commanding officer, a short, square-shouldered man with the features of a young Jon Voight but lines that said fifty and a haircut that said George Armstrong Custer. Even from a distance, what set him apart from his company was that he looked like an actor who'd been digitally matted into the scene. The effect caused Raszer to blink and check through Dante's binoculars. Face to face with his Kurdish counterpart at the crossroads, the CO was engaged in heated argument. His alpha body language suggested he was winning, but the Kurd, for his part, was holding his ground with less display. On both sides, there seemed to be a lot of tension. Things looked ready to blow.

"Mercenaries," Dante hissed.

"And they're not natives," said Raszer. "American or European. Can you make out the patch on the CO's jacket?"

"Green River Security," said Dante. "The A-rated Blackwater. The top guys are renegades who broke away from PMCs like Jax and DynCorp 'cause they thought they'd gone soft on the teat of the U.S. government. The foot soldiers are mostly Salvadoran and Columbian. The top gun—"

"Does not look friendly," Francesca said.

"No, he doesn't," Raszer agreed.

Ruthie came to his side. "If they're Americans, maybe they'll—"

"Oh, for fuck's sake, girl," Dante blurted.

"Enough," said Raszer. "We're not going to announce ourselves, but before we move on, I need to get an idea of what the issue is down there. I'm going to follow that gulley to the outcropping about twenty feet from the road and find out what I can hear."

"Too dangerous," said Francesca. "And unnecessary."

"I disagree," said Raszer. "Respectfully—but I disagree."

"Then I'll go with you," she said. "I'm light on my feet . . . and I know Kurdish."

Raszer gave her a steady look, and nodded.

It took them more than ten minutes to work their way down to a vantage point. They had reasonably good cover for most of the way; the danger lay in setting loose the scree that covered the mountains. Halfway down, Raszer lifted his binoculars and confirmed what he'd both suspected and hoped: The Kurdish captain was none other than the young soldier with the piercing blue eyes. His men were a racial mix. Some were dark as Egyptians, others almost as fair as Dante. The Kurds claimed the lineage of the ancient Assyrians, but trade and conquest had long since had their way with the gene pool. Kurdish people were bound together by land and shared history—and the solidarity that comes with being the common enemy of their neighbors.

The gulley carved its way to within about fifty feet of the road, at which point they scrambled up the side to a large, jagged outcropping with chinks affording a view. The problem was the absence of flat ground; in order to see, they had to lock their toes against the steeply angled slope and lever up to position.

The first words Raszer was able to make out were in English, from the mercenary leader: " . . . think you can hold that pass with twenty men, you're both a martyr and a fool. I'll be happy to prove my point if you like . . . but why not let us take a look around? If it's clear, we'll turn it back over to you. Or"—he turned and swept his arm across his own company and its arsenal of fully automatic weaponry—"you can die today."

The Kurdish leader replied in carefully measured English.

"No. We cannot stand against your guns. But you cannot kill us, either. If you do, and then bring your men into the Buzul pass, there will be three hundred more of us raining fire down on your heads. By midday, you will be food for buzzards."

"Don't count on it, Mustafa," the leader sneered. "Another few hours, and the air strikes'll clear those hills out for us. Enjoy the last days of Kurdistania, friend, because by May 1, the ground you piss on will belong to El Mirai, along with your whore wife and whore daughters." The CO spat and parked a hand on his gun.

There was no movement on the other side. The Kurdish chief's fighters were well trained, indeed, for they remained as undemonstrative as he was and would have altered their posture only if he had. He took a quick count of the mercenaries. "I see thirty whores here. You make it thirty-one. I'm sure you are the best paid whore of all."

"You've got fifteen minutes to stand down, and then we cut you to pieces." The leader gave a nod to the man on his right, and rifles were raised to hips.

Raszer watched the Kurdish commander battle with himself, and saw his blue eyes flash. "My orders are not to die defending the pass. Not today. Go ahead. We will not stop you. The snipers will pick you off." With that, he stepped aside.

With his attention squarely on the unfolding scene, Raszer hadn't noticed that Francesca was about to lose her footing and was now clawing at the rock. In an effort to regain her purchase, she involuntarily dislodged a stone the size of a grapefruit, which skittered down the gulley wall and hit bottom with a sharp *clink*.

The two adversaries turned, as did most of their men. Raszer quickly scanned the rock formation for a hiding place. He worked his way over to Francesca, gave her his hand, and helped her to a more solid foothold. She apologized with her eyes, but he only put his finger to his lips and motioned to a small chimney in the rock. Barely large enough for one grown man, it would be a squeeze with the two of them. He got her in first, then wedged in beside her and pulled her down until they had become one featureless form, unmoving, hardly breathing.

A few seconds later, the two commanders arrived, each with a gunman at his back. They stood on the far side of the outcropping and continued their argument while their deputies began to search the area.

"Could have been a coyote," said the American. "Or one of those fucking opium peddlers."

"A stone rolls every second in the mountains," the Kurdish captain replied.

The gunmen simultaneously stepped around the rear of the outcropping, where Raszer and Francesca's hiding place was in plain sight but grayed down by shadow. Had the soldiers not been keeping an eye on each other, they would surely have picked them out. Raszer buried his face in Francesca's hair. He felt her heart beating like a bird's against his. One of the gunmen—he could not tell which—approached. Raszer drew a single breath and held it. There was an unforgiving pause. It sounded as though the Kurdish leader had come around the west side of the rocks.

"Nothing here," the American called out. "But I don't like what my nose tells me, so I've modified the plan. You save face for today, Mustafa. You and your men fall back. After you're out of sight, we'll do the same. It's only a reprieve. In twenty-four hours, we're coming in with air cover."

"I will believe that when I see it. Until then, be assured that the Kurds in the Buzul will pay no more tribute to your lord. And when we stop, the rest will soon follow. Even those jackals in Iran who bow to you." He shot a question to his scout.

"Like I said," the merc said scornfully, "enjoy it while it lasts." A pause. "Let's go."

Raszer and Francesca waited a good ten minutes, until both forces had begun to withdraw into the hills. Then they extricated themselves and took a last look through the chinks. It was difficult to fathom what they saw: From the roadway leading directly to the fortress, two long black Lincolns had rolled down into the crossroads. The driver of the first got out to consult with the men from Green River Security. He removed his dark glasses and ran a finger across his blond mustache. Then he muttered something Raszer couldn't catch the whole of, but that concluded with two words he did pick up: "Greenstreet.

Motherfucker." The episode had the immersive mise-en-scène of a dream in which events are seen simultaneously from all angles.

If Raszer needed evidence of Philby Greenstreet's wildest assertions, there it was. The driver, standing there in a navy blue suit and tie, would have no trouble boarding a plane at LaGuardia. This man looked like a Mormon.

"That was way too close," Dante said upon their return. "I hope it was worth it."

"I think it was," Raszer replied.

Ruthie was wide eyed. "I can't believe they didn't see you."

"I'm not sure the Kurd didn't see us."

"What's going on, then?" Dante asked.

"I think we should talk to him," Raszer said calmly.

"Talk to who?"

"To the blue-eyed Kurd," Raszer answered. "I think we have common interests. Look, if I do get Katy out, it probably won't be tidy. It'll require some kind of trick, and those always have short fuses. We're unarmed, and we're going to need some protection to get her clear. From what I heard down there, things around here are about to get noisy, and we may be able to slip out under that cover."

"Noisy how?" asked Dante.

"The Kurds in the Buzul are refusing to pay the Old Man's tribute. That's not going to go down well."

"It's about time," said Francesca.

"So I'm going to try and catch Blue Eyes before he disappears into these hills."

Francesca nodded. A moment later, Raszer was gone with Shaykh Adi.

⬥ ◆ ⬥

His name was Dostam Ahmid Rahim, but to all in the Buzul Dagi, he was known as Mam: Uncle. The moniker was more than honorary; he claimed to have no less than forty nieces and nephews in these mountains—an impressive fact, given his age. He was thirty or thirty-one—he'd forgotten which—but he'd already lived three lives fighting Iraqis, Turks, and rival warlords. Raszer's overture had been received with raised guns and wary curiosity, the presence of Shaykh Adi at his side attenuating the sense of threat.

Raszer liked the commander instantly. More than once, he felt the urge to drop the charade, the French accent, the labored English, the monkish docility. But he couldn't, because once a ruse is practiced, dropping it only makes its target feel like a fool, and then a doubly cautious one.

Adi stretched between them as they sat by the embers of the breakfast fire, drinking coffee thick as oil. Where the operational details were concerned, Raszer told the leader everything he had in mind, except exactly how he intended to bring Katy Endicott out. Even if he'd known, it wasn't germane to their discussion. What was critical was that once he had her out, he be able to turn her over to an armed unit for escort to a helicopter waiting in the nearby village of Hadad, a chopper that would transport Katy, Ruthie, and the Fedeli back to the cars in Ispiria.

The unresolved detail was money. Raszer had proposed that $5,000 from his personal account be wired to a bank his host specified, as payment for the protection he and his men would provide. But Mam would hear nothing of it. Conducting an innocent young woman to safety was a mission of honor. To accept money would make his men no better than the whores the Old Man employed. But beyond that lay a more personal matter of honor—and vengeance.

One of Rahim's nieces, a seventeen-year-old from Cukurka, was believed to have been taken to El Mirai. Her abduction had caused such great rage and shame among her kin that there was no guarantee they would take her back. Still, Mam had sworn to her father that the rape would be avenged. It was far bigger, he told Raszer, than one girl. Villages from here to Diyarkabir were missing young women. The future mothers of Kurdistan were being devalued. It was, the leader pointed out, a novel form of ethnic cleansing, for no honorable Kurdish man would ever take one of these girls as his wife.

In the end, Raszer accepted Mam's pledge. To have questioned it would have been a grievous insult. There was no guile in the Kurdish leader's mien. Beyond that, it was clear as his cobalt eyes that his men would honor his agreement. Still, Raszer's own sense of symmetry called for a reciprocal gesture. He reached into his pack and brought out the fragment of age-polished black stone that Henry Lee had stolen from the Old Man's mysterious recruiter and carried back to Los Angeles.

He set it on the woven blanket before Mam Rahim and said, "In the eyes of the world, it may be of great worth or no worth at all. But I believe that for our adversary, it has a special value. If what I have been told is true, it is a fragment of the original *al-Hajar al-Aswad* of Mecca, the pilgrim's stone of the Ka'ba. If it is needed to secure the girl's freedom, use it. If not, it will remain in your family's possession forever."

Mam Rahim picked up the stone, weighed it on his palm, put it to his lips, and held it to the sky. He pressed his hands in acceptance.

After discussing the logistics of the escort, Raszer told the Kurd that he would need a few hours of "sanctuary" with Katy after bringing her out, ideally in a safe location somewhere between El Mirai and the village; at the least, Rahim could provide armed protection. Raszer had to assume Katy's psychic condition would be ragged; he could not pluck her from one reality and drop her into another without allowing her a period of decompression.

As Raszer prepared to leave, Mam Rahim stood, holding the stone in one hand. He stooped to give Shaykh Adi a scratch, then looked at Raszer and said, "If God had not chosen you for his army, Frère Deleuze, you would have made a good soldier."

Raszer shook his hand and said, "Only for a cause like yours."

✦ ✦ ✦

As HE MADE HIS WAY back to his companions, Raszer felt for the first time in more than a year that he'd earned back a measure of grace. This turned his thoughts to Monica, and he decided that while he was on the high ground, he'd attempt again to reach her. They hadn't connected for twenty-four hours. He got through for a scant three minutes before the signal dropped, but what she told him in that time backed up his decision to entrust the black stone to his new ally.

"Don't lose me, Raszer," she said breathlessly. "This is good. You asked to open a file on the Ka'ba stone. Well, I've been all over it—mostly misses. But *this* is a hit: We know the stone was an object of pilgrimage before Islam. We know the legend is that it fell from heaven, outer space, whatever. We think it was associated with the pre-Islamic triple goddess. Well, check this out: Around 928 AD, the Ka'ba stone was stolen from Mecca by a splinter Ismaili sect called the Qarmatians, serious Muslim anarchists who said they lived in the resurrection body. They took the stone to Bahrain and kept it for twenty-two years. When they returned it, it was in pieces, and some pieces were missing. The stone that's in Mecca now is a patch job. But here's the best part: There's a theory that the Qarmatians secretly worshipped Atargatis, the goddess on your coin, only they worshipped her as Al'Uzza, the mother aspect of the triple goddess of Mecca! And Al'Uzza links to Isis, who links to Inanna and Cybele, and all of them inspired castration cults." She paused. "So maybe that's something?"

"More than something," Raszer responded.

THIRTY-FOUR

"EASY FOR SHAMS TO SAY," Raszer muttered, contemplating the eight-hundred-foot wall of rock he had been instructed to climb. "He could just beam himself up."

"She's no easy scramble," said Dante. "It's like El Capitan times three."

"El Capitan's got marked routes," said Raszer. "This . . ." He stepped back and tipped his head as far as his neck would allow, still not able to see the top. " . . . worries me." The wall rose sheerly up from the ledge and teetered back at an obtuse angle.

"Well," Dante said, taking the monocular from his eye after scanning the ascent, "if it's any consolation, it doesn't look as if the last two hundred feet will be any harder than the first five hundred." He pulled out two thick coils of rope. "Let's harness up."

The previous night had been a sober one in every sense. They'd been over the plan many times. Each round, one or more of them brought up something they hadn't yet considered. Katy's rescue had begun to look like one of those many-worlds scenarios from theoretical physics—too many possibilities, and always the stark probability of failure. Raszer had to keep reminding his companions that what they were attempting was not a hostage rescue. They were neither trained nor equipped for that, and he made it clear he wanted to see no acts of heroism. This was more akin to visiting the judge on the eve of sentencing to plead for the life of a son. The court held all the cards; all you could do was argue that the consequences of a harsh decision might come back to haunt the judge.

Or kill him.

If the Old Man were merely some wildly inflated, mysticized version of a territorial crime boss, Raszer would have to figure that the chances of his walking out with Katy were miniscule. He was wagering everything on the hunch that his adversary was something more than a thug, because, against all odds, his only card was the faith that if the Old Man did indeed see himself as a lord, he would also grant the occasional mercy.

Raszer had been painfully aware since the twin meetings in Colorado and Iskenderun that this was a one-man show. He was a human gambit, presenting his opponents with a classic dilemma: They could kill the pawn and risk opening their flank to a bishop or a queen, or they could gamble on extending their domination of the board by letting Raszer claim some small victory. In this sense, his mission was exactly like that of the character he portrayed: the petitioning priest, sent by the king to the enemy lines to negotiate for the princess's release. He might return with her; he might return without his head. Either way, as Greenstreet had said, the presence of one man altered all the variables.

The sanctuary Mam Rahim had offered for Katy's debriefing seemed more than ideal. There was a network of caverns deep inside the fortress mountain, used by the Kurdish fighters to cache arms and evade Turkish attacks. Ruthie had begged to wait there with Dante for Raszer's arrival, rather than accompany Francesca to the village. She wanted to be the first to see her sister free, and though Raszer's every instinct fought the idea, he found himself unable to say no. If he couldn't grant such a request, how could he expect the adversary to grant his? If Katy's release took place by day, they'd proceed with their escort to Hadad. If it were at night, they would await the sunrise before moving out.

On the outskirts of the tiny hamlet, Francesca would wait with Raszer's satellite phone to relay news to the soldiers fanned out along the road between her and town, and to Monica. Splitting up their meager forces was designed not only to facilitate the conveyance of information, but also to increase the chances that in the event of a trap, at least one of them might be able to get away and bring help.

Where that help would come from was uncertain, but Monica was a resourceful woman.

At this moment, while Raszer and Dante secured their climbing harnesses, Ruthie, Francesca, and the wolfhound looked on from thirty feet below, on an overlook that aproned off the main path. Their instructions were to wait until Raszer was on the wall and Dante had descended before moving out. Francesca had his journal and all his documents; Dante had the rest of his belongings. Raszer had taken nothing with him but a liter of water, his cigarettes and Zippo, a photograph of Katy, and a paperback copy of the Qur'an. It never hurt to cite scripture or sura when arguing for the unthinkable, even when the hearer was only nominally pious.

Preparing for the ascent was painstaking. Dante placed a top anchor at about eighty feet, where the first serviceable ledge was located, and belayed Raszer up. They were able to make another hundred feet that way, ledge by ledge, before the wall began to bulge out at something in excess of twenty degrees. There were entire hours when they were barely able to cover twenty feet.

The composition of the rock was inconsistent: Most of the steel stoppers held firmly in good cracks, but a few tore brutally through surfaces that looked and felt solid but proved to be little more than sun-kilned clay. That meant finding much deeper fissures and placing the much larger cam anchors, of which they had only a modest complement. On top of this, Raszer was making a vertical climb at the age of forty-four and after a strenuous four-day trek across mountainous terrain, and, as fit as he was, he felt it.

At 260 feet, with only the tiniest dimple as a foothold and little more than a hair's width for his fingers above, his strength gave out, and with a shout he flew back from the wall, watched the closest of his stoppers pop out with the force of shrapnel, and then dangled in clear blue over the chasm, well beyond the overlook where his companions waited, and probably a quarter mile from the closest landing. If the second anchor did not hold, he was gone. And that would be the end of it.

Below, Ruthie screamed, and Raszer's gut froze. The whole point of this rear entry was surprise, even mystification. If someone threw a spotlight on him before he'd made it to the top, he might as well have rung the doorbell.

"Okay," Dante said, from ten feet above, "this is what you need to do. You need to trust that stopper, the one on the overhang, just above your head. It won't fail—it's in a good, solid crack and it can handle 2,500 pounds of pull. You're going to need to start swinging and build up enough of an arc to get back on the wall. Once you're on and you can give me a little bit of help, I can belay you up to me."

"Which means," said Raszer, not moving, "that you figure the stopper might not hold if you try to pull me up from a dead hang." The words came with difficulty. His mouth was bone dry.

"That's the physics of it, aye," said Dante. "Sorry."

"Okay. Just wanted it straight. Now, you want me to swing . . . even though every swing will put about 1,200 pounds of strain on that anchor?"

"That's about a thousand pounds less than if I try to pull you. Check out the angle. D'ya have a better idea?"

"No," said Raszer. "I guess I don't."

"Lean back, straighten your legs . . . then push forward and pull your knees up."

"Oh, Christ."

"What?"

"I just looked down."

"Don't. The rock is life."

"Do me a favor?"

"Anything but a lap dance."

"If you have to scratch or shift your stance, do it now, before I start swinging."

"I'm good."

"Okay. Here goes."

"I've got you."

"Fuck."

"What?"

"My legs won't move."

"Fire one neuron at a time, mate. Lean back . . . "

He saw and heard it all. Saw the rope go taut and zing the air like a violin string. Heard the anchor bite into the rock, and the atoms of steel ping with strain. Watched the fingerhold shift in and out of focus as he reached for it, just a little closer with each swing.

The air whistled past his ears. Finally, he felt his toes touch the wall.

"Go!" said Dante. "Don't wait. Power up and over. Now. I've got you."

In the end, it was less Raszer's grit than his refusal to consider rappelling back down to the ledge that did the trick. He was up.

There was a shelf of generous width eighty feet below the top, which was where they'd agreed Dante would leave him. The final leg was textbook climbing, the incline of the rock now at last in Raszer's favor, and they could not risk a second man's being sighted if Raszer's plan for arriving out of a cloud was to be realized. They took a break to catch their breath, and spent a few minutes in that silent appreciation of each other's presence that stands for sentiment among men. Then the boy began his descent, and Raszer, with a hundred feet of rope and a small belt pouch of climbing hardware, set his sights on the ancient wall of quarried brick above.

The voice came when he was still thirty feet below the base of the wall, scraping away at a shallow fingerhold. Because it was nasal in timbre, melismatic, and issued from an open-air loudspeaker, he first thought it might be a muezzin's call to prayer. Soon enough, it became apparent that it was a woman's voice, and that her summons was not to prayer. He recognized enough of the Arabic to hear a kind of exhortation: *Rise up, young warriors*. The drums began to pound in the echoes of her last utterance. It was a rhythm of carnal command. There was a shout and a mass of voices in unison, followed by the *ccrrraack* of a multitude of palms clapped together.

This, Raszer thought, must be the equivalent of field exercises at El Mirai.

On the one hand, he was grateful for the cover of sound. On the other, the presence of a very large group of people on the other side of the wall meant that his arrival would hardly be unnoticed. He could hang here until the crowd dispersed or, as Shams had suggested, make an entrance. Time to rethink. Time to be in the game.

The stronghold's original builders had not anticipated attack from the steep side, but neither had they scrimped on its fortification. The wall was not less than thirty feet high and was, in terms of climbing difficulty, a virtual model of the rock itself. Wind had worn away the edges of the enormous bricks, leaving just enough room for fingertips, though precious few places to get a toehold.

The climb was as lateral as it was vertical. Worse, no place was secure enough to allow Raszer to pause to restore his strength, so by the time he was finally able to chin himself up to a crack wide enough to offer a view of the spectacle below, all of his sinews had been stretched to the fraying point. The ligaments in his right shoulder could not have supported the arm of an infant. He knew well this exhaustion, this place where there is nothing left but a spark in the mind, where flesh is simply dragged along by the engine of the spirit.

This would be Raszer's state for whatever remained of his journey, but he couldn't allow it to dull his edge. Even when his body was out of fuel, his mind's pistons would have to be firing.

What he saw assembled on the vast, open parade ground of the fortress were the Old Man's acolytes, the fedayeen of this new order of assassins. There were no fewer than a thousand young men and women, most within a few years of Scotty Darrell's age. It might be a small army, or a very large cell. Their formation was a military rectangle, two equal groups of males flanking the smaller contingent of females. All wore the red-sashed white robes that Scotty had worn on the rooftop in Hollywood on the day of Harry Wolfe's murder. They were barefoot, and not one was out of step.

The men had pivoted inward so that their collective line of sight formed an equilateral triangle with a raised reviewing platform at its apex. The women stood with feet apart and eyes forward. There were, at that moment, six individuals on this dais, which adjoined the main structure of the fortress. Five of the figures were draped in a finer, pale green version of the garment the supplicants wore, and the sixth was in black. The headdresses were distinctive, not the common *kaffiyeh* but something resembling the chain-mail helmets worn by Crusader knights. The robes draping the man in black weren't those of a traditional sheikh or sharif, but more like those of a thirteenth-century papal legate. There was a green curtain at the rear of the platform.

The music was savagely propulsive, but the movements of the faithful were as tightly choreographed as a Middle Eastern Falun Gong, and some appeared to defy gravity. One movement, at which the women were especially adept, required shaping the spine into an S-curve, with the hips far forward, the midback bent just as far to the rear, and the shoulders and head nearly aligned with the pelvis. It had the look of an evasive maneuver for a knife fight. The most remarkable, however, began with a crouch, followed by an extraordinary upward surge of energy, at the peak of which the *fidais*' feet left the ground and remained in midair for a full count of five. The collective clap Raszer had heard from the rock face was what brought them down to earth again.

If this was Islam, it was a very exotic sort. But then, the faithful were far from typical. They might be fearsome as a group, but not one looked individually threatening, which, Raszer supposed, was precisely the idea. Any of them, without raising the slightest alarm, might pass through the gates of the Magic Kingdom with a bomb strapped to their belly. *Physical beauty, native intelligence, and a certain malleability.*

The curtains at the rear of the dais were drawn apart, and the portal was flanked by two more forms in black. Into the breach stepped a magnificent figure in robes of lustrous green silk, his face masked by a full veil. A roar went up.

The figure to whom the *fidai* were pledging allegiance could only be that of the Old Man of the Mountains himself.

Summoning up the last measure of strength in his right arm, Raszer pulled himself higher into the gap in the wall—and lost his foothold in the process. As he sought to regain his position, he looked down briefly. Returning his eye to the notch, he received a shock to the brain stem. Standing opposite him on the parapet, his own eye to the chink in the wall, was one of the black-robed lieutenants.

Raszer's fingers lost their grip, his toe slipped from its crack, and he fell backward, the slack rope only barely breaking his fall.

Near the base, scrambling to avoid the precipice, he slammed headfirst into the stone. With his legs dangling helplessly over the edge of the cliff, the lights in his mind dimmed, sputtered, and then went out. Raszer went limp in the harness. He was semiconscious when they reeled him in.

THIRTY-FIVE

HE KNEW THAT SOMEWHERE, it must be spring, and that he had a large lump on his head. It didn't hurt, although it should have. Nothing hurt, but he knew he wasn't paralyzed because he was able to feel the soft ground beneath him. There was birdsong above and a bright light in his eyes. Raszer closed them and tried to remember himself.

When he did, what he spoke was a single word. "Katy?"

Now there was a scent, up close to his nostrils, bittersweet and familiar. He opened his eyes and saw only a kind of splotched, wet redness. His vision was occluded, his depth perception way out of whack. The red object seemed to be located in the center of his skull. Finally, he fixed the scent. Pomegranate. He was being revived with the perfume of a freshly cut pomegranate. The hand holding it was attached to an arm, and beyond the arm was a face, blurry but feminine.

"Katy?" he said again.

He tried alternating between right eye and left, and was finally able to fix her nose with his right. Then he closed both lids. Time passed. He might have drifted.

When he opened his eyes again, the hand and the face had left his frame of vision. Raszer laughed softly, and then wondered where the laugh had come from. Then he realized he was high. Very high. How had they gotten him high? And when? He felt a trickle of panic, but it ebbed quickly in the blossom-scented warmth.

There was some rustling, and the sense of a new presence. He glimpsed a face, and, as with the first scent of the pomegranate, it was foreign and familiar at the same time. There was a hand on his thigh. Warm breath. Suddenly, a series of neural circuits closed and he registered the nose, the mouth, and the hair, as if digitally reassembling a face from a damaged photo. He pushed himself up and took her head in his hands.

"You're Katy," he said.

She shook her head. "Am not," she said, and began to caress him.

"Are too," he said. "You answered to it."

"My name is Aïcha."

"It suits you," he said. "Did you choose it?"

She shook her head no.

"That's too bad. A person should choose her own new name."

A scarlet macaw preened its feathers on the branch of a plum tree not six feet from where she sat. Beyond that, a small, clear stream trickled over crystals of green quartz. On its near bank were varieties of orchid he had never seen before, and on the far side, a skinny young man lay curled into a bare-breasted girl.

The garden appeared to have no boundaries. It was a superb optical illusion, an overturned bowl with a cyclorama of pale blue sky stretched from horizon to horizon and a sun—or what looked like a sun—pulsing heat through cirrus clouds near the zenith. No physical structure, no matter how grand, could ever have enclosed such a space. As Raszer's pupils contracted and returned some depth of field to his vision, he realized there were hundreds of pairs of eyes on him, staring like jungle creatures from the extravagant undergrowth. It was Polynesia as imagined by Henri Rousseau.

"This can't really be heaven," he said, "or they wouldn't have let me in."

He thought he saw a smile. It revealed itself stealthily, like the royal blue underplumage on the macaw's wing. Like new skin beneath a bruise.

"Do you want something?" she asked, as she had probably been taught to.

"Like what, Aïcha?"

"You know," she said, and moved her hand a few inches up his thigh.

"Oh, that," he answered, shaking his head. "No. But I am thirsty."

She rose and padded over to the stream. A cacophony of birdsong burst from a nearby kumquat tree. A few of the more curious girls had ventured closer to observe the stranger. He felt like a sailor beached after a shipwreck. It was unsettling—the natives could eat him if they chose—but, at the same time, not entirely unpleasant.

Katy returned with water in a scooped-out pomegranate shell. It was sweet and cool, with the faintest alkaline undertaste. He took one swallow, rinsed the rest, and spat it out. He became aware of the lulling, almost musical sound of trickling water everywhere. It was as if the quartz over which the water flowed was tuned to consonant frequencies and resonated by the current. "I can see how this place—and whatever they put in the water—could weaken your memory." He drew himself up to a sitting position and took her hand.

"Listen, Katy," he said. "They're not going to let me stay here long. There are some things I need you to know. I've seen your mother . . . "

A muscle twitched beneath her left eye.

"She's keeping a safe place for you. She hasn't forgotten you. Do you remember her, Katy?"

She shook her head and rocked back. From the far side of the little stream, two girls with plaited hair drew near enough to listen and sat down cross-legged on the mossy ground. Very soon, a third emerged from beneath the kumquat tree, while a boy of Dante's age and build looked on protectively. Katy appeared to have an entourage.

"I'm a queen, you know," she said, matter-of-factly.

Raszer smiled. Now that his vision had cleared, he saw how she both was and wasn't like Ruthie. The structural beauty of the face made them close kin, but where Ruthie was the wench, Katy was every bit the lady in the high window. Her skin was the color of cream; her eyes were large but heavy-lidded and languid.

"Who made you a queen, Katy?" he asked.

"Why do you keep calling me Katy?" she asked. "Katy's dead."

"No. I'm looking at her. But if you'd rather I called you Aïcha, that's fine."

"I couldn't rather because I am," she said. "Or, rather, would be if you'd quit trying to stumble me."

"Ah . . . there you go: 'stumble' you. That's from the Witnesses. That's when an outsider comes and tries to trick you out of your faith. You're remembering."

"No. I'm forgetting," she recited. "Forget to remember, remember to forget."

"Is that what they've taught you here? What else have they taught you?"

She gave no answer but looked around, as if for approval to continue the dialogue. Raszer kept his eyes on her, but was peripherally aware that he had attracted a small audience. He'd have to move quickly. "Ruthie's here," he said.

Katy narrowed her eyes. "Where?"

He motioned beyond the false sky. "Where I came from. Outside."

"What are you then . . . God?"

"Not by a long way. But a priest gets to borrow God's eyes once in a while."

She drew back. "You're a priest?"

"Don't be ashamed. Priests are men, too."

"Not here."

"What do you mean?"

Circumstances permitting, she might have chosen to answer the question, or she might not have. As it was, Raszer saw her eyes widen as the words left his throat, and an instant later he was seized from behind and dragged to his feet by two men in pale green robes. A third stood by, holding a Kalashnikov. In a muffled tenor, he ordered, "Bring him" in Arabic.

Raszer looked back over his shoulder as he was taken away, hoping to make a parting connection with Katy. If he was now to be granted an opportunity to make his plea for her, he wanted to feel that in some small way she might be complicit. She had risen to her feet. Behind her, the other girls who'd been listening in had come forward, and a group of the males flanked them jealously.

A few things became marginally clear as Raszer was removed from the Garden: Despite her altered state, she knew who Katy Endicott was, even if only in the third person. The entire conversation had likely been witnessed from somewhere beyond the perimeter. She was alive, and real enough, but she was also a game piece and had been used to bait him. This he had to remember: Play the game.

They passed through a small grove of persimmon trees, then into a darker stretch of junglelike foliage, and finally into total blackness. When the light returned, they had left paradise behind and were in the bowels of the castle.

He couldn't get a fix on the time of day. The corridor was narrow, and the walls of ancient rock sweated with damp. He assumed they were in a subterranean level of the fortress, within the mountain itself. There was an acrid smell of urine and other effluents: the odors of fear. Raszer's mood went black. He wasn't being led to the throne room to share mint tea with the monarch. He was to be interrogated.

◆ ◆ ◆

It was a small room. If your aim is to squeeze someone, you don't want to give them a sense of space. The odor was stronger here, inseparable from the mineral scent of the stone. To his relief, there were no visible instruments of torture. There were two crude wooden chairs, and a rear door of rusted iron. They led him to one of the chairs and stood back. Presently, the iron door swung open heavily and a fourth man entered and sat down opposite him. He was not what Raszer had expected, and then again, he was.

He was five feet, six inches of compact flesh in a Green River Security officer's uniform, had graying blond locks, and was pushing sixty. He wore a Maltese cross around his neck and had "Jesus Loves Me" tattooed on his right forearm. Heavy folds of skin dropped over his eyes. He was the mercenary commander from the crossroads.

"American?" he asked in a Midwestern accent.

"*Canadien*," Raszer answered.

"Doubt it," his questioner shot back. "But you do speak English, right?"

"*Oui*. Yes."

"Excuse me, but go fuck yourself, Padre. We don't exactly go by military convention here, but for the record, who is it you say you are and why are you here?"

"My name is Gilles Deleuze. I am a Franciscan priest from the Taize community in France. We received a petition from a Catholic lay organization that works to retrieve missing girls believed to have been trafficked. My travel was arranged by International Refugee Relief in Iskenderun. I have all the documents."

"I really don't give a rat's anus about your 'documents.' And just who is it you think's been trafficked?"

"The young woman's name is Katy Endicott. American. I—"

"Right." He drummed his fingers on the table, stood up, and walked around to Raszer's rear. "Fuck this. Did Greenstreet send you?"

Raszer considered his answer for perhaps a second too long. The interrogator nodded to the robed men, both of whom came forward and grabbed Raszer's arms. The mercenary leaned in close enough for Raszer to feel the breath on his ear, reached between his legs, and clamped his testicles in the vise of his right hand.

"Believe it or not, my friend, I'm the good cop. Now, if you force my hand, I'll pop your balls out like peas from a peapod."

"That"—Raszer swallowed hard as the sweat broke—"would not be wise."

"And why is that?"

"The U.S. State Department knows of my mission."

"Oooh," replied the interrogator, squeezing harder. "The State Department!"

"And others. But you are interfering with my memory."

The interrogator released just enough of his grip to allow Raszer fleeting relief. "Play smart. What's the point in holding out when we already know who you are?"

"I've told you who I am," Raszer said. "But there *is* something more."

"And what's that?" Finally, the mercenary took his hand away.

"I have something the Old Man wants. Something that was stolen from him."

The interrogator glanced at his three accomplices, then glared at Raszer. "Okay, 'Jill.' I'll be Jack, and you and I will go fetch a pail of water." He stood up and nodded to the robed guards. "Take him in. Call for me when he starts to leak."

"You seem a clever man," said Raszer. "So you must know that my being here changes the game. Let me walk out with one girl, and you keep the advantage."

The mercenary nodded to the iron door. "We'll talk after your baptism," he said.

The robed guards hoisted Raszer from the chair and took him into the adjoining room, while behind him the mercenary commander wiped his hands with a white rag. The door closed heavily. Raszer stared mutely at the device parked against the opposing wall. A museum piece, vintage 1550, kept in good use.

For just a moment after he'd seen it, he became a man without moorings.

The thought that he was going to be tortured into a "confession" seemed almost ludicrous until he reminded himself of the game. In the second and third levels of The Gauntlet, as originally devised by the Fraters, the player was pursued through cyberspace, and eventually via emails, text messages, and even phone calls, by a Grand Inquisitor intent on making him disavow his creed. Of course it made sense that in this demonically hijacked version of the game, a player like Raszer would have to come to such a moment as this. Lunatics always literalized their fantasies.

The robed men stripped him of his clothes.

From studying what allowed rational people to believe in irrational things, Raszer had learned this essential about faith: 10 percent of it came from being shown something—maybe a miracle, more likely a beauty never seen or a message never heard. The other 90 percent came from the will to believe that the thing shown is what it's claimed to be. A water stain or the face of Jesus? A dust mote caught by sunlight or a faerie? Raszer had discarded the agnosticism that argues that such a willing suspension of disbelief amounts to self-delusion. It wasn't delusion; it was replacing one form of seeing with another. It was accepting the possibility of the sublime.

The Philby Greens had given him an implement of survival. A second self. The question was, could he figure out quickly enough how to operate it?

The men led him to the table. He knew better than to put up a fight.

The sloping platform was made of solid oak and had the dimensions of a single bed. The head end was approximately three inches below the foot, which put the subject at an incline known as Trendelenburg position. The physics of it had all been worked out over time with that exquisite acuity of thought that characterizes the design of all instruments of torture. There were steel brackets to secure feet and hands, and straps for the torso. Once the men had secured Raszer's legs and midsection, they stretched his arms fully above his head and locked them down at the elbow.

He waited for the water.

A third man entered the room, this one in the multilayered black garment of the order's sharifs. He wore a veil across the lower two-thirds of his face—a head surgeon from Hades. He smelled of some aromatic balm, and his eyelids and lashes were darkened with kohl. Raszer had seen three of his rank on the reviewing platform, all of the same height and build. Had one of them been the Black Sheikh of Shams' fable?

With what seemed a single motion, the new inquisitor pinched Raszer's nostrils shut, inserted an eye dropper in his reflexively opened mouth, and dosed the back of his throat with a burning tincture. Raszer felt paralysis spread instantly over the length and breadth of his body, along with a sickening familiarity: It was a variant of the same dope with which Layla had incapacitated him in Hollywood.

He could feel everything, but he could not move, except to talk or scream.

"Let us begin," said the leader. His voice had a quality that Raszer—had he not been stone terrified—might have found ridiculous. Where had he heard it before?

Again, he waited for the stream of water to hit his face. Instead, he felt a spike enter the back of his neck just below the skull, and something pressed to his scalp above each temple. *God help me*, he thought. *They're going to mix water and electricity.*

"Would you like me to stop now?" the inquisitor asked. He must have felt Raszer tense, as a sensitive dentist does when he's gone too close to the nerve.

"Yes," Raszer gurgled.

"Who are you?" In Arabic. "What is your name?"

Raszer repeated what he'd told the mercenary.

"Who is Philby Greenstreet?"

"A djinn," Raszer answered. "Nobody."

The sheikh nodded to the others, then stepped back with a rustle of silk.

It was suddenly dark. Not dark as if someone had turned out the lights, but dark as in blindness. As in a total absence of stimulation to the optic nerve. Whatever they'd stuck in the back of his head had short-circuited his vision. A series of images snapped across his brain, not like sporadic video signals, but like dreams. Impossible things.

He saw Monica in the mirror, but from an angle that suggested her point of view. She stroked the mascara onto her lash, and so did he. She stepped lightly into her pumps, and so did he. He saw the assassin enter the bathroom, snap her head back, and plunge the knife into her heart, and felt a deeper pain than he had ever felt.

"Jesus!" he screamed.

"Don't call for Jesus," the inquisitor said in Arabic. "He *is* nobody."

The light flooded back into Raszer's eyes, and he saw his tormentor. The pain was still there, and all warmth had begun to drain from his center.

"*J'ai froid*," he said.

"*Désolé*," replied the sheikh. "Would you like me to stop?"

"*Oui.*"

"*Qui est* Philby Greenstreet?"

"*Personne.*"

The lights went out again.

Now he was at a rain-streaked window, his little palm pressed against the pane, as if to feel the torrent through her fingertips. He could see her reflection in the glass, pensive, waiting. She called for her father, and a man in a duster appeared in the room behind. He took her from the stool, his enormous copper-stained hand over her mouth, and folded her roughly over the back of the sofa. He was strong enough to do it with one arm; the other lifted her dress. The man stank, and he was wet from the rain.

"*Oh, God! Oh, God! Oh, God! Oh, God!*" Raszer screamed. "*Brrriiiigggiiittt!*"

He felt himself entered, and violated, and torn, and bleeding, and there was no one there to stop it. No father. No mother. Not even Monica, because she was dead. The sounds that came from his throat were not sounds that he could associate with himself or anything human. They were the sounds you'd hear if you put your ear to the wall of hell. The lights came back on, but Raszer couldn't see because his eyes were full of tears.

"Would you like me to stop?"

"Fuck you."

"Who is Philby Greenstreet?"

"*Je suis Philby Greenstreet.*"

✦ ◆ ✦

SOMETHING HAPPENED in the time between. He figured out what he needed to do. If the dreamlife of his second self was suffering unendurable torture, he would seek a lesser hell in the dreamlife of the first, the primary self. If that's what it was. Another time, another table, another group of robed practitioners, and death hovering close by.

His heart had stopped, though that wasn't how the attending doctors had put it. Like all priestly elites, they spoke in code. The place inside his head became a big, noisy room suddenly emptied of people, in which an alien sound, heard only faintly below the previous din, was now very much audible. The sound—which might have been the drone of the heart monitor—began to separate into strands. Other voices in other rooms. He rose from the gurney and walked, pulling the IV cart along with him. He turned a corner and saw the floor nurse, slipping his personal effects into a plastic bag. He stepped through a door into a room without walls. The voices there were louder. A young woman was in the Muslim posture of prayer, toes curled under, forehead pressed to the ground. She looked at his face and then at his wrists, which were cut and dripping large amounts of blood onto the floor. Her wrists were bleeding, too. "How could you do this to us?" she asked him. He bandaged the girl's wrists, then staggered back and doubled over in pain.

The sudden jolt of the defibrillator panels then obscured all sound and light. There were flashes of illumination—comic-book lurid. Pow! Zap! Sizzle! His spine whipped. The room began to fill again. The doctors were back. He felt a searing pain in his left eye, as if a blown ember from a nearby fire had entered it. "Look," said the nurse. "Do you see that? His eyelid is burning." The doctor leaned in, then leapt back, a hand on his cheek. "Jesus! What the hell is that?" Another voice said, "He's on fire from the inside. Impossible. Turn off the lights."

◆ ◆ ◆

A CURTAIN WAS MOVED ASIDE. "Let him cool off," said a voice in Arabic. "Then we will proceed." Raszer felt hardness rise up under him with the color red.

There was something warm on his shoulder blades. It was the only part of him that felt relief. The warmth, he realized after opening his eyes, was the sun. He was alone on a balcony that protruded from the base of the fortress out over the chasm, and he was face down in a pool of his own sweat. The floor was of some dark-age amalgam, painted a faded red, and the walls rose to his solar plexus. They had dressed him in a pair of drawstring muslin pants, a nominal concession to modesty. He stood with difficulty and walked slowly to the wall. He rested his arms on it and remained there for quite a while, bending to cough out phlegm and bile when the urge came.

Far below, through the valleys beneath the serrated mountains, the Silk Road caravans had traveled, laden with peppercorns and coffee—things men had once killed for. The position of the sun made it midday. Raszer was there an hour before anyone came.

The curtains parted.

"Are you feeling better?" the man asked, in an unnervingly delicate voice.

"That's all relative, isn't it?" Raszer replied.

"As all things are," answered the sheikh.

The voice, the robes, and the bearing were similar—identical, in fact—to those of his torturer, but it seemed possible that this was a different man.

"All things? Even Allah?"

"If by Allah, you mean that which presides over the machinery of the universe, this is coeternal with the universe . . . but its interpretation by man is relative."

"The Qur'an—some would say—is also an interpretation. Is its truth relative?"

"The truth of the Prophet's revelation is not in the text. One must have eyes to see it. Most see only words, and no word can be read without prejudice. Worse, men try to divine moral law from them, and there is no kinship between law and revelation. The truth of the Qur'an is that there is no truth but God, and God is incomprehensible."

"I wonder what truth you hoped to divine from torturing me."

"Truth is not the point of torture."

"Truly," said Raszer. "Are you the god of this place, who determines who will suffer and who will be granted pardon?"

"Anyone can be a god," replied the sheikh. "Consider the dog taken from its mother and placed in a strange home. It has been stripped of the familiar, and will offer unqualified devotion to the first person who provides it with sustenance . . . even though that person may in the next moment beat it severely. Shall I demonstrate?"

"It wouldn't have effect, and I know that's what you're after. I've been to the well of nothing, and found it wasn't empty. You can take everything, and God will still be there. That is the reason to develop faith: to survive monsters like you."

"And if the monster you see is a mirror of your own self?"

"Then I know which mirrors to smash."

"Ha!" said the sheikh. "Fortitude you have. But passion blinds you. Let me show you the world as it is." He whistled through his teeth, a long, trilling tone with a scoop at the end. Presently, a young man—one of those Raszer had seen in the garden—came through the curtained doorway and stood before the sheikh. "What is your name?" his master asked.

"My name is yours to give," the young man replied.

"Son of a whore," said the sheikh. "Where were you born?"

"I was born in the Garden."

"Remove your robe."

The young man—now seeming far more a boy—did as he was told, and stood naked before the wall. A shiver ran the length of his body. Instinctively, he cupped a hand over his groin, but not quickly enough. Raszer was at first moved to pity, the way he might have been moved by an animal missing a limb, or a child with a cleft palate, but quickly the milk of pity soured to anger, and then to fury.

Between the young man's legs was only a vestigial organ.

He had been cut to the root.

Maybe it was the memory of the mortally wounded soldier, twitching spastically in the road, and maybe the outrage of the waking nightmares they'd only an hour ago projected on the white walls of his mind, but finally it was too much. Raszer turned on his tormentor and took hold of the veil that covered his face.

"*Fils de merde,*" he spat.

"Poor comportment for a priest," said the sheikh, freeing himself. "Have you heard what science has found? Ninety percent of the human genome is identical to that of an earthworm. And what is fornication but the worm in human nature? And what is law but the boot that keeps the worm pinned to the ground? If we wish to be free of the boot, we must be prepared to sacrifice the worm. Only then can the will triumph."

"Very tidy," said Raszer. "Very clean. But you've destroyed the fruit to cut out the rot. Man and the earthworm share genetic lineage because both are the products of a single idea: the Word made flesh. An essential current flows through the sex parts; if you break the circuit, we lose our connection to the power source. If I call myself a priest, it is because each day I strive to transform this current into love, and this service is by choice. Deny this choice, and I'm no longer a servant—I'm a slave."

The sheikh uttered a command that Raszer didn't comprehend, and without the slightest hesitation, the naked boy had vaulted the wall and leapt to his death. Raszer followed the descent to impact eight hundred feet below with a shout stopped in his windpipe and a hand impotently outstretched.

"There are a thousand more like him inside," said the sheikh. "Do you truly believe that your world can survive an order such as this?"

"And what is your place in it?" Raszer asked. "If there's no truth, and everything is permitted, it's difficult for me to see the 'order' in it."

"We are . . . what has always been in these highlands. We are like the wind, and want only what the wind has: pure existence, without constraint of law or social order. To go where we please, invisibly. The only God on Earth is will. The only law is will expressed as power. Men once knew this, but have been tricked by sentiment. Tell me, where is pity in the world? The God of this world demands discord, not community."

"I think you're a few thousand years late . . . maybe a few hundred million. Even orangutans form communities. You can't will the world to jump when you say, 'Jump.'"

"Perhaps not. But we can will the world to fear, and in fearing, it will form boundaries and stand one side against the other. We will occupy the neutral ground. We will hasten the world's division and reap the space between."

"What you'll reap is the whirlwind . . . "

"Have you come to preach to us, Father?"

"No. I've come for one girl. One girl is surely worth keeping your castle."

"Perhaps more. She is a special girl. What do you offer?"

"What can one American girl be worth to someone like you?"

"Let me answer your question with a question," said the sheikh. "What quality in woman is most valued by man?"

"Why don't you tell me," said Raszer.

"A beautiful emptiness, upon which he may project his desire."

Raszer said nothing.

"What will it mean for your world if her face becomes the face of terror?"

Again, Raszer stayed silent.

"So I ask you again. What will you pay for her?"

"Something worth a thousand souls to you. The missing piece of the Ka'ba stone, *al-Hajar al-Aswad*, taken from Mecca when your forebears sacked it. That's the history, isn't it? They returned it in pieces after twenty-two years. But of twelve fragments, only seven were restored. Four of those remaining were hardly more than chips, but one was of a size great enough—in the hands of a master—to evoke Atargatis. The stone was yours until a boy named Henry Lee took it from under your nose."

"The whole of this fortress is built upon sacred rock. Why should we bargain with a Christian for a fragment of what we already possess?"

"Because it's a very special fragment, and because you understand that cracks lead to catastrophes. Once it's widely known that the stone of the Ka'ba is *not* intact—and that the Satanic verses have a basis in history, the Islamic world will erupt . . . and the conflict you hope to profit from may never occur."

"How would you propose to deliver this stone to us?"

"As soon as the girl is on her way home, it will be handed over to you."

"By whom?"

"By me."

The sheikh said nothing, but stepped to the wall and surveyed the sweep of the canyon. After a few moments, he spoke. “This matter is not for me to decide.” His voice trailed off as he left the balcony, saying, “I will send someone for you.”

If the story went where stories are wont to go, Raszer was about to meet the Old Man of the Mountains.

THIRTY-SIX

IT WAS AN ORDINARY DOOR of uncertain age, pale green with a knob of tarnished brass. Raszer stepped through into a small, square space that resembled a museum re-creation of a late-eighteenth-century European sitting room. There were in the room a love seat with fat cushions upholstered in striped silk, two high-backed chairs of dark, ornamented wood, two matching hutches of the same dark wood, and an oil painting of a small cottage in a deep forest. Nothing about the room was especially inviting, or forbidding. Nothing made him feel that he was expected to linger there. But he felt out of place and uneasy, as if he were the wrong-size doll in a dollhouse.

Raszer had been given no instructions by his attendant, other than a gesture and the words "Through there." On the opposite end of the room was another green door, identical to the first.

He walked to the door and was about to open it; then he paused and turned. It was then that he perceived the truth of the room: The scale of everything was just slightly—almost imperceptibly—smaller than life. That's why he'd felt too big.

He turned the green door's tarnished knob and stepped into a larger square room with precisely the same furnishings. The placement was identical, as was the position of the green door on the opposite wall, only now he felt smaller, as if a lens had been flipped or the floor had dropped. Oddly, the possibility that the furniture was larger seemed the least likely. He tried to access the first room so that he could compare the scale, but the door had locked behind him. He did not want to stay here, either, so he proceeded to the next door. Again, he turned just before leaving, and noticed that smoke was rising from the chimney in the painting of the little house in the woods. He didn't think it had been there before, but he might not have noticed it.

The third room was larger still, although the relative proportion and placement of every article in it were exactly the same. This time, Raszer allowed himself to gather his thoughts for a minute, sitting on the love seat. The pause did him no good. His bearings were off; he felt vulnerable. He reasoned that the interrogation had taken a lot out of him, and now they were fucking further with his head. If his senses were to be believed, he had lost about six inches of height in two minutes. He knew now, of course, that the scale of the rooms and furnishings must be gradually increasing—that it was some kind of optical riddle—but this was not at all what he *felt*.

What he felt was that he was shrinking. Once again, the door locked behind him. He glanced at the painting. The front door of the cottage had now opened, and a blond child was coming out. She seemed to be upset. He thought immediately of Brigit.

The fourth, fifth, and sixth rooms continued his diminution, but in increments so finely calibrated that his mind couldn't get a fix on the change in scale. Someone with a mastery of geometry—and the science of human perception—had mapped this out.

In physical stature, he was now about ten years old.

On entering room number four, having learned his lesson about the self-locking doors, he determined to remain at the threshold with the doorknob in hand, looking both ahead and behind, until he'd figured out the ratio. But he found that he was unable to see the space ahead without stepping fully into it—and that the door shut smartly the moment he stepped away from it.

By room six, the expression on the face of the girl in the painting had become one of distinct panic, and the open door of the cottage revealed an adult figure, flat on a cot at the far end of the room, his arm dangling listlessly over the side, as if he were either drunk or dying.

Raszer denied the implications at first, but now they were unavoidable: The girl was coming more and more to resemble his daughter, and the enfeebled figure on the bed to resemble him.

He knew that a good optical illusion could be so deeply disorienting that you lost track of ordinary things, yet he was surprised to find that by the time his physical sense of himself had shrunk to about forty-two inches and the high-backed chairs towered over him like skyscrapers, he'd forgotten how many rooms he'd been through.

He didn't think it could be more than a dozen, but why, then, was he so many worlds away?

How had they done it? A couple of ideas had taken root in Raszer's mind, both based on the effect the experience was having on him. The first was that he was being taught to mistrust his perception. The second was that he was being diminished so that his ego would not present an obstacle to whatever sort of dark enlightenment they had in mind. Both seemed to be ways of preparing him for his destination. Weirdly enough, his altered perception and its inside-out quality lent him a kind a balance. That is, until he saw what was happening in the painting.

It was no longer a naturalistic landscape of quaint cottage and leafy trees, but a hyperrealistic depiction of death in the forest. The girl had moved into the extreme foreground and stood with her hands clapped over her open mouth, eyes wide in terror. A third of her form had passed outside the picture frame. The dying man in the cottage, jaundiced, horribly gaunt, and seemingly much older, was clearly meant to be him. The man had lifted his arm with what must have been a last reserve of strength, and appeared to be summoning. His cracked lips were parted as if calling.

Raszer stepped closer.

Did you say something? was what he thought. He stepped closer. *Come again*? He was in close and could now see—almost feel—the paper-thin skin stretched over the cheekbones, the sharp ridge of the avian nose, a strange glassiness in the right eye.

And then, suddenly, he found himself looking out from the skull of the man in the painting.

What he saw was a simple plank floor, swept clean, and a room in which he could make out only the chair beside the bed (where the child had probably kept her vigil), a wood-burning stove, and an easel on which the girl had painted the cottage in watercolors. Everything else was flared out by the light that spilled through the open door. The light was like gold mist. Raszer felt that if he could get to it, he might be young again. He would not be feeble.

But it was hard to tell how far away the door was. There was something wrong with his depth perception. One at a time, and with difficulty, he lowered his eyelids. With the right lid closed, he could see as he had before. With the left lid closed, he could see nothing. He opened his good eye and crawled from the cot onto the floor, remaining on all fours until he reached the door, which was, in fact, quite a long way away. When he arrived, he took hold of the knob and pulled himself up.

He had returned to his present self and stood in a room the size of the very first room, but empty of furniture and painted the same pale green as the doors. A fissure bisected the floor on a diagonal from corner to corner, and in the fissure ran a clear spring from which vapors rose. On the wall, where the painting had hung, there was now a large mirror with a gold frame, and inside the mirror, a peacock sat on a golden stool, preening its glowing feathers. It was both more real than a hologram and less real than a photograph. No matter which direction Raszer moved, he could not eclipse the bird. It had not seemed to notice his arrival, so he decided to speak to it.

"Hello," he said.

"Hel-lo," the bird said back. The voice struck Raszer immediately. It had the usual avian graininess, but behind that, something else: the quality of a marionette's voice, thrown by the puppeteer. Hadn't he'd heard this in the kitchen of the Kingdom Hall in Azusa, in the voice of Elder Amos Leach? A neither/nor quality.

"Do I hear an echo?" asked Raszer.

"In a manner of speaking," said the bird.

"Who's the fairest of them all?"

The bird said nothing. Clearly, it felt it was.

"You've mindfucked me and shrunk me, and shown me my own death. Now do I get the girl?"

"You have one more task to perform."

"What's that?"

"First, a question: Who is Philby Greenstreet?"

"Can't tell you what I know. Only what I think."

"That will do."

"Philby Greenstreet is the Preserver. Like Shiva. You're the Destroyer, right?"

"What is it he seeks to preserve?"

"For lack of a better term, civil society. Pluralism."

"And this is your ideal? A 'civil' society?"

"Not ideal, maybe, but the base condition for anything better to happen."

"What *is* ideal?"

Raszer hesitated. He knew he was being engaged in a dialectical exchange, preplotted by his avian interlocutor.

"I can't believe I'm having this conversation with a bird."

"You are having this conversation with Melek Ta'us. What is ideal?"

"The peace which passeth understanding," Raszer answered warily.

"And where is this peace to be found?"

He saw where the interrogatory was leading. The correct answer was "death."

"Nowhere," he replied.

"Nowhere?" the bird repeated, cocking its plumed head.

"Na-Koja-Abad. Nowhere-Land."

"And how does one reach this wondrous place which is no place?"

"I won't presume to teach hermeneutics to one such as yourself, Lucifer."

"I was once an angel, yes. Now merely a god. But there is always more to learn."

"Well said. Have I told you how beautiful you are?"

"You have no idea," said the bird, opening its glorious fan. "Get to the point."

"Look closer."

"What?" asked the bird, unused to being directed.

"Na-Koja-Abad is the pearl in the oyster. A world enfolded, as the physicists say, in an extradimensional matrix. The seeker must use *ta'wil* to see past *zahir* to *batin*, the inner reality of things. If he's successful, he enters through the door of imagination to *alam al-mithal*, the intermediate realm of subtle matter—things that haven't yet become. He can do this only in the subtle body, the *jism mithali*. In this, he achieves *dhawq*, perception of the sublime. Finally, if he hasn't been frightened away by what he sees, he achieves *ilm*, the gnosis that the world is the imperfect embodiment of the pearl, of perfect forms conceived in the mind of God. And there lies the peace I spoke of."

"How Platonic," said the bird, puffing its feathers. "But how does a man return to the ugliness and pointlessness of the world after seeing such sublime things?"

"In truth, he never left it. He has arrived at the Mountain of Qaf, where the point of departure and return are one and the same. The world, however, has become new to him, and he will never see it again with the same eyes. The beauty coexists with the world, however flawed its external manifestation."

"Just so. The world is a mere representation. A facsimile! What is lost if it ends?"

"Nothing will be *lost*," said Raszer. "But we will have failed. And if a man can't see the form of heaven on Earth, there's no reason to think he'll recognize it later."

"You are clever, but you are wrong," the bird said, "and living in vapors. We, too, have created a place that many see as heaven, but this does not make it so. You are no less fooled. There is no heaven on Earth, and no God in the lotus. Worldly existence has no purpose other than the acquisition of advantage. You have, however, seen the shadow of the real, which is that Qiyamah is here for those who can dispel illusion. We are not many. We draw from a great well of power at the base of the world mountain, which connects in turn to all the wells of all the mountains of all the worlds. Let the human cattle play their games. We are the GamesMasters. We will enter heaven."

"Then pull some strings for me," said Raszer. "I want the girl."

"Why save what is already lost? Why settle for a trinket . . . "

Raszer said nothing, but watched as the peacock's image flickered—

" . . . When you can have emeralds?"

—and was replaced by the magisterial figure of the Old Man, robed in vibrant green, at first materializing in the illusory space inside the mirror, then finally taking his place as a mere reflection, seen over Raszer's left shoulder.

"Do not turn around," said a voice richer than the bird's but of the same unsettling ambiguity. "Regard me only in the mirror, or you will die."

"Whatever you say," Raszer agreed.

The Old Man stepped closer. An inch or two shy of Raszer's height, his head was entirely covered except for the eyeholes, and his body was draped in so many layers of silk that it was impossible to determine what sort of frame was underneath.

"You may take the girl, but only after you have pledged fidelity to me."

"I'm already pledged to another."

"Do you not know that I can see through your disguise, priest?"

"You can never be entirely sure, though, can you? That's the beauty of disguise. All it asks is a grain of doubt. And besides, the purpose of disguise isn't only to fool others. It's to allow the wearer to be someone else."

"What will you give me, then?"

"I'll give you the black stone. I'll walk out with the girl; she'll be handed over to a Kurdish unit outside the gates and held at a location close by until it's in your possession. I doubt Mam Rahim will break the rules, because he knows your mercenaries will play polo with his head and most likely slaughter his family if he does."

"And how can you be sure that we won't . . . 'break the rules'?"

There was a lengthy pause.

Raszer's sensors began to tick. In the air surrounding them was a distinct electricity. "Come closer," he said, "and I'll tell you why I trust you."

He heard the slippered foot move across the stone floor and felt the toe against his heel. He heard the soft shifting of fabric and felt the arms encircle his hips. The hands fluttered to rest, one atop the other, over his groin. He froze.

"Leave the world," the robed figure breathed, "and be immortal with us."

From the breath carrying the words came the scent of methyl salicylate. Oil of wintergreen. He glanced down at the slender hands caressing him, and saw that on one of them, a digit was missing where a ring finger should have been.

"Layla?" he said. In a heartbeat, the figure folded into thin air like a time-lapse sequence in reverse and returned to the mirror. The red walls lifted like painted flats, and Raszer found himself in an expansive court, watching three black figures—the puppet masters of his new fate—approach him from a colonnade on the far end. In light of what he'd seen, he ought to have been awed by their mastery of the game.

But Raszer was beyond awe, beyond exhaustion, beyond anything but wanting to make the right move.

THIRTY-SEVEN

HE WAS ALLOWED TO collect his belongings before being taken to Katy. He'd been told that she'd been informed of his coming, but it was clear when they arrived in the garden that she hadn't exactly packed her bags. He watched from a distance as two of the guards tried to martial her. He grew concerned when she shook her head and began to scoot away from the stream bank where she sat with some of the other girls. When they tried to pick her up, she kicked desperately, broke free, and tore off toward a far grove of plum trees. One guard took off after her; the other turned toward the black-sheathed figure standing beside Raszer and gestured, as if to say, *What now?*

Katy's behavior was not at all atypical of the children, wives, and husbands Raszer had been hired over the last decade to spring from various prisons that most had walked into with eyes open, and it should have ceased to confound him. She flailed wildly, and he flinched when the guard struck her to the ground.

"This won't do," he said firmly.

"I will take care of it," said his robed companion.

"Please," said Raszer, pressing his luck. "Give me a few minutes with her . . . "

"A few minutes," said the GamesMaster. "The clock is running on this move."

Katy spotted him when he crossed the stream; she stilled, her expression as wary as a cornered animal's. Raszer stopped eight feet short of where she sat beneath the tree.

"Aïcha?" he said.

She turned halfway.

"Do you remember who I am?"

Just the slightest nod. Mostly in the eyes.

"I want to take you home."

A question formed on her face. *Where?*

"No. Not where you came from. Where you belong."

He moved a couple of steps closer.

"I have to leave for a little bit, but I'll be back for you. With Ruthie."

He sat down beside her, and she didn't move away.

"Aïcha was born here," she said quietly. "She'll die outside."

"That's probably true," Raszer said. "But there's another woman waiting. None of us is ever just one person. The thing is to choose the one you like best and settle in with her. It won't be the one your father or mother knew. If you choose wisely, it'll be the one that most resembles the reflection of God's face in your heart."

She rolled her eyes up to the false sky. "But the world is gone. They told me so. All in flames."

"After the fire, Katy, things grow again." He paused. "Silas, your father, died a few weeks ago. So you're free to be whomever you imagine yourself to be."

She didn't seem to know how to connect to the information.

"Listen," he said. "You know about the game, right? The boys told you?"

She nodded.

"All I'm asking . . . is for you to let me be your guide."

"But I don't know how to play," she said.

"That's all right," he said. "I'll teach you."

Raszer left her there, beside the tree, in the counterfeit garden, beneath the counterfeit sky, and made his way out. The minute he set foot on the rocky ground outside the enormous iron gates, things resolved for him in a stark and sobering way. He understood why Ruthie had come, and why he'd allowed her to stay. He saw that she, too, had a character to portray in the "chaotic fiction" of his current enterprise. In truth, she might in large measure be its author, given that she had brought him to Shams, and Shams had ushered him into whatever sort of gamespace he now occupied.

TINAG. *This is not a game.* Not like any he'd ever played, anyway.

And though he might have wished for the cup to be taken from his hands, he also understood that whatever Ruthie had set in motion had already fixed certain probabilities.

A detachment of Green River mercenaries accompanied Raszer to the place half a mile down the access road where he'd previously arranged to meet Dante and Ruthie. Raszer couldn't be sure if the guards' silence was a consequence of orders from their captain, or of the fact that a number of them appeared to be Central or South American, with the high cheekbones and sculpted fierceness of jungle fighters. In any case, they weren't the talkative sort. These were the new model soldiers of fortune, drawn from death squads in places like Chile and El Salvador. They also represented a new kind of colonialism, since their commanders were mostly American or British—some Belgian or even Dutch. The East India Company lived. The empire never ended. The pan-Islamic wars had built them into a global private army, at the calling of anyone with a fat enough purse.

"We'll stop up here," said Raszer, pointing to an overlook up ahead, "and wait."

The gunman who seemed to be nominally in charge asked, "How long?"

"As long as it takes," said Raszer. "They'll come."

✦ ◆ ✦

THE MERCENARIES REMAINED at arms. They didn't banter, or squat in the white soil to share cigarettes or pictures of girls back home. They were, after all, professionals.

After about twenty minutes, Dante's sun-bleached head cropped up from the boulders, on the side of the ridge opposite the sanctuary entrance. This was good. Had he shown up too quickly and come from the right, the gunmen would have quickly deduced the location of the cave. Dante hesitated when he saw the battery of automatic weapons, and ducked out of sight until Raszer had called out a second time.

Cupping his hands, he shouted the prearranged all clear: "The king is dead!" And then, when the boy had come within twenty yards, "Bring Ruthie!"

"It'll take some time!" Dante called back.

"That's all right! I need her here! Katy needs her!"

When Dante had gone, Raszer finally sat. It didn't matter that the ground was hard, or that two muzzles were trained on him. It didn't matter that they'd just as soon saw off his head. The sun was warm, he was bone-tired, and after he had smoked a cigarette, he lay back against an angled rock and slept.

In his dream, he'd misplaced a set of keys and could not enter his own house. Other doors of other houses were unlocked, but not his. He was making tea in the kitchen of one of the houses when a woman appeared. It was his wife, but he didn't know her. She pointed at him and asked, "What's wrong with your face?"

When he woke, it was to the prodding of the head gunman's toe.

"Wake the fuck up," he heard the man say.

Ascending the rocky path from the right was a figure whose form vibrated in and out of register, like a desert mirage. Long strands of auburn hair whipped across her round face. At first glance, she seemed a runaway from his dream.

What the hell is this? he said to himself.

It was Ruthie as he'd seen her the first time, waiting on the deck of her stepfather's trailer. It was Ruthie as Katy.

How long, he wondered, had she been preparing for this entrance? How remarkable, to have thought to bring the wig and the dress to the other side of the world, to carry them, secreted in her pack, across a mountain range. For a long time, she seemed to be moving in place. If he was not mistaken, she was smiling.

He said, when at last she stood close, "You think we're playing dress-up?"

"*You* are, aren't you?" she replied.

Dante now appeared in the brush on the left, and Raszer signaled him over.

"We're on," he told the boy. "Everything as planned. I'll be at the gates in an hour. Once things are in motion, go back and wait for us. We'll meet you there."

He turned back to Ruthie. "Let's go. I'll explain on the way."

THIRTY-EIGHT

THE PARTY MADE ITS WAY from the garden, slowly threading the maze of corridors, and finally entered the vast atrium inside the fortress gates. Raszer had Katy's right arm, Ruthie her left, and they were flanked by the gunmen, with the American and the three black-robed GamesMasters in the rear. Katy's gait was uncertain, like that of someone leaving a sanitarium after a long period of bed rest. Her eyes, after more than a year in the Garden's unceasing light, could not adjust to the dimness of the halls.

Outwardly, she was in pretty good shape, though all her muscles had gone slack. Psychically, it was another story. She kept looking back toward the garden as if she'd forgotten something. Most likely, she'd been taken there initially in a drugged state, as he had, and, because it presented such an extraordinary illusion of limitless space, had never even considered that it might be contained within the walls of a stone box.

When they reached the inner gate, Raszer turned to the American. "If your men have nervous trigger fingers, tell them to park them. You may think you know the score, but you don't. Just let me walk away with Katy, and not a shot will be fired."

The first gate rolled open, and when blue sky appeared through the second, heavier gates, it was picketed with the rifle barrels of the Kurdish unit.

In their midst stood Francesca, cradling a small wrapped bundle. Raszer gave her a nod and she stepped forward. The Kurds leveled their rifles, and the mercenaries of El Mirai responded in kind. Taking Francesca's package with one hand, Raszer handed Katy off to her with the other.

In the immediate wake of the exchange, Katy cast an anxious glance at her sister, who'd stepped back from her place at Raszer's side. She stood now in the crossed shadow of the mercenaries' rifles. He couldn't read Ruthie's face, but caught the almost imperceptible shake of her head. Before he could reflect, other shadows swept across and the sound of massed boots on scree signaled the arrival of a second unit of Green River mercenaries. He counted eighteen of them, and they surrounded the Kurdish unit, pinning them between their guns and the castle gate. Raszer turned to the black sheikh nearest him. He presumed it was his own tormentor, but could not be sure.

"If one shot is fired, we all will die," he said.

After a beat, the sheikh turned to the mercenary leader and gave a nod. It was barely more than a tic, but it served its purpose, and tension dropped a notch. Raszer put the parcel into his hands, took a step back, and turned briefly to check Ruthie. She hadn't moved. He narrowed his eyes and motioned for her to join her sister. For the second time in fifteen seconds, he saw that same faint shake of the head. He kept his eyes on her as his pulse rose and his mind raced to decipher her body's code.

The sheikh unwrapped the bundle, put the stone to the sky, and turned it until the idiosyncratic dimple revealed itself. He handed it to the second of his rank and motioned him inside. After the man had disappeared, the GamesMaster raised his palm and said, "Wait."

After a few minutes, there came from within the fortress the sound of fervent incantation. Raszer reasoned—if reason had a place here—that the chant was addressed to the stone, and that a servitor was being summoned. Magick, like expensive drugs, had to be tested before the buy was made. And bluffs had to be called.

Raszer looked to Ruthie. Her eyes were on her sister. He couldn't help but wonder now, remembering the snapshots he'd seen that day in Detective Aquino's office, if that look said, *Let's play the game we used to. You be me, and I'll be you.*

There was a sharp cry of affirmation from inside, followed by the shout "*Atar'atah! Hi-yae Ho-nae!*" The robed man nearest Raszer nodded, and Raszer motioned for Francesca and the Kurdish detail to move out. The two remaining Masters slipped through the gates as they began to roll shut on massive iron casters. He walked to Ruthie and held out his hand, and when she gripped it, he thought for an instant all might be well. The rear gates would be sealed in another ten seconds, and the outside gates had already begun to close. She released his hand, put her arms around his neck, and kissed him on the mouth before backing through the line of gunmen and into the crack that remained between light and darkness. He lunged for her, but found a muzzle in his face and the ranks closed. An instant later, the gates came together with a gnashing of steel teeth.

Raszer cursed the sun, and had momentary reason to wonder if it was any more real than the one that shone on the Garden.

They had switched places.

✦ ◆ ✦

WHEN THEY HAD REACHED the sanctuary and stationed their guard, he sat down with Katy not far from the vertical cave entrance, a man-size rabbit hole that offered just enough light for her to see him. He chose not to question her about the mechanics of the exchange. He didn't question her at all, because he didn't yet know what answers he was looking for. He could see that her own gates were drawing shut, and might remain closed for a while. He'd seen it in so many of his strays: this icing over, this pulling into the shell. There was shame to deal with, and rage, and fear, and, most confusing of all, there was missing the devil you knew—in this case, a devil with an opium fix—and the captivity you had come to trust. And so Raszer took her hands in his, and after a while began to hum a tune to her. Francesca and Dante sat nearby, their backs against the cavern wall, while the Kurdish retinue covered the entrance. It would be dark in an hour, and Raszer had decided they'd wait for morning.

Her pulse, felt faintly through her palms, was as slow as a yogi's. Her newly dilated pupils made her eyes almost black, and soft. She seemed to like the humming. He knew why: There was no drug quite like opium, nothing that made a person feel as cozy and safe. All things became haloed with soft, diffuse gaslight. None of this placidness, however, would survive Katy's inevitable crash. Soon she'd be climbing the cavern walls, clawing the dirt, and probably kicking him. He began thinking about a new plan.

After a long time, she decided to speak.

"Where're we going?" she asked.

"Eventually . . . America," he answered. "After that, where *you* want to go."

"I don't know about that." A pause. "I guess I'd still like to see Washington?"

"Washington . . . " he repeated. "D.C.?"

She nodded. "We were going there. For Christmas. Does it snow there?"

"Sometimes," he said. "A field trip. Nice. Were they always that nice to you?"

She kept her eyes on him for a long time in the fading light. Then she dropped her head, shook it from side to side, and began to cry softly. He held her hands firmly, feeling her pulse begin to spike up a little. After a while, he said, "Listen, I'm going over to talk to Francesca for just a minute. Dante over there, he'll keep watch over you."

He stood and nearly toppled over. He was dizzy from hunger and exhaustion. He motioned for Francesca to walk with him.

"What did they do to you in there?" she asked, seeing him stagger.

"I'm not ready to talk about it yet," he replied. Beneath the cave entrance, he lit a cigarette and fell back against the rock. "I can't believe I didn't think about this . . . "

"About what?" she asked.

"They got her strung out on high-grade black opium, and she's going to crash real soon. If she wigs out, they're going to find this place, and I'm not the least bit sure they won't kill us all."

"What do you think?"

"I think we send you and Katy ahead to the village with the soldiers. Dante and I will keep two of them behind to guide us down later."

"I don't understand. Why don't we all go?"

"Two reasons," he said. "The first is the separate-boats strategy we've already agreed to. The second is that I need to think . . . about Ruthie. About what to do."

"*What to do about Ruthie*?" she repeated, moving in close on him. "She walked right in there, as she undoubtedly intended to from the start. She made her choice. Excuse me . . . but *fuck her!*"

"I know I should go with your gut, Francesca. I agree, her staying didn't look coerced. That's just the problem. There has to have been some kind of deal made, but when . . . and with whom, and for what?"

"*Stupido uomo!*" she said. "It's not enough to survive. You have to figure it all out. You don't even see the answer right before your eyes."

He exhaled a long plume of smoke and regarded her steadily. "Oh, I *see*," he said. "Believe me, Francesca of the Fedeli d'Amore. I *see*." He stamped out the cigarette. "What time did Monica say the helicopter would be there?"

She looked at her watch. "In a little less than eight hours: 4:00 AM."

"I want you to go. You speak Kurdish. I want you to ask the unit leader to radio ahead to Rahim and ask him to meet you halfway. Then stay with him until the chopper comes."

"When will I see you?"

"I'll be there by four, if not earlier. I just need to work some things through."

"And if you are *not* there?"

He took her head in his hands. "I will be. But no matter what, you get her—and Dante—into that helicopter before sunrise, back to the vehicles, and back to your base. You promise me, okay? Monica will get me out. Promise me, Francesca."

She reached up to touch the scar she'd left him, then sucked in a breath and nodded.

It took Raszer an hour to prepare Katy to leave without him, and it felt like the rush job it was. He'd earned a small measure of her trust, only to turn her out into a harsh world on her own. He was cutting corners with her soul. He did as much of the restoration work as he could, but came up short. At some point, he muttered words of apology. She looked at him oddly and said, "Just please don't put me in a truck, okay? I don't like the dark."

"A truck?"

"If you sell me or trade me to someone. Wherever it is I'm going."

"You're not being traded to anyone, Katy," he said, taking her hands. "You're going home."

✦ ◆ ✦

WHEN THEY HAD GONE and it was just Dante and Raszer and the two remaining soldiers, Raszer sat down beside the boy and let out a long, low moan.

"It must take a lot out of you," Dante said, "someone that damaged."

"I'm pretty wrung out. But there's so much more to do."

"I don't know how you got her out of there so fast. I mean . . . I've *been* in there."

"Well, if they knew they were getting Ruthie, I may not deserve much credit."

"There's always a trade-off, isn't there? What matters is breaking even."

"I don't think even's going to be enough," Raszer said, looking long and deep at Dante. "But I wish I'd thought so when I was your age." He paused. "You're way ahead of my station. You're going to have a very interesting life."

"Shit . . . I hope it's half as interesting as yours."

Raszer laughed softly. "Why don't you try to get a little sleep while you can?"

✦ ◆ ✦

IN HIS MIND, Raszer went back over every frame of the time Ruthie had spent inside the fortress. He didn't believe he had ever fully taken his eyes off her. Yes, he'd left the sisters alone in the Garden, but they'd always been in his sight and had never been with a third person. Yet Ruthie had stepped into her sister's place as seamlessly as an understudy replaces an actor in a Broadway production. Raszer was stuck on the why. And in the far chambers of his mind, he was trying to figure out some way to avoid the consequences it implied.

There was the slightest ripple of sound around his ears, but not enough of a signature for his brain to subject it to analysis. The Kurdish soldiers—who knew, as hill fighters, that an unsuppressed sneeze could draw a bullet—made no sound. He scanned the area surrounding the narrow slit of a cave entrance and saw no movement. Dante was curled up nearby, but Raszer was certain he hadn't stirred. Now came another sound, this one defined enough for his mind to replay: a stone skittering down the steep mountainside and landing with a *plunk*. Every hair bristled. There was trouble. Raszer rose to a crouch and crossed the cavern to Dante.

"Hey!" he whispered, and kept some distance so the boy wouldn't wake with a shout. "Listen to me now. You've got to go, got to get out of here."

It took a few seconds for Dante to put things in register. "What? Why?" he asked.

"No time. Is there another way out of here? When I saw you this afternoon, it looked like you'd . . . is there a rear exit?"

Dante nodded, troubled. "For a skinny guy like me. But—"

"Then go. Now. And whatever happens, make sure Katy's on that first chopper out." The boy hesitated, and Raszer gave him a push. "Wake up. Go." He paused. "And live."

Once Dante was out, Raszer climbed into the main entrance, a near-vertical shaft on the boulder-strewn mountainside. The moon had now risen level with the opening, its pale glow illuminating his face. He hoisted himself into the chimney and boosted himself up to its mouth, keeping his eyes at ground level. A second later, he heard a whispered but percussive *pffftt-pffftt*, followed by an exhalation and a thump. The first was probably the sound of a high-grade silencer, at least 90 decibels of attenuation. The second was unmistakable: a body hitting the hard earth.

There was suddenly open gunfire, the second Kurdish soldier's defense. A cascade of silenced gunshots followed, and then the call, "He's down."

It was the voice of the American mercenary.

It was a nightmare's conundrum. Raszer didn't want to go back down, because he'd be cornered like an animal. He didn't want to run, because in open country he would be too easy a target. And if he remained where he was . . .

His neck was suddenly in a vise grip. They pulled him out of the chimney and tossed him roughly onto the rocky ground.

"Right where she said he'd be," said the American, a gray lock of his center-parted hair over one eye. "Six more weeks of winter for you, my friend. I hope you brought a coat." He dropped to one knee, leaned in, and said, "A piece of advice: Never, ever trust a whore."

THIRTY-NINE

THE PLATEAU FROM WHICH the fortress of El Mirai commanded the landscape had been heaved up from the earth a hundred million years before. Its highest point, a mere 2,700 feet above sea level, made it one of the lesser formations in the range, but its monolithic form—along with the remarkable land ramp leading to its summit—more than compensated for its size. Its reputation as a seat of supernatural (and malevolent) power stemmed from a history enhanced by centuries of legend.

This much was known: At some point in human memory, a meteor the size of a house had slammed into the valley floor at the mountain's base, throwing up a titanic amount of earth and creating the land bridge that led to the gates. In the annals of Islam, the fortress had over the centuries been host to more than one form of exotic heresy, sometimes nominally Muslim, mostly not. The mountain's location in a remote wasteland claimed by everyone, but deeded to no one, had made long tenancies possible. As far back as the tenth century, Islamic cartographers had been known to say, "The land to the east belongs to the Sassanids of Persia, and this to the north and west to the Seljuk Turks. This to the south is Urartian, but this—this land in the center—belongs to Shaytan."

Finally, there was the light that gave the fortress its name. At certain times of day, under certain conditions, one could look across the broad canyon from a nearby vantage point and see nothing but brown rock and blue sky where the castle had previously been. Inevitably, this vanishing act occurred when the viewer was pointing out El Mirai to a skeptic.

In times past, a party approaching El Mirai from the south would have seen—if the light was right—the fortress spread like a medina in shades of pale green and saffron yellow across the rocky crown. Below its massive walls, the cliff face was sheer and striated, and dropped nine hundred feet to the slope. At a certain point when ascending the land bridge, the angle of view would reveal the scaffold—beside and below the enormous iron gates—where the enemies of El Mirai were hung from the cliffside, sometimes headless or limbless, and left as offerings to the huge black vultures who were the true gods of this place.

On this particular day in the present time, a smuggler or arms merchant climbing the path to that same vantage point—seeking a good price for contraband, or looking to purchase dated stocks of old Soviet-bloc munitions and sell them back at a markup to the U.S. and Britain—would have been greeted by a similar horror. Stopping in his tracks, mouth agape, he would think, *Poor bastard.* Then, recovering, he would say to himself, *Better him than me.* If he chose to proceed, he would do so knowing to be very careful, so that he did not end up, like this man, dangling over an abyss and crying out the thousand names of God.

Raszer had been on the wall for three hours by the time the sun began to bleed over the eastern horizon. He was suspended by a heavy leather strap from an ancient iron spike that had been hammered centuries ago into the rock. It was clear from the vintage of the spike and the wear of the leather that he was not the first to have hung here. He did not know yet whether it had been an act of mercy or practiced sadism for them to have left his body intact. That would depend on how long it took him to die.

The strap had already bitten deeply into his wrists and arrested the circulation of blood to his hands. He knew this because he couldn't feel them. The angle of his suspension guaranteed this because, although the cliff face appeared perfectly vertical from a distance, it was in fact just slightly oblique. In order to brace his feet against the rock and bring any relief to his arms, Raszer had to arch his spine and kick back until his heels found some tiny notch to rest in, and they never held for more than a few seconds. This action put even more strain on the strap and on his arms, and with a gasp he would feel his heels lose their purchase and the panic rush in as he found himself once again dangling over the chasm, praying that the spike would hold.

He couldn't have dissuaded them. He had nothing left to offer, and nothing of value to confess. Besides, as he'd been reminded, truth wasn't the point of torture, much less of execution. They'd spelled it out before they took him out to the cliff.

"Before you die, you will come to a realization: Your life had no meaning. You mattered to nothing and no one, least of all to God. Whatever god you choose as a buoy in life will abandon you when death is near."

"Can I ask you a question?" Raszer had said.

"Yes, of course."

"When you conjure your servitor from the stone and demand that she work your will on the world, aren't you admitting the possibility of grace? If supernatural agency can move the machinery of the universe, doesn't that suggest a power source?"

"You misread us if you take us for agnostics. There are powers in the universe, or the stars would never have flared into being. They are there to be used. What there is not is anything that *cares*. What there is not is anything that remotely resembles *love*."

"I would trade one moment of my existence for a thousand lifetimes of yours."

"We'll see if you feel that way after eight hours on the wall."

✦ ◆ ✦

THE LAST HOURS OF NIGHT, for all their agony, had offered a kind of hope. With the sun, at least he wouldn't be so cold. With the sun, he could be seen, and if seen, pitied, and if pitied, saved.

But when the sun came, it only spread light on the bleakness all around him: ridge after gray ridge of treeless, grassless, lifeless rock. What sort of angel could be summoned from this landscape? What kind of terrible djinns had the prophets of old invoked to do their bidding, only to have them turn on their masters and demand worship? Marduk? Baal? Yahweh?

Raszer's right heel, already bruised and raw from the night's kicking and flailing, slipped out of its temporary pocket, and as he swung free, the canyon floor rushed up at him. He felt a spasm, then a bolt of pain in his chest, and convulsed, drawing his knees up sharply and causing the spike to ping from strain.

He surmised that his death would come from heart failure. That was probably how this execution worked. If it was to be, he hoped it would happen before his spirit broke, though it was usually the other way around. A prisoner in the Soviet gulag had once written in his journal that the number of hours a man could withstand torture was directly proportional, by a factor of .333, to the weight of his soul, a weight that ranged from nine to twenty-seven grams. The man had probably lost his mind, but the idea made a certain kind of sense. Raszer began to think that his soul might be of insufficient weight.

What he was feeling was the onset of despair. It came with the sun.

About eighteen inches to his right, and a foot or so above his head, there was an indentation in the rock, a kind of natural alcove with a narrow ledge. He'd noticed it after dawn and thought that if somehow he could swing his feet up to it, he might get some blood flowing back into his trunk. Of course, doing this would put strain on his tether, and even the slightest movement made him reel with vertigo. Still, he kept his eye on the ledge, and in what might have been an hour or might have been an endless minute, he heard the *thwup, thwup, thwup* of massive wings beating the air and watched a black buzzard—an old-world vulture—come in for a landing.

The creature weighed at least forty pounds and had a wingspan of at least seven feet. Its top feathers were black and granite gray; its breast was buff colored. The head was bald and came to a point in a great raptor's beak that could probably scoop the beating heart out of a man. Its nearness made him shudder. The bird did not appear to be the least bit frightened, and seemed only mildly curious. Though Raszer had no way of knowing, he guessed that it was a female, and that the ledge was its nesting place.

Over the next two hours, the bird provided his only diversion from agony. The pain in his shoulders, where muscle was tearing and ball joints were grinding like a mortar and pestle, was so deep that he began to lapse into brief periods of unconsciousness.

When he came around, the pain was still there, but so was the bird.

Army nurses know to hold a mortally wounded soldier's hand. A small comfort, but no man wants to die alone. In the absence of better company, the vulture became a fixture, a companion, in Raszer's dramatically reduced world. It perched with as much dignity as an ugly animal can, preened itself, and paused every so often in the midst of its toilet to cock its head at Raszer, not in a reproachful way, but as if to say, *What do you make of me?*

In view of his experience with the peacock, Raszer half expected the buzzard to talk, maybe to engage in some great dialogue about truth and death. But the bird revealed nothing, and this was the thing that began to peck away at the tiny egg of spiritual fortitude Raszer had left.

If God would not grant him a talking bird, even at death's door, then maybe the jig was up. If there was to be no illumination at the end, then maybe there had never been light. Pain can take a man's mind to such places. But what finally pierced the last membrane of spirit was an idiot's epiphany about why the vulture had kept him patient company for so long, a realization that an ordinary man would have come to far earlier.

It was going to eat him.

The habit of coming to the ledge had undoubtedly been bred into the birds over centuries of seeing corpses hung out like suet for their consumption. The vulture was doing what it had always done: It was waiting for him to die.

You'll be waiting a long time, Raszer said without words.

The bird looked him up and down, as if to say, *Maybe not. You don't look so good.*

Appearances can be deceiving, Raszer replied.

Not to a scavenger, the bird seemed to answer. *We know*. In a single, practiced motion—as if casually plucking a grape from the recess of a vine—the vulture extended its long neck, thrust its open beak into Raszer's right eye socket, and, with a shake of its head to loosen the sinews, removed his right eye.

It sat for a moment with the organ held delicately in its beak, then swallowed it in one gulp.

Raszer's system immediately entered salvage mode. It hadn't happened. No. It could not have. Delirium. Time could be reversed. Yes. Go back, go back. And if it had happened—if his right eye were in the vulture's stomach—he would get it back, the way fishermen retrieve arms from sharks' bellies.

All these thoughts occurred as adrenaline coursed through his arteries and bootstrapped him into a panicked state. Fight or flight—only, he could do neither.

He began to taste blood and feel wind in the orifice.

As long as the bird remained there, sated and self-satisfied, Raszer's sense of affront would grow. That, he couldn't stomach. He braced, arched his back, and pumped out from the wall, swinging his legs up to the ledge and kicking furiously to dislodge the interloper. The vulture fought back, pecking his calves and feet, tearing off bits of flesh and fabric, but then, after brief battle, flapped its big wings twice and took off.

For a few moments, Raszer's bloodied feet rested on the ledge, his body in a strange hammock position. Then his heels slipped off the stone, and with a terrifying jerk and a creak of leather, he swung back to a dangling stop. Through the clouded lens of his left eye, he saw that a party of armed men was ascending the path to the fortress gates and appeared to be flanking a prisoner. The summit of the path was about thirty feet to his right, and level with the position of the spike that held him to the wall.

Once his remaining eye had cleared and focused, he saw that the armed men were the Green River officer and his posse, and that their captive was Dante.

And this was when the draining of Raszer's hope became a hemorrhage. Not the merciful flow from the cutting of a major artery, leading quickly to unconsciousness and death, but the steady oozing from a thousand small internal cuts.

Dante. In the space of a four-day trek, this highlands Huck Finn, with his skinny body and nest of golden hair, had become for Raszer a counterweight to the anomie of the Scotty Darrells and Henry Lees of the world. And during their climb of the north wall, something had passed between them that, once given, couldn't be taken back.

Dante's wrists were shackled, and he looked to have been beaten around the face. The American had him by the arm, and pulled him roughly to the edge of the path, where the slope raked steeply down to the floor of the canyon. Dante's face creased in sympathy as he looked on Raszer, half-dead and half-blind. His lips began to form words. A repeated phrase, something he wanted Raszer to know. *It's over*? No, not that. *It's okay*? Almost. No. *She's okay. She's okay.*

The commander pressed the muzzle of his pistol to the back of Dante's skull, fired once, and shoved the body over the edge. He wiped his hands on his cavalry-blue trousers, parked them on his hips, and gave Raszer a nod.

The most awful thing of all was that Raszer couldn't summon a response.

None of this enterprise had been remotely worth its price in grief. None of it. One girl might have been pulled from the wreckage, but another had crashed and made the tally a net zero. Three people—all of whom Raszer might have treasured as friends—were dead. Scotty Darrell was dead. And the beast roared. Fuck it.

So he hung his head, and he wept. From the eye came tears, and from the empty pocket of flesh came blood, mixing as they ran over his lips. His body jerked and heaved as he was wracked with a grief that came in bolts from the center of his belly. Raszer didn't pray for death—that wasn't in his repertoire. What he prayed for, and finally cried out for, was to be known to someone, and, in being known, to have worth.

For a long time, it was very quiet. He didn't let his eyelid drop, because there was no longer any comfort in darkness, or any point in trying to concentrate his will. Instead, he kept his good eye on Dante's corpse, believing that somehow his vigil would keep the scavenging birds away. The feeling had left his shoulders and hands, and he knew that was a bad sign. It became apparent to him that he was going to die soon.

What was that, again? It became apparent to him that *he* was going to die. Yes, that was it. Simple enough. So why did the two pronouns contained in that thought not seem to refer to the same person? The object was clearly the man hanging from an iron spike. The subject, to whom this man's imminent death was apparent, occupied another country. It wasn't a Cartesian split; to oppose mind and matter presumes that both occupy the same pocket of existence, but separately. What was flickering like a discharged neon sign in front of Raszer's eye was the consubstantiality of two worlds.

The feeling couldn't be caught and held down for examination. Not when pain was present. When he tried, it went away, and he was left with only a poor description of it. He knew that it must be related to the inverted vision he'd acquired in the grove, and to the sense of displacement he'd had since Iskenderun. He knew that what Chrétien and Dante had told him about the advanced levels of Gauntlet play somehow described who and where he was. He just had no idea where to go with it.

He, of course, didn't need to go anywhere. Anywhere came to him.

Raszer felt warmth and gentle pressure against his midsection. The strain on his arms was suddenly relieved, and for a time, keeping his heels on the wall required no effort. He shifted his focus from the rocky slope to the space immediately in front of him, and found that he was in the embrace of a small but evidently very sturdy female person wearing a Mongolian herdsman's wool cap. Her breasts were against his breast and her hips were against his hips, and as she had come from nowhere and was managing this feat while holding on to nothing, he figured her for a phantom.

Shit, he thought. *It's the angel of death. Has it happened already? So fast?*

"Shhh," she said. "Don't talk crazy. I told you you'd see me again."

"Shams?"

"Shams I am."

"Where'd you come from?"

She looked up at Raszer, and he saw all the beauty of the man in a woman's face.

"Do something for me," she said. "Look west, toward home. Just beyond the three jagged peaks—only, when you see the peaks, see them *on the inside*."

When he did as she had told him, he felt the pressure and piercing sensation in the iris of his left eye that always preceded the light. When it broke through, it flared momentarily, and only after his monocular vision had stabilized did he see the city. Its outline was familiar, for it was the same one he'd seen at the Kurdish wedding in Ispiria. Its brightness was as great compared with the day's as the day's was with the night's.

"Na-Koja-Abad," he whispered.

"Yes."

"Nowhere-Land."

"Yes."

"Am I going?"

"You're already there," the angel said, and slipped from his body like a sheet.

A shadow fell across the face of the rock. Something large and looming. Raszer looked up, but the glare from the object's corona was too intense. A beating of wings. The air made waves against his eardrums. "Fuck," he said out loud. *The bird is back. Out of the way, you motherfucker. Just let me see the city again. Let me see . . .*

"Hang on," said a male voice from above. "We'll get as close as we can and send a man down for you."

The helicopter was black as a raven, and its familiar dreadlocked pilot was only a few shades lighter. In the open bay, holding a megaphone, squatted Rashid al-Khidr, and over his shoulder, Raszer thought he might have spotted the second Mr. Greenstreet. A third man in a harness was preparing to lower a rescue cable. In the cabin's rear and in shadow, Raszer saw the outline of two forms, one female and one canine. The chopper tipped and veered, its blades slicing precariously close to the cliffside. A burst of automatic-weapon fire issued from the fortress wall, forty feet above.

A second flying gunship, as black as the first and similarly unmarked, dropped down—seemingly from nowhere—and returned the fire, peppering the parapets with machine-gun bursts and raining stone dust on Raszer's head. The chopper carrying Rashid and Francesca dove steeply to evade the barrage.

"Give us a minute!" Rashid called out. "We are expecting help."

There was a great grinding of steel, and to Raszer's right, the forward gates of the fortress began to retract. The guards emerged in pairs, occupying both sides of the land bridge and immediately directing a volley at the helicopters. The gunship ascended and returned fire, while the rescue chopper repositioned itself for a second attempt.

Up the steep sides of the bridge streamed Mam Rahim's hill fighters, blasting as they ran, alternatively diving behind small boulders and rising to get off another round. It was exactly the kind of fight they'd trained a thousand years for. When he heard fire and shouts from the west side of the slope as well, Raszer knew that the *pesh merga* must have come at the gates from both sides.

Caught between the fusillade from above and the Kurdish crossfire from below, El Mirai's forces were temporarily neutralized, and the rescue chopper was finally able to get its harnessed man lowered into place, about forty-eight inches from Raszer's limp form. Raszer looked into the face of his rescuer and saw a young Special Forces officer of twenty-six or twenty-seven, square-jawed and resolute but worried underneath.

He looped the harness under Raszer's arms and had begun to thread it between his legs when a burst of fire came at them from below and chipped away the rock just overhead. Hurriedly, the young soldier dropped the loose end, removed his knife, sliced through the leather strap, and pulled Raszer's body against his, shouting, "Go!" to the men above. Raszer's arms remained extended above his head for a moment, as if unable to accept their release. Then they dropped limply around the soldier's neck. The chopper pulled rapidly away from the wall in an almost perfectly lateral maneuver, and carried its dangling catch to a gentler slope before attempting to reel it back in.

A bullet passed his right ear.

"Shit!" the soldier shouted. He shook the cable and yelled "C'mon!" to accelerate their ascent, but Raszer only saw his lips mouth the word.

But the helicopter was under fire, too, and could not orient itself. The pilot began to pull away from the barrage. A second bullet fired from almost directly below grazed Raszer's ribs and buried itself in the soldier's chest. He saw the soldier blink twice before a helpless expression covered his paling face and his grip weakened.

The chopper dropped precariously and veered toward the canyon. Twenty feet below, in the eye of the melee, the American mercenary commander took aim. An instant before he pulled the trigger, Raszer slipped through the half-engaged harness and dropped to the slope. He heard more than felt his kneecap crack against rock.

There was a cry from above, and Raszer looked up to see the underbelly of the wolfhound known as Shaykh Adi as he leapt from the open bay. On the dog's heels came Francesca, briefly restrained by Rashid until gravity got the better of his grip on the girl. He did not hear or see either of them land. The chopper tilted, its engines howling and its runners scraping stone. The sound of gunfire rose in escalating waves, and the propeller blades beat the air around Raszer's ears into a thick foam of noise.

Then, suddenly, the air stilled.

The rescue helicopter withdrew, and the gunship dropped into its place, its fire pinging the iron gates of the fortress. From the parapets above, a small anti-aircraft missile was launched, and the gunship tilted at what seemed an impossible angle. Below, the American took dead aim at its pilot. Raszer crouched beside a boulder, his damaged kneecap pulled up to his chest. He was out of the firestorm, but it wouldn't matter if the chopper crashed. None of them would get out alive.

The mercenary was eighteen feet up the steep slope from where he hid. Raszer searched the ground for a rock large enough throw him off his aim but small enough to hurl with his wracked arms. He had it in hand when his enemy fixed the target.

The American never got the shot off.

From the far side of the land bridge came a blur of raven-black hair and blue eyes. In the time it takes to say goodbye, Mam Rahim had cut the mercenary's throat from ear to ear.

Raszer rose slowly and painfully to his feet. Not a centimeter of his flesh was free of pain, but as far as he was able to determine through the screen of shock, nothing was broken. He looked around for Francesca. The firefight had been pushed west by the Kurdish forces, who were evidently trying to create a safe zone for the rescue chopper to make another attempt.

That was—or should be—good news, he reasoned. Could he let himself think so? He tried to straighten his spine, but his entire frame had been torqued out of shape. The wisest thing to do under the circumstances was to find Francesca, seek cover, and wait it out. A small avalanche of stone skittered past his feet. He looked up.

What he saw robbed him of what little breath he had.

Poor Emmett Parrish had painted a stripe on his bedroom wall to protect him from the egregore conjured from Henry Lee's little rock. But Raszer did not have so much as a piece of chalk. There was a shriek, and then there was only the wind.

It materialized as air and dust in cyclonic motion. A dust devil. But even at first glance, there was more. Its white-noise roar swallowed all other sounds. It had a shape, and the shape impelled it to move from side to side, like a dancer. An electrical storm seemed to rage at its center. It descended the slope, moving toward Raszer, and enveloped him in a matter of seconds. Just before that, he caught a fleeting glimpse of Francesca and the dog. Immediately, they became a memory no more real than myth.

He was in the eye of the twister. It was absolutely quiet, and absolute quiet—like total darkness—is a terrifying absence filled with the whispers of ghosts and gods. He looked up toward the mouth of the funnel and saw a face as passive as that of a sphinx. Lips parted, and lightning flashed. Current streamed down the cone. After the glare subsided, the lips had become a crack, and through that crack was the end of the world.

Rashid had called it the nunc—the gap between form and substance.

The place where things get lost and never found.

Raszer felt his feet leave the ground as his body began a slow, spinning ascent. The interior walls of the vortex became walls of flesh, yielding as he approached the mouth. He gasped for breath. The cyclone had sucked all the air out of him.

"You can still choose me," he heard her say from all directions.

"Not in a million years," he answered. "Let me go so I can kill you."

His feet suddenly hit the ground, and he fell to his damaged knee. There was a great weight on him, and no air in his lungs. He staggered to his feet and lurched left and right, trying to dislodge the parasite from his back. Her arm was at his throat, a leg coiled around his midsection. He couldn't see the face, but he knew from the scent that Layla Faj-Ta'wil had emerged intact from the vortex. He peeled her fingers from his neck for long enough to swallow a gulp of air and asked, "Who the hell are you?"

"I'm the one who knows you," she answered. "I'm the one who *wants* you."

For a frightening instant, it felt good to be wanted that badly. Then he said, "I'm not available."

"Then no one will have you," she breathed, and slipped from his body like a sheath of skin, coiling at his feet and flicking an adder's tongue. The snake drew back its head and readied its attack. Raszer looked up and saw that the Kurdish forces had contained the fortress guard, and that the first chopper had landed.

"Goddamnit!" he howled. "Will somebody kill this thing?!"

From his right came a bristling blur of limbs, muscles, and fur. Shaykh Adi opened his jaws and sunk his teeth into the soft tissue behind the adder's head. The snake whipped furiously, but vainly. Adi had it where it lived, and after enduring a minute of ferocious shaking, the serpent—to all appearances—decided to play dead.

Adi bounded down the slope toward the canyon floor, dragging the limp reptile over the sharp rocks. At a distance of fifty or sixty yards, Raszer saw the snake begin to writhe again. A few seconds later, dog and prey vanished behind a small ridge.

Francesca had come to his side, and lent her shoulder to support his battered body. They waited, hearing and seeing nothing for an agonizing minute. Rashid and Rahim joined their party. The Kurdish unit formed a phalanx behind them, allowing El Mirai's splintered forces to fall back into the fortress.

A dark cloud rose from the desert floor and spun itself into a shape like smoke from a stack on an arctic winter's day. As it rose, it became a shadow on the barren ground; the shadow traveled over the ramparts of El Mirai and grew until its darkness blanketed the citadel. Shortly after that, the dog came trotting back.

Raszer turned to Rashid. "You wouldn't have a cigarette, would you?"

"If you don't mind Turkish tobacco . . . "

"Any kind," Raszer said. "As long as it burns." He eyed the helicopter, then the surrounding area. "Where's Greenstreet?"

Rashid offered a cigarette to Rahim as well, and lit both. The question went unanswered, or perhaps unheard.

"Forget it," Raszer said, half to himself. "Let's just get Dante's body . . . and get the hell out of this place."

FORTY

A LIGHT SNOW FELL on Massachusetts Avenue, making cocoons of light around the streetlamps in the embassy district. It snows infrequently in Washington, D.C., and two inches slow the city's works considerably. Raszer was on foot, having come from a meeting in a room at the Mayflower Hotel. The subject had been Kurdistan, and certain impediments to its nationhood, and none of the attendees had been there as a matter of record. Raszer had been invited, but he had other business in town as well.

In the street and lined up all the way to Wisconsin Avenue and beyond, police barricades had been erected, diverting traffic from the National Cathedral and making the city even more of a mess to get around. That was one reason he'd decided to walk, rather than taxi to the Cathedral. He walked with a limp and wore a black silk patch over his right eye—or, more precisely, over where his right eye had been. He'd always been told that to lose an eye is to lose depth perception, and that made sense. But depth perception was the least of Raszer's problems, as now he saw the external world as a re-creation—and not an entirely convincing one—of the world he saw internally. It required some legerdemain, but he had found that if he superimposed one image on the other and observed the interference pattern, he could recapture depth.

A Mercedes limo navigated around the barricades and pulled up to the curb beside him. Raszer stopped but did not flinch. He knew the car. He lit a cigarette and waited. The rear door opened and the first Mr. Philby Greenstreet, resplendent in a black cashmere topcoat, swung his six-foot-two frame out and crossed the snow-dusted parkway to Raszer's side.

"Sure you wouldn't like a ride?" he asked.

Raszer nodded toward the cathedral, its spotlit spires looming less than a quarter of a mile away. "Thanks, but no. I'm close, and I love snow on Christmas Eve. Besides, I've developed a phobia about limousines."

"Probably a phobia worth keeping," said Greenstreet. "Nasty things happen in limousines." He glanced at Raszer's bad leg. "You sure you're ready for this?"

"Never better," said Raszer. He cocked his head. "Didn't I see you twenty minutes ago? Do we have a problem?"

"I've just gotten word. All three of the young men are in custody. They were apprehended separately, two hours apart, wearing suicide jackets containing enough explosives to take down a row of flying buttresses and a few hundred parishioners."

"So it's only the girl in there?" Raszer asked.

"Only the girl. We don't know for certain that she made it into the church, but we'll assume she did. And that she'll burrow in and stay there."

"Right. Just reassure me that the bomb squad's best is doing its thing. If the FBI has the other three, then some genius should've figured out by now how the jackets are wired." Greenstreet nodded. "And in case things go badly . . . the police have to keep pedestrians and cars at least a hundred yards back on all sides."

"You have my absolute assurance," said Greenstreet. "It's all been handled with a degree of discretion I wouldn't have expected in this town. The service has been canceled. The president and his family will spend their Christmas Eve at home. The foreign dignitaries are in their hotel rooms, under heavy guard. The SWATs are in place near the nave and transept doors."

"How long before the media get wise to all this? I'm concerned she might have a phone with Internet access. If she knows they know she's in there, she may—"

"As far as the media know . . . at this moment," said Greenstreet, stepping back into the Mercedes, "the carol service is still on for ten, and the police presence is more than warranted by the guest list. Merry Christmas, Mr. Raszer. And good luck."

"Merry Christmas," Raszer replied. "By the way . . . something I never sorted out: That crack commando team that showed up to pull me out, the exotic choppers, the guns—who paid for all that? Not the taxpayers, I'm guessing."

"Just one taxpayer," Greenstreet replied. "The same man who paid for the jet. And the technology we used to track you. You remember my mentioning a wealthy veteran of The Gauntlet?"

"Sure, I remember," Raszer answered. "What's his name?"

The elegant spook gave a wink. "Philby Greenstreet's his name."

He began to raise the tinted window.

"Wait," Raszer said, stepping forward. "I'd like to know, in case I don't . . . in case things don't work out: Has anything we've done put the brakes on what these people intended?"

"We've set them back for now," the spy replied. "We're slowly weeding them out of Defense and State and the NSA. But they always find a way to crawl back in. And tonight is important. The National Cathedral is as potent a symbol as any. If it blows, there'll be a massive reaction—which is what they want. Whenever collective fear can be induced and chaotic factors set in play, they regain control of the game."

With that, the window was sealed, and he was gone.

Raszer walked on until he stood beneath the church.

Like his cast iron stove and his home's steampunk decor, the National Cathedral was a beautiful anachronism, and for that reason, if for no other, Raszer was fond of it. In a city of eighteenth-century marble, it was a granite throwback to the Middle Ages. Commissioned in the late 1900s and finished a hundred years later, it had been painstakingly constructed, vault by vault, buttress by buttress, to the specifications of High Gothic architecture.

Gothic design excited something in Raszer: it was an architecture of the impossible, designed to prove to man that God could hold up the sky with one finger. In one sense, it was a mere replica, built out of its time and native place, but Raszer found it beautiful and a thing worth preserving. Just as the world—also a replica—was worth preserving.

If the cathedral came down, there would be hell to pay.

But while his adversary's designs were grandiose, Raszer had learned to keep his more modest. There was a girl inside the church who was also worth preserving, though whether her mangled psyche could be restored was anybody's guess. It was true that she'd betrayed him to his enemies and was accountable for Dante's murder. If anything, this only put a keener edge on Raszer's resolve.

Because he still didn't know *why* she had done it.

Once he was inside the cathedral close, and after presenting himself to the coordinator of the joint security force, Raszer sought out a man named Davos, the FBI liaison to the guys on the bomb squad. He'd been told they were bringing in a certified explosives genius, a guy nervy enough, they'd quipped, to "defuse a nuclear payload on its way down and then parachute to safety." He wanted to meet this prodigy, and he also wanted to know what sort of device they'd found the three young Ishmaels carrying.

"That's just the problem," said Davos, watching the snowflakes melt on his palm. "They weren't carrying. Seems they were s'posed to pick up their kits at four different locations—one in each quadrant of the city. That way, if one of them was nabbed—"

"Wait a second," Raszer broke in. "Greenstreet just told me they were loaded for bear when they were caught . . . that each of them had enough to bring down the church."

"Who's Greenstreet?" the FBI man asked, wiping his palm.

Raszer stared. His scalp prickled as the sweat broke.

"Whoever he is had the wrong intel. Or he read it wrong. We got a *description* of the device from one of the three, but we still don't have the hardware. Based on that description, we *think* it's the same rig that took out Bernard Djapper and Douglas Picot in Los Angeles. If it is, the main thing you need to know is that it's not detonated by the carrier, and it's not on a timer of any sort. It's radio-triggered from a long way off . . . "

"Which means," Raszer said, his gaze drifting up to the stained-glass rose window between the two towers of the west nave, "that she could be wired for sound."

"Could be," said Davos.

"Where's your genius?"

"He's not here yet."

"Jesus. Where the hell is he?"

"He's on his way. Stuck in Dupont Circle. It's the friggin' snow. A sprinkle, and the town falls to pieces. And the D.C. cops have roadblocks everywhere."

"I can't believe I'm hearing this. He could jog from Dupont Circle. I'm going in."

"You'll want this," said Davos, offering what appeared to be a designer flak jacket, complete with logo.

"And what's that going to do?" asked Raszer. "Keep my guts from spilling out when the bomb goes off?"

"Suit yourself," said Davos, tossing the jacket back onto a pile.

The bells in the high tower began to ring out "Adeste Fidelis," on what cue, Raszer couldn't guess. There was no one in the church to hear, save for a renegade Jehovah's Witness girl for whom the tune would have little meaning and little chance of inducing a change of heart.

"Do we need the bells?" Raszer asked.

"Everything as usual," said the FBI man. "Hey, before you head in . . . can I ask you something?"

Raszer nodded.

"*Why*?"

"Why what?"

"I know you've been cleared to go in. I'm not questioning that. But why would you want to when there are guys who do this for a living?"

"I've got a thing about closure," Raszer said.

"Not much of an answer."

"Best I've got. You've got my cell. And you'll call me as soon as your guy gets here, right?"

There was silence.

"*Right*?"

Finally, a nod.

Raszer entered from the east, as instructed, through a subground service door that led to a vast open space beneath the chancel. The bells were muffled, but still quite audible. *O come let us adore him. O come let us adore him.* He'd had plenty of time to study the cathedral's floor plan, and knew that there were three ways into the upper chamber. The one he wanted led via a retractable stairway to a hatch that opened into the crossing, where the transept intersected the nave. If she were in the chancel, the choir, or sitting in a random pew halfway back from the altar, she'd see him.

His thinking was sound, but when he stepped quietly up into the heart of the great cathedral, he felt no eyes on him. It shouldn't have surprised him. It was a place anyone could disappear into, a place to make anyone feel small. The intricately ribbed vault of the nave arched to heaven, 140 feet above. The polished oak railings of the choir and clerestory, luxuriantly wrapped with twinkling evergreen boughs, were high enough to induce vertigo.

Far above the choir, the massive pipes of the organ rose to lengths of more than twenty feet. In the stillness of the place, Raszer could hear the pipes breathing as imprisoned air whistled softly through them. Everything was prepared. Everything as usual.

Except for one thing: A candle was burning on the altar.

He stood at the crossing and watched its flame strobe at the tempo of a bird's heartbeat. The lighting of candles was sacramentally proscribed. No acolyte, much less a priest, would leave one burning in an empty church. He padded up the broad, thickly carpeted steps to the altar. The candle's penumbra formed a circle eight feet across, but within the circle, there was little light. Stepping carefully into the dark center, Raszer moved behind the altar. Despite his caution, he kicked something light and metallic. It chimed like a copper kettle, and in the aftermath, he heard the swishing of liquid.

He froze. "Ruthie?" he said softly. When there was no answer, he took the candle from the altar and brought it down to the floor.

The sound had come from a brass washbowl, used by the celebrant to ritually cleanse his hands before administering Holy Communion. Some of its content had splashed onto the carpet; it had an acrid odor. Raszer knelt and put his nose into the bowl, and his nostrils closed reflexively. Urine. "Jesus, Ruthie," he whispered.

In the pulsing light, he saw further evidence of her ceremony. She'd jimmied open the cabinet containing the Communion wine and downed at least one carafe. The chalice lay overturned nearby, and scattered around it were a few white Communion wafers. It wasn't the obvious sacrilege that stunned him so much as the feral urgency of it. She had accomplished her own transubstantiation: holy wine into piss.

He stood, taking up the candle and spreading its light into the sanctuary. If she'd been following the apostate's path, that's where she would have headed next: to the holy of holies. He thought he might find her passed out there, but he did not.

Raszer set the candle back on the altar and descended to the nave's central aisle. He called her name again. The tower bells had begun to chime *O come, o come, Emmanuel*, when he heard a distant siren. A stray headlight illuminated the rose window above the west entrance. He counted off each row of pews, passing his hand over the smooth, scrolled wood as he walked. He had now left the candle's outer ring, and the nave fell into shadow.

A shape registered a second after he saw it. He stopped, backed up two rows, and revisited what he'd seen. It was a body, prone on the pew on his right, about halfway down the row. He heard the deep, measured breathing of sleep.

She was on her side, her right hand beneath her head, her left resting protectively on the bulky explosive pack she wore against her stomach. He said her name again, so as not to alarm her when he got close.

Then he sat down beside her and waited.

"Still trying to save my soul?" she asked after a few minutes.

"You tell me, Ruthie. Does it want to be saved?"

"Oh, I don't guess so. My daddy sure didn't think it did. He said I was beyond salvation. Said there was never a teaspoon of good in me, even when I was a baby."

Raszer shook his head. "You spend the first twelve years of life seeking your father's blessing. If you're still looking for it after that, you're in trouble. Grace has to come from somewhere else."

"Bless me, Father, for I have sinned." The sarcasm was there, but halfhearted.

"Yeah, I'd say you have. But that's not the end of it." He slipped a worn copy of the Book of Common Prayer from the back of the pew and began to leaf through it. When he'd come to the Reconciliation of the Penitent, he read: "The Lord be in your heart and upon your lips that you may truly and humbly confess your sins."

"There are too many of 'em," Ruthie said.

"Katy's with your mom in Taos," he told her. "She's working at the inn."

"That's perfect. Clean white sheets every day. That's where she belongs. This is where I belong. Some girls answer to heaven, some girls answer to hell."

He paged again through the prayer book, looking for something. He found it in rite two of the Daily Evening Prayer.

"If I say, 'Surely the darkness will cover me, and the light around me turn into night,' I will despair. But the darkness is not dark to you, O Lord; the night is as bright as the day; darkness and light to you are both alike."

She lifted her head and looked at him, noticing his eye patch for the first time.

"What happened to your eye?"

"A little bird had it for breakfast."

"Did they . . . do that to you?"

"To tell you the truth, I think I got off easy. They blew Dante's brains out."

She sat up, wobbled, and rubbed her head. "*What?*"

"You can't be surprised, Ruthie. You're a long way from naive." He turned to her. "Why did you do it? Why did you tell them about the cave? What was the deal?"

"The deal was you or me. That prick Djapper had so much shit on me from when I hung with Henry. Interstate transport of illegal weapons. Drugs. Stuff we blew up. He only played me because he figured sooner or later he'd get to use me. And he did. He used me in the usual ways, and he used me to get you taken out."

"Djapper put you up to that?"

"He bought my fuckin' ticket. Told me how to find you."

"And if you'd said no—"

"I'd go to jail . . . maybe worse. Couldn't take prison. No way. And I couldn't stand it hangin' over my head. Can't take that shit, either."

"But Djapper was blown to bits before we even made it to El Mirai. You sold me out to a dead guy."

"I didn't know he was dead. And anyway, who were you? Just some guy who'd fuck me and walk away . . . the way everybody walks away."

"Yeah," Raszer said softly. "So that was it? Life sucks and then you die?"

"Pretty much," she replied, then leveled her eyes at him. "Except that he told me if I didn't cooperate, he could see to it that Katy was raped by dogs, cut into a thousand pieces, and fed to them for dinner."

Raszer closed his eyes and the prayer book and let it wash over him.

After a moment, she spoke again. "Johnny and Henry told me the stories about the Garden. It sounded like some kind of peace."

"And peace is what you wanted?"

"I wanted a whiteout. You know, like how in the movies sometimes everything goes white? No complications. No fucking choices. I wanted to white out the world."

He glanced at the bomb pack. "And that's what you intend to do tonight."

"Damn straight," she said. "So why don't you get out of here?"

"Not without you, Ruthie," he said.

"Why? What am I to you? I fucked you over, mister. Wise up."

"Shams asked me to look after you. Said you had a soul worth tending."

She stared for a few moments, then lowered her eyes. "Shams said that?"

"Yeah."

"Shams was a dreamer. Look where it got him."

"Right. Look where it got him. Flowers spring up where he steps." He waited. "Walk out with me, Ruthie. This whole thing with the Old Man is coming apart. Your testimony will be worth something, maybe immunity. These guys killed Johnny and Henry, Dante and Shams. Don't throw yourself on the pyre for them. Don't—"

Without preface, she laid her head against his chest, and he held her close for what seemed a small eternity. "Guys like you screw up everything for people like me," she said. "You make it seem like there's a reason for things. Take me out of here before I see through your con."

Lightly, almost chastely, she kissed him, then took his hand.

They made their way breathlessly up the aisle toward the western door. She squeezed his hand tight and let out a sob of anxiety as he reached for the big handle.

He pulled the door open and called out. "Davos! I'm bringing her out. Get everybody back and get your man ready to go to work. Are we clear to walk?"

"You're clear," he called back. "Come ahead and then move away from her."

Raszer stopped and squinted into the police lights. "Move away? Why?"

"Like I told you," came the reply, "we don't know how it's triggered!"

He squeezed her hand. Arc lights cast the snow in shimmering relief as they stepped out together. It looked like a movie set. The bells had begun to play "O Little Town of Bethlehem." Raszer's hand was torn from Ruthie's and he was moved hurriedly toward a bomb shield and restrained, while Ruthie stood alone, blinded, on the uppermost step.

The massive door swung shut behind her, leaving the cathedral in near darkness. A few seconds later, an explosion ripped into the doors and sent shrapnel eighty feet into the air, shattering the rose window and littering the pews with shards of brilliantly colored glass. The wind gusted down to the altar and snuffed the candle out. The tower bells stuck on the first syllable of *Beth-le-hem*, and kept ringing out the same note.

It was a long time before anyone stopped them.

EPILOGUE

THE JANUARY RAINS PELTED the picture window with a staccato rhythm. Each rivulet took its own form on its way down to the sill. Some looked like rivers Brigit knew from her maps, and others looked like anacondas. She turned away, thinking that the rains wouldn't be as bad as last year, and that this was all right. There had been enough bad weather. She saw Dr. Schoeppe coming out of the bedroom and knew that this meant she could go back in. Brigit approached her with a certain hopefulness.

"He's better today, don't you think, Dr. Schoeppe?"

"I think you can call me Hildegarde," said Raszer's analyst. "Yes, better. Not great, but better. Great will take some time. What about you?"

"Mmm. Okay, I guess. Sad a lot. My dad's always been, you know, excited about things. Like, 'Brigit, check this out!' or 'Brigit, guess how the ancient Gubi-Wubi tribe made the sun stop!' It's hard to see him not be excited."

"I know. For a while, you may need to be excited for him. It's contagious, you—"

There was a knock at the main door—the door Silas Endicott had walked through almost a year before.

"Should I open it, Monica?" Brigit called into the office.

"I'll be right there, Brij," Monica answered, rising from her workstation. She wore a gray wool tube dress and had newly streaked her hair. She peeked through the window, then opened the door for Lieutenant Borges.

"*Buenas tardes, señorita,*" said the lieutenant, with a courtly tip of his head. "As always, your beauty is a cure for the stormiest of Mondays."

"*Buenas tardes*, Lieutenant," said Monica. "Lorca couldn't have said it better."

Borges looked past her shoulder. "Ah, he has a visitor . . . "

"That's all right," said Hildegarde. "I'm just leaving."

"Dr. Schoeppe," said Monica, "this is Lieutenant Luis Borges, of the LAPD."

Hildegarde stepped forward to shake his hand. "It's a great pleasure, Lieutenant. Stephan speaks very highly of you. He says you keep the city sane."

Borges chuckled.

"And this is Hildegarde Schoeppe," Monica continued. "She's Stephan's, er—"

"Hildegarde is my dad's shrink," Brigit piped in. "But she's a Jungian."

"She is, is she?" said Borges. "In that case, I will escort the doctor to her car. I have never met a real . . . Jungian."

"I'm not sure I believe that," said Hildegarde. "But I'll accept your escort." She turned back to Monica and Brigit. "I'll see you on Wednesday. Call me if—"

Monica nodded.

"I'll be right back," said Borges.

"Okay," Monica replied with a soft smile. "I'll leave the door open."

When they had reached the end of the front walk, Borges spoke. "Would it be a violation of doctor-patient privacy for me to ask how he is doing? He seems very much a changed man."

Hildegarde turned to him and thought for a moment. "I'll speak to you as his friend. I think he'd be all right with that. He's the same man. Older, I think . . . in the sense that he left years behind over there. He's shaken, that's for sure. It would be glib to sum it up as post-traumatic stress . . . although there is certainly that. It's not psychosis. He's perfectly lucid. He can't seem to get out of this 'place' he's in. He calls it 'seeing outside-in.' Parts of his description of it make it sound like autism . . . but it's not. And there's grief—deep grief. A real connection with this girl. The one who—"

"Who blew herself up," said Borges.

"Or was blown up. Yes."

"Well, you know . . . he always suffers when he can't bring them back."

"Oh, I know," she said. "Believe me, I know. This is deeper."

"I have a theory," said Borges. "I won't ask you to endorse or refute it. You know, I'm sure, that he had a couple of brushes with suicide when he was a boy . . . " She gave the slightest nod, but that was all he asked. "I think every time he pulls one of these people out of the darkness, he pulls himself out. And when he can't . . . "

She nodded. "The city is lucky to have you, Lieutenant. Keep us sane, will you?"

"Do my best," he said, and opened the door for her. "But remember, this is L.A."

✦ ✦ ✦

BRIGIT WAS AT RASZER'S BEDSIDE when Monica showed Borges in. Raszer was prone on his old futon—the same he'd had since the divorce—and Brigit sat cross-legged on the Persian rug, looking through a photo album. She glanced up.

"Does this mean I have to leave again?" she asked Monica.

"Just for a few minutes, angel," said Borges. "If that's all right."

"I know," Brigit said, rising. "Police business."

"C'mon, Brij," said Monica. "I'm making ginseng smoothies."

Borges scanned the room for a place to sit. Raszer, lying on his left side under a pale green bedsheet, motioned to a high-backed chair in the corner. With evident pain, he sat up and reached for a cigarette. He wore drawstring pajama bottoms and was wrapped in bandages from waist to chest. He groaned and lit the cigarette.

"When do those bandages come off?" Borges asked.

"Another week," said Raszer, exhaling smoke. "And every time they change them, I go back there, Luis. I have to watch her . . . come apart."

"It's just a damned good thing they pulled you behind that flak shield when they did, amigo, or you wouldn't be here to relive the horror."

"She was all alone on those steps. So fucking scared. The look on her face—"

Borges sighed deeply and dropped his chin to his chest.

"So, what do we know today, Luis?"

"Not much that we didn't know yesterday. Except this, and it's unconfirmed; it will probably never be confirmed. My guy with the FBI's counterterrorism group says they did have one of the other bomb packs in hand two hours earlier. Found it in a gym locker in Foggy Bottom. A government building. An employee handball court."

"Foggy Bottom," Raszer repeated. "The State Department?"

"He wouldn't say. He did say that they took it apart, they knew it was cell phone activated, and they had the number. Now, that doesn't mean it was *her* number . . . "

"Yeah, but Christ, Luis . . . they could've dropped a radio shield over her and blocked the call the minute she walked out of there. I've seen it. I know they can do it."

"Maybe there just wasn't time."

"I don't want to tell you what I think."

"Why not?"

"Because you'll write me off as a nut job," said Raszer.

"I did that a long time ago," said Borges, "and I'm still listening."

"I need to think before I rant," said Raszer. "I just wish . . . I just wish . . . " He stubbed out the cigarette and lay back down with a groan. "God, I'm tired. I hope this isn't what getting old is like."

"I know where you're coming from. Conspiracies, when they're real, don't work like assembly lines. They're about gambling on probability; a series of on/off switches that may operate and let the thing happen. Or may not. Nobody ever touches the switches—that's how they keep their hands clean. I see it here all the time. And if there were people moled into the U.S. government who wanted to see the sky fall, this is the way they'd go about it. If it doesn't happen this time, they just snap their briefcases shut, slip off quietly to some high-priced lobbying or consulting firm, and wait for another day. The good news is, thanks to you, that day is not today."

"Not to me," said Raszer. "I'm a foot soldier. But there is a guy—"

"Don't tell me," said Borges. "I like being at least a little dumb. Not you. You'll never close your eyes. You'll never walk away from a door you can jimmy open. So, my friend, you'd better figure on a long ride on the edge." He stood up. "Speaking of eyes," he said, pointing to his own right, "I know a guy downtown, on Jeweler's Row, who makes the most beautiful glass eyes you've ever seen. He uses gemstones—sapphires, rubies, emeralds—for the iris. He did one for a partner of mine. Want his number?"

"Maybe later. I'm going to stay with the pirate patch for now."

"Okay, friend. Rest up. And rest a little easier. Detective Aquino called me this morning. That JW Elder, Amos Leach? He's been charged with six counts: two sexual battery, two contributing, one statutory, and one obstruction. And all that without any cojones. Your boy Emmett Parrish came out of his shell to give a statement."

✦ ◆ ✦

After the cop had left, Brigit crept back in with her smoothie and two straws, and took her place beside the bed. For a long time, their exchange was wordless. Raszer gazed at the stained-glass window he'd commissioned some years before, a depiction of Sir Galahad's vision of the Holy Grail. The golden rays issuing from the Grail were runnels in the glass, and had been cut at angles so as to trap and refract the late-afternoon sun.

Brigit could, up to a point, hop aboard her father's train of thoughts, but not when he went to the outside-in place. There, she couldn't follow.

"Tell me again about Francesca and the Fedeli d'Amore," she said.

"Francesca," he said softly, easing back. "I want you to meet her one day. She's quite a lady. And she has a dog that isn't really a dog at all."

"Shaykh Adi," Brigit said.

"That's right. The kindest, wisest eyes you've ever seen."

"And you'll take me there . . . to the place that isn't really a place at all?"

"Na-Koja-Abad."

"Nowhere-Land."

"Maybe someday," he said. "After they clean up the neighborhood."

"Do you go there sometimes, Daddy . . . even when you're here?"

"I think so, yeah. I'll try to keep the visits short."

"That's okay," she said. "I'll keep an eye on you here if you want to go. In your mind, I mean. Or whatever—"

"Thanks, muffin. It's always good to know someone's waiting."

"I'll be waiting," she said, and touched his arm. Her expression froze.

"What?" he asked.

"I just had one of those . . . that weird feeling."

"Déjà vu?"

"Yeah. When I said, 'I'll be waiting.' I've said that before." She smiled—a little epiphany. "You know how you said that sometimes you feel like you're still in that game? That you're just playing and the real you is someplace else?"

He nodded.

"Maybe that just comes from knowing that there's a story made up for all of us, way before we're born. And we just sort of walk through it—like a game—until we figure it out and start playing for real. Then it's not a game anymore, is it?"

He laid his head on the pillow and aimed his good eye through a stained-glass rose to the sun, now golden and sinking. Brigit took her book and curled up on the rug, close enough to take his hand if he had a nightmare. She would stay the long night, and be the first thing he saw when he opened his eyes in the morning.

ACKNOWLEDGMENTS

THOSE WITHOUT WHOM, nothing: My publisher, Charlie Winton. My editor, Michele Slung. My agent, Kimberly Cameron. Copy editor, Annie Tucker. Managing editor, Laura Mazer. My protectress, Dorris Halsey.